Martin G Jordan (signature)

Moth

Martin G Jordan

This novel is dedicated to my wife Aoife
and our children, Patrick, Niamh and Michael.

To order a signed copy of the novel;
to contact the author or to leave comments;
please to visit:
www.martingpjordan.com

Published in the Republic of Ireland by:

Diggy Duffy Publishing [Reg no 591628]
W91 EFY8
diggyduffy@gmail.com

A CIP record of this book is available from the British Library.
First printed May 2017

Cover design concept by Claire Casey
Moth-eye rendering by Michael Linehan

A very special thank you to Agnete Lundetræ Jürgensen
(www.lundetrae.com).
For her kindness, enthusiasm and most critical eye.
I hope that all fledgling writers find such wonderful support.

ISBN 978-0-9956148-1-9

The elephant hawk-moth, (Deilephila elpenor)
a native of many parts of Ireland,
has trichromatic colour vision
and can see colours that the human eye cannot.
Studies have determined that the elephant hawk-moth can
even see and distinguish colours in the dead of a black night.

Prologue

"Mummy?"

"Yes dear?"

"Daddy's dead."

The boy's voice was just above a whisper but something in the way that he spoke, rather than what he had said, caught his mother's attention. To the obvious annoyance of his boorish grandmother who had been staying with the family for the last three weeks and whose presence was the reason for the visit of his two great aunts, his mother turned and smiled at her son. He knew she was feeling sorry for him because she knew he was unhappy and bored and would rather be somewhere else. Sitting in the stuffy front room, on a sunny summer afternoon with his mother and three octogenarians, was not the place for a ten-year-old boy, but the bang on the head that he had received that morning had been severe. He had been unconscious for nearly twenty minutes and he still looked pale. Despite his tearful protests and those of his more vocal twin brother, the family doctor had insisted that he stay in-doors and be 'kept an eye on', and most certainly could not go as planned with his father and brother to the football match in Dublin.

"What was that, darling?" said his mother.

His grandmother eyed him suspiciously. He thought about a phrase the old woman liked repeating whenever either he or his brother spoke up or tried to attract their mother's attention when she was in the room. *In my day, we didn't pander to children. They should only speak when spoken to.*

The boy hesitated. Something told him that he had made a mistake. He shouldn't have said anything, but he knew it was too

1

late now. Something bad had happened and he was sure he'd be blamed.

He shouldn't have said anything.

When he raised his head he saw that they were all looking at him.

"What did you say, darling?"

"Daddy is gone, Mummy."

"Yes, but your daddy and your brother will be back soon. The match is over. They will be home soon. They probably stopped to get you a surprise on the way. That's why they are late."

His mother looked worried.

"No...but...d...addy's dead," he said.

"Why would you say something like that?" she said.

There was a hint of annoyance in his mother's voice.

He shouldn't have said anything.

"What is that silly boy saying, Kay?" said his grandmother.

He pointed at his father's empty armchair in the corner, between the window and the fire place. It still held the shape of his father's bottom in the worn seat and the dark marks on the arms of the chair where his father rested his elbows when he read his newspaper, but the colour traces of his father were gone.

He'd seen them vanish and the boy knew what that meant.

"The colours are gone. They aren't there anymore Mummy. That means Daddy's dead."

The boy began to sob, but he kept on talking.

"Just like when Patsy died. All his colours were gone from his tractor and from the buckets in the yard."

He knew his mother was thinking about what he'd said; remembering the day last year when she'd found the old man's body at the edge of the potato field. The boy had said the same thing then, about Patsy's colours disappearing.

He shouldn't have said anything.

Children should only speak when spoken to.

The phone in the hall rang. Everyone jumped. The elderly sisters looked at his mother. The phone kept ringing. It seemed louder than usual. His mother rose and went out.

"I'm sorry Mummy," he whispered.

His grandmother blessed herself.

"Sweet Jesus Mary and Joseph, what was that child babbling about?" she said, as if he had left the room with his mother.

Her two sisters looked at each other and then at the boy. They could all hear his mother speaking on the telephone because she'd left the door slightly ajar. Her voice sounded strange. She sounded like she was choking. When she returned to the living room she was shaking and her face was wet from crying.

"There's been an accident. John crashed the car coming back from the match, at McLaughlin's cross. There was another car involved. Garda Flynn is on the way over to take us to the hospital," she managed to say before she started to wobble and had to grab the door frame. His two great-aunts stood as one and rushed to her side. They took an arm each and led her back to the couch. His grandmother didn't move. She just stared at him. He tried as hard as he could to look away but he found it impossible. It was like her eyes were talking to him, accusing him.

"How could you know?" she said in a tiny voice.

He didn't answer her. He pretended he hadn't heard her.

"I'm talking to you, boy. How could you know this?"

One of her sisters turned on her.

"For God's sake, stop it Chris. We don't know if he's..." her words trailed off into nothing.

"He knows. Don't you, boy?" said his grandmother. She spat the last words at him.

"You know that they are dead!"

Part One

"Béidreach."
"Bitch."

Chapter 1.

C *oncentrate on the colours*, he told himself, because he knew that concentrating on the colours would take his mind off what was to come and stop him thinking about the terrible pain in his head.

Michael X stood waiting at the back of the television studio with his eyes closed. Like the lights, his headache was blinding. It was always that way just before he went on. He'd be walking from his dressing room to the back of the set and a switch would be flipped somewhere at the front of his brain and the pain would arrive fully formed and at full volume. The soothing power of the prescribed pain-killers he'd taken thirty minutes earlier, would be instantly neutralised by the migraine's dreadful noise. By the time he reached the top of the short flight of steps that led down to the studio floor, the pain would be so bad that it felt like his eyeballs were being squeezed together.

Michael slowly opened his eyes, the action of lifting his eyelids adding to the pain at the edge of his cranium.

Concentrate.

Albescent, azure and ochroleucous sand. A hippy van perched on a dune overlooking a deserted beach at dusk. They are the colours of Stephanie, the make-up lady. She'd left her colour marks on the stainless steel handle of the door leading to the dressing rooms. There are many other colour marks on the door handle, but when Michael concentrates he only sees Stephanie's colours. For Michael it is like focussing on a familiar face in a large crowd of strangers. Seeing her colours brings to his mind vivid memories of Stephanie. All of his senses bristle with the thoughts of her. He can smell her perfume and feel the warmth of her breath as she applies foundation on his cheeks with a thick soft brush. It tickles his face. He can hear her voice.

"Stops your face from glowing like a lollypop under the studio lights. Ya don't wanna look like a lollypop on telly do ya Michael?" she whispers to him as she flicks the soft dense bristles across his forehead, brushing away the pain.

Concentrate.

Minium, tan and topaz yellow. Strawberry sauce and melted chocolate dribbled down the petals of a dying daffodil. The colours of a palm print on the wall beside the water-cooler left there by Brendan Best, the host of the show. Michael can imagine Brendan leaning over the pretty young receptionist as she fills her cup with chilled water. Brendan is talking and joking but not really talking to her, just listening to himself speak. Brendan's colours are everywhere in and around the studio. Not surprising, thinks Michael, after all, the television studio is Brendan's kingdom.

Concentrate.

He stares at the chairs in the Green Room, where the celebrities go to wait before being called out. They are all so stained with nervous colour that Michael finds it hard to see the fabric underneath, yet in the blur of colours he spots Tanya's vibrant sage and celeste cream, like lipstick on a popsicle. Tanya was only in for the summer months, a work experience student from the local comprehensive, but she touched all the chairs and left her marks everywhere.

Clive, the security guard, had been in the Green Room too and he had left his burgundy and bottle green finger smudges on the glass wall that separated the famous from the ordinary. They reminded Michael of tiny portholes of sunlight reflected in a forest puddle.

There are familiar colour marks everywhere and if he concentrates hard enough Michael can find them amongst the fog of everything else and see the person in the flesh, hear their voice and feel the calming heat of their presence beside him.

Concentrate.

The colours are points of focus and words to be remembered. They are memories and living photographs. They are the traces left behind by people Michaels knows. They are all around him and they, literally, colour his world. And they have the power to take his mind off his terrible migraine. So, Michael concentrates on the colours until it is time to go on.

"Concentrate on the colours," he whispered to himself, "because I know if I concentrate on the colours they will take away the pain."

*

With his usual exaggerated enthusiasm, Brendan Best, the suave young presenter of *Good Afternoon Norwich*, finally got to Michael's segment of the show. Michael was sure that Brendan was taking longer and longer in his build-up, teasing the audience and the viewers, whilst adding to Michael's discomfort. Michael didn't complain. He never mentioned it. After every show Brendan was ebullient.

"They love you Michael. The audience, the viewers, the sponsors, everybody loves you. And who can blame them? That boyish face of yours. Those killer blue eyes. That soft Irish drawl. Even that edgy nervous energy you give off, always bubbling just beneath the surface. It feels like anything could happen, at any moment. Sooo appealing. It feels authentic, you know? That's the key, Michael. That's what television is all about. Feeling real! They believe you. That's the key. You're a genuine superstar, Michael."

Michael could not deny that his fifteen-minute guest appearance twice a week, every Tuesday and Thursday, on the afternoon magazine show for BBC North East had upped the viewing figures of Good Afternoon Norwich dramatically. Michael was a ratings star on an otherwise ordinary television show and his appearances were enough to make Good Afternoon Norwich a bit of a television phenomenon. The show in its entirety was repeated after midnight and as the word spread clips of Michael's segment were uploaded to the internet. Michael X was on the verge of becoming an international sensation and Brendan Best could see it and was intent on rising along with him. For Brendan, Michael was his discovery and at every opportunity he referred to Michael as, "my Irish mystic."

For Michael, the worst bit was waiting to be called out. He always got the jitters and always had a pounding headache. He had been doing the TV appearances for over two and a half years but standing in the wings waiting to go on never got any easier for him. He still got butterflies in his stomach and sometimes the pain in his gut was so bad that it almost took his mind off the migraine. He often wondered if he was getting a stomach ulcer. He perspired so much during the fifteen-minute slot that he had to change his shirt after every appearance. Yet every Tuesday and Thursday Michael returned to the couch to face a member of the two hundred strong studio audience brave, or stupid enough, to expose themselves to Michael X's piercing gaze. Michael would offer advice and insight but he was really only there for the money. The members of the audience had their own reasons for volunteering. Some came to the couch for their shot at fifteen minutes of fame. Others came for the dare or to catch Michael out. One or two came with genuine requests. The latter Michael tried to help, but he knew in his heart that he was fooling them. Good Afternoon Norwich was nothing more than show business and in his role as Michael X, the Irish mystic, he was nothing more than an actor.

That particular Tuesday afternoon seemed no different to any other.

Brendan Best was speaking to a woman via a video link to her living room in Birmingham. Her narrow bird-like face filled a large screen that hung on the back wall of the studio set. Michael was quite sure that he had never seen the woman before. The studio audience seemed enthralled by her and was becoming increasingly boisterous. The woman had been the subject of one of Michael's readings the previous year and was now back on the show to explain how her life had changed since meeting Michael. She was waving a set of car keys and she trembled with excitement.

"How lucky have you been Shelly Sealy?" said Brendan.

"Becos of what Micol told me I stawted doin' competitions. I do 'undweds of them every week an' I've won loads o' stuff. I won a caw," she said excitedly.

"Wow Shelly," said Brendan.

"Yes an' it's all thanks t' Micol X."

"Well that's what we are here for Shelly," said Brendan, before Shelly could say anything else, "We are so glad we have helped you. Well goodbye Shelly Sealy and…well…good luck!."

Michael watched as Brendan milked the studio audience for a noisy response. It amazed Michael how Brendan could remain so calm and how he could slip so easily from one persona to the next without batting an eyelid. One minute he'd be all sincere and concerned, the next he'd be joking with the audience. Brendan was the shallowest and most insincere person Michael had ever met and yet despite that Michael could not help but like him. Brendan's colours reminded Michael of funfair lollipops and the chocolate toppings on an ice cream cone. They made him smile.

Shelly's image disappeared and the screen went blank before rising silently into the empty space above the studio.

Michael had a memory flash.

He is sitting opposite a young wiry haired woman with too much make-up. She is wearing a garish low cut braless top and a tight leather mini-skirt. She has ugly high heel shoes and green fishnet tights. She speaks with a harsh East End London accent. She pronounces most of her "r's" as if they are "w's". In the lowered lights of the studio Michael barely hears her voice. She is yapping on about not being able to find her "Mistew Wight". She seems confident enough, but Michael is certain that this is just a rouse. The colours that gently pulse about her bony frame, the colours that only Michael can see, are dull and lifeless. They remind him of oily newspapers at the bottom of an emptied garbage bin. Browns, muddy greens and dark greys.

Michael remembers thinking that her colours betrayed loneliness and possibly suggested self-delusion. They were not unusual colours, but the combination was unique to her, just like her fingerprints, or the hidden lines in the retinas of her small desperate eyes.

But Michael also remembers seeing something sparkle, in amongst the dirty tones. He's not surprised by this. In his experience everyone contains something magical. In her case it is a bluish red and it winks at him from around her abdomen. He thinks the dominant colour is called carmine. It brings to his mind a fire on a distant hillside after a thunderstorm.

So Michael speaks to the woman in a low voice and in vague terms. He always speaks in vague terms to the people that come down from the audience. It makes it easier for everyone. For a lot of people what Michael does is nothing more than a cheap carnival trick and most of the time this opinion is correct. He throws in a little bit of what he can genuinely decipher in the limited time available, but does so using words easily interpreted

11

in many different, often contradictory ways. He tells the young woman that she possesses a lucky gene. This, he is sure is rubbish because what he sees has nothing to do with anything physical or biological. Michael believes that what he sees is a manifestation of a person's essence and that the colours he sees is the aura of their life-force.

His brother says that what Michael sees is a person's soul, but Michael isn't convinced. What he is certain of, is that everyone's colour aura is as unique as they are and that the aura is the colour of their life. It rises from beneath their skin like smoke and it trails behind them, leaving traces on furniture and walls. It is alive and the colours have meaning. Michael tells the young woman that if she is more positive about herself, her future will be better. She looks at him as if he has just imparted some great ancient secret just for her. It pains him that his lies no longer bother him as much as they did when he first started the TV gig. He doesn't tell her what he really sees; that the dark colours out-number the light ones. He doesn't say that he doubts that she will ever acquire anything with the power to take away the loneliness or to lessen the underlining greyness of her life. Nor does he share with her his opinion that none of the many men that she chooses as her Mr Right will ever leave her with anything other than regret. These thoughts make Michael sad. Looking into her expectant excited eyes he wishes that there was some way he could teach her to focus on the fire that lives within her. But Michael is no teacher. He is only an observer and most of the time, a fraud.

"I think you have a lucky gene," he remembers telling Shelly Sealy, "I see a lucky spark."

A roar from the studio audience drags Michael away from thoughts of Shelly Sealy and back to the present. Brendan Best had just called him out.
"Come and join us Michael. Ladies and gentlemen, let's give it up for…the one…the only…our very own…Michael X."

*

As soon as the applause had died down and Michael had taken his usual seat in the centre of the couch closest to the steps, Brendan Best declared that it was now time to meet this week's lucky participant; the man or woman who would have their future revealed by his Irish mystic. Brendan reached for the cue card, but before he had time to call out the name written on it, a well-dressed couple in their early thirties stepped up from the front row. The tall handsome man turned back momentarily and waved at the audience, as if acknowledging an old friend and then he followed his attractive partner up to the couch opposite Michael.

"A couple, this week?" said Brendan with surprise.

Michael noticed that Brendan looked momentarily flustered, but it didn't last long. The cheery smile returned quickly and his narrowing eyes ran up and down the young woman's shapely body. As she lowered herself beside him on the couch one of her knees softly caressed one of his and Michael saw Brendan gulp and then lick his lips.

"Well, who do we have here?" he said "and what have you to ask of Michael X?"

Michael could tell that Brendan was ignoring the flapping arms of the assistant floor manager over his shoulder and what seemed to be a minor scuffle at the back of the studio. Brendan moved a little closer to the woman. Although there was a coffee table between the two couches Michael could smell the woman's perfume. It was sharp and sweet but pleasantly intoxicating.

"I'm Jane and this is my husband Peter," she said in a soft middle-class English accent. "We want to ask Michael if he can help us find our daughter. She's been missing for almost ten months now. Someone took Ally, Michael. We want to know if she's still alive. You help the police to find missing people, don't you?"

Jane stared at Michael and he held her gaze.

Brendan Best looked shocked and some people in the audience gasped. It took Brendan a moment or two before he recognised who the couple were. Michael continued to look at Jane. The pain behind his eyes was as bad as he'd ever experienced it.

"You're the Wesley's, aren't you? Allison Wesley's parents?" said Brendan. His flustered look had returned. Michael knew who the couple were. Allison Wesley was the first in a series of abductions of little girls in the north east of England. Since Allison's disappearance four more had been taken. The abductions happened in broad daylight and the case had become worldwide news. All the girls were aged between six and eight years old and all were blond and particularly pretty.

"You're our last hope, Michael" said Peter.

"I'm not sure about this," said Brendan, "this is not..."

"We have her quilt!" said Jane ignoring Brendan's protests. She withdrew a small chequered blanket which was loosely tied around the handles of her handbag and without looking at it she stretched her arm out over the low glass table toward Michael. He reached out and took it from her. For a split second their hands touched and when they did Michael saw a strange shadow cross in front of Jane's already dark eyes. His migraine slammed into his forehead like a lump hammer. The pain was so intense he almost dropped the blanket.

"How old is Ally?" Michael asked, ignoring the pain in his head. The blanket swirled with a myriad of human colours.

"Eh, six," said Peter. "She was five when they took her."

Peter's voice seemed strained, his emotions exaggerated. Michael looked at him and he immediately thought of Brendan Best. Brendan had gone quiet. Someone in the control room had decided to let the show go on and without warning the lights in the studio were lowered. A camera focussed on Michael's face.

He looked again at Jane Wesley. Her dark eyes appeared like polished opals. He thought of the word obsidian, but settled on opaque.

No light, he thought. No colour.

He caressed the blanket then turned back and looked at Peter Wesley.

"Well then, okay?" whispered Brendan. "Let's see what Michael X can do."

Still staring at Peter Wesley, Michael X, slowly closed his eyes.

Chapter 2.

Detective Chief Inspector Wally Griffin of the North East Division of Serious Crimes was sitting up in his bed feeling miserable. The bright afternoon sunshine made the partially drawn floral curtains almost transparent. His wife Hattie had just taken away the lunch tray without a word about the half-eaten sandwich. He was weak and hot and uncomfortable. He'd spent most of the morning and almost an entire box of man-sized tissues attempting to quell the flow of warm sticky goo that oozed continually from his throbbing nose. The used tissues were scattered around him on the bed and floor. His hopes of using the time in bed to catch up on reading had come to nought. He could not find a comfortable position; nor could he concentrate for more than a page or two. It was ten past three. With a resigned sigh, Wally reached for the TV remote. Afternoon television... a different bloody world, he thought. Entertainment for the elderly, the infirm and the unemployed. Television for bored housewives and hung-over students. Television for the zombie class – the bloody undead. Not his type of television. DCI Wally Griffin was a News at Ten or period-drama type of guy. He certainly wasn't one to watch afternoon television. He sighed. He couldn't remember the last time he'd been struck down with the flu. He'd had very few sick days in his nearly forty years in Her Majesty's police service and being bed-bound was unfamiliar and very unpleasant territory.

The small flat screen in the corner of his bedroom stuttered into life. A news report from North Korea popped up. Wally pressed his thick sweaty thumb on the programme back button and watched the images change in rapid succession: motor racing~ wildlife~ tele-shopping~ cartoons~ more wildlife~ a game show~ a chat-show of some kind~ a repeat episode of a popular US police drama~ an American sit-com~ Italian soccer.

Wally took his thumb off the button. The channels kept changing for a short while. Something had caught Wally's eye but it had taken time to register in his bunged-up brain. He pressed the programme forward button, this time one channel at a time, until he arrived back at the chat-show. He raised the volume. The camera zoomed in on a face that he recognised. It was that spooky Irish psychic that Detective Inspector Brian "Horse" Hopkins used as a consultant on a few of the missing persons cases. Wally saw it as a waste of valuable police time, resources and money, but DI Hopkins was convinced that the Irishman was useful and Wally had to admit that there had been some positive results. Wally had known that the Irish psychic appeared on television but he had never been interested enough to find out when or on which channel.

"Afternoon television!" thought Wally, "I should have guessed!"

It had not been Michael's face though, that had caught Wally's eye on the channel flyby, but instead the faces of the couple sitting opposite him.

"What the fu...?" said Wally to the television when the image switched back to Jane and Peter Wesley. Jane was staring at Michael.

"You help the police to find missing people don't you?" she was saying.

"Bloody hell!" said Wally, and he kept on saying it as he rummaged among the bed covers for his mobile phone.

*

"Afternoon Guv. How are you feeling? You better now?" said Detective Inspector Brian "Horse" Hopkins when the call was put through.

"No I'm not better. Do I fuckin' sound better, Hopkins?" Horse heard a loud sneeze followed by a muffled, "bloody hell" before his boss continued.

"Are you at your desk Hopkins?"

"Yes sir."

"Then turn on the television and go to channel, eh, 256, Here and Now, Good Afternoon Norwich and hurry up."

"What's this about sir?"

"Just do it and you'll see."

"Okay. Hold on a second."

Horse laid the phone on his desk, found the remote control and switched the television on to channel 256. He raised the volume. The other detectives in the incident room looked over. Horse stared at the screen in disbelief. He picked up the phone.

"Holy God, Guv! What's going on?"

"You tell me Detective. He's your man. Do you think that Irish fuckwad set this up?" The DCI was angrier than Horse had ever heard him.

"No way, Guv. He doesn't even know Peter and Jane Wesley," protested Horse, "Michael's only being looking into the most recent girl, Sandra Short. Sandra's parents approached Michael and he came to us. There is no way Michael has anything to do with this Guv."

"Well someone's fuckin' with us Hopkins and I don't like it. Get onto the station and get them to stop this now! Tell them they are interfering with the investigation of a serious crime and..."

Before Wally Griffin finished what he was saying the lights in the studio dimmed and Michael's face filled the screen. Then, after a moment or two Michael closed his eyes.

"Bloody hell," said the DCI but Horse was no longer listening. The other detectives in the incident room gathered under the screen. No one spoke. Even the audience in the television studio seemed to be holding a collective breath. Everything went eerily silent. It was as if someone had hit the mute button on the television.

The image on the TV screen in the incident room changed to a wide shot of Ally's parents. As if on cue they looked at each other and then turned and stared directly at the camera. Peter Wesley appeared to be blinking in slow motion and Horse thought he looked wired, like a skittish child trying hard not to giggle at a funeral. In stark contrast, Jane Wesley was a picture of controlled calm. Her eyes seemed solid black. Cold, thought Horse. Her mouth was shut tight in a wide pout and the touching lips made a perfectly straight line, with just the slightest, barely discernible downturn at either end. In any other circumstance Horse would have said she was smirking.

The camera returned to Michael. He held a child's comfort blanket in both hands and seemed to be studying it intently. He moved his head from side to side as if he was listening to music through hidden earphones and then very slowly closed his eyes.

What happened next made everybody in the police station jump. Down the phone Horse heard his boss curse loudly, sneeze and then curse again. Horse lowered the phone onto his desk and watched aghast as the bizarre scenes unfolded on the television screen in front of him. In the television studio Brendan Best verbalised his shock with an inappropriate word and then, as a camera zoomed in on his face, clasped both hands over his mouth as if to hold back a possible tide of further expletives. At the same time the studio audience let out a loud theatrical gasp. The sound they made was like the sudden release of air from a blocked water pipe. The camera that had been focussing on Michael shunted backwards sending Michael's face in and out of focus.

It started when Michael opened his eyes.

This time the action was not slow and measured but instead his eyelids flipped open like they were on a spring-release. He looked completely different. The pupils of his soft blue eyes were fully dilated and his face was filled with rage. His lips parted and his jaw tightened. He bared his teeth like a rabid animal and when he stared at Peter Wesley, Michael looked almost feral. One woman, who Horse interviewed afterwards, and who had been sitting near him in the front row, said Michael X looked possessed and several members of the studio audience said they heard him growl.

Horse watched in amazement as Michael stood up and, with a clenched fist, flung the comfort-blanket as hard as he could into Peter Wesley's face.

"Where are they?" he hissed at the man sitting opposite him. "You took the children. You have them! Where are they?"

Before Peter Wesley had a chance to speak, Michael lunged at him across the low glass table, knocking Peter off the couch and onto the hard studio floor. In front of a cowering Brendan Best and a stunned studio audience, the mild mannered Michael X locked his hands around Peter's neck and started to squeeze the life out of him.

"Where are they? Where are they?" he shouted again and again.

*

Pandemonium erupted in the television studio. Jane Wesley howled and threw herself onto Michael's back. Her sharp fingernails tore into the flesh of his cheeks and her bony fingers crept across his face as she searched for the soft jelly of his eyes. Brendan Best dropped onto the floor and scurried away from them like a frightened puppy. The audience screamed and yelled but none of them left their seats. Finally, someone somewhere cut the broadcast signal and station security guards moved in to take control.

With his mobile phone pressed hard against a hot sweaty ear, Wally Griffin could hear Horse Hopkins shouting down another phone, "No one leaves that studio. Do you understand? I don't care if you have to chain the doors. No one leaves until we get there. Yes, we're on the way!"

As the image on the screen changed to a test card which read WE APOLOGISE FOR THE TEMPORARY LOSS OF SERVICE, Wally Griffin began to undress. Moments later he stood exasperated and naked on the landing.

"Hattie. Hattie," he shouted down the stairs, "Where are you, woman? For God sakes Hattie, what have you done with my clothes? I need my clothes Hattie. I need to leave, now!"

Chapter 3.

The night was cold and as damp as a dishcloth. A gusty wind played with an empty beer can, rattling it to and fro across the narrow empty street. It was two in the morning. Detective Inspector Brian Hopkins, Police Constable Richard Cannings and Detective Chief Inspector Wally Griffin sat in a parked unmarked Audi with the cabin light off. It was so dark in the car that they could only see each other as silhouettes. Wally Griffin sat in the front passenger seat and sniffled loudly between every angry sentence. From the back seat, where Horse sat, it sounded like his boss was sobbing.

"What the fuck have I let you talk me into, Hopkins?" said the DCI without turning around. Constable Cannings fiddled with the steering wheel but said nothing. Horse leaned forward and pushed his head between the two front seats as if preparing for a group photograph. Nothing moved outside the car.

"He'll be here." Horse whispered reassuringly.

"He'd better be," barked Griffin. "Why did I agree to this? Another fucking fiasco, just like earlier at the Wesley's house… Absolutely nothing! Your mystic didn't exactly shine there did he? And now this. The Middle of Norwich, ten past two in the morning and on a hunch? I'm telling you Hopkins, five O clock tomorrow afternoon the Wesley's walk, and then there'll be hell to pay. She's claiming he broke her nose…"

"It was self-defence, Guv," interjected Horse, "she was trying to gouge out his eyes. Michael punched out in self-defence."

"We won't have a fucking leg to stand on if we have to let them go. False arrest, harassment, police brutality, not to mention what the press will make of the fact that Scotland Yard's finest rely on the visions of a fucking Irish fortune teller for leads in the most high-profile child abduction case in the history of Her Majesty's police service. Fuck Hopkins! What have you got me into?"

"Sir, you've come this far, there is no point in pulling out now. This could be the break we've been looking for."
Cannings spoke before the DCI could start again.

"A car's comin' Guv. Is that 'im?"

"Yeh, that's him. I'll go talk to him. See what he needs," said Horse.

"He needs a fuckin' straight jacket. We all do," said Griffin.

Horse slid out of the back seat and quietly closed the door as Michael's old Vauxhall pulled up to the kerb. Michael sat in the car for a short time before getting out.

*

"How's your face Mikey? I hope you got a tetanus jab. You'd never know what diseases that bitch had," said Horse as he approached Michael.

"I'm fine," Michael lied. His headache was still as bad as it had been all day and behind a mask of calmness, his mood was sombre.

"Why are we here, Brian? "Do the Wesley's own a place in this part of the city?" Michael said.
Michael looked around. The narrow streets were squalid and deserted.

"Not that we know about. Long-story-short Mikey, this is the best location we could come up with, once their house proved to be clean."

"Oh? How's that?" said Michael.

"I've been mulling things over since this afternoon. Something has been nagging at me about this case for a long time," said Horse.

"Only one something? Listen Brian, it's him, Peter Wesley, and I know at least some of the girls he took are still alive. But, what I don't understand is why he did it? Go on the show I mean. Why would they do that?" said Michael.

"Shit, mate. There's no point asking me. Maybe it was some sort of game for him, part of a power play? Maybe it was an opportunity to interfere with our investigation. A chance to make the coppers look like idiots or expose you as a charlatan. God only knows. But if you say Peter Wesley has the girls then I believe you," said Horse.

Michael winced.

"You sure you're okay mate?"

"Yes. Just tired, that's all. There's something else Brian."

"What?"

"I'm sure it's not just him. She's in on it too."

"I had the same feeling. That's why I had them both arrested."

"Right. So why here then?" asked Michael again.

"When Alison Wesley went missing back in January, we didn't know that her abduction was the first in a series, so our focus was on Peter Wesley. Daddy is always the first and prime suspect when a daughter goes missing. Peter had a watertight alibi of course. Jane Wesley provided that. But, as you know I'm an old-school policeman. I believe in the power of a hunch. Truth is, I never liked Peter Wesley. Actually I liked her even less. From the beginning I felt there was something wrong, so for a while we tailed him."

"Really? You never mentioned that," said Michael.

"Well, it wasn't actually legal so keep it to yourself alright? Official channels can be slow and cumbersome. Anyway, myself and a couple of the lads watched the Wesley's house and we really thought we'd hit the jackpot too. Every couple of nights – late, always after midnight – Peter left the house and drove here."

"They do have a place here then?" said Michael.

"Eh, I'm not sure. This is an old red-light district and it appears Peter Wesley is fond of a bit of street skirt. More than a bit, actually! As I said, he came here two or three times a week."

"But now you think there was some other reason for him coming here?"

"Possibly. It's possible Jane knew what her husband was doing and she gave him a false alibi because she was ashamed. That's what my governor thinks."

Horse glanced over his shoulder at the parked Audi.

"But not you?" said Michael.

"No, and my hunch extends to both of them. I don't see him doing anything on his own, not without consulting the boss. I reckon Jane wears the trousers in that house, don't you think?"

"Yes, she is definitely the boss," said Michael.

"Anyway, when it became a serial abduction we backed off Peter Wesley. Liking a bit of street rough isn't a crime."

"I thought it was, but you're the policeman so you should know. Anyway, it's not much to go on, is it?" said Michael.

"It's all we've got, mate. This is the last throw of the dice. In fifteen hours' time we will have to charge them or release them. My governor who, by the way, doesn't like you, has informed me that there's a bunch of highly paid lawyers waiting in the wings to eat us all alive. If we don't come up with something tonight, we'll both be looking for new jobs. You could do time for assault. Like I said, the last throw of the dice. If we don't get something out of this, we are all fucked."

The two friends stood in silence for a moment and then Michael said,

"Well I hope you're right then, Brian."

"God so do I. Fuck the job Michael. If the children are here somewhere, we need to find them and stop whatever is going on. If they're here, you can find them. I know you can!"

"Did Jane Wesley ever come here? With her husband?" said Michael.

"Not that we know of. They do have two cars though, so I suppose she could have followed him here separately. They seem cunning enough. Jane Wesley was never on our radar. She's the girl's mother for God's sakes."

"I know. I know. But your hunch is telling you that they are both involved?"

"Yes. But I'm only sharing that thought with you, Mikey. If my Governor thought I suspected Jane of being anything other than an accessory, he'd have me committed to an asylum before you could say nut-job."

"Jane is very strange," said Michael. He didn't add that the colour aura he'd seen around her was extremely odd and more than a little disturbing. At first Michael had thought it was the light in the studio, but after what happened, and the way she had reacted, he thought differently. Even when the lights came back on, Jane Wesley's aura appeared to him as a series of overlapping blacks, almost entirely without colour.

Just like her eyes, he thought.

"Anyway, it's the girls. That's why we are here. Go find the girls Michael."

"I'll try Brian," said Michael.

"Good. I better leave you to it then," said the detective.

"Yes."

"Do you need anything?"

"No. Just to be left alone."

"Righto. We'll be in the car, if you need us."

"Grand," said Michael.

Before Horse returned to his colleagues in the dark Audi he took Michael's arm.

"Don't be a hero, mate, okay? We're the cops. You're the...well, whatever. Just don't be a hero."

"Sure. Don't be a hero. Sure," repeated Michael as he watched Horse walk away.

Chapter 4.

The street stank of burnt rubber, rotting vegetables and something like stale soy sauce. The wind had picked up and now it carried droplets of icy rain that quickly wet Michael's hair and face. Instinctively he clung tighter to the plastic supermarket carrier bag which was tucked under his arm. He'd retrieved the bag from his car once Brian had gone back to his colleagues in the Audi. Michael moved forward slowly and once he was a good distance from the watching policemen he stepped into the doorway of a boarded-up shop and removed the comfort-blanket and a teddy bear from the shopping bag. He was sure he wouldn't need either of the items. He already knew the colours of two of the girls, Sandra and Allison, but whilst the teddy bear was all Sandra, the blanket had the colours of other children too. In the confusion of the studio bedlam he had managed to retrieve Ally's blanket and no one had noticed that he'd taken it, not even Jane. He was sure he wouldn't need either of the objects tonight but now, alone in the dark deserted streets, their softness gave him comfort.

He pulled up the collar of his trench coat and with the teddy bear in one hand, and the comfort-blanket in the other, he stepped out onto the dark empty street and began his search.

Up and down he walked scanning the two storey buildings on either side, his head moving as if in a trance. Up one side, down the other, stopping here and there before moving on, but he found no trace of the girls.

It was a shopping street in one of the oldest, most run-down parts of the city. Time and progress had passed it by. The area had not seen good times in many years, if ever at all. It seemed that every second shop was boarded up, and those that still traded during the day were now hidden behind ugly rusting security shutters padlocked to the pavement. There was no life here and as Michael continued his search, his mood and headache worsened. The cold rain continued to spit at him.

There is no life here, he thought.

No life.

In the distance, a rumble of thunder warned of heavier rain to come. When a woman spoke, Michael jumped. He had been sure the street was empty.

"Is the nice gentleman looking for someath? Maybe Mary can help the nice gentleman find wha' he's looking for."

"What?" said Michael, as the young woman stepped out from the shadow of a doorway in front of him.

"There's no need to be shy. Ten for a hand, fifteen ifs you'd like Mary to go down on you and for thirty-five we can go back to your car."

She winked and smiled. He saw that one of her front teeth was chipped.

Mary was wearing a blue imitation leather low-cut top with an ill matched lime green mini-skirt. Her fishnet tights clung to her short beefy legs like taut spider webs and she wore impossibly high stilettos that added at least six inches onto her height. Even with the heels she was still about a foot shorter than Michael. When she saw the teddy bear and blanket she said,

"The weird stuff costs extra, but I don't mind. I'll dress up like a baby if that's what turns you on."

"What? No! I…I'm not here for that. Thank you, but no…thank you."

Mary was the colour of rusty metal and blood-blue beetle shell. She seemed tired and cold. Michael gave her a warm smile.

"Maybe you can help me though," he said, adding quickly, "I'll pay you, of course."

Mary narrowed her eyes suspiciously and stepped back.

"You a copper, are you?" she asked.

"No. No. I'm not the police."

Michael avoided looking in the direction of the parked Audi at the far end of the street.

"I'm looking for someone who has a place around here, or at least I think it's around here. His name is Peter, tall dark haired chap. Posh bloke," said Michael.

Mary continued to squint at him suspiciously.

"I might know where he lives. What's it worth to you?"

Now Michael's eyes narrowed.

"Could be worth a hefty reward if the information is good. But I'll start with a tenner and you won't even have to take your hands out of your pockets."

"I ain't got any pockets, Irish," said Mary sullenly.

Michael took out his wallet, which Mary eyed with what looked like lust, and he passed her a crisp ten-pound note. He slipped the wallet back into the inner pocket of his coat, but kept two twenties in his hand, pinched between finger and thumb, making sure Mary knew that there was more to come if her information was good.

"Well, what have you got then Mary?" he said, the two twenties held just out of her reach.

"Peter, did you say? Yeh I knows Peter. He don't live around here though. He works the docks. I wouldn't call him posh either. I think he's a Jew boy or one o' them Muslims."

"No. That's not the guy I'm lookin' for. My guy is a sharp dresser, has a posh voice and I'd say he likes it rough." If Peter Wesley came here so frequently for sex Mary must have met him, thought Michael.

"He owe you money does 'e Irish?" asked Mary.

"Something like that. He's got something that doesn't belong to him. Never mind. It doesn't matter. Here Mary, get yourself something to eat and get indoors. It looks like it's really going to start raining soon."

Michael leaned forward and handed Mary the forty pounds. When he did so he noticed other colours around Mary. There were soft oranges and lemons radiating from her. They were warm and they shimmered around her eyes and they pulsed below her heart. They were beautiful and arresting and were far stronger than the blues he'd seen earlier.

Michael raised an eyebrow and smiled.

"Seen something you like, Irish?" she said snatching the money from his hand.

"Yes," he said mysteriously.

Mary looked stunned. She seemed unable to speak, or move. She just stared at him. Michael noticed a change come over her. It was as if she'd been wearing a mask and the mask had suddenly fallen away. The woman was gone and he now looked into the face of a little girl, an innocent face full of joyful hope and excited promise.

Mary lowered her eyes.

"Thank you for trying to help me Mary," he said.

There was nothing here. The search had been a complete waste of time, he thought.

He turned and began to walk away.

"Hey, Irish," Mary called after him, "this guy, Peter, 'e into threesomes, is 'e?"

Michael stopped and turned around.

"What? What do you mean?"

"'e the sort of guy, who'd bring his girlfriend along for the ride, is 'e?"

"I'm not sure I understand, Mary."

"His names not Peter, I know that for sure. Jack's 'is name and 'er name's Jill. Posh both of 'em. Both like it rough. The bitch nearly strangled me with 'er claws. Real psycho bitch that one. Still have the marks on me, see?" She lifted her head and Michael saw claw marks on either side of her throat.

The hairs stood up on the back of Michael's neck.

"They came here?" he said.

"Hey!" said Mary, "Jack 'n' Jill, 'ow about that? I never did notice that before. Jack 'n' fuckin' Jill. Like them two kids that went up the hill."

"They came here?" Michael said again.

"Oh yeh. They had a little spot they liked, in the alley behind."

With a flick of her head she pointed to a dark recess on the other side of the street that Michael had taken for a recessed doorway. Her large gold coloured earrings sparkled in the soft rain as she did so.

"That's an alley?" he said.

"Yeh. You want to see Irish?"

Michael thought for a moment. It might be a trap. If he followed her he'd be out of view of Horse and the other policemen in the parked car and she could mug him for the rest of the money in his wallet or maybe she had a pimp waiting in the shadows with a knife. In his mind Michael heard Horse's parting words: Don't be a hero.

"Want to see where Jack and Jill liked to 'urt Mary, Irish?"

Michael thought of Mary's colours and the little girl that was there beneath the garish make-up and gaudy outfit.

He nodded.

"Sure, Mary. Lead the way."

With that, Michael followed Mary into the shadows, under an almost invisible archway and into a dark secluded service yard at the back of the shops.

*

The yard smelt worse than the street and it was much darker too. There were only one or two working lights and these had yellowed over the years. There were tall metal bins everywhere. Those under the yellow lights cast long ominous shadows that looked like fallen gravestones on the wet stone floor. The service yard was a swirling wind-trap and there was a sickly stench that Michael found almost vomit-inducing. There was a scuttling sound coming from somewhere toward the back which Michael guessed were rats. He tried to block out the noise. He wasn't fond of rats.

Mary made her way toward one of the lights which was located high on the wall above a set of concrete steps that lead down to an unseen basement. Michael followed her cautiously.

"They liked to do me on these stairs, 'im behind and 'er above me," Mary was saying.

When he caught up with her Michael stopped. Mary continued to tell him about the unusual sexual habits Jack and Jill but Michael was no longer listening.

On the wall at the top of the stairs leading down into a shadowy pit, Michael spotted splashes of colour he recognised. There was more colour on the painted metal handrail that ran down the side of the stairs and more again on the wall. Mary didn't see the colours. She couldn't. Only Michael could see them and to him they were unmistakable. The colours on the handrail were Amanda's. The colours on the wall belonged to Allison Wesley. Amanda's colours were fading. He knew he'd have to hurry.

Instinctively he squeezed on the teddy bear and approached the top of the steep steps.

"Mary," he said. His voice was low but commanding.

"Listen to me Mary. There are three men sitting in a parked Audi up the road. I'll give you one hundred pounds if you go get them and bring them back here now."

She looked at him.

"Wha?" she stammered.

"Mary. You are not in trouble. I promise you. They are policemen, but they aren't interested in you. Tell them Michael sent you. Tell them that we've found the girls. Please Mary bring them back here and run Mary. Please hurry!"

Without waiting for a response Michael grabbed the wet and slippery handrail and descended carefully into the darkness.

Chapter 5.

A re you sure? There are no lights and no sounds coming from in there," said DCI Wally Griffin. He sounded both annoyed and sceptical.

The five of them were huddled at the bottom of the concrete steps with only two torches between them. The yellow glow from the wall light above their heads was useless. Wally had his ear to the solid timber door. There was a metal bracket above his head securing the door to its frame with a heavy duty padlock. The padlock was shiny and looked new. It seemed quite out of place amongst the squalor. Wally banged his fist on the door for a second time. The action caused him to sneeze. There was still no sound from inside. Before anyone could reply Mary spoke up. Confident now that these policemen were not here to arrest her for soliciting, Mary had relaxed considerably, but nonetheless, she stayed close to Michael. Michael was still her client. He had given her one hundred and fifty pounds, which she stashed in a secret hiding place beneath her lime green skirt, and she would stay with him as long as he wanted her to. She liked Michael. She trusted him and although she had no idea what was hidden in the cellar or what these men were after, she was now as curious as they were to find out what was behind the door.

"Oh yeh, I'm sure," she said in answer the DCI's question, "This is the place alright, this is where they liked to do me." It's quiet here. No one ever comes into the yard at night. Rats and stink. But *they* didn't mind. It was quiet and they like to scream. Like wolves they were, both of them! Howling so loud, they'd wake the dead. Just like wolves. Yeh and laughin' too, all the time. They liked to hurt me. I still got the marks. Oh yeh. This is the place alright".

"Did they ever go inside" asked Horse. He didn't look at Mary when he spoke, but continued to scrutinise the padlock.

"Naw. We waz only ever out here on the steps. It's the only light in the courtyard," she said. "It's always on. I think it's busted. I suppose they wanted to see what they were doin'."

"Did you ever see the door open?" Horse asked.

"No. It was always dark down here. Scared me to tell you the truth, but they paid well. Honest though, I 'ope I never see them again."

Mary moved closer to Michael.

"This is it. The girls have been here Brian. We need to hurry," said Michael.

"Right. Go get the crowbar from the trunk Rich and call for back up."

Before Constable Cannings started back up the stairs DCI Griffin spoke up.

"Hold on a minute Hopkins, we don't know what's in there, if anything at all. I don't want half of Norwich woken up in the middle of the night on a wild goose chase, based on the visions of Mystic Meg here. I'm not sure we should even consider ￠ forcing entry. Let's think this through."

"Get the crowbar Cannings or do I have to get it myself?" said Horse with a snarl, "Go on."

Cannings hesitated but when the DCI didn't stop him a second time he climbed the concrete stairs, taking two at a time.

Cannings got back just as Wally Griffin was saying "…and you can consider yourself suspended if you attempt to force that lock DI Hopkins."

Cannings passed the heavy crowbar to Horse.

"Well Sir, if you don't want to be an accessory to the fact I'd look away now," said Horse and then he wedged the short end of the crowbar between the door frame and the metal bracket and, with one strong yank, ripped the bracket away from the timber. Then he turned around and shone the torch directly into Mary's face.

"Mary? That's your name isn't it?" said Horse, turning to Mary.

"Yeh?" she stammered. She squeezed against Michael.

"We found the door like this, okay? You're a witness Mary. It was busted when we got here. Okay?"

It only took Mary a moment to understand what the big policeman had said.

"Oh yeh! The door. Yeh, that's right. It was busted when we got here. I'll swear to that in court of law," she said with a smile.

"Good girl, Mary, good girl," said Horse.

They entered the basement room in single file and what they found there suggested that DCI Wally Griffin had been right and that there was nothing to find. It was an innocuous if untidy storeroom filled with display dummies, boxes of coat hangers and other clutter commonly found in the back rooms of small businesses. They only thing they couldn't find was a light switch.

"You see Hopkins. I told you. There's nothing here," said Wally Griffin. There was anger in his voice.

"Wait," said Michael. He pointed the torch to the back corner, "look over there, behind those boxes. There's another door."

"And another padlock," said Cannings, who'd hardly said a word since getting back from getting the crowbar.

"That door leads probably leads into the back of the shop. This operation is over Hopkins. We go no further I will not be party to this, breaking into a shop," said the DCI and he turned to leave.

"Not so fast. If that leads to the shop, which by the way must be one floor above us, why is the padlock on this side of the door?" said Horse.

Griffin stopped in his tracks and turned around. The group shuffled forward, with both torches trained on the new padlock. Mary clung to Michael's arm.

"Well Guv? In for a penny in for a pound?" said Horse and then, without further ado, ripped the second padlock away from the door. It clattered noisily across the floor.

The door swung out toward them and came to a stop against the back wall. Michael noticed that it was much thicker and heavier than the outer door and that rubber seals had been fixed to the frame to give the door an airtight seal when it was closed. Like a freezer door, he thought. Beyond the door was a short corridor that curved away to the right. There was a light switch on the wall. Horse stretched out his hand and flicked it on. Fluorescent tubes stuttered noisily into life, both in the corridor and in the unseen room beyond. When lights stopped banging,

Horse and the others heard the whimpering. It sounded like frightened animals. Horse looked at Wally Griffin who suddenly looked frightened. Without warning, he sneezed loudly. From somewhere beyond the bend in the corridor they heard a child scream. Horse moved forward. The others followed close behind.

"It's the police. Don't move. We have the place surrounded," shouted Wally over Horse's shoulder.

That's when all the girls started screaming.

*

The six little girls were huddled together at the back of a large animal cage that occupied a third of the cellar floor. Most of the girls were semi naked, all of them continued screaming.

"It's okay. It's okay. You're safe now," said Horse as he grappled with a third padlock on the door of the cage. Once that door was opened and it was clear that the girls were too frightened to come out, Mary climbed into the cage and went to comfort them.

"Go get help, Rich. Everything," said Horse.
Constable Cannings looked at the Wally Griffin for approval. The DCI nodded weakly. Wally looked ill. All the blood seemed to have drained from his head, which was wet with sweat, and glowed under the harsh fluorescent light. When Cannings headed back down the corridor, Wally followed him, but stopped when he reached the outer room. Once Canning was out the door and back up the stairs, Wally dropped to his knees and began to hyperventilate. Then he started to cry.

Horse and Michael checked out the rest of the inner cellar. The air in the room was thick with the smell of fug and bleach that seemed to rises from bare concrete floor and ooze from the rough crumbling brick walls. Everything in the room containing the cage was filthy. Within the cage there was a single cracked toilet bowl fixed to the back wall. Next to it there was a low matching wash-hand basin. On the floor were three large stainless steel bowls, containing bits of bruised fruit and old vegetables.

"It's like an animal holding pen," whispered Horse, "Why Michael? Why do this?"

"Look, Brian, there's another door," said Michael, pointing back toward the corridor.

The door was hidden in a shadowy corner behind the entrance door. On the floor next to it, was a large pile of mouldy blankets covered in yellow fur. Michael could see insects scuttling about between the folds of heavy material. He and Horse moved forward cautiously. The girls in the cage, over their shoulder, went quiet. The door was not locked. Horse turned the knob carefully and pushed it open. A light flickered on automatically. What lay beyond was even more shocking than the squalor of the cage cellar.

The second room was smaller than the first and was dominated by an ornate king-sized bed which was covered with beautifully pressed satin sheets and matching pillowcases. The wall behind the bed was wallpapered and included a large framed painting of a beautiful coastal scene. The floor beneath and around the bed was carpeted. Trendy lamps sat on trendy bedside tables and a phone and a digital clock completed the illusion of normalcy. It reminded Michael of the television studio of "Good Afternoon Norwich" and the illusion of a studio set was reinforced by the addition of an expensive looking digital camcorder that sat on a tripod at the foot of the bed. Under the legs of the tripod were two boxes containing neatly arranged recordable DVDs.

On one side of the bed, hidden behind an ornate hardwood Japanese screen, was a hanging rail containing various leather costumes and masks. Behind these was a wall-rack holding whips, studded bondage straps and what looked like medieval implements of torture. Michael felt ill and when his imagination began to flood his mind with images of what might have gone on in the bedroom, he had to get out. He went back to the girls and found them all huddled around and clinging to Mary. She was crying but he could hear her whispering to them.

"It's okay Sweeties. It's okay. You're all safe now," she was saying in a voice he didn't recognise.

*

The rain, that had been promised all night, arrived with a vengeance, shortly after Constable Cannings reached the concrete steps and he was soaked to the skin before he reached the Audi.

The rain was thick and loud, pounding the cobbled streets and slate roofs of the old city, and it did it's best to extinguish the red and blue flashing lights of the emergency vehicles that came rushing to the scene. The ambulances rattled under its terrible onslaught, and the heavy black sky held back the approaching dawn.

Within two hours of the discovery, Horse stood wide-eyed and defiant at the centre of the service yard, letting the rain wash the tears from his upturned face. His hands were balled into tight fists and he shook with anger. To the paramedics and policemen that moved up and down the steps with focussed determination, he looked like a boxer preparing to enter the ring for a fight. Arc lights cast long shadows in all directions. Near the archway, two figures were huddled together under the inadequate protection of a trench coat. Mary clung to Michael and squeezed Amanda's teddy bear. Michael hugged her and she sobbed and gulped like a child. None of the people who moved purposefully in and out of the white rectangular tent that had been quickly erected over the steps leading down to the crime scene, paid them any attention.

*

The six surviving children were taken away in three separate ambulances, whist the remains of two little dead girls, whose bodies were found under the filthy pile of blankets in the corner, had been removed by a police van to the coroner's office. The cordoned off crime scene extended to an area a quarter of a mile in every direction.

The crimes committed by the Wesley's, to their own daughter and the daughters of others, changed the lives of the five witnesses forever. DCI Wally Griffin became a national hero. He was awarded a medal of commendation. During his many press briefings and television appearances, in the weeks that followed the grim discovery, he never once mentioned Michael's involvement, saying only that the police had been acting on a reliable tip-off. Whilst the completed DVDs found in the box under the legs of the tripod had been produced to such an expert degree that the identity of the two adult participants was impossible to prove, a discarded DVD, found under the remains of one of the dead girls, contained *outtake* material which showed both Peter and Jane Wesley with their masks removed. How the DVD had found its way into the hands of one of the dead girls was never satisfactorily explained. Mary Angela Price received the financial reward offered by the families for information leading to the discovery of their missing girls and with the money, she left the streets of Norwich forever. Brian Horse Hopkins requested, and was granted, a transfer to narcotics. Within three months he had moved to the south coast. Constable Richard Cannings suffered from post-traumatic stress disorder and retired from the police force on medical grounds. A year after the incident.

When Horse called to Michael's flat, a week or so after the terrible night, he was informed by Michael's landlady that her nice Irish tenant was gone and that he had left no forwarding address. She added that she would miss him very much.

Michael X, television mystic and sometime police consultant left Norwich days after the discovery without a word to anyone, and he disappeared so completely, it was as if he had never been there at all.

Part Two

"Tá an fharraige míshuaimhneasach inniu
tar éis na gaoithe móire."
"The sea itself is unsettled today after the storm."

Chapter 6.

Fourteen Months Later

The early April mid-morning sky was clear of any clouds and the day was unusually sunny. Despite a gusty wind that came and went like stuttered applause, the sea between the mainland and the island appeared to be sleeping. With a noisy report the open-topped ferry trundled forward at an even steady pace, although the waiting secluded harbour, the only safe landing place on this, the mainland side of the island, was still completely hidden from view.

"At least another fifteen minutes," said the pilot gruffly without being asked. Despite his words some of the passengers near him began arranging their baggage ready to disembark. One or two even edged towards the break in the railing where the gangway would be positioned. There was a general air of anticipation and relief. The ferry smelt of rotting seaweed, diesel and sea sickness.

Given the usually wild and unpredictable weather experienced off the North West coast of Ireland, an open-topped ferry seemed wholly unfit for the purpose of safely taking passengers the more than four mile journey to and from the island, and yet it had been continuing on its way, defying the odds, non-stop for almost twenty years. The St. Kevin was old, rusting and very noisy but it persisted, day in day out, just like the two men that travelled with her, twice a day, all year around.

The *St. Kevin* could legally carry one hundred passengers, but during the summer months it regularly carried more than that. It had no interior space, unless you counted the tiny engine compartment under the pilot's feet. Even the small bridge was nothing more than a partially covered rusting wind shield, with a long slit window of Perspex which had yellowed so completely that it was now almost opaque. The overweight pilot spent most of the journey with his body bent to one side so that he could see around the pillar that formed one end of the bridge wall, although he did so more out of habit than necessity. He was so familiar with the routes to and from the island he could probably have made the journeys with his eyes closed.

All the available seating was on the wide rear deck behind the bridge. There was a small amount of standing room at the front of the ferry, but this space was usually only ever populated by brave noisy children.

The seating was in the form of back to back timber slated benches in three rows, separated by two wide aisles. The aisles were often packed tight with standing passengers, but on this April day there was a lot of room to move about. The seating and aisles were covered by a single taut orange and white striped awning that rattled violently eight foot above the wet deck. It defused midday sunlight, when there was any, and gave limited protection to the travellers in light vertical rain. The sides of the boat were completely open and for most journeys, when Atlantic winds and rain joined forces, the coloured awning was next to useless at keeping any of the seated passengers dry. Regular travellers wore heavy coats or wind-breakers. The uninitiated often arrived on the island soaked to the skin. But today it was sunny and the sea appeared calm. The ferry was only half full and most of the travellers were comfortable.

The ferry's ticket collector, and self-appointed tour guide, stood beside the pilot at the bridge. He held a microphone and spoke, virtually non-stop for most of the fifty-minute journey. He read from a script, most of which he'd been reading from for nearly two decades. His voice, distorted by tinny loud speakers fixed to the awning support posts, contained neither conviction nor enthusiasm.

"As I mentioned earlier, the island of Skellig Éin was first visited by St Áedán at the beginning of the sixth century and it was on the wild desolate rock, a mile off the north western coast of Ireland, that he built his hermitage and, with the help of newly converted mainlanders, laid the foundations for a chapel dedicated to Our Lady of the Gentle Sheppard. As you may know, this is a very special year in the history of Skellig Éin, being the fifteen hundredth anniversary of the founding of the Christian mission on the island. The current Prior of the monastery, Father Francis will lead a weeklong celebration of prayer and reflection in June, culminating on the 20th with the famous candle-lit midnight procession, which begins at the gates of the Priory and ends at the site of the old chapel and holy well in Ballyhoary. The procession takes the dangerous clifftop walk, a route St. Áedán used to evade capture by marauding villains, many of whom fell to their death in their efforts to catch the saint. We expect the island will be overrun with pilgrims and tourists for the week in June, but you are coming at a quieter time," the guide said with a disinterested smile.

He was a bird-like man, tall and gangly with a long pointed nose and a slight permanent stoop. When he moved, which was rarely, he did so in slow manoeuvres, like a wounded ostrich. He spoke with an affected accent, his words pinched and precise, like a television newsreader, but every so often he'd say something that betrayed his west of Ireland country roots. He'd talk of "demon beeests" and "the wawters from de migic well." Only a very few of the passengers ever listened to him. Most of the travellers were pilgrims who generally came in excited groups and who, more often than not spent the journey chatting amongst themselves. The priests and nuns on the boat, which there was always a few, knew the story well already not to bother listening to him, and any student or lecturer from Galway University, which had a large campus on Skellig Éin, dismissed the stories of holy wells, demon monsters and a saint that apparently had lived to be over a hundred and fifty years old, as just religious hocus-pocus. There were always one or two locals on every crossing, frequent travellers who had heard the spiel so many times that they could, if asked to, probably recite it word for word.

Every now and again the human ostrich raised his head and surveyed the passengers under the awning. His eyes invariably focussed first on a particularly beautiful woman sitting on her own against the railing in the first row of seats. She was an island woman and a regular on the ferry. Whenever she travelled she always sat on her own, in more or less the same place, at the end of the bench against the rail. She was in her mid-thirties but she wore an old woman's head scarf and a heavy ugly duffel coat, neither of which could disguise her beauty. She ignored him, and all the other men on the ferry watching her, and instead stared blankly out across the ocean for the entire trip.

After a little while the guide returned to his recital.

"It has been estimated that St. Áedán lived to the ripe old age of one hundred and fifty-three. Legend has it that the holy man found the secret of eternal youth on Skellig Éin. Over the centuries travellers and pilgrims, like yourselves, have braved the unpredictable currents of the wild Atlantic Ocean to reach the island. Some come in search of sanctuary, others in search of miraculous cures attributed to the black waters of the holy well. A drop on the tongue has been known to cure many ailments. There is a great deal of documented scientific evidence that strange and wondrous things have happened on the island of Skellig Éin."

The guide continued to drone on and on and neither he, nor the rotund pilot standing beside him, noticed that trouble was brewing on the benches directly behind the beautiful woman in the head scarf.

*

Michael Eustace did his best to pretend he hadn't heard her, but when the young woman sitting on the bench opposite him kicked him hard on the shin with the scuffed toe of a pointy shoe, he had to sit up and take notice.

"Hey! Rick's tawkin ta yez. Didn't ye hear him?"

She spoke quickly and with an inner-city Dublin accent. Michael tried to focus, but his mind was elsewhere. The ferry rolled forward and sea spray raced across the side of his face. He was sweating profusely, despite the strong cool sea breeze. The woman, in her mid-twenties, leaned forward and held her face less than a foot from his. Michael stared at her and she smiled vacantly at him. She raised her left hand and pointed to someone sitting to her right.

"Rick asked you a question. Didn't ye hear him?" she said again. Her strawberry blond hair wobbled slightly when she spoke.

"I said, do I fucking know you from somewhere, old man?" said the one named Rick. The blond sat back so that Michael and Rick could face each other. Rick had a cruel face but soft baby-blue eyes that were as pale and unusual as Michael's own. They made him look kind, thought Michael. But looks can be deceiving. Rick's colours were greys and silvers. Cold. Cruel. Calculating.

He spoke like the woman but slower, emphasising every syllable, as if he was speaking to idiot. A nervous snigger rose from the rest of the group sitting around Michael. There were three other men, none of them older than twenty five, and Michael guessed that all five were together. Michael was certain that none of them were locals, pilgrims nor university students. He dropped his eyes and stared at the wet floor, and wished he was somewhere else. Anywhere else.

"Well?" snapped Rick.

"Kick'em again Megan," said one of the other young men and the whole group laughed.

"Do...I...fuckin'...know...you...from...some...where?" said Rick again. There was anger in the Dubliners' voice.

Michael slowly raised his head. He felt ill and was nursing one of his very bad headaches. And he didn't like boats. He looked at Rick again, then grimaced.

"I...doubt...it," he whispered, then lowered his head. The gesture appeared dismissive. Rick got to his feet, towering over Michael.

"What did you say?" he hissed.

The man sitting next to Michael, a freakish blond monster covered in tattoos and piercings, slid sideways along the bench, leaving space for Rick to sit down. As he did so he nudged the smallest of the group off the end of the bench and onto the wet floor. There was another explosion of laughter.

"Ha ha. Good one Mo! Yah Rats, ye fuckin' eegit," said the brute who had been sitting on the other side of Rick. Rats stood up quickly, wiped the back of his pants and sat back down, red faced.

"Sorry 'bout dat Rats," said the blond monster called Mo, before bursting out laughing too.

"Fuck off Mo, and fuck you Lash," sneered Rats. Their laughter quickly died away when Rick slumped down on the bench beside Michael. Rick put his lips close to Michael's ear.

"What did you fuckin' say to me, cun'?" he spat.

Michael turned and saw Rick slip a hand into the pocket of his trousers and withdraw what looked like a closed flick-knife.

Michael opened his mouth to speak just as the ferry pitched forward over a rising wave. The boat lurched quickly into the deep basin left in the wave's wake and then shuddered almost to a complete stop, before being scooped up at the other side of the swell. Michael's stomach heaved in response and bitter bile rose in his throat. He knew what was coming so he tried to turn away but wasn't quick enough. His gut clenched and he retched all over the shoes of the young woman who had kicked him earlier.

"Agh fuck, me fuckin' shoes," Megan screamed. Rick jumped away, knocked into Mo who, in turn, sent Rats off the end of the bench again. Megan continued to scream.

"Shut the fuck up Megan, will ya, it's only yer fuckin' shoes. I'll buy yiz another pair when dis fucker gives me 'is wallet," said Rick.

Megan ignored him. She didn't move and would have stayed like that, hunched over and wailing, had Michael not thrown up again. This time some of his vomit splashed onto the ends of Rick's trousers. This time Rick screamed.

"Fuck! You did that on purpose, you fuckin' cun'. You're goin' ta fuckin' pay for dat!"

When Michael heard the click of the opening flick-knife he squeezed his eyes shut, pressed himself tight against the railings and braced himself for the imminent assault.

Chapter 7.

Two tall, well-built men, wearing similar coloured suits, made their way up the aisle. When they reached the scene of the commotion, the older of the two tapped Rick on the shoulder.

"What's that you got in your 'and mate? I 'ope you're not thinking of doin' somethin' silly now." The man spoke with a pronounced London cockney accent.

Rick turned around and looked up at the two men. They both stared down at him. He narrowed his eyes, defiantly. After a moments consideration, he retracted the blade and let the flick-knife slip back into his pocket.

"I wiz doin' nothin'. Just talkin' to the man" he said.

"Better be nothin', cos' if I have to turn out your pockets and I find something I shouldn't, there is no knowing what I might do," said the Englishman.

"You a Garda are yiz?" said Rick.

The Englishman didn't reply.

"Fuckin' Brit. That's wha' ya iz," she Megan. "Look at me fuckin' shoes. They're ruined. I can't wear dem now, they're mingin."

The younger of the two men, who was perfectly groomed and looked, for all the world, like a wealthy business executive, approached Rick.

"Why don't you and your friends go sit down there at the back of the boat and there'll be no trouble. You don't want trouble, do you?" he said, just above a whisper.

Unlike his companion he spoke with a posh Dublin accent. Rick stared at him for a little while, then signalled to his friends with a flick of his head. The three young men, Mo, Lash and Rats, stood up. All eyes were on Rick who had returned his attention to the Englishman. Although Rick was a head shorter than the Londoner, he stared defiantly up at him, just long enough to show he wasn't frightened or intimidated, before pushing past him and heading for the back of the ferry. His three friends followed without a word. Passengers, standing in the aisle, moved aside to let them past.

The young woman called Megan was last to get to her feet. Before standing up, she whispered something into Michael ear. He didn't respond or even move, but remained hunched over, with his head almost in his lap. Before following her friends to the back of the ferry, Megan stopped and looked up at the Englishman, just as Rick had done. He smiled at her. She didn't smile back.

"Yez nothin' bu' a fuckin' English prick," she hissed.

*

Soon the ferry passengers went back to doing whatever they had been doing before the incident had begun, and the two men sat down, opposite each other, on the seats vacated by Rick and the other three men. The Englishman sat on the bench opposite Michael, but down from him, so as to avoid stepping in the vomit on the floor. The Dubliner took the seat next to Michael. As soon as he sat down he tapped Michael gently on the arm.

"You should drink some water, it will help," he said.
Michael slowly turned and, raising his eyes rather than lifting his head, looked up at the Dubliner. After breaking the seal and removing the cap, the Dubliner handed Michael a bottle of Ballygowen.

"Thank you," said Michael taking the water with a shaky hand. He drank in slow measured gulps, without raising his head.

The Englishman hardly registered the exchange between his companion and Michael. His full attention was elsewhere, distracted by someone on the seat behind him.

As soon as he sat down, the Englishman stretched his arms out across the back of the slated bench, which he now had to himself, and one of his fingers accidently caressed the neck of the woman sitting behind him. He felt her flinch. When he turned to apologise he came face to face with the most beautiful woman he'd ever seen. She had the face of an angel. She looked cross and seemed to be about to say something, but then didn't. Instead, she just stared at him. Before she averted her eyes, the look of anger on her face was replaced by one of frightened bewilderment. When the Englishman tried to speak he found himself tongue-tied and dry-mouthed, like a teenage boy in the presence of the prettiest girl in the school. She turned away from him before he said anything and left him staring at the back of her head. After a while, he sighed and then turned back to face his companion. When he did so, he saw and recognised Michael. The Englishman gasped.

"Well, fuck me said the queen bee, is that you, Michael X?" he said.

Michael lowered his eyes to the floor. His cheeks were red and his face was wet. He looked like he might get sick again. When the sky darkened, he shivered.

"That is you, Michael Eustace. I know it is. It's me. Horse!" declared the Englishman, with gusto.

When Michael didn't move Horse leaned forward and brought his head down to Michael's knee level, then looked up at Michael, as if examining him over the rim of a pair of invisible spectacles. Michael raised his head in the same slow motion he had used when addressing Rick, and offered Horse a weak smile.

"Hey, Brian," he managed.

"Jeez, Michael, that's no way to greet an ol' mate. How have you been? You look like shite, by the way," said Horse.

"Thanks, Brian. I see you've lost none of your English charm," said Michael.

"Jeez Michael, where did you go? I thought you'd died or something."

The Dubliner sitting beside Michael looked at Horse and raised his eyebrows.

Horse smiled.

"This is Michael X, Paul. My Irish friend, from Norwich, the one I told you about? The consultant I worked with in England, back in the day. Remember, I told you about 'im? The TV celebrity?"

"Oh right," said Paul, unconvincingly.

Michael lowered his head again and drank some more water.

"Oh yeh, now I remember. You're the psychic!" said Paul.

Horse stared across at his colleague and gritted his teeth dramatically.

Michael sat bolt upright and looked angrily across at his English friend.

"I'm not a psychic," he snapped.

"Hey, I never called you a psychic," protested Horse, raising his hands in a gesture of submission, "I only ever use the scientific term *spooky Irish mystic* when telling people about your wondrous abilities…at dinner parties and the like."

Horse's face lit up with a cheeky grin.

Michael guffawed a little.

"Seriously though Michael, one day you're 'ere and the next you're gone. Not a word. Not a postcard. Not even a *Dear John* letter? It's been over a year."

Michael spoke slowly.

"I had no idea you cared so much, Brian. Anyway, after what happened, we all got blown in different directions, didn't we? The simple truth is, I had to get away. I'd had enough. I don't think the BBC was sorry to see me go, either. I got out before I became famous for the wrong reasons. Something else came up and I had to come home. I did try to contact you, once, a few weeks after, but they said you had left. Stationed elsewhere; reassigned; something like that. Then, life got in the way, you know how it is, Brian."

Horse just nodded.

Michael stared up at the massive cliffs of the island that now towered above the ferry and blocked his view of most of the sky. The harbour was nowhere to be seen.

"Are we nearly there?" he said, as a rolling wave seemed to drain the blood from his face. The earlier clear blue sky had vanished completely and the sea suddenly looked angry. Heavy clouds, that seemed to have come from nowhere, looked swollen and ready to release their load.

"We'll be there in about five minutes" said Paul.

"I hate boats" said Michael, almost to himself.

"It's probably the sea you hate" said Paul, then added, "apparently your body thinks it's being poisoned and reacts by forcing you to throw up."

"This is Superintendent Paul Creagan," said Horse with a wave of his hand, "and as you can see, he's the comedian of the partnership. Paul, this is Michael Eustace, sometimes known as Michael X."

"That was a long time ago. That person no longer exists, Brian," said Michael, taking another mouthful of the water. Michael smiled at Paul Creagan and said,

"Thanks for the water and nice to meet you Paul," and, with a nod toward Horse, he added, "and can I just say, how very sorry I am, for all your troubles."

"Huh?" said Paul.

"Ha, ha!" said Horse with a jaunty shake of his head, "now that's the old Mickey I remember. Well, well, well, isn't this turning out to be a most interesting day."

*

At the back of the ferry Rick Kavanagh stood in stony-faced silence. His crew, with the exception of Megan his girlfriend, stood slightly apart and were not talking either. Megan was bent over trying to clean the sick off her shoes with a wad of wet tissues. She was still cursing and complaining.

Rick turned his back on them and stared into the foaming wake of the boat. The ocean was as black as the sky above it and the mainland of Ireland had vanished behind a dark horizon. It looked like it was going to start raining.

That was the least of Rick's worries.

Kavanagh knew they were going to be late and Mr G was not going to be happy. He'd hold Rick responsible, even though it wasn't Rick's fault. The ferry had left forty minutes later than it was supposed to. *Engine trouble*, according to the fat-fuck pilot. Kavanagh had wanted to punch him and the creepy ticket collector and then the puke guy. Rick really wanted to hurt somebody. Mr G would be angry and, worse still, disappointed. He might even want to hurt Rick, to make an example of him, so that the others would understand that there is no messing with Mr G.

Rick imagined the scene in his head. He could hear Mr G's voice.

"When I say, be here at ten, I mean ten. Not ten past ten. Not five past ten. Not one minute past ten." Mr G's spoke with a mid-Atlantic accent, a mixture of inner-city Dublin and American east coast gangster. Mr G, the *Tony Saprano* of Sheriff Street. The accent was derisory and comical, except that no one would dare laugh at Mr G, not if they wanted to continue breathing. "So, how do you think it makes me look, when you stroll in here forty minutes late, with not a care in the world? You see how disrespectful that is to me? How do you think it makes me feel? And tell me, Rick, how do I make this right? What do you think I should do? How do I make this right?"

And then Mr G. would give a sign, just like they do in the gangster movies, and one of his goons would step in, maybe that big blond psycho Russian guy, and then something bad would happen, something real bad.

In the distance there was a rumble of thunder. Rick shivered. He knew it had little to do with the sudden drop in temperature. A chilly wind had come out of nowhere and a storm was definitely brewing. If it started to rain they'd have to move back up the boat to the cover of the awning, back toward the policemen. Rick wondered about them. Why were they here? Why were they heading to the pilgrim's island? Rick didn't recognise the Englishman but the other man, the Dubliner, looked very familiar. He was sure he was a cop and that he'd seen him in Dublin. Rick took out his phone and turned back to face the front of the boat. When he was sure no one was watching, he stole half a dozen photographs of the two suits. He thought that the photographs may be something Mr G would be interested in; something of a distraction; something to take Mr G's mind off thoughts of disrespect or of *making things right*.

*

Marie Joyce hadn't moved when the commotion started over her shoulder, but instead made a point of ignoring it and continuing to stare out to sea. Once the young woman sitting directly behind her had started screaming, the lady sitting on the bench beside Marie stood up and took her young son to the front of the boat. No one occupied the two vacant places left behind, which suited Marie just fine.

As soon as the commotion really got going the man sitting opposite Marie lowered his head and fixed his eyes on the floor. This pleased her too because he'd been staring at her since they left the harbour. She had spent most of the journey avoiding his lascivious attention. She found him disgusting. He was in his forties but was trying hard to look younger. He wore very revealing luminous yellow skin-tight Lycra leggings and the type of hoodie only teenagers wear. Marie had seen him slip his wedding ring into one of the skinny pockets of his pants before he sat down opposite her. She immediately wanted to get up and move seats but didn't because she didn't want to have a creepy man forcing her to do so. So, instead, she stayed, scowled at him and then ignored him completely. She would have loved to tell him to "fuck off" but that was not an option when a woman and her little boy sat down beside her.

Marie Joyce was used to the unwanted attention of strangers. Like most young women, Marie was constantly being looked at by men. But, in Marie's case, most men didn't just stare, they leered at her. She was stunningly beautiful and her dark brown eyes were hypnotic. Even other women stared at Marie. Despite, or because of this, Marie was obsessively self-conscious. When she looked in a mirror she didn't see beauty, she saw flaws. In her opinion her nose was crooked and her nostrils too wide. She was obsessed with a permanent, but tiny, skin blemish under her left eye and she hated the sight of her large pouty lips. She kept her brown hair cut short, tom-boy fashion, because, if left to its own devices, it grew wild and unruly. She made a point of wearing dowdy clothes, which hid her fit slender body. When someone looked at Marie, her instinctive reaction was to look away. She knew that doing this made her appear rude and she was aware of the fact that people thought she was stuck-up, haughty and odd. At first this bothered her, but over time she convinced herself that other people's opinions didn't matter. Martha, Marie's older sister and her business partner in M & M's Coffee Emporium, a thriving café in Ballyhoary, and an elderly retired doctor, were her only real friends. Marie kept to herself and found comfort and pleasure in oil painting and rock climbing, both of which were very solitary pursuits. Although a fiercely independent woman, the truth was that Marie Joyce was shy and lonely.

Marie continued to stare out to sea and went on ignoring what was happening over her shoulder even when the two men in suits came to break up the trouble. When the older of the two men flopped down behind her and spread his arms out wide across the top of the bench, one of his hands momentarily touched the collar of her coat and a stray finger gently brushed the hairs on the back of her neck. She flinched, and so did he. She turned around and got ready to release a tirade of angry invective. The man turned too. He opened his mouth, but said nothing. When their eyes met

Marie found she couldn't say anything either. He looked familiar, particularly his eyes, and Marie suddenly thought of someone else; someone from her past. Time seemed to slow and Marie held the stranger's gaze for much longer than she wanted to. Finally, she reverted to instinct, turned and looked away.

Staring out into the dark ocean Marie felt tears well up. When she raised her hands to cover her face she found that they were trembling.

It is only the salty wind, Marie told herself.

It's only the wind.

*

The ferry finally thumped and scraped against the side of the stone pier and the pilot quickly tied her up. Within ten minutes the boat was empty, save for the captain, the guide and the slowly emerging figure of Michael Eustace.

Michael had taken business cards from both Brian and Paul, with a promise to meet them for a drink over the next few days. When they left him for their shuttle bus, he was feeling better. As the boat emptied the guide finished his story. Only Michael was listened. The guide spoke of a great battle between St Áedán and the Devil, in a dark world that exists somewhere between Hell and Earth, deep in the caves under Skellig Éin.

"The island of Skellig Éin is home to some of the deepest caves anywhere in the world. It is estimated that less than ten percent of them have been discovered, and fewer again, fully explored. There are stories told of demons and monsters that dwell in the deepest parts of the caves, hiding in the darkness, waiting for Satan's return. St Áedán brought Christianity and enlightenment to the island of Skellig Éin, but he didn't manage to rid the inhabitants of their ancient beliefs in vampires, banshees and winged satanic beasts."

Although feeling better, Michael was unsure on his feet as he finally moved forward toward the gangway. Before disembarking he apologised to the pilot and the guide. Neither of the men said goodbye or offered to help him with his luggage. Michael concluded that both men were glad to see him off their boat and, all things being considered, so was he.

Chapter 8.

Brother Benjamin skipped dangerously fast down the wide steps leading from the carpark to the harbour and pier. He held the hem of his cassock above the top of his woollen ankle socks, as if tiptoeing across a shallow stream. His rubber-soled sandals made very little noise as they padded down the hard, sandy surface. The dark clouds that had, not half an hour earlier, threatened a terrible storm, were now completely dissipated and the sky was once again clear and brilliant blue.

Below him the last of the mini buses began to climb the winding tarmac road that led from the small harbour to the inner part of the island. The convoy of packed buses would snake up to the carpark behind him, noisily dropping gears and revving engines in response to the steep incline and narrow winding turns, each one mimicking the actions of the vehicle in front; stopping, starting and stopping again. For those passengers who had found the boat journey difficult, the introduction to solid ground brought little relief. From the plateau carpark, the mini buses would spread out in different directions, descending into the valley below. Most of the convoy headed south towards the lake and Ballyhoary, the urban centre of the island. Two went west to the university campus. A single bus travelled north onto a vast open limestone plain, (a marshy flatland criss-crossed with narrow raised roads and isolated houses), heading for the tiny fishing village of Boolin, known locally as *Howlin* because it suffered the onslaught of regular and spectacular storms. Boolin sat at the end of a narrow unprotected promontory which jutted out into the wild North Atlantic Ocean and the wind that raced around its narrow streets, changing direction at every turn, sounded like the village was being attacked by a hoard of angry dragons. People in Boolin often had to shout above the wind to have their words heard. During the winter months Boolin was often cut off from the rest of the island when the single link road became flooded. In the terrible winter of 67 Boolin became another island for the best part of six weeks.

The monastery was situated half way between the university and Ballyhoary and therefore travellers visiting the monastery, if not being met by someone with a car, would take any one of the buses going to the urban capital of the island.

An attractive woman in a colourful head scarf, one that reminded Brother Benjamin of something his mother might wear, was the only other person on the steps and as they passed each other, she neither acknowledged him nor returned his cheery smile.

Brother Benjamin hardly noticed. He was late and, because he was late, he was annoyed. Fr Prior had told him not to worry; he would have no trouble recognising Michael. But Brother Benjamin did worry, it was in his nature to worry and on top of it all, he was late. He couldn't see anyone on the dock and the ferry was tied up and the two crew members were gone. What if Michael had got fed up waiting and had climbed onto one of the buses to Ballyhoary? How embarrassing. Brother Benjamin could spend the rest of the morning searching the island for someone he had no way of recognising or describing.

At the bottom of the steps Brother Benjamin looked around. There was no one in sight. Near the boarded-up ticket booth, the only building in the small harbour, two large suitcases sat, side by side, like guard dogs at the mouth of the pier. Brother Benjamin walked towards them and as he approached a familiar figure stepped out from the dense foliage behind the building. Brother Benjamin raised his eyes in shock, "Fr Francis... Fr Prior?" he stammered.

"Ah," said Michael, smiling at the young monk, "you must be my ride."

*

The mini bus with "International Conference on Cross Border Co-operation" written in childish writing on large pieces of white cardboard in the front and back windows, came to a juddering halt and threatened to slide back down the hill and into the bus behind.

"Well," said Horse loudly, once he had settled himself into the seat beside Paul Creagan near the front of the bus, "that was an enjoyable boat ride, wasn't it?"

"Hmmm. That friend of yours didn't look very well," said Creagan.

"True enough, mate. Some people just don't like boats."

"I think there was something else wrong with him," said Creagan.

"Oh?" I hadn't noticed. Hey, whatcha think of the American pair? Now there's a happy couple, if ever I saw one."

"Which ones?" asked Creagan, knowing full well that Horse was referring to the Texan and his crew-cut partner that they'd spoken to before getting on the bus.

"You know who I'm talking about, Paul. The black guy and his short-arse partner," said Horse. Horse turned around in his seat and nodded at the big black man sitting at the centre of the back seat. The black man's partner, an all-American GI Joe type, was staring blankly at the back of the seat in front of him, with a face that could turn milk sour. When Horse caught the liverish man's eye, he winked at him with a theatrical shake of the head. The GI Joe ignored him. Seeing the exchange the black detective guffawed loudly, then boomed,

"I do hope you've made your will, Red, 'cos there's a mighty good chance we aint goin' to make it to the top of this hill and if you've left anything to me, whatever it is will be going to the dog shelter."

"Fuck. I fuckin' hate this place," said Red, as the little bus jumped forward another couple of feet. Horse smiled and nodded at the big black American, who had introduced himself as Harry Buckingham from Houston, Texas, in the U.S. of A Horse then turned back and faced the front of the bus before closing his eyes. Once again his thoughts returned to the image of the head-scarfed angel on the ferry.

Each of the mini buses carried twenty people with ease and none of the buses was more than two years old. They were as comfortable as any large coach, with leather seats, air conditioning and ample leg room. The centre aisle was wide and there was a TV screen hanging from the ceiling at the front. The windows were tinted and were fitted with colour co-ordinated sun shades.

The journey to the Tara Cove Hotel and Conference Centre in Ballyhoary took the southern road from a small carpark that sat on a high plateau overlooking the small port. Once the bus emerged from under a canopy of dense trees, the high road was relatively straight and the views spectacular. Even the cynical Gerry "Red" Redinski, Harry "Buick" Buckingham's partner, was impressed by the view of the valley from the high road. With cell phone in hand, Red leaned across the back of Buick and took as many pictures as he could. He tried hard to steady his hand and properly frame each shot. He snapped the ruined abbey and round tower. He photographed the enormous black lake from every angle. The lake was surrounded, on all sides, by dense forests and for photographers the only opportunity to capture the full scale of it was from the top of the mountain road. The lake was full of islands, some of them conical in shape, like miniature volcanoes. All of the lake islands were overgrown with tall trees and dense vegetation. None of them looked inhabited or very welcoming. When the bus descended to the valley floor Red took photographs of the traditional cottages along the road that skirted the lake and the low whitewashed stone walls that separated one field from another. He fiddled with the on-screen controls in an attempt to improve the picture quality but only managed to get himself into a tizzy. He cursed under his breath.

"Me? I'm jus' goin' buy a pack of postcards 'fore I leave. Professional photographers do them, Gerry. Know what I mean?" said Buick.

"Fuck you Buick, and stop movin' about, you're fuckin' with my focus!"

"Oh you'd be so lucky, cranky Polish white boy. When was the last time you got anyone to fuck with your focus?"

Someone sitting nearby chuckled. Red scowled.

Two Dutch policemen in the seat behind the driver were also taking pictures with their phones, and a big blond Norwegian detective stood in the aisle with a Canon digital SLR taking hundreds of shots per minute, the click, click, click of the shutter adding to Red's growing anger.

Horse and Paul sat in silence with their phones in their pockets.

Horse tried to focus his mind on the job in hand and the reason he was here at the "International Conference on Cross Border Co-operation". The goal of the conference was to promote and improve co-operation between the various European law enforcement agencies and the Americans, and to provide a forum to consider new ways of strengthening existing border control measures. All this in an effort to stem the tide of illegal traffic - drugs, counterfeit goods and illegal immigrants- and the free movement of religious radicals from one jurisdiction to another. Horse had heard it being variously described as part of the ongoing war on drugs, the war on terror or another step in securing European borders in the face of a new Cold War with Russia. Ireland held the presidency of the European Union and therefore the international conference would be held in Ireland. At first, the choice of Skellig Éin as the venue seemed odd, but on reflection Horse thought it made a good deal of sense. The island was remote and therefore easily secured. The Tara Cove Hotel and Conference Centre was state of the art and boasted four stars with a Michelin star restaurant. There were one hundred and eighty rooms in the hotel and a further two hundred or so available in Bed and Breakfast accommodation around the island. From a strategic point of view, it made sense too. It was well known that Central American drug cartels still used the relatively unguarded west coast of Ireland to land their drugs, before distributing them to the rest of Europe. Skellig Éin had over ten miles of wild and, seemingly inaccessible, coastline looking west to the Americas, so that if any of the foreign delegates were unsure of the scale and complexity of the problems they faced all they had to do was look out their hotel bedroom window.

Detective Inspector Brian Hopkins of the London Metropolitan Narcotics Division and Superintendent Paul Creagan from Garda Síochána Head Quarters in Dublin had been partnered for the conference weekend. They had been together for the last two months and would be for the next four. Brian had been seconded to Garda head-quarters for six months to provide assistance in an investigation centred on a Dublin gangster known as Mr. G, (real name: Maurice Gimple), who was on the island for the Summer. Mr G had legitimate business interests on the island, operating a laundrette, a tattoo parlour and a nightclub, called Studio 54, in the town of Ballyhoary. Mr. G. spent April to September every year living and working on the island. Brian and Paul's presence at the International Conference on Cross Border Co-Operation was a cover. They were on assignment. A reliable tip-off, had led the Dublin police to believe that there was a large consignment of Columbian drugs being smuggled into Ireland, somewhere along the north-western coast. The fact that a known Dublin gangster was on summer vacation on Skellig Éin seemed too much like a coincidence, so Brian and Paul were sent to the island to investigate.

Paul seemed to have no problem playing chaperon to the older English policeman. Horse suspected that Paul liked him. If it was true, the feeling was mutual. Horse liked the way Paul dressed and had started to emulate the younger man. Before leaving the mainland, he'd travelled to Galway and purchased a suit, a couple of shirts and three Jon Snow ties from Louis Copeland & Sons. Horse had never spent so much money on clothes nor had he ever dressed so well.

Horse ignored the amateur photographers in the mini-bus and stared blankly out the window. He tried hard to focus on the case but he couldn't. The bus had become loud and the detectives in it, boisterous. In the end he gave up, took out his phone and took a photograph of a donkey in a field.

"One for the kids," he said when his colleague gave him a curious look, "if I ever have any kids."

Chapter 9.

Rick Kavanagh and his crew made sure that they were first onto the mini bus with a sign in the front window which read Ballyhoary Direct - via Lake Drive Road. Rick wanted to get going as soon as possible and was hoping that the shuttle bus might make up some of the time lost on the ferry crossing.

"How long does it take to get to town?" Rick asked the elderly driver as soon as he climbed on.

"Twenty-five minutes, once we get going," said the cheery driver.

"Well whatcha fuckin' waiting for? Let's get goin' then," said Rick.

"As soon as everyone is on board. It won't be too long," said the driver, nervously.

"Shit," said Rick, giving the driver a seething look. He stomped down the aisle and sat in the centre of the rear bench seat. Megan followed him. She had to squeeze passed him to sit down. Rats and Lash each took one of the double seats on either side of the aisle, one up from Rick and Megan. Rick watched as the last of his gang, Damien "Mo" Smallhouse got on. Rick thought how appropriate his surname was. Mo was the size of a small house. He was Rick's muscle man. Big and vicious-looking, Mo had a flat head, cauliflower ears and small closely spaced eyes. The muscles under his left eye twitched regularly, giving him the appearance of a wild animal primed for attack. He had an army style crew-cut which was dyed albino white. It made the top of his head look like it was covered in a thin layer of snow. Most of his skin was tattooed and he had piercings everywhere. There were studs, pins and rings in his cheeks, eyebrows, lips, neck and ears. On all of his fingers, including his thumbs, he wore gold and silver rings.

"Our very own Mr T", thought Rick.

The bleached hair, tattoos and piercings made Mo look stupid, but Rick knew that first impressions can be deceptive. Whilst he was as vicious as he looked, Mo certainly wasn't a fool. Rick was fully aware that, next to himself, Mo was the smartest of the gang members. Rick suspected that Mo's vicious moronic persona was cultivated - an act to divert attention away from his true character and motivations. Rick was naturally suspicious of everyone, but recently he was most suspicious of Mo.

Mo stopped at the top step, leaned forward and pushed his ugly head into the driver's cabin. The driver pulled back in shock.

"Whatcha waiting for, old man? We're all on now, so you can get fuckin' movin'," he snapped.

Mo put a big hand on the steering wheel and smiled dangerously at the driver. Rick thought Mo looked more frightening when he smiled.

"Mo!" shouted Rick from the back of the bus.

Mo either ignored Rick or pretended not to hear him, and leaned closer to the driver who had retreated as far as he could, and was now pressed hard against the door.

"Mo!" shouted Rick again, this time with anger in his voice.

Mo reluctantly retrieved his head from the cabin and stared defiantly down the aisle. Before he had time to say anything else, a strange looking middle-aged woman mounted the steps behind him and tapped him hard on the shoulder with the handle of her umbrella.

"You mind your language, young man. How dare you speak to our driver like that! You should be ashamed of yourself," she said in a stern voice. Mo turned around with a raised fist ready to strike the woman, but when he saw her he hesitated. From where Rick was sitting he thought Mo looked genuinely bewildered.

The woman was as tall as Mo but nowhere near as big and yet there was something about her that was frightening. She was dressed like someone from the 1950's. She wore a woollen skirt, woollen tights and brown leather laced brogues, polished to a mirrored sheen. She had on a heavy drown duffel coat, a thick woollen scarf, that completely covered her neck, and a pair of soft black leather gloves. Her face was caked in make-up and her blue eye-liner, which looked like it had been applied with a child's crayon, managed to darken rather than brighten her already black eyes. Although her face was thin, accentuated by a long crooked nose, her permed golden hair was full and thick. Whilst her face suggested that she was not a heavy woman, her breasts seemed more than ample under the thick coat. Rick, who was becoming more agitated by the minute, thought she looked like a witch. He'd noticed her on the ferry because she seemed to be watching them. Unlike the other ferry passengers, who'd all looked away when Rick and his gang had made their way down to the back of the boat, she'd continued to stare at him, even when he returned her gaze. She'd shown no fear then, and was showing no fear now.

"Do you think I'm afraid of you?" she said to Mo, as if reading Rick's mind.

When Mo hesitated she said,

"Well then, go sit with your friends so we can all get on and get moving."

Rick stood up.

"Leave it, Mo!" he shouted angrily. Mo looked down the aisle at him. So did the odd-looking woman. When she smiled, Rick shuddered.

"Leave it, Mo. Come here and sit down," he said again, this time with less authority. Finally, and without a word, Mo turned from the woman and shuffled down the bus. He plonked onto the seat beside Rats Egan, who had moved in to make way for him. Rick continued to watch the strange looking woman. He wondered if she *was* a witch. She was particularly ugly, and yet, he thought, there was something about her that made her interesting – almost attractive. He'd heard of the dangerous charms of witches. She turned away from him and began speaking loudly to the driver.

"Where do I get off for the late Dr Greene's surgery please? I'm the new district nurse. It's my first time on the island," she said.

The driver, whose face was now as red as a tomato, gave her a weak smile.

"You can get off at Leahy's Cross. The surgery is just around the corner. I'll tell you when we are there and point you in the right direction," he said nervously.

"You are a dear, thank you...eh..?"

She raised her thick eyebrows.

"Eamon," he said, as he composed himself.

"Eamon. Thank you, Eamon, and I'm Eileen Fancy," she said, offering him a gloved hand.

He hesitated before shaking it, but then did so with gusto.

"Nice to meet you Eileen. I'm Eamon Regan."

"Nice to meet you too, Eamon Regan," she said, holding onto his hand for a little longer than seemed appropriate. Then, and with a shake of her head, she turned and headed down the bus. Rick was sure the conversation with the bus driver had been for his benefit, but he couldn't think why. For a moment, he wondered if she would keep coming, and try to squeeze in between himself and Megan. The thought made him feel ill. Thankfully she didn't. Instead she took a seat near the front but, before she sat down, she stared directly at Rick, giving him another toothy grin. A tingle of ice ran down his spine and he had no option but to lower his gaze. Somewhere outside a wild creature screamed. When he looked down at his hands Rick thought he could see them shaking.

*

Marie Joyce placed her holdall on the car roof and opened the driver's door of her Renault Clio with the key. It was an old car and had neither remote control nor central locking. She had parked it under a large bushy tree, hoping that the canopy of thick leaves would provide a degree of protection if the torrential rains returned while she was away. The car leaked in heavy rain and the carpet on the front passenger's side was usually soggy. She always left one window slightly open to prevent the front and back windscreens fogging up and also in a vain attempt to remove the musty smell that permeated the cabin. Every time Marie sat in her little Clio she told herself, in no uncertain terms, that it was time to replace the car, but then she'd turn the key and the little engine would fire up, the blow heater would hum into life and she'd feel guilty and think of all the reasons for keeping things just the way they were. Marie had found that accepting the present situation was preferable, (no matter how difficult it made her life), to the inevitable trouble that accompanied change. Keeping things just the way they were, was just how she liked it.

The roof of the car was sticky with gum deposits from the overhanging branches and the bottom of her bag left coloured hairs on the off-white paint.

"Damn," she said to herself.

She got into the car and threw the holdall onto the passenger seat. An envelope with *Galway Private Hospital Oncology Department*, stamped on the top left hand corner, poked out of the bag and winked at her. She ignored it, started the car and left the carpark. She headed down the southern road after the last of the mini buses. She decided that she would visit her old friend before going on to town. Once her little car reached the bottom of the long winding descent she took a sharp left onto a hidden side road that snaked through a dense forest of silver birch. Marie knew all the short-cuts and rat-runs on the island, and this way was a quicker, quieter and a more beautiful route to Dr French's pink two-storey cottage on Lake Drive Road.

The CD player, which she guessed was worth more than the car, and which was nestled safely in the boot, was playing a piano piece by Ludovico Einaudi. She liked the music so she turned up the volume as loud as she could, in an effort to hear it clearly above the rumbling road noise. Sunlight danced through the long white legs of the surrounding trees and the cabin of the little car flickered and pulsed with light and the gentle touch of piano keys. As the music rose and filled her ears, Marie thought of the news that sat in the brown envelope in her bag; she thought of Dr French and her sister Martha and she thought again of the big man on the ferry and his pale blue, familiar eyes. She gripped the steering wheel tightly and, despite her best efforts, Marie Joyce began to cry. For the first time in so very, very long, Marie felt afraid.

Change was coming and change frightened her.

*

"It's the swell after all the rain we've had," said the young priest as the two of them made their way up the steep bank towards the carpark. Michael was surprised at how strong and fit

Brother Benjamin was, given that he looked like he would benefit from a few good Irish dinners. His face was gaunt and his skin had an unhealthy pallor. He wore a long unkempt black beard and had a bald pat on the top of his head. If Michael was asked to describe him he would have said gangly and undernourished. His colour aura however was alive and vibrant. There were a lot of oranges and lemons, reds and greens. The aura filled out his skinny frame and Michael guessed that if he narrowed his eyes Brother Benjamin would look solid and strong. Despite Michael's protestations Brother Benjamin had insisted on carrying both suitcases, which contained most of Michael's worldly possessions, and did so with surprising ease. It was Michael who was getting short of breath and the one having trouble keeping pace. The compacted sand steps, each faced with a plank of roughly sawn timber, were wide enough for the two men to ascend side by side. The young priest talked as he climbed. Michael huffed and puffed loudly in response.

"It rained here for the past fourteen days and nights, only stopped yesterday afternoon. Like on the mainland, but much worse. This morning it is glorious, hardly a cloud in the sky. But last week, long hard heavy rain. And winds, like you wouldn't believe! But today, all calm and beautiful. There has been flooding and the sea was wild. And then of course there was the earthquake. An earthquake! Can you believe it? You heard about that, of course. It was reported on RTE and Sky News and CNN. They said it's centre was close to the Priory. We felt it. The walls shook and furniture moved. It was exciting and frightening at the same time. Who would have thought it? An earthquake, in Ireland, and here, on Skellig Éin, of all places."

"Hmm," said Michael, envious of Brother Benjamin's energy, "and this swell you mentioned?"

"Oh yes," continued the priest, slowing his pace a little to allow Michael to catch up, "after a rough storm the surface of the sea looks calm, but the ocean is rolling underneath. For people who get sea-sick it's the worst kind of sea and it can be very unpleasant."

"Tell me about it," said Michael as they finally reached the top step and a large expanse of tarmac opened out in front of him.

"Gosh, but you look so much like our Prior, Father Prior, Father Francis, I mean, your brother. Father Prior told me I'd recognise you but I didn't know how I would, you know," chuckled Brother Benjamin, repeating, almost word for word, what he had said when they introduced each other at the pier.

"Twins," Michael repeated. "You didn't know your Prior had a twin brother?"

"We knew Fr Francis had a brother. He talks about you often, but he never said you were twins." Brother Benjamin shook his head and smiled.

"He told me I'd recognise you but I didn't know how I would."

The empty carpark sat on a plateau that momentarily broke the rhythm of a high rocky mountain range. The mountains ran in a horseshoe shape around three sides of the islands, buffering the inner valley plains from the worst of the Atlantic storms. Only the northern part of the island was without this protection and therefore, apart from a small fishing village of Boolin and some isolated houses, the northern third of the island was sparsely populated and least visited. Michael thought the car park was a lonely and unfriendly place and he imagined that most travellers experienced the same psychological chill when they first saw it. He didn't think it was the kind of place you'd think about setting up camp. On the other hand, had the plateau not existed access from the shore to the inner part of the island would have been virtually impossible unless you brought rock climbing equipment with you in your boat. All the roads leading from the carpark, (there were four including the one going back down to the pier), dropped quickly into the shelter and obscurity of dense ancient forests.

"We're over here," said Brother Benjamin, as he headed off toward a strange looking vehicle parked near one of the exits. Michael's jaw dropped when he was close enough to see where Brother Benjamin was leading him.

"You...you want me to travel in that? But...but what about my suitcases?"

It was a motorbike and side-car and the side-car looked home-made. The side-car sat frighteningly close to the ground even before Michael climbed in, but when fully loaded with the two suitcases, one strapped to the side of the contraption and the other perched in front of him, Michael felt sure it's metal bottom must be touching the tarmac.

"Loads of room! No problem," said Brother Benjamin. "Solid as a rock. We'll be grand, and you'll love her. She's a flyer," he declared.

They smiled at each other. Whilst Michael's smile was more of a grimace, Brother Benjamin's was boyish, full of excitement and bursting with pride.

"Keep your hands inside at all times, and you'll probably need to put these on."

Brother Benjamin handed Michael what looked suspiciously like a pair of World War II fighter pilot goggles.

"For the flies," he added with a wide smile.

Before they left, Michael took one last look around the deserted car park in the vain hope that some other option was available to him. There wasn't any. The carpark was empty. Resigned to his fate, Michael held onto the suitcase on his lap and closed his eyes. After a moment, he closed his mouth too. With a roar of the engine and the upward flick of Brother Benjamin's sandaled foot, the bike jumped forward, violently dragging the side-car and its terrified occupant down the steep mountain road and into the forests below.

When Michael and Brother Benjamin reached the ornate front doors of the Priory twenty minutes after leaving the plateau car park, Michael stumbled out of the sidecar, pulled off the sweaty goggles and, leaning over a well-tended raised flower bed, threw up the remaining contents of his stomach.

Chapter 10.

Marie Joyce wiped her face on her sleeve before getting out of the car. She was met at the gate by a big black woolly mongrel who announced her arrival with deep booming *woofs*. The frantic wagging of the dog's bushy tail seemed to reverberate through it's old body and the sound of its barking brought the house owner to the door.

Daibhí French was a big man in his early seventies, but could easily have been taken for a man ten years younger. He stood upright and filled the door. A retired British Army doctor, Daibhí had never looked anything but the army man he would always be. His skin was a healthy West of Ireland shade of strong milky tea and his smile was warm and commanding.

"Good boy, Hound," he said to the dog, "you show her the way."

Marie smiled. Her eyelashes felt sticky.

"Welcome, my dear. Come on in, I have the kettle on."

"Hello Daibhí, how are you? A coffee would be lovely, so long as you don't put a shot of brandy in it, like the last time. The island is crawling with police".

"Oh?" said Daibhí. He kissed her on the cheek and gave her a hug. She felt the strength of him. Despite his age he was a fit man.

"There's some sort of Garda conference on at the Tara Cove. There was a load of foreign policemen on the ferry."

Daibhí French stood back. She could tell he was assessing her. She wondered if his assessment was as a doctor or a friend. Probably both, she decided.

"Come on in. Is everything alright Marie?"

"Great. Yeh, great. Suffering a little from hay-fever. My eyes are watering. I forgot to take my anti-histamine tablet this morning. I brought you some Stilton from Galway and I found a book you might like."

"You shouldn't have, my dear. You are very thoughtful. Come in, the fire is on."

"It's a bit warm for a fire, isn't it Daibhí?"

"I know, you're right, but I was up early and we are men of routine, are we not Hound?" The dog looked up excitedly at the sound of its name. "And the house wouldn't be the same without the smell of burning turf. It's just a little fire."

Marie was always surprised at how neat and tidy the house was, given that it's only occupants were an elderly man and his equally elderly dog. Since Daibhí's wife had passed away several years before, he and his dog had been the cottage's only inhabitants. A local woman came in once a week to clean the place and unload her troubles. Daibhí was patient and kind to her, despite the fact that the cleaning lady did more talking than cleaning. Marie had to agree that there was a something familiar and comforting about the smell of burning turf. The front room was warm but not uncomfortably so. There were two old armchairs placed either side of the fire, one considerably more aged than the other. The better of the two was kept for visitors. Hound instantly sat himself down on the rug between the two chairs.

When Dr French returned with the two coffees, they both sat down. Marie smelt the coffee before putting the mug to her lips. Daibhí French smiled but said nothing. One of the many reasons Marie Joyce and Daibhí French got on so well was that they felt comfortable and at ease in each other's company. Nothing was ever forced between them. No subject was broached unless it was clear that the other wanted it discussed and they never used small talk to fill a silence. If Marie didn't want to speak, she didn't have to. If Daibhí was maudlin, he did not have to explain why. From their very first meeting at the hospice, where Daibhí came every day to visit his dying wife and where Marie came every day to teach his dying wife to paint, they silently acknowledged a mutual bond. From a shared sorrow their friendship grew and over the years they came to depend on each other for companionship and support. Each one filled something that was missing in the other, and during difficult periods, they gave each other the strength to go on.

For a long time, the two friends sat sipping their coffees without saying anything.

"Oh, I nearly forgot," said Marie eventually.

She placed her mug on the mantelpiece, then rummaged through her holdall, which she had dropped on the floor beside her chair, and removed a small wheel of cheese in wax paper and a hardback book, on American Civil War battles. She had to tug at the book, to free it from the bag, and when it finally popped out, it brought with it the brown envelope with the hospital stamp on the front. The envelope landed on the rug and Hound sprang to his feet and inspected it with a big wet nose. Marie quickly snatched the letter with her free hand and shoved it back into the bag. The old man gave no indication that he had spotted the letter. She handed him the gifts over the head of the dog, the wheel of cheese supported on top of the book.

"Ah, but you're the best girl, and you spoil me Marie."

After quickly glancing at some of the glossy illustrations and old photographs in the book, Daibhí put the presents on the floor beside him, taking time to centre the cheese over the battlefield image on the front cover. Hound eyed the cheese for a while but then slumped back onto the rug, turning his head from Daibhí to Marie and back again. After a moment of hesitation, Marie retrieved the envelope from her bag.

"I got the test results," she said.

Daibhí French nodded, but his blank expression didn't change. She passed him the envelope. Hound wagged his tail. The retired doctor rocked the manila envelope up and down in his hand, as if trying to guess it's weight, as if doing so would somehow reveal the contents within., All the while he watched Marie.

"You were right, Daibhí" she said, "it was nothing. Just a lump of dry skin. That's all. You were right."

"But you were right to have it checked out," he said.

He opened the envelope and read its contents.

"Good. Thank God," he said.

"Thank *you*," she said.

"Tell me Marie, was that why you were crying, when you got here?"

She relaxed and smiled.

"Nothing gets passed you, you old codger. Yes, that was it. I suppose it was a delayed reaction," she lied.

How could she tell him the truth? There was no point in mentioning the real reason for her tears. It was silly. A strange coincident. Nothing more than that. How could she explain to him that, on the ferry back from the mainland, she'd thought she'd seen a ghost.

*

Rick Kavanagh hadn't been able to get a signal on his mobile phone since he'd left the mainland, despite the promise of full coverage from his telecom provider, and therefore couldn't contact Mr G to tell him they'd be late. The internet on his phone was super-fast but the phone signal was crap.

"Fucking lying bastards", he said to himself.

He was standing at the entrance to a night club. Golden letters saying Studio 54 were on the curved stone lintel over two black painted steel doors. One of the doors had a discreet spy-hole located at the centre of the gold painted image of a snake swallowing its own tail. There was a matching image on the other door, but no spy-hole. The entrance to the night-club was half way down a narrow stepped pedestrian street, five minutes from the bus stop and the busy town square. Megan stood beside him and she looked small and nervous. Rick had left the other three, Mo, Lash and Rats, sitting on a park bench in the square, with instructions not to draw attention to themselves. It was probably an impossible request. The centre of Ballyhoary teemed with tourists, groups of pilgrims and the odd islander and the three guys looked nothing like any of them. Rats and Lash wore hoodies and they both looked stoned because, most of the time, they *were* stoned, or were thinking about being stoned, whilst Mo would stand out if he was covered in soot and hidden in a pitch-dark cellar. In fact, Mo made a point of standing out. Whilst Rick didn't care if people stared at his three amigos, he didn't want them causing a scene or, more to the point, getting themselves arrested. He warned them not to talk to anyone and not to fight amongst themselves, which Rick accepted was the biggest risk. Rick knew that Rats and Lash despised each other, whilst Mo didn't seem to like anyone, but especially not Rats or Lash. Rick knew Mr G wouldn't be happy if there was any kind of a scene, and would, of course, blame Rick if there was. Being late was bad enough.

Rick took out his useless phone and noted that there was still no service. He went to the messages folder and scrolled back to the message he received from Mr. G earlier in the week. He read the message again, in case he'd missed something the previous hundred times he had read it.

* STUDIO 54 * 11.30AM SHARP * THURSDAY *
* CALL PETE * BRING 4 * G *

It was written in the style of an old-fashioned telegram. Kavanagh knew that Mr G wrote it like this on purpose. Although he rarely used mobile technology, or any computer technology at all, Mr G. believed that there was a proper text-messaging etiquette and, just because texting was a new form of communication, there should be no reason to write in an abbreviated form. Abbreviations, Mr G had told Rick, were for people who couldn't spell or worse, people who were too lazy to look up a dictionary to find out how to spell the word.

When Rick had first read the text he was confused. He didn't know where Studio 54 was (he'd searched Google for nightclubs in Dublin named Studio 54, but couldn't find any) and he didn't know why he had to ring Pete Mercer.

Pete Mercer was a well-known Dublin drug dealer and all round "psycho" who had spent several periods in Mountjoy Jail for various misdemeanours, his most recent spell being 18 months for a violent assault on a young architectural student on Abbey Street early one morning. Apparently, Pete's defence for almost killing the young man was *because he looked at me funny, Your Honour.* Along with being a vicious thug, Pete Mercer was, more importantly, Mr G's guard dog and right-hand man.

Pete didn't like Rick and the feeling was mutual. When Rick called Pete, after receiving Mr G's cryptic message, he was greeted with a, "an' wha' de fuck do you want? I've no time for girl talk. I'm fuckin' busy here fuckin' your ma, Kavanagh, ha, ha, ha."

Rick ignored the taunt. He tried to remain calm and composed. From experience Rick knew that not letting Mercer wind him up was the best way to deal with him. He suppressed his rising anger and spoke as calmly as he could.

"I have a message from Mr G." he said, and he read it out over the phone.

"So?" snapped Mercer.

"What does it mean?"

"Don't you understand English, you dopey cun'?"

"Where's this Studio 54?" said Rick.

"Can't you work it out smart boy, or are you thicker than your mama's lips?" Mercer made some gurgling noises. "Oh yeah. That's it, mama. You know you love it big and hard."

"Maybe," said Rick, "I'll just text Mr G and tell him I couldn't find you. Yeh, that's what I'll do."

Mercer suddenly stopped play-acting and started shouting down the phone,

"You listen here, you little shit: I'll fuckin' cut you in two an' feed you to the fish in the Liffey, you little cun'. I better not see you ever again, or I'll fuckin' do you. I swear I'll fuckin' do you."

There was a pause and then Pete said,

"Studio 54 on Skellig Éin Island, and you better not be fuckin' late, you little cun'. And don't fuckin' bother comin' back". The line went dead.

It was now just after twelve. The Angelus bells from the monastery chapel had just announced the hour. Rick was a half an hour late and was, like Megan, nervous. He took a deep breath, walked forward and hammered loudly on the metal doors. He had the strangest idea that he if he knocked again he might wake one of the circular snakes. They suddenly looked evil.

One of the doors opened and Rick was met by the giant Russian blond called Stefan. He was so big, he made Mo look like a midget.

"Are you Reek?" the man said in a deep foreign accent.

"That's right."

"Weel, you ar late, Reek. You know dis?"

Rick didn't reply.

"Weel, I tell you Reek. Mr G, he iz not happy. So, you better come in."

Chapter 11.

"Father Francis."
"Brother Michael."

The well-worn joke still made them both smile. They hugged.

"How are you Michael? I'm sorry I wasn't here to meet you when you arrived. I was in Galway all day. I take the morning mass there two or three times a week. The parish priest is very old and should have retired years ago, but the Catholic Church is terribly understaffed as you know, so we all do what we have to."

"No problem. You are a busy man. What happened your eye?" asked Michael.

They were standing in the Prior's timber panelled study. Two floor-to-ceiling French doors on either side of an ornate fireplace opened out onto a large, well-tended garden and cast a grid of afternoon sunlight on the carpeted floor. A fire had been set in the hearth, but had not been lit. The room smelt of furniture polish and old books, but was airy and full of light.

Michael took a seat in one of two leather armchairs in front of the Prior's mahogany desk. Father Francis took the other.
There was a soft tap on the door.

"Come in," said the Prior.
Brother Benjamin entered, carrying a bunch of envelopes."

"This morning's post, as you requested Father Prior."

"Thank you, Brother Benjamin."
Father Francis smiled warmly at the young priest.
Benjamin smiled at the Prior and then left without a word. He didn't look at Michael. Michael raised his eyebrows and looked at his brother.

"Brother Benjamin is a very sensitive soul, Michael. I think he feels he did you a wrong, making you travel in his side-car."

"He might have a point," said Michael.

"He couldn't get the car to start and was afraid he'd be late and miss you, so he had to take the bike. He has been looking forward to meeting you and now he feels responsible for making you sick and angry. I know that he wanted to make a good impression on you."

"He didn't make me sick. I had one of my bloody headaches. Actually, the bike ride was quite exciting."

"Well, maybe you could tell him that. It would mean a great deal to him, and to me!"

"Sure. No problem."

Father Francis glanced at the post but didn't open any of the letters. He dropped them on his desk.

"So, what happened the eye?" asked Michael again.

"Oh this?" The Prior gently stroked the bruise under his left eye, but then quickly removed his hand, as if caught in an indecent act. "Somebody punched me this morning, in Galway."

"Oh? I hope you didn't punch him back, Father Francis."

"Of course not."

Michael smiled.

"Anyway it wasn't a *him*. It was a *her*," said the Prior.

"Really? Is there something you want to confess to me, Father?"

"Ha! Very funny. I have nothing to be ashamed of, if that's what you mean? In fact, I'm sure I never met the woman in my life. She just walked up to me outside the church, said "Father Francis", emphasising the *Father*, called me a name I won't repeat, punched me and then walked off. She'd quite a right hook. Nearly knocked me over."

"A compliment, coming from you. By any chance did she have an emaciated drugged-up look, scraggly hair and pointy shoes? Did she liken you to a certain part of the male anatomy? If so, I think I had a run-in with her myself, on the ferry over."

"As a matter of fact, no. That's the strangest thing. She was very classy. In fact, very attractive and very well dressed. And she had the most unusual pale green eyes. When she walked up to me I thought she must be new to the parish and she'd come to say hello."

"I see. Very strange," said Michael.

78

He lowered his eyes and shuffled his feet. The Prior narrowed his good eye so that it matched the other.

"I don't suppose you know anything about this, do you Michael?"

"I have nothing to be ashamed of, if that's what you mean," said Michael, repeating his brother's words.

"No? Maybe you are becoming rebellious in your old age."

"Steady on with the old bit. Remember, I'm the younger brother here."

They both laughed.

"So are you ready for the big week then?" said Michael.

"Yes I am. My first year as the Prior and I get to host this. I can't believe it really. Three of the old priests from Africa are coming over for it."

"You know mum was so proud of you? She told me so before she died. I am too, you know? I always have been. I always looked up to you brother."

"Thank you. It means so much to me that you came."

"I wouldn't have missed it for the world. Anyway, now that I've sold the house, I've nowhere to live. The buyer virtually chucked me out on the street. Still, he paid way over the odds and I could have been waiting years to shift it. Mullingar is hardly New York."

"Well you can stay here for as long as you like," said the Prior.

"We'll see. I'll stay until the end of June and then I'll see about a place of my own, maybe in Galway. With all this money from the sale of the house, I can pick and choose."

The Prior touched his eye again.

"If I'm lucky this swelling will have gone down before the celebrations begin."

"Oh, it's nothing that a bit of make-up wouldn't take care of. I used make-up a lot in my celebrity TV days," said Michael.

"Maybe you could stand in for me, Michael? I'm sure you get mistaken for me all the time and, I suppose, I probably get mistaken for you too, what do you think?"

Michael looked sheepishly at his brother.

The Prior touched the bruise again.

"And how are your migraines, Michael?"

"The headaches are much the same. If you are asking if I still see the colours, the answer is yes. I've stopped trying to analyse what I see, but I can't help noticing, you know? If you forgive the pun, they colour how I see people."

As if to mimic the actions of his brother, Michael touched the side of his forehead with two fingers. It was something he did whenever he thought about his headaches, a habit he'd had since childhood.

"And a headache was the reason you were sick in our flower bed?" asked the Prior.

"Yes. That, and the boat trip. A hidden swell, according to Brother Benjamin," said Michael.

"He's right."

Changing the subject Father Francis said,

"Did you know that Primrose Kyle lives here on the island?"

"I had no idea. Scout is here? It's funny because I had been thinking about contacting her. I haven't seen her for so many years."

"Well yes. She lives here, with her daughter."

"Didn't she marry a wealthy economist or banker, or something like that?"

"Yes, a man named Brennan. His family were bankers in London. Old money and new. Of course, she always had her own. Her paintings still sell for big money. Primrose and her daughter live in a large country estate overlooking the lake."

"Scout was always a country gal at heart, wasn't she?" said Michael.

"They had only one child, Hanna. She's about twenty-four now and the spitting-image of her mother. When Hanna was ten her father died. Collapsed on a golf course, I understand. A very young man. A heart attack, I think. Anyway, Primrose and Hanna stayed on the island. She has a small art gallery in the town. I see her at mass every morning and she helps in Care for the Elderly. She has retired from the international art scene."

"I see," said Michael. A mischievous smile crossed his face.

"Damn it, Michael. That's the second time you've accused me of mischief with female parishioners."

"Sorry. I can't help it. You and Scout were an item once," said Michael.

"That was very long time ago. We were teenagers. Another time. We were all different people back then." After a pause the Prior said, "Anyway, when I told Primrose that you were coming to stay with me for the celebrations, she asked if you'd call in to see her. She wants your help or advice, on something or other."

"Did she say what it was she wanted?"

"It's about Hanna. She's gone missing," said the Prior.

There was another tap on the door. It was Brother Benjamin again. "Dinner is being served Fr. Prior."

"Goodness it's nearly half past six. Thank you, Brother, we will come straight away."

The two brothers rose together. Even after forty four years, the brothers were still strikingly similar in appearance, the only difference being the way they dressed and the Prior's black eye. Once Brother Benjamin was out of ear shot the Prior said,

"Make good with Benji as soon as you can, will you Michael? He's is a sensitive soul," said the Prior, adding,

"Often too sensitive for his own good."

"At the earliest opportunity, I promise," said Michael.

"Thank you. Actually, Benji reminds me of you when you were a kid. You were always so innocent."

"Huh. Well maybe I've changed in my old age," said Michael.

"Anything's possible," said the Prior, giving his brother a toothy grin.

As they left the Prior's study Michael's thoughts strayed to the memory of a recent encounter he'd had with a beautiful woman, with the most unusually pale green eyes.

Chapter 12.

"I wish I wuz back in Dublin. This place gives me the fuckin' creeps," whispered Seánie Rats Egan, as much to himself as to Jimmy Lash Pierse who was standing uncomfortably close to him. Lash was listening intently to Rick and the Russian. Rats was only half listening. The night was as black as the bottom of a sack of pitch and the lonely road was full of moonlight noises. Gusts of icy wind rolling in from the ocean spat salty sea-spray into his face, making Rats shiver.

They were standing together between two parked cars, fifty yards from the edge of a cliff, and a hundred-foot, sheer drop, to an isolated rocky beach below. Rats felt uneasy. The darkness was solid, and Rats thought it was like he had a black hood pulled over his head. He found himself regularly gasping for breath, as if the night was trying to smother him. He could hardly make out Rick's face, even though Rick was standing no more than six feet away. Now and again gaps appeared in the clouds, letting the pale moon peep through and then, for a few brief moments, Rats could just about see the other four people standing near Rick. When the moon hid behind the clouds his companions appeared as nothing more than recognisable shadows. No one moved. Megan stood close to Rick, Mo between the Russian and the other driver. Even without the light of the moon Rats always knew where Lash was. He could smell Lash and, if for some reason he couldn't smell him, he could always hear him. Lash didn't go in for personal hygiene, and his open-mouth breathing was like listening to a snoring horse.

"Haaw."

"Haaw."

"Haaw."

Rats hated everything about Lash. He hated his viciousness, his foul odour and his moronic attitude. But most of all, Rats hated Lash's stupid fucking breathing.

Rats leaned against the second of the two cars, the one that wouldn't start, and thought about their predicament. The driver of the second car had left his iPad charging on the seat, whilst they were all down in the caves, and it had somehow drained the car battery. When Stefan, Mr G's Russian doorman, realised what had happened, he went absolutely mental. Rats thought there was going to be a fight between Mr G's two henchmen, but there wasn't. Instead the second driver, a mouthy smart-arse from Belfast, went really quiet, which wasn't like him at all. Stefan was the bigger of the two men and Rats guessed that in a showdown the Northerner wouldn't stand a chance. Stefan looked cold and vicious. He had small baby blue eyes in a large square face. He was permanently tanned and his teeth were pearly white. Whenever Rats looked at Stefan, which wasn't very often, he thought of the soulless robotic killer he'd seen in a sci-fi movie. Also Rats thought Stefan was a fake and suspected the Russian spoke, and understood, English far better than he let on.

"Eez fuckin' no good. We can't even push her start. De car eez on de sand. Anyway, if we try, we make loud noises, which weel attract attention. I weel return to town in my car and get battery to bring back. Two of you to stay here with de car and de drugs."

Rick immediately volunteered Rats and Lash to remain with the stranded car. It annoyed Rats that Rick hadn't bother asking him for his opinion on the subject.

"...stay with the car and stay oura sight, right? Are yeh fuckin' listenin' Rats?" snapped Rick.

"Yeh. Rick. Stay with the car. Yeh Rick, I'm listenin'," said Rats with little enthusiasm.

"An' don't be fuckin' seen, we don't wan you two drawin' attention. There's a lot a Mr G's valuable stash in dat boot. Stay in the car and keep your fuckin' heads down. Don't play with yer phones either, someone might see de light. Aw righ?" said Rick.

"If someone comes, you can pretend yer lovers, fuckin' in de back, like a couple o' fuckin' queers, ha ha," said the second driver.

It was the first thing he'd said since they found out about the flat battery.

"Fuck you, ya stupid nordy bastard," said Rats. Rats knew the driver wouldn't start anything in front of Stefan.

Megan giggled. Rick suppressed a laugh.

"Enough talk," said Stefan angrily, "Come. We go now. We come back very soon."

Rick stepped closer to Rats and Lash.

"Y'understand what I'm saying?"

"Yeh," said Lash.

"Don't fuck around, dha hear?"

"Yeh, no, yeh, righ'," said Lash.

"Yeh righ'," repeated Rats.

Rats didn't think they'd be right. He didn't want to stay with Lash and, just for a moment, before Rick climbed into the car with the others, Rats thought about asking Rick if Mo could stay with Lash instead him, but in the end he decided not to say anything. Everyone was in a pissy mood and Rats was sure if he spoke up it would only make things worse - if that was possible!

*

Together Rats and Lash watched the car drive away. As soon as it was out of sight the wind rose and howled at them, as loud as it had done all night. Rats shivered violently then hurriedly climbed into the front passenger seat of the stranded car and slammed the door. After some hesitation Lash climbed into the back seat.

"Fuck, it's freezing," said Rats. Lash sat in silence for a while and Rats knew that Lash was thinking. Lash was definitely the dumbest member of Rick's gang and the process of working things out in his thick ugly head was very slow. Rats knew that Lash was wondering if Rats had somehow managed to get one over on him, by taking the front seat. Finally, Lash spoke.

"If yer dat cold, why don't you pu' on the hea'er, you little dumb fuck?"

"Wha?" said Rats

"Turn on de fuckin' hea'er. Are yeh def?"

"The battery's dead," said Rats.

"So wha?" said Lash indignantly.

"So the fuckin' heater doesn't run without the fuckin' battery, does it?"

Rats wanted to add "you big dumb fuck," but decided he better not get Lash too angry. The threat of physical violence was always present and Lash didn't need much of an excuse before he lashed out!

The cabin of the car got progressively colder. Rats balled up in his seat and tried to sleep. His teeth began to chatter. After a while Lash started breathing loudly. It sounded like Darth Vader was in the back of the car.

"Haaw."

"Haaw."

"Haaw."

"Fuck, can you shut your mouth when you breathe?" said Rats.

"I'll shut your fucking mouth for you ya little cun' ......"

Lash stopped in mid-sentence when the car shook violently.

When it stopped rocking, Rats whispered,

"What the fuck was dah?"

"I don't fuckin' know, do I?" said Lash. Rats detected a tremble in Lash's voice.

"Maybe Rick's back an' havin' a laugh," said Rats.

"We wooda have heard de car," said Lash quietly.

Rats was trying to think what could have caused the car to rock when it happened again, this time with even more force.

Lash yelped like a kicked puppy.

His "haaw, haaw" was replaced by whispered mumblings.

Rats thought he heard a muffled "Hail Mary" from the back seat.

Rats lifted his head and peered out the side window into dark night. Not such a big man now, are you Lash?

An idea formed in his head.

Before he said anything the cabin exploded with light. Rats dropped his head below the dashboard until the car passed by. Just as it did Rats raised his head and looked out to see if he could see what had caused the car to rock. All he saw was flat fields and whitewashed low stone walls. The walls sparkled in the beam of light from the passing car. Rats came to the conclusion that the violent rocking must have been caused by strong gusts of wind.

"Hey Lash, maybe it was a Banshee. Whatcha' think? I seen a ting on de telly 'bout dis island, dat said a Banshee lives here." He scraped his nail along the underside of the glove compartment.

"Fuck sake, wha was dat, Lash?"

Lash said nothing.

Rats made the scraping noise again, louder this time.

"Oh shit, she's outside the car, Lash. She's trying to get in. Oh fuck Lash, what are we going to do?"

Still no reply from the back seat. Without warning the car rocked again, just as violently as before.

Even though Rats was sure he knew the cause, the suddenness and force of the rocking shocked him. He held his breath. "Just the wind," he told himself. Once he calmed down, he said,

"Hey Lash. There's a crowbar in the boot. I seen it, earlier. I'm going to go get it. I'm not fuckin' lying here waiting for that Banshee bitch to come get me."

"Don't get out of the car," moaned Lash, "don't Rats".

This is priceless, thought Rats. Big, dumb-fuck Lash sounded like a frightened little girl.

"We gotta do something, Lash. We gotta."

Checking that the cabin light was off, Rats opened the car door.

"Don't do it Rats. I'll tell Rick."

"But you want me to get the crowbar don't you Lash?"

Lash didn't reply.

Rats climbed out.

The air outside the car was much colder than inside the cabin, and the night was quieter than he'd expected. There was, surprisingly, little wind.

"Strange," whispered Rats under his breath.

Leaving the passenger door wide open, he moved to the back of the car and quietly opened the boot. The slabs of coke had been stacked to one side under a heavy high visibility builder's jacket. Lying next to the jacket was a crowbar. Rats was considering his next move when he heard the car door slam shut and the central locking system engage with a loud clunk.

"Fuck Lash, ye fuckin' bastard," screamed Rats when he realised what had just happened. When he lowered the boot he saw Lash's face pressed up against the rear window, a cruel inane grin plastered all over his face.

"Hey Rats, you little fuckin' twat, say hello to the Banshee bitch for me, ha, ha, ha."

Rats was furious. Lash, of all people, had out-witted him. How could he have been so stupid? To top it all off, it was freezing and the fear he'd dismissed when he'd been in the car now returned with a vengeance. He shivered.

"Fuck. Stop fuckin' messin' Lash. Open the fuckin' door."

"Go fuck yourself, Rats. Yer not getting' back in."

Rats thought about smashing one of the windows with the crowbar, but when he considered how Rick would react he decided it wasn't a good idea. He thought about climbing into the boot. He opened the lid again and sized it up. It was big enough for him to get in beside the coke but he'd have to shut the door and again he wondered how he would explain that to Rick. Anyway he didn't like the idea and a vision of a black hood returned again. He shivered violently. Rats knew that if he didn't do something, he'd freeze to death. He looked at the high-visibility coat. It was padded and heavy. He decided to put it on, but he turned it inside out, so that he wouldn't stick out like a Christmas tree, especially if another car came along. The lining was matt black. Once on, only a small portion of the coats cuffs and collar were still the luminous yellow and Rats could quickly cover these if another car came along. The inside-out coat was hard and cold against his body and it took a long time before he stopped shivering.

Rats closed the boot with a loud bang. An animal bellowed in response and made him jump. He looked at the locked car and cursed his own stupidity. When he looked in the side window he saw that Lash was lying along the back seat with his hands behind his head. He was smiling.

"You goin' ta open de door, Lash?"

Lash shook his head.

"Well I'm walkin' back t' town. I might even meet Rick an' de Russian on the way, gha know wha' I mean? You can explain to them why you locked me out. Open the fuckin' door. I fuckin' swear, Lash. I'm gonna go."

Lash just kept on smiling and shaking his head. Rats thumped the top of the car as hard as he could. The unseen animal squawked again. It sounded closer now.

"Fuck you Lash."

Rats shivered again, but this time not entirely because of the cold. He thought about what he should do. He had to do something. There was a break in the clouds. In the distance he could see the outline of a two storey house perched on a hill. It seemed to be the only house for miles. Rats thought about taking a look. He figured that if it was empty he could break in and take shelter and if it wasn't, it probably belonged to a lonely old farmer, and Rats knew that lonely old farmers were known to keep all their cash at home.

⁂

Rats started to move from the car, putting one foot carefully in front of the other, until he felt hard asphalt road under his feet. With one last look over his shoulder, and making sure Lash was watching him, he started off in the direction of the house.

The road was narrow, with no margins or kerbs, and was hemmed in, on both sides, by thick high brambles. The road rose into the distance. Rats knew, from the journey out, that it was full of deep dips and steep rises and that approaching cars would appear, disappear and appear again. He'd have to be careful and be ready to duck for cover if a car came along in either direction.

The night seemed noisier now. There was still very little wind, which was very peculiar given the strength of the gusts that had violently rocked the car. Rats stopped and listened. He was sure he heard the car door opening and the sound of footsteps. "Ha. Lash is coming after me," he thought. He considered turning around but instead he picked up his pace. He'd decided to put as much distance, and darkness, between himself and Lash, and as quickly as he could. The brambles on either side of him creaked. Although it was impossible to hear or see Lash, Rats was sure he was being followed. He could sense Lash behind him. Rats picked up his pace and then almost stumbled off the side of the road and into the hedge.

"Fuck," he yelled, as he fought with the thorny bushes in an effort to remain upright. He just managed it. The edge of the road was not as straight as he thought. He rummaged in his trouser pocket and retrieved his mobile phone. Switching it on, he pointed the screen toward the ground in front of him. Immediately an owl screeched in the hedge behind his head.

"Fuck, shit, fuck," he said out loud.

After a moment he composed himself and slowed his breathing. He noticed his hand was shaking again. He tried to focus on the sounds around him, but could hear very little above the rustling of the brambles and the thumping of his own heart. The road behind seemed to be empty, but he was still convinced that Lash was back there, hiding in the shadows.

Should he go back or go on, he wondered? He was now quite some distance from the car and closer to the gates of the house. He decided to go on. He'd let Lash follow him. Then at some point he'd hide and wait until Lash passed by. Then he'd jump out, and scare the shit out of Lash, or even better still, get back to the car and lock Lash out!

Rats moved forward toward the gates. He stomped his feet and made as much noise as he could. The sound gave him comfort. He got into a rhythm and soon relaxed a little. He could sense Lash behind him, could hear his footsteps, just perceptible above the sound of his own. Rats slowed. So did Lash. Rats picked up his pace. So did Lash. Rats thought that was strange. Could Lash be purposely keeping time with his footsteps? After all, Lash had proved to be not as dumb as he looked. A car approached. Rats ducked into the hedge. He pulled the black jacket about himself and made sure none of the luminous edges were exposed to the light. He turned his head away from the oncoming car and in its strong head beam he searched for the crouching figure of Lash. There was no one on the road behind him and, as far as he could see, no one crouched in the hedges on either side of the road either.

Where was Lash?

As soon as the car had passed, Rats pulled himself out of the hedge. He stretched, turned and looked up the road. There was movement up ahead. An animal had come out from one of the fields near the entrance gates to the house. A dog, maybe?

"Fuck," he said. Rats didn't like dogs. Time to go back, he thought. Maybe this had not been such a good idea, after all. He felt scared. Suddenly there was a blood-curdling scream from something far away. It sounded like the raucous laughter of an hungry dogs.

Definitely time to go back, he decided. He crossed the road and hurried quietly back the way he had come. If Lash was coming along, Rats would soon reach him. If Lash was hiding somewhere in the hedgerow, then *he* could jump out and Rats would surely piss himself.

"I seen you. I fuckin' seen you," Rats shouted into the approaching darkness.

There was no response.

A gust of wind rustled the brambles on the opposite side of the road. Rats stopped and listened. He thought he saw movement, between the hedge and the road.

"Ya know, I can fuckin' see you, Lash. I seen you from back there."

Nothing moved on the other side of the road.

Rats thought about going over to take a closer look but then thought better of it. He looked over his shoulder. The animal that had come out onto the road, was a shadow in the distance, but now it was on his side of the road and was moving, purposely, after him. Rats couldn't make out what it was. If it was a dog, he thought, it was a big one, or maybe it was a small horse or a cow. A very fuckin' quiet cow, he thought.

"Fuck, fuck, fuck," he whispered.

He got moving again, away from the shadow crouched in the hedge and away from the approaching animal. He entered a hollow. The moon came out and the road in front clearly visible, but Rats could see nothing but dark sky beyond the rise in the road. He quickened his pace, but couldn't bring himself to run. Rats was convinced that once he reached the top of the hill, he'd be no more than fifty yards to the car. He decided not to look back to see if the animal was still following him. Suddenly he heard a familiar sound coming from behind him.

"Haaw."

"Haaw."

"Haaw."

Rats turned and braced himself for Lash's attack.

"I seen you, Lash, I seen you," he whimpered as loudly as he could. There was no one behind him. In the pale moonlight the road, for as far as he could see, was empty. And it was also very, very quiet. Even the brambles seemed to be standing still.

"Too fuckin' quiet," thought Rats.

"I seen you, Lash, I seen you," he whispered.

His heart was banging so fast he thought it was about to explode. He turned and moved forward again. Despite the cold night air, he was aware he was sweating. The coat was heavy and now felt like a wet rug. When he reached the brow of the hill he saw the car. A wave of relief washed over him and he began to run. It was less than thirty yards ahead. The car looked empty.

"Fuck you Lash," he gasped.

When Rats had got to within ten feet of the car he slowed and then stopped altogether. His heart was pounding and his breathing was short and very loud. As if on cue, a cloud crossed in front of the moon and the impenetrable darkness returned. From over his shoulder he heard the familiar sound again, before something gently nudged the side of his head. Rats felt a warm breath caress the side of his face.

"Haaw."

"Haaw."

"Lash? Is that you Lash?" whispered Rats, although, for some reason, he was certain it wasn't Lash behind him.

"Haaw."

"Haaw."

Rats felt weak. He couldn't move. He *knew* it wasn't Lash. It was the Banshee and it didn't matter that he didn't believe that Banshees were real, this one was real and she'd come for him.

"Haaw."

"Haaw."

He was nudged again, harder this time, and now he noticed a strong smell of rotting fish.

"Haaw"

"Haaw"

Whatever was behind him, was also above him. Something warm and sticky dribbled down his forehead and into his eyes. Whatever it was, it stung his face. He tried to scream. Instead, he wet himself. The next nudge was more like a punch, straight between the shoulder blades, and the force of it threw Rats forward onto his knees. He began to cry. He scurried forward on all fours, the car now no more than ten feet away, but before he could reach it, the animal grabbed him and, digging it's claws into his back, lifted Rats up into the air. Rats felt his legs dangling beneath him and, as he rose, the moonlight returned and he could see the outline of the car below him. It seemed smaller now. Something like large claws ran down the front of his jacket - like hungry spiders - searching, probing. Rats heard a ripping sound and felt a tugging on the thick jacket, and then at his clothes underneath. When an icy chill ran across the skin of his belly he knew what was coming next. The claws were sharp and brutal. They slashed and tore at his belly flesh and his cold skin was warmed by his spilled blood. Something heavy and wet splashed onto the ground below him

He tried to close his eyes but couldn't.

"Haaw"

"Haaw"

The moonlight was now as bright as a torch. Rats looked down at his dangling feet. His shoes were wet and red. Panic was replaced by a degree of coherent thought. He must try to escape the clutches of the Banshee. If only he could shake himself free, he thought, it was not such a big drop to the ground and then the safety of the car. But her grip on his spine was vice-like. Maybe if he could turn and face her, blind her with his torchlight, she'd let him go. He still had his mobile phone clutched in his fist. He twisted his head and somehow managed to switch on the phone light. He pointed the light upwards. When he saw what had him in its clutches his heart missed a beat and he blacked-out.

A sudden piercing pain in his right shoulder dragged him back to full agonising consciousness. He was looking down at the road again, staring at his phone. It was still in his hand and the powerful torchlight was still shining upwards at the thing that had him in its grip. It took Rats a moment to realise that his phone and his hand, and most of his right arm, were lying on the road, ten feet below him.

For the first time since the thing took him Rats started to scream. His screams turned to gulps and then became gurgled, when something thick and wormlike climbed into his mouth and bit off the a large lump of his tongue.

The last thing Seánie Rats Egan saw, before his face hit the front windscreen of the stranded car, was Lash's terrified eyes staring at him from the back seat. When the windscreen smashed, and his nose broke, tiny beads of glass pierced his cheeks and jabbed into his eyes. When his face hit the steering wheel the force sent two of his front teeth down his throat. When he was dragged back out, his limp bloody body slapped twice off the bonnet of the car, before landing heavily onto the road.

For a moment, there was no sound. It was as if the wind and the ocean had been shocked into silence. Then and without warning, the driver's air bag exploded and Lash, crouched down behind the front seats, started to scream.

For Rats Egan, the agony was over in an instant. It was like someone had hit a switch and immediately all the terrible pain was gone. He could still see and hear, but he no longer had any feeling. It was good. When he looked down he saw that he was rising again, higher and higher, up into the night sky, above the car and the island, and away from Lash and the horrors below.

Rats was fully lucid and he felt at peace.

It is over and I am dead, he thought.

But Rats was wrong.

It was not over and he wasn't dead.

Chapter 13.

Michael woke up smiling.

He got out of bed and pulled back the large heavy curtains, then looked around the room. He hadn't seen it in daylight. The ground floor bedroom was beautiful and perfect. It looked out onto the monastery gardens through a set of French doors like the ones in his brother's study. Beyond the gardens were reed-covered sand dunes and beyond them the ocean. The high-ceilinged room smelt of fresh paint and floor wax. He thought it was a healthy smell. On a writing desk near the French doors was a large vase of freshly cut flowers. Against one wall was a tall mahogany double wardrobe that looked strangely familiar. After a moment, he recognised it as the one from his mother's bedroom, from the family home in Mullingar. In front of the wardrobe stood his unopened suitcases. An ancient iron radiator clanked intermittently and was very hot to touch, but the room retained a background chill. Michael scurried back to bed. He had fallen asleep thinking about his meeting with Susan and now, curled up again under the many layers of warm blankets, he let his mind wander to their encounter less than a week earlier. Despite an ignominious end to the brief affair, the memory of Susan brought both pleasure and hope. He closed his eyes and let his mind revisit it, for the umpteenth time.

It had been late in the afternoon, the Friday before Michael set out for the island. He'd been in Galway city all day, tying up the last of the legal matters concerning the sale of the house and then meeting with his old friend Thaddeus O Sullivan for a very long lunch. The sale of family home had been completed in record time and the monies now sat in his bank account. His brother had insisted that Michael take it all, even though their mother's will split her estate equally between her two boys. For the first time in his life Michael felt, and was, a relatively wealthy man. After bidding his friend farewell, he wandered aimlessly about, alone and at a bit of a loose end. Michael was considering how he might best waste the weekend, when he walked into Susan.

He had been crossing the busy junction of Tower Walk and Castle Street, when a taxi swerved across the road in front of him, forcing him to jump onto the footpath. Before he had time to express his annoyance at the driver, or even ponder the cruel irony of being knocked down and killed at this precise moment in his life, an attractive woman stepped into his path and commandeered the cab. Her movement was swift and precise. Her outstretched arm clipped his chest and very gently, but firmly, stopped his forward momentum. Once her other hand had grabbed the door handle of the cab, she turned towards him and smiled sweetly. Her smile said,

"Sorry mister, this one's mine."

The look of confusion on Michael's face clearly surprised her. She stared at him, wide-eyed. He remembered feeling an urgent need to say something; to explain himself; to tell her that he hadn't been competing with her for the taxi; to tell her that he was only trying to cross the road and then avoid being run over; to tell her that he was happy for her to take the car and good luck to her because the cabbie was a nut-case; to tell her that he thought she was quite the most beautiful woman he'd ever seen. Michael opened his mouth, but none of these thoughts materialised into words. Instead, he just managed to shrug and smile back.

Her beauty was disarming. Her eyes were a smoky hazel-green and they sparkled when she smiled. He found himself fawning like a teenager. She noticed his discomfort and it made her smile.

She wrinkled her brow. Her eyes still sparkled.

"Maybe we could share?" she said, the rear door of the taxi open and inviting.

The question was charged with sexual tension.

"Where are you heading?" he managed to say, without sounding too excited.

"To my hotel room," she said.

"I think that's the way I want to go," he said, and then with her unspoken permission, Michael followed the beautiful woman with the hazel eyes into the back of the cab.

He paid the taxi man and went after the woman into the Great Lion Hotel. As soon as they reached the foyer she turned and, with another firm but gentle hand on his chest, blocked his progress forward.

"There are rules," she said in a quiet voice.

"There are?" he said. He had relaxed and wanted her to see that.

"First names only. No lies. I'll know if you are lying. Best if we don't talk too much. As soon as I say go, you leave. It is a one-time-only event. We never meet again. If we ever do, I will not acknowledge you. I will ignore you and expect you to do the same. Do you understand? Are we clear? A once in lifetime event. Are we clear?"

She was three or four inches shorter than Michael but, in her expensive heels, they stood almost eye to eye. He liked her voice. It was cultured and natural. There was nothing fake about it. Nothing put on. He liked her teeth and her smile, her high cheekbones and her small nose. He liked her mouth and her full luscious lips. But most of all, he liked her eyes.

Michael was entranced by the colour of her eyes. They seemed to draw in the surrounding light and turn it into green smoke. They were jewels and they gave her a remote and mysterious appearance. She was extremely sexy. Whilst there was nothing exceptionable about the physical attraction he felt towards the woman, any man would have found her attractive, Michael's interest in her eyes was something else altogether. What struck him most about her hazel eyes was that they contained within their hazy swirl, colours that he had never seen before. The effect was both shocking and captivating.

They were magical.

"Are we clear?" she said again.

"Yes. Once in a lifetime," he replied.

"One-time event," she said again.

"I can go with that," he said, knowing that, whatever happened, it was a lie.

"Good. Meet me outside the lift on the fourth floor in five minutes."

The hotel room was warm and spacious. It was both a bedroom and an office, a junior suite aimed at the busy executive guest. In the corner, at one side of a set of glass doors that led to a small balcony, was a writing desk with a stiff-backed chair and a modern table lamp. At the other side of the doors was a low coffee table and two comfortable armchairs. A king-sized bed took up most of the rest of the room. A medium sized ensuite, complete with both separate shower and bath, occupied a space to the right of the entrance door. There was a large flat screen TV fixed to the wall above a dressing table at the end of the bed.

"If you would like to freshen up there are disposable tooth brushes in the bathroom," she said.

It was more of an instruction than a suggestion, so Michael entered the ensuite and closed the door. For a moment, he wondered what the hell he was doing. He was both thrilled and unsure. He felt young again, but when he looked in the mirror he saw a familiar and *very* middle-aged man staring back at him. As he removed the blue plastic toothbrush from its sealed sleeve he noticed that his hands were shaking.

"Get a grip. What are you afraid of? It's not as if it will ever matter," he whispered to his double in the bathroom mirror.

He flushed the toilet, washed and dried his hands and went back into the bedroom, smelling of peppermint and soap.

She was standing at the balcony doors looking out across the city. Without turning around, she said, "I was afraid you'd died in there. I might have difficulty explaining that one, if you had!"

"No. Not dead yet," he said as she turned towards him. He could have sworn his heart missed a beat. She laughed. It made him relax. He thought it was a particularly lovely sound.

"Glad to hear it. Well then, I'm Susan" she said. She walked up to him and began to remove his jacket and unbutton his shirt.

Michael wasn't sure what to do with his hands. He was forty-four years old, had been married and divorced, had had a few, relatively brief and desperate, sexual liaisons in the lonely period following the break-up of his marriage and had recently ended a three-and-a-half-year relationship with someone more than ten years his junior. He was experienced and mature, yet here, with this beautiful stranger, he felt awkward and shy.

"So, what's your name?" she asked, "and remember, no lies. I'll know if you're lying."

"Francis" he said, unblinking.

Susan narrowed her hazel eyes.

"Francis?" She rolled the name around her mouth, like it was a ball of sugar.

"Are you called Frank?" she said.

"I'm called a lot of things, but Frank is not one of them."

"Well, tell me Francis, have you ever made love to a stranger before?"

He was glad she hadn't used the other term.

"No," he said. He touched her face. "No," he said again.

"Aren't you going to ask me if I have?" she said.

He ran the back of his hands down the front of her silk blouse. Her body responded to the touch.

"No." he whispered and he kissed her on the lips.

"Hmm," she said, "a romantic."

He smiled and freed the blouse tails from beneath the waist of her pleated skirt. Her skin was warm and she shivered slightly at his touch.

"Romantic or not, you'll be wearing a condom," she said, as she opened the buckle of his belt and, in one swift movement, tugged both his trousers and briefs down to his ankles.

When they were both fully naked they fell together onto the bed. Susan had spent some time gently fitting on the condom. Michael had been surprised that, despite how excited he had become by her gentle caresses, he had succeeded in controlling himself. At first she dominated him, astride his body, legs wide across the bed, pelvis rocking forcefully, pulling him further and further inside her. Susan's shoulder length hair flicked forwards and backwards with her every thrust and sigh. Her hands pressed down on his chests, fingernails digging gently into his skin, her tanned body arched upwards above his smiling face. Michael let Susan lead. He lay on his back and watched her watching him with her searching green eyes. His hands roamed her body and he reacted to her every quiver and subtle sign. When she slowed her rhythm, they rolled over and he took command. The union was like nothing he had ever felt before. He had heard of sexual compatibility but had never given it much thought. But here, with Susan he believed that it was possibly true.

Their love-making seemed to go on and on. The frantic beginnings and cautious excitement of the first act, was replaced by something slower and warmer, something more private and, somehow, familiar. They kissed and caressed, like old lovers reunited after a long separation. Michael had a notion that he knew Susan from somewhere in a forgotten past-life, and that she knew him; that they had a shared history, maybe in some other century, some other world, and the engine of their love-making had brought the shadows of its hidden memories into view. When they came, together in fierce and tortured bliss, it was electric. She gripped him inside herself so tightly that he thought he would never pull himself free. In the wild delirium of the final pulsating act, before Susan fell asleep beneath his wet body, Michael felt so alive and free that the joy he felt overwhelmed him and threatened to make him cry. Everything that had been dark was light. Everything that had been dying was rising into life. The hotel bedroom was filled with colour.

Susan slept for nearly twelve hours. At first, Michael lay beside her, watching her beautiful features slowly curl up and morph into the sleepy little girl that she once had been. After about an hour, he dragged himself free, covered her with the blankets and then went into the bathroom to shower. Her words rattled around in his head as the water washed his face and eyes: "When it's over, you leave. Are we clear?"

Should he go now, or wait until she wakes up? he wondered. In the end, he got dressed, sat down in one of the armchairs and, all through the night and into the morning, watched he./////////˜r sleep.

When Susan woke, and saw him there, she looked confused. When she saw that he was fully dressed, her mood turned to anger. Why was he still here? How had he dressed so quickly, without her knowing? Had she dropped off for a moment? What time was it? Quarter to eight? He needs to leave.

"I was thinking of going for breakfast, at that little café overlooking the harbour," he said, nodding over his shoulder, "I know it's against your rules, but I'd love you to join me. No strings attached. Just breakfast and small-talk."

"You need to leave," she said again, standing now, the blankets wrapped around her body, "I want you to leave. Anyway, I don't know where I will be tomorrow morning."

"Tomorrow morning?" Michael said, looking bewildered, "I meant breakfast now, in the next half hour. I'll wait for you. If you don't come, I'll understand. No strings."

He rose from the chair, grabbed his jacket and moved towards the door.

"What do you mean, now? Who has breakfast at eight at night?"

Michael made a face. "It's morning," he said, "you slept through the night."

"What? That's impossible," she said, "Impossible! I don't sleep. I haven't slept more than two hours in a row, any night, in the last ten years." She seemed genuinely troubled.

"Well you slept for nearly twelve hours solid, and you slept well. I just watched over you, that's all. I'm sorry if I frightened you by staying. I should have left but…" he thought he saw fear in her eyes, "…I'll, I'll go now."

When he got to the door he turned around and faced her. He wanted to say something else, something important, but he couldn't collect his thoughts. He had a childish urge to say "thank you", but resisted. He left her room and made his way back down to the hotel lobby. His mouth was dry and he had a strange aching in his chest…

A loud knock on the bedroom door made Michael jolt out of the dream memory. He managed a hoarse "yes?" The person knocked again. "Yes?" Michael said, louder this time.

"May I come in?"

It was his brother, the Prior.

"Of course. Come in. I'm awake."

Michael sat up in the bed. The Prior entered with a hearty smile. "Good morning. Did you sleep well?" he said.

Michael could tell that his brother had been up for quite some time.

"Yes I did, thank you. What time is it?"

"Just after half past eight. It's a beautiful morning."

"I can see that," said Michael, looking toward the French doors.

"Did you sleep with the curtains open?"

"No. I was up a while ago, but I got back into bed."

"Ah, right. I just came in to tell you that I have to go out, and that I won't be back 'til this evening. Will you be okay?"

"Sure. I plan to go into town and call on Primrose," said Michael.

"Good. It's going to be another nice day. Make the most of it, while it lasts," said Father Francis.

Michael smiled at his brother. "I love the room," he said, " and I noticed mum's wardrobe. It looks like it belongs here."

"I'm glad you think that. There is something of mum in almost every room in the monastery." Father Francis stared at the wardrobe for a moment and then said, "Well, there's a shower room at the end of the hall and you know where the toilets are, don't you? Off the main hall. Breakfast is self-service, in the refectory again. Do you remember how to get there?"

"Yes. I'll be fine," said Michael.

"Bother Benjamin will take you to town, and he knows where Primrose's gallery is. She will probably be there."

"I thought I might walk in," said Michael, climbing out of bed for the second time that morning, thinking how the second time is always much harder than the first.

"It's much further than you think, over four miles, and the road is narrow in places, there is no footpath and it has a lot of sharp, blind corners. Not great for walking. There is a coastal path, which is longer, but safer, unless the weather changes, which it does, frequently and without warning. Until you are more familiar with the island and it's strange and unpredictable weather, I suggest accepting local knowledge is the best option. I know how you like your long walks, Michael, but today let Brother Benjamin take you. He is in the cellars with Father Bernard. It's the door under the main stairs. You will have to go down. They won't hear you from the hall. Anyway, I'd better get going or I'll be late for Mass. Can't have that. There could be a riot. See you this evening. Call me if you need anything. Okay?"

He emphasised the "anything".

"Sure. Thanks. See you later, bro. And thanks, for everything."

Chapter 14.

Dr Susan McCarthy had just opened the doors of the island's only medical clinic, when her mobile phone began to ring.

She lifted the flap and saw the image of the Wicked Witch of the West from The Wizard of Oz on the small screen.

"Hello mother," she said with a sigh.

Her mother began to argue. Susan interrupted her.

"No this doesn't mean that I'm *not* going to Canada. I just have eight weeks to kill, so I agreed to take this posting."

Her mother began again and Susan interrupted her again.

"I told you on the voice-mail I left. Didn't you listen to it? Skellig Éin. Yes. The pilgrimage island. It's a temporary locum. I'm doing it as a favour for a friend. The island doctor, Brendan Greene, died suddenly. Stroke, I believe. He was old and he should have retired years ago, and then his long-suffering nurse took off and she hasn't been heard of since. So the island is without a permanent doctor or a nurse and it seems the HSE is having trouble finding any replacements, so, as I was at a loose end, I agreed to stand in. They're paying me well and it's something different."

Her mother reverted to the old subject. Susan repeated what she'd said.

"It doesn't mean I'm staying here. It's only for eight weeks, that's all and then I'm off. I'm going to Canada, mother. You know that, and we've discussed this."

Her mother said something about being left on her own.

"We've discussed this. Look, I'm here now. I'll be back on the mainland in two weeks' time. I'll call down. We'll go for lunch. Okay? Yes. I'm fine. I'm staying in the Tara Cove Hotel.

It's absolute luxury and the HSE is paying. Yes, I'm eating and even sleeping a little. What? Yes, I said sleeping. It must be the sea air. I'll see you in a couple of weeks. Okay? Yes. Bye, mother. Bye."

She disconnected and closed the flap.

Immediately, the phone started ringing again.

This time the caller ID said unknown number.

The voice on the line was strange.

"Hello. Yes, this is Dr McCarthy speaking. Oh, yes. Hello Mrs Fancy. Yes. Yes… Great. When can you start? Tomorrow? Great. I'll see you here at eight thirty. Do you have somewhere to stay? Oh, that's handy. I'm at the hotel. Well, I'll see you then. Bye. Goodbye, Mrs Fancy, Eileen. Okay. Grand. See you then, Eileen. Bye."

Susan closed the flap of her mobile and slipped the phone into her pocket. A district nurse, what good fortune, she thought. She put the key in the front door and entered the late Dr Greene's surgery for her second day of work on the island. The place still felt cold, despite the heat rising from the storage heaters that she'd remembered to switch on before she'd left the previous night. There was something odd about the atmosphere in the place and for the briefest moment, Susan wondered if Dr Greene's ghost haunted the little building.

As she closed the door a gust of wind whistled in and tickled the hairs on the back of her neck and she had the sudden memory of a recent kiss.

*

Mr G was not having a good week and, to top it all, he had just been summoned to an urgent meeting with the monstrous Sylvester Parker.

Mr G had often fantasised about ignoring the calling cards when they were hand delivered to his nightclub, but his business sense, and an innate instinct for survival, told him that it would not be a wise move. Mr G hadn't got to where he was by being stupid or by biting the hand that fed him. He had not survived in his particularly brutal world, by messing with his superiors. Whilst Sylvester Parker was an extremely wealthy and generous client, Mr G had no illusions about what sort of person he was. He knew that his infamous client was an extremely dangerous man and, if Mr G was totally honest with himself, Parker frightened him.

There were many stories told about Sylvester Parker's methods that were shocking, even for someone with Mr G's propensity for violence. But talk is cheap. It was not the hearsay that made Mr G's blood run cold. Unlike most people, Mr. G had actually met Sylvester Parker and the man gave him the creeps. From the moment he'd set eyes on Parker, Mr G knew that he was dealing with a force much more dangerous than anything he could muster, a very twisted and evil monster. Mr G recognised a psychopath when he saw one, and Sylvester Parker was a definitely a psychopath. He was a Devil.

Parker even looked like a Devil. He had a sickly pallor, small black eyes and a sharp cruel face. His long dark hair was greasy, pulled back from his forehead and tied into a tight pony-tail. Mr G was sure he wore face powder, eye-liner and rouge. His teeth were stained and crooked. He had bony fingers and long dirty fingernails, and his voice was loud and raspy. He looked unwashed, and gave off a sickly sweet smell of something chemical and something long dead. The thought of having to sit in the same room with him, made Mr G shudder, but once summoned, there was no getting out of it.

As usual the card had been hand-delivered by Parker's man servant, O'Hara, in an envelope with an elegant M.G. centred on the front in black ink. The envelope smelt of aniseed and must, and reminded Mr G of Parker. The cream-coloured card inside had rounded corners and gold-leaf edging, and could easily have been mistaken for an invitation to a garden party. It wasn't an invitation. It was a summons and, because it was unexpected, it carried a severe health warning. Today the message consisted of three words, written in the same hand that had addressed the envelope:

House -Twelve - Today

In the top left hand corner was another elegant M.G. and, centred under the short message, was an intertwining S and P. which looked suspiciously like a serpent climbing a lob-sided tree. The snakes head was formed by a small blob of ink, where the fountain pen had been left on the paper for a moment too long, becoming the body as the ink narrowed into the first curve, thickening in the middle and then narrowed again for the second curve, before ending at a sharp withdrawn point, like the tip of a fish hook. Mr. G was convinced that if he stared at the signature for long enough, the black snake would slither off the page.

O'Hara was a curious and odious creature, who showed no fear and seemed to find everything about Club 54 distasteful, including Mr G. In stark contrast to his master, O'Hara was fastidiously clean and, as Mr G noted on several occassions, made a point of not touching anything or anyone during his short visits. He never sat down, always wore gloves and, although about the same height as Mr G, managed to always be looking down on Mr G, both figuratively and literally. And O'Hara never said much. Mainly he watched and waited, until the drama was over. Sometimes Mr G watched back. O'Hara was as creepy as his employer. He was unnaturally skinny and he had pointed, feminine features and thin lips. Mr G was convinced that O'Hara wore a woman's corset under his tight-fitting waistcoat. When his mouth was shut, which was most of the time, the touching of his lips made a perfectly straight line. It made him look smug. Which he was. Fearless and smug. Given the opportunity, Mr G would be only too happy to strangle the little bastard with his bare hands. But that wasn't ever going to happen. O'Hara was to remain unmolested.

The routine was always the same.

As soon as he entered Mr G's wood panelled office O'Hara would carefully remove a small silver tray with a domed lid from the satchel he carried over his shoulder. The satchel was the only thing Stefan, Mr G's doorman and bodyguard, was allowed to search. Mr G took the tray without a word.

"Until you feel the heat on your fingers," O'Hara reminded him, with a cruel smile. Mr G didn't need reminding but, again, he held his tongue. As always, he placed the tray on his desk and removed the tightly fitting lid. In the centre was a small box of safety matches. As instructed by Parker at their first meeting, Mr G lit a match and set fire, first to the envelope, and then the calling card. In both cases he was forced to hold the corner of the burning paper until it was nothing but ash, only letting go when the flames blackened at his fingers and the pain made his eyes water. As usual he was careful to ensure that all the ashes fell into the tray. When the drama was complete and the lid replaced, Mr G handed the sealed tray back to O'Hara, without looking at him. He knew if he did, he'd find him smirking.

It was only after O'Hara had left, and Mr G was alone again, that he put his stinging fingertips into his mouth.

*

Brian Horse Hopkins was sitting in a comfortable armchair in one of the small alcoves dotted about the reception area of the Tara Cove Hotel and Conference Centre, thinking about the beautiful woman from the ferry, when she walked across the room in front of him. She was following a tall man wearing a chef's white apron. She was talking rapidly. When she saw Horse she stopped in mid-sentence and seemed to lose her train of thought. Horse smiled and nodded at her. She narrowed her eyes and frowned. He thought it made her look more beautiful. He broadened his smile. She shook her head dramatically; turned back the way she was going and followed the man in the apron through a set of swing doors into, what Horse guessed, was the hotel kitchen. He watched the doors until Paul Creagan arrived. To his great disappointment, the beautiful woman didn't re-emerge.

"Ah, there you are, Brian," said Superintendent Creagan as soon as he entered the hotel lobby.

"Here I am. The question is, where were you? I've been ringing your room since I got up. I was sure you'd gone native and run off with one of the lovely island ladies," said Horse.

"What?" said Creagan indignantly. He took the chair opposite the Englishman and furrowed his brow. Horse noticed that the Dubliner was wearing a new suit and wondered if the younger man had a different suit for every day of the week.

"I thought you'd run off on me, you know, to live in a cave like the founding Saint, whatever his name was, to make a rake of children with one of the local beauties, and spend your days teaching the little brats how to live off the land and master the dark art of sharp dressing?"

"You're in a good mood this morning Brian. Did something happen I should know about?"

"No, nothing happened. I had a good breakfast and a good sleep…well…that is, until about five thirty, when I was woken by a bunch of rowdy seagulls. I've never heard anything like it. Sounded like the battle of Bird Hill was happening outside my bedroom window."

"Skellig Éin," said Paul mysteriously.

Horse gave him a quizzical look.

"It means island of the birds or Bird Island," explained Paul.

"Oh I see. Well they don't put that in the hotel brochure, do they?"

"Ha," said Paul.

"So why were you out and about so early or can you tell me? Meeting this mysterious American contact that you are not allowed to talk about? By the way, please call me Horse. Everybody else does."

"Well, Horse, I was at a meeting, but it wasn't with an American. I have Irish contacts too, you know. I got a call early this morning from one of them. It appears someone dumped something into the ocean late last night, in a very remote part of the island."

"Drugs?"

"No. A 2011 Volkswagen Passat, actually"

"Huh?"

"Yeah, and they knew what they were at, too. They choose a very secluded cove, surrounded by high cliffs and very deep water. Up to five metres deep, actually. Whoever dumped the car, didn't want it found. They pulled the licence plates off before they sank it, but that was all. They forgot, or didn't bother about, the log-book. It was still in the glove compartment and, fortunately for us, inside a water-tight sandwich bag. The dumpers probably figured any paper in the car would quickly disintegrated, long before anyone found the car, if ever anyone did find it."

"So how did your man know about this?" asked Horse.

"Actually, he watched it happen. He was out fishing, heard the splash, and watched the car sink. Apparently, cars do take a bit of time to sink, just like in the movies. Well anyway, my man got some divers to go down to check it out."

"What sort of a fisherman is he?"

"A local, with a conscience. Back in the day, he was a look-out for the Gardaí, when the Provos were bringing guns and explosives in from Central America. Now he looks out for drugs."

"Handy man!" said Horse.

"Indeed."

"So what's the significance of this car then?"

"It's registered to a Mr Gregory Kelleher, an accountant with business interests here on the island."

"Get on with it, Paul. The suspense is killing me."

"Patience in a virtue, Horse."

Horse glanced at the doors of the kitchen and Paul continued.

"Gregory Kelleher is a chartered accountant and a man of some means. On the face of it, all his money is legit. Married for eight years, has two children and keeps very much to himself. Likes golf and attends Mass with his family every Sunday. Enjoys two family holidays a year, always to the same part of Portugal, one in early spring and one in September. Rents the same apartment. A family man, who likes his routine. He and the family spend the rest of the summer on Skellig Éin. He has a second office here. His main business office is in Galway. He drives a black Mercedes S Class which he changes every eighteen months. His firm owns a few other cars for the use of clients visiting the island. The 2011 Passat was one of these pool cars."

"Well," interrupted Horse, "so far, he sounds like a prime candidate for the Most Boring Islander of the Year award. I suspect there is a fly in this accountant's butt ointment?"

Creagan furrowed his brow again.

"Have you been drinking?" he said.

"Why? Are you buying? Seems a bit early in the morning, but if you're having one yourself, I suppose I couldn't let you drink alone. You Irish. Huh!"

"I was warned about you," said Creagan.

"Were you really? What did they say?" said Horse.

"Just that you can be a bit of a handful. Cavalier attitude, unorthodox and a bit of a comedian," said Paul with a smile.

"Thank God! I thought it was going to be something bad. Anyway, get back the riveting story of the accountant and his butt ointment."

"Yes, well, Gregory Kelleher won't be winning islander of the year, boring or otherwise, because it appears that he has a few secrets."

"Oh?" said Horse.

"It seems that Gregory has a liking for prostitutes and he regularly *plays away from home*, as you English might say. His preference is for young prostitutes, and, seemingly, the younger the better."

"At last! Our accountant is a sleeze-ball. Why didn't you say that at the beginning?" said Horse.

"It gets better. Gregory frequents the same brothel whenever he visits Dublin, which is at least once a week. As I said, he is a man who likes his routine. His wife thinks he's at client meetings."

"Let me guess. By any chance would this brothel be owned by a certain Maurice "the gimp" Gimple?"

"First prize to the English detective. Our very own Mr. G," said Paul.

"Well, well, well, you have been a busy little bee. This is news, indeed. Paul my son, things maybe lookin' up after all. The lights are comin' on and, even though our dance partners still smell funny, at least they aren't a couple of blokes, if you know what I mean."

"I have absolutely no idea what you mean, and I'm fairly sure you don't either, Horse."

"Ha. Fair point, Superintendent Creagan, but it's a nice image, isn't it?"

"If you say so, Horse."

The door behind Paul opened and the beautiful woman re-emerged carrying a box overflowing with vegetables. Horse was sure she glanced at him before heading out through the front doors. He stood up. "So what do say we call in on Mr Kelleher, and see what's up with this sunken car of his?" he said.

"I rang his office. He's away in Dublin today," said Paul getting to his feet.

"Dublin? At an away match, do you think?" said Horse.

"Most probably," said Paul. "He'll be back on the island tomorrow."

"Well, we'll call in on him then."

Horse went to the window and looked outside. The beautiful woman was climbing into a tiny car. He wondered would she look around; hoping she'd look around; willing her to look around.

She didn't.

Chapter 15.

After O'Hara left Studio 54 Mr G made his way down the two flights of stairs to the basement bar. It was the largest room in the club and included a stage and a dance floor. Most of the time the room was in semi-darkness, but now all the lights were on.

Stefan, the Russian doorman, caught up with him on the stairs. They didn't speak. After his encounter with O'Hara, Mr G was seething and he needed some way to vent his anger. Hurting people made him happy and, experience had shown him that satisfying his vicious tendencies, was the surest way of relieving tension. He pretended it didn't. He convinced himself that it was a necessary part of being a crime boss. How else, he'd asked himself, if not by violence, was he to show his minions who was in charge. The fact that hurting people gave Mr G a hard-on, was beside the point.

Rick Kavanagh and his crew were lined up against the back wall of the dance floor. When the club was open and the lights were low, the wall looked shiny and precious. With the lights on it revealed its true self, a greasy brown wall, with patches of peeling paint and missing plaster. Mo stood on Rick's left, whilst Megan and Lash stood, a bit apart, on his right-hand side.

Rats Egan was missing.

No one had been able to find Rats when they returned to the car with the new battery. What they did find was a battered bonnet, a smashed front windscreen and the front of the car covered in blood. They also found a trail of blood along the road. No one could fathom what had happened. Rats was gone and they all assumed the blood in the car and on the road was his.

Lash had been no help. They found him crouched on the back seat of the Passat, his face covered in tears and cocaine. He was uninjured but was so stoned that he was almost unconscious. He'd soiled himself. Somehow Lash had managed to rip a hole in the back seat to get to the boot of the car, and then pull through a large bag of Mr G's cocaine. He'd gorged himself. Despite the missing windscreen, it was hard to breathe inside the cabin. Not only did it stink of Lash's shit and Rats' blood, but particles of coke floated about in the confined space like talc. Rick, Stefan and the other driver had to drag Lash out from the back of the car by his legs. He put up a desperate fight and kept kicking and screaming at them, pleading with Rick not to let the Banshee get him. Lash got himself into such a state that he began hyperventilating and almost died on the drive back to Ballyhoary. Stefan and the other driver then had to make a third trip back to the Passat to clean up the evidence and get rid of the car. Mr G was woken, at two in the morning, to be told the news. He wasn't happy. He told Stefan to make sure Rick and the others reported to the nightclub first thing next morning. Once they arrived the Russian was to take them to the basement, for a team meeting.

O'Hara's surprise visit had delayed him but now Mr G was ready to see them. Stefan had got them to line up against the back wall. Rick looked wary. The big blond tattooed and pierced gang member named Mo, was trying to look hard, but Mr G knew he was scared, just like the others. Megan looked terrified and Lash looked stoned. He was smiling at nothing in particular.

The bright beams from the track-lighting over the dance floor had been directed unto the back wall, so that Rick and the others had to drop their heads to avoid the glare. They looked like prisoners awaiting execution by firing squad. It was exactly as Mr G would have wanted it. It was almost as if Stefan could read his mind, he thought. The idea that he and the Russian had similar ways of thinking made him happy. Finding Stefan had been a stroke of good fortune. He was a powerful bodyguard, an excellent doorman and, in Mr G's opinion, a kindred spirit. He understood Mr G.

Mr G walked over and stopped a foot from Rick Kavanagh. Stefan came and stood beside him. Rick continued to stare at the floor. Mr G reached out his left hand and gently lifted Rick's chin.

"What am I to do with you?" he said.

It was a rhetorical question. Rick opened his mouth to say something. The Russian stepped forward and, without warning, punched Rick hard in the stomach. When Rick dropped to his knees Mr G grabbed him by the hair and pulled his head back, forcing him to look into his eyes.

"Did I ever show you the ruby ring I got given by my Sicilian friend, Juan Carlos?" Mr G raised his right hand and made a fist. On his index finger was a gold ring with one enormous red stone.

"An unusually large ruby, don't you think? Very tough, with very, very, sharp edges. Beautiful, is it not? A gift from a friend. A man who keeps his promises. A man of honour!" said Mr G. He brought his fist close to Rick's face. Before Rick had time to consider whether he should answer any of Mr G's questions, Mr G drew back his arm and punched the ring into the socket of Rick's left eye. Kavanagh recoiled but Mr G, who still had him by the hair, slowly reeled him back toward him and punched him again. Both hands worked unison. Punch, recoil, reel back in and punch again. Again and again and again. Kavanagh's body squirmed and slipped on the polished timber floor, but Mr G kept a tight grip on his hair. With one last punch, Mr G let go. Rick collapsed into a pool of his own blood. He moaned and gulped for air and then started screaming. Megan started screaming too. Stefan stepped forward and kicked Rick viciously in the stomach.

"Shut dee fuck up, unless you want to lose dee other eye."

"It's okay Stefan, let them scream, no one can hear them down here," said Mr G.

The Russian took another swing with his heavy boot in Rick's direction. Mr G held out his hand.

"That's enough Stefan. It is done," he said.

Mr G. turned to the others. The earlier bravado was gone from Mo's face, replaced by a look of fear. Mr G. thought Mo might try to make a run for it. He didn't. Instead, he shuffled sideways, as far from Rick as he could, without being too obvious. Megan was shaking uncontrollably and she began to sob. Jimmy Lash Pierse, who was standing beside her, had watched Ricks' beating with the same vacant expression he'd had all along. He smiled when he saw Mr G looking at him.

Mr G scowled.

"Heeze become a retard," explained Stefan, on seeing Mr G's reaction, "since he overdosed. His mind is completely gone."

Mr G narrowed his eyes and regarded Lash suspiciously.

"Are you sure?" he said. Before the Russian answered, Lash nodded vigorously and broadened his smile.

"Sure," said Stefan, "'e's a retard now."

Mr G fiddled with his ruby ring. He'd gotten a lot of Rick's blood on his hands. He could feel it between his fingers. He turned and looked back at Mo. Mo's face had turned ashen, and was now almost as white as his hair. Mr G smiled at him then moved over and stood in front of Megan. Stefan moved with him. Megan flinched. Mr G leaned in and lifted her chin, just as he'd done with Rick.

"Do I frighten you?" he whispered.

She stared at the floor and nodded.

"You must know, I would never raise my hand to a woman," he said, "even to someone as wretched as you. Make yourself useful and tend to your boyfriend's injuries. He is your boyfriend, isn't he?"

Megan nodded again.

"Well then. It's your job to look after him, isn't it?"

Megan didn't move.

"What are you waiting for?" snapped Mr G. Megan dropped to her knees, beside Rick. Mr G. turned to Stefan.

"Get some bandages and bring two basins of warm water Stefan. And soap and towels."

Stefan looked annoyed and, just for a moment, Mr G thought the big Russian might disobey his instructions.

"Stefan?" said Mr G in his most dangerous voice. He watched as Stefan considered the instruction. Maybe, thought Mr G., Stefan was sorry that the beatings were over. Maybe Stefan would have liked to have hurt on of the others too. Mr G smiled at him. "The lesson is over, my Russian friend. The leader takes the punishment for the mistakes of his men. That is as it should be, is it not? We are done here, Stefan."

Stefan scowled, but then, did as he was told. He went away and soon returned with two basins of warm soapy water, and two large face towels. One of the basins he placed in front of Rick and Megan, and gave her a towel. She began gently cleaning Rick's eye. The second basin the Russian held out to Mr G so he could wash the blood off his hands. As he did Mr G said,

"Lord wash away my iniquities and cleanse me from my sins." Then he looked down at Rick and said, "Someone always pays. This time, it was your turn. An eye for an eye, Rick. It was your turn."

Before he left the basement, Mr G addressed them all.

"You will all stay here at the club until Pete Mercer arrives. Stefan will look after you. When I get back, you will return to the caves, and you will stay there until I have forgiven you. You have let me down twice, but I know that now, the lesson is learnt, and I am certain that you will not let me down again."

Lash smiled and nodded frenetically at Mr G., who made a point of ignoring him. Mr G handed the ruby ring to Stefan.

"Polish it and put it back in the box on my desk. Pete Mercer will be arriving later today. He should be here before I get back. He may have someone with him. He will take charge of this lot."

Mr G turned back and looked at the balled-up figure of Rick Kavanagh on the floor, "and make sure she knows what she's doing. I want him cleaned up. He's no good to us if he gets an infection and decides to die. And I don't want any nosy doctors having to be called out either."

"Okay," said Stefan, with little enthusiasm.

"And Stefan, let me know if Rats turns up, will you?"

"Okay. You go. Everything weel be okay. You go. Nothing to worry about, boss."

"Yes. I need to go. I should be back, sometime after one," said Mr G.

Mr G climbed back up the stairs, this time on his own. As he went, he thought about Stefan's words.

The Russian was wrong. Mr G did have a lot to worry about, most of which, began and ended, with a man called Sylvester Parker.

Chapter 16.

Mr G stood outside the tall iron gates, waiting for them to open. The gates were totally out of proportion to the two-storey house that sat in a hollow at the end of a long gravel drive. If the ornate gates were at odds with the house, it in turn, was totally at odds with its surroundings. Not only was it the only man-made structure in the flat featureless landscape, but it looked like someone had transplanted an English village rectory into an Irish bog. The house sat on about three acres which was bounded on all sides by an eight-foot-high mesh fence. Mr G despised the ornate gates, he hated the alien house and wanted to bulldoze the ugly fence. He hated everything about the place, and hated coming here. His spine ached from travelling in the back of the small stuffy van, and O'Hara's nasally voice, coming from the gate intercom, grated on his nerves.

"Wait for the gates to open fully, before proceeding," said the tinny voice from the intercom.

"I'm on foot, as you very well know, you creepy little moron," thought Mr G, but managed to hold his tongue.

"Someone will be waiting at the front door to greet you," continued O'Hara.

"Someone? I'm sure there is only you and him in there," Mr G wanted to scream, but instead let out a feeble "okay," before he could stop himself.

Mr G had followed procedures, as always, and was on time, as always, too. It was five minutes to twelve. He had left the club and walked to the laundrette. Mr G had an office at the back of *Crisp & Clean* which, together with the nightclub and a small tattoo parlour, constituted the legitimate side of his operations on the island. Mr G spent most of his working day in one or other

117

of the two offices. The laundrette was four doors down from the club, in the middle of a long terrace of two storey buildings. All the buildings in between were vacant and owned by Mr G. Each of the buildings, between club and laundrette, was secretly connected to its neighbour by a well disguised door in the party wall at either ground floor or basement level. The garden behind the laundrette backed onto a lane leading to a walled yard at the rear of his tattoo parlour, *The Devil's Ink Well*. The owner, Zero Mann, an Albanian refugee, did odd jobs for Mr G. These included transporting goods around the island and acting as a kind of chauffeur. Mr G travelled in silence in the back of Zero's old van, whenever he had to visit Mr Parker's house in the country.

As he made his way, on foot, up the gravel driveway, Mr G. thought about how much he hated everything about visiting Sylvester Parker.

He hated the initial threatening manner of the summons; he shuddered at the thought of having to slink about in the back of Zero's cold and uncomfortable van, sharing the same air with the great unwashed *tattoo artist*; and he despised having to cow-tow to the weirdo O'Hara, Parker's manservant. But mostly, Mr G hated his powerlessness in the face of it all - the fact that he had no choice in the matter. When he was given the order, he was expected to jump to attention. If he didn't, there would be consequences. It had to be done. First and foremost, Mr G was a businessman. Sylvester Parker was his employer, and one who paid handsomely, and this deal had a very special and unique prize, one that Mr G could not afford to let slip away. Business was business and what had to be done, had to be done.

Before he pressed the doorbell, Mr G checked his watch. It was a minute to twelve. O'Hara opened the door just as the bells of the Angelus called the pilgrims and parishioners of Skellig Éin to noon prayers.

"You made it, and *just* on time. He's expecting you," said the unnaturally skinny manservant.

"I'm never late, am I?" said Mr G. angrily, wanting to add, "of course he's expecting me, he summoned me, didn't he, you stupid little ponce," but, once again, he held his tongue.

"Well, you know what's good for you then, don't you, Gimple?" said O'Hara letting the snide remark turn to a smile.

His thin waist quivered when he stepped back to let Mr G into the hallway.

"This way," he said, directing Mr G toward the door of the sitting room that stood slightly ajar.

As Mr G passed O'Hara he noticed that the manservant smelt strongly of talc and women's perfume. Before entering the room, he turned and sneered at him, sniffed the air and shuddered dramatically.

Chapter 17.

Parker's study was unnaturally hot, although the source of the heat was not obvious to Mr G. It was exactly as it had been the last time Mr G visited, and the time before that. The room was gloomy and stank of body odour and fug.

Mr G entered slowly and took in as much of the surroundings as he could, without being obvious. He was always looking for something that he could use to his advantage. So far he'd found nothing. Parker sat behind his large mahogany desk watching him. An old-fashioned desk lamp, the only artificial light that was on in the room, cast a yellow glow and gave Parker's long face a jaundiced pallor. Heavy velour curtains were drawn across the bay window, blocking out most of the early afternoon sunlight. Mr G thought that they may once have been burgundy in colour, but were now so dirty they were almost black.

There was a squat limestone fireplace which was empty, and looked as if it hadn't been used in years. A cobweb covered the firebox and tiny dust motes, agitated by Mr G's arrival, bombarded its trembling silk. Scrunched up balls of cream writing paper littered the floor around an empty coal scuttle. The walls of the room were dirty, the colour of wet mushrooms, and cluttered with oil paintings, in ornate, old fashioned frames, African tribal masks and the stuffed heads of curious and, sometimes, unrecognisable animals. The floor was carpeted, the pattern of which would only ever be fully revealed, after hours of aggressive cleaning. It felt sticky under Mr G's shoes. Mr G guessed that he would have felt uncomfortable in the room even if he'd not been in the presence of Sylvester Parker.

One of the painting was particularly disquieting. It hung on the wall behind Sylvester Parker and it seemed to encapsulate the dreadfulness of place, and the room's only occupant. Mr G did not let his eyes linger on it.

It was the portrait of a mediaeval nobleman, seated in front of a landscape of horrors. His pose reminded Mr G of that of the Mona Lisa and, like with the Mona Lisa, the viewer was instantly drawn to the subjects' peculiar smile. Although bordering on cartoonish, the artist had managed, with a good deal of competency, to give the nobleman's face a personality which conveyed both cunning and menace. His eyes were gleeful and sly. His smile, evil. In the fields, that fell away behind him, there were graphic depictions of torture, rape, bestiality and murder. The nobleman was gloating and Mr G was convinced that if he spent too long staring at his wicked face, the nobleman might wink at him. The thought gave Mr G goose bumps. It was the darkest painting he'd ever set eyes on.

Sylvester Parker sat upright in his leather chair and smiled. It struck Mr G that Parker adopted much the same pose as the nobleman in the painting behind him, and exuded much the same air. Parker motioned to a stiff hard-backed chair that had been placed in front of the desk.

"You may sit," he said.

Mr G sat down. His hands felt hot. He wiped them on his trouser legs, before crossing them on his lap. He could hear faint noises that seemed to be coming from below the floor. He thought he could hear people screaming. He glanced up at the painting of the nobleman and thought he saw movement.

"It has been a very troubling week and I have been forced to consider whether my faith in you, Maurice, has been misplaced." Parker pronounced Mr G's first name as *Mawreece* and he paused momentarily between the *mis* and *placed.* It was theatrical and rather silly, but Mr G wasn't laughing. Parker wasn't speaking either, he was hissing. As he spoke, he lobbed a ball of cream writing paper from one hand to the other, whilst never taking his eyes of Mr G or seeming to blink.

"What am I to do with you, Maurice? Eh? What should I do?"

"I have it under control, Mr Parker," said Mr G, as firmly as he could. His mouth was dry, his words rushed. He found he needed to explain.

"It was a mistake. Two of the crew from Cork Street. I've dealt with it. It's all under control. It won't ever happen again. I can assure you of that, Mr Parker. Nothing like this will ever happen again. You have my word."

"Really? I don't think you know the meaning of control Maurice, or what it is, to give your word. Don't lie to me Maurice or I'll take more than just your *eye*. You may have dealt with your subordinate, but where is the *rat*, Maurice?"

Mr G stared at Parker. How could he have known about Kavanagh's beating. Parker read Mr G's shocked expression.

"Ha! I know everything you do Maurice. Everything! I make it my business to know. Your assurances mean nothing. Your lies are insulting. Betrayal will be punished."

"I would never lie to you. I would never betray you. Never! It is true that we haven't found Rats Egan yet, but we are searching, and we will find him - I can assure you of that - and when we do, he will pay for this, and then he will go missing again, permanently. I promise you that, Mr Parker!"

Parker continued to toss the ball of paper from one hand to the other, but now with added venom.

"Assurances. Promises. All very well, Maurice, but they are only words. I cannot tolerate loose ends. You must know that."

Before Mr G had a chance to respond Sylvester Parker flung the ball of paper he'd been playing with, hard into Mr G's face. Mr. G flinched and drew back on his chair, almost toppling over. The stinging ball of paper landed on his lap.

"You have twenty-four hours to deal with this. Twenty-four hours, or *you* will disappear, just like your rat, Maurice. Then I will have my fun. If you are lucky, I may find it in my cold heart to let you die, but I will have to think long and hard about it. I may decide to keep you alive. I can keep my playthings alive for a very, very long time, Maurice."

As if on cue the screaming sounds coming from under his feet, became louder by a couple of decibels.

"Am I making myself clear, Mister G?" said Parker with a cruel smile. Mr G's squeezed the ball of paper and clenched his buttocks. He had a sudden urge to empty his bladder.

"Of...course," he stammered.

"Find the rat before twelve tomorrow, and I will let this incident pass. You and I have work to do. Our foreign friends will be very displeased if we have to postpone the pick-up any longer."

Sylvester Parker stood up and turned around. Mr G didn't move. He wasn't sure his legs would hold his weight, if he tried to stand. Parker began to admire the painting of the nobleman.

"You may leave," he said.

Mr G stumbled from the room and through the already open front door. He didn't look at O'Hara, nor did he remember getting to the gate. The sunny morning was gone and layers of clouds swept in from the ocean, a lower band racing faster than the blanket of grey floating above it. His bladder ached but he knew he wouldn't be able to relieve himself until he was back in the tattoo parlour yard.

It was only when Mr G climbed back into the waiting van and shut the back doors, that he realised that he still gripped the ball of cream coloured writing-paper that Sylvester Parker had thrown at him. Without looking up, or saying anything to Zero Mann, his temporary driver, Mr G surreptitiously slipped it into the pocket of his jacket and closed his eyes.

Chapter 18.

After breakfast Michael found Brother Benjamin where his brother had said he would be, in the cellar with Father Bernard, the bursar.

The stone stairs leading to the basement was narrow and steep. Two flights of sixteen steps each, brought Michael to a long narrow corridor that sloped further down towards a heavy door in the end wall. From the bottom step of the stairs Michael could clearly hear the familiar nasally voice of the bursar, the same man who had quizzed him incessantly at dinner the previous night. For some reason, Father Bernard had taken an immediate dislike to Michael, which seemed odd given his obvious admiration, bordering on a fawning adulation, of the Prior. It had seemed to Michael that all of Father Bernard's self-regarded questions at dinner, had less to do with gleaning answers from the Prior's twin brother, and much more to do with making Father Bernard appear clever and funny. Michael found this irritating, but he smiled and nodded at the man's questions. "Of course, in your line of business…" Father Bernard would begin, with a knowing smile to the others at the table, or "You being a television celebrity, I would have thought…" and finishing with a "…wouldn't you agree?" or a "…surely not?" Each question was rhetorical and accompanied by a theatrical look of surprise. Michael had dealt with this interrogation with a polite nod or friendly shrug of his shoulders. In Michael's experience, the best way to deal with intellectual bullies was not to take their bait, and not engage in their arguments. His strategy had had the desired effect. When Father Bernard saw that he was failing totally in his attempts to rile Michael, he asked to be excused and left the table shortly after finishing his meal.

Michael guessed that by the end of the evening he had acquired, by no fault of his own, an enemy in the monastery.

From behind the heavy cellar door Michael could hear Father Bernard's voice. He was shouting and seemed to be annoyed with Brother Benjamin.

"Can't you put them in order, like I told you? If they are not in order, I will never be able to find them again. Sometimes I wonder if you're a help or a hindrance, Brother Benjamin. I can't think why our Prior puts so much trust in you."

"But they won't fit Father, and you said not to force them into place," Michael heard Benji say.

"Oh give them here, I'll show you. Of course there's room, didn't I arrange the cans there myself earlier?"

Michael knocked, but the conversation behind the door continued. Father Bernard raised his voice in exasperation.

"Oh really, now look what you made me do. Really, Brother Benjamin, you are no use to me at all. I'd be better off doing it myself."

Michael knocked louder and when there was still no reply, he decided to go in. The hinges screamed in protest as he pushed the heavy on the door, the sound silencing the men within. Michael entered and, to his surprise, stepped onto a metal gantry that looked down onto the cellar floor, five feet below. A curved stone ceiling hung a foot above his head. The gantry had a ships galley-ladder and a waist high guarding. Michael leaned on guarding and looked down.

"Hello! Brother Benjamin! Are you down there?" he said, pretending that he had heard none of the men's conversation.

The two priests stepped out from behind a row of shelves and looked up at Michael.

"Ah, there you are. And Father Brendan, how are you?" said Michael with a smile.

"Father Bernard," snapped the bursar.

"Bernard, sorry, yes, of course. Father Bernard. And how are you both today?

The two men seemed genuinely surprised, but before either could muster more than a grunted response, Michael went on.

"Brother Benjamin, I was wondering, when you have time, if you could bring me into town, sometime this morning? That is, if you're not too busy, of course. I'd love to have another go in the side-car," he added with a smile.

"Really? Em, well yes, of course," said the young Brother excitedly. His face lit up in the gloom of the stone room.

Michael looked around. It appeared as if the cellar had been hollowed out of solid rock, rather than built by the hard labour of Irish monks, hundreds of years before. The walls were constructed of stone rubble, the floor of flat stone slabs and the ceiling looked like the underside of a railway tunnel. Everything was grey. Even the white cassocks of the two priests seemed to be coated in a fine layer of dust. The cellar was cold, but not uncomfortably so and, despite all the greyness, and lack of natural light, it was not stuffy. It smelt of apples and garlic.

Had the room been empty, it may have looked enormous, but from Michael's vantage point, looking down from the gantry, it seemed small, almost cluttered. There were rows of floor to ceiling high shelving units, running front to back with narrow aisles in between, all laden with cans, jars and bottles.

Down the centre aisle, against the back wall of the cellar, Michael could see a dark rectangular hole in the stone floor. It looked like, and was about the size of, an open grave. From where he was he could just make out a short flight of stone steps leading down to another door in the back wall, which stood ajar. Michael could just make out the tops of other shelves in the room beyond. He guessed that the floor in the next room must be another five or six feet below the floor of this cellar.

"Down and down and down again," he said to himself.

"What was that?" said Father Bernard.

"Nothing Father. Just thinking aloud," said Michael.

Father Bernard gave him a dismissive look, then said with a curt smile,

"As for your request, I'm afraid I don't know if I can spare Brother Benjamin. We're very busy with the stock-taking today. No, no I'm sorry, but it's impossible. I can't spare him. Maybe later this evening?"

"B...but Father..." began Benji, before Michael interrupted him.

"Oh. I'm sorry. I must have misunderstood the Prior," said Michael. "It was Father Francis who suggested it. He must have been mistaken about the work that Brother Benjamin had to do for you. Never mind, I'll call a taxi. I will have to give my brother a piece of my mind when he gets back, making me climb down all those stairs, on a fool's errand."

Michael turned to leave. He saw Brother Benjamin's faced drop. Michael winked at him.

"Wait," said Father Bernard, "Maybe there is something I can do. I know I have some rearranging to do, which I can do on my own, and we can finish the stock-taking when Brother Benjamin gets back."

"Well if you're sure, Father Bernard? I wouldn't want to be a nuisance," said Michael, adding "I promise to send him straight back. Thank you, Father."

Michael gave Benji a secret triumphant smile.

"I'll meet you in the courtyard in ten minutes, if that suits you, Brother Benjamin?" he said.

"That would be great. Ten minutes. Yes!" enthused the young priest.

Michael hurried back out the door. The smell of garlic was making him feel ill and he didn't think Brother Benjamin would understand if he were to throw up again, on the way in to town.

*

Brother Benjamin left Michael at the doors of the gallery with a hearty backward wave of his hand, and a promise to return for him, whenever he needed a lift back to the Priory. As he headed off up the road Michael knew the young priest was smiling. Michael had shown enthusiasm from the get-go and was genuinely exhilarated by the hair-raising journey from the monastery to Ballyhoary, something he shared with Benji, as soon as he climbed out of the side-car.

"That was great. I haven't had so much fun in ages," he said when he took off the helmet and goggles, and handed them back to the young priest.

"I'll come and get you when you want to come home. You can ring the monastery," said Benji, adding, without thinking, "and if you say that Father Prior said that I should come get you, Father Bernard won't be able to say no." After thinking about what he'd just said, Benji blushed. Michael thought about teasing him, but decided not to.

"Thank you Brother Benjamin, you are very kind."

"Please call me Benji. Everyone does."

"Will do, and thank you again, Benji."

When Brother Benjamin was gone, Michael walked over and knocked on the blue front door of the gallery. No one answered. When he tried the handle, he found the door locked. He cupped his hands and peered through one of the side windows. There were no lights on inside. He stepped back, and then kept going until he reached the edge of the road. Everything was quiet. The building looked deserted. Michael cursed. He had no way of contacting Primrose. He was annoyed at himself for not asking his brother for her number before he left, and didn't dare call the Prior now, in case he was in the middle of mass, or confessions.

Michael looked around. The gallery building was set well back from the road and was surrounded, on three sides, by giant ancient trees. There was a small gravel carpark at the front, with a low timber post and rail fence, separating it from road. Over Michael's shoulder, on the far side of the road, was a wild lawn which ran down to the shore of the lake. It was a secluded location for a gallery, he thought, although no more than a ten-minute walk to Ballyhoary.

The gallery was housed in what appeared to be a converted school house, but this was an architectural conceit. When Michael looked in the window he saw that the interior was open-plan and modern. Great care had been taken, in both the design and execution, to make the building blend in with its wild surroundings. A rampant Virginia Creeper, which was just coming into leaf, covered everything bar the glass in the windows. The only indication that it was a business premises was a small double sided sign which hung from a pole at the entrance to the car park.

An eight-foot-high brick wall, which was also covered in the green creeper, separated the carpark from the back garden of the gallery. There was a hidden painted door, half way along. Michael walked over to it and, as he drew near, he could hear the faint sound of music coming from somewhere beyond. He tried the latch and found the door unlocked, so he pushed it open and entered another world.

Behind the door was a large well-tended landscaped garden which stood in stark contrast to its wild rugged surroundings. Michael was immediately struck by its beauty. It was an oasis of calm. A hidden sanctuary of peace.

With the exception of a large irregularly shaped lawn, there were flowerbeds everywhere. The secret garden was a symphony of dappled sunlight, dancing in the morning mist. Michael closed the door by gently lifting and replacing the latch, in the hope of not waking anything sleeping in the garden. Along with the music, which was a little louder now, Michael could hear the tinkling of water, although he couldn't see a fountain or a pond. He stepped to the edge of the lawn and looked about.

In the far corner, a timber bench sat in the shade of a weeping willow. At the centre of the lawn was a brick barbeque on an island of stone flags, reached by way of a series of stepping stones buried in the lawn. Next to the barbeque was a large clay oven. Between these two was a slated teak dining table with six wicker chairs. The table was covered by a rectangular umbrella. Among the shrubs and bushes, in the raised planters that bordered the lawn, there were stone and metal sculptures of various sizes. Some of the smaller pieces were on tall, purpose-made plinths, whilst the larger sculptures stood directly on the ground. There were discrete up-lighters around each piece of art, buried up to their necks in bark mulch.

"An extension of the gallery space," thought Michael.

The garden was an exercise in harmony and Michael recognised his old friend Primrose, everywhere he looked.

When he turned away from the garden and looked back at the building, what greeted him was both curious and unexpected. Unlike the traditional cottage-style of the front, the back of the building was two-storey and built in a very contemporary style. The walls were clad in raw galvanised steel, that seemed to be floating in the air, held together by a series of thin copper cables, like the stitched sails of a foreshortened galley. Now and then, the steel panels were punctured by large rectangular holes of dark glass. To one side, there was an odd-looking extension that jutted out about twenty feet into the garden. It looked, for all the world, like the front end of a glass-hulled steam liner that had, somehow, crashed through the building and dry-docked on the patio. The allusion to a ship's hull was due to the fact that the glass walls of the extension sloped outwards, from bottom to top, and its roof consisted of a hodgepodge of stepped overlapping materials that could, from a certain angle, appear as the different deck-levels of an ocean liner. The roof of the extension was bizarre. Sheets of corrugated tin sailed over stepped irregular panels of different coloured glass; a series of perforated circular trays of greening copper drained onto, what looked and sounded suspiciously like, rigid cardboard; and fans of bamboo thatch stood, like broken inadequate umbrellas, above the lot. It looked as if it had been made from discarded materials, or bits and pieces washed ashore after a storm. Michael could see that a large portion of the floor of the extension was glass too, under which a pool of crystal clear water shimmered in the colours from the roof above.

"The rain room," said Michael with a smile, "Primrose built her rain room."

Following the sound of the music, Michael found the brightly painted back door, tucked in behind one of the galvanised steel panels. He could hear Julie Andrews singing, *My Favourite Things*, from The Sound of Music.

He knocked. A little while later the music died away and, after what seemed like an age, the door opened and Michael stood face to face with his old friend Primrose Kyle.

*

"Francis," said Primrose, "it's you!"

"Michael," he corrected.

He smiled boyishly.

"Michael. Yes. Of course. Michael. Sorry. Come in. Come in. How are you?"

"I'm fine. And you? How are you, Primrose? I thought for a moment that you were out, but then I heard the music."

Before he'd crossed the threshold, she grabbed him, pulled him into her arms and hugged him so tightly that he thought she was angry and wanted to hurt him. When they pulled apart he saw that she was crying.

"Oh Michael, it's been so long. Too long," she choked.

She wiped her eyes then looked then looked him up and down, like a mother about to send her youngest off for his first day at school. She furrowed her brow.

"Are you really okay? You look thin," she said.

"I'm fine. Honestly. I still get my migraines, but they don't seem so bad, most of the time, anyway. So really, I'm much the man you remember, just older, much older."

She gave him one of her happy-sad smiles.

"Come in, come in," she said, closing the door.

"You look wonderful, Primrose. I swear, you look younger than you did twenty years ago, on the day we graduated."

"Twenty-one years ago," she corrected him, "It's so long ago. God, to be twenty-one again."

"Well, you really do look wonderful."

She continued to scrutinize him. Her colours were so familiar, he thought. They made him happy.

"It's been too long. We should have kept in contact. We should have made an effort."

"Life got in the way. I find it has a habit of spoiling plans, don't you?"

"Yes. You don't need to tell me that," she said.

Michael had a fleeting glimpse of the wild independent Primrose Kyle he used to know, before she became Primrose Brennan; before she became a wife and mother. He wondered about the big decision that she had made, twenty one years ago, the decision that had changed the course of her life so completely and had brought here to Skellig Éin and, ultimately, this reunion. In final year in art college in Dublin Primrose Kyle achieved a high distinction for her portraiture and was offered a place at the prestigious Goldsmith College of Art in London to continue her studies. It was a dream come true and an opportunity that very few art students from Ireland were ever offered. Primrose was ecstatic and, for a short time, became a minor celebrity - the talk of Mullingar. But then, life got in the way. She found out that she was pregnant. Against the advice of her tutors and many of her friends, and to the great relief and joy of her Catholic parents, Primrose decided to stay in Ireland and keep her baby. She turned down the place at Goldsmith, left Dublin and returned to her parents' house in Mullingar. After a hastily arranged and very private family wedding, Primrose married the father of the child and she became Mrs Paul Brennan, a loyal wife and, by all accounts, a doting mother.

"No, I don't suppose I do," said Michael.

She took his hand and led him into a large sitting room and kitchen that looked out into the garden. An open door at the far end of the room led into the two storey gallery space. A staircase in the corner led to a mezzanine floor above them.

"Sit down," she said, pointing to a couch. "Would you like a coffee, or something stronger?"

"A coffee would be grand. Black ,with a splash of cold water, please," he said.

Primrose put the kettle on.

Michael didn't sit down. Instead, he hovered about, gravitating toward a group of framed photographs on the granite mantelpiece above a wood-burning stove. Almost all of the photographs were of Primrose's daughter, Hanna. At all stages of her life Hanna looked like a miniature version of her mother.

"You made the right decision," he thought.

When he turned around Primrose was staring at him. Without a word, she dropped her eyes onto a neat pile of things that had been placed on the coffee table between them. Michael followed her gaze. There was a cardigan, a university scarf and a novel.

"Can you see her?" she whispered.

Michael walked over and picked up the novel. There was a leather bookmark, two-thirds of the way through. It was a tattered copy of "Emma" by Jane Austen.

"Yes," he said. He touched the soft cardigan.

"She has beautiful colours. They are so much like yours, Primrose."

Chapter 19.

Primrose gave Michael a tour of the art gallery. The ground floor was in two halves, the double height gallery at the front, which included a small artist's workshop, and the two-storey residence at the rear. The two sections were divided by a frosted glass-block wall, which rose to the first floor only. The wall was smoky white but was interspersed with blocks of colour – reds, blues and greens. It supported the mezzanine floor and was topped with a series of railway sleepers that in turn supported an ornate railing cast from bronze. The mezzanine level was part of the living quarters but also a viewing balcony into the art gallery below.

"How do you get into the Rain Room?" said Michael, scanning the blank wall that separated the kitchen from the glass extension for signs of a door. There was none.

"You'll see," said Primrose, smiling mysteriously.

She led him up the stairs to the mezzanine level. It was a library cum office cum sleeping quarters, but mostly a library. There was a large sofa-bed, a writing desk, several easy chairs and other bits of furniture. But mainly, there were books. They were on shelves, on the desk, on the chairs and on the floor. Full height bookshelves ran the entire length of two side walls. One half of one was devoted entirely to paperback novels. The taller, lower shelves, housed large books on art and artists. There was an eclectic mix. Michael spotted books on history and philosophy beside comedy and graphic novels. There were gardening and design guides along with the autobiographies of the famous and books on scientific studies and technology. Cook books seemed to be scattered randomly about.

"I need to sort them out," said Primrose, when Michael began to browse. He took down a book called "Birds of Ireland and Britain," by Father Michael O Donovan. It was published in nineteen forty-two and was full of exquisitely hand-painted drawings of birds in their natural habitat.

"They don't publish books like this anymore," Michael said absent-mindedly.

"It belonged to my grandfather. He loved birds and he knew the author, a teacher and artist. He did the drawings too. It's quite rare."

"It's beautiful," said Michael.

"Some people find birds frightening," said Primrose. "Hanna did for years, ever since a large seagull attacked her on a beach when she was a little girl. It swooped down and snatched the ice-cream cone, right out of her hand. Seagulls are big and brazen. I can't say I like them mush, but I adore the little birds. They bring music to my garden."

Michael carefully replaced the book and looked around.

The hi-fi, that had been playing Julie Andrews, sat on a low table at the centre of the back wall. Beside the hi-fi was a curiously shaped door, recessed into the wall.

At first, Michael thought the multi-coloured door was a piece of art. It's dark blue frame looked twisted, with one corner higher than the other, whilst the top section of the frame bowed upwards in the middle. The door itself, which was bright red, looked like it had being submerged in boiling water for long periods and had shrunk. Parts of the it's red face were cracked and stripped away, revealing a vivid yellow core. The green handle was large and awkward, and seemed too far from the edge of the frame to be of any use, and the elongated keyhole underneath, was straight out of a Salvador Dali painting. Like the roof of the glass extension in the garden, the whole assembly looked like it had been put together from old bits of timber washed up on a beach. Michael imagined he was seeing the door reflected in one of those wobbly mirrors in a fairground. It looked like something a toddler might draw.

A tilted sign above the door read:

Where there is Rain,
There is always
An Abundance of Life.

"Want to see?" said Primrose.

She opened the door.

Michael could hear the sound of trickling water again, much louder now. He followed Primrose.

Immediately inside the door there was the small circular metal landing of a spiral staircase that led down to the floor of the Rain Room. The staircase was sculptural, and appeared to be made from cast iron gutters, semi-circular channels and pipes.

"You get in from up here. Everything in my Rain Room enters from above," she said with a smile.

Michael followed Primrose down the tight spiral stairs.

When he reached the bottom, he gave out a silent gasp.

There was water everywhere; running across the various levels of the haphazard roof; trickling down the glass walls; dripping into small pools or splashing onto hard and soft surfaces. The room, which was much bigger than it looked from the garden because of the sloping walls, sparkled and sang. Despite all the water, the air was fresh and the room was surprisingly dry. Michael felt like Alice entering Wonderland.

It was magical and musical.

Primrose directed him towards one of two old armchairs positioned either side of another pot-bellied turf-burning stove. This one was much older than the one in the living room. There was a lot of other furniture in the room, but the space wasn't cluttered. There was a large couch, two more arm chairs, each with its own standard lamp, a small writing table with a leather chair, a tall free-standing double-sided bookshelf and a side board which housed a kettle, a coffee machine, crockery and cutlery and a compact fridge. The smooth stone flagged floor, which continued out under the glass wall into the garden, was covered with large Turkish rugs. There were plants everywhere too. The Rain Room was an extension of the garden, but separate from it, and part of the house but also, not part of it. It was the most amazing space Michael had ever been in. Being there had a curious effect on him. It demanded a primordial reaction. He wanted to laugh. It was inexplicably comforting. He imagined he was inside the body of a living creature – inside a womb.

"Now it is sleeping. The water you see and hear is coming from a containment tank in the attic. This place is something else completely, when it rains. If you are lucky it will rain while you are here. Then you'll really see my Rain Room, Michael."

They sat down.

"Is it just as you imagined it, all those years ago?" Michael asked.

Primrose had spoken of building a Rain Room for as long as he could remember. It was her response to the fashion of building sun-rooms and conservatories, on the back of Irish houses. Primrose argued that it was ridiculous for Irish people to build monuments to the sun, when the sun only showed up for a couple of weeks every year, when instead, they could glorify the rain, which was a constant and loyal companion, no matter what the season. No one took her seriously. But Primrose was always independently minded and she was convinced that her idea was a good one. If others didn't listen, then it was their loss. Someday, she promised herself, she'd build a Rain Room and, true to her word, she had done it.

"Yes and no. I had it built after Paul died, so I never got to share it with him. But the result is better than I ever imagined it. It is my place to read, and think and relax," she said. "A friend asked me to design one for him, but I declined. It's mine. I don't want to share it."

They sat for a while in relative silence. Michael noticed that, after a short time in the room, he stopped hearing the trickling water, just like the ticking of a clock or the sound of a lover breathing next to you in bed, become part of your aural landscape. He fingered Hanna's cardigan, which he had brought with him from upstairs. Her pulsed weakly.

"Tell me what happened to Hanna, and how I can help," he said.

Primrose told him about her life on the island.

She said she no longer sold her own art. Her gallery displayed the work of local artists. To pass the time, she gave art lessons, to children on Saturday mornings, and adults, two evenings a week. She sat on the board of the local primary school and painted for herself, as a form of relaxation. The paintings she made were personal and unusual. Even if see wanted to sell any of them, she probably couldn't. Tourists wanted Irish landscapes, Paul Henry-esque, not three dimensional geometric collages. Maybe if she lived in Dublin, there would be a market for her art. It didn't matter. Financially, she was very well off.

Michael thought Primrose looked tired. When she talked about Hanna her voice changed.

"We have been through a lot, in the past few years," she said. "There were bad times, but things are getting better. I believe a lot of the problems we had were a result of Paul's early death, and, in particular, how we both dealt with it. Her father's sudden passing, when Hanna was only fourteen, was devastating for her. Being an only child made it much worse. She clung to me. We clung to each other. But a fourteen-year-old should be thinking of other things, rebelling against their parents, breaking away, not clinging to them."

"Like we rebelled?" said Michael.

"Yes. Exactly. But I had to be strong for Hanna, Michael, and, for the first time in many years, my life had a real purpose. My focus was Hanna and I can't deny that I enjoyed the role of being a comforter for my grieving daughter. But I was being foolish and selfish. I see that now. Pretending everything was okay. Believing that I could fill the void that Paul had left. We were both suffering, but when I look back, I think I was taking advantage of the situation. You see, Hanna had always been much closer to her father. They talked a lot, probably kept secrets from me, not important ones, but secrets all the same, and I remember sometimes feeling excluded. Hanna adored Paul. Her grief was immense and, in truth, I was in no position to deal with it properly." Primrose lowered her eyes and swallowed hard. "In the years following Paul's death, Hanna buried herself in her studies. She did exceptionally well in her Leaving Certificate and got a scholarship to Galway University, to study marine biology. She has always loved the sea. Of course, accepting a place in Galway meant moving away from home, and it was during her first year at university that the cracks in our relationship began to appear. We rowed whenever she came home, so she stayed away, more often than not. On the few occasions that she did come home, she brought ghastly young men with her, who were only interested in her for one reason. She is a beautiful young woman. The rows got worse and worse. I accused her of being childish, acting like a teenager, which is probably what she was doing, making up for the lost years; and she accused me of using her as a crutch. We even rowed in public, out on the street."

Primrose spoke quickly. Her voice faltered now and again, but she always managed to compose herself just before the tears arrived, and went on.

"It finally came to a head about a year ago. I threw her out, her and her guest, a man almost twice her age. I told her if she was going to throw away her life, she could do it on her own. She accused me of being glad that Paul had died, that I had never loved him. She said that he'd told her that my parents had forced me into the marrying him, and that I had never loved him. Oh God Michael, it wasn't true. I did love Paul and I missed him so much. Her words were so hurtful. It was the final straw.

"That row happened here, at the gallery, on the opening night of an exhibition for a local artist. I had been trying to get her to put on a show since I came to the island, but she'd always resisted. Finally, she agreed. I had arranged for a critic from the *Irish Independent* to come to the opening, and I invited the great and the good from the Dublin art scene. Hanna and her middle-aged boyfriend turned up, uninvited. They were drunk and very rude to the guests. Hannah and I nearly came to blows. The night was ruined. The local artist, a shy talented woman, didn't speak to me for months afterwards. I couldn't blame her. The review in the newspaper devoted two lines to the artist's work, and three and a half paragraphs to the mother and daughter cat-fight. Thinking about it, always makes me cringe."

Primrose closed her eyes.

"Hanna and her man-friend left the next morning and I really thought I'd never see my daughter again. She had been left a very large inheritance in Paul's will. She didn't need me and so she stayed away. We were both so stubborn. We are so alike."

Primrose could contain herself no longer, and started to cry. Michael rose from his seat but she held up a hand to stop him.

"I'm fine," she insisted.

After a moment, she continued.

"Despite everything, Hanna continued to do well in college and achieved a first-class honour in her masters. I was so proud of her, but my stupid pride prevented me from telling her how I felt. She got funding to do a PHD. Ironically, it was her research for this that brought her back to the island. Galway University has an annex here. Did you know that, Michael?"

"Yes. I saw it, on my way in," said Michael, "Big annex!"

"Oh yes. Mostly marine courses, but also geology, speleology, ornithology and certain archaeology courses. I believe they also have a small theological and history studies department. A lot of international students come here, some even from the Vatican, to study the life of St Áedán."

She wiped her eyes.

"Anyway, thanks the intervention of a mutual friend, actually, it was the artist whose opening night had been ruined by our cat-fighting, if you can believe that, we made up, and Hanna agreed to come home. Oh Michael, I can't tell you what it meant to me. This year has been the best year of my life. I'd almost lost my daughter, but she came back to me. But now, I've lost her again."

Primrose started to cry again.

This time Michael got up and went to her. He knelt in front of her and held her in his arms until she was spent.

"I need to go on," she said.

Michael waited.

She sniffled and wiped her eyes.

"Six days ago, Hanna was here. It rained hard and we sat here, drank wine, played *Scrabble* and laughed so much, it hurt. It was wonderful. The next day Hanna went missing and she has been missing ever since."

Primrose looked at Michael.

"We had planned to meet for lunch on Saturday. When she didn't turn up, I knew there was something wrong. I tried to find her, but nobody knew where she was. So I reported her disappearance to police headquarters in Galway. The Garda station here on the island is mostly unmanned. Part of the governments cost saving measures. Sometimes a Garda is sent over from Galway, but most of the time the station is empty and closed."

"It's happening all over rural Ireland," said Michael. He went back to his seat.

"When the Galway police found out about our legendary public fights, they simply stopped looking for Hanna. People are saying that Hanna has run away with a middle-aged lecturer from the university. The only one who believed me is the Prior. He said he'd help. He said you'd help."

"He was right. I will do everything I can."

"I knew you would," she said.

141

Michael's mobile vibrated in his pocket and then started to ring. "Sorry, I forgot to switch it off," he said. He retrieved the phone and flipped open the cover. An unknown number appeared on the screen. Michael narrowed his eyes.

"Take it, it's fine," said Primrose.

The old-fashioned ring tone persisted.

Michael answered.

"Hello?" he said.

"Michael? I have the right number, haven't I?" said an English voice."

"Brian? Yes it's me," said Michael, making a face at Primrose.

"Great. I wasn't sure you had given me the right number. Thought you might have done another runner mate, after I left you on the ferry," said Horse.

"No. I'm through with running, Brian. Anyway, I'm not smart enough to think of doing something that devious," said Michael smiling now.

He mouthed the words "old friend", when Primrose looked quizzically at him.

"You around for an afternoon pint, mate? There's some lovely pubs in the village," said Horse.

"Ballyhoary is a town, Brian. Actually, because it has a cathedral, it may, technically, be a city," Michael said.

"Only in Ireland mate! Anyway, the pubs in the village are what I'm interested in. What'd you say? I've got a car. I could come pick you up from the sanatorium, or wherever it is you're been held. I'm sure they'll let me take you out for the afternoon, me being a policeman, and all."

"Hold on a sec, Brian, and I'll ask matron if it's okay. By the way, I've given up the booze. Trying to lose a few pounds," said Michael. He lowered the phone, but could still hear Horse talking. "Lose a few pounds? You're a fackin' skeleton mate. You could be the poster boy for the front of a charity box…"

"Hold on a sec Brian, will you?" said Michael, cutting him short. He covered the mouthpiece with his hand and spoke to Primrose.

"Brian is a British detective. He's here on the island, attending a conference on cross-border co-operation, or something like that, at the Tara Cove. We worked together on *missing person* cases, in England. That's how I know him. It's purely by chance that he's here, but maybe he could help us find Hanna. I'm sure he'll help, if I ask him. Is there somewhere we can meet?"

"We could meet him at M&M's. It's on the main square."

"Is it a pub?"

"No. A coffee shop. Fantastic food. Beautiful homemade cakes. And you can speak to Marie. She's the artist I spoke about, Hanna's friend, well if she'll talk to you. She mightn't. She can be, at times, well, a bit odd. Artists! You know what we're like."

"Say, in half an hour?" said Michael.

"Your friend can't miss it. It's on the main square," said Primrose.

Michael made the arrangement. Horse seemed genuinely happy to help, but something told Michael that his English friend would have been much more enthusiastic had M&M's served beer and pork scratchings.

Chapter 20.

The three of them sat at a table behind a low wind breaker that separated the front garden of the coffee shop from the footpath. M&M's was on the southern, sunny side of the main square in Ballyhoary. Across the park they could see the ocean. Michael introduced Horse to Primrose when they arrived and Martha, one of the two "M's", took their order of cream teas and home-made scones. When Primrose enquired about Marie, Martha told them that her sister was away getting supplies, but that she should be back soon. After hearing Primroses' story Horse asked about the investigation.

"There is no investigation," said Primrose bitterly. "The Guards investigated Hanna's disappearance, when I first made my complaint, but as she is an adult and there were suggestions that she may have gone off with a married man, they simply dismissed my concerns and stopped looking."

"Could it be true, that Hanna was seeing this married lecturer?" said Michael.

"No. It's all rubbish," she snapped.

Michael and Horse looked at her.

"Sorry," she said.

"What's this geezer's name?" said Horse.

"Professor Larry Kearns. It seems he went missing at the same time Hanna did. He was known to have a thing for pretty young students and, apparently his marriage was on the rocks. He was Hanna's tutor, but she despised him. She told me herself. She said he was a creep."

"And Hanna was last seen on Wednesday morning at the university campus, is that right?" said Horse.

"Yes. A friend, Carroll Lenehan, met her in the corridor. Carroll told me Hanna was in an awful hurry and that she was on the way to meet Professor Kearns. Of course, that suited the polices' theory that they'd run off together."

"I see," said Horse, "well, we'll start there then. Carroll Lenehan."

"Hanna was very excited about the research she was doing, how life can exist in the most extreme conditions, places where there is no oxygen or no sunlight. Kearns was the top man in the field, so she had no choice but to work with him. He may be a letch, but he was also a brilliant scientist," said Primrose.

"And you're sure that there is nothing in the rumours? said Horse.

"I'm positive," said Primrose in a calm voice. "Hanna had recently met someone. A young man her own age. I think he may even be a couple of years younger than her. Kevin. I haven't met him. But I think it is serious. She was very happy, Detective Inspector Hopkins."

Horse nodded. His face was expressionless.

"Okay," he said, matter-of-factly. "The university is our first port of call, and I'll see what I can find out from the boys in Galway. My colleague, Paul Creagan, worked in Galway for a while and he knows the Chief Superintendent over there. I think his name is Sutton. Can you give me a list of Hanna's friends? We'll need to speak with the last people to see her, and find out, whatever we can, about this Professor Kearns fellow, and see if there is any connection between their disappearances. There mightn't be, of course. Can we see Hanna's room? She lived with you, didn't she?"

"Only the weekends. She has rooms in the University. It came with the scholarship. I'll do a list of her friends – the ones I know. I don't have a number for Kevin. I don't even know his surname, but I'd guess Carroll would know. As for Chief Superintendent Sutton, he's the one who said Hanna had run off with Professor Kearns. *It happens all the time*, he told me. I have no faith in him, or any of his people, for that matter," said Primrose.

"Oh. Okay. Well, leave it with us. I can't see the Garda in Galway having a problem with us casting a fresh pair of eyes over the file," said Horse.

Michael knew Horse was lying. From his experience working with the police force in England, he knew that policemen didn't like the idea of an outsider interfering in one of their cases, even if, in their opinion, there was no case there, in the first place. He also knew that an English policeman nosing about would not be welcomed either. However, Primrose seemed to be impressed by Horse and Michael knew that Horse would be discrete and thorough.

When Martha returned with the teas, Michael enquired about a bathroom. He felt a headache coming on.

"You'll have to use the downstairs toilet in the house," she told him. "The recent torrents caused the café toilets to flood and Barty O' Brien still hasn't gotten around to fixing them. It's through the green door marked private, then down the hall on the right, under the stairs. Mind your head; it used to be a broom cupboard."

"Did you 'ave it converted, when 'arry Potter moved away?" enquired Horse, giving Martha a cheeky grin.

"Oh no! Harry left years ago. It was only when Norman Bates and his mother were arrested, that we had it converted into a toilet," Martha said, before moving on to another customer.

*

When Michael re-emerged from the tiny under-stairs toilet, his face and hands were wet. He had tried to take a strong pain-killer for his headache, but there was no glass next to the small wash basin and he couldn't bend down in the tight space to get his head under the tap. In the end, he resorted to hastily scooping water with his hands into his mouth, before the bitter tablet had time to dissolve on his tongue. It was only when he had successfully managed to do this, that he noticed that there was no towel in the room either.

Standing in the hallway dripping water onto the carpet, Michael noticed that the kitchen door opposite was slightly ajar, so he tapped on it gently, with a wet finger.

"Hello?" he called out.

There was no answer.

He pushed the door open and immediately spotted a roll of kitchen towel on the counter.

"Hello," he said again.

The kitchen was empty, so he went in. He pulled off three sheets of paper towel from the roll, dried his hands and face, and then looked about for a bin. He couldn't see one.

The kitchen was large and bright and homely, with many feminine touches. There were oak *Shaker* units with a cream granite worktop; there was a large *Stanley* range with two comfortable armchairs in front of it; and, at the far end of the long room, a pine dining table with six chairs and a matching free-standing dresser, containing colourful hand-made crockery. All this was very traditional and not uncommon in many Irish country houses. If it wasn't for the unusual paintings that covered the magnolia walls, it could have been any kitchen in Ireland. But, the dark canvases changed the room completely.

The only difference between any of the paintings seemed to be their size. All were portrait-style, and all un-mounted, the thick paint extending to, and beyond, the wrap-around edges. They were almost three dimensional, with globules of paint, criss-crossed with lines and deep furrows. At first glance, they appeared to be paintings of grey rock, but on closer examination, and a little concentration, they revealed their true nature. Michael wondered if, for most viewers, each painting looked identical to the ones next to it, and that the only colours they saw, were different shades of grey. But that wasn't how he saw them. To Michael, each one was quite unique and he could clearly see colours among the greys. When he focussed, he could also see other things too.

Faces.

The paintings were portraits.

He was amazed.

"Very clever," he said. He walked over to a large portrait of a woman, who might have been an older version of Martha, the lady who had served them their tea. Next to this was a smaller portrait of a sad young man with eyes that looked very familiar. It might have been a portrait of Horse, when he was a teenager.

"What do you think you're doing? This is a private house. Didn't you read the sign on the door?" said a voice from the end of the room. Michael turned to see a very irate, but an extremely beautiful woman, standing at the open back door. He hadn't heard her come in and, before he had time to explain, she put down the bags she was carrying and picked up a poker from the coal scuttle.

"If you don't leave, I swear, I'll hit you with this," she said.

"I'm sorry. I was using the toilet and there was no towel. I just came in to take some kitchen roll. Please don't hit me. I was just admiring the portraits."

Michael held up the crushed paper towel, as proof that he was telling the truth. The beauty narrowed her eyes and lowered the poker a little. She looked somewhat like Martha.

"Is that your mother?" he said, pointing to the big painting.

"Who are you? Do I know you? You look familiar," she said.

"I'm Michael Eustace. I don't think we've ever met. You may know my brother, though, Father Francis? We look alike."

Her expression didn't change.

"You can see the woman, in that painting?" she said.

"Yes. I can see them all, if I concentrate. It's very clever. Are you the artist?"

"This is a private house, not an art gallery. I want you to leave," she said. Michael thought she looked frightened.

"I'm sorry. I shouldn't have come in. I'm sorry," he said.

When see said nothing more, he turned and left the way he'd come, taking the lump of wet kitchen towel with him.

When he returned to the table, he explained to the others why he had taken so long, and then called Martha over, as she was cleaning a table nearby.

"Is everything alright? Would you like some more tea?" she asked. Michael explained to her what had happened and apologised. He asked if she would speak with her sister for him, and to see if she could get her sister to join them. He explained why they were there and he introduced Horse to her. Martha said she'd do her best, but couldn't promise anything, explaining that her sister, Marie, usually didn't give people second chances. When Martha went inside, Primrose said,

"She'll come. I know she will. She's the artist I was telling you about earlier. She gave me a second chance, didn't she? And she's a friend of Hanna. She gave me a second chance. I'm certain she'll give you one too."

Chapter 21.

Daibhí French found Seánie Rats Egan, whilst out walking with his dog. Given that the elderly man was quite some distance from his, or any other house, he had no option but to use the mobile phone that Marie had given him, to call for help. Marie had insisted that he carry the phone with him always, but especially when out walking and, despite his abhorrence of the new technology, he respected her wishes. However, he had never actually used the phone and now was forced to try to recall her instructions. He remembered that the phone contained one stored number, hers, and so it was Marie that he called. He recognised her voice immediately, although she sounded slightly flustered. Somehow, she knew it was him because she didn't say "hello", but said, "Daibhí. Is everything alright?" As soon he explained that he and Hound were fine, she calmed down. As soon as he told her that he had found a dead body in the woods, she got agitated again. She told him to remain calm. He told her he *was* calm and that it was *she* who was getting excited. She told him that, by a curious coincidence, she was, at that very moment, sitting next to a policeman. She told him she'd put the policeman on. A confused Englishman came on the line.

"ello. This is Detective Inspector Brian Hopkins speaking. *Dotty,* is it?"

"Dr Daibhí French speaking. Are you a Garda?"

"Eh, no sir. I'm a Detective Inspector with the British police service. I'm here at a conference on the island, but I can arrange to get a Garda out to you, sir. What seems to be the trouble?"

"I've found a dead body, Detective Inspector Hopkins, in the woods at Seven Springs."

"Seven Springs? I'm afraid I don't know where that is, sir."

Daibhí sighed. The little phone felt funny at his ear. He could hear Marie's voice. She was telling the Englishman that she knew the way.

"Detective Inspector Hopkins?" said Daibhí.

"Yes Dotty?" said Horse.

"I'd prefer if Marie didn't come with you. The body is in a bad way. Quite cut up."

"I see. I understand," said Horse.

Marie came back on the line.

"Daibhí. Make your way down to the road and wait for us. We'll come to you straight away. "

"I'd rather you didn't come out here, Marie," he said.

"Don't be silly. Now make your way down to the road, and we'll be there soon," she said.

He said nothing.

"Daibhí," said Marie into his ear.

"Okay. I'll meet you in the lay-by, on Highfield Road."

Daibhí didn't head down to the road straight away. Instead, he found a seat in the mossy rotting trunk of a long-ago felled tree, and sat down. He needed to catch his breath. Using the mobile phone had annoyed him for some reason, although he couldn't say why. Hound sat on the ground beside him. The big dog was uncharacteristically quiet. Hound's usual canine curiosity, which had initially led Daibhí up the steep path to the clearing and the discovery, had completely deserted him. He lay at the old doctor's feet, with his head between his outstretched front paws, staring at a piece of ground just beyond his nose, making a point of not looking up at the body hanging in the tree.

"Sweet Jesus Christ Almighty, what in God's name happened?" whispered Daibhí.

Hound didn't reply.

Looking up at the flayed body, which dangled from a high branch of an ancient beech tree, Daibhí French found it impossible to imagine what could have caused such injuries or how the person had got up there. Even for a man with his medical background, it was difficult to be sure of the gender of the husk that hung like a slab of meat on a butcher's hook. He guessed that it was the body of a small man, by the width of the hips, but only a detailed examination would reveal the truth.

The injuries were extensive. It looked like the person had been torn to pieces before being hung in the tree.

The left arm and leg were missing entirely, as was the flesh and muscle from the left side of the head and face. The rest of the facial skin had been completely peeled back, exposing muscle, gristle and torn blood vessels. The one remaining eye sat precariously in an otherwise empty socket, like an abandoned bird's egg in the hollow of a gnarled tree. A handful of hair sprouted from a single clump of scalp. A large part of the right arm was missing too, and the skin over the chest, stomach and groin hung in a flap, like a bloody apron. A long section of intestine had burst free from the exposed gut and dangled down toward the forest floor, as if to take the place of the missing leg. A *Dr Martens* boot was the only item of clothing that had survived whatever had happened.

It was a surreal sight, made more curious for the fact that there was very little blood on the body, and none at all on the leaves of the surrounding trees, or on the ground underneath. If anything, thought Daibhí, the body looked jaundiced, as if it had been drained of its blood.

Even from his vantage point, twenty feet away, Daibhí could see that flies, and other insects, had begun to explore and lay their eggs inside the body. There was movement behind the ribs that made Daibhí flinch. A rat, or some other animal, must have managed to climb up and burrow inside.

Daibhí crossed himself and said a silent prayer, then he rose from his seat and climbed back down the wooded incline toward the road. Hound stayed close to his master, seemingly quite happy not to venture off on his own again.

*

"Holy fuck," Horse heard himself say, as soon as he stepped into the clearing and looked up at the body hanging in the trees. He turned quickly toward the old man standing behind him and apologised for the profanity.

"That's perfectly alright and understandable, Detective Inspector Hopkins," said Daibhí, who was panting slightly after the climb back up through the trees. "This is as far as I came. Hound went up there, directly under the body, but returned to me immediately. I think the old fellow got freaked-out by it. I've been wondering if it could have been an aeroplane accident, but…there's no debris. Oh, and I sat for a moment over there," continued the elderly doctor, pointing towards the felled tree behind them.

"Interesting," said Horse, not really listening to the old man. "Is Michael behind you? Where is he?" Horse stepped around the doctor and called back down the hill. "Michael! Where, the hell, are you?"

"I'm c…oming," gasped Michael, when he finally pushed through the trees and reached the clearing.

"Bloody 'ell, you're unfit, mate," said Horse.

Michael spotted the tree-trunk seat and went over and sat down. It took a while before his breathing slowed to a reasonable rate.

"Really Mick, you look like shi…terrible. You sure you're okay?" said Horse. He smiled apologetically at the doctor.

Michael nodded.

"I'll be fine in a moment," he said.

"Has your 'eadache gone?" Horse asked.

"Not yet. The tablet I took at the café should kick in, any time soon," said Michael, lowering his head.

"Arrgh," shouted Marie.

Horse turned around. Marie Joyce had joined them in the clearing and was staring up at the horror in the trees.

"Marie! You promised me you'd stay with the car," implored Dr French. Horse was happy to see her. He liked looking at Marie. He liked being near her.

"Really Miss. You should go back down," he said, with little conviction. He stepped in front of her, in an attempt to block her view of the body. "Really, Miss Joyce, we need to cordon off the crime scene," he continued. He tried to sound authoritative. He was close enough to smell her perfume.

"Crime scene? You mean someone did that to him?" she said. Marie twisted her body so she could see around Horse.

"Well, we don't know that for sure yet, but, for now, it's a crime scene and the fewer people 'ere the better, Miss."

Horse mirrored Marie's movement, stooping until she was looking squarely into his eyes. "Please Miss Joyce. Maybe you should take Dotty back down to the car?" he said. He had a terrible urge to kiss her.

Michael was calling his name. He was saying something important. The timbre of his voice was insistent. Horse had to work very hard to drag himself free from the spell Marie Joyce had cast upon him. Finally, he straightened up and turned around. Michael was on his feet and was looking up at the body in the trees.

"He's alive." Michael was saying.

"What? Who?" said Horse.

"He's still alive," said Michael again, "the man in the trees. He's still alive."

*

"Impossible," said Daibhí indignantly, "No one could be alive, in that state. The movement you see in his chest is …," Daibhí hesitated and looked at Marie, before finishing his sentence, "insects under the skin, and the release of trapped air within the body cavity. That's all."

"Uggh" said Marie.

"It's not the movement. He's still alive," insisted Michael, his eyes never leaving the body in the trees, his voice steady and calm. "He's dying, but he's still alive!"

Marie looked at Michael and then up at what was left of Rats Egan.

"How do you know?" she said.

"I can see it, his life," said Michael.

Marie looked back at Michael and she made a strange face.

"Are you sure, Michael?" said Horse.

"That's totally impossible," interjected Daibhí French, "no one could live with such injuries."

"I'm sure, Brian. I'm sure," said Michael, ignoring the old man.

"Well, this changes everything," said Horse.

Marie and Daibhí looked from the detective to Michael and then at each other.

"This is ridiculous, totally ridiculous," scoffed Daibhí. "Are you a medical man, sir?" he said to Michael. There was anger in the old man's voice.

"No," Michael said.

"I didn't think so. Think of the blood loss, for God's sakes. Two major limbs severed at the torso, not to mention the damage

155

to the groin and head! The poor man, if it is a man, would have drained of blood within a matter of minutes. And then there's the severe trauma and shock to the heart! That alone, would be enough to kill him." Daibhí's voice was raised. Marie gently squeezed his arm.

"Oh, I'm sorry dear," he said, turning towards her, "I didn't mean to disgust you." Horse saw that the look on Marie's face surprised the old man.

"I think he could be right, Daibhí," she whispered.

"What? Marie, dear, I may be old and going senile, but honestly, any one of these injuries is enough to...there is just no way he's alive."

"Let's leave it to the detective. You have done as much as you could. Will you bring me back down now, Daibhí? I don't like it here," said Marie.

"Yes, of course, my dear. Hound will be wondering where we've gotten to," said Daibhí.

Before they headed back down, Marie turned to Horse and gave him a knowing smile. He wanted to kiss her so much, it hurt. He smiled back.

He kept watching her until she and Daibhí were out of sight. Then he got out his phone and began to pace in a small circle. He called Paul Creagan. He spoke quickly and replied to Paul with short "hmm"s and "okays". He agreed that Paul would inform one of the senior members of the Irish police force attending the conference, and then get on to the island emergency services and let them know that a full incident team would be required. In the meantime, he and Michael would do what they could. If Michael was correct, and the victim *was* still alive, getting him down from the tree and to hospital was the priority. The story of how he got up there, would have to wait. Cordoning off the site would require ropes and ticker tape. Getting the body down from the tree was something else altogether and Horse hadn't yet worked-out how they would do that. At the very least they would need sturdy ropes, pulleys, step-ladders and some sort of scaffolding. It would be dark soon, so arc lamps and a generator may also be needed. Paul suggested contacting the university for equipment and manpower.

"Great idea, Paul, then get here as quick as you can. And find a doctor. Bring him with you. Okay? As quick as you can. Someone will meet you at the road. Cheers mate. Hurry now."

*

Dr Susan McCarthy was tidying her desk and getting ready to leave for the evening when there was a persistent assault on the intercom buzzer. Her district nurse, cum receptionist, Eileen Fancy, had left for the evening, trusting the temporary locum to lock up the surgery. Susan suspected another emergency and so she rushed to the door. Her stomach rumbled as she went. She hadn't eaten since breakfast and had been looking forward to trying the interesting looking Indian restaurant she had seen on her drive in, that morning. Food would have to wait.

"Well I told you didn't I?" Susan could hear her mother's voice, "If you must be a doctor like your father, then you'll have a doctor's life. And where did it get him? Never a moment's peace and an early grave, that's where."

The tall man standing on the doorstep was just about to press the bell again, when Susan opened the door.

"Is the doctor in? I need to speak with him urgently," the man said, in a posh Dublin accent.

"Are you looking for Dr Greene?" she said.

"Ehh...yes, I suppose so," he said.

"I'm afraid Dr Greene passed away recently. Are you a friend?"

"No. I need a doctor, eh...any doctor."

"I'm Dr Susan McCarthy. I'm the locum here, until a permanent replacement can be found. Do *you* need a doctor?"
The handsome man looked flustered. Susan could see he was embarrassed by his earlier sexist faux pas.

"It's not for me, Dr McCarthy. I'm Superintendent Paul Creagan. There's been an accident. We need a doctor to attend."

"A traffic accident?"

"No. I'm not sure. It's quite serious, from what I understand. The victim is in the woods, off Highfield Road, not far from the junction with Lake Drive."

He took out his badge and held it out to her. She didn't take it and gave it only a cursory glance.

"I believe you, Superintendent Creagan," she said.

"Well. I could be anyone," he said.

"I suppose so," she said.

"You will come then?"

"Yes, but I don't know the island Superintendent Creagan. Is Highfield Road far from here?"

"Actually, to be perfectly honest, Dr McCarthy, I don't know. I'm only visiting. I think it's a bit of a drive. I'll get directions as we go. You can come in my car," he said.

She raised her eyes. He was handsome, in a movie-star kind of way, all sharp edges and perfect teeth. He dressed like he was modelling his expensive suit.

"Maybe I should see that badge of yours again, just to be sure," she said, giving him her best smile.

He went to his pocket and retrieved his badge.

"I was joking," she said dryly.

"Oh," he said.

"I'll follow you, in my car. What are the injuries, do you know, Superintendent Creagan?" her tone matter-of-fact, her smile gone.

"No, but fairly extensive, I believe," said the Superintendent, "I just got the call from my colleague. He's with the bod...victim."

"Okay. No matter, I'll get my bag. Did you call emergency services?" asked Susan, "They're based on the university campus."

"I was on to them. They have only one ambulance and the island's two fire engines are tackling a blaze at a pharmaceutical plant in the valley. The ambulance is on route to the airport at the moment. An American tourist had a heart attack. They will be with us, as soon as they can."

"Yes I know about that. They left about fifteen minutes ago. Give me a minute to lock up. My car is around the back."

Three minutes later Susan got into her hire car and closed the door. It had a hollow smell, of new plastic and upholstery wax. Her stomach grumbled again. She had a quick look in the sun shade mirror. When she saw how tired she looked, she sighed. Her large hazel eyes had lost their usual sparkle. When the detective's car pulled up in front of her, and then moved off up the road, she turned on the engine and followed after him.

Chapter 22.

Susan reached the top of the steep climb through dense trees, feeling quite good about herself. She'd followed Superintendent Paul Creagan along a muddy rising path, silently thanking God she'd worn flat shoes to work. The Superintendent was panting loudly in front of her, whilst she was breathing normally.

"Bloody 'ell Creagan, you're in a worse state than Mick," said an Englishman, who was waiting for them at the top of the path. "Once you get your breath back, mate, I'll show you something that will take it away again,"

"This is...Doctor...McCarthy," Paul said, still panting, "Detective Inspector Brian Hopkins, of New Scotland Yard."

"Dr McCarthy? Hello," said Horse with a big smile. He stretched out his arm and offered her his hand. Susan wasn't sure if it was as a greeting or for support.

She shook it, with excessive vigour.

"Thank you so much for coming, Dr McCarthy," he said.

"Susan, please," she said, then, raising an eyebrow, "You're quite a bit outside of your jurisdiction, aren't you Detective Inspector Hopkins?"

"I suppose I am, Dr McCarthy, ha, ha. I'm here for the conference on cross border co-operation. At the Tara Cove Hotel. I happened to be with the lady who got the call about this, and I agreed to accompany her here. As soon as I saw what we were dealing with, I contacted Paul and asked him to find a doctor, and arrange a rescue party."

"Please call me Susan, Detective Inspector Hopkins. I had a quick chat with Dr French, before I came up. He says you believe the victim is still alive? Dr French told me he doubted it was possible, given the man's injuries." Susan adjusted the strap of the bulky bag she had slung over one shoulder.

"Let me take that for you, Dr Susan" the Englishman said, "and please call me Brian, or Horse. My friends call me Horse."

"I'm fine. It's not heavy. Thank you, Brian," she said.

"Righteo! Well, this way, then. Mind the brambles…Susan," he said.

Before Horse had taken two steps," Paul stopped him.

"Wait up, Horse. The people from the university are here."

Susan could hear other coming up the path.

"Who are they?" said Horse.

"With luck, they are cavers and rock climbers. I spoke to a professor. He agreed to bring whatever he could, for a mountain rescue. Hopefully, they'll have ropes and ladders and other equipment. We should talk to them," said Paul.

"You find out who they are and what they've got, then follow us. It's just through here. There's a large clearing. You might want to warn them though, Paul. It's not pretty back there," said Horse, "Come along, Dr Susan. Let me show you the subject of your next peer-group paper."

Behind Susan a portly middle aged man bounded up to the top of the path. He wasn't carrying anything. Behind him, she saw four heavily laden young men. The two at the back were carrying what looked like a large folded aluminium table.

"Are you Professor Darby?" said Paul.

"The very man! Kieran Darby at your service. And these are my four trusty Sherpa."

"Very good. I'm Garda Superintendent Paul Creagan. Nice to meet you. So what have you got for me, Professor?"

Susan recognised one of the students. He'd been in her surgery earlier in the day, accompanying a friend who'd had been bitten on the hand by some sort of animal, possibly a large dog. The student smiled at her. She smiled back.

"Are you coming or not, Doctor?" Horse called from the bushes up ahead.

"Coming," she said, then followed him along a short path into a clearing. Behind her she could hear Professor Darby laughing.

Once they were out of the cover of the bushes, Horse pointed upwards. "So Doc! You ever seen anything like that before?" he said.

Susan brought her hand to her mouth to stifle a gasp.

"Oh my God," she whispered. Despite a surprising degree of revulsion, she couldn't take her eyes off the horror in the trees. She saw the movement behind the ribs. It must be an animal, she thought. The idea made her shiver.

"Detective Inspector Hopkins…I mean, Brian. I agree with Dr French's opinion. This person is…*has* to be…dead."

"Under any other circumstances, Doc, I'd agree with you, but if Michael says the man is still alive, then I have to take it seriously. And Michael says, he's sure of it."

"Michael? Who's Michael?" she said.

The Englishman turned toward the back of the clearing, then shook his head.

"Huh? He was here a moment ago. He must have gone back down to the car. Michael's not great with the blood and guts stuff, but I trust his judgement. Believe me Doc, if Michael says this guy is alive, there's a pretty good chance he is. Don't ask me to explain. It is, what it is. Michael is never wrong about these things."

Susan wondered if it was some sort of joke, some sort of island initiation, a wind-up of the new female doctor. If it was, it was a hell of an elaborate rouse, and almost as unlikely, she concluded, as the person hanging in the tree being still alive.

Her eyes were drawn to the movement behind the rib cage. It bothered her, a lot.

"Well, I can't tell from down here. I'll need to take a closer look. So how do you want to do this, Brian?" she said.

"I don't think the guy is held up by much at all. That large branch seems to be hooked under his right arm – or, what's left of it – and that lower branch might be wedged up his…well, you know. With luck, the students will have brought some sort of scaffolding with them. If we can set up something under him, maybe a few of us could gently lift him off the branch, and lower him down. If he *is* still alive, we can make him comfortable here in the clearing, until the ambulance crew get here. I don't think an airlift is an option. The forest cover is too dense. But, we'll see. First we need to get up there, and get him down," he said.

"If he *is* alive, which I still very much doubt, lifting him off the branch penetrating his anus, will surely kill him. We will need to leave the branch where it is, so we'll need a saw," said Susan.

"Of course, you are right, doctor. What was I thinking?" said the Englishman.

"Okay. Set up your platform, and then I'll go up and take a look. If that's a rat in his chest, Inspector Horse, I won't be hanging around. If that's a rat up there, I'm gone. Are we clear?"

"Fair enough Doc. You go sit over there, and I'll call you when we're ready."

Susan didn't argue. She went over and sat on the felled tree-trunk and watched Paul Creagan come into the clearing, followed by the four students, carrying their gear. Behind them, came a very chirpy Professor Darby.

"I 'ope you have strong stomach, Professor," said Horse.

"Don't you worry about me Sir. I've seen my fair share of dead bodies in my time."

Not like this you haven't, thought Susan.

*

Professor Darby's stomach proved not as strong as he'd thought. As soon as he got a close look at what was left of the man in the tree, and then saw the movement in the chest cavity, he turned deadly pale and threw up into a hedge. Susan didn't bother to react. Better out than in, she thought. Darby moved away and sat on the ground looking miserable.

Susan watched with fascination as they erected the platform. When assembled, it became a large aluminium table with four strong adjustable legs. Once positioned under the body, each leg was braced to the nearest tree by a length of rope. There was an integrated ladder in one corner. The whole thing was up and in place in less than ten minutes, positioned centrally under the victim, so that the top of the table was less than a foot from the dangling *Dr Martens* boot. Before he called her over, the English detective asked Professor Darby if he'd go back down to the cars and get coats or blankets, if he could find any. The Professor seemed delighted to do so, and was gone before anyone had a chance to say *cheerio*.

"You're up, doc," said Horse.

Susan stood up, adjusted the shoulder-strap of her bag and headed over to Horse.

"After you," she said.

"Righteo," he said. Before going up the ladder, Horse turned to the group of students. "I think it's safe to say that this thing will take four of us. I need a volunteer. Which one of you chaps would like to go up there with us. The student that Susan recognised, stepped forward.

"Good man. What's your name?" said Horse.

"Kevin."

Horse climbed the ladder.

"Hi Kevin," said Susan, "How's your friend doing?"

"Paul? He's fine. He's a bit of a drama queen. He said you did a great job, sewing him up," said Kevin.

"Hey. Are you comin' up doc, or have you lost your nerve?" said Horse from the platform. She looked up at him. He was smiling at her.

"Remember what I said about the rat, Inspector Horse," she said.

"I remember. I remember," he said.

Susan climbed. Kevin followed her. Paul Creagan went up last. With the four of them, and the body, there wasn't much room. It was awkward to move about and the drop to the forest floor was close to eight feet. Just high enough, thought Susan, to look dangerous. She ended up behind the body, along with Kevin. Horse stood on the victim's left side, Paul on his right. Horse moved his face close to the movement in the chest cavity.

"Dr McCarthy, can you come around here and take a look at this. I'm sure it's not a rat."

"You'll have to shuffle along, Inspector," she said.

Everyone moved one space clockwise. Susan took Horse's place at the front of the body and he moved into the space vacated by Paul, who joined Kevin at the back. Now that she was up close, Susan could see that the movement behind the ribs had a regular rhythm.

"What do you think it is?" whispered Horse.

"I think, it's his heart," she said, "but I have never seen one beat so fast. It's impossible."

Horse leaned closer to her. All the skin and a fair amount of the muscle around the victim's chest was missing. He raised

163

himself up on his tiptoes and peered through a hole in the victim's breast plate.

"I can see it. It *is* his heart. Michael was right. He *is* alive."

"We'll have to get this man down and to hospital, Inspector," Susan said, "but I'll need to try to slow that down, before it explodes!"

Horse dropped back unto his heals and moved back. Susan went down on one knee and opened her bag. She found a syringe and a small vial of a bluish liquid. With practised ease she transferred the medicine into the syringe, tapping the sides, to release any trapped air bubbles. Then she stood and squirted a little of the liquid into the air. Dusk had arrived. It would soon be getting dark.

"This might help to slow it down a bit. I'll have to inject in straight into the heart. I can't be sure which of the veins are still connected," she said.

"OK. Let's do it then," said Horse.

"Everybody hold the body, just in case," Susan said. She didn't explain what she meant by *just in case*. Horse, Paul and Kevin held onto whatever they could. Susan gripped the syringe like a dagger.

"Are we ready?" she said.

"Not really. Be careful. If he kicks out, you could be sent flying, Susan. I don't want two bodies, okay?" said Horse.

She smiled at him.

"Well, you make sure he doesn't kick out then, Brian," she said. "So? Are we ready?"

Before anyone had a chance to answer, Susan jabbed the syringe into the victim's racing heart, and squeezed down on the plunger.

Nothing happened.

She withdrew the needle. As she did, she felt the pulse of the slowing heart reverberate along the needle's length. A tingling sensation ran, from the tips of her fingers, up her arm. It was a strange feeling, like a series of tiny electric shocks, or a short intense shot of *pins and needles*. Horse released his hold on the body. Paul and Kevin did likewise.

Susan thought she could hear something. She put her ear close to the victim's throat. It was a low gurgling noise, barely audible, even in the quiet forest. She raised her head and looked at Horse in amazement.

"He's breathing," she said, "and look, his heartbeat is slowing down!"

"His arm moved," said Kevin.

"We need to get him down. Do you have a saw?" said Susan.

"There's a small hack-saw with the tools," said Paul.

"It'll have to do," said Horse.

"I'll get it," said Kevin.

They shuffled clockwise again and Kevin climbed down the ladder. When he was gone Susan noticed movement in the victim's abdomen. She leaned closer, to take a look. Paul, who now stood next to her, leaned in too. She could smell him and recognised his expensive aftershave. In any other circumstance, she would have complimented him on his choice.

Susan stretched out a finger and gently pushed one of the victim's lower ribs. She felt something move behind the bone.

"Have you found something?" said Paul.

"Will you help me please, Paul?" she said.

"Eh…sure. I guess," he said.

"Do you think you could gently prise those two ribs apart? Very, very, gently. I need to take a closer look," she said.

"Eh...okay," said Paul. He didn't sound enthusiastic about the idea. Horse twisted his head around the body to see what was going on. "What is it?" he said.

"I'm not sure," said Susan, taking a flat head tweezers from her bag. Paul looked worried. She tried not to smile.

"You okay, Superintendent?" she said.

"Sure," he said.

With the index finger of his right hand, Paul pushed on the upper of the two ribs. Then, with the index finger of his other hand, he gently pulled the lower rib downwards. A gap in the gristle appeared.

"A little more please," Susan said.

Paul pushed the bones further apart. Something white moved within. Susan inserted the tweezers and pinched on soft white flesh. The thing reacted with lightning speed. Susan jumped backwards, as if she'd been electrocuted. Paul tried to pull away, but the creature grabbed his finger. Susan stumbled backwards and fell off the edge of the table, crying out as she went, knowing the hard ground was rushing towards her. She slammed her eyes shut and braced herself for the crash. Someone grabbed her wrist, and yanked her back, stopping her downward momentum. She swung widely to the right. When she opened her eyes, she saw that Horse had her. He was very strong and with one heave he hauled her back onto the table. At the same time Paul cried out and fell backwards off the table too. Dangling from the end of his finger was a long white worm, like the trailing tail of a diving kite. He crashed heavily into a thick hedge. Horse and Susan raced down the ladder after him. Paul emerged from the hedge like he was being attacked by a swarm of bees, his arms flailing about in every direction. The white worm was gone.

"What, the fuck, was that?" he shouted

His finger was bleeding. Susan took his hand, while Horse searched the undergrowth. The worm had bitten Paul hard enough to draw blood. The bite was circular, the size of an old one cent coin. Around the edge of the wound was a strange gummy liquid. It was milky coloured, with veins of almost luminous green running through it.

"What the hell," said Horse, when he joined them. "You ever seen anything like that before, Dr McCarthy?"

"As it happens, Horse, yes I have," she said.

"You 'ave? What is it?"

"I have no idea, but I saw the very same stuff around a bite wound, at the surgery, earlier today. Apparently it was caused by a large dog."

Chapter 23.

Sylvester Parker found out about Seánie Rats Egan's death almost immediately, even before the waiting medical team at Galway University Hospital were told to stand down, because the emergency case from Skellig Éin would not be arriving, after all. Rats died in the ambulance, as it made its dash to the airport.

A fire crew had arrived at the clearing not long after Paul had his accident. They brought ladders, harnesses and proper cutting equipment, and managed to get Rats down from the tree in one piece and alive. They left part of the branch that held him suspended, inside him. After clearing a wide passage through the trees, they stretchered him down the hillside and transferred him to the waiting ambulance. Susan suggested she go with the two-man ambulance crew, but they declined her offer, telling her they'd be fine and didn't need a doctor on board. The driver was a big man and his paramedic companion, bigger again.

The ambulance had gone no more than two miles down the road when Rats suddenly woke up. The paramedic had been installing a saline drip into his remaining arm, when he began to convulse violently. Because he wasn't strapped down, he threw himself around the confined space, like a beached fish gasping for oxygen. First he knocked the burly paramedic over and then, with wild spasmodic jerks, he kicked the floored man several times in the face with his steel toe-capped *Dr Martens*. On hearing the commotion in the back the ambulance, the driver pulled over. When he went around the back of the vehicle and opened the back doors, Rats Egan tumbled out and was dead before his mutilated body hit the cold hard asphalt.

Later that evening, O'Hara delivered another note to Mr G, in the usual form and the usual envelope. The message was contained in three lines and ten words. As usual the card was signed with the same snake-like "S" and, as custom demanded, once read, the card and its message went up in flames.

Rat in morgue.
Clean up – post haste.
Bring indisputable proof.

*

Susan left Marie and Daibhí at the gate of the retired doctor's pink two-storey cottage, did a three-point manoeuvre on the narrow road, and then headed back for the turn which would eventually bring them to the priory. Susan had offered to bring the three of them home because Horse and Paul Creagan had to stay at the crime scene. Marie insisted on staying the night with Daibhí. The old man was cold and he looked exhausted. When Marie got out of Susan's car she suggested to Michael, who had travelled without a word in the back with Daibhí, that he take her place in the front passenger seat. He did so, reluctantly.

When the road widened, at the base of the mountain, Susan steered the car onto the gravel verge and slammed on the breaks. The car skidded and moved sideways, but eventually stopped, throwing up a hail of dust and pebbles. Michael instinctively grabbed at the dashboard. Wide-eyed, he turned towards Susan. He found her twisted sideways in her seat, staring angrily at him.

"So what do I call you? Mystic Michael or Father Francis?"

When he didn't reply, she hissed at him.

"Well?"

"I'm Michael. My brother Francis is a priest. He's the Prior of the monastery. *Father* Francis. We are identical twins."

"You mean...wait...were you...?"

"It *was* me in Galway. Not my brother. It was me, Susan."

"Then you lied to me. You said your name was Francis."

"Does it matter?" Michael said.

"Does it matter? Of course it matters. You lied. You used your brother's name and I attacked him outside church. If you had to lie, why use his name?"

Michael couldn't answer her.

"I'm sorry," was the best he could do.

She looked like she might hit him. He thought of his brother's black eye and winced.

"I have a good mind to throw you out, and let you make your own way back," she said.

"I really am sorry, Susan. I wanted to tell you, but then...well, things just got out of hand."

The anger on her face softened and he saw the unusual colours dancing at the back of her perfect hazel eyes, the same ones he'd seen when they stood, face to face, in the hotel lobby.

Susan said nothing. She waited.

This was his opportunity, he knew, his last chance. He spoke quickly.

"When I saw you again Susan, back there in the clearing, I had to leave. I didn't want to cause you any trouble. But, well, I've been thinking and, I know it's against your rules, but I'd like to see you again. The truth is, I haven't been able to stop thinking about you, since that night," he said.

"You are un...believable," she said.

"Look, Susan, I'm too old to beat about the bush. I was going to try to find you. Really, I was."

"And how were you going to do that, exactly?" she said.

Michael looked at the colour marks her hands had left on the steering wheel.

"I have my ways," he said.

She shook her head dramatically, but he caught the shadow of a smile.

"Won't you give me another chance?" he said.

"How can I be sure that you are not lying to me again? You've lied to me before, Michael," she said.

"I'm not lying to you. I promise, I'll never lie to you again." He paused.

"Not everything is as it seems, Susan," he said.

"That's for sure. On the subject of *things not being how they seem*, how did you know the man was alive? That could have been an animal, moving about behind his ribs," she said.

"I could see his life."

Michael shrugged his shoulders, as if to say, isn't it obvious? When she gave him a dumbfounded look he said,

"It's my party trick, Susan. I see life!"

"What do you mean, you see life?"

"I see an aura of colours around people. It has something to do with their life force. Sometimes it's like a thin layer of smoke. When the person dies their colours disappear, but when they are alive, the colour aura is there on them, and I can see it. I could see his colours and that meant, he was still alive."

"Really?" she said.

"Really! I've been seeing the colours all my life, or at least, for as long as I can remember."

"Is it some sort of synaesthesia?" she said.

He shrugged his shoulders.

"If you are asking if I'm somewhere on the autistic spectrum, I don't think so. It's just something I've always been able to see. I have spoken with some autistic savants, people who see the world in terms of colour, but I've never met anybody with *my thing*," he said.

"Your thing? And you see these colours, around everybody?"

"Yes, but just people, not animals or trees or fish. Just people. The colours of human life."

"And everybody has a colour aura?"

"If they are alive, and everyone's colour aura is individual to them, like their fingerprints," he said.

"Wow. That's some trick," she said.

"I suppose," he said.

"And you've never met anyone who didn't possess this colour aura?" she said.

"Well, one person," he said.

"Only one? In all your life? Who was it?" she asked.

"Me," he said.

"Oh?"

"Yes. I don't have a colour aura or, if I do, I can't see it."

*

It was the Prior who opened the door to them. When he saw it was Michael, he gave him a toothy smile.

"Ah, there you are. We were getting worried about you, Michael. Brother Benjamin has been beside himself because you never called for him to come and collect you," he said.

"I managed to get a lift. This is Dr Susan McCarthy," he said, stepping aside, "but I believe you two have already met."

170

Susan stepped forward into the light. She was mortified and couldn't stop staring at the Prior's black eye. She covered her mouth with her hand.

"Oh God, Father. I am, so, sorry," she said.

Father Francis looked at Susan and then at his brother. His welcoming smile was gone, replaced by a stern look.

"How could you, Michael? Dr McCarthy, it is I who should apologise to you, for the actions of my brother. I am sure you have nothing to be ashamed of. It is Michael who should be apologising, to both of us."

The Prior offered her his hand. Susan shook it. His handshake was strong, his grip firm but gentle.

"I am delighted to meet you, Dr McCarthy. Have you taken over Dr Greene's practice?" he said.

"Please, call me Susan, Father. To answer your question, no I am only the temporary locum, until a permanent replacement can be found, or until my visa comes through."

"Are you going abroad, Dr McCarthy?" said the Prior.

"Yes. I have a job waiting for me in Canada," she said, "once my visa comes through."

"Well, I'm sorry to hear that," said the Prior.

"So am I," said Michael, with a frown.

Susan smiled at him.

"You two are quite the double act, aren't you?" she said.

"I suppose, we are," said the Prior.

"Speak for yourself," said Michael.

They all laughed.

"Won't you come in, Dr McCarthy?" said Prior.

"Not this evening, Father. I must to get back to my hotel."

"Well, maybe another time then?" he said.

"Yes. Well, I best be going. I'm sure we'll bump into each other again, Father, before I leave. Hopefully next time, under better circumstances," she said.

"Oh?" said the Prior, looking confused.

"I met your brother at the scene of an accident, and I gave im a lift back," she said.

"A *car* accident?" said the Prior.

"No. An attack of some sort," she said.

"Good God. Was it serious?" said the Prior.

"Yes, but the injured man is on his way to Galway. Once he is stabilised, he may be able to tell us what happened," she said, adding, "It was quite bizarre."

Michael nodded in agreement.

Susan stared at the Prior's black eye again.

"Would you like me to look at that eye for you, Father? It's the least I can do," she said

"No, no. It's fine. It looks much worse than it is," he said.

"I am so sorry," she said again, "I'm not usually so aggressive."

"My brother has a habit of making people do some very strange things," said the Prior, his smile back on his face. "Are you sure you won't come in, doctor? We'll be sitting down for evening meal, in the next fifteen minutes or so? Dr Greene often took a meal with us, after his visits around the island!"

"Thank you very much, but I've already eaten," she lied, "Really, I must be going now, I've had a long day. Some other time?"

"I'll hold you to that, Dr McCarthy" said the Prior. He took her hand again. "I'm so glad we had a chance to meet."

"*Susan*, please. Call me, Susan."

"Good night then, Susan. I look forward to meeting you again," he said. The Prior turned, and went back inside.

"I'll walk you to your car," Michael said.

Susan didn't object.

"I'd like to take you out to dinner tomorrow. What do you say, Dr McCarthy?"

"But, what about my rules?" she said.

"I think we've broken them already, don't you?"

She turned and faced him.

He hesitated for a moment, then kissed her.

She kissed him back. She felt warm inside.

"I have to go," she said.

"The Red Orchid at eight thirty? Lincoln and the Fish is playing later on, at Studio 54. They're a mixture of traditional Irish and blue grass. Supposed to be *the next big thing*. Studio 54 is having an over 35's night. So what do you think, Susan? We could sneak you in."

"Ha. I think you are precocious and persistent, but I'm not doing anything tomorrow night, so I suppose having you buy me dinner is better than eating on my own."

Her stomach grumbled at the thought of food.

"I have to go," she said.

"Tomorrow then?" he said.

"Tomorrow," she said. She knew her eyes were sparkling. They always sparkled when she was happy.

Susan climbed into the hire car and closed the door.

She drove back to Ballyhoary without seeing the road, being bothered by the plasticky smell in the cabin or listening to the grumbling of her stomach.

It was nearly five miles.

Susan smiled all the way there.

Chapter 24.

Rick Kavanagh sat in the front passenger seat of the small white van, attempting to stifle a yawn. Pete Mercer sat beside him, behind the wheel. Mo was crouched in the back. The engine had been off for fifteen minutes, but it still ticked regularly, as it cooled down. The inside of the van was cooling down too. Rick shivered. No one spoke. They just silently stared at the action happening in a pool of light on the far side of the carpark. They watched, and they waited.

It was past midnight and the night was particularly dark.

The morgue was housed in a single storey red brick building with long narrow windows at high level. It had one entrance, a set of double doors at the back. It had a low pitched slate roof and white plastic gutters. With its one oversized chimney, on the southern gable, it looked like a badly proportioned bungalow. The building sat awkwardly, in a sea of car parking, at the back of a complex of modern concrete and glass four storey university buildings, that housed various science departments. The morgue was dwarfed by these at the front, and by a forest of mature forty foot evergreens, at the rear. The parking spaces directly outside the double doors were reserved for staff, ambulances and the hearse. These spaces were usually empty. By 6.30pm every evening, most of the rest of the car park spaces were empty too. As there were no street lights, the small white van, sitting in the shadow of the trees, was completely invisible to anyone in or around the morgue building.

A small ambulance was backed up against the doors, which were thrown wide open. The doors of the ambulance were open wide too. Light spilled out from the building, and from the ambulance, but very little of either spread to the surrounding car park. Rick had visions of Red Indians watching cowboys around a camp fire. He fiddled with the thick bandage over his eye. His other eye twitched. He watched as the paramedics carried the body of Seánie Rats Egan into the building.

"Jah think they'll leave a guard wi' im tonite, Pete?" whispered Mo, leaning forward from the back of the van.

Pete turned on him.

"Shut the fuck up. Keep your fuckin' mouth shut dha' hear? I'll fuckin' cut your throat, so I will. An' that goes for you too, Popeye. You fuckers talk too fuckin' much."

Rick ignored the dig. He went to scratch at the big white plaster again, but resisted the urge. Mo sat back down on his make-shift seat and kept his mouth shut. Rick was sure Mo was sulking. Rick glanced sideways at Pete Mercer. Like his voice, Pete's face was hard and cold. He had a flat boxers' nose, small eyes and a cruel smile. His thin black hair was receding, so he combed it over and used wax to keep it in place. Rick guessed that Mercer, who was not much more than thirty years old, would be bald in a couple of years.

Rick hated Pete and, he knew, the feeling was mutual. Rick returned his attention to the action across the car park. Once they'd made their delivery, the ambulance crew switched off the lights, locked up the morgue and headed away. After a suitable interval, during which, nothing happened, Pete got quietly out of the van and told the others to do so too.

"An' be fuckin' quiet," he snarled.

Pete made Mo carry two jerry cans that looked heavy and smelt of petrol. He gave Rick a crowbar and a medium sized leather holdall. The bag felt empty.

Pete took the only torch and walked ahead of the others. Rick walked a few steps behind him and Mo took up the rear. It was a slow and silent procession. The smell of petrol was powerful in the chilly night air. At one point Mo stumbled over the edge of a raised kerb, and almost fell over. Pete didn't seem to hear and Rick acted like nothing had happened.

The building was not alarmed - who'd want to break into a morgue, thought Rick – and although the doors appeared to be strong, they weren't. The crowbar had little difficulty ripping apart the dead lock. The timber split open with a loud screech, but the noise lasted only a moment. Once silence returned, Pete opened the doors. Inside was a sparse empty lobby and a pair of half glass swing doors. These opened into a large white room which, with the exception of a small toilet and a big walk-in freezer, constituted the rest of the building. There was a strong smell of chemicals which, combined with the petrol fumes, made Rick feel queasy. Pete turned on his torch and focussed its narrow beam on a large black plastic bag that was perched on top of a shiny stainless steel table, in the middle of the room. But for the sparkle of a chrome zip, that ran from top to bottom along its length, it looked like an oversized sack of rubbish.

"That's gotta be 'im. There's nothing else in here, unless our geezer's in de freezer, ha, ha" Pete said with a loud chorkle.

Neither Rick nor Mo laughed at Pete's joke.

Pete scowled, then walked over to the table and pulled down the zip of the black bag. When he focussed the torchlight inside he jumped back in shock.

"Oh, the fuck sake!" he said.

Rick approached cautiously.

"The fuck sake," Mercer repeated.

Even with one eye, which was blinking frantically in the sticky chemical atmosphere of the torch-lit morgue, Rick could see the full horrors of the body in the bag. It didn't look like Rats. Mo put the jerry cans on the floor and came over.

"That's not Rats," he declared.

"How' gha fuckin' know it's not? Looks like yer ma, does it, Mo?" said Pete.

Mo stepped back.

"I'm just sayin' dat it doesn't look like Rats, dats all," he said.

What was left of the body was lying on its side, with its head twisted at an impossible angle. Had there been eyeballs in either of the empty sockets, they would have been staring straight up at the ceiling. The broken jaw, half of which had been stripped back to the bone, drooped to one side and the gaping cavity, that once had been his mouth, was empty of tongue and teeth. In the flickering torchlight, it seemed a twin to the dark hollow that marked the place where once there'd been a nose.

It looked like some animal had taken an enormous bite out of the side of the neck. Through the gap, Rick could see the upper part of the spinal column.

"C'm here Mo an' turn 'is head aroun'," said Mercer, holding the torch over the table.

"Wha?" said Mo.

"Turn 'is fuckin' head aroun'. Giz a look a' de back of his head! Go on yah fuckin' pussy. We havin' gaw all nite. He won' fuckin' bite."

"That's 'cos he doesn't have any teeth," said Mo, laughing raucously at his own joke.

Mercer looked angry

"Turn 'is fuckin' head, or you'll be in the fuckin' bag with him!"

"Calm down. I was only jokin'. He can't bite me. He's got no fuckin' teeth. Get it?" said Mo.

"I swear, if you don' fuckin' turn his head, *you'll* have no fuckin' teeth, you fuckin' stupid cun'."

"Alright. Alright. I'm turnin' his fuckin' head. Calm down," said Mo sullenly.

Mo took a deep breath and stretched out his arms. He slowly touched the head. Rick thought the bloody skull looked small in Mo's big hands. It surprised Rick how careful Mo was, almost respectful, like he was touching something precious.

Rick had an urge to bless himself, but thought better of it.

"Go on den, turn it, so's we can see de tattoo," said Mercer, shining the bright light into Mo's eyes.

"Oh right! His tattoo! Yeh. Okay!" said Mo.

Mo lifted the small head off the table and twisted it to one side. It moved with surprising ease. When he twisted it more than he should have been able to, there was a horrible squelching noise. Pete focussed the torchlight on what was left of the collar line. At the base of the skull there was a tattoo which read *Mum*, drawn in a gothic script.

"That's Rats alrigh! I want me mummy," sneered Mercer.

He turned the torch and pointed it at Rick.

"C'mere Popeye. Is this your boyfriend, the late Séanie *Rats* Egan?"

Rick looked at the tattoo.

"Yeh. That's Rats," he said.

"Then that means, you're up. Push back there Mo, and give 'im room. Popeye's got some operatin' te do. You'll find a hacksaw in de bag there, Kavanagh. Mr G wants de head - with de tattoo. So fuckin' watch where you're cuttin', okay?"

"You want me to cut off his head?" said Rick aghast.

"That's fuckin' righ, smart boy, an' be fuckin' quick about it, or you'll be doin' it blind, gha know wha' I mean?"

Mercer looked particularly vicious in the shadowy light. Mo moved well back and out of Rick's way. When Rick stepped closer to Rats he thought he might collapse. His hands shook and the chemical smell made his head spin.

"Get, the fuck, on with it. We haven't gaw all nite!" snapped Pete.

Although he could no longer see his face, Rick knew that Pete was smiling.

Ten minutes later the white van crossed car park, in total darkness. Only when they reached the road did Pete turn on the lights. Rick had stopped shaking, but he still felt sick to his stomach. He sat bolt upright on the front passenger seat and stared blankly through the rear view mirror. The sports bag containing Rats Egan's head, sat on the floor between his feet. He barely registered seeing the angry flames, as they ripped open the roof of the morgue building behind them. His field of vision narrowed. Something else caught his eye in the rear view mirror. It was much closer to hand, and it winked at him. When he focussed on it he saw that there was something on the white bandage over his damaged eye. He'd been scratching the eye patch with his bloodied hands and had left traces of Rats' blood and other stuff on the bandage. The *other stuff* was creamy white, with veins of green running through. It reminded Rick of the colours of Connemara marble. The green substance was almost luminous and, as he stared at it, it slowly soaked into the cotton bandage and disappeared. He touched the bandage and found it was saturated. When he pressed on it a line of the milky substance dribbled down his cheek and onto his top lip. It tasted like fish. He rubbed his mouth with the back of his hand and then looked in the mirror again. The luminous green goo was completely gone. There was none on his face or on the bandage. Rick wondered if he'd imagined seeing it. By the time they got back to the small car park behind the tattoo parlour, the bandage over Rick's eye was completely dry.

*

179

When evening meal was over, Michael and Father Francis retired to the Prior's study. Despite Brother Benjamin's happy countenance, Michael had been poor company at dinner and had asked to be excused before the dessert, saying that he was quite tired after his long day. Word of the incident in the woods had travelled fast and there were many questions and much discussion among the priests in the refectory. Michael tried his best to be polite and give the monks as little information as he could without being rude, while the Prior watched on with a look of concern. Father Francis followed Michael out and asked him to join him in his study for a nightcap.

They sat opposite each other at the smouldering fire. Michael refused the offer of a whiskey, so the Prior didn't take one either.

"Is there something wrong? Has something happened?" Fr. Francis said.

Michael stared into the flickering flames, but said nothing.

"It's that woman, Dr McCarthy? She's got to you, hasn't she?" said Father Francis.

"I can't hide anything from you, can I brother?" said Michael.

"She seems very nice. I think she likes you. There is a great passion in that woman. I have the black eye to prove it," said Father Francis

"It's not her. Yes, she lovely and yes, I really like her."

"I'm glad. She's beautiful too," said the Prior.

"Isn't noticing passion and beauty something you priests are not supposed to do?" said Michael.

"You really know nothing about Christianity, do you Michael? All those years going to mass every Sunday morning, and none of it got through to you. Christianity is *all* about passion and beauty."

"Really? Well in that case I'll have to start going to mass again. I've heard there is a very charismatic preacher on the island, so maybe I'll give it a go, while I'm here."

"I'd like that very much. But come for your own sake, not mine."

Michael leaned forward and lowered his head. The heat from the turf fire warmed the side of his face. His headache was back. This could be one of the big ones, he thought.

"She's leaving for Canada, is that it? You could try to change her mind, you know? You can be very persuasive, when you want to be Michael," said the Prior.

"You mean, I could kidnap her and lock her in the attic? Anyway, it's not about Susan," said Michael. He hesitated.

"I met Primrose," he said

"Oh yes, of course, I forgot," said the Prior.

Michael looked troubled.

The Prior's face fell.

"Oh God, is Hanna ...?

"No! She's not dead," interrupted Michael, "but she's in trouble, big trouble. Her colours are very weak."

"You must find her. You must," he said.

"You know that I will do everything I possibly can."

Michael turned and faced the fire.

Wherever Hanna was, he thought, she was dying..

Chapter 25.

Brother Benjamin slept fitfully and was woken several times by howling winds, booming thunder and, finally, by an urgent need to use the bathroom. The bedroom floor was cold under his bare feet, but the floor in the long corridor outside his room was colder still. As soon as he was ten paces from his bedroom door he thought about going back for his sandals, but his bladder insisted that he keep on going. The hall was dark and full of shadows but Benji decided not to turn on the lights, in case he woke anybody and caused a fuss. Michael's room was on this corridor and Benji knew it wouldn't do to wake up their famous guest.

With every rumble of thunder, Brother Benjamin's heart skipped a beat. He hurried along, as quickly as he dared, until a tremendous clap of thunder shook the walls and stopped him in his tracks. Once again he thought about going back, but the further he went, the greater became his need to use the bathroom. He moved forward, but slower than before. The silence between the booms of thunder was almost worse than the racket they made. His imagination started to play tricks on him. He felt that he was no longer alone in the corridor and that his presence had woken something, some kind of night demon, something from one of those horror comics he like to read, and Brother Benjamin was sure that, if he dared listen hard enough, he could hear giggling just below the sound of his own pounding heart. The hairs on the back of his neck stood up and his mouth went dry. His bladder began to hurt.

"You are a silly-billy Benji," he said. It was his mother's voice, and the thought of her gently scolding him, made him smile.

The double doors at the end of the corridor drew near. Michael's room was just before them. Benji stopped for a moment, and put his ear to Michael's door. He thought he could hear Michael talking to someone. Maybe he's up late, saying his prayers, thought Benji. The idea gave him comfort.

He quietly pushed through the double doors and entered the large entrance hall. The front doors, at the far end of the hall, rattled in the wind, but looked solid and secure. The toilet was half way down on the left, across the hall from the door leading to the cellar. The main staircase loomed large overhead and, in the flickering light, its spindly balustrades made it look like the skeleton of a monstrous snake. Lightening flashed through an enormous skylight above the stairwell and the rain on the glass sounded like handfuls of pebbles being thrown into a metal tray. Benji shivered and hurried along. He opened the heavy bathroom door and quickly found the light switch. The fluorescent light stuttered into life, as it usually did, but on this occasion refused to settle down.

On, off, flicker. On, off, flicker. On, off, flicker.

"I'll need to replace your tube tomorrow," Benji said to the annoying light. As if hearing what he'd said, it stopped flickering and settled into a warm yellow glow. It hummed nosily. Brother Benjamin found the sound of it, strangely comforting.

If the parquet floors of the corridor and stair hall had been cold, the tiled floor of the little bathroom was freezing, so Brother Benjamin wasted no time getting to the nearest of the two toilet cubicles. He was in such a desperate hurry he didn't bother to lock the door behind him.

After relieving himself and flushing, he dropped the heavy wooden seat, turned around and sat down on it. Carefully, he pulled his knees up to his chest, positioned his heels on the edge of the toilet seat and, after adjusting his heavy woollen cassock, cupped his hands over his cold feet and messaged them vigorously until they began to warm up.

Benji sat in silence and stared at the back of the cubicle door. As he watched, it slowly opened and thudded against the thin partition that separated his cubicle from the one next door. Now, with the door open, Benji could see his own reflection in the mirror behind the row of wash basins opposite. With his face between his spread-eagled knees, he thought he looked like a large brown cat perched on a gate post. The idea made him giggle and he felt foolish for being scared. There was nothing to be scared of, he told himself, this time in his own voice; it's only a storm.

Benji didn't move. He found being perched on the timber toilet seat surprisingly comfortable and was certainly in no hurry to head back across the icy floor or down the long corridor of whispers. He was seriously considering staying there until morning, when something heavy crashed into the small high-level window above his head. The noise was so loud, it almost knocked him off the seat. He turned his head and looked up over his shoulder. Thankfully, whatever had hit the window hadn't been strong enough to break the glass.

Benji held his breath. For a moment, it seemed that the storm held its breath too.

Then there was another bang against the glass, this time much harder and louder. The glass held, but the shock of the second assault, propelled Benji off the toilet seat. He was just out of the cubicle and in the process of turning to look back, when the third bang smashed the window and the force of the crash threw Brother Benjamin onto the floor. He was showered with broken glass. When he finally managed to look up he saw, to his horror, that the thing that had broken the window was reaching into the room. It looked like a long thick branch from a fair sized tree, but it moved from side to side with purpose, as if it was searching for something. The light flickered again. The thing above Benji's head became agitated and attacked it, causing the stuttering fluorescent tube to explode with a loud pop. More glass rained down on Brother Benjamin as everything went black.

Benji lay on the floor, paralysed with fear.

He could hear his heartbeat and the sound of his own breathing, which seemed particularly loud. He closed his eyes and then his mouth. He could still hear breathing.

"Haaw. Haaw."

He realised that it wasn't his own breathing that he could hear.

"Haaw. Haaw."

There was a roll of thunder, which was immediately followed by a long flash of lightning. Everything in the room became light. Benji opened his eyes and watched in horror as the long branch-thing, hovering above his head, split in two, revealing the outline of two rows of jagged teeth.

In a moment of sheer terror, Benji scrambled to his feet, found the door handle and was back in the main hall before he knew what he was doing. He ran through the double doors, down the dark corridor and didn't stop until he was inside his bedroom. He locked the door, then started to cry. His feet were bleeding and he was trembling violently. He was more terrified than he had ever been in his whole life. Instead of getting into bed, he crawled into the corner, furthest from the door, and squeezed himself into the space between the wardrobe and the wall. There, curled up into a ball, he buried his head in his hands.

Brother Benjamin tried to close his eyes, but he couldn't. Every time he did, he saw a large white triangular eye looking down at him and heard the heavy breathing of the monster, as it moved in for the kill.

*

The next morning Fr Francis visited Michael in his bedroom and told him how he'd found Brother Benjamin in a desperate state, after following a trail of bloody footprints from the bathroom to his bedroom door. The janitor had to break the lock to get into Benji's bedroom, as the young priest was hysterical and refused to come to the door. When they finally managed to calm him down, Benji told them that, during the night he had been attacked by a demon in the ground floor bathroom. His feet were badly cut up, after standing on broken glass from a shattered window. Father Francis told Michael that he would call Dr McCarthy and ask her to come over.

"Maybe you could go visit him, before you go out this morning, Michael. He's in the infirmary. It's on the third floor. I'm sure you'd cheer him up and you may be able to talk some sense into him," said Fr. Francis.

"Of course I'll go see him. I'm not sure about talking sense into him. He thinks I'm magical or something," said Michael.

"That's good. I think you're magical too, you know," said the Prior.

On hearing that Susan was coming over, Michael decided to make an extra effort when getting himself ready for the day. He'd shave, put on a new shirt and one of the new pairs of Chinos he'd purchased in Galway, the day before he'd set out for the island. He even decided to splash on some *Ferrari Black* aftershave, something he only ever did on special occasions, like weddings or funerals. As the Prior turned to go, Michael stopped him with a sudden exclamation.

"Wait!"

Father Francis turned at the door.

Michael lifted up the scarf and cardigan that he'd taken from Primrose's gallery, the ones belonging to Hanna. He'd left them on top of his suitcase before getting into bed the night before. When Father Francis saw what was in his brother's hands, his face dropped. Michael knew what the Prior was thinking.

"No! The colours - her colours – they are very strong. Hanna has recovered. She's okay. She's better than she was yesterday, much better."

"Oh, thank God. Our prayers have been answered."

Michael smiled at him.

"Please find Hanna Michael, and bring her home to Primrose," said the Prior before he left.

Chapter 26.

When Dr Susan McCarthy got the phone call from the Prior, asking if she could visit the monastery at some point because one of the monks had had an accident, she had just sat down at her desk and was about to review the notes before her first appointment. She had had a large fried breakfast in the hotel and now felt bloated and sluggish. The thought of climbing back into the car and driving into the country, didn't appeal to her. Once the Prior assured her that the monk's injuries were not life-threatening, she agreed to come as soon as she could, but said it would probably be later in the day. Susan normally ate muesli and fruit for breakfast, but had been so hungry going to bed the previous night that, for once, she'd abandoned her healthy morning routine. She ate quickly and she ate a lot, and now felt guilty for enjoying it so much

A vigorous run around the lake at lunchtime was on the cards.

At first she'd thought the voice on the phone had been Michael's. Not only did the brothers look alike, but they had the same soft Irish country accent and strange way of speaking. Unlike most of their compatriots, they pronounced their *th's* and both spoke slowly and clearly, completing each word before moving on to the next. But it was the curious inflection in tone that was particularly unusual and distinctive. It was almost musical. The effect of this odd accent was to give Father Francis's voice a certain gravitas whilst, in Michael's case, the way he spoke made everything he said sound mysterious. Susan guessed that, to foreigners, the brothers sounded unquestionably Irish yet, to their fellow countrymen, their accents must have seemed foreign. She liked the way they spoke, but she wished that one of them had a lisp, or a stammer, or something that would help her to tell them apart, on the phone.

When she said goodbye, and returned the receiver to its cradle, the guilt she felt from her excessive breakfast was replaced by a feeling of sadness. She had been momentarily thrilled when she had thought it was Michael's voice on the phone, and the acknowledgement of this fact bothered her. Why was she feeling like this, she wondered? She had no future here, no future with Michael. She was leaving for Canada in a few weeks and it was very likely she'd never come back. And yet, meeting him again had affected her. She hadn't stopped thinking about him since they kissed at the car and she had slept wonderfully, despite the storm, her empty stomach or her supposed insomnia. She'd woken with mixed feelings, happy that she'd slept so well, but sad that he wasn't there, in the bed beside her when she woke.

"What is the matter with me?" Susan said, just as Eileen Fancy entered the room, without knocking.

"Did you say something, Dr McCarthy?"

Susan looked up and furrowed her brow. She consider the district nurse, with a mixture of surprise and annoyance. The odd-looking woman looked different today, she thought. Mrs Fancy seemed to read Susan's mind. "I've had my hair done. Do you like it? she said in a low cracked voice.

Susan didn't think that the difference was her hair. It was something about her face. Whatever it was, escaped her.

"Yes. It suits you. I thought there as something different about you, today," said Susan.

"It has a bit of colour. Just a tint darker," said Mrs Fancy.

"Yes. You look nice," Susan lied.

Although Susan hated the term, she could not deny that the best word to describe Eileen Fancy was *ugly*, and she seriously doubted that there was anything that her district nurse could do, (to her hair or anything else), that would change that fact. Moreover, it didn't bother Susan in the slightest that she was having these unkind thoughts about a woman that she hardly knew. The truth was, from the moment they'd met, Susan didn't like Eileen Fancy. There was something false about her, something secretive, and Susan's instinct for spotting a liar, which had only ever once deserted her, was on high alert when she thought of Eileen Fancy.

"I came in to tell you that our first appointment is here, doctor," said Eileen, almost impatiently.

"Oh. Right. Please send him in," said Susan, adding, "In future, could you please knock before you come in, Eileen. Thank you."

*

Brian Horse Hopkins slept like a baby, although his head didn't hit the pillow until well after two thirty in the morning. He was never a man to be kept awake by loud storms or bad dreams. He fell asleep quickly with the image of Marie Joyce's beautiful face on his mind. He woke at eight thirty to the sound of his mobile phone ringing on the bedside table. On seeing that it was Superintendent Sutton on the caller ID, he was tempted to ignore it, turn over and go back to sleep.

The conclusion of the previous night's affairs was still a vivid memory. He mulled them over in his mind, before answering the phone.

A little after midnight, a Garda team from the mainland arrived at the hillside crime scene and quickly assumed command. Paul introduced Horse to Superintendent Brendan Sutton and then gave the Superintendent a brief report on what they'd found, and what actions had been taken. Sutton was accompanied by an overweight red-faced Sergeant Solent. Both men looked like they had been drinking. Sergeant Solent said little, nodded inanely and murmured "dat's rite" after almost everything his superior said.

Superintendent Sutton scowled at Paul and made a point of ignoring Horse. From the off, he was angry and insisted that this was a *local* matter and would be dealt with by the *local* police. During their conversation, Sutton's phone rang and, without apologising, he took the call. It was the desk clerk from Galway Garda station and his voice was loud and clear enough for the others to hear what he was saying. He was calling to inform the Superintendent that they had just got word that the victim had died in the ambulance on route to the airport. Sutton cursed and growled. When he ended the call, he looked like if he wanted to spit. He gave Paul a dirty look.

"You make sure I get everything you have, Garda Creagan. Notes, photographs, names and contact numbers for every one of those people you let crawl all over our crime scene. I now have to spend the night on this God-forsaken rock, so you make sure you get me your completed report to the station in Ballyhoary, first thing tomorrow morning, do you hear me? I don't want to spend one minute longer than I have to on this fuckin' island. You got that, Creagan? I don't know what you people in Dublin, or in London for that matter, get up to, but here, we follow proper procedures and protocols."

Horse ignored the insult. Paul couldn't hide his annoyance, but didn't argue with the Superintendent. They exchanged mobile numbers. Horse logged Sutton into his phone as *Mutton*.

"I want your report, first thing, do you hear? And I don't care if you have to stay up all night doing it."

Horse saw Paul grit his teeth.

"First thing in the morning, Superintendent," he said, before climbing into the car and slamming the door. Horse smiled at Sutton and Solent and then, with a theatrical nod of his head, climbed in beside Paul.

For the entire journey back to the hotel, Paul ranted about Sutton. Horse let him at it. Finally, Horse interrupted him.

"Who cares Paul? We have our own fish to fry. Let Sutton deal with this."

"But what if it has something to do with our case?" Paul said.

"Do you really think that's possible, Paul? Why would you think that?" said Horse.

"I don't know. It's just odd, don't you think?"

"Hey, everything and everyone on this island is odd, Paul. Just because it's odd, doesn't mean it's got anything to do with Mr G and our drugs. I can't say I see a connection."

Horse's mobile phone continued to ring, vibrate and crawl across the bedside table. *Mutton* continued to flash on and off on the screen. Horse snatched it up, just before it toppled off the edge, and put it to his ear.

"Hopkins," he said with a yawn.

"Superintendent Brendan Sutton here. I'm glad to see someone got some sleep." The Superintendent sounded more annoyed than he had the previous night. Horse ignored the sarcasm, yawned again and said,

"Good morning, Superintendent Sutton. What can I do for you?" putting on his cheeriest voice.

"What's good about it? I'm looking for Garda Creagan. Is he there with you? He's not answering his phone."

"We decided to get separate rooms, sir. Paul is in room 327." Sutton huffed loudly.

"I want my report. I expected it here, first thing this morning."

"I understand it is on its way to you, as we speak, Superintendent. Paul is probably at your door right now, finger on the bell, as it were," said Horse, maintaining his jocular style.

When Sutton didn't respond, Horse said,

"So, any progress in the case, Superintendent?"

"That's none of your business. Just tell Garda Creagan I called, do you hear me?"

The line went dead.

"Nice talking to you too, Mutton," said Horse to the silent phone.

Horse threw the mobile onto the bed, lifted the receiver of the hotel phone and dialled room 327. He let it ring for about two minutes, before hanging up. He redialled and, again, let it go on ringing, just in case Paul was in the shower. Finally, he gave up and rolled out of bed.

Horse showered, dressed and went down for breakfast. He took a table set for four, at the far end of the dining room. Most of the other, thirty or so, tables were occupied. It seemed he had arrived at peak time. There was a clatter of plates and cutlery and the general buzz of morning conversation. He ordered a pot of black coffee and a plate of scrambled eggs with toast. There was no sign of Paul, so he ate alone. As soon as he rose to leave a group of young adults, who had just entered the dining room, spotted his imminent departure and made a bee-line for his table.

Chapter 27.

Standing in the hotel lobby Horse rang Paul's mobile, just as the Dubliner came through the front doors. Horse was struck by a feeling of déjà vu.

"Ah, there you are, Creagan. Off on another one of your early morning escapades, were you?"

"I've been up a couple of hours. I printed the photos and prepared my report on the incident in the woods."

"You are an extremely excellent man. I've had Superintendent Mutton on this morning, looking for you and your wonderfully enlightening report. He sounded like he had a bee up his ass. I get the feeling he doesn't like me - or *you*, for that matter. I can understand him not liking a smartly dressed Dublin dude like yourself but, what did I ever do to get up his fat nose?"

"Eight hundred years of oppression?" ventured Paul, almost absentmindedly.

"Not that old chestnut again? Maybe I could say sorry to every Irish person I meet, begging their forgiveness for the sins of my colonial forefathers? Do you think that would help?"

Creagan smiled.

"It might be a start," he said.

"Huh," said Horse, "and there was me thinking, all was forgiven. Aren't you Irish and us Brits BFF's now?"

"I'm not sure everyone got that memo, Horse," said Paul.

They moved into a small empty lounge off the reception area and closed the door. It was much darker than the hotel lobby, but suited them perfectly. It was a late-night room, for guests who couldn't sleep and needed somewhere quiet, to read in peace. Scattered about was a mishmash of odd but comfortable armchairs, arranged in a haphazard fashion around a series of small coffee tables. There were built-in bookcases on either side of an ornate fireplace, stacked with old books that, Horse imagined, no one ever read. They sat down at a table under the tall window that looked out onto the gravelled drive at the front of the hotel. The entrance area was alive with activity. A tourist bus was being loaded with hotel residents heading off for a day's sightseeing around the island. Nearby a group of pilgrims were listening intently to a local guide who was shouting at them from a raised kerb. Taxis came and went at regular intervals. As Horse watched, a heavy cloud scudded across the morning sun and momentarily cast a shadow over the proceedings.

"Do you want to have a look at this, before I submit it to Sutton?" said Paul.

"Thank you, Paul," said Horse.

Creagan passed him the rather thick report. Horse took his time perusing it. Most of the report was photographs. One or two showed Marie, on the periphery of the main action, and Horse lingered on these. When he got to the close-ups of the victim hanging in the tree, he flinched.

"Fuck sake, Paul, it looks worse in the photograph," he said.

"Yes. I had the same thought. Probably because of the flash. Highlights everything. What sick bastard could have done that?"

"I've seen some terrible things, but this is something new, for sure. If it was torture, it has plumbed new depths of depravity. Had the old doc not stumbled on him, God only knows how long he could have hung there. Death for this guy was a release," said Horse.

"Sutton confirmed that the victim died, did he, when he spoke to you, this morning? Did he say if they identified who he was?" asked Paul.

"Mutton told me nothing. I told you, he doesn't like us and anyway, he doesn't strike me as the sharing type. It wouldn't surprise me if he sent some of his boyos around here, to escort us out o' town. Don't you hate not being loved, Paul?"

Horse returned to one of the images showing Marie.

"He's a petty-minded bastard," said Creagan.

"The report looks good, Paul. I can't add anything useful."

"Thanks."

They went quiet for a while, both men lost in their own thoughts. Paul reached out and took back the report.

"How's your finger?" said Horse.

Creagan looked at the plaster.

"It's fine. Hardly a mark. I was more worried about my back, but that bush broke my fall. What, the fuck, was that thing?"

"You tell me. I thought I saw a worm. I've heard of tape worms living inside people and growing to over ten-foot long. Maybe it was one of them."

"Oh shit," said Paul and made a face like he'd bitten into a lemon.

"What did the lovely doctor say, when she was kissing your finger better?"

"What?" said Creagan.

"Oh come on Paul, you must have noticed the beautiful doctor? Those gorgeous green eyes? She had my pulse racing, that's for sure," Horse said, then immediately thought of Marie and felt a sudden and inexplicable pang of guilt.

"Oh! Yes, she is very beautiful and I imagine she was glad she wore her flat shoes."

"That's what you noticed about her, Paul? Her shoes?"

"Anyway," said Paul dismissively, "I have some news, if you're still interested in our case?"

"Right. Out with it, then," said Horse.

"I met my American contact. I wanted a second opinion on this, before I handed it over to Sutton."

"What? You showed the report to your American friend?"

"He's law enforcement too," Creagan said defensively.

"Hey. I've no truck with that, Paul. This is your business. I'm only a consultant but, all I'd say is, if Sutton finds out, there'll be hell to pay."

"Yeh well, as you say, this is my business. Sutton doesn't bother me," said Paul.

"Okay. So, what did the American say then?"

"He told me he's seen something like this before."

"What? Like the guy in the tree? You have got to be kidding me!"

"No. There's was this Bolivian ex-army doctor, who became an enforcer for the Columbian drug cartel. A real psychopath! Got his rocks off, torturing people. Men, women, children - it didn't matter to this guy. His speciality was skinning his victims and then, keeping them alive for as long as possible. Apparently he killed a female DEA undercover agent, late last year, the result of which was to bring a shit-load of heat onto the cartel. There were raids, arrests and all the rest. It cost the cartel, big time. Soon after that, this guy drops off everyone's radar. Vanished, into thin air. It is commonly believed that the cartel dealt with him, had him killed and buried in a lime pit somewhere. But not everyone is convinced he's gone. Some believe that he was too valuable to the cartel, and so rather than having him executed, he was shipped out to Europe, to help control the growing competition from the Russian mob."

"And your guy thinks our man in the woods could be part of this Bolivian doctor's handiwork?" said Horse.

"Maybe. If it is, it might tie him into our deal," said Paul.

"In what way?" said Horse, trying not to sound sceptical.

"Well, maybe it was a warning? A message from the Columbians to Mr G?"

Horse sat back in the armchair and brought his hands together under his chin.

"It doesn't make sense. Our man was pretty-well hidden in those woods. If Dotty and his dog hadn't found him, I don't suppose anyone else would have."

"Well, maybe Daibhí wasn't the first to find the body?" said Paul. "Mr G might have been told to meet someone in that clearing and, when he gets there, that's what he finds waiting for him."

"Huh. You have been thinking about this, haven't you, Paul? It's possible, I suppose. This Bolivian psychopath, has he got a name?" said Horse.

"Oh yes, sorry, I forgot," Paul rummaged through his note book. " Yes, here it is. He called himself Dr Augusto Lafuente, but, it's probably not his real name. No such person was ever enlisted in the Bolivian army. Anyway, he was better known by his nick-name, El Pelador. Apparently, just the mention of this, was enough to scare the shit out of most people."

"El Pelador?" said Horse.

"The Peeler," said Paul.

The two detectives sat for a while in gloomy silence. The dark clouds had moved on and the morning was bright and alive with noise and light. A screaming raucous child caused both men to look out the window.

"Come Creagan, let us deliver that report to Superintendent Mutton and then, how about you and I pay a visit to that accountant fellow, George Kelleher, was it?" said Horse, struggling out of the armchair, "Let's see if we can find out how he's connected to all this. Then I need to spend some time with my old friend, Michael Eustace."

"*Gregory* Kelleher, not George. The offices of Kelleher and Blunt is not far from the Garda station. I can drop this report in on the way. Are you not going to make an appearance at the conference this afternoon, Horse? You might like it, and I'd like you to meet some people."

Horse watched Paul rise out of his chair with ease. As soon as he was upright Paul straightened his jacket and, with the tip of the un-bandaged index finger, gently flicked a hair from its chest pocket.

"We'll see. I promised Michael I'd meet him at the university. I said we'd help him find out what happened to the daughter of an old girlfriend of his."

"Have we time for that?" said Paul.

"I do. I'm only here as an observer, remember? This is your gig, Paul. Anyway, she probably ran off with her randy lecturer. It wouldn't be the first time something like that happened, would it?"

*

Michael took another deep nervous breath, checked again that the bike was in neutral, tightened his helmet strap for the twentieth time and finally plucked up the courage to start the engine. It had been a couple of decades since he had last ridden a motor bike, and he had never ridden one as large as this, or one with a side car attached. His satchel, containing a notebook, his digital SLR camera, some fruit and a small hardback book on the life of St. Áedán that Brother Benjamin had given him to read, was sitting snugly on the seat of the side-car beside him.

Brother Benjamin had insisted that Michael borrow the bike, saying it would be an honour to lend it to him.

"You'll be doing me a favour by taking her out. She needs a run every day, or she gets restless. I won't be able to ride her for a while," he'd said from his infirmary bed.

Michael relented and promised to look after Brother Benjamin's bike, until he was well enough to ride it again.

"I'm glad you're getting back to your old self, Brother Benjamin. I will visit you this evening, when I get back, and tell you all about my adventures, if you'd like that?" said Michael.

"I'd like that very much, Michael. And thank you for coming in to see me this morning," said Benji.

"Well, we are *neighbours*, aren't we? Why wouldn't I?"

"Neighbours? Yes, we are neighbours. I think I'll write a long letter to my mother and I will mention your kindness. She will be very impressed that I have a famous TV personality for a neighbour," said Benji with a smile.

Michael had stayed with Brother Benjamin for nearly an hour, but Susan never came. In the end he decided he'd better head off to the university. He'd call Susan at the surgery later, to confirm their date. When Brother Benjamin gave Michael the keys of his motor bike, he also gave him a small illustrated book on the life of St. Áedán, which included lurid illustrations of demons and sea monsters. Michael felt duty-bound to accept.

With the roar of the engine held to a decibel level just below intolerable, and with his whole body shaking, Michael nudged the bike into gear. Slowly he released the clutch and twisted the throttle. With a rumble of rubber on stone, the heavy three wheeled lump of metal moved cautiously across the cobble driveway, passed under the entrance arch and headed out through the wrought-iron gates. Michael moved the bike into second gear. As his confidence grew and the road opened up in front of him, he went up to third, then fourth and fifth. Within fifteen minutes the bike was at full throttle and Michael was breaking and accelerating with ease, taking corners like he'd been doing it all his life. When he hit the open countryside, that led north towards the university campus, he leaned back as far as he could and, from behind the sun tinted visor of his helmet, started howling like a lunatic.

Chapter 28.

What exactly is this about?" asked an angry Gregory Kelleher. He rose from his chair and glared at the two policemen. "You come to my office on a false pretence and now declare yourselves to be police officers, with no need of my accountancy services. I really must object."

"You will understand and appreciate the reason for our subterfuge, if you let us explain, sir" said Paul Creagan, "Please now, sir, sit back down and hear what we have to say. We are seeking your assistance with our enquiries into some very serious matters."

Kelleher remained standing, his small eyes moving from one policeman to the other.

"I'm not sure you would have been very happy, had we introduced ourselves properly to your receptionist Mr Kelleher. Two detectives, from the Vice Squad?" said Horse.

Kelleher's face seemed to change colour. Horse wasn't sure if it was a reaction to his English accent, or to the mention of the word *vice*. He sat back down.

"We are making enquiries sir, into some very serious matters, relating to child exploitation and rape, following the discovery of some video tape material," lied Paul.

Paul acted cool and Horse hoped that Kelleher believed his story.

"Vi...ideo tapes? C... child exploitation? R... rape? What's has this got to do with me?" said Kelleher. His eyes twitched.

"The tapes in question were discovered in a squat, next door to a brothel, in Dublin city, sir. They are, how can I put this, very revealing about the goings-on in the bedrooms next door, if you get my drift?" said Creagan.

There was a long silence.

Horse could see that Kelleher was thinking, working out how bad this was for him.

"As I said sir, this is a very serious matter, but we are only at the beginning of our investigation. For now, we are trying to build a case," said Creagan.

"A case? I still don't know what this has to do with me," said Kelleher, although now sounding far less sure of himself.

"Don't you, sir?" said Horse, tightening the screw.

"I think I need to speak to my lawyer. This interview is over gentlemen," Kelleher said, with as much bravado as he could muster. He stretched his hand out toward the phone on his desk.

"Suit yourself, Gregory, but we would prefer if you didn't do that. It is not in either of our interests to have this go public, but as soon as lawyers get involved this discussion we are having right now becomes official, and well, once official unfortunately that's the way it will go." said Paul.

He stood up and nodded at Horse.

"Come along, Brian," he said.

Horse began to rise.

"Wait. What do you mean go public?" said Kelleher

"Well, sir", said Creagan, "if you were to make this an official visit then, of course, we would have no choice but to bring you in for official questioning, you understand." Paul gestured toward the closed door. "If that were to happen, it would be very difficult to keep the details of our investigation out of the newspapers. Neither you nor I would want that to happen, I can assure you. At this moment in time Mr Kelleher, it is better that our enquiries are kept very secret."

"We have bigger fish to fry. You are not our target, Gregory. You misunderstand. We want your assistance, your co-operation, that's all," said Horse.

Keller looked from Paul to Horse and back again.

"Our interest is in the person who made the tapes, Gregory" said Paul.

"I..." stammered Kelleher.

Paul sat back down.

"You are not the only one compromised, Gregory," said Paul.

"It was just the once," Kelleher began to blurt, "I...I was very drunk. She took advantage of me. I felt terrible in the morning. I would never…I have never done anything like this before. I was very drunk. Oh God. I am married. I have children."

Kelleher's breathing became heavy and he spoke quickly. He was a terrible liar. According to the real Dublin Vice Squad, Gregory Kelleher was a regular visitor to Mr G's emporium of lust.

"Did you enquire about the age of the young woman, Mr Kelleher, before you went to bed with her?" said Horse.

"She told me she was nineteen. She looked nineteen," he almost shouted.

"And it was only the one occasion, sir?" said Paul

"Yes! Yes, of course. That's what I said. I was drunk. The little bitch took advantage me."

Horse gritted his teeth. He wanted to climb across the table and beat the truth out of the smarmy little prick. Instead, he made a fist under the table but kept a straight face.

"That's what we thought, sir. Now, I must ask you this. Has anyone been in contact with you? Perhaps someone you don't know? Someone threatening you? Blackmailing you?" said Paul.

"No….no one," Kelleher said.

Kelleher was a very bad liar.

Paul looked at Horse. They made cryptic faces at each other.

"Are you sure about that? We have reason to believe the tapes are being used to blackmail rich and influential men."

"I'm quite sure, detective Creagan."

"Well, we believe that it's only a matter of time, before someone does contact you. They'll probably be after money. That's the usual thing," said Horse

Kelleher turned in his seat and looked at Horse

"Are you a Garda?" he said.

"Inspector Hopkins is from Scotland Yard. There are a lot of people co-operating on this. It is much bigger than you can imagine, Gregory," said Paul.

Kelleher looked ill.

"If you co-operate with us, we will do our best to keep you out of this. If you co-operate, there may be no need for your involvement to ever get out. As it was only the one time and, as you say, you were very drunk, you are a victim in this. It was clearly a matter of entrapment."

"Yes. That's what it was. Entrapment," said Kelleher.

"But, if you don't co-operate, we will have to treat you as a hostile witness, disrupting our investigation and perverting the course of justice. You understand our position, don't you, Gregory? So, will you co-operate or do we have to make this official?"

"Yes. No. I mean…I will co-operate. It was entrapment. I am the victim." Gregory's face had reddened considerably and his forehead began to glow.

"Good," said Paul, "As soon as you are contacted, and we are sure you will be contacted Gregory, I want you to let me know. Do you understand? Here's my number."

Paul passed Gregory his business card.

Paul and Horse stood up. Kelleher stayed seated. The interview was over.

"Please don't come back here," said Gregory.

"Would you prefer if we called to your house?" said Horse.

"Of course not," yelped the accountant.

"Well then, if we need to speak to you again, we'll come here," said Horse.

I'll be waiting for your call, Gregory. I hope you don't let me down," said Paul.

He turned and went out the door.

Horse hesitated. He stood for a moment and stared at Gregory Kelleher. The accountant looked frightened. Horse clicked his teeth and then followed Paul out of the offices of Kelleher and Blunt.

They walked back to the car in silence. Horse hopped into the driver's seat and rummaged in his pockets for the car keys.

"Shit. Gimme yours, will you Paul? I must've left mine at the hotel," he said.

"Do you think he'll go for it?" said Paul. He passed Horse his car keys.

"He looked genuinely scared, but I don't know. He's not stupid, that's for sure. Maybe Mr G doesn't have anything on him. Maybe Gregory is one of Mr G's associates, you know, like a silent partner, or something like that? I've seen it before. If that is the case, then he knows we were bluffing and he was playing with us. But, like I said, he looked scared," said Horse.

"You think he was scared of us? said Paul."

"No. I think he's just scared. And he was lying about not being contacted. I'm sure of that."

"I guess he's got some thinking to do," said Paul.

"Guess so. Given the opportunity, I'd be happy to beat the truth out of him, if that sort of thing is still allowed in this jurisdiction," said Horse.

"No. I don't think it is, but I know how you feel. The guy's a creep. So where are we going now Horse," said Paul,.

"Back to university, Paul. I got a call from Michael and have agreed to meet him. You okay with that, or you want to spend the morning at the conference?"

"No. I'll go with you. I'm sure whatever your friend Michael is up to, it is far more interesting than whatever is being discussed at the International Conference on Cross-Border Co-operation," said Paul.

"Good God, I think I've turned your head, Garda Paul Creagan. Soon you'll be talkin' and dressing like me."

Paul looked Horse up and down.

"Can't ever see that happening, mate," said Paul doing his best impersonation of the Englishman.

*

The university campus was a sprawling complex of modern buildings surrounded by vast areas of surface car parking and a regimented one-way system, that seemed to take you the longest way possible between any two points. There were signs everywhere, which Michael found confusing, so instead of following the strict road markings, he headed diagonally across the car park toward a small group of students. He stopped the bike, removed his helmet and asked them for directions to the Reed Chambers. Primrose had told him that Hanna shared an apartment in a student's residency of that name. A pretty girl, who seemed to Michael to be about thirteen, pointed to a four-storey block close by, where another group of students were gathered at the front door, conversing with a stout middle-aged man who Michael recognised.

"Thanks," said Michael.

He parked the bike and walked over. As he got near he caught the end of joke a dirty joke being told by the Professor.

"*Not*, says Sister Bernadette, if we go back through the woods the same way we came!" Kieran Darby roared with laughter at his own joke. The male students standing around him joined in.

Michael noticed that the female students in the group were less enthusiastic about Professor Darby's humour.

"Good one, Professor," said one of the young men. Michael saw Darby wink at a small pretty girl, whose cheeks redden under his gaze.

"Excuse me Professor Darby, could I have a word?" said Michael when he was near enough. Professor Darby turned. Michael could tell that the Professor was having difficulty remembering where he'd met Michael before, so he said,

"We met briefly last night, when you were assisting the police at the incident in the woods? I'm Michael Eustace. I don't believe we were formally introduced, Professor."

Michael held out his hand.

"Oh yes, of course. Michael, how are you? Terrible thing. Really, really terrible."

Darby clasped Michael's hand in both of his and shook it vigorously. The jolly demeanour quickly left his face.

"Terrible thing," he said again.

The group of students became childishly quiet.

"I am sorry to interrupt," said Michael, "but I was wondering if any of you can help me? I'm looking for friends of Hanna Brennan. I believe this is where she lives. I'm at the right building, am I not?"

"Yes you are," said a tall blond at the front of the group, "I'm Carol Lenehan. I'm one of Hanna's room-mates. Our rooms are on the fourth floor."

"Ah Carol, yes, Primrose mentioned you. Great, I was hoping to have a word with you. I'm an old friend of the family. Hanna's mother has asked me to help her find her daughter."

"Are you a private detective?" asked Carol.

"You're that TV psychic, aren't you? I remember you from the telly," piped up a young man with a pronounced English accent.

"I'm not a psychic," said Michael tetchily, "I'm a friend of the family, that's all."

"Yeh, that's right," continued the English student, ignoring Michael's response. "You're Michael X. I remember you. My Gran thought you were great. She tried phoning in to the show, to see if you could find Washington her cat. When he went missing, we told her that Washington was probably stolen by an international gang of cat thieves, because he was so unusual. We told her he'd probably been sold to an oil sheik and was living the high life in Arabia or somewhere where they worship cats. Actually, Washington was just a scrawny ginger moggie, but Gran had him forever. My dad reversed over him in the Range Rover, but hadn't the heart to tell her. Gran was sure the famous Michael X could find her beloved cat, but the woman from the BBC wouldn't let her talk to you. Anyway, Gran's gone the same way as Washington now."

"Your dad reversed over your Gran in his Range Rover? That was harsh, Harris," said another of the students.

The group laughed. Even Michael smiled. The English student named Harris went red.

"No, you twat, Brew. She died. She's with Washington in heaven, or wherever."

After a moment, all eyes returned to Michael. Carol Lenehan's expression gave little away and, for a moment, Michael thought that she was looking at him suspiciously.

Professor Darby broke the silence.

"This has nothing to do with the thing in the woods? You don't think that...that was Hanna...do you?" he said nervously.

"Oh God no. No Professor. Not at all. They are not connected in any way. No. No," said Michael decisively. He smiled at the professor and then at Carol.

Darby's expression changed to one of relief.

"A TV personality, eh? Well, well. When are you on?" enquired the Professor with a smile.

"I gave that up a long time ago. It was just a bit of fun," Michael lied.

"The shows are on YouTube Professor," said Harris, adding "I knew you were a fake, but Gran wouldn't listen. You psychics are all the same,"

Michael ignored him.

"Well, I don't know about that, Harris. What Mr Eustace did last night was bloody impressive. I really don't understand how you knew that poor man was still alive, I..." said Darby, but then stopped in mid-sentence. Professor Darby had promised Horse that he would say nothing of what he'd seen in the woods. He smiled apologetically at Michael.

"Would you like to visit our apartment?" said Carol Lenehan.

"That would be great, thank you Carol. It would help me a great deal," said Michael.

"Get 'im to show you his crystal ball, Carol. I bet it's not as big as it looks on the telly. Everything looks bigger on the telly or so I've been told," said the student named Brew, the one that had made the joke about Harris' grandmother.

The male students burst into raucous laughter again.

"Oh really," said Darby, as if shocked by the remark, but when he saw Michael smile, he chuckled loudly.

"Well, come along then, if you're coming," said Carol.

"Grand," said Michael and he followed Carol to the front door of the apartment block. Professor Darby followed them. The other students hesitated. One of the young men stepped out of the crowd and went after Michael. In response, the rest of the group followed him.

The honking of a car horn stopped everyone in their tracks. Michael turned around and saw a familiar car making a diagonal bee-line for them across the car park. It approached at speed and skidded to a dramatic stop.

The two male occupants climbed out at the same time, in what looked like practiced synchronicity.

Michael smiled.

"Who is it?" said Carol.

"It's the cavalry," Michael whispered.

"Well, 'ere we all are then. Have you found her yet Michael?" said Horse, straightening his jacket as he approached.

"Detective Hopkins," said Darby.

"Ah, good day to you, Professor, and how are you feeling today? Better now, I 'ope," said Horse. Darby blushed.

"I'm fine thank you Inspector," he said.

Horse turned to Michael.

"Well? Any news of our missing girl?"

"Not yet Brian. But you're right on time. We're about to visit Hanna's apartment."

"Excellent. Well, lead on then."

Chapter 29.

No one paid any attention to Paul Creagan when he entered the apartment, fifteen minutes later, and declared that he knew where Hanna was. Horse was in the living room, in animated discussion with Professor Darby. Michael was in Hanna's bedroom. Carol Lenehan stood watching him. Michael had his eyes open but gave the appearance of being in a trance. He was holding a gold locket belonging to Hanna and concentrating on it, with the intensity of a man threading a very small needle. He'd found the locket on her bedside table. It contained a photograph of her mother and father. It was also covered in her colours.

Paul repeated what he said, louder this time.

"I've found Hanna. I know where she is!"

Carol Lenehan grabbed Michael's arm and shook him.

"Did you hear that? They've found Hanna," she said, excitedly.

Michael stared at her, but his dulled expression didn't change. He looked at the locket again and frowned. Hanna's colours were very faint.

"Hey. Listen. They've found Hanna," said Carol, squeezing Michael's arm. Michael blinked. Carol pulled him toward the door. "They've found Hanna," she repeated. Michael broke free of her grip and followed her into the living room. All eyes were on Paul.

"They're in the caves, most probably trapped, and it's not just Hanna and the Professor, either. Apparently, a whole class of students is missing. How the hell does a whole class of students go missing, for the better part of two weeks, and no one notices they're gone?" said Paul, casting a critical eye on the only university employee in the room. Professor Darby looked genuinely confused.

A young Asian student stepped into the room behind Paul and sneezed loudly.

"Sorry," he said. His voice was shallow and nasally.

"This is James Wong," said Paul. "He is one of Hanna's classmates. He was due to go on the cave expedition with Professor Kearns and the others, but he came down with pneumonia. He's been in the infirmary until this morning."

"Bloody 'ell Creagan, that was quick work," said Horse.

"Just good old-fashioned police work, mate. I just knocked on a few doors" said Creagan. "James has the whole story, don't you James?"

All eyes turned on James. He sneezed again and smiled weakly. Michael thought James still looked ill. He also thought he looked concerned.

"They must be in trouble," said James, "Since the earthquake, all the usual entrance routes into the cave network have been closed off. There have been rock collapses and some of the shoring has been damaged. It all has to be checked, before anyone's allowed back in."

"Are you saying Professor Kearns ignored the warnings and went in anyway?" said Darby.

"We're not children. Professor Kearns was our tutor, not our school teacher. We found something exciting. It couldn't wait. We had to go down there, to see for ourselves."

James Wong took a moment, before continuing.

"We had been surveying an area of the flatlands, near Seven Springs, using deep earth sonar equipment, and we got some real interesting readings. Very odd. The equipment lets us determine the density of the rocks, up to a mile below the surface. It's slow and laborious work, but the results are great. It's like we're x-raying the island. Real deep, x-rays. It allows us to map the different layers of rocks and locate the cave systems and water courses underground, and all that, from equipment on the surface. As I said, it's slow work, but the results can be fantastic. If our readings were right, it was more than fantastic. It was monumental. We did the survey again and then cross-checked the readings three times from different station points, but we kept getting the same thing. Our survey suggested that there was an enormous cavern, more than a kilometre below the surface. I

210

mean enormous! Like nothing any of us had ever seen. Larry was very excited. We all were. We agreed that the only way to find out, for sure, was to go down there. Professor Kearns suggested getting Paddy Gallagher to go down with a team of experienced cavers, but we were all against that. We found it, and we all wanted to go down. Everyone was very excited about going. I wanted to go, but then I got bloody pneumonia. They went in through The Devils Throat. It was the closest entrance to the find, and like I said, all the other entrances were closed off."

He sneezed again, sniffled, apologised and shivered.

"Not *The Devils Throat*!" declared Professor Darby. "Oh good God, no! Nobody has used that entrance in years. I was sure it was sealed up. What was Professor Kearns thinking?"

"We are all competent climbers and cavers. We knew what we were doing," said James defiantly. Michael thought about Hanna being underground. He wondered if it explained the odd readings he was picking up, from his own form of sophisticated x-ray.

A tall, well-built man, in his early thirties, entered the room. Michael recognised him as one of Darby's team of scaffolders from the woods. He was accompanied by another of the young men from the night before. It was the one named Kevin, who he knew had helped Susan with the victim in the tree.

"Ah Paddy, the very man," said Darby.

The tall man spoke with a flat country accent.

"It seems they did go in through The Devils Throat, Professor. Their ropes and lanyards are still there. A walker spotted the gear earlier today and reported it to Mountain Rescue," he said, then he nodded at the Asian student and said, "How'ya James?"

"Hi Paddy," said James.

Kevin acknowledged Michael, with a worried smile.

"Oh God, this is terrible," said Professor Darby.

"What's The Devil's Throat?" asked Michael.

"It's an extremely dangerous entrance into the cave system. It's located about thirty feet below the top of one of the tallest and wildest cliffs on the island," said Darby dramatically, adding, "Foolhardy climbers have fallen to their death, just trying to reach the Throat. Climbing up to it from below is impossible. There is nothing down there but deep ocean, and the waves are over fifteen feet high."

"And that's on a quiet day," added Paddy.

"Some climbers who did manage to make it inside, were never heard of again," continued Darby, "*Swalleed up be the divil himself*, as the locals would say. Whatever you say about not being children Mr Wong, using The Devil Throat is prohibited and incredibly foolhardy, and Professor Kearns knew that. His students are his charges. If Professor Kearns had said no, none of you would have gone down there. What was he thinking?"

"We'll have to send a rescue party down, Professor," said Paddy, "However well they planned the expedition, they are going to be down to the last of their food and water by now. Nine days in the darkness is bad news."

"Oh God," said Darby again, "nine days. Oh dear sweet Jesus, I fear the worst."

"Hanna is alive," said Michael.

Everyone turned and looked at him. He held up the golden locket, as if the others could see what he could see.

"She's alive," he repeated, "and if you can get me into the caves, I know I can find her."

*

Horse called for order.

He told the students, who had gathered around the door of Hanna's apartment, that the drama was over and that it was time to go back to doing whatever they were meant to be doing. Horse suspected that, for most of them, that meant hanging around somewhere else. Professor Darby, Paddy Gallagher and James Wong were asked to stay. Despite Paul's attempts to ferry him out, the boy named Kevin insisted on staying too. He looked to both Carol and Michael for support. He argued that he had been part of the hillside rescue, was an excellent climber and was a very close friend of Hanna. Carol whispered something into Michael ear and Michael told Horse to let Kevin stay. Kevin sighed with relief.

When Paul closed the door, calm settled over the room.

"So, we need to send in a rescue party," said Horse. "How many are we talking about, down there?"

"Four students and Professor Kearns" said James Wong. "Eric, Axel and Gitte, and Hanna. Five in total. They are all experienced cavers and divers. They brought SCUBA gear and provisions for six days, maybe a little longer. They were going deep, so they were carrying a lot of rope. Hauling all the gear was the biggest thing. If the way was clear, they could reach the cavern in one day. They'd mark the route, take some photo's, do an outline assessment of what they found, leave as many markers as they could, then return to the surface. Once the route was laid out, others could return later, for more detailed exploration."

"So, if it was a two-day expedition, why bring provisions for six days?" said Horse.

"They had no idea what they'd find. The cave system behind The Devil's Throat is mostly unexplored. Also, there was no way of knowing what the earthquake had done. It's likely that they would have to follow water courses or swim across underground lakes. Progress might be very slow. There was no way of knowing. Also, if something happened, having extra supplies is vital. They would set up base stations along the way, and a camp somewhere, for sleeping," said James.

James looked very pale. Horse offered him the armchair.

"Sit down lad, before you fall down," he said. James didn't argue. Paddy Gallagher spoke.

"Okay. We'll get help from the mainland, Professor. No disrespect to anyone here, but this is a job for the professionals. Heading into the caves of Skellig Éin is not for amateurs. Certainly, attempting to get in using The Devils Throat would be crazy. I've never gone in that way. Gareth Lavelle is the only person I know who climbed down to the Throat. He told me the climb down was difficult enough, but getting in, he said, was near impossible. You could only get in, if you knew what you were doing. Gareth can't help us, though. He emigrated to Australia, last year."

"You're right, Paddy," said Professor Darby. "We need to inform the authorities. This is a job for the professionals. It would be foolish to think any of us could seriously form a credible rescue party."

"No," shouted Kevin. Everyone turned and stared at him. "No, it won't work. It will take them ages to set things up," he said, "and even then, they will insist on going in through one of the main entrances. They won't attempt to go in by The Devils Throat. You know they won't, Paddy. They'll spend most of the time moving rockslides and securing collapsed tunnels. It could be a week before they find her."

"Well, we don't know that for sure, Kevin, and anyway, maybe Professor Kearns and the students are fine. We just don't know, one way or the other. Paddy's right. The risk is just too great for any of us to attempt something so dangerous," interjected Professor Darby.

Horse held his hands up to his face and nibbled at the skin of his index fingers. Michael rubbed the side of his temple.

"So what do you say, Michael?" said Horse.

"I don't think she has much time, Brian. I think she's in trouble. Whatever we decide, the rescue has to happen, as soon as possible. I'd say, we should go now," he said.

"How can you be sure Hanna is alive, or that she's even in trouble?" asked Carol.

"Trust me," said Michael, "I just do. If you want my advice, I say, go now! We've not got a moment to lose."

"Right," said Horse, "that's that, then. We go in immediately." He looked at Darby. "Isn't there anyone else on the island who could show us how to get into the caves through this Devils Throat, Professor?"

"I don't think so."

Paddy Gallagher whispered into the Professor's ear."

"Of course. I forgot. Double D. But, what's the chance she'd help us, Paddy?" said Darby.

"Who's Double D?" said Horse.

"The local woman - the climber who discovered The Devil Throat. She was the first person to get into there." said Paddy.

"Great. Please tell me that this Double D person is still alive and *not* living on the other side of the planet," said Horse.

Paddy and the Professor looked at each other.

"Yes, Inspector, and she lives on the island. That's not the problem," said Professor Darby mysteriously.

"What *is* the problem?" asked Michael, before anyone else.

"Well, firstly, I doubt she's been down there for years, but that's not it. The fact is, well, she might not want to help us," said Paddy.

"And why would that be?" said Horse.

"Well, besides the fact that we're all amateurs and could die in the process, which actually, probably wouldn't bother her too much, it's just that, Double D can be difficult," said Paddy.

*

214

Darby continued to object to the idea of going it alone, but finally acquiesced and agreed to contact the mysterious Double D. He called her on Horse's mobile, while the others stood around and watched him. Once the Professor had introduced himself and told her that he was using the phone of an English policeman, it seemed to Horse that Double D did most of the talking. Darby's half of the conversation consisted mainly of *uh huh's*; and *righty ho's*.

To everyone's surprise, Double D agreed to take them in to The Devil's Throat. Darby wrote down her instructions and, as soon as she hung up, relayed them to the gathering.

She would meet them at 4.30am at Hangman's Cross. This would be the first and last opportunity, for some time, to enter the Throat, as the island weather forecast had predicted an easing of the westerly winds toward dawn. Everyone would need to be ready. She would bring five climbers down, get them safely in the Throat and that was all. A sixth person would be required to stay up on the cliff, to man the ropes. Horse noted that Professor Darby didn't tell Double D that their party would include at least one novice climber.

"Well, that's sorted. It's an early start for all of us," said Horse.

"I really do think we should talk Mountain Rescue," said Darby. He looked at Paddy for support. Paddy shrugged his shoulders. "I think I'll have to agree with Kevin, Professor. Mountain Rescue will do it *by the book*. If this man is right," he said, looking now at Michael, "we don't have the time for that."

"I agree," declared James, who was slumped in the armchair with his head almost between his legs.

"Right. It's agreed then. So, let's get organised," said Horse. He spoke directly to James Wong, "Firstly, you need to get back to bed. Paul will take you back to your apartment. Tell him everything you know about the expedition. Everything that's relevant. Okay?"

James looked up at Horse and nodded weakly.

"I'll go with you," said Carol.

They stayed in Hanna's apartment for nearly an hour, making plans and agreeing the arrangements. Paddy Gallagher, who was the most experienced climber among them, would lead the party.

He would call on another experienced caver named Denis Healy, a sergeant in the local Territorial Arm, to be his right-hand-man. Denis climbed with Paddy regularly and would bring first-aid and survival skills, which may turn out to be invaluable. Brian Hopkins, Kevin Carr and Michael Eustace would complete the five. Kevin liked rock climbing and he knew the cave system of Skellig Éin well enough. Horse had some climbing experience from his university days and regularly used the blue climbing wall in his local gymnasium in Charring Cross. Michael admitted that his only experience of climbing was up trees, when he was a boy.

"But you're our bloodhound, Mikey. You gotta come," said Horse.

"I'll be fine, knowing you'll be there to look out for me," said Michael.

"Right you are, mate," said Horse.

It was agreed that they would meet at Hangman's Cross at 4.15am. Paddy would bring gear for Horse and Michael.

"So what's this Double D gal like, Professor? A big manly lass, is she?" said Horse.

"What? Oh no, not at all. In fact, you've met her, Detective Inspector Hopkins."

"I have?" said Horse.

"Yes. Double D is only a nickname. That's what the climbing community call her. Dare Devil! Her real name is Marie Joyce. She was with the elderly doctor, on the hillside last night," said Darby with a smile.

Part Three

"Na haoinne is a neamh-meabhairín bheag féin air."
"Each of us is odd in our own little way."

Chapter 30.

Mr G sat behind his desk fiddling with a Biro. He had been fiddling with the Biro for almost an hour. He was thinking. Fiddling with the Biro helped him to think. He had been thinking a lot recently, and thinking too much made him tired and angry. Mr G didn't need to think. He knew all he needed to know, to run his considerable criminal empire, and what he knew was sufficient. He could add and subtract and had a rudimentary grasp of percentages, in so far as his 95% cut was always mountainous next to the 5% left for the other parties to any deal. He could read and write and had an excellent memory for names and faces, a very useful trait for a man who never forgave an insult nor forgot a debt.

Mr G was not married and hadn't fathered any children, and the fact that, at the age of fifty-four, he was still a virgin, didn't bother him in the slightest. He never pondered the nature of his sexuality. He had no brothers or sisters and since his beloved mother passed away last year, no parents either. He had a couple of uncles, on his father's side of the family, living in England but they didn't know him and he had no interest in knowing them. And, with the exception of the terrible grief he felt at the sudden death of his mother, Mr G spent very little of his time thinking about his isolated existence either.

The business was his life, and the vast piles of money and lavish lifestyle he derived from it, was all Mr G needed to feel fulfilled and happy. Money was power and power allowed him to satisfy the one desire that gave him most pleasure: controlling and, sometimes, hurting people.

Despite his average height Mr G had always been a strong boy who grew up to be a fit man. And he had always been a bully too. In the classroom as a child, and in the boardroom as the main man. It was a trait he'd inherited from his violent father, along with a fierce temper and an almost insatiable appetite for causing other people pain. He liked to say that his father had beaten the boy he once was, into the man he had become. Most problems in Mr G's world could be solved with the sharp end of a crowbar into the top of the skull or a long serrated knife twisted into the soft flesh of a quivering belly. More recently, disputes were settle from the barrel of a gun, discharged at close range into the back of the head. It was Mr G who took care of the business. He was the one to swing the crowbar, to twist the knife, and he was the one who, after taking lessons from a hapless Lithuanian refugee, pulled the trigger. For minor matters, or final warnings there was his ruby ring.

Violence gave Mr G his money and the money gave him power. Power and violence made him happy and they fed on each other, like a serpent devouring itself and becoming stronger by doing so. Mr G had come across the snake-image in a book on mythical creatures. The Ouroboros – the perfect circle, formed by a snake swallowing its own tail. He was so taken by it, that he adopted the Ouroboros as his business logo. It was the masthead for Studio 54 and the symbol was painted in gold on the front doors of the nightclub. The image was repeated in artworks dotted around the rooms of the club and on the smoky mirror behind the bar. When he looked at the Ouroboros it reminded him of the keys to his success and the sources of his control over others.

Recently however, Mr G had noticed a change. Something had happened that had made him feel different. Suddenly there seemed to be a great deal that was *out* of his control, and he attributed the changed circumstances to the arrival of Sylvester Parker. For the first time in as long as he could remember, Mr G felt afraid, and it was Sylvester Parker who frightened him. It was as simple as that. Parker frightened him.

Mr G had not witnessed Parker doing any of the things that he was said to have done, but he knew that all the stories were true and that if he ever attempted to attack Parker, the consequences would be unimaginably bad for him. Even trying to find anything out about Parker was dangerous. Mr G had heard of skinnings, dismemberment and cannibalism. Parker apparently took torture to a whole new level. If half the stories were true, then Parker was ten times worse than Mr G; ten times as cruel and ten times as vicious. Like Mr G's father, Sylvester Parker was a man to fear. Mr G fantasised that Sylvester Parker was the Devil himself and he regretted the day he ever agreed to go into business with him. He had been lured by Parker's charm and the promise of riches and power beyond his wildest dreams. He had dived headlong into Sylvester Parker's wicked world foolishly believing that he had found another wealthy patsy to exploit and control. But Parker had tricked him, and now he was doomed, a laboratory rat running in a maze of Sylvester Parker's making. A laboratory rat - watched and controlled.

Mr G was sure that as he sat at his desk, fiddling with his Biro Sylvester Parker was sitting at his desk, in that dark musty room in the isolated house, watching him. How else could he have known about the beating of Rick Kavanagh in the basement or that Rats Egan was dead. Mr G guessed that there must be cameras and microphones, phone taps and intercepted post, satellite surveillance and computer hacks. Maybe even spies in his organisation. Thinking about Sylvester Parker consumed his waking hours and affected his sleep. Because of his suspicions, Mr G could confide in no one, could trust no one. He was on his own and for the first time in his life, his precious isolation frightened him. He felt as vulnerable as a shaved rabbit, strapped to the scientist's table, waiting for the scalpel.

But Mr G had no intention of letting Parker win. It was time to act, and act he would.

It took Mr G over an hour to devise his plan of action and, as the pieces came together in his head, and his anger abated, he wanted to smile. His enemy had inadvertently given him a weapon that Mr G could use to defeat him, or at least to chase him away. It sat in the top drawer of his desk, within touching distance of the hand fiddling with the Biro. Mr G had carefully flattened it out and placed it in a protective plastic sleeve. He had read it, over and over, until he could recite it by heart. It contained so much power, it was frightening. Like a bottle of nitro-glycerine perched on a rickety stand, the single page letter, written with a delicate hand on thick expensive writing paper, was a bomb ready to explode in Sylvester Parker's face.

Mr G believed that the curious letter, which literally dropped into his lap, had the power to defeat the Devil himself.

*

Once the plan of action had been agreed, the rescue party left Hanna's apartment and split up.

Horse offered Michael a lift back to the Priory.

"Naw, you're grand," said Michael, "I came on the bike."

Horse squinted at the bike and side-car.

"You are kidding me, mate. You came on that?"

"Yes I did! Want a lift back? Paul can take the car. The side-car is surprisingly comfortable," Michael lied.

"Eh, no, that's okay, thanks," said Horse.

"It's not mine, obviously, so I'm extra careful with it. Haven't gone over a hundred and twenty yet. You sure you wouldn't like to chance it? Live a little Brian. What do you say?"

"Naw, mate, I'm sure. Live a little *longer*, is what I say!"

"Suit yourself," said Michael

Horse climbed into the car and started the engine. Once Michael got going, Horse followed him out of the car park and did his best to keep up with him, but soon lost sight of the bike along the windy roads.

Horse drove over a humped back bridge and, a hundred yards further along, saw Michael's bike and side-car pulled over to the side of the road.

"Oh, here we go, Paul; he's probably run out of petrol or fucked the engine up, or something. I suppose we'd better stop," he said. They drew up behind the motor bike and both men got out of the car. Michael was standing in front of a pair of tall iron gates, set back and hidden from the road.

"What's he doing?" said Paul.

"Don't know?" said Horse.

Michael stood quite still. He went from looking through the tall cast-iron gates at the large two storey house that sat in a hollow at the end of a long gravel driveway, to staring at the stainless-steel access control pad, located half way up one of the gate posts, and then back again. He seemed to be lost in thought.

"You break down or what?" said Horse.

"No. Just curious. Almost missed it. Didn't spot the house or gates on the way out. Almost impossible to see from the road. Did you notice that? The house is in a hollow. It's almost as if it's hiding," said Michael. He moved to the access panel and stared at the key pad.

"Are you looking to buy, Michael? Looks like a bit of a money pit, if you ask me. I'd say that old heap hasn't seen a lick of paint in forty years. You'd be buying a pig in a poke, with that heap," said Paul.

"Yeh. Some ol' codger probably lives in there in one room, heats the place with a candle and eats road-kill. Spends his nights oilin' his chainsaw and looking at dirty postcards he's been collectin' over the years. Place probably stinks of cat shit and dead things," said Horse.

Paul laughed.

"Ha. A pretty sophisticated looking intercom system and security gates for a psycho-cat man, don't you think, Brian?" said Michael pointing to the polished stainless steel plate buried into the old stone gate post. The fish eye camera lens twinkled in the sunlight.

"And there's an eight-foot high fence around the whole site," he added.

"So what? The owner wants privacy. Who wouldn't want security out here in the middle of nowhere, with gangs of thieving thugs targeting old people living alone?" said Paul.

"Well, why don't we see if anyone's at home," said Horse.
He walked up to the intercom and raised an index finger.

"No, wait! Don't!" said Michael, rather too forcefully.
Horse stopped and turned around. Both he and Paul looked at Michael.

"I mean, forget it, I'm just being silly. As you said Paul, these people just want privacy. Three strangers calling to their gate, probably terrify whoever is in there. We should go," he said.
He smiled half-heartedly before returning to the bike.

"Really Brian. We should go," he said again.
Horse stepped away from the intercom, took one last look up toward the house and then headed back with Paul to the car.

"Your friend's a little odd," whispered Paul.

"Just a *little*?" said Horse with a smile.
Michael heard what they'd said.

"Sorry. I was just curious. I need to get going. I need to visit Primrose and tell her what we've found out and tell her the plans. Then I need to speak with my brother and try and arrange breakfast for three in the morning. You absolutely sure I can't give either of you a lift?" he said, hopping back on the bike and donning Brother Benjamin's distinctive helmet.

"Not bloody likely mate. You go easy now and keep your eyes on the road. Never mind the bloody scenery. We'll pick you up at the Priory at about three thirty, okay?" said Horse.

"Okay. See you later then," said Michael before turning the bike back onto the road and heading away.

When Horse and Paul got back in the car Paul said,

"What was that all about?"

"I have no fucking idea, mate. When you are dealing with Michael Eustace, you must be prepared to embrace the bizarre. What you and I might find strange, Michael finds significant. I have learnt to trust Michael and his odd behaviour. You would be wise to do so too."

*

Sylvester Parker returned to the series of crystal clear monitors and sat down. He fiddled with the cordless keyboard and toggled through the three different views of Mr G's office above Studio 54. He'd been watching Mr. G for the best part of an hour and had to take a bathroom break. When he returned, he found nothing had changed. The images on the three central consoles were three different views of the same thing: Mr. G, sitting at his desk, fiddling with a pen. Sylvester Parker was not happy. He had been watching Mr G since Mr G returned from his afternoon walk and, despite the three high definition cameras and the two microphones hidden about the room, Parker was sure that there was something he was not seeing. The volume was turned up to its highest level so Parker could hear Mr G's breathing above the grating noise of the Biro being twirled on the desk.

At the beginning Mr. G. had seemed worried, almost frightened. He appeared to be sweating and the fidgeting with the Biro was like a nervous tic. Parker had enjoyed watching Mr. G like that. But as time went on, Mr. G's mood visibly lightened and, as it did, Parker's own mood darkened. He even thought that he detected a repressed smile on the Dublin gangster's face.

"What are you up to?" he said to the image on the screen.

Parker focussed on the view from the hidden camera over Mr G's shoulder, but could see nothing significant.

There was movement on one of the monitors on Parker's left, but he ignored it. He focussed on the screen in front of him and tried to see what Mr G was doing with his other hand. It was resting on his lap, out of sight of any of the three cameras. A face filled the screen on the left but, once again, Parker ignored it. Mr G stood up, walked around to the front of his desk and stared directly at Parker, directly at the camera hidden on the bookshelf behind the door. Parker gawped at Mr G and was convinced Mr. G pouted at him, before opening the door and leaving the room.

Parker huffed angrily. He turned to the screen on his left, the one that had been trying to catch his attention earlier. It was the view from the fish eye lens of the gate intercom. It showed an empty and quiet road outside the gate. Parker frowned. His thoughts were still with that sly parting smile on Mr. G's face.

He pressed some keys and the image from the screen on the left changed places with the one in front of him, replacing the one of Mr G's, now empty, office. He pressed more keys and the gate-image began to rewind. Figures appeared and moved backwards and forwards in robotic double time. Three became one and then the one walked backwards out of the cameras line of sight. Parker pressed the *Play* icon. A man walked from the road and as he approached the camera he removed his biker's helmet. He stopped and stared through the gates to the house beyond. The intercom camera was not high definition, so Parker could not get a good look at the man's face. Just another nosy tourist, he thought. He was just about to fast forward the image to real time again, when the man at the gate turned and stared directly into the intercom camera. Sylvester Parker gasped and stood up with such force, that his chair toppled backwards onto the floor.

"Michael Eustace?" he said, "It's just not possible. How the hell did he find me?"

Chapter 31.

Rick Kavanagh appeared to be asleep, but he wasn't. On the contrary, he was fully awake and fully alert. With his un-bandaged eye, he watched the goings-on in the cave and pondered his escape plan. Megan lay beside him. She hugged him. Despite her best efforts to stay awake, Rick knew by her breathing and the stillness of her body that, like all the others in the cave, she had succumbed to the power of exhaustion. It didn't matter. If they were going to escape, it would have to be tonight and if he had to carry a sleeping Megan in his arms, then that's what he would do. They would escape together. She was his girl and he wasn't leaving her behind, to be the plaything of Pete Mercer or the cigarillo-smoking foreigner whom Rick referred to as the Creep.

The Creep had turned up the day before and, to the clear annoyance of Pete Mercer, immediately took charge of the operation to rescue the buried drugs. He spoke with a Spanish or Portuguese accent and, Rick guessed, was probably a member of the Cartel. He had a flat head, a long nose and a thin wiry moustache that he twisted and tugged whenever he watched Megan from the side of his eye. He was creepy and dangerous-looking and Rick didn't like him from the start. Given the opportunity, Rick would have gladly punched the smile off the foreigners smug tanned face.

Just before dark, Rick and the other workers finally broke through to where the drugs had been buried by a rock slide caused by the recent earthquake, so Mercer and the Creep left the cave to report the good news to Mr G. They placed two guards at the entrance before they left. Within an hour of them leaving, both the guards were, like the rest of the workers, sound asleep.

The dampness of the cave had seeped into Rick's clothes and the thought of spending another night lying on the wet sand made him feel more determined than ever to get away. His plan was simple. Once past the sleeping guards and outside, he and Megan could climb up to the top of the cliff and hide in the woods, or maybe even find an empty cottage, where they could hold out until all the fuss died down. It would be dangerous, possibly suicidal, but it would have to be now. Time was running out.

Whatever hope Rick had had of becoming Mr G's favoured lieutenant, was now dashed, torn to pieces, just like the body of his childhood friend, Seánie Rats Egan. Rick had disappointed Mr G too many times, and the punishment for his failures would be final. The drug stash had been located and would soon be transferred to the arriving trawlers. After that, a clean-up operation would be undertaken. All evidence of what had gone on in the secluded cove would be expunged, and all the witnesses silenced forever. No trace of their bodies would ever be found. Rick and Megan, Mo and Lash, and all the other rock-shifters, would disappear. Mr G would return to Dublin, with Mercer at his side, and the Creep would scuttle back into the shadows.

Rick had no illusions about their future. Unlike the other workers in the cave, who were sure that their hard labour would be rewarded with a percentage of the spoils, Rick knew the truth. He had known Mr G for many years and knew his modus operandi. The worker-bees were expendable. Their disappearance was part of Mr G's grand scheme. It had always been that way and Rick had gone along with it, when it hadn't affected him. But Rick and his crew had been demoted to the ranks of the expendables, and now there would be no question of any of them ever leaving the cave alive. So, escape was the only option and it would have to be tonight.

By all accounts, Rick Kavanagh should have been scared. Megan certainly was. These men were dangerous and they frightened her. Since the incident in the basement, Megan had become a quivering shell of her feisty self, prone to sobbing and whining. At times, it seemed that she might break-down completely. But she trusted Rick and knew that he would protect her. When he confided in her his plans for escape, she swore she'd follow him to the ends of the earth. She told him that she loved him and, although Rick was not the type to buy his girl flowers and chocolates, or show affection in any way at all, he was sure he needed her and imagined that this must mean he loved her too. She was *his* girl and he would look after her.

Rick wondered *why* he didn't feel scared, or tired, for that matter. If anything, he felt stronger and braver than he ever did before. The beating Mr G had meted out, and the subsequent beatings Mercer had administered, at every opportunity since coming to the cave, had had little effect. His damaged eye was almost completely healed, although he still wore the bandage, to avoid drawing unwanted attention. The resurrection of his dead eye was a miracle that he couldn't explain, but attributed it to Megan's gentle care.

Then there was his heightened energy.

Since coming to the cave Rick had felt fantastic. He had the energy of a teenager, but without the need of long periods of sleep. The work of clearing the rocks had been hard, and for most of the other men, back-breaking. They were all exhausted by the end of every shift. In contrast, Rick didn't seem to need rest and worked voraciously, as if working to save his life. He worked faster and moved more rocks than any of the others, and the results of the physical labour were beginning to show on his body. He made do with the measly food rations and he hardly slept at all. Since arriving in the cave he hadn't slept more than a couple of hours. He simply didn't need to sleep. Rather than being drained at the end of the days' hard labour, his body was restless and excited. It was as if the harder he worked the more energetic he became. The work that exhausted the others, seem to charge Rick's battery. He felt strong and he fantasised about being invincible.

*

Once the noise of snoring and heavy breathing had reached a constant, predictable pitch and rhythm, and he was sure the two guards at the mouth of the cave had fallen asleep, Rick released Megan's vice-like grip and quietly stood up. Nothing was stirring except the stale air rushing in and out of the sleeping workers' tired lungs and the gently flickering flames of the few candles that were permitted at the rear of the cave. After a short pause, to inhale the sweeter air at standing level, Rick bent back down and lifted Megan up into his arms. She had lost a good deal of weight since coming to the island but he was still surprised at how light she was, and how little effort was required to carry her. Once she had settled into a comfortable position, with her arms wrapped around his neck and her head snuggled into his chest, he made his way to the mouth of the cave, gingerly stepping over and around the sleeping bodies on the floor.

Rick knew that if they were to escape, they would have to climb back up to the top of the cliff as quickly as they could, taking the same winding path that had brought them down. He would have to wake Megan. He could not safely carry her up in his arms. The path was steep, very narrow and very dark. They would have to climb it, in single file. There was no other way. And to stray from path would be lunacy, even in daylight. On one side a dense thicket of prickly furze hugged the cold rock face; on the other, a sheer drop to the rocks below. Rick was sure they could do it, if Megan was quiet and held onto the back of his shirt. His only fear was meeting Mercer and the Creep on the path. If they did, all would be lost.

Rick carried Megan past the sleeping guards with ease, but negotiating the rocky terrain, between the mouth of the cave and the start of the rising path, was painfully difficult. Whilst the sea air was sharp and chilly, and therefore a refreshing relief from the stale air of the cave, it stung Rick's cheeks and watered his eyes. He made slow progress, stumbling from one slippery rock to the next, but finally felt hard sand under his shoes and, as soon as he did, he picked up his pace. In no time they reached the start of the rising path. The cliff loomed menacingly above them.

The night was much darker than Rick had imagined it would be, and the crashing waves much noisier than he remembered, and it was the noise of the ocean and the blackness of the starless sky that prevented Rick hearing or seeing the approaching figures of Mercer and the Creep, until they were almost on top of him. Had Pete Mercer been facing forward, rather than looking back arguing with his foreign companion, he would have seen Rick at the same moment Rick saw him. Rick reacted quickly, taking two large sideways steps into the brush under the cliff wall. In the darkness, and still holding a sleeping Megan, he slowly lowered himself onto his hunkers.

This proved to be a mistake.

As Rick squatted, his knee-joints cracked loudly, and Megan mumbled and threatened to wake up. Rick held his breath. The two men on the path stopped arguing. Pete raised his arm and looked around. A gust of wind pushed aside a blanket of cloud and a half-moon peeped out and cast a weak light onto the spot where the two men stood, listening.

"What eez it?" whispered the foreigner.

"I heard sometin'," said Mercer.

Pete squinted and stared directly at Rick. Megan stirred again, but then settled in Rick's rigid arms.

"Whatcho hear?"

"I dunno. Sometin'," said Mercer, He sounded annoyed.

"Tis de fucking sea. There iz no one here," said the Creep.

Mercer rummaged in his pocket for his phone.

"What you doing?" snapped the foreigner.

"My mobile...my *cell* phone, has a good torch," said Mercer as he located the phone.

Rick squirmed. The game was up. He wondered if he could reach his flick knife. Megan kept it hidden at the bottom of her small shoulder bag. He didn't think so. He thought about jumping up and rushing at the two men. In front of him Pete Mercer raised an outstretched arm and got ready to flip on the phone torch. Suddenly, the foreigner lurched forward and violently forced Pete's arm back down, almost knocking the phone out of his hand.

"Wat are you doing, you stupid Irish fucker. You want to tell evereebodeee we are here?" snapped the Creep.

Mercer yelped and swung around, ready to strike the other man, but when he saw the flicker of a blade in the moonlight he held back. The Creep was holding a long serrated knife and he was smiling at Pete.

"You want to try me, Irish fucker? I will gut you and leave you for the seagulls. Go on, Irish fucker. Try me." The final words were whispered. In the pale moonlight, Rick could see Pete Mercer's face. Pete wasn't smiling.

"Yer roite, amigo. I wasn't thinkin'. Fuck't. It was only me fuckin' imagination," he said.

"Gooode," said the Creep.

"Come on de fuck, it's fuckin' freezin' ou' here. Only one more poxy day in that fuckin' cave, an' it'll be all over. Thank fuck. Come on, de fuck," said Pete. He forced a smile. When he turned away from his companion, the smile became a sneer.

Rick could tell that the Creep frightened Pete, something he found surprising given what he knew about Pete, and the fact that the foreigner didn't look that strong. The Cartel was clearly calling the shots now and Pete knew it. Maybe, thought Rick, Pete wasn't going to be going back to Dublin, after all. Maybe, in the eyes of the Creep Pete too was one of the expendables. The idea pleased Rick.

When the two men moved on and continued across the dark beach, Rick let out a stifled breath and stood up. He had to think and act quickly. He knew that it wouldn't take long for Mercer and the Creep to notice that something was wrong and realise that he and Megan were missing. When that happened, all hell would break loose. Pete's suspicion, that someone had been hiding in the undergrowth near the base of the cliff path, would be confirmed and a search party would be sent out, and Pete would know exactly where to look. Finding the guards asleep when they returned to the cave, would only hasten these inevitable events. Pete Mercer was as tenacious as a pit bull terrier and twice as vicious. He would be angry and frightened and, given his hatred of Rick Kavanagh, would not rest until they were both caught and severely punished.

Despite the fact that the situation appeared hopeless, Rick remained surprisingly calm as he considered his options.

Climbing up the path was now out of the question. It would be the first place that Pete's search-party would look. Hiding in the undergrowth, with the view to climbing up at some later point, once the coast was clear, was not an option either. Rick knew that Mercer would immediately place guards on the clifftop to prevent anyone escaping that way and then, when the sun came up in a couple of hours, anyone on the side of the cliff or hiding among the rocks would easily be discovered. On the other hand, escaping seaward was also impossible. Firstly, the freezing ocean was wild and treacherous, and, even if you were a good swimmer, as Rick was, he wasn't sure there was anywhere to swim to. Secondly, the jagged rock promontories that enclosed the tiny cove were enormous and unclimbable, just like the walls of a prison yard. So, on the face of it, their situation seemed dire. But Rick had a plan and, if luck was with him, it could prove to be a perfect path to freedom.

He slowly lowered Megan to the sandy ground, holding her until she found her feet, then gently shook her awake. She wobbled a little and, for a moment or two, had difficulty recognising where she was. The cold night air, and the look on Rick's face, quickly brought her out of her sleepy stupor.

"Do you trust me, Meg?" he whispered.

"Wha?" she said, shivering as she spoke. The word echoed.

"Do you trust me, Meg?" he asked again.

She looked around.

"Well? Do you or don't ya?"

"Yeh. O' course I do. Have we go' away, Rick? Are we free?"

"No, not yet. Come on now, as quietly as you can. We have to go back. Trust me, Megan. We gotta go back into the cave."

*

As they approached the mouth of the cave, Rick and Megan could hear loud angry voices and the sound of shuffling feet, followed by the stifled cries of the two guards being rudely woken by Mercer and the Creep. Rick had to drag Megan forward. When they reached the entrance, he pulled her to one side and pressed her flat against the cliff wall.

"Shhh," he whispered, his face inches from hers. They could hear Pete. His voice was loud and angry. He was ranting.

"Y' lazy fuckers. I should fuckin' cut yer balls off. Y' lazy fuckin' bastards."

There was the sound of a boot swishing across the sandy floor and one of the guards yelped.

"Yeh fuckin' stupid fucker," Mercer continued.

Rick chanced a quick look into the cave.

He saw Pete Mercer kick out at a man lying on the sand, catching the man full in the face with the toe of his boot.

The Creep had the other guard by the hair and was viciously dragging him across the floor on his hands and knees, towards an opening in the opposite wall which led into a make-shift toilet used by the workers. It was a deep, dark and narrow alcove with a bowl-shaped pit in the centre of the floor, perfect for squatting over when nature called. The pit was regularly overflowing with human excrement but, because of the room's proximity to the mouth of the cave, most of its pungent odours dissipated in the sea breeze before ever making it into the cave. When the tide came in and the floor of the alcove flooded, the human waste was flushed out to sea. But the tide had been out for hours and the pit in the floor was full and the smell at the entrance to the cave was obnoxious. Even Rick and Megan could smell it, from where they stood.

Still holding him by the hair, the Creep dragged the guard halfway into the alcove, so that the man's face and upper body hovered over the pool of shit and urine.

"You are sheet and you will be dee lesson for all deese other sheets," said the Creep.

He jerked the man's head backwards and upwards. Rick saw the knife before the terrified guard did. With a vicious thrust of his arm, the Creep slit the man's throat. Blood gushed in every direction as the man's body jerked and kicked out. When the Creep let go of his hair, the guard flopped face-first into the pool of excrement, flapping about like a drowning dolphin.

Rick drew back his face and closed his eyes.

After a while, and as soon as he thought it was safe to do so, Rick chanced to look into the cave again. Pete, the Creep and the surviving guard were gone. Rick could hear a loud commotion coming from inside the cave. A roll-call was under way. He knew their time was short. He took Megan's hand.

"Don't make a fuckin' sound, awright? Not a fuckin' sound," he whispered.

Megan nodded. Her hands were trembling.

"Awright?" he said again.

She nodded again.

"Okay. C'mon."

Ducking down, Rick dragged Megan across the cave entrance and into the stinking make-shift toilet. Once inside, he lifted her over the body of the dead guard and pushed her into the darkness against the back wall. He followed her, using the body of the dead man as a stepping stone over the shit-pool. As soon as he reached Megan she grabbed him and clung to him, as tight as she could. He didn't object.

"Not a fuckin' word," Rick whispered, "not a fuckin' sound, awright?"

Chapter 32.

Susan left the clinic a little after three o clock. She was excited at the prospect of seeing Michael again. As soon as she got to the front door of the Priory she heard raised voices coming from the hallway behind. Straightening her skirt and pursing her lips she pressed the white porcelain door bell, and kept her finger on it longer than was polite. The ringer was loud and shrill and, as she suspected, the sound of it silenced the voices behind the door. Once again it was the Prior who opened the door to her.

"Ah. Dr McCarthy. Hello, how are you?" he said with a forced smile.

"Father Francis, I am so sorry I'm getting here so late. I have been extremely busy. We seemed to have had one emergency after another, all day long. I am so terribly sorry."

"Oh, never you mind. Brother Benjamin's injuries are not life threatening. I think your presence will have more of a psychological benefit, than anything else. Do come in, Dr McCarthy?" said the Prior.

"Susan. Please call me Susan," she said cheerfully.

The Prior seemed distracted and Susan was aware of someone standing behind him.

"While I'm here, I was wondering if I might have a private word with Michael, and then maybe a chat with both of you together?" she said.

"You most certainly can, Susan. Maybe you can talk some sense into him. The Prior stepped to one side and revealed Michael standing behind him.

"Hi there," said Michael awkwardly.

"Oh, hello," said Susan.

For a moment, no one spoke. Susan broke the silence.

"Right then. Firstly, to the wounded patient, and then, maybe a word with you both."

"Right, well this way then, Susan, and when you're finished with Brother Benjamin, we'll be here in my study," said Father Francis, pointing to the panelled door to his right.

After visiting Brother Benjamin, Susan returned to the hall. Before going to the Prior's study, she ducked into the toilet to freshen up. The room was clean but dark. The light switch didn't work and she noticed that a large piece of plywood that had been fixed over one of the high-level windows. She guessed that this must be the place where Brother Benjamin had had his accident, so she didn't stay a moment longer than was necessary. Back in the hall she straightened her skirt, for the umpteenth time, and then gently knocked on the study door.

"Come in," said the Prior or, at least, she assumed it was the Prior's voice.

When she entered both men stood up. Michael had been sitting across the desk from his brother and she wondered if they had been sitting in silence before she came in.

"How's Brother Benjamin?" asked Michael, offering her his seat.

"He's fine. I changed his bandages and gave him a tetanus shot. He asked about you, Michael. He said he thought you looked tired, when you got back this evening," she said.

"Did he ask about his bike?" said Michael.

As soon as Susan sat down, the two men did likewise. Michael found a hard-backed dining room chair against the wall and placed it beside her, tilting it so he could look at her without turning his head. Susan felt her cheeks redden.

"Bike? No I don't think he mentioned a bike," she said.

Michael's face lit up.

"My brother has been acting like a child, Dr McCarthy," said the Prior, "He borrowed Brother Benjamin's motor bike and now he thinks he's Evel Knievel."

"Have you been jumping ravines, Michael?" said Susan.

"It has a side-car attached, so, no, but it's surprisingly nippy around corners. Quite a thrill. Maybe I could bring you for a ride sometime, Dr McCarthy?"

"Hmmm. I'll have to think about that. Maybe," she said. She looked down at the floor. She had a sudden flashback to the hotel room in Galway. She fiddled with her fingers then raised her head and looked at the Prior.

"Do you think, Father Francis, I could speak with Michael alone, for a few moments?" She clutched her medicine bag, to suggest her discussion with his brother would be of a professional nature.

"Of course. I need to look in on Brother Benjamin and draw the curtains about the place. I'll see about arranging your early breakfast," he said, giving Michael a pointed stare.

Susan thought she detected annoyance in the Prior's tone.

"And I'd like to speak with you too, Father Francis, before I go," she said.

When they were alone, Susan opened her bag and removed a thick grey folder bursting with papers and notes. A lined sheet of paper was stapled to the front cover and, among the various typed numbers and dates, Michael saw his name written on the front.

"Is this a professional call, Dr McCarthy?"

"In part, yes. These were sent to my predecessor, Dr Greene, from Mr Thaddeus O Sullivan. Is he your oncologist, Michael?"

"Teddy? My oncologist? No! He's an old friend and my doctor. But *not* my oncologist."

"I see. I thought that…your headaches, might have been ..?"

"Cancer? No! He's an old friend and he just happens to be a cancer specialist, that's all. He has always been our doctor."

"I know of Mr. O Sullivan, although I've never met him."

"We grew up together. Best friends. We still are. He's a good man. You'd like him. He'd like you. I'll introduce you sometime," said Michael.

Susan played with the cover of the folder.

"So, these headaches, they're just migraines then?"

"Well, I wouldn't say *just*. I always have a headache, of one sort or another."

"That must be very debilitating?"

"I've gotten used to it. Most of the time it's just like background noise, but sometimes the pain gets so bad, I start seeing things."

"These colours you told me about? Is that what you mean?"

"No. I see them all of the time. I'm not sure the headaches and the colour auras are connected. No. I see weird stuff. Just weird stuff. It's hard to keep my eyes open when the pain gets really bad," said Michael.

"Are there ever times you are not in pain?"

"Sometimes. It's quite rare and there doesn't seem to be rhyme or reason to why the headaches go away, or why they return either," he said.

"When was the last time you had a respite?"

She noticed Michael hesitate.

"The longest spell was a four or five-hour period, about a week ago."

"What were you doing?"

"Most of the time, I was just sitting quietly, doing nothing."

He hesitated again.

"If you could find out what the circumstances were that led to that respite, then maybe you could repeat it," she continued, sounding very much the doctor.

"I'd like that," he said and smiled.

Susan felt her face flush.

"Was it when you were with me, in Galway?" she said.

"Yes," he said.

"Is that why you stayed?"

"No. I stayed because I wanted to. I liked being with you, watching you sleep."

"I went to the restaurant, for breakfast. You weren't there," she said.

"Did you? Oh. I didn't think you would. I'm sorry, Susan. Soon after I left the hotel I got the mother of all migraines. It seems the hours watching over you was the *quiet before a hurricane*. I had to find a pharmacy and then lie down. I took a handful of pain-killers, found a park bench and fell asleep. I didn't wake up until after noon."

"You liked watching me sleep?" she said.

"I like everything about you, Dr McCarthy."

She tried not to smile. She wanted to touch him.

"I booked the restaurant and got two tickets to *Lincoln and the Fish*," she said.

Michaels face dropped.

"Oh," he said.

"Oh?" she said, raising an eyebrow.

"I might have to skip the concert," he said.

"Why?" she said.

There was a knock on the door.

"Eh...come in," said Susan with a sigh.

It was Father Francis.

"Just in time," said Michael.

"What's going on here?" said Susan.

"So Michael hasn't told you yet, Susan?" said the Prior.

"Told me what?" she said, looking from one to the other.

"That he is climbing down a cliff-face later tonight, along with a bunch of like-minded amateurs, despite the fact that he has no climbing experience and, from what I remember, is terrified of heights."

"Is this a joke?" she said.

"I only wish it was," said the Prior.

*

Horse and Paul called to the Monastery at a half past three. Michael and Father Francis were waiting at the door. The night was at its darkest, but the earlier gusty winds had died down considerably. A slight breeze whistled though the tree-tops and a single grey cloud scudded across a cold clear sky. It was ominously quiet. Despite the hour, Michael seemed surprisingly upbeat.

"You seem chipper, mate," said Horse, "manage to get some shut-eye, did you?"

"Eh, not really, but I'm fine, Brian."

"Hello Father," said Horse. He introduced Paul Creagan.

After the niceties were exchanged, they stood watching each other for a moment in awkward silence.

"Right," said Michael, "enough of this, time we got going."

He hugged his brother.

"Look after yourselves," said the Prior.

"We will," said Michael.

"God Bless you all," said the Prior. He smiled at Horse and Paul.

"Thank you, Father. Don't worry, I won't let anything happen to him," said Horse.

Michael looked at his brother.

239

"I have to go. You know that. Hanna is in trouble and I might be the only one who can find her," he said.

"Be careful. All of you," said Father Francis.

"Don't rent out my room," said Michael.

The Prior managed a weak smile.

"Come on you two, we need to get going," shouted Paul from the car.

"God Bless," said the Prior.

"God Bless, Father," said Horse. He climbed into the car.

"See you, soon," said Michael, giving the Prior another hug.

Michael sat quietly in the back of the car. Thoughts of his brother, and Primrose and Hanna, were quickly replaced by thoughts of Susan. He stared out into the black night and let his mind return to their evening together.

This time, he'd left her sleeping.

They had had a lovely meal in a small lakeside restaurant and afterwards had gone out to the garden and down to the large gazebo beside the jetty. The evening was cool and windy, but not cold. Susan looked beautiful in a pale blue taffeta dress, her bare shoulders covered in a large pink shawl. She wore a delicate gold chain necklace and dangerously tall high-heels shoes. The sparkle in her eyes was electrifying. The colours behind her eyes, alive.

They had the garden and gazebo to themselves. The music from the bar was piped outside and Michael asked Susan if she would like to dance. She surprised him by saying *yes*. They slow-waltzed to Leonard Cohen's *You got me Singing* and soon found themselves in a tight embrace. When the music stopped, they sat down on the bench-seat still holding on to each other.

"I need to use the bathroom? You won't go away, will you?" Michael said.

"I'm not going anywhere?" she said

"Good. Back in a sec. I'll see what happened the music," he said.

Michael returned quickly.

"Where were we?" he said and held out his hand to her.

"But the music has stopped," she said.

"I have a feeling it might get going again, any minute now."

Susan stood up cautiously. As soon as she did, the music started and Michael dragged her into his arms. I was Cyndi Lauper's *True Colours*.

Susan smiled.

"Is this your doing, Michael?"

"Naw. Purely coincidental, Dr McCarthy."

She kissed him, held his face close to hers and forced a smile. Michael thought she looked beautiful, but a little sad, too.

When he paid the restaurant bill they went back to the Tara Cove Hotel and made love in Susan's room like they were young lovers exploring sex for the first time. A little after one o'clock Michael took a taxi back to the Priory. Before he left her, he scribbled a note on a sheet of hotel headed paper, that he'd found in the top drawer of the bed-side table. As he quietly scribbled in the half-light, Susan slept soundly, her soft breathing mimicking the beating of his own heart.

Susan,

You know that my strange ability allows me to see your true colours? Well, I wanted to tell you what I see.

Your colours are beautiful, just like a rainbow.

But, I see something else too, something I've never seen before. It's very unusual and it has been haunting me, as you have, from the moment we met.

I think I can see a trace of myself in your eyes. Not a reflection. A part of me. Maybe, something I thought I'd lost, or something that has always been missing. I know, that doesn't make sense but, what I'm trying to say is, I think we are meant to be together.

I think I love you. I think I always have.

Please wait for me. I will come back for you.

I promise.

Michael

x

"You okay back there? You're very quiet," said Horse.

The car heaved and jerked, as Paul dropped gears, to climb a steep winding hill.

"Just great," said Michael.

Chapter 33.

Hangman's Cross was a lonely isolated spot overlooking the open plains of the northern island. It was not a crossroads, as Paul Creagan had expected, but instead a grassy plateau, in off the road, on a severe right-hand bend at the top of a long steep climb. Paul had had to drop down to third gear, and then rev the engine noisily, to ensure that his hire-car did not stall as they neared the top of the rise.

Hangman's Cross was backed by a dense ancient forest that shielded it from the worst of the weather roaring in from the Atlantic Ocean behind. Except for a stone obelisk, topped with a rusty iron cross, it could have been mistaken for a small car park at the edge of a forest walk. Paul drove in and parked next to a muddy unattended *Land Rover*. Nothing moved in the low beams of his car lights. He switched off the engine and then, as a matter of habit, turned off the lights too. They were immediately buried in a blanket of solid darkness. The night was as black as the bottom of a coalmine. Paul turned the lights back on.

"Well, we're not the first. Should we wait, or get out?" he said.

"I don't know. We might be early. Whoever owns the *Defender* must be out there somewhere," said Horse, "What do you say, Michael? Should we get out and explore?"

"We're here now, so let's get out," said Michael. The ride in the back of the car had been comfortable but stuffy and Michael needed some air. He opened the door and climbed out. The warmth of the cabin was instantly replaced by an icy wind that stung his face. He gasped and hugged himself. He realised he wasn't wearing a proper coat. Whilst Horse and Paul both wore heavy duty Garda high-vis padded jackets, Michael had on nothing more than a flimsy wind-breaker over his woollen Aran jumper, cotton shirt and short-sleeved vest. His heavy Chinos kept his legs reasonably warm and Father Francis had managed to find him proper hiking boots which, along with a pair of thick woollen socks, were surprisingly comfortable, but the rain jacket was wrong. He needed something much heavier, to hold back the cold sharp wind.

He adjusted his eyes to the darkness and looked around.

Hangman's Cross, or what he could see of it at a quarter to four in the morning, had little going for it. The place was cold and eerie. It felt like the scene of a crime and, given its name, Michael suspected it probably had been, at one time or another. Beyond the reach of the beam of light from Paul's hire-car, that quickly dissipated into the night like misty rain, he could see very little. The shadowy trees that lined the edge of the forest looked like crouching beasts, their protruding branches like fingers pointing into the distance. All of them looked *good for hanging* and Michael was sure that, on a clear day, a body hanging from any one of them, could be seen for miles around.

"Spooky place, isn't it?" whispered Horse.

"Yes, it is. I don't suppose the *Jeep* driver is a tourist either," said Paul.

"It's a *Land Rover*, not a bloody *Jeep*. One is an unrivalled British classic, the other is...well...American," said Horse.

"Whatever," said Paul dismissively. He turned away and bellowed into the darkness.

"Hello. Hello."

No one replied. Before he called out again there was the sound of two vehicles dropping gears and revving their engines, as they climbed the hill.

"Here we are," Horse declared, "the troops have arrived."

Two cars drove in and parked side by side, one facing the *Land Rover*, the other facing Paul's car.

Paddy and Kevin got out of the first car. Two unknown men got out of the other. They all came together in the pool of light from the three cars. Michael smiled at Kevin. Paddy Gallagher introduced Denis Treacy. Denis had brought a younger man with him, Hughie Nagle. Michael thought Hughie looked like a smaller version of Denis. They wore matching khakis and were fully kitted out for the climb, with similar backpacks and peaked caps. Michael couldn't be sure if the logo on the front of the caps showed a snow-boarder, a skate-boarder or a surfer. The words underneath were clear however. *Living the Extreme.*

"Hughie's my right-hand man. He wasn't going to miss out on an opportunity to tackle the Throat, were you, Hugh? And the more the merrier, eh?" said Denis, by way of an introduction. Michael thought Hughie looked a little scared. His colours were subdued and lifeless.

Paddy Gallagher didn't look pleased that Denis had brought an extra man. Kevin Carr ignored the conversation and got on with organising his equipment.

"So where's this famous Double D?" asked Denis. "I can't wait to meet him."

Before Paddy had a chance to explain, Marie stepped out from the shadow of the trees, walked up behind Denis, and whispered in his ear.

"She's right behind you."

Denis jumped with the fright.

"Shit, Christ, fuck," he said, moving away from her.

"Bit edgy, aren't you?" she said.

Horse tried not to smile. Ignoring him, she glowered at them all and soon made her feelings clear.

Firstly, they were all late and the window of opportunity to get into the Devil's Throat was almost gone. If they were to have any chance of getting into the cleft safely, they would need to be ready to drop over the edge of the cliff as soon as the first rays of dawn appeared, in less than fifteen minutes' time. The way she saw it, it would take them that length of time just to make their way through the forest and get to the edge of the cliff. She said that there was a storm coming in from the Atlantic. The wind had been increasing steadily over the last hour and it was a gusty swirling wind, enough to challenge the most experienced climber. "It'll have some fun with you lot on the cliff-face," she said. There was no humour in her voice.

She directed most of her ire at Paddy. He had not followed her instructions. They were late and there were too many of them.

"This is a stupid idea," she said, "I expected more from you Paddy. I expected competent climbers, not this. Honestly, I'd say you lot attempting this is as good as suicidal."

Horse tried to calm her down. She continued to ignore him. She referred to Denis and Hughie as *Rambo and Son* and belittled

Paddy with a sarcastic tongue. Michael tried to remain inconspicuous and out of her firing-line, but it proved impossible because the only padded jacket that Kevin could offer him was phosphorescent green. In the car-light he looked like an over-sized glow worm. He was sure that, at that moment, he could be seen from most parts of the island.

"And look at you two," she said, "What are you like? The chuckle brothers, PC Plod and Luminous Lenny."

Michael started to laugh. Horse joined in. Kevin spoke up.

"I know we're probably not the ideal rescue party, but we're all Hanna has. I'm not leaving here until she's safe and if this man says she's still alive, and that he can find her, I believe him. If you won't help us, then we'll go on our own," he said.

"What's Hanna to you? The love of your life, is she?" sneered Marie.

"As a matter of fact, yes she is," said Kevin with as much confidence as he could muster. He looked young but determined. He stared at Marie. She looked embarrassed. Horse spoke up.

"Look, Miss Joyce. We need your help. Michael says time is running out for Hanna. So we need to go now. Tonight!"
Still looking at Kevin, Marie said,

"Okay. Suit yourselves. I will get you in, but then you are on your own. We need to go *now*! Like I said, the wind is picking up. Every minute counts."

"Thank you, Miss," said Horse.

Marie turned and looked directly at Horse for the first time since she arrived.

"Stop calling me *Miss*, Englishman. My name is Marie."

"I'm Brian, but if you wish, you can call me Horse. My friends call me Horse," he said.

"You just make sure you do what I say, Englishman, you and the rest of your merry band of mental patients," she said, then turned and headed off into the dark forest.

"And now means *now*!" she shouted over her shoulder.

*

They moved in single file, along a barely discernible path, through the dense ancient forest that skirted Hangman's Cross. Marie was soon out of sight. After stumbling forward for almost ten minutes they spotted a bright white light up ahead. Michael thought it must be a clearing of some sort. It turned out to be a fifteen-foot wide wind-swept ridge at the top of a massive cliff looking down into a fierce rolling ocean. The light was coming from an arc lamp suspended from the stout branch of one of the trees, wired to two car batteries tucked under a heavy plastic sheet. Beyond the reach of the light, an ominous black sky hung like a tarpaulin, sending misty rain to saturate the mossy ground in front of them.

They gathered side by side under the canopy of wet trees and watched Marie, who had continued out onto the cliff edge. None of them seemed to be in any great hurry to follow her.

The noise from the ocean, battering the unseen cliff wall, was deafening. Michael thought it sounded like hundreds of angry lions trapped in a pit. Sea mist wet their faces and droplets of rain, that had collected in the bowls of upturned leaves, spat at them at irregular intervals. Despite his heavy coat, Michael shivered. The rocky ridge was mossy and coated with an oily film that sparkled in the light of the arc lamp. It looked treacherous. The light on the ridge was cold and blinding and, for the second time that night, Michael had the feeling of arriving at a crime scene.

Marie had everything set-up to go.

Four rope-lines, looped around the trunks of sturdy trees, ran across the ridge and over the edge of the cliff. Two of them were taut, the other two, slack. Other ropes were coiled on the ground. A system of ratchets and crampons, attached to the taut ropes, allowed the haulers at the top of the cliff to control the speed of descent of the climbers. Michael assumed that one pair of ropes was for a member of the rescue party, the other for Marie.

Marie came back from the edge and shouted instructions. She told them that she would accompany each climber down and, hanging beside them, guide them into the hidden opening known as the Devil's Throat. Once a climber was safely inside, she would be hauled back up and accompany the next one down. Each manoeuvre should take less than ten minutes. Paul Creagan would stay on the clifftop and do the hauling. Paddy would help him, until he himself was ready to go down. Once the entire rescue party was in the Devil's Throat, Paul would haul Marie back up and together they would secure the site. Before leaving for home, Marie agreed to help Paul erect a tent in the forest, where he could wait in shelter and watch the ropes. Professor Darby had promised to send students out to relieve Paul, the first tranche of which was due mid-morning.

Being the least experienced, and given the fact that the weather was steadily deteriorating, Michael was first to step backwards over the cliff edge. Marie stood beside him shouting instructions. He tried to ignore the sounds of the ocean below or the creaking of the rope as it strained under his weight. He decided that the best option was to trust Marie, and do exactly what he was told.

They descended slowly.

There wasn't much climbing, except just at the end, when Michael had to scramble unto the lip of the narrow cleft at the entrance to the Devil's Throat. This final manoeuvre was terrifying, as it meant swinging into the open mouth of the cave, grabbing at a vertical crack in the rock face and then, hanging on until the haulers on the surface released more rope. Once there was enough slack Marie shoved Michael from behind and he tumbled, unceremoniously, onto the floor of the cave. It took Michael two attempts at the swing and grab and he knew he could never have achieved it on his own. Marie remained cool-headed throughout and Michael was surprised at just how strong she was, for such a slight woman. Once they were both inside, Marie uncoupled Michael's rope-line and directed him to the back of the cave, where the soft yellow glow of an oil lamp illuminated a pile of rucksacks, ropes and other climbing equipment. Before heading back out, Marie instructed Michael to sit and wait with the gear. She told him that, under no circumstances, was he to attempt to help her when she returned with the others.

"Stay where you are and don't interfere," she said.

"Yes Mam," he said. He refrained from saluting.

*

The wait in the cave seemed much longer than Michael had anticipated and he started to worry that there may be problems on the surface. Through the mouth of the cave, and intermittent flashes of lightening, he could see the dawn's horizon. The sky above the ocean seemed to be darkening, rather than brightening, with the coming of the new day. The mist had been replaced by heavy rain and the growl of the ocean had risen by several decibels. Michael was tempted to move forward and look out, but decided not to. He felt safe and the flicking light from an old-fashioned oil lamp, one that Marie must have placed there before they arrived, gave the cold grey space the perception of warmth. He stared at the rock walls and thought he could see faces in the shadows. They were not threatening and they never turned their hollow eyes in his direction. He rummaged through his pocket and found Hanna's locket. He took it out and held it to the light.

Her colours were fading again.

At last, two dangling bodies came into view and, after a bit of manoeuvring, Kevin rolled onto the floor. He released himself and stepped backwards away from the entrance, then joined Michael at the back of the cave. With a thumbs-up gesture and a smile Marie ascended out of view. Next came Horse, followed by Denis and Hughie. Hughie looked pale. This time Marie swung into the cave but did not undo her harness. Taking off her helmet she spoke to them.

"Once Paddy comes down, you can set off. I have given him directions to the main tunnels. There are supplies in those rucksacks behind you, enough for four or five days. Hopefully you will not need it all. Professor Kearns's line is back there too. It seems they were making their way to the main tunnels. Their line should lead you to them. Good luck to you all. Be careful," she said.

"Are you not coming with us, Miss? I mean...*Marie*?" said Horse, with a hang-dog expression on his face.

Marie tried to give him an exasperated look but it didn't work. She reddened a little.

"I've done my bit. I said I'd get you in, which I have done. The rest is up to you," she said.

Michael noticed that Marie had difficulty holding Horse's gaze.

"I think, Marie," said Horse, "we'd all feel safer if you came with us."

"Paddy Gallagher is a very experienced caver and guide. He knows these caves as well as I do. You are in good hands," she said.

"Still and all, I for one would much prefer to be in yours, Marie," said Horse. He kept a particularly straight face when he said it.

Marie huffed loudly. Michael thought he saw her smile. If she did, it didn't last long.

"All of you, stay back from the edge. Wait for Paddy and then you can go," she said curtly, but then added in a softer tone, "Good luck to you and be careful."

Before she left the cave, Marie looked at Michael.

"Good luck," she said again, as if speaking only to him.

*

Marie found the climb back up more difficult than before. Not only did the worsening winds and pelting rain make getting a good grip more difficult, but her visibility was down to a couple of inches. Along with that, her mind kept straying from the job at hand. The Englishman had distracted her again and despite her well-rehearsed inclination to feel annoyed, she had to admit that she liked his attention. When she first saw him on the ferry he reminded her of someone, a ghost from her past. But that was then and different. Now she'd gotten to know him a little, she liked him and she was quite sure he liked her. She tried not to think about him and to concentrate on getting back onto the ledge, but he kept invading her thoughts. She even began to worry for his safety.

As Marie approached the clifftop something heavy crashed into her and knocked her sideways. Had she not instinctively raised her legs she would have slammed face first into the cliff wall.

"What the hell..." she shouted into the wind. There was no way to tell what had struck her but, whatever it was, it had the effect of forcing her up the last few feet. She scrambled over the lip and onto the ledge. A rumble of thunder greeted her and a fierce gust of wind tried to push her back over the edge. Paul pulled on her rope and dragged her toward him.

"You okay?" he shouted once they were a foot apart.

"I'm fine. Something heavy hit me. Must have been something in the wind, debris from the ocean, or something, I'm fine," she said.

"What," shouted Paul.

"Never mind," she shouted back.

Paddy approached. Marie looked into his eyes. She thought he looked worried.

"You better get going Paddy. The wind is getting worse, every minute. The others are all safely in and waiting for you," she shouted.

Paddy nodded.

"Are you okay with this? Are you sure you're okay on your own?" Marie shouted at him. "Do you want me to go down with you?"

"Yes. No. I'm fine. I know what I've to do," he shouted back.

"Then, you better get going. Get down and in there, as quick as you can. Use the rocks to pull yourself in before releasing. Remember what I showed you," she shouted above the wind.

"Right," said Paddy.

She accompanied him to the cliff edge.

"You sure you don't want me to go with you?"

She had to scream above the noise of the ocean and rising wind.

Paddy shook his head and leaned back over the edge. As soon as he dropped out of sight, Marie moved away from the edge and back to where Paul Creagan stood straining with the rope that now carried Paddy's weight. It was less noisy under the trees.

"Are you okay?" she said.

"Sure," said Paul, "I got the easy job."

Marie smiled and began to remove her harnesses.

"Hey, Marie?" said Paul suddenly, "Should Paddy's rope be doing that?"

Marie turned.

"What?"

"Look at the rope. It's jumping all over the place, but Paddy's not looking for slack. There was a sudden strong tug on it, and now it's stopped moving altogether. He can't be down yet. I haven't released enough rope," said Paul.

"Are you sure?" said Marie.

"Yeh. And now it feels like he's stopped. I think he's stopped ascending," said Paul.

"Shit. Something must be wrong. I'm going to have to take a look," she said, "Tie up his rope and then take mine. Hold it tight and I'll go to the edge and see what's happening. Just don't let me fall, okay."

"You're jokin' me, right?" said Paul.

"Come on man, you can do it. A big Garda like you. Come on, I won't lean far. You just make sure you don't let me fall," she said. Before he had time to argue Marie grabbed the end of the slack rope, wrapped it around her thin waist and started walking purposely back out to cliff edge.

"Oh shit," said Paul.

"You good?" she shouted back over her shoulder

"Wait...okay...yes...I got you," Paul shouted after her.

He clasped her rope in both hands, wrapped it twice around his left arm and braced himself, as if about to begin a tug-of-war competition. Marie waited until Paul gave her a nod, telling her he was ready, before she moved her feet toward the cliff edge. Paddy's rope was now quite still. Paul took her weight. With a raised right arm, she indicated for him to slowly give her more and more slack. When he did, and with the balls of her feet beyond the edge, Marie leaned out and shone her torch downward. Slowly, inch by inch, she leaned further out. When she was far enough to see down the cliff face, she raised her hand and Paul stopped releasing rope.

The storm lashed the top of Marie's helmet and icy water ran down her nose. She had to shake her head to clear the droplets from her eye. She moved the torchlight from side to side and followed Paddy's rope down the wall. She could just about see his top half through the rising mist. The air smelt of salt and sea. It stung her face. Paddy wasn't moving and he hadn't reached the Devil's Throat. With a wave of her raised hand she indicated to Paul to pull her back up. As she rose she thought she saw an enormous shadow dart in and out of the darkness, just above the rolling waves. She guessed it must be more ocean debris, a large sheet of tarpaulin, or something like that. It always amazed her what the ocean storms manage to drag up and blow about.

Once fully upright and back on steady ground, Marie moved quickly to put back on her harness.

"Paddy's in trouble. He looks unconscious or dazed. He might have bashed his head on the cliff wall. He's hanging about six feet above the Devil's Throat. You will have to lower him down for me to get him in," she shouted to Paul above the storm.

"Can't we just drag him back up?" he asked.

"No. It's too dangerous. I'll go back down but I won't be able to get back up, until this storm has passed, so don't wait for me.

Once we're in, I'll tie one of the ropes to something down there and you can draw up the others. Don't wait. It'll be alright," Marie said.

"Are you sure you want to do this, Marie?" he said.

"I don't think I have a choice, Garda Creagan. Do you?"

Chapter 34.

Mr G. met Gregory Kelleher in the bus shelter at the bottom of the lane that ran behind the offices of Kelleher & Blunt Accountants. The two men sat next to each other on the narrow blue plastic bench and stared out into the swirling grey rain. For a long time neither of the men spoke, seemingly content to sit and stare into the nothingness of the early afternoon. Anyone familiar with the men's routines would have assumed that the meeting was a matter of chance. Mr G had stepped in out of the driving rain, during his daily lunchtime walk, whilst the accountant was on one of his regular cigarette breaks. Kelleher's pretty secretary had insisted that her boss comply with the law banning smoking in the workplace and so, when the urge came upon him, he was forced to go outside to smoke. On rainy days, he would sit at the bus stop, have a cigarette (or two) and wave away the one island bus, on the very odd occasion that it threatened to stop for him. Every day, hail, rain or snow, Mr G went for a long lunchtime walk. He had taken up walking to lose some weight and his efforts had been a spectacular success. He had lost nearly thirty pounds in less than a year. Despite walking a different route almost every day, it was not unusual for Mr G to pass the sheltered bus stop, on the way back to his office.

Their meeting at the bus shelter was not a matter of chance.

"How are you Gregory?"

Mr G didn't look at the man sitting beside him when he spoke, but instead, continued to stare out into the storm.

"I'm alright. Work's a pain though. More and more regulations. Hard to keep up with it all. Why did you want to meet? I thought you said we'd never meet again," said Kelleher.

"Where you are concerned, Gregory, I can do what I want. That includes changing my mind about our arrangement. You, on the other hand, must do what you are told and not ask silly questions. Just listen and do what I tell you," said Mr G.

Kelleher said nothing. He wanted to spit. He hated the way Mr G spoke. The Dublin thug liked to sound American, and the accountant found it pathetic, but Mr G was dangerous and he scared Gregory, so Gregory kept his opinions to himself.

"But, we are good, Gregory. I like you and you have always done what I have asked of you. I appreciate that and, as I said, I like you. Really, I do. We are good."

Mr G continued to stare out across the road and talk into the driving rain. He never once turned or looked at Gregory, and Gregory suspected that Mr G was acting out a scene from some old spy movie or TV gangster show. Whilst Mr G continued speaking, the accountant fiddled with his hands and puffed on his cigarette.

"And because I like you, Gregory, I have a very special job for you. Only you and I will know of this and, when you get me what I want, I will reward you well," said Mr G. "*Very* well!"

Gregory tensed and was sure Mr G sensed the change in his demeanour.

"Don't worry, Gregory. It's nothing illegal or dangerous. It's just...paperwork. You are a paperwork man, are you not?"

Gregory waited. Mr G stood up, as if to go. He stretched out an arm with an open palm, seemingly to measure the weight of the rain, then shook his head dramatically and sat back down. Anyone watching him would have assumed that he had decided against continuing with his journey.

"It is a private and delicate matter of the utmost importance to me, Gregory," Mr G continued.

There was a long pause. Gregory lit a second cigarette from the dying butt of the first. He didn't want one, but knew it would annoy Mr G. Mr G hated smoking, in any circumstance.

The Dublin gangster wrinkled his nose, before going on.

"I have a letter in my pocket, which I will give to you. It is in a plastic sleeve and, under no circumstances, should it be removed by you. You are not to touch the letter. It contains two sets of fingerprints, mine and those of a second, unknown, man. I need you to tell me who the second prints belong to, and anything else you can find out about him. That's all. Simple as that, Gregory."

"Fingerprints? Fingerprints? How am I supposed to do that? I'm an accountant. Fingerprints! How can I do this?" said Gregory.

"I don't know, Gregory, but you'll think of something. I know you have connections in the police. Isn't your brother-in-law a Garda? And that friend of yours in the State Solicitors Office, she might be able to help you. But Gregory, this has got to be done with the utmost discretion. Tell no one where you got it and under no circumstances are you to remove the letter from the protective sleeve. Keep it well hidden until I ask for it back. I'm sure that a man with your peculiar tastes has a secret hiding place, for documents and other things, that you don't want others to find. Don't you?"

Gregory winced. The second cigarette tasted bitter at the back of his throat.

"So, there we have it, Gregory. As far as you are concerned, this letter is evidence in a crime and it should be treated as such."

"But, but…" stammered the accountant.

"You can do this, Gregory. I know you can. I know you won't let me down."

Mr G stood and pulled up the collar of his trench coat.

"I will contact you, this day week. That should be enough time. There is a card containing my fingerprints in the sleeve with the letter - for *discounting purposes*, you understand? I'll want that back too. In another envelope, you'll find a small token of my appreciation. Let's call it, the first instalment. There will be a lot more where that came from, when the job is done. I know you won't let me down, Gregory. We are good, Gregory. We are good."

Before Gregory Kelleher had time to say anything else, Mr G was gone, striding off into a swirling storm that showed little sign of abating. For quite some time Gregory just sat on the bench shaking. He tried to think, but he felt dizzy from the second cigarette. What could he do? How could he possibly do this and what would happen to him if, or when, he failed? He began to panic. His world was falling apart and he felt like an animal caught in a double snare. Whichever way he moved, one of two sharp wires tightened around his neck and threatened to strangle the life out of him. A smiling Mr G held the end of one of the wires, the posh cop from Dublin, with his cockney sidekick, held the other. Despite the cold, Gregory Kelleher started to sweat. His lips became dry and his small eyes darted about, as if unable to focus on anything for more than a second or two. Finally, and as if by chance, his eyes came to rest on a brown padded A4 sized envelope sitting on the bench beside him. He had not noticed Mr G leaving it there. Only after making his way through a third, hurried cigarette did Gregory Kelleher find the courage to pick the envelope up and tuck it inside his jacket.

Then, threatening to throw up at any moment, Gregory Kelleher stumbled back to the office.

*

Sylvester Parker was angry.

He was fed up watching Mr G and was annoyed that he'd missed Michael Eustace at the gate. He cut opened the large brown envelope he'd been holding and let the red folder slide out onto his desk. On the cover were the words:

Private & Confidential,
Almost Fully Verified.

As expected, the first few pages contained a summary of the detailed report within. Parker began to read and as he did so, his mood lifted.

Family Background.

Michael Eustace is forty-five years old. He has an identical twin brother Francis, who is the Prior of the monastery on the pilgrimage island of Skellig Éin. Michael's parents are both dead and he has no other living siblings. A younger sister died of leukaemia at the age of six. Michael's father died in a car crash when the boys were ten. Michael was in the car with him at the time*. [The footnote read: *95% verified.] Patrick Eustace had a massive heart attack at the wheel and drove, at high speed, into an on-coming car. The ten-year-old Michael sustained serious head injuries in the crash, but after a period in intensive care, fully recovered.

The Eustace brothers have been described as being like chalk and cheese. Whilst Francis was a sensitive and shy boy, Michael was angry and aggressive, with a tendency towards violence.

"And I have witnessed first-hand those aggressive tendencies of yours, Michael Eustace," said Sylvester Parker to the empty room. He read on.

Teenage Years.

As a teenager, Michael was constantly in trouble with his teachers and later, with the police. It seems he has a problem dealing with any form of authority. At sixteen he was expelled from school when, in a schoolyard fight, he nearly beat another boy to death. The incident was considered so serious that, had a local Garda Sergeant, Terence Flynn (a family friend) not intervened, Michael would have ended up in a young-offender's detention centre. Sergeant Flynn became Michael's sponsor in a rehabilitation programme. The policeman found Michael a place in the local VEC school and got him involved with a boxing club. Michael proved to be smart and for a period excelled in his studies. He was also a natural boxer, with a legendary left hook. In the ring, Michael's aggressive nature was controlled, but not contained. His fights were notoriously vicious and bloody affairs. He was fearless and cold, not stopping until his opponent (or sparring partner) had conceded defeat. There was even talk of Michael fighting at a national level, but nothing came of this.

Parker smiled. This information was music to his ears.

Early Adulthood.

On his seventeenth birthday, a year before he was to sit his Leaving Certificate (State exam) Michael left home, made his way to Dublin and got on a ferry to England. Within days of his arrival he had enlisted in the Royal Marines. The army life suited him. He completed the Commando thirty-two-week course and was immediately sent to fight in northern Iraq. At the age of twenty-four Michael Eustace was sent to West Africa with a *small covert task force, code name Company K. They were sent there to assist local government forces in disrupting the activities of anti-government militia groups. Company K operated below the radar, in a moral and legal vacuum, and was given a free hand to achieve their objectives by any means, fair or foul.*

Parker turned the page. There was a grainy photograph paper-clipped to the top of the second page of the summary. It showed a small group of soldiers standing in a jungle clearing. One man stood slightly apart from the others. It was a young Michael Eustace. Parker studied the photograph for a long time, before continuing to read the report summary.

Company K acted with impunity for fifteen months. On the fifteenth of November 2002, the men of Company K walked into a rebel ambush. Those not killed, were taken prisoner and the rebels showed little mercy. The men of Company K were tortured and, one by one, executed. The details are in the appendix of this report. The men's bodies were mutilated and used to taunt the authorities. Their heads were stuck on stakes and placed outside the gates of the British Embassy; their severed limbs nailed to the doors of government buildings; and their dismembered torsos gutted and stuffed with explosives, becoming gruesome roadside IED's. Michael Eustace was the only one spared. The reason for this is unclear. It may have been because he was the only member of Company K to hold an Irish passport.

Three months after his capture, the rebel party holding him were intercepted by a small force of Irish U.N. Peace-Keepers. On hearing that the rebels held an Irishman captive, the commander of the Irish force negotiated for Michael's release. He was close to death and was hospitalised for over a year, firstly in Kinshasa and then in Nairobi.

It was in Kenya that he was reunited with his brother Francis.

Given the extent of his injuries and the clandestine nature of the operations, the British authorities thought it best to quietly close the files on Company K. All the other members were dead. Michael Eustace was given an honourable discharge and all links with the Royal Marines were severed, all records expunged.

After a long recuperation, Michael returned to Ireland to live with his mother in Mullingar, while his brother Francis remained in Kenya, took his vows and was ordained a Roman Catholic priest five years later.

The time spent as a dog soldier in Africa changed Michael Eustace in a dramatic way. His aggressive tendencies were gone or repressed, although his restlessness and wanderlust remained. A year after returning to Ireland Michael left home again and began, aimlessly, travelling the world. The main report details this period, which appears of little interest.

Four years ago, Michael turned up in England with an Australian girlfriend, a foreign correspondent with the BBC. She managed to get him a job as an Irish mystic, on an afternoon television show for BBC North East. The relationship with the Australian did not last long. She moved back to Sydney. Michael stayed in England. His relationship with the BBC didn't last long, either. Following an allegation of assault, which occurred during his last live television appearance, his contract with the BBC was terminated and he once again returned to Ireland to live with his now elderly and ailing mother.

She died eight months ago.

Three days ago, Michael arrived on the island of Skellig Éin and is staying with his brother Father Francis at the Priory. Michael is on the island to attend the fifteen hundred year celebrations of the founding of the Christian missionary on Skellig Éin. Michael intends to stay on the island until the end of June.**

[The footnote read: **92% verified]

Parker carefully read through the rest of the detailed report. The research was thorough. When he was finished, he returned to the photograph clipped to the top of the second page. He stared at the young soldier standing apart from the other men of Company K.

Parker touched the photograph. His finger was bone dry and it left no mark on the glossy paper. He caressed the young soldier's face.

"There you are, Michael Eustace. There you are! It has taken me time to find you, to find *all* of the players, but now we are here and it will not be long before we are together, you and I, and then Michael Eustace, you will feel the power of my vengeance."

Chapter 35.

Soon after Marie returned to the Devil's Throat, Paul Creagan set about making camp in the woods beside the mossy ridge. It took him ages. Firstly, he had to find a suitable open space among the trees large enough to take the tent but also close enough to the edge of the forest so that he could watch the ropes. Then he had to erect the two-man tent on his own, and make sure it was properly tied down. This took him the best part of an hour. By the time he'd finished his heavy Garda coat was soaked through, and twice as heavy as it had been when he'd begun. He was exhausted and hungry. Paul knew that if he climbed under the canvas he'd be asleep in minutes so decided to stay outside, and upright, until help arrived. He leaned against a stout tree and watched the storm abate. When the sun finally made an appearance, it was half way up the sky and its bright light blinded him. He thought about Horse and his strange friend Michael Eustace. He watched the ropes and tried not to think of sleep.

Just before noon three students, all classmates of Kevin Carr, turned up at his cliff top watch. One of them, a very handsome well-dressed blond student named Henry Troy, brought a large expensive picnic basket and a second, much larger tent which seemed to erect itself. Paul gathered his gear, ready to leave. Henry looked surprised.

"You must stay for brunch, Inspector Creagan. I insist," he said.

"Thanks, but I better be off. I'll be back at some stage tomorrow. Stay away from the edge and watch the ropes. All of you, stay away from the edge."

"Yes, sir," said Henry. He gave Paul a small salute.

"Ha. Thanks for the offer, though. But I really need to go."

"Any time, Detective Creagan," said Henry.

Paul left them, went back to the carpark and climbed into his car. He yawned and squeezed his eyes shut. He thought about going to sleep in the seat. His phone rang.

"Hello," he said.

"Is this Garda Paul Creagan?" said the man on the other end of the line.

"Yes. This is Paul Creagan. Who is this?"

"This is…eh…Gregory Kelleher, of Kelleher and Blunt Accountants. You said to ring, if someone got in touch."

"Mr. Kelleher? Oh yes, Mr Kelleher, of course. Has someone been in contact with you, sir?"

"I think they're watching me. They could be bugging my phone. Can we meet, Garda Creagan?" said Gregory.

The accountant sounded agitated.

"Calm down, Mr Kelleher. I can meet you now, if that suits you. Where would you like to meet me? I can come to your office."

"No! Not my office. I think they are watching me. I'll meet you…eh…upstairs in M&M's. It's a coffee shop on the square. Upstairs is quiet. There are private booths. Can you be there in half an hour?"

"I think so. You did the right thing, contacting me. I'll be discreet," said Paul.

When Gregory cut the line, Paul looked at the mobile before slipping it into the cradle fixed to the dashboard. He thought about calling Horse, but then dismissed the idea. There would be no coverage underground. He turned on the engine, looked over his shoulder before reversing out of the space. In the rear-view mirror he caught a glimpse of Henry Troy standing at the edge of the wood. Henry was watching him. Paul thought about it for a moment and smiled.

"Yes, sir," he said into the mirror and gave Henry a hearty salute, before driving away.

*

The meeting with Gregory Kelleher in M&M's was not what Paul expected. Gregory was nervous and twitchy and Paul knew

264

from the start that he was lying to him. The accountant passed Paul a stiff A4 sized envelope and explained that inside was a letter given to him by a man he'd never met before, with instructions to find out who the fingerprints belonged to. Paul showed Gregory a photograph of Mr G and, after some terrible amateur dramatics, Gregory agreed that Mr G *might* have been the man who gave him the letter.

As soon as Gregory left the café Paul made a call. Ten minutes later he met Harry *Buick* Buckingham in the quiet room next to the reception foyer of the Tara Cove Hotel. Harry was intrigued and told him that finding out who the fingerprints belonged to would be easy enough, if the owner had form, and was on the system.

"The system?" said Paul

"Well, everybody is on the system these days, even the good guys," said Harry mysteriously.

"Really?"

"Oh yeh. Even your mother is on the system, Paul. If I asked, I could probably find out what your mother had for breakfast this morning," said Buick.

Paul frowned.

"So why bring this to us? You think it could be connected to our thing?" asked Buick.

"I don't know. Possibly. I don't see how, but it came from Mr G, I'm sure of that. And Gregory Kelleher knew very well who Mr G was. As to why I'm asking you, everything that's going on here is strange, don't you think? And, if it is connected, isn't it better to keep it under wraps? Besides, you guys have better resources, you will prioritise it for me and you are here now. And if you know what my mother had for breakfast, this will be a walk in the park for you."

Buick raised a quizzical brow.

"Look, if I sent this to Dublin, I'll be waiting three to four weeks for a response."

"Okay. I was just asking. Can I take a look?" said Buick.

"Sure. It's just a letter. It's in a plastic sleeve, so go ahead, be my guest."

Buick opened the envelope and let the letter in the plastic sleeve slide onto the table. They both leaned over and stared at it.

"Huh," said Harry.

Paul yawned and studied the letter. The hand-writing was precise and neat. Paul rubbed his eyes and focussed. He hadn't studied it properly in the coffee shop, when Kelleher had handed it to him. In the subdued light of the small ante room the letter looked beautiful, almost artistic, he thought. In contrast, the language was awkward and grating.

Sylvia Locklead
Ashford
UK
TW15 3JZ

My Dearest

We were so upset to hear about P, because of what he meant to you my love. Are you like him? - not at all! Almost as surely as the monster mansion is not for one like you. Finished off, he was, by fear and cowardice - not love.

Soon we will be triumphant and together - you need never doubt my love. You are ever in my thoughts, my sweetness.

Will we three be together again? Be sure of it, if of nothing else my darling. Free to express our feelings, a family again. Wait and we will come for you. For the players are assembling. My greatest work will soon be at hand. Sign my name forever into your precious heart.

S

"Bloody odd letter, but the handwriting nice. You think it might be a foreigner?" said Harry.

"Odd for sure. I didn't really study it, when Kelleher slipped it to me. It could be bad English, I suppose," said Paul.

"Well, I'll get our boys to see what they can dig up. By the way, you look like shit, Paul. You been up all night nailin' one of those lovely female Garda beauties I keep bumpin' into in the corridors upstairs?" Harry winked at Paul and chuckled, then slipped the plastic covered letter back into the envelope.

"What? No! I mean, I'd never be that lucky, Buick," said Paul awkwardly. "I was…never mind."

"All right! Only jokin' with ye, man. Well, I better hit the road. We don't want your English friend seein' us together, do we Paul? He might get the wrong idea."

Buick stood up.

"See you Harry, and, thanks," said Paul, then closed his eyes and sighed.

Chapter 36.

The group of seven descended in single file, even when the cave was wide enough to go side by side. They had developed a sort of rhythm and the amateur cavers took comfort from having an allocated place in the line. Denis Treacy led the way and a forlorn Patrick Gallagher brought up the rear. Hughie, Denis' sidekick, stuck close to Denis's shoulder, with Kevin a few steps behind him. Then came Horse, Michael and Marie. They had been moving along for almost four hours, following the guide ropes left by Professor Kearns and his party. Their way was lit by the rocking white light from the torches fixed to the side of their climbing helmets. Every hundred yards or so along the passageway, a ribbon of tiny blue LED lights had been wrapped around the Professor's guide rope. A tiny compact waterproof battery pack, containing two button batteries, dangled from the end of each ribbon. In areas of particular danger – an unseen hole, uneven ground or lowered head height - the blue LED's ribbon lights were replaced with red ones. It was a simple method of path-finding. If all the torches were extinguished, a climber could find the guide rope by way of the little LED's and make their way back to the surface holding onto the rope. Treacy demonstrated this soon after leaving the Devil's Throat.

"Everyone turn off your torches!" he said. "It's important for those of you who do not cave regularly to know how dark *dark* is down here. Fucking dark – that's how dark! Without lights or the rope, you'll never find your way out, an' the darkness will drive you fuckin' mad. The darkness maybe only one of the enemies lurking in these caves, but it's a big fuckin' enemy!"

Michael thought Denis's speech was rehearsed. He also detected the hint of an American accent during the overly dramatic delivery.

Denis had appointed himself the rescue-party leader, once it became clear that Paddy was not himself, since he'd cracked his head on the descent into the Devil's Throat. Paddy complained of headaches and dizziness, but insisted on staying with them. No one at the time voiced any objection to Denis assuming command, although Michael guessed that several the group harboured concerns about his leadership qualities, not least of all, Paddy Gallagher. Denis insisted on carrying the largest haversack. Horse Hopkins carried the next heaviest. The rest of the supplies were shared among the others. The massive pockets of Michael's ultra-luminous jacket were stuffed with bits and pieces, including extra torches and a bag of LED ribbon lights. Into one of the button-down pockets Horse had stuffed an extremely large bag of boiled sweets. "For the adventure," Horse had said with a smile. With all the pockets full to bursting, the already bulbous jacket seemed to double in size and Michael knew that he looked even more ridiculous. It wasn't long before Horse was making fun of him, repeating Marie's label of Luminous Lenny, but Michael didn't mind. The jacket was surprisingly comfortable and warm. It was like travelling in a thick, but relatively light, sleeping bag.

After four hours of trekking, everyone was tired and Michael noticed that, apart from Marie, they were all puffing and panting loudly. Denis said little and whatever he did say seemed only for Hughie's ears. Denis and Hughie raced forward with a degree of cocky confidence that worried Michael, but when he felt like asking them to slow down, or even stop for a break, he thought of Hanna and kept his mouth shut.

As Michael plodded along his thoughts turned to Marie Joyce. He found Marie curious and interesting. She was strikingly beautiful but, he noticed, she played down her beauty in many ways. She dressed in drab colours, had her hair cut in an unflattering tom-boy style and seemed to hold her face in a permanent scowl. She acted shy and reserved but Michael was sure she was single-minded and, probably, as tough as nails, and he guessed there were very good reasons why the caving community on the island called her Dare Devil.

Michael liked Marie. Even her colours were beautiful. They were strongest around her hands and between her forehead and eyes. The dominant colour he saw was turquoise, in a cloud of ice blue, umber and gold. He was reminded of the Virginia Creeper clinging to the front wall of Primrose's art gallery. Despite their difficult first meeting in her kitchen, he was sure she liked him too, and he fantasised that it was because of him that she had agreed to go with them, in their search for Hanna. It certainly hadn't been her original plan to go along. Once she'd got Paddy safely down off the cliff face, she told them that she would wait in the Devil Throat until the storm had passed and then climb back out.

Michael had pleaded with her to come with them, telling her that they all would feel better with her as guide, even though he was sure that Denis did not. Denis had not liked it when Marie had crept up behind him in the car park or her referring to him and Hughie as Rambo and Son. Michael overheard Denis tell Hughie that the Double D nickname stood for Dick-Dodger.

"She's a skinny little dick-dodging lesbo, Hughie, that's what she is. Everyone on the island knows it. What a fuckin' waste, eh?" he declare said it, as they made their way through the trees, on the way to the cliff edge, and Michael was convinced that Marie had heard Denis say it. If she had, Michael had to concede that it may have been the real reason she had a change of heart and agreed to go with them - just to annoy Denis.

"Oh, very well, I'll go with you, if that's what you *all* want," she'd said. Michael remembered that Denis did not join the chorus of approval from the others.

They walked, crawled and climbed, always moving downwards, deeper and deeper, away from the Devil's Throat, and into the Devil's belly. They squeezed, one by one, through tight crevices, sometimes having to remove their bags or even their jackets to allow them through the narrow gaps of damp cold limestone. They shuffled, heads bent, in low corridors, like the large Alice running down the rabbit hole, and they scuttled on hands and knees like a line of crabs. There was no sound in the caves, bar that of their own breathing, the scuffing of their boots and knees on the dusty floor and the squeak from their straining backpacks. If anyone spoke, their voices sounded odd, almost alien. Words were muffled in the still icy air. The cold in the

271

caves was as solid as the rocks and the air smelt of nothing but emptiness.

"We should take a break Denis," shouted Horse up the line. His voice seemed hollow. Michael was relieved that his English friend had spoken up.

They'd reached a relatively wide low cavern where they could sit and remove their haversacks. The ground had levelled off too. Ahead of them the tunnel was low and narrow and they would have to walk with their backs bent.

Denis stopped and turned. Hughie almost walked into him.

"Fifteen-minute break everyone. Don't get too comfortable, people," Denis shouted like a drill sergeant, as if the idea to stop had been his.

Haversacks and travellers flopped to the floor.

Even in the relatively small space Michael noticed that Marie managed to find a spot on her own. She removed her backpack and sat down in small alcove. After removing his gear Horse walked over to her and offered her a wrapped sweet. She surprised everyone, but especially Horse, by accepting it with a smile.

"I haven't had one of these in years," she said.

"Rhubarb and custard," said Horse, "my personal favourites. Nice spot you found there."

"It's call an exedra. Nature's very own park bench," she said and slipped the sweet between her lips.

Horse held out his hand and after a moment Marie handed him the empty wrapper.

"Thanks," she said.

"Well, we don't want to litter the place, do we?"

There was room for one more person on her rock seat, but Horse didn't ask if he could join her. Instead, he went and sat on the floor beside Michael, who was in an animated conversation with Kevin and Paddy. Kevin quizzed Michael relentlessly.

"But how can you know that they are still alive? If you are not a psychic, what are you then?" Kevin said.

"I don't know what I am Kevin," said Michael gently. "I just see things. Signs of life, you might say. I always have done and for a long time I assumed everyone else saw the same things I did. Maybe I am a psychic but I have never liked the term or its connotations. Psychics claim to see dead people. I see life."

"What does that mean? What do you see?" asked Paddy.

"Colours. I see colours. They are in the air. They come from people. Every person has a colour or, to be exact, a collection of colours, that together make up something unique, an aura particular to that person. I see these colours and I can distinguish one person's colour from someone else's, the same way you can distinguish me from Kevin, if you know what I mean," he said.

"You see an aura around everyone?" said Kevin.

"Yes. But not like in the movies. It's not just around the person, it runs through them as if it's from somewhere inside them and sometimes it pulses like a heartbeat."

"Is it a person's soul that you see?" asked Paddy.

"Maybe? That's what my brother thinks," said Michael.

"But, I still don't understand how you know they are alive," said Paddy.

"People leave traces of their colour on personal objects and, sometimes, on walls and other things that they have touched. Some of it sticks and stays. I don't know why. Most times it doesn't stick. It seems arbitrary actually, but when a person dies all the colour traces of them disappears. Like magic," said Michael.

He bent his head and grimaced. He never liked talking about his gift because he could never do so without thinking of all the times he watched the familiar colours of the ones he loved disappear before his eyes. His father, his little sister and most recently the familiar colours of his loving mother.

"Magic? What a load of crap," said Denis Treacy. "Is this why we're here, on the say-so of this guy? Christ on a bike, I've heard it all now. Do you believe this shite, Paddy?"

"Hey watch your mouth," said Horse, "You just do what you're good at, and keep your opinions to yourself."

"Or fucking what?" said Denis standing up and visibly puffing out his chest.

"You do not want to go there, mate," said the Englishman standing up in response.

"I'm not your fucking mate," said Denis with a sneer.

"Calm down everybody," said Paddy. He moved between the two men.

He turned to Denis.

"I asked you to come along Denis to help us rescue our friends because you are an experienced caver. If these guys can help us find them, then that's all the better, right?"

Denis sneered again.

"I don't need some fucking freak and a lesbian to show me how to track a bunch of inexperienced university ponces. They've been down here for more than a week, Paddy. You know what that means. We're searching for dead bodies. The end of this amateur adventure is a pile of cold dead students and their dumb ass professor."

"Hanna is not dead," said Michael.

His voice was weak. He knew that this could only partially be blamed on the thinness of the air. The climb had taken its toll on him and his head hurt. As soon as he sat down he had felt dizzy. Hanna's colours were fading and he knew time was running out for her.

"That's it? Spooky speaks and we all fall in line? For fuck sake, Paddy!" said Denis.

Paddy cringed.

"Come on Hughie, break-time is over. Time to find the bodies," said Denis.

He grabbed his haversack, slung it over his shoulders and headed on into the caves. Hughie looked at the others before picking up his backpack and heading after his friend.

"That's just great. They've taken the majority of our supplies," said Kevin.

"Rambo and Son ride again," said Marie.

Michael raised his head and looked at her.

"Hey. If it's any consolation Spooky, I believe you."

Michael was sure Marie winked at him.

Chapter 37.

Just as Rick had guessed, it didn't take long for Pete Mercer to notice that he and Megan were no longer asleep with the others, and a quick check would confirm that the two were no longer in the cave. Rick could imagine Pete's mind racing and recalling the incident at the bottom of the cliff path, and the feeling he had had that there was someone hiding in the shadows. Pete started shouting.

"All o' yous, get the fuck out there and find them two fuckers, before they get away," screamed Pete. There was an angry desperation in his voice.

Then the Creep spoke. Unlike Pete, his voice was calm and menacing, but there was anger too.

"There will be no lights and they are to be kept alive, do you understand? I want them both alive. Quickly now. Find them."

"Fuck, fuck fuck. I fuckin' told you there was someone out there. I fuckin' knew it. I'll kill that fuckin' cun' Kavanagh, and his bitch. I swear I'll fuckin' kill the two of them," shouted Pete.

Rick and Megan stood like statues at the back of the stinking toilet. Rick imagined Mercer running around in erratic circles, like an mad dog chasing its own tail. The thought gave him pleasure. Despite his precarious predicament, Rick was as calm as the foreigner sounded.

"You can keel them both when I finish with them. I weel not let them die, I promise you that," said the Creep.

Rick felt Megan tense up.

There was the sound of shuffling feet, as the workers hurrying out into the cold dark night and then voices, directly outside the toilet entrance.

"Wait. You stay here with dee retard," said the Creep.

Rick heard Mo's voice, but he couldn't make out what Mo was saying.

"You heard him. We can't have that fucker out there, making noise, an' it'll have to be you Mo, 'cos 'e clings off yer, like yer his fuckin' mammy," said Pete.

"I need to pee, Mo," said Lash. Lash sounded excited rather than concerned or annoyed at being referred to as a "retard".

"Why do I have to stay with him, Pete?" said Mo, ignoring Lash's pleas.

"Cos I fuckin' said so, righ'? Now get back inside where no one can see you, an' fuckin' stay there," said Mercer.

"I need to pee, Mo," said Lash again.

A shadow crossed in front of the entrance to the make-shift toilet. Megan tighter her grip of Rick's arm. Lash stepped in and stopped. He stared directly at Rick and Megan.

"There's someone in here," he shouted. "Mo, I can't pee. There's someone in here."

"What?" said the Creep, coming to the doorway of the latrine. Lash moved aside to let the foreigner look in.

"I can't pee with someone watching," he said again.

The Creep leaned forward and squinted into the gloom. Rick held his breath. The Creep smiled.

"Ha! I see him. Don't worry, 'e won't watch, will you?" said the Creep and he kicked out at the body of the dead guard lying in the pool of excrement. "You have your pee, den you go back inside with your friend, okay? I promise you, he won't watch you."

"Are yez comin' or not?" Rick heard Pete say.

The Creep went out. Lash stepped forward and, still staring at Rick, unzipped his flies and urinated onto the back of the dead man. When he was finished, he wiped his hands vigorously on his trousers and then went back into the cave.

After what seemed like an age, Rick chanced to look out. Mercer and the Creep had followed the workers outside and were no longer in view of the entrance. Mo and Lash had gone back in to the sleeping area of the cave.

"Come on Meg, time to get out of here," he whispered.

Hand in hand they stepped over the dead body lying in the filth pool. They used his back as a stepping stone and their weight on his body made it rock in the foul water causing the liquid beneath him to suck and squelch.

"Where are we goin' Rick?" whispered Megan in a terrified voice.

"You'll see, Meg. You'll see," he said.

*

Rick had known that there was no way that he and Megan could have reached the clifftop without being caught, especially after their near miss at the bottom of the climbing path. The wild ocean and the high promontories that enclosed the secluded cove ensured that any escape along the coast was out of the question. Their only option was to go deeper into the cave system and hide there or, with luck, find another route to the surface. Rick was banking on the fact that the cave would be emptied once the search for them was set in train. He figured that at least one man would be left behind with the drugs and had resolved to kill whoever it was, as quickly and quietly as he could. The guard, or *guards*, left behind would have to die, if he and Megan were to get away. If Mercer or the Creep stayed behind, that would pose a much more difficult challenge, but Rick didn't care. He wasn't afraid anymore. He was ready to face either of them. In the end, luck was on his side. The fact that Pete left Mo and Lash behind meant he wouldn't have to kill anyone. As soon as he returned with Megan to the sleeping quarters Rick got straight to the point.

"They mean to kill you, Mo. You know that. Pete Mercer is a lying two-faced fuckin' bastard. When the drugs are on de boat, they plan to kill all of us. Only Pete and de fuckin' Creep will leave here alive. That's de truth. You know it is. Me an' Megan are getting' outta here now. Yer either with us or against us. What's it goin' te be Mo?"

Mo didn't spend too long thinking about it.

"I'm fuckin' with you, Rick. You know me. Always have been, always will be."

"Always will be," repeated Lash.

Lash smiled at Megan.

Rick took Mo to one side and explained his plan for their escape, which included taking a share of the drugs and burning the rest. They discussed what to do with Lash. Should they take

277

him, or leave him behind? They agreed that they couldn't leave Lash, at least, not alive. Lash clung to Mo like Megan clung to Rick. If Mo were to leave him, Lash would start screaming. Since the incident with Rats and the Banshee, Lash had become withdrawn, childlike and fidgety. He shadowed Mo everywhere he went. He even followed him to the toilet. If Lash started screaming, he would alert Mercer and the others. When Mercer got back to the cave Lash would lead them straight to Rick's secret escape route. If they didn't take him along, they'd have to kill him, but neither Rick nor Mo seemed to have the stomach for that.

"Anyways, he'll come in handy in a fight," said Mo.

"Yeh, righ," said Rick.

And he's a handy drug-mule too, thought Rick.

"Right. So here's what we gonna do," Rick said, loud enough so that Megan and Lash could hear him. "We're goin' further inta de caves. We can hide there, or better still, find anudder way out. Come on, quick now, an' no messin', an' no fuckin' talkin, righ?"

*

During the first day of rock clearing Rick had come across a horizontal crevice, just above floor level, which was virtually invisible in the subdued light of the cave. When Rick first saw it he thought it was nothing more than a shadow. The cave walls were full of shadows, formed by shallow intents or stretches of different colour, darker rock. But, it wasn't a shadow. It was a crawl-space under the wall and it led into another tunnel behind. Even when the rock wall was illuminated by torchlight the narrow opening could only be seen if you were looking for it. Rick had found it by accident. He had been taking a leak against the rock wall and noticed that there was no pooling at his feet, as he might expect. His piss ran down the wall and disappeared. When Rick was sure no one was watching, he dropped to the ground and shone his torch under the wall and saw glimmers of a large tunnel within. The crawl-space was tight, at best no more that eighteen inches off the floor, but it was tall enough for a person to squeeze through. Rick decided, there and then, that this would be his *Plan B*, if an escape up the path proved impossible.

Now it was time to put his Plan B into action. Rick instructed the others to move a pile of the cocaine to the back of the cave, just enough packets that they could carry between them. Whilst they did that, Rick explored. He discovered a holdall, hidden under the Creep's make-shift bed in the alcove that he shared with Pete Mercer. Rick emptied its contents onto the cave floor and stamped on most of the items, as if they were cockroaches. He took pleasure smashing a framed photograph of a dark hair woman holding hands with little blond girl. He wondered if it was a picture of the creep's wife and kid. Rick thought the woman looked hot. He took the photo from the broken glass and shoved it into his pocket. He didn't smash everything belonging to the Creep, but instead, put somethings back into the holdall, to take with him. There was an unopened packet of cigarillos and a book of matches and a set of bone handled skinning knives in a velvet lined mahogany case. One of the bigger knives was missing from its slot and Rick guessed that the Creep had taken it with him when he went outside. It was probably the knife the Creep had used to cut the guards throat outside the worker's toilet. The photograph, the box of knives and the cigars were part of the Creeps identity and taking them was better than destroying them. Rick knew that losing them would make the guy mad as hell, and that thought made Rick happy. With luck the Creep might even take his anger out on Pete Mercer.

"Fuck you, you fuckin' grease-ball, and fuck you Mercer," Rick said under his breath.

When Rick got back to the others he packed the Creep's holdall with as many slabs of cocaine as he could manage to stuff in, twelve blocks in all. Filled to bursting, he figured that the holdall was worth more than a million euro, more than enough *get-away and disappear-forever* money. The drugs would be Rick's ticket to a better life. With the proceeds from the sale he could change his name, move abroad and disappear forever. He'd go somewhere exotic, somewhere warm, some place where no one would ever find him.

But taking *just* what they could carry wasn't enough for Rick. He wanted Mr G to pay, too. So, before he left, Rick lit up one of the cigarillos and with the lighted match set fire to the gauzy corners of the hessian bales that held together the remaining slabs of cocaine. It took surprisingly little time for the fire to get going.

"Explain that to the Cartel, Mr G you fuckin' twat. Maybe they will want to teach you a lesson. An eye for an eye! Or maybe they'll want one of you balls instead."

Rick turned to the others.

"Come on then. Wha'cha waiting for? Let's get de fuck ou'a here."

Rick, followed by Megan, Lash and Mo crawled under the wall at the back of the cave. Behind them a dense putrid cloud tumbled and rolled across the caves' ragged ceiling, as millions of Euros worth of the finest South American cocaine went up in smoke.

Chapter 38.

"What?" said Detective Paul Creagan, shouting into his mobile phone. He'd returned to the cliff-watch as promised, and was enjoying a coffee with Henry Troy, when the call came in.

The rain had stopped but the wind, coming in from over the ocean, was vicious. It howled like an angry dog.

"I can't hear you. The reception is awful. Wait a moment and I'll go back to the car. Hold on, okay? I can't hear you." Paul made a face at Henry and mouthed a silent "sorry."

The other two students had left them an hour before and, since then, Henry and Paul had sat together in the make-shift camp, drinking coffee and talking. Henry had agreed that the other two students could go and had given them his car. Paul said he would give Henry a lift back to the university when the next lot of students turned up to relieve them of their vigil.

Paul stood up and made his way through the trees to the car park at Hangman's Cross. He kept the mobile pressed to his ear. When he climbed into his car and shut the door the drop in the noise level was startling.

"Hello, Paul Creagan speaking. Sorry about that. Who is this?"

"Hey Paul. Where you at man?"

"Hey Harry. What's up?"

"Where you at? You need to get back to the hotel, and bring the Englishman with you. There's someone here wants to speak with you both, urgently."

"What are you talking about?" said Paul.

"Your love-letter, that's what? It's fuckin' incendiary, man!"

"What? What do you mean *incendiary*?"

"Like a bomb, incendiary. All I know is, as soon as our techies got goin' on that letter, red lights started flashing all over the place. I'm not kiddin'. CIA, FBI, National Security, Interpol, Homeland Security, the whole world and his fuckin' mother. I shit you not. My phone's been goin' crazy all morning. I've had some five-star general screamin' at me for the last fifteen minutes. My instructions are to bring you guys in. You'd swear to God I'd sent them dirty pictures of the First Lady. You two wise guys got to get over here now Creagan!" said the American. His tone was serious.

"There's no way to contact Horse, Harry. He's underground. I don't know when he will be back. There's no way to contact him. What the hell is this about, Harry?" said Paul.

"That fuckin' letter. You're not listening to me, man. The fuckin' letter you gave me. I'll wait for you in hotel bar. Don't fuckin' delay and don't speak to anyone in the meantime. How long will it take you to get back?"

"I donno. Fifteen, twenty minutes?"

"Make it ten," said Buick, then abruptly hung up.

Paul quickly made his way back to the camp, his mind racing and his ears red. He apologised to Henry, telling him he'd have to leave immediately and that he had no idea when he'd be back. He was annoyed and he wanted Henry to know it. He apologised to Henry for that too. Henry said that he understood and that he would remain at the camp until reinforcements arrived.

"James Wong and a couple of other students are on their way over," he said with a weak smile.

"Thanks. I owe you one, Henry," said Paul as he headed back to the carpark. Before climbing into his car he looked over his shoulder. Just as before, Henry had followed him to the edge of the wood.

"I'll come back for you, one way or another, okay?" he shouted above the wind.

"I'll be waiting," said Henry. He gave Paul a coy smile.

"I'll buy you a pint, when this is all over," Paul shouted.

He wasn't sure if Henry heard what he said.

Chapter 39.

As soon as he stood upright Rick removed the bandage from his damaged eye. In the light of the two torches the eye looked like it had changed colour during it's revival. The iris was a much paler blue and had a marbled effect that, at certain times, made it sparkle. None of the others commented on it. Getting away seemed the priority.

There was only one way to go, down along a narrow tunnel that brought them further and further from the burning cave behind. Rick had no idea where he was going but knew that they had no option but to keep going. Forward was their only option now.

The tunnel varied in height but was never so low that any of them had to crouch. The floor sloped gently downward, a fact that bothered Rick. He had hoped that the secret tunnel would lead them to the open air somewhere beyond the secluded cove, but knew that, for that to happen, they should be climbing, rather than descending. The more they progressed along the sloping tunnel, the deeper they went below sea level.

Rick wasn't overly worried. *Lady Luck* was with him and he felt confident that wherever the tunnel led, it would ultimately set him free. Foremost on his mind was the desire to put as much distance, and as quickly as possible, between them and their angry murderous pursuers. Megan clung onto his arm and seemed more frightened than she'd ever been. She shuffled forward on unsteady legs and clung to him as if she was drunk. Mo dragged Lash along by a rope tied around both their waists. Lash kept muttering to himself and smiling inanely at the taut rope in front of him. Mo heaved and grumbled but somehow managed to keep up with Rick and Megan. Rick and Mo both carried torches that they had found among the Pete Mercer's stuff. Everyone carried shrink-wrapped slabs of cocaine. Megan had one block under her arm, like a brick sized handbag. Mo had his pockets full and Lash carried eight slabs around his waist, tucked under his belt. Rick thought they made Lash look like a suicide bomber.

Taking some of the drugs and destroying the rest had not been in Rick's original plan. Nor had bringing Mo and Lash along either. But when the opportunities presented themselves, these decisions seemed obvious and ordained. Taking the drugs and the two boys, and burning the remainder, was going to cause a hell of a shit-storm and the thought of the likely consequences for his enemies gave Rick's a mental hard-on.

"Fuck you Mr G. Fuck you Pete Mercer. And fuck all you foreign arse-wipes. Fuck you, 'til yer all fuckin' dead," he whispered.

They had travelled for about fifteen minutes, along the descending passageway when they turned a corner and found their way blocked by a wall of rock.

"Shit," said Rick. Megan whimpered at his side.

"A fuckin' dead-end. Shit, fuck," said Mo.

"Shit, fuck," mimicked Lash.

"Whata we goin' do now, Rick?" said Megan.

"Now, Rick?" mimicked Lash.

Rick said nothing. He ran his torchlight along the line where the wall met the floor. This time there was no deep shadow or hidden entrance.

"Shit," Rick said again.

"Shit," mimicked Lash.

"What's that up there?" said Mo. He pointed his torchlight up to the top of the wall five foot above their heads.

"Up there," said Lash, who continued to stare down at the rope connecting him to Mo.

Rick looked up. In the top left hand corner there was the deep shadow of a possible crevice.

"That might be something," said Rick.

"Something" said Lash. He raised his head and smiled at Megan.

Rick moved closer. Megan tugged at his arm.

"Fuck, Megan. Let fuckin' go of me, will ye?" he snapped.

When she didn't let go, but instead gripped his arm even tighter, he turned on her. For a moment he thought of punching her in the face with his free hand, but something inside of him, which he didn't understand, made him pull back at the very last moment. He was sure it had nothing to do with shame or pity. He feigned a smile.

"Sit down Meg," he said, as if speaking to a child, "It's okay. I'm just goin' take a look. You can see me, righ?" He prised her fingers off his arm and pushed her roughly aside. "You'll be okay. You mind this bag. I won't leave without it, now will I? I won't go anywhere without that, now will I, Meg? I promise. I've looked after you, haven't I? So sit, the fuck, down, an' relax, righ?" he said. He gave her the Creep's bag and turned to Mo.

"Give us a leg up Mo, an' I'll have a look," he said. Mo did so, without a word.

It was a deep shelf much the same height as the floor-level crevice that had led them into the tunnel. Standing on Mo's shoulders, Rick shone his torch into it. He couldn't see if it led to another tunnel. As far as he could tell it was a eighteen inch high horizontal crack that went on and on, as far as he could see. There was no way of knowing that it led anywhere other than into the heart of solid rock. If he managed to climb in, which would not be easy, he would have to shuffle forward on his stomach with his head turned to one side, and his cheek touching the floor and the rock ceiling two inches above him. It would mean moving forward blind, using only his outstretched arms to find his way. If he got stuck, because the crevice narrowed rather than opening up, he could become wedged in the darkness, stuck forever and buried alive! The further he crawled in, the greater the risk of getting stuck. There would simply be no way of turning around and crawling back out if the crevice led to a dead end. Even reversing would be nearly impossible, especially if he crawled in too far. The thought of getting stuck in the darkness made him squirm.

Had *Lady Luck* deserted him, he wondered. Had she tricked him? Would they have to turn around and go back?

"Let us back down," he said.

Mo lowered him back to the tunnel floor.

"Can we get through, Rick?" said Mo.

"Get through, Rick?" said Lash.

"Can't you shut him, de fuck, up? I can't hear meself fuckin' think," snapped Rick.

"Can't we keep goin' Rick? We can't go back. They'll be comin' for us. They'll find the entrance and they'll come after us. We shouldn't have takin' de drugs, Rick," said Megan. "I told yah, we shouldn't take dem."

Rick looked at Megan as if was only seeing her for the very first time, as if she was a total stranger to him. This wasn't the Megan he thought he knew. His girl would never question him. Why didn't she believe that he knew what he was doing? How could she say she loved him, if she couldn't see him for what he really was? He was a winner. He couldn't lose. Why couldn't she see that? He wanted to scream. He wanted to punch her. Instead he gave her a cruel smile.

"Sure we can. We'll get through, Meg. You'll see," he said. He watched her for a little while. When she drew near, he backed away. When he stared at her with his different coloured eyes, she looked away.

Megan had lost a tremendous amount of weight over the last year. Drugs, drink and her obsession with body-image had all taken their toll. Her skin was pale, almost translucent. Next to the three men, she looked like an emaciated doll and reminded Rick of a victim from a Nazi concentration camp that he had seen in a TV documentary about World War Two. She was no longer the beauty that had caught his eye, back when they were still in school, or the twenty-year-old who turned envious heads whenever he brought her out on his arm. This was not the Meg that made his heart race or his cock hard. The woman in front of him *was* a stranger. Rick wondered why he hadn't seen it before. None of these people know me, he thought. They are all strangers.

"We can keep going, O' course we can, Megan. We only need to climb through another hole up there, an' then we'll be free. Mercer an' the others will never fuckin' find us." he said. "And, 'cos you're de smallest, Meg, you'll go first."

"Wha? I don't want to go first. I can't," she screamed, "Please Rick, don't make me go first."

"Don't make me go first," mimicked Lash, in a surprisingly good impersonation of Megan's terrified voice. Rick shone his torch in Megan's face.

"You're the smallest. It has to be you. Don't be a baby. We'll be right behind you. Once you get through, we'll follow you. Like you said, Meg, we can't go back and they're comin' for us. So up you go now."

"Please Rick, don't make me go on my own, please," she pleaded.

"Tie the rope around her Mo and give 'er yer torch. We haven't time for any more fuckin' chit chat. Come on."

Mo pushed Megan up the rock wall and kept pushing until she reluctantly gripped the lip of the crevice. His big hands cupped her small Converse sneakers. She began to shake violently.

Rick stood on Lash's shoulders. Lash didn't seem to mind even when Rick moved his feet about. Lash seemed happy just to be standing next to Mo.

"I can't do it," said Megan when she saw how narrow and dark the crawl-space was. "I can't see where it goes. I'll never fit in there, Rick. Please don't make me go first."

"Sure you will. Fuck sake, you could sit up in there, Meg. Anyway, you got a rope around you. Once you get through, tug on it three times and then I'll come after you. Make sure it's into another tunnel okay. Just keep going 'til you get to another tunnel. Go on and get, the fuck, in there," he snapped.

Rick and Mo pushed Megan. She had no choice but to crawl into the crevice. Rick put the torch in front of her.

"I can't, Rick. Don't make me do it, I don't like small spaces. You know I don't, Rick." Megan was getting herself into a panicked state. She tried to release her feet from Mo's grip but couldn't. Rick shoved her further in.

"Go on, to fuck," he snapped. He pushed firmly on her bony backside. When she was almost fully in, he took hold of her legs and pushed her forward, as far as he could.

He could hear her sobbing and thought she was hyperventilating.

Finally, she began to crawl forward.

As he watched her go, Rick found himself smiling.

What he really wanted to do, was giggle.

Chapter 40.

Paul drove from Hangman's Cross like a demon. He had a very bad feeling. Any joy he had felt, having spent the morning in the pleasant company of Henry Troy, was well and truly gone. He suddenly felt alone and wished that there was some way he could get a message to Horse. Almost as soon as the car reached a steady sixty miles per hour, twenty miles per hours faster than was sensible on the winding island roads, Paul's mobile went off again.

"Paul Creagan," he answered in exasperation, fighting with an extremely sharp bend on the narrow road.

"Is this Superintendent Paul Creagan?" said a woman's voice.

"Yes," snapped Creagan, "who is this?"

"Are you alone, Superintendent Creagan?" she asked. Her tone was dismissive. Her accent, northern.

"Yes? Who is this?" he asked again.

"Please hold for Commissioner Whelan," she said, ignoring his question.

Paul pulled the car onto what passed for a soft margin and slammed on the breaks. The car didn't skid but stopped with a jolt, causing his safety belt to bite into his broad chest.

Garda Commissioner Luke Whelan was being put through to his mobile. The idea was almost comical and for a moment Paul thought it was a wind-up. But as soon as the Commissioner spoke, Paul knew it was the man himself. Paul had attended one or two press conferences given by the Roscommon native and knew the Garda Commissioners distinctive voice very well.

"Superintendent Creagan?" said the Commissioner.

"Yes sir," said Paul. He turned off the engine. A strong gust of wind caught the side of the car and rocked it, noisily.

"Are we on a secure line, Superintendent? Are you alone?"

"Yes sir, yes. I'm in my car, sir, alone," said Paul. His ears became hot.

"And, you are still on the island?"

"Yes sir."

"Well Superintendent Creagan, would you like to explain to me what the hell is going over there?" The Commissioner sounded extremely angry.

"I'm not sure that I can, sir," said Paul, regretting it as soon as the words left his mouth.

"Well, Superintendent Creagan, you'd better start finding a way, and fast. I've just had a call from the director of U.S. Homeland Security, who happens to be an old friend of mine. He was enquiring about our progress in some top-secret operation involving American law enforcement. He mentioned you by name Creagan. So find the words. Explain to me what, the fuck, is going on over there."

Paul composed himself before he replied. He knew he had to be very careful. His phone started to beep, alerting him of another call. Whoever it was could wait, he thought.

"Sir, myself and Detective Inspector Brian Hopkins, from New Scotland Yard, are working together on a drugs case, which led us here to the island of Skellig Éin. We believe there is a large shipment of cocaine arriving from Central American in the next few days. The original tip-off was from Baltimore Narcotics. We arrived three days ago and we have been staying at the Tara Cove Hotel. The International Conference for European Cross Border Co-Operation, being held at the Tara Cove, is our cover. Baltimore PD have two detectives at the conference as well. We have been liaising with them. We are particularly interested in a Dublin criminal named Maurice Gimple, known as Mr G, and…"

"I know all this, Creagan. Mr G is nothing but a small-time pimp. Isn't he one of our informers? Why are narcotics looking at him?" interrupted the Commissioner.

"I believe he is an informer with vice squad in Dublin. We are interested in him because we believe he's moved into drug trafficking, sir."

"What has this got to do with anything, Creagan? What has it got to do with Homeland Security?"

The police Commissioner's anger wasn't abating. An expression Horse liked to use popped into Paul's head: *As angry as a bear with his balls in a beehive.*

Paul almost laughed.

"We...are convinced, sir, that Mr G is involved in this drugs shipment, sir. He is here on the island, now."

"I'll ask you again, Superintendent Creagan; what has this to do with Homeland Security?" said the Commissioner.

"Well, sir, as I said, we have been liaising with the narcotics division of the Baltimore Police Force. It was Baltimore that contacted New Scotland Yard initially about the possibility of drugs being channelled through Ireland on their way to the UK and Europe. It was Inspector Hopkins who made the connection between Maurice Gimple, the drugs and the island. The international conference is our cover, a fortunate co-incidence. Baltimore have two narcotics detectives at the conference. We have been liaising with them for the past few days."

His ears were red again.

"Liaising? It appears Creagan you've been more than liaising. What I'm trying to get you to explain to me, Creagan, relates to some document that you passed over to the Americans, which somehow ended up on the desk of my friend at Homeland Security?"

"Oh that! Well, yes sir," said Creagan, his voice suddenly cracked, his new-found confidence gone. The beep for call waiting stopped for a while and then started again.

Paul's mind raced. He started to talk quickly.

"One of our informers, here on the island, a local accountant, acquired a letter from Mr G. It seems to be written in a code of some sort. I gave it to the Baltimore detectives to see if it meant anything to them, sir. I..."

Paul suddenly felt sick in his stomach.

"You gave it to them? What, in God's name, did you do that for? Is this *our* investigation or are we now working for the Americans? Was this Inspector Hopkins' idea?"

"No sir. I couldn't reach Inspector Hopkins. It was my decision, sir."

"By the way, where is Inspector Hopkins? My office has not been able to reach him all morning," said the Commissioner.

Paul knew his next words would be crucial, if anything could be salvaged from this fiasco.

"Detective Inspector Hopkins is following another lead, sir. He is un-contactable at the moment, sir," said Creagan.

"Un-contactable? What does that mean? Is he undercover?" asked an increasingly exasperated Commissioner.

Paul wanted to say "in a way, sir, yes," but decided now wasn't the time for witty wordplay.

"He's gone into the caves sir, with a search party. They are looking for a group of missing students," he said, and continued quickly before the Commissioner could interrupt again, "Inspector Hopkins believes that the drugs may be in the caves somewhere too. He thinks the missing students may be linked to the drug shipment, sir."

"Hopkins believes the students are involved with Mr G, is that what you are telling me Creagan?"

"No. No, sir. He thinks that the missing students may have stumbled in on something, maybe disturbed the gang. Inspector Hopkins joined the search party to see where it would lead," said Paul, hoping the lie would be convincing.

"A bloody long-shot, isn't it?" said the Commissioner.

Paul said nothing.

"Well," said the Commissioner, "Hopkins is well respected and has a good record for getting results. He came highly recommended. My late predecessor, God rest his soul, had nothing but good things to say about Detective Inspector Hopkins, so I can only assume there may be some validity in this notion of his. So, Hopkins didn't know about this letter?"

"No, sir," said Paul.

There was a long pause. Paul wondered if he should say something, but decided not to.

"I still don't know why Homeland Security is interested in the letter. Do you Creagan."

"No, sir."

"What are you doing now Creagan?"

"I'm on the way back to the hotel, sir. I have arranged to meet with the Americans," said Paul.

"Not on your own, you're not. Who's the senior Garda on the island?"

"The Garda station is unmanned, sir. The island is policed from Galway," said Paul, doing his best to avoid sounding contemptuous.

"Yes, of course," said the Commissioner.

"Chief Superintendent Sutton is the senior officer, sir," said Paul, closing his eyes as he said the name.

"Ah yes. Brendan Sutton. A good man. Do you know Chief Superintendent Sutton, Creagan?"

"Yes sir. I spoke with him yesterday about another matter, sir," he said.

"What other matter?"

"The body that was found in the woods, two nights ago."

"Body? What body? Has this anything to do with this letter, Creagan?"

The Commissioner was shouting.

"No sir. We have no evidence to suggest that the two matters are connected. Chief Superintendent Sutton is running that case. We are not involved. We were just the first on the scene. It's Chief Superintendent Sutton's case, sir.

"Good God. What the hell is going on over there?"

It was a rhetorical question. Paul felt weak. He almost wished he had gone with Horse into the caves. The climb down to the Devil's Throat suddenly seemed inviting.

"Creagan!"

"Yes sir."

"Go back to the hotel and wait for Chief Superintendent Sutton to contact you. Speak to no one. Do you understand? Sutton will ring you. I've just been told he's on the island. Under no circumstances are you to speak with the Americans on your own. Do I make myself clear, Garda Creagan? You are only to meet with the Americans with Chief Superintendent Sutton present. Do I make myself clear?"

"Yes sir. I'll wait for the Chief Superintendent to contact me. We will meet the American together. I understand sir. Thank you, sir."

The phone went dead.

"Fuck," said Paul Creagan, "Fuck, fuck, fuck."

His mobile rang. He looked at caller ID.

Unknown.

"Hello?" he said. Please let it be Horse, he thought.

It wasn't.

"Paul? It's Buick again. Where are you, man? The cavalry has arrived."

"Listen Harry, I can't meet them yet. I need to see you first. Make some excuse; say I'm on the way. Meet me in ten minutes, upstairs in M&M's. It's a coffee shop on the main square. Order me a double espresso, will you? Ten minutes. Don't bring your friends. Thanks. Ten minutes, and on your own Buick, okay?"

When Paul put the phone down and started the car, his hands were shaking. He switched off the engine and tried to calm down. He was in the middle of a shit-storm. It had always been a possibility, but things seemed to be slipping more out of control than he could ever have imagined. He wondered what he had got himself into, agreeing to be part of all this. He never felt more alone.

Since coming to the island of Skellig Éin strange things had happened and events had moved in directions none of them could have predicted. Nothing felt right, everything felt dangerous. First there was the mutilated body in the woods, then the missing students and now Mr G's curious *incendiary* love-letter. Could it be possible that they were all somehow connected, and connected to their investigation?

It still didn't seem credible.

Something crept forward from the back of his mind and whispered in his ear, but not loud enough to be heard. When he tried to concentrate on it, to drag it from his unconscious to the lucid part of his mind, it evaded his attempts and melted away like smoke drawn up a chimney.

He tried to relax. Whatever his brain was trying to tell him, he was sure it was important. He closed his eyes and took long slow breaths, in through his nose, out through his mouth. The image returned and materialised as a face. The voice at the back of his head whispered a name.

Michael Eustace.

Chapter 41.

Not long after the five had set off in pursuit of Denis and Hughie, Professor Kearns's guide rope came to a sudden and abrupt end, at a double knot of LED ribbon lights. From then on the Professor's route was mapped out with just the LED ribbons lights, still positioned on corners and at changes in level. Some were wedged into crevices, others left on the floor of the tunnel. It was clear that Professor Kearns had run out of rope and rather than turn back had decided, recklessly in Paddy's opinion, to continue into the caves using only the LED's as markers to find their route back to the surface. Climbing in dark caves without a rope-line was tantamount to suicide. Leaving the ribbon lights to compensate for the lack of rope was a risky and foolhardy strategy. Michael wondered what Kearns would do when he ran out of the little lights. Would they continue, with nothing more than a vague notion of their way back? Paddy Gallagher was livid.

"Those stupid bloody amateurs," he said, holding up the bunch of LED's dangling from the end of Kearns's rope, like they were the remains of dead animal. "Bloody amateurs - all of them!"

"We must keep going, Paddy," said Horse.

"Why? Denis is right. They're probably all dead by now anyway," Paddy said.

"No they are not. Hanna is alive, and the others too," Michael said. "I'm sure of it."

"Then we go on," said Kevin.

"We go on," said Horse.

Michael saw Paddy look at Marie.

"We go on!" she declared.

Michael couldn't be sure if Marie was being sarcastic or serious. Sounds in the still cave air were distorted and the normal inflections in a person's voice, the tell-tale signs of true intent, could not be trusted. Paddy gave a resigned sigh and pushed on.

They had been following the path of tiny lights for about three quarters of an hour, when they first heard Hughie's cries. He sounded frightened and very far away.

"Help. Help. Help. Pleeeese. Help meee."

"Fuck," said Paddy, "now what?"

They all picked up their pace which didn't suit Michael. The earlier break had not revived him. He was tired and despondent and his head pounded. Added to that, his feet and calf muscles were sore, and his mood was black. He noticed he was breathing louder and each breath was short and raspy. Only Marie seemed to notice that he was struggling. She put a hand on his shoulder and turned him around to face her, just as more of Hughie's cries reached them.

"Please help meee."

"What a bloody fiasco," said Paddy from the front. "From the very start, it's been a disaster. First I get knocked into the cliff wall and crack my fucking head. Then Denis and Hughie storm off like a couple of spoilt brats. Then we find out Professor Kearns and the others think it's perfectly okay to continue without the safety of a rope-line. And now this. A total bloody disaster. And, for what? I really think Denis is right. We've gone far too deep already and there is still no sign of them. Nearly two weeks they've been down here. Denis is right, we will only find their bodies. That's what awaits us."

He looked back to Marie for support. She ignored him. She was concentrating on Michael.

"You need to rest," she whispered.

"I'm okay. We need to go on. If the lights run out you will need me to find them. I'm the only one." He stretched out his arm and touched a colour mark on the rock wall beside him where, at some time in the past, Hanna had touched it. He knew none of the others could see what he was seeing but didn't care. Marie smiled at him.

"I didn't say to stop altogether, but you need to rest. Okay?" she said in a very quiet voice, so Paddy couldn't hear her.

Michael saw genuine concern on Marie's beautiful face.

"I have a slight headache. Maybe if I sat down and closed my eyes for a while, it will go away," he said.

He wondered if Marie could tell that he was lying, that he was ready to collapse. His headache had been getting progressively worse since they'd set off from the Devil's Throat. It was now so bad he thought his head might soon explode. The pain made breathing difficult and he longed to be back on the surface, standing under a clear blue sky in acres of crisp clean air. Since entering the caves he'd avoided taking any painkillers because he'd taken one before leaving the monastery.

"You need me," he said.

"Help meee," called Hughie from the darkness up ahead.

"Sit for a while and catch your breath, Michael. You need to rest," said Marie.

She steered him toward a low flat topped boulder to one side of the trail. Michael flopped down with a sigh. Marie helped him remove his haversack and then she removed hers and sat down beside him.

Horse turned around.

"Hold up, Paddy," he shouted up the line.

Horse trudged back to Michael and Marie.

"You guys okay?" he said.

Michael's knew his head was red and shiny with perspiration.

"We need to rest," said Marie.

Paddy and Kevin came back too.

"We have to go on. We can't stop Marie," said Paddy.

"You three go ahead. We'll catch up. We need to rest," said Marie forcefully.

Michael dropped his head. Marie touched his hand.

As if aware of her thoughts, Michael raised his head and whispered to her.

"I'm just a little light-headed, a bit dizzy, that's all. I'll be okay in a little while."

"Go on Paddy. You three go ahead. We'll catch up with you. Keep fixing the rope and we'll catch up. I'm not used to all this exercise. Michael has agreed to stay with me. Go on then," she said.

Horse stood over them. Marie looked up at him.

"Go on now, Englishman. We'll be fine. I'll look after Michael. We'll be fine," she whispered, so only he could hear.

Horse was worried, but nodded at Marie.

"Okay," he shouted over his shoulder. "We'll push on, Paddy. These two need a break. They'll catch us up."

Horse winked at Marie then turned to go.

"Hey, Englishman?" she called after him.

Michael raised his head.

Horse turned back. Michael could tell from his face that Horse was bracing himself for another of Marie's smart remarks.

"You be careful," she said

"What?" said Horse, taken aback.

"I said, be careful," she said.

"Oh. Right. Yes. I will then. We will. You too."

"Well, are you coming or not?" snapped Paddy.

"Yeh. Hold yer horses, I'm coming," said Horse with a big smile.

"Thank you, Marie," said Michael as soon as the others were out of earshot.

"Don't mention it. Anyway, I was hoping I'd get a chance to speak with you on your own," she said, "So, that worked out very well, didn't it?"

*

All four, Megan, Rick, Mo and Lash, managed somehow to squeeze through the long tight fissure. They crawled for more than half an hour before finally making it to somewhere they could stand up. It was a terrifying ordeal. They shuffled along with an island of suffocating rock inches above their heads, crawling from one tight spot to the next, never knowing where they were going or if they would ever get out. The dreadful, and not unlikely, possibility of being trapped forever in the sandwich of rock played heavily on Rick's mind. He was sure the others were thinking the same thing, except maybe Lash who, despite being the biggest of the group, seemed the least fazed by the experience. Bar the sound of Lash's heavy breathing and Megan gulping noises, they shuffled along without a sound. By the time they finally got out Megan was hysterical. She choked and wailed. In stark contrast Rick was ebullient and almost punched the air in triumph when he stood upright. He thought about punching Megan again.

They emerged onto a narrow ledge near the top of a cliff wall that formed one side of a deep canyon. The floor of the enormous space was more than a hundred feet below the ledge. When Rick stood upright he could touch the flat rock ceiling with the tips of his outstretched fingers. It was cold but dry.

The ledge, which was never more than four-foot-wide, was relatively level. It sloped gently downwards to Rick's right for about a hundred yards before suddenly coming to a broken end and a sheer drop. Below it was another ledge that sloped gently in the opposite direction.

Rick carelessly leaned out and shone his torch as far down the cliff wall as was possible. He was sure he could see more ledges of various lengths and widths all the way to the canyon floor. Rick imagined himself floating out from the wall and looking back at himself, seeing the ledges, one over the other all the way down. It brought to his mind the memory of a coin machine he'd played with in a hospital waiting room when he was a kid. Drop a coin in the slot at the top and watch it roll and drop, roll and drop, from ledge to ledge, roll and drop, zig-zag all the way to a neat pile of coins at the bottom.

"Can't I have me penny back, Gran?"

"Naw. Your penny's goin' off to feed the little black babies in Africa, Ricky. Now come on, yer mammy's been waitin' te see yez all week."

"But I can see me penny, Gran. I want me penny back."

Roll and drop, roll and drop, zig-zag, from ledge to ledge all the way to the big pile of drugs money at the bottom.

"We're going down," Rick said. No one argued. There was no going back. Not now. The crawl through the confined space had been terrifying and for three of them at least, it was a great relief to be out and standing upright. And there was no going up. They were at the top of the wall.

"We're going down," repeated Lash with an exuberant grin.

Rick secretly wished they could climb up, rather than always having to travel down, but he kept this thought to himself. Not that he had any intention of sharing any of his inner musings with his companions. Mo, Lash and Megan were drug mules. Nothing more than that. For most of the crawl through the solid rock Rick had fantasised about his future life and his fantasies no longer included any of his three companions. On the contrary, he had

299

resolved that he would have to kill them all, as soon as the opportunity arose.

They were losers and they slowed him down.

Megan had shown her true colours and Rick despised her for her cowardice. How it was that he'd never seen the real Megan before was now beyond his comprehension. Her constant whining and whimpering drove Rick mad. She hung off him and dragged him back. Rick was Superman. Megan was nothing more than a victim. He knew now that she could never match up to him. She could never be Superman's gal. Megan was a bit-player in the movie that played in his twisted mind. She was no longer his leading lady. Rick was the hero, the cunning trickster who managed to outwit the local drug lord and pull off the greatest sting in history. Megan was one of the unfortunate expendables. She was an extra, the disloyal girlfriend who gets her comeuppance before the movie ends.

Then there was Mo.

Rick never trusted Mo. He had always been just a little too close to Mr. G. for Rick's liking. Since their agreement to escape with the drugs, Rick had been suspicious of Mo's motives. Hadn't Mo been a bit too quick to agree to change sides? And he'd been genuinely shocked when Rick set fire to the rest of the drug stash. Well, Rick thought, as soon as the opportunity arose he would cut Mo down. Of course, he'd have to do Lash first. Who's to know what that big fucking dope would do, if Rick knifed Mo in front of him. So, it would have to be Lash first, then Mo and then...Megan. For the moment, Rick needed them all. They were his drug mules. But as soon as the time was right and the opportunity presented itself, which he felt certain it would, Rick would kill them all. Lash and Mo and Megan.

No witnesses and no regrets.

The climb down from the ledge at the top of the canyon wall was much more difficult and dangerous than Rick had imagined it would be, even for someone as fearless as Superman. The drops between the ledges varied considerably. At times the distance between the ledge they were on, and the one below, was as much as ten feet. To get down they had to shuffle backwards on their hands and knees over the edge, and then hang and drop. Getting Megan to even move toward the edge was a struggle. In the end Lash dropped down first and stood below to catch Megan when one of the other two lowered her down. It was dangerous but Lash seemed buoyed by his role in the proceedings. Whatever had happened to Lash back on the road, when Rats Egan went missing, was a mystery. Rick guessed that whoever took Rats left Lash as a warning. Maybe they made Lash watch as Rats was being mutilated. There had been a lot of Rats' blood on the road close the car. An awful lot. And maybe Lash tried to kill himself by overdosing on the cocaine from the boot, but only succeeded in scrambling his brain. Whatever happened, Lash now had the mind of a five-year-old, albeit in the large and powerful body of a fully grown man, with no regard for danger or his own safety. He would scamper over the edge and dangle above the precipice without a second thought, smiling up at the others like a cheeky child. He led the way and the others followed. Sometimes the next ledge wasn't directly below the one they were on, so rather than dangle and drop they had to jump out and down, across a terrifying gap. As always Lash was eager to go first and he hardly took two steps before jumping out, regardless of the distance. Once, he didn't jump far enough for his feet to reach the lower ledge and ended up hitting the protruding lip with his stomach. Hardly winded or perturbed by the fact that he was on the point of falling to his death, he swung an arm about like a monkey, while clinging to the ledge with the other, until he found solid purchase and could drag himself up to safety. Once on the lower ledge, Lash stood at the edge with open arms, ready to catch the others when they jumped. He made it look easy.

On and on they went in this fashion, ledge by ledge, down and down until they finally reached the canyon floor. As soon as they got there, everyone started to talk. Megan began to cry. Mo quizzed Rick and complimented Lash. Lash giggled and kept mumbling something that sounded like "peas."

"Will you all shut, the fuck, up. I can' fuckin' think," Rick snapped.

They all fell silent.

Lash whispered "peeease."

"Sssssh. I can hear something. D'you hear it? Ssssh," snapped Rick.

They all listened.

Lash lifted his big head as if to sniff the air. Rick noticed how cold it was. Lash started to breathe through his mouth.

"Haaw. Haaw. Haaw."

"I think I can hear someone calling," said Rick.

"Haaw."

Rick gritted his teeth and tried to concentrate on what he thought he'd heard.

"Help meeee, peeeeeese," Lash whispered between exhales of breath. Rick turned and shone the torch in Lash's face.

"What'd you say, Lash?" he said.

"Help meeee peeeeeese," repeated Lash.

"You can hear it too? Yeh, that's it. Someone is calling for help. Down there," Rick said. He swung the arc of his torchlight behind Megan and down into the canyon. Mo followed with the other torch. They couldn't see anything.

"Help meeee peeeeeese," repeated Lash.

"Yeh, I heard it. There is someone down here and if there's someone here, then there must be another way out." said Rick in triumph.

Chapter 42.

Marie and Michael sat together in silence. Michael's breathing had slowed considerably. He took large mouthfuls of water from his canteen and closed his eyes. Marie said nothing. She had moved to a rock opposite and he knew that she was watching him.

"I'm grand. I just needed a break. I have a bit of a headache. I've got some pain relief tablets that will do the trick," he said, rummaging blindly in the side pocket of his haversack. When his fingers located the packet of tablets he popped three of the yellow capsules from their foil card and swallowed them quickly in a large mouthful of water.

"I'll be grand soon," he said, wondering to himself if taking three was altogether sensible. A warning on the packet said no more than one tablet to be taken every six hours.

"Will you? Good. I thought we were about to lose you there for a minute," Marie said casually.

"I'll be right as rain in no time," he said. He still felt dizzy. His forehead was hot and he felt like he'd had one too many beers. He wanted to close his eyes, curl up on the floor and go to sleep.

"You said you wanted to speak to me?" he said without looking at her.

"Yes. About my paintings. How were you able to see the people behind the grey?"

"I don't know? Can't everyone?"

"No. You're the first."

"Oh? Can you not see them?" he asked without raising his head.

"Obviously *I* can. I painted them!" she said, sounding slightly annoyed. Michael was sure she wanted to add "stupid," but she didn't. He felt stupid.

"Sorry. Of course, you can. What I meant was when they are finished?"

"Yes. But maybe I know what to look for? You saw the faces straight away. Sometimes I have to concentrate," she conceded.

"Maybe it's not just me. I don't suppose too many people get the chance to see them, do they?" he said.

"What does that mean?" she said defensively.

"I just mean, they are not on public display, that's all," Michael said quickly.

"Yeh well..."

"I think they're wonderful. You certainly have an artist's eye Marie."

"Thank you."

When he raised his head, he found her smiling.

"I'm sorry I threatened you in my kitchen. I knew from the moment you spoke that you were alright," she said.

"Oh?"

"I'm a good judge of character. Maybe I'm psychic like you?" she said.

Michael began to protest.

"I know, you're *not* a psychic. Don't get excited, I was joking," she said. She leaned forward and touched his hand.

"Are you sure you're okay, Michael?"

"I will be, in a little while, once those big yellow babies do their magic. Thanks for staying with me."

"No problem," she said with a smile. She left her hand on his. He closed his eyes again.

She started talking.

"I am a very good judge of character. For example, I could tell straight off that Denis that he was a grade A asshole," she said.

"Hardly insightful," said Michael.

She giggled.

"Fair point. Okay, then how about, I think Hughie is in love with Denis. Did you notice the fawning adoration in everything he does? He acts like Denis's puppy."

"What?" said Michael.

"You must have noticed that they dress the same, right down to the colour of their socks? My guess is that Denis brings Hughie shopping and picks out the clothes for him. I can see Hughie modelling his new gear in front of Denis and loving every second of his hero's attention. Probably means Hughie is gay, God love him."

Michael opened his eyes and squinted at Marie.

"I wouldn't have taken you as a homophobe!"

"I'm not. No! I mean, I think it's likely Denis is the homophobe. Very likely. He's a misogynistic mammy's boy. My point is, imagine what it must be like if Hughie is in love with Denis?" Michael dropped his head again and sighed.

"Do you analyse everyone like this, Marie?" he said.

"I suppose I do, now that you mention it, but I usually keep my thoughts to myself."

"So what's your assessment of me then?" said Michael

"Actually, I like you. I particularly like your fashion choices. That *Mr Blobby* jacket really suits you, although I suspect the glare from it, has contributed somewhat to your headache. It's given me a headache travelling behind you," she said.

Michael raised his head and looked at her wide-eyed. They both started to laugh.

"You like me?" he said.

"Don't tell anyone, will you?" she said.

"As we're being honest with each other, I have a question for you, Marie," he said.

"Fire away," she said.

"Okay. Why did you decide to come along with us? And don't give me any of that crap about having no choice. You could have stayed in the Devil's Throat."

He was feeling better. The cave had stopped spinning. He was alert and his headache had begun to subside.

"Maybe I feel I owe Primrose and I know Hanna. She's nice. If I can help her, I will," she said.

"And that's all? No other reason?"

"No," she said unconvincingly.

"I was thinking of Brian," said Michael.

"Who?"

"Detective Hopkins. Horse. The Englishman."

"Why would I have come along because of him?" she said indignantly.

"Because you like him too? I've seen you watching him, Marie. And I know he likes you."

"He reminds me of someone I once knew, that why I stare at him."

Michael remembered that one of the grey paintings in Marie's kitchen was of a young man who had Brian's eyes.

"An old boyfriend?"

"He's…well, he died many years ago…he…"

Hughie cried out again. His voice sounded pathetic.

Marie stood up and shuffled her feet.

"If you are better now, we should go. Time to save the world, Michael," said Marie. "Are you better now, ready to go?"

"Yes. Much better," he said. The conversation was over.

"Well come on then, *Luminous Lenny*. Destiny is calling."

*

Hughie's cries were very close. Horse, Kevin and Paddy could see a flickering light in the tunnel up ahead. It was a torch being turned on and off in a steady rhythm. A distress signal.

"Thank God," said Paddy Gallagher.

"Amen, to that. I feel like the meat in a rock sandwich," said Horse. His feet were cold and sore and his socks were wet through.

"The sooner we're out of this bloody place the better. It gives me the creeps" said Kevin.

For the last ten minutes the three had been making their way down a very narrow fissure. It was slow going, difficult and dangerous. Paddy led the way. Horse followed and mimicked Paddy's every step. Kevin brought up the rear and followed in Horse's footsteps. Finally, an end was in sight. The flashing torch light ahead suggested that the bottom of the fissure was close at hand and that they had found Hughie. Since leaving Michael and Marie, and before entering the fissure, they had made steady progress, following the trail of Professor Kearns's way-finding lights. For the most part, they continued along as before, in single file. Much of the journey was along a spacious and airy tunnel, the floor of which was dry and relatively flat. Horse was conscious of the fact that they were always descending but the slope in the floor was so shallow as to be almost indiscernible. The ceiling too was far above their heads so they could walk upright, which was a great relief to the tall English policeman. Horse found it relatively easy going and could control his breathing. But for Hughie's cries, he would have begun to enjoy himself. Even the air seemed better than before. It was crisp rather than cold and it lacked the bitterness of the air closer to the surface. He even thought he could feel a slight breeze on the side of his face. As if to support this idea motes of dust rose off the floor in front of him, and danced in the light from his helmet torch.

When they filed passed the entrance to the dark fissure, the one that they would eventually have to climb down, none of them gave it too much notice. It appeared like nothing more than a long vertical shadow in the side wall of the tunnel. The only evidence that it was more than just an alcove was a distinct rush of warm air on the side of the face as they walked by. Horse stopped momentarily and shone his torch into the gloom but then moved quickly on after Paddy. Ahead, the tunnel turned sharply to the left. Paddy reached the corner first and stopped. Horse almost walked into him. Their way was blocked by a solid wall of boulders and rubble.

"Shit. A dead-end," said Paddy.

Horse looked at the wall of stone. Among the scree on the floor was a torn ribbon of LED lights.

"Looks like the roof of the cave collapsed," said Horse.

"And it's recent," said Paddy.

"The Professor and the others must have got trapped by the rock slide," said Horse, adding "we'll never move this. We'd need dynamite."

"You think Denis and Hughie are under all that?" asked Kevin, once he caught up.

"Help me. I'm here," shouted Hughie, as if to answer Kevin's question.

His voice was coming from behind them, over Kevin's shoulder, and not from beyond the wall of collapsed rock.

"Help me, I'm here. Please."

"Back this way," said Horse, "I think I know the way they went."

"Wait," said Paddy. "Let me go first."

They entered the narrow opening in the same order that they had reached it. Once inside, Paddy hung a ribbon of red lights on the nearest available ledge.

307

"For Marie and your man," he said, although his explanation was unnecessary.

"We'll trail the rope along the floor for now. I think he's close. I'll come back and fix it properly, if needs be," Paddy said.

"Whatever you say, boss," said Horse.

There was no sarcasm in his voice.

At its widest point the fissure was no more than eight foot across but most of the time it was so narrow that they had to remove their back packs, in order to squeeze through. Before they got to the bottom, they had to remove their jackets too. The crevice was a vertical tear through the rock. When Horse shone his torch upwards he could see that the crack continued beyond the torch light. The floor of the crevice was a series of steps, formed by lumps of fallen rock that had dislodged when the crack had opened up. Progress down was slow and hair-raising. Paddy used the walls for support, pressing the palms of his hands against opposite walls before exploring the uncertain floor with an outstretched foot. The other two followed his lead. On a few occasions the floor fell away and they had to use the rope. Paddy left red LED's almost all the way down.

Finally, they reached a relatively level rocky floor and took time to catch their breath before moving on. Horse looked back up the crevice. He tried not to think of the climb back up. He was sore from the climbing and his mood had changed since entering the crevice. He didn't like it and the further in they went down, the worse he felt. He had the strange idea that they had entered somewhere they shouldn't, that they were trespassing. He sensed danger. Goose bumps rose on his arms and he shivered, although he was not particularly cold. He imagined the rock walls slamming together and crushing them, like flies between clapped hands. He wanted to climb back up and warn Marie and Michael not to follow.

The walls of the fissure were saturated. In the torchlight, they were black and shiny. When Horse touched the wall he found that it was sticky. The liquid wasn't water and it had a smell that was neither pleasant nor recognisable. He rubbed his fingers vigorously on his trousers to remove the strange substance. At first Horse couldn't work out where the wetness was coming from, because the rock face looked dense and solid. He directed his torch upwards again and saw, six feet below the entrance to the crevice, what looked like a high watermark, a horizontal line separating the shiny surface from the dry rock above it. If it was a high waterline, he thought, it meant that the fissure had recently been flooded almost all the way up to the tunnel floor. He decided he'd keep the thought to himself, or at least, for the moment.

"Come on, let's get going. I don't like it in here," he said.

"Me neither," said Kevin.

Hugh cries were amplified and distorted in the narrow space. It sounded like he was giggling. When his cries turned to a choking sound and then stopped altogether, Horse gasped.

"Shit," said Paddy.

They moved on as fast as they could, but it wasn't easy. The bottom of the fissure was an obstacle-course of scattered rocks, boulders and black pools of the same liquid goo that coated the walls. Some of these pools were large and they had no option but to wade through the icy liquid. Paddy said that he suspected that the fissure was newly formed and, like the collapsed ceiling in the upper tunnel, most likely a result of the earthquake.

It was with a sense of great relief when Paddy, Horse and Kevin finally emerged from the crevice. What they found, when they stepped out onto a cliff ledge, defied logic.

Paddy gasped.

"Impossible," he whispered.

Horse could only gawp at the vast unimaginable vista that opened out in front of him. He was not a caver and therefore had no real notion of what to expect, but he was quite certain that what he saw was indeed, nothing short of impossible.

Chapter 43.

"Impossible," gasped Paddy, when he finally found his voice, "fucking impossible." He was breathing heavily, almost forcing the words out of his mouth - panting with excitement.

"Are you seeing what I'm seeing?" he said, "Can you believe this?"

Neither Horse nor Kevin answered. Horse thought that what he was seeing had to be a trick of the light. An illusion of some sort.

They had emerged onto a narrow ledge at the base of an enormous cliff and they looked down into the floor of a chamber of bewildering proportions. The cliff ran round, in both directions, as far as he could see and rose to meet a flat rock ceiling more than a hundred and fifty feet above their heads. In front of them was a gigantic ocean, and ten feet below them, its beach and shore.

"Insane," said Paddy.

"Impossible," repeated Kevin.

"I don't like it. It doesn't feel right," whispered Horse.

Horse's first impression was that they had somehow managed to make it back to the surface and that he was once again looking out onto the North Atlantic, under a heavy starless sky. Was it possible, he wondered, that they had unwittingly doubled back on themselves or had emerged somewhere further along the western coast of the Skellig Éin?

He knew it was a very unlikely explanation.

Firstly, they had been descending continuously since leaving the Devil's Throat and had travelled for more than six hours. Not long before reaching the fissure Paddy had suggested that they could be as much as a kilometre underground. Was that not the same as a kilometre below sea level, thought Horse? How could they be back on the surface, if they were under the sea? It hurt Horse's head just thinking about it. Secondly, the place was much too dark to be anywhere above ground. Even on the darkest of nights on the surface of the earth, there was always some light, no matter how faint. But not here, he thought, wherever here was. Beyond their torchlight, the darkness was as thick as clay. It was singular and monotonous. There was no contrast and no variation. No reflected flicker from a hidden moon through a thinning cloud, no ghostly outline of something familiar, as the eye adjusts to the gloom. There was no adjustment. Beyond the reach of the three helmet torches there was simply no light. Horse felt that they were standing in a place as far away from the sun as any human had ever been, and that the light they brought with them was as much a stranger down here as they were.

And then there was the silence. It was eerie.

"I don't like it," Horse said again.

He found that he was whispering. It felt like he'd entered a church. The silence was oppressive and, like the darkness, unnerving. In Horse's mind, the darkness and the silence had substance, were almost tactile and together, they thickened the air.

Halfway down the beach, Hughie lay slumped over, as still as a rock. Horse's first thought when he saw him thee was that they were entering a trap and that Hughie was the bait.

"I don't like it. It doesn't feel right."

If Horse was wary and concerned, Paddy, in stark contrast, was ecstatic. He stood aghast and wide-eyed, with his hands on his hips.

"Amazing. Truly bloody amazing. I just can't believe this." he gushed. "This must be Professor Kearns's hidden chamber, the one that James Wong told us about. No wonder the Professor chanced entering by the Devil's Throat. He must have known it was something like this. Bloody amazing!"

"How could anyone imagine such a place existed?" said Horse.

"I don't like it either," said Kevin.

Paddy directed his torchlight onto the beach, casually running the light over the still and prostrate figure of Hughie and then on toward the shore. The beach was a series of level tiers, stepping down three times between the base of the cliff wall and the water's edge. From cliff to ocean was about a hundred yards and there was about a four-foot drop from one tier to the next. Giant steps, thought Horse, or steps for giants. The end of the last tier acted like a sea wall, holding back the weight of the ocean. There was a slow tide but the surface of the ocean was as still as a lake. Hughie lay at the centre of the second tier, his torch lying in front of him on the gravelly sand. It had fallen from his outstretched hand. It lay at the edge of a small quarter circle of its own yellowing light, just out of Hughie's reach. It looked as if Hughie had given up trying to reach for it, but had left his arm out, seemingly not having the energy to pull it back. His hand hovered inches above the torch but his fingers were rigid and lifeless. Horse saw a terrible resignation on Hughie's stiff face, a look he'd seen before on the faces of car crash victims, just before they let go their grip on life. There was no sign of Denis.

"We need to get down to Hughie," Horse said although he had little desire to climb down from the ledge.

Kevin directed his torchlight along the wall to their left.

"Look. There's Professor Kearns's climbing rope," he said.

Paddy and Horse turned around. About fifty feet above them was another ledge and further along, the mouth of another cave, one much larger than the exit from the fissure. Horse guessed that it was the end of the cave system that they had been following before being stopped by the landslide. A taut knotted rope ran from within the cave and down the cliff face to their ledge and then on down to the beach below. If they moved along their ledge they could use the Professor's rope to reach the beach.

If this was Professor Kearns's hidden chamber, thought Horse, then they should be very close to finding Hanna and the others. He guessed Kevin was thinking the same thing. Paddy, on the other hand, seemed to be in a world of his own.

"What's that, Paddy?" asked Kevin, focussing his torchlight on a small motor sitting on the beach, not far from where Hughie lay.

"That's a mobile generator," answered Horse, "How the bloody 'ell did they lug that all the way here?"

"Two men could carry it down here without too much difficulty," said Paddy dismissively.

"And the arc lights? Did they carry them all the way down here too?" said Horse dubiously. He ran his torch light along a line of cable that snaked across the ground, from the generator to two separate lighting stands, both of which carried large rectangular lamps eight foot above the beach. The generator was not running, and the lamps were not on.

"You'd be surprised the lengths we cavers will go to, in pursuit of our goals. Those lamp frames are aluminium and demountable. Actually, they're quite light," said Paddy.

"I thought you said the Professor and the students were amateurs, Paddy?" said Horse.

"Well, I've changed my mind. Actually, I think the expedition was well planned. I think they might even have had a very good idea what they would find and knew the only way to reach it was by climbing in the Devil's Throat. This has got to be one of the greatest cave discoveries of our time," said Paddy.

"Well, I don't like it. It's weird and smells rotten down here," said Kevin.

Horse nodded in agreement.

"As far as I'm concerned the sooner we're out of here the better," he said. He noticed his own breathing had become short and raspy, "but first we need to help Hughie and then find Denis and the others. Come on, we'll use the Professor's rope. The sooner we find them, the sooner we can get out of here."

They climbed down to the beach. Their feet sank into the wet gravel and the crunching noise it made, when they walked forward, was loud and angry. Horse thought of Marie and Michael. He knew they would not be far behind. Just as before, he wanted to warn them not to follow, not to come any further than the ledge. He imagined that the black ocean as a crouching monster, watching and waiting, ready to pounce as soon as they moved far enough away from the safety of the cliff and, no matter how hard he tried, he couldn't shake off a feeling of unease. In his mind they had entered monster's lair.

Horse considered himself a rational man, although he would freely admit to being surprisingly open minded, for someone in his chosen profession. His belief in Michael's strange abilities was proof of that. But here, every inch of instinct screamed danger. He knew from experience that first impressions were generally correct, despite any evidence to the contrary. Something either felt right or it felt wrong, and this place felt very wrong. Standing on the strange beach, looking out across the ebony surface of an impossible underground ocean, all of Horse's instincts for survival told him to run.

They made their way over to Hughie. Each step was a loud announcing crunch. Pools of black liquid filled the hollows left by their footprints. Horse noticed that the surface of the beach wasn't sand or pebbles. It looked like tiny bones. Paddy picked up a handful and held it under his torchlight. Without saying anything he emptied the material into a small plastic sample bag which he then shoved into one of his pockets.

Horse noted puzzlement on Paddy's face.

"What is it, Paddy?" he asked.

"Not sure, to be honest," said Paddy.

Standing on the beach, the ocean looked larger and even more menacing. Horse thought he saw movement, a hundred yards from shore, as if something enormous was rolling just beneath the surface, but when he shone his torch out across the surface his light revealed nothing. There were no tell-tale ripples or sudden splashes, no reflected sparkle from the silver belly of a rising fish. The surface was unnaturally still, like an opaque motionless mirror.

Hughie had fallen asleep. When they woke him, he whimpered like a wounded dog. The lower half of his right leg was completely buried in the strange gravel, as if he was being slowly eaten by something hidden beneath the surface.

"You any good with engines Detective Hopkins, being an Englishman and all? I know how you English love your motors," said Paddy pointing his torch at the generator.

"In our blood," said Horse, adding "Probably the sparks need drying out. I'll see what I can do. You two see to Hughie and find out what happened to Denis."

Horse shone his torch out to sea again. This time he was sure he could see the surface rising and falling at irregular intervals. When he mentioned it to the others, Paddy suggested that it might be boiling springs pumping plumes of hot water up from the seabed, a common enough phenomenon in large cave pools. Horse wasn't convinced. He imagined a giant fish darting about just beneath the surface. The more he looked, the more he was convinced that something was living in the giant sea.

"Could there be something out there? Creatures, I mean. Humpbacked whales or something?" Horse said.

"Not in a million years," said Paddy. "It's too dark and too cold and we're too far below the surface."

"What about the creatures that live in total darkness, at the bottom of the Atlantic Ocean, along the Mariana Trench? Isn't that more than seven miles down?" said Kevin. His voice seemed raspy.

"Look, if there is some life down here, it's going to be pretty bloody small, isn't it?" snapped Paddy.

Kevin knelt in front of Hughie.

"Hey Hughie. We're here now," he said.

Hughie said something. Kevin couldn't hear him. He leaned in.

"What's that, Hughie? I can't hear you. It's okay. We're here now. Where's Denis, Hughie? What's did you say?"

Horse noticed that Kevin was whispering now.

"Don't go near..," said Hughie. He stopped to catch his breath, then didn't finish the sentence.

"The air seems strange; don't you think?" said Horse.

They all focussed on their breathing.

"Yeh. It's salty, or something. Tastes like lime or aniseed," said Kevin.

"Please," whispered Hughie, "I can't move..."

Paddy shone his torch into Horse's face.

"See if you can get the lights working, will you," he snapped.

"Yeh. Okay. The lights," said Horse and he set off toward the generator.

Kevin put his ear close to Hughie's mouth.

"I can't hear you. What did you say, Hughie? What happened to Denis?"

Paddy had directed his torch onto Hughie's buried leg. His trousers were ripped and one of the larger veins on his leg looked like it was just about to burst.

"It's okay, we're here now, Hughie. I can't hear you. Say again?" said Kevin.

"There, that should do it. The sparks were just wet," declared Horse, adding, "Let's fire this baby up."

"What was that? Say it again, Hughie. Don't what?" said Kevin.

Hughie finally managed to get the words out, just as the generator chugged into life, and the chamber was flooded with a cold white light from two large halogen lamps standing eight feet above the bony beach.

"Don't let them see you and don't go near the water!"

Chapter 44.

Rick, Megan, Mo and Lash made their way along, following the sound of the crying voice.

They moved toward what seemed like the entrance to the canyon, where the sheer walls on either side abruptly ended and beyond which there appeared to be a vast open plain. At least, that's what Rick told the others he could see. None of them argued with him. In truth, he couldn't see any further than the others, but Rick had fixed an image in his mind and despite the limited reach of their torches, he was confident that he was right. Rick marched forward with his head held high. The other three followed with their eyes trained on the canyon floor, taking great care not to stumble or get their feet wet. Rick mumbling something under his breath. He had been mumbling to himself a lot since entering the canyon. "Keep an eye out for the Injins," he whispered, then glanced up the high canyon walls and gritted his teeth. In his head, Rick was in one of those American Westerns he watched on television every Saturday morning, when he was a little boy. His granny had a small house and she had the only telly on the whole street. His ma only had a shitty two bed apartment and she didn't have a telly. On Saturday mornings Rick was sent to his granny's house, while his mother went to her house-cleaning job. There was always American Westerns on the telly on Saturday morning, and there were always lonely canyons and open plains, and a mysterious stranger who saves the stranded pilgrims and tricks the crooked ranchers and kills all the savage Indians. On the old couch in his granny's front room, Rick was the fearless gunslinger, leading his small band to safety. His Gran bought him a cowboy hat and a metal Colt six-shooter which came in a holster with a silver star on the side. She'd ruffle his hair and she teased him.

"Keep an eye out for them Injins, Ricky. If they catch you, they'll scalp you."

Rick Kavanagh smiled at the memory.

"Keep an eye out for the Injins," he whispered.

Rick thought he heard an echo. It was Lash. He was walking directly behind him.

"Eye out fir d'injins," Lash said.

Another memory came to Rick.

He saw Rats' severed head in front of him, still dripping with the stinking slime that had been so difficult to wash from his skin and clothes. Pete Mercer had made Rick hold the head up for Mr G. to see the tattoo. Even Mr G baulked at the sight.

"Christ Almighty," was all Mr. G. could say, before waving them out of his room.

"You know what I think?" Pete Mercer had said to Rick, after they left Mr. G's office,

"I think he scalped Rats. Can you believe that fuckin' sick bastard? Cut 'im to pieces, plucked out his eyes an' scalped 'im. Sick fuckin' bastard. Like a fuckin' red injin. Scalped 'im 'e did. Sick fucker."

"Eye out for the Injins," he heard his granny say, again and again. Each time, her voice changed a little. As the words tumbled around in Rick's head, it no longer sounded like his granny speaking. It sounded like Pete Mercer, whispering in his ear.

"We'll have your other eye out, Popeye. Eye out for de injins."

Rick noticed that the air had an unnatural yet familiar odour. He thought it smelt like bleach or cleaning fluid. It reminded him of the smell of his mother's hands when she came to pick him up, late on Saturday evenings. Thoughts of his mother convinced him that they were following the right track and he was sure they'd soon be free.

They moved quickly, keeping the torches trained on a small area of floor directly in front of them. Rick insisted that they stay close to the base of the canyon wall. Despite his confidence he was nevertheless cautious and the wall gave them a fair degree of cover. He couldn't dismiss the possibility that they were walking into a trap. The Creep was a smart little fucker. It could be his voice they were moving towards.

The truth was they had little choice but to stay close to the wall, unless they wanted to get their feet wet. Running down the length of the canyon was a wide expanse of dark water, the edge of which meandered in and out along its length. Sometimes the river almost touched the base of the wall and Rick and the others had to jump from rock to rock to avoid getting wet. The water was perfectly still, black as the night and looked very cold and very deep, even near the base of the wall. It made crossing to the opposite side of the canyon impossible.

"Big fuckin' river," said Mo.

"Big fuckin' river," repeated Lash.

"What way is it flowing?" asked Rick.

"It's not flowing," said Mo. "maybe it's a lake?"

"Not flowing," repeated Lash.

"It looks evil, Rick," said Megan.

"Evil," said Lash.

"Shut, the fuck, up Megan. Rivers aren't evil, you stupid cow," Rick said.

"Stupid cow," said Lash and he began to giggle.

The canyon widened, as its mouth approached. When Rick reached the end of the canyon wall he stopped, switched off his torch and made faces at Mo to do the same. Darkness enveloped them. Megan moaned. Rick leaned forward and looked around the corner. He could see well into the distance thanks to two powerful lights that sat on tall stands three hundred yards away. There was no open plains, as Rick had thought, but instead, a wide raised beach which stepped down to the shore of a vast silent ocean.

The steps ran along the beach like tracks, forming three separate level platforms, like a viewing gallery around the edge of the sea. There was a drop of four or five feet from one level to the next and the surface of the beach was not sand but a curious gravel that looked like the weathered bones of tiny birds.

Rick turned and faced the others, now nothing more than barely discernible silhouettes in the darkness behind him.

"The plains are fuckin' flooded," he whispered, "bu' it doesn't matter 'cos we'll be out of here soon."

He turned and looked back up the beach.

He could see three people under the strong lights. One of the figures seemed to be lying in the sand with the other two standing over him. Rick was sure they were all men. The one lying down was probably the one that had been calling for help. It had been a man's voice they had been following. The other two stood and moved like men. Rick could never explain why, but even from a long distance, men and women looked distinctly different. Women stood and moved differently to men. He was certain that the three figures were all men. They had on heavy padded jackets and wore helmets with torches on the side. They didn't need the torches because of the two powerful arc lamps. One of the standing figures had a large haversack on his back.

Rick knew immediately that it was not Pete Mercer or the Creep, or any of Mr G's people. These three were professional cavers and Rick knew that they could lead him back to the surface.

Rick took off his back pack and hunkered down into a squat position. The others hunkered down around him. Rick turned back on his torch but kept his fingers over the front to subdue the light. Mo didn't turn on his torch but held it at the ready.

Rick unzipped the bag and rummaged through blindly with his free hand. He retrieved the ornate box that he'd found under the Creep's bed and set it gently on the ground under the light of his torch. When he lifted the lid the neatly arranged knives sparkled in the torchlight.

"Okay, listen, here's what we're goin' ta do," he whispered, "There's three of dem I can see, but there might be more, so we gotta be careful. They look like cavers. They might have weapons, but I don't think so. If we rush them, we can take them down. They got bags and ropes and probably food and water." He passed a knife to each of them. Megan didn't seem keen to take the one Rick handed to her. It looked large in her small hand. Rick hesitated before passing a knife to Lash, but finally gave him the second largest knife in the box. It looked small in Lash's bear-like paw. Rick took it back and swapped it for the biggest one. Lash smiled at the knife and then at Rick.

"Follow my lead, an' keep your fuckin' heads down 'til I say so. Alrigh'?"

No one said anything.

"Alrigh'?" Rick said again, louder and angrier.

"Yeh, alright," said Mo.

322

Megan just nodded. It looked more like an exaggerated shiver.

"Alrigh'?" said Lash, perfectly mimicking Rick's inner city Dublin accent.

Rick shone the torch in Lash's face. Lash was smiling, but it was not a smirk. Rick looked in Lash's eyes. There was no arrogance or threat. Lash didn't even blink.

"Come on. We're goin' to go out toward the sea, to the lowest level near the water's edge, then we'll sneak up on them. If we keep our fuckin' heads down, they won't see us until we're on top of them. Alrigh'?"

"Alright," said Mo.

"You stay behind me Megan, and don't make any fuckin' noise, d'hear? An' you make sure he keeps his big head down, an' doesn't make a fuckin' sound 'til I give the signal, Alrigh'?" Rick said, pointing his torch at Lash again.

Mo nodded.

"Yeh, no problem Rick. Heads down, no sound. No problem Rick. Let's do it."

"Let's do it," repeated Lash.

Rick switched off his torch.

In single file they scurried across the beach toward the ocean, dropping down each step as quickly and quietly as they could, until they reached the edge of the shore. The last step was the steepest so that, with their heads lowered, they were completely shielded from the men gathered under the arc lights on the middle tier.

"Righ, let's go. Follow my lead, single file. Keep yer fuckin' heads down and keep fuckin' quiet, righ?" said Rick.

When he turned away from the other three he smiled.

He couldn't help himself.

Chapter 45.

When Michael and Marie finally emerged from the fissure, into the brightness of the enormous chamber, what Michael saw left him speechless. Marie gasped. The white light from the two arc lamps was focussed on a small group of people huddled together at the centre of an endless beach that stepped down twice before reaching the shore of an enormous ocean. The ocean was black and its surface turbulent. As a backdrop to the smallness of the huddled group, the ocean appeared impossibly large. Michael's first thought was that they had somehow ventured onto the set of a sci-fi movie and that the alien ocean in front of him had been generated on a giant blue-screen. It seemed just too large to be real. The towering cliffs didn't help. After the stillness of the caves this place was noisy and terrifying. Above the hum of a small generator there was a faint, but distinct hissing sound, like steam escaping from a cracked radiator.

"What's happening?" Michael finally said.

"I don't know," said Marie. He thought she sounded worried.

I don't like this," said Michael.

"Neither do I," said Marie.

Their voices sounded funny.

The air was thick and cloying and it made Michael feel ill. Coupled with that, his headache had returned with a vengeance. His eyes watered. Things wandered in and out of focus and he felt dizzy. When he looked out across the beach he no longer saw bone grit but instead, a carpet of mould. Plumes of puss coloured dust rose from the beach and dissipated like smoke in the air, like puffs of mushroom spores rising from a damp forest floor. The air smelt of fug and rot. It was a nightmare vision and Michael was sure Marie could not see it.

"We need to get down there," said Marie, pointed at the huddled group.

"Okay, but we need to be quick, Marie. I think this place is poisonous," he said. His voice was croaky.

He tried to focus on group on the beach. They were people he knew, colours he recognised.

Kevin and Paddy were lying across a prostrate Hughie. Hughie's colour aura was fading. None of the three were moving. In a dark corner of his mind, where he was sure his present headache had been born, Michael saw the beach as an ancient, breathing, hissing thing. Something feral and angry, something that had been hiding in the darkness, waiting to be woken, waiting to be fed.

"We need to get out of here, Marie," he said in a small voice.

In the corner of his eye he saw movement. A small group of people was heading towards them, across the sand, moving very slowly, making little progress. Marie didn't notice them. She was concentrating on the huddled group under the lights.

"Paddy! Kevin!" she shouted.

Neither men moved.

"We need to get down there. I think that tide is coming in?" she said.

Michael looked out to sea. Marie was right. The water was rising, although he could see no tide.

"How did they climb down?" said Michael.

They both looked along the ledge and up the cliff wall but could see no rope. The ten-foot drop, whilst not too far, was far enough to be dangerous and certainly too high to climb back up without the aid of a rope.

"Strange?" said Marie.

"Everything is strange; don't you think?" said Michael.

"Never mind, we'll drop our own lines. Come on, help me," she said.

They went back into the crevice and secured three ropes around outcrops of rock. The Marie began attaching the crampons and pulleys, and while she was doing that Michael went back out to the ledge and scanned the cliff wall above them. He noticed a patch of colour on a higher ledge, at the entrance to another cave twenty feet above them. The colours looked familiar. There was no rope dangling from this upper cave either.

"We need to get out of here," he said again.

When ready, Marie abseiled down to the beach. Michael followed her, but with a lot less gusto and enthusiasm. As he descended he kept his eyes fixed on the entrance to the higher cave entrance, expecting at any moment to see someone he knew poke their head out and wave down at him.

No one did.

The surface of the beach gave way under his weight. Although at a distance it looked like grit or gravel, up close it looked like tiny bones. It was wet and difficult to walk on, and his feet continually sank into pools of dirty coloured liquid. Marie reached the group first. Paddy, Kevin and Hughie appeared to be sleeping. There was no sign of Horse.

"Oh shit," said Marie.

"What?" said Michael.

"It's the air. It's poisonous," she said, dropping to her knees.

"I've been telling you that, since we got here," he said.

Marie ignored him and removed a small canister from her haversack, pulled out a concealed face guard and inhaled deeply.

"Oxygen," she said. "Where's Paddy's haversack. He has one of these too."

They both looked about, but could see no bag on the beach.

"Maybe they're lying on it," said Michael.

"I don't think so. I think that's just Hughie under there," she said. Michael looked down the beach. The approaching group of people had almost stopped moving.

"That's Horse," said Michael, pointing toward them. "There are people with him. I don't recognise any of them. I can't see Denis or Hanna. Maybe Horse took Paddy's bag?"

"We've got to get out of here Michael, before we all succumb to whatever is in the air. And look! The water is rising too. We'll drown if we don't get back up to the tunnels." Marie took another lungful of oxygen.

"We'll get this lot awake then you go help the Englishman. Okay? Take some oxygen and then help me wake them. Quickly now," she said.

Michael took two large lungful's and then passed the canister back to Marie. He looked down at the sleepers. Kevin was slumped over Hughie and Paddy looked as if he had fallen asleep on his knees. His chin was on his chest with his forehead pressed into Kevin's shoulder. It was as if Paddy was praying over two dead companions.

Marie knelt beside Paddy and shook him violently.

"Paddy. Wake up, Paddy."

She pressed the mask against his mouth and nose.

"Breath Paddy. Come on. Breath."

Paddy's eyes rolled behind fluttering eyelids as he slowly came back to life, gulping the oxygen as he did so. For a moment or two he seemed lost and frightened but soon came back to life.

"What...happened?" he stammered.

"It's the atmosphere. It's poisonous. Where's your oxygen?" asked Marie.

"What?" It was...here beside me. Where is it? What's happened?" he said.

"Never mind that now, we need to get out of here, the tide is rapidly rising. We need to get out of here, now," said Marie.

They woke Kevin. His haversack was missing too.

Reviving Hughie was a different matter. He seemed to be in a comatose state and only barely alive.

"We'll just have to carry him out," Marie said. "Come on. Paddy. Kevin. Help me now. Michael, you take the oxygen over to the others. Once we get Hughie back to the fissure I'll come back for you. And hurry Michael! Everybody hurry! That tide is coming in fast."

Before Michael left, they all took some oxygen. Paddy and Kevin revived quickly. The four of them carried Hughie to the upper tier and then Marie gave Michael the oxygen canister.

"Go Michael. Your English friend will need this. Get them back here as quickly as you can. Hurry, we're running out of time."

Michael saw that Marie was right. The ocean was rising and the beach was disappearing fast. He watched as the black water crept quickly toward the legs of the lighting gantries. Michael looked back at the generator.

"It won't be long before the water reaches the generator," he shouted at Marie.

"Well stop talking and get going then. What are you wating for?" she said. There was panic in her voice.

Chapter 46.

Michael watched as the ocean rose up and swallowed the beach. He thought of the high-water line he had noticed in the vertical crevice, just below the entrance to the main tunnels. He knew it was a long way back up and if they didn't hurry they would be caught by the rising water and would surely drown. He decided to run.

It wasn't easy. He took more of the oxygen. It helped with the pain in his head too. He was sure the stale air in the chamber was contributing to his headache. The bursts of fresh oxygen held the pain at bay. He drew closer to the approaching group. They were at a standstill, fifty yards away, watching him. He suddenly became aware of a subtle change. The background hissing noise had become a whisper. From somewhere beyond the reach of the lights, somewhere beyond the unseen horizon, Michael thought he could hear a voice, like someone calling him.

It sounded just like a drawn out "H...hey."

The voice said "H...hey. H...hey. H...hey."

"St...ay"

"H...hey."

"St...ay."

He tried to ignore it, knowing the voice he was hearing was not real, but coming from inside his own head.

"St...ay." Michael picked up his pace.

The group being led by Horse turned and began to move towards the wall of the upper tier, away from the approaching ocean. Michael too, moved inland. His legs were heavy but somehow he found new strength. He looked for Hanna in the group, but knew she wasn't there. Maybe he couldn't see her, he thought. The colours rising from the beach were distorting and distracting.

"Please God, let Hanna be with them," he said to himself.

He looked over his shoulder and saw that Marie, Kevin and Paddy were up on the last tier of the beach.

Michael reached Horse at the edge of the upper tier. Horse looked exhausted and about to drop. There were three people with him. Hanna wasn't one of them. Neither was Professor Kearns. Michael tried to remember how many had gone on the expedition but his headache was getting in the way of any attempt to concentrate.

"This is all that's left," gasped Horse, before taking the oxygen mask and inhaling deeply.

"I'm sorry, Michael," he said between gulps, "The others are dead. Hanna is dead. She drowned. Professor Kearns too."

As Horse took the oxygen, colour seemed to come back to his face. He passed the canister around.

"This place floods every day, Michael. This is Gitte and Axel, and this is Eric. They survived by climbing into an air pocket in a cave back there. There is poison in the air. We have to get out," said Horse.

Gitte, a pretty blond woman in her early thirties held the hand of the man named Axel. She took the oxygen without letting go of him. Michael could see that they were a couple and that Axel was happy for Gitte to take as much of the oxygen as she wanted. Gitte thanked Michael then passed the mouth piece to her partner. Both spoke in broken English.

"Tank Good you came for us. Tank you," Gitte said.

Michael thought she might cry. Axel gorged on the oxygen. The other man, whom Horse had identified as Eric, waited his turn with sullen eyes. He was older than the other two. He tried to remain composed but once he got going, he gulped and gagged at the oxygen too.

"Take it easy," said Horse, "we might need that again before we're home."

"We need to get back to the ropes and up to the ledge, Horse. As quick as we can." said Michael.

"But what about the roof collapse? Did you break through? We got trapped down here," said Eric.

"We found another route, onto the lower ledge. Come on, there is no time to explain. If we hurry we can get back to the tunnels. Come on, let's get to the rope," said Michael.

They moved with surprising speed, once revived by the oxygen, but Michael couldn't help wondering how long the small canister would last, with so many hungry lungs to feed. The shale on the higher tier was more compact and moving across it was easier than on the lower tiers and it was not long before they reached the rope. Paddy and Marie were waiting on the top of the ledge at the mouth of the fissure.

"We need some oxygen," said Marie.

Horse passed the canister up to her. Once she and Paddy had taken some, they began hauling the group up, one by one. First Gitte, then Axel and then Eric. Horse and Michael assisted from below.

"Hurry Paddy, get them into the fissure and get climbing, as high as you can, as quickly as you can. I'll help these two. The air is better the higher you climb," shouted Marie, then turned and looked down at Horse and Michael.

"You first," said Michael.

Horse didn't argue. With Michael pushing him from below, Marie hauled Horse up beside her. Almost as soon as Horse had climbed onto the ledge there was a loud crack, a bright orange flash and then everything went black, as the generator spluttered and went silent. An echo of the spark lingered for a moment on Michael's high-viz jacket, but quickly disappeared.

Without the hum of the generator the hissing sound rose considerably. The voice returned.

"St…ay."

*

Marie's turned on her helmet torch and Horse followed suit. Both of them directed their torchlight down to the spot where Michael had been standing, but Michael was gone.

"Shit," Marie screamed. "Where is he?"

Horse said nothing. They both scanned the beach with their torches, hoping to catch the tell-tale glow of Michael's luminous jacket. The steps had vanished and the cream coloured beach had darkened considerably. Finally, Marie spotted him.

Michael had moved away from the cliff and out towards the approaching ocean.

"What's he doing?" she said. When she saw something move to Michael's left she grabbed the rope and, without a word to Horse, dropped back down onto the beach.

The bony gravel was saturated and soft and she sank up to her ankles. She tried to move but found it was nearly impossible. Her boots were heavy. It was like wading through deep wet mud. She kept hold the rope with both hands and pushed out as far as she could. Darkness filled the space behind her, the rope her only life-line to the others.

"Michael," she called out.

He didn't respond.

"Michael, it's this way. We've got to...get...out...of...here," she yelled.

He wasn't even looking at her. He was staring at a thin figure stumbled slowly toward him. Marie could tell that it was a woman but she was too far away to recognise who it was. What she could see, terrified her. The woman had her arms raised and in one hand she held a knife, in the other, what looked like a large white rock.

"Look out, Michael," screamed Marie.

The person kept coming toward him, but he didn't move. He just stood and waited for her to reach him.

"Look out, Michael," Marie shouted in desperation, knowing he couldn't hear her because the hissing noise had become a din. It drowned out everything. Marie tried to continue out but found it impossible to raise her feet from the clawing sand. She felt weak and the poisonous air was making her breathing difficult again. She needed oxygen, she needed the Englishman and she needed Michael to hear her. She wanted to sleep.

"Look out," she said again, but now her voice was gone.

Eventually, Marie dropped to her knees and began to cry.

Chapter 47.

Twenty minutes earlier.

*L*ash was really getting on Rick's nerves.

"..n' go back for Mo an' Megan, Rick. ..n' go back for Mo and Megan, Rick."

On and on, again and again, like a skipping record.

"..n' go back for Mo an' Megan, Rick."

Each time he said it, it sounded like the idea had just popped into his head.

"We'll go back for them soon, Lash, once we find the way out. You wanta get outa here, don't you, Lash?"

"..n' go back for Mo an' Megan, Rick. "

Rick tried not to sound exasperated. The hulk of a man that lumbered behind him was agitated and nervous and Rick didn't fancy his chances in a fight, not now that he had foolishly given Lash the biggest knife from the box.

Rick Kavanagh should have been happy, the fact that he wasn't, weighed heavily on his mind. Rick couldn't shake off the feeling that *Lady Luck* had deserted him and that his destiny had been handed to someone else. And yet, on the face of it, everything appeared to be going Rick's way. Firstly, he still had almost all of the drugs they had taken from the cave, despite being two mules down. The fact that Megan and Mo were gone was a good thing too, even if they had taken some of the stash with them. What they had been carrying was small fry compared to the amount of drugs that Lash now had in a haversack on his back and Rick had in the Creep's holdall, more than enough to set Rick up for life, once he made it to the outside. Secondly, Rick was pretty sure they were on the way out. The ribbons of blue and red lights that now guided them, were proof of that. And thirdly, if Pete Mercer and the Creep were still on his tail, which Rick very much doubted, there was no way they could follow him up from the beach. Once he and Lash climbed onto the ledge Rick secretly cut the rope, preventing anyone from following them up. Rick should have been happy, but he wasn't and he wasn't sure why. Something had changed and the journey across the beach had freaked him out. A layer of his self-confidence had been stripped away. He was no longer so sure of his own invulnerability and, to top it all, he was certain he had heard whispering voices speaking to him from across the ocean. The voices were cold and cruel.

"H...hey, He....ey," they hissed at him in an accusatory tone.

"..n' go back for Mo an' Megan, Rick."

"Yeh, soon, Lash, soon, we'll go back for them."

Of course Lash hadn't seen Rick cut the rope. The knife had been quick and silent. And the hissing noise, that came from somewhere far beyond the shore, had drowned out the sound of the rope-end clumping onto the beach below. Lash was the first onto the ledge and immediately moved towards the tunnel mouth, his attention drawn to a bunch of LED lights sparkling in the gloom. Once Rick had struggled onto the ledge he saw his opportunity and without a second thought cut through the thick rope. So even if Rick had wanted to go back for Megan and Mo, which of course he didn't, there was no longer any safe way back down to the beach.

"..n' go back for Mo an' Megan, Rick."

"Soon, we'll go back. Quiet now, an' let me fuckin' tink, will yah?"

Lash took a moment to consider Rick's words and then said,

"..n' go back for Mo an' Megan, Rick. ..n' go back for Mo an' Megan, Rick."

Rick tried to work out what had just happened on the beach, but the monotonous chatter from Lash made it almost impossible to concentrate. Nothing made sense. One minute, the four of them were running along the water's edge towards the group of cavers under the arc lights, with their heads and backs bent below the step and being as quiet as the scree beneath their feet would allow, and the next moment, Megan was screaming hysterically and Mo was gone. They had been no more than twenty feet from the three men on the middle tier when Megan started screaming but, by some miracle, they cavers hadn't heard her. When Rick chanced a look above the step he saw that it was because the cavers had stopped moving.

"What, the fuck? I think they're asleep," he said.

He turned around.

"Will you shut, the fuck, up, Meg. Where the fuck is Mo?"

Megan dropped to her knees and curled into a ball against the gravel wall. Mo was not behind her, nor was he anywhere to be seen. Rick shone the torch out to sea. The water was no longer still. It looked angry and the tide was coming in. Mo was not in the water either. It was then that Rick noticed the hissing noise. It made him think of the gush of steam that announced the arrival of a train in one of his Saturday morning Westerns, except that this sound was constant and unrelenting.

"Where, the fuck, is Mo?" he said again.

Lash ignored the question.

"The...thing...took him," shrieked Megan.

She pointed toward the ocean with wide eyes.

"Wha?" said Rick.

"In de sea. It grabbed 'im and dragged 'im ...in," she said. She choked before continuing. "The ting took Mo... the ting from de ocean," she said again. She began shaking violently.

"What thing?" said Rick.

"One a does tings with eight arms an' legs," she said, as if it should have been obvious.

"An octopus?" said Rick.

"Bu' wi' claws. Mo touched it, an' it grabbed 'im, an' dragged 'im inta de sea, Rick. I seen it. I swear, Rick."

"That's impossible, Megan."

"I swear Rick. It was an octi...pus."

"Octopuses don't have claws. What are you talkin' 'bout, Megan?"

"I swear, Rick. The octi...pus got Mo. Rick, I swear."

"Where's Mo?" said Lash.

"He's just gone back for something, Lash. He'll catch up soon. Come on we need to get up there, before those lads sees us," Rick said. He turned his back on Megan.

"Don't leave me, Rick," she pleaded.

"Lift Megan up to the next level Lash, an' then follow me. We got to get up there."

Rick watched as Lash went back, knelt down and took Megan gently into his arms. She didn't resist. He carried he up to the next level and carefully deposited her onto the shale. She resumed the foetal position and closed her eyes.

"Don't leave me Rick," she whispered. Lash smiled down at her and then turned toward Rick.

"Come on Lash. Leave her, she'll be fine. She needs her sleep."

Rick and Lash found the three cavers slumped over each other. Rick had been right. They were asleep. He nudged the nearest one with his foot, causing the sleeping man to topple onto his side.

"They're fuckin' drugged or someth'," Rick said, as much to himself as to Lash. "Help me with their haversacks and check their pockets, Lash. They must have food, an' somtin to drink," he said

Lash kept looking over his shoulder to where Megan lay on the sand. She hadn't moved.

"Where's Mo, Rick?" he said.

"He'll catch up soon. Com' on. Help me with these three."

After they had searched the three sleeping cavers and searched their haversacks, Rick emptied out the largest one and gave it to Lash.

"Put the drugs in dat, Lash," he said.

When Rick spotted the knotted rope dangling down from a cave entrance, high on the cliff wall, he smiled.

"Up an' out. Up an' out," he said to himself.

"Come on Lash, we're goin' up there," he said.

Lash looked at Rick then looked over at Megan. He frowned again. Rick knew what Lash was thinking.

"Megan will wait for Mo an' then they'll follow us up. Come on. Once we're up we can pull 'em up after us, can't we? Megan needs to wait for Mo. Com' on, Lash."

"Where's Mo?" said Lash again.

Rick had no idea. The hissing had got louder and the tide was coming in, faster and faster.

"He's comin' Lash. He'll be here soon. We got to be up there, so we can pull 'im up when he gets here. *You* can pull 'im up, Lash, Megan too. Com' on Lash, come on."

Once on the ledge Rick cut the rope and followed Lash into the tunnel.

"..n' go back for Mo an' Megan, Rick. ..n' go back for Mo an' Megan, Rick."

"Yeh. When we find a way out, then we'll go back for Mo and Megan."

Rick gritted his teeth. "If you doesn't stop going on and on, I'll knife you sooner than I planned," he said under his breath. He looked back at Lash and at the heavy haversack he had on his back like a school bag. The mule and the getaway money. There was no way Rick was turning around. No way was he going back to that place. He could still hear the whispering hiss from the beach and, despite his bravado, it frightened him.

"H...hey. H...hey"

"..n' go back for Mo an' Megan, Rick. ..n' go back for Mo an' Megan, Rick."

The tunnel twisted and turned and the floor rose steadily as Rick and Lash moved further from the entrance and further from the beach. Once they had gone about four hundred yards Rick turned and shone his torch into his Lash's face.

"Okay Lash. Give us the haversack an' go back for them. I'll wait here for you. You go back for Megan and Mo and pull them up. I'll set up camp. We need to rest. They'll be there by now, at the bottom, waiting for you. Can I trust you to do that, Lash? Can I? Or do I have to do it myself?"

Lash looked hurt.

"I'll go back for Mo and Megan, Rick. I'll go now."

Lash turned and began to set off in the dark.

"Wait. Give me the bag," said Rick.

Lash turned and narrowed his eyes. Rick could see that Lash was suspicious.

"I'll go now," said Lash.

"Leave the haversack. You'll have to carry Megan, Lash. She won't like you to get dirt on her skirt or on her lovely blouse. The straps of de haversack are very dirty, Lash".

Lash licked his lips.

"You wouldn't want 'er blouse to get smudged, would you, Lash? You'll have to carry Megan, Lash. You saw her, she's very sleepy."

"I'll go back now," Lash said again. "I'll leave the bag."

"Good man," said Rick as Lash dropped the heavy haversack onto the cave floor and headed back down the tunnel.

"Hurry back. I'll be waitin' fer you here," Rick called after him.

Rick picked up the haversack and watched Lash go. Then he turned around and headed on along the twisting tunnel. As he went, he collected all the LED ribbons that were fixed along the route and shoved them into his pocket, leaving nothing behind but solid, hissing darkness.

Chapter 48.

Michael stood at the edge of the ocean. He could hear Marie's voice, but could no longer see her. The plumes of dirty colours rising from the bony sand obstructed his view back to the cliff base. He moved forward to meet the approaching figure.

When he'd first seen her, he thought it might be Hanna. Now that they were no more than six feet apart he saw that it wasn't but, instead, the young woman who had kicked him on the ferry over to the island. She had her arms raised and her face was alive with fear. She had a knife in one hand and something white and heavy in the other, but her movements were slow and Michael didn't think she meant to harm him. He could see that she was frightened and had been crying. When she got within touching distance she stopped and lowered her arms. Michael leaned forward and took the knife. He dropped it into one of the pockets of his jacket. He ignored the white package in her other hand. Whatever it was, it didn't look much like a weapon. When he moved forward and wrapped his arms around her, she fell against his chest and began to sob.

Michael had spotted her when the lights went out. He hadn't seen her, but in the moment of total darkness, when the arc lights had gone out and before Horse and Marie had time to switch their helmet lights on, Michael had seen a distinct mass of colour among the dirty fug that rose from the surface of the beach. He knew immediately what it meant. Someone alive was still on the beach and he had no choice but to investigate.

The ocean was rising at a ferocious rate. The water raced up the beach on either side of Michael and the young woman, and the gravel hissed as it passed by. Michael noticed that they seemed to be standing on the last bit of ground still above the water line, but he knew it was a rapidly diminishing causeway, and that if they didn't move soon, they would be engulfed.

"We have to go," he shouted into the young woman's ear.

She clung to him, but didn't make any effort to move. He would have to carry her. The pain in his head had moved to an area behind his ears. He lifted the young woman off her feet just as the ocean washed over his boots and soaked his socks. She wrapped her legs around him and linked them behind his back. Once sure of his balance, he turned and headed slowly back towards the base of the cliff and Marie's rope.

The woman was surprisingly light. In contrast, his legs were incredibly heavy. The submerged beach clung to him. As he pulled one foot free the other sank further into the slush, making each step more difficult than the last. It was tortuously slow going. The icy water gripped his ankles and drenched his lower legs. Michael tried to avoid gulping the pungent air. As the water rose, the hissing became louder, and the whispering more distinct.

"H...hey. St...ay."

The water rose above his knees. Michael could see the cliff wall and the light from the helmet torches, but they seemed to be moving away, rather than getting closer. Without the relief of fresh oxygen, he found it difficult to breathe and his legs felt like jelly.

"St...ay."

And his headache was spreading and getting worse. The inner lining of his skull felt like it was on fire, as if his brain was floating in a pool of acid. Every movement cause pain somewhere new. Even his cheeks hurt. Had he not been carrying the young woman Michael might have given up and let the ocean take him.

He trudged on.

Suddenly he felt a strong hand on his shoulder. When he raised his eyes, Horse was standing in front of him holding out the oxygen mask. He slipped it over Michael's nose and mouth.

"Breathe," he said.

As Michael filled his lungs with fresh air, Horse grabbed him with both hands and pulled him and the young woman out of the water and over to the cliff wall.

"You still up there, Marie?" shouted Horse, shining his torch up the wall.

"Of course I am. For God's sakes, hurry up. The ocean looks wild," she shouted down at him.

"Okay. First her, then Michael, then me," he shouted back.

Horse tied the rope around the woman's waist and lifted her up as far as he could. Marie dragged her up the rest of the way.

Water rushed over Horse's boots. He jumped back.

"Shit, something touched my leg," he said.

He grabbed the rope when it came back down.

"You go first," said Michael. "You're stronger than me. Once you're up there, you can haul me up after you."

Horses jumped again and then kicked out.

"Fuck. What was that?" he said.

"Go on Brian, we haven't time," said Michael.

"Okay. But don't you go anywhere this time, okay?" said Horse.

"I won't. I promise. Go," said Michael.

Before Horse hauled himself up, he tied the end of the rope around Michaels waist with a strong double knot.

"See you in a minute," he said and then scampered up the wall.

Michael was alone in a pool of yellow torchlight.

The freezing water quickly reached his crotch and then his waist. Soon it reached his chest and covered the rope. Michael looked up. The ledge was no more than five feet above him, but it might as well have been fifty. The water was rising faster now and would soon be over his head. Something heavy touched his leg. He looked down and was surprised that he could see through the water, down to the beach below. The plumes of colour dust were still visible, but they looked different. They were vibrant and strangely beautiful. They looked almost like human colours.

"Strange," Michael said.

He moved his head from left to right and then he turned around. The colours were everywhere.

A wave splashed water onto his face and as he cleared his vision he saw a large shadow in the water approach him at lightning speed. Whatever it was, it rammed into him and smashed him toward the cliff wall. He lost his footing and would have gone under had there not been a strong tug on the rope around his waist. Horse and Marie were hauling him upwards.

The rope tightened and pinched his back and under his arms. It caused excruciating pain.

Michael began to rise up but then, suddenly, he stopped.

Something had him by the ankle and was trying to pull him back down again.

Horse and Marie tugged at the rope with added force. The pressure on Michaels back and chest was immense and he found it difficult to breathe. He could no longer feel his legs. When he looked down he was shocked to see that his right leg was up off the sea bed and stretched out behind him. Whatever had attacked him was still holding on, and trying to drag him out to sea. Michael could hear Horse screaming. The ocean rose and then poured over the collar of his luminous jacket. He shuddered as icy water ran down his spine. He knew the water would soon be over his head and he would drown.

He wanted to scream. He was being pulled apart like a rag doll. From above, Brian and Marie were pulling the rope with all their might, whilst from beneath the ocean, some unseen force had him by the ankle and was trying to drag him under. The torches from the ledge blinded him, but he was sure that Horse and Marie couldn't see what was happening. He tried to shout up to them, tell them to stop pulling, but couldn't find his voice.

He knew he had to do something quickly. The water reached his chin and the pressure on his chest was so great that he was sure, at any moment, he would lose consciousness.

In a final moment of clarity, Michael looked up at the desperate faces of his friends on the ledge and mouthed, "I'm sorry," before rummaging in the pocket of his jacket, finding the knife that he had taken from the young woman on the beach and, with one clean slice with the razor-sharp blade, cut through the rope that was tearing him apart. In an instant, he was gone.

He hit the beach with tremendous force, then bounced down the steps and out to sea at a frightening speed. Before he lost consciousness, Michael thought he saw something that he recognised.

It was Hanna's colours.

Part Four

"Gáirdin an Ollphéist."
"The Garden of the Sea-Monster."

Chapter 49.

Soon after Lash left in search of Megan and Mo, Rick emptied the contents of the Creep's satchel and filled the haversack he'd taken from Lash. In one of the side pockets of the caver's haversack he found, what looked like, a small oxygen tank, complete with face mask and regulator. In another, there was a flask of water and a bag of boiled sweets. Rick popped one of the sweets into his mouth. It was sugary and strangely comforting. It made him feel warm. For some reason the taste of it reminded him of his mother. He felt his earlier confidence return. He took another sweet, put the bag back where he'd found it and, with the haversack on his back, moved on.

"Up and out," he said to the wet tunnel walls. "Up and out."

The hissing from the ocean had become a din and it spurred Rick on. The haversack was heavier than he expected but he didn't care. The cocaine was his ticket to a new and better life, and the ribbon-lights were his sign-posts back to the surface.

Rick noticed that the further he moved into the tunnel the louder the hiss from the ocean seemed to be, and at one point, the noise brought him to a standstill. In a moment of panic, Rick wondered if he had somehow turned around, and was now heading back towards the beach. But the incline in the floor told him he was still go up and therefore, he must be going the right way.

"Fuckin' dumb pussy," he mumbled to himself and tried to smile. It was a trick, that's all, an echo amplified and thrown forward by the shape of the twisting tunnel, he told himself.

"H...hey."

The hiss sounded like an animal breathing.

"H...hey."

He walked faster. Nothing moved up ahead, save for the shadows scurrying away from his searching torchlight.

"H...hey."

"Ah, fuck off! I'm not fuckin' listenin'!" he shouted back down the tunnel.

"H...hey."

Finally, the floor levelled off, easing the strain on his tired legs. He turned a sharp corner and the tunnel became a straight line as far as he could see. He decided to run. There was something up ahead, something shiny and bright.

Was it daylight?

Was it the exit from the caves?

In his haste, Rick tripped and fell forward, the weight of the stuffed backpack propelling him, face first, toward the dusty floor. He threw his hands out, to cushion the fall, and let the torch fly out of his hand. It crashed onto the floor before he did, bounced twice and then went out.

Total darkness enveloped Rick. There weren't even ribbon lights to puncture the blackness.

"Fuck," he said.

"H..hey."

The bright and shiny thing he'd been heading toward was gone too.

"Fuck."

He scrambled onto his hands and knees and scuttled forward in the blackness. The weight of the bag on his back shifted forward and almost toppled him onto his side.

"Fuck, fuck, fuck."

Panic rose from a pit in his stomach.

"H...hey."

"Fuck off," he yelled over his shoulder.

He shuffled forward on sore knees, reaching blindly for the torch. The darkness was solid and felt heavy. He became disorientated, no longer sure what was forward, what was back.

"H...hey."

The hissing was all around him.

"H...hey."

Ricks fingers touched something metallic. He snatched at the torch, rolled onto his backside and cradled it to his chest, like it was a wounded bird.

"H...hey."

The torch felt different, maybe lighter he thought. Rick had the terrible notion that the batteries had fallen out during the fall, but as he fumbled with it in the dark he could find no evidence that anything was missing. He flicked the button. Nothing happened.

"Oh fuck. Oh fuck."

"H...hey."

"Fuck, fuck, fuck," he whispered.

He stood up and shook the torch. Nothing happened. He banged it against his thigh several times, each time harder than the last. He ignored the pain.

"H...hey."

He thought he could hear giggling.

"He...he....H...hey"

The torch finally came on, it's stuttering light mimicking his shaking hand.

"Thank fuck," he said.

The tunnel looked different now. The air seemed thicker, the light of the torch no longer as penetrating as it had been.

The fall must have damaged it in some way, he thought. Something moved in the shadows behind him.

"Dat you, Lash?" he shouted.

Lash didn't answer.

Rick knew it wasn't Lash.

"H...hey. H...hey."

Rick turned back to where he had seen the bright and shiny light.

It was there again, fifty yards ahead. No more than that.

He began to run again, but this time, taking care where he put his feet and trying not to shake the torch too much. The torchlight was essential and comforting, and Rick knew that he'd be lost without it.

"H...hey."

He kept running, not knowing what was coming up behind him, but certain it wasn't something good.

Rick was twenty feet from the source of the bright and shiny light, when he recognised what it was, and the realisation almost made him cry. From a distance, it had looked like daylight or light from another tunnel. But up close, it revealed itself to be nothing more than a dry patch of rock at the top of an otherwise wet rubble wall. The upper portion was lighter in colour than the wall below and was sprinkled with tiny pieces of quartz that flickered in the torchlight.

"Shit."

But that wasn't the worst of it. The wall in front of him, two thirds wet and one third dry, was a dead end. Rick had reached the end of the tunnel.

"Oh shit...no," he said.

He looked around for some other way out, but there was none. How could this be? he thought. Hadn't he been following the caver's lights? Why would they have led him into a cul de sac? It didn't take Rick long to work it out. The wall in front of him was the result of a ceiling collapse. It must have happened after the cavers had passed by, on their way to the hidden beach. It was definitely a dead end, and there was no way of knowing how thick the rock fall was. He was trapped. There was no way forward and now, no way back.

"H...hey."

*

Rick spun round and looked back down the way he'd come. He thought he could see someone, or something, moving in the shadows just beyond the reach of his torchlight, but couldn't be sure. What was certain was that the tunnel was filling up with sea water. Just above the hiss and whispers, was a gurgling sloshing sound, as the ocean rushed up the tunnel. At any moment, it would come around the last corner and race up the passageway toward him. He had to move up to ceiling level or he would drown. He turned back to the wall of rock that blocked his way and surveyed the dry top portion. The high tide mark was a couple of feet above his head and then there was four feet to the ceiling. He wondered if he could climb up and cling onto the wall in the dry zone, then maybe he could wait out the tide. It seemed his only option. He was sure he must get away from the water.

"H...hey."

He thought about the thing Megan had said about Mo being attacked by an octopus with claws.

"Fuckin' stupid dumb bitch," he shouted down the tunnel. "Octopuses don't have claws!" His voice sounded weak. When he thought of Megan he felt a sudden pang of regret. He wished she was still with him. He was *Superman* when she was with him. Why had he been so cruel? She was his gal. Why had he left her to die on the beach?

"I'm sorry Meg. Really I am," he whispered.

"H...hey."

He started to climb. The confidence that he had relied on since entering the caves was gone again, but so too was his strength and stamina. The climb proved difficult and tiring. He fell several times, but fear and determination spurred him on and he finally managed to get his hand into a large crack between the ceiling and a sizable boulder at the top of the wall. Rick raised his legs above the tide mark and searched for footholds. He would need both his arms and legs to support his body and the heavy haversack on his back. Just when he felt secure, with both his feet wedged into cracks in the rock and both hands clinging to the top of the boulder, something grabbed him and pulled him backwards. The boulder came loose, dislodged completely and toppled forward after him. Rick jumped backwards onto his attacker and the boulder crashed harmlessly on the tunnel floor. Rick jumped to his feet, turned around and came face to face with Lash. Over Lash's shoulder Rick could see the water rushing up the tunnel.

Lash looked distraught.

"De men took Megan," he said, "and de Banshee took Rats an' Mo."

Lash sounded hysterical. His big frame quivered and Rick noticed that he was holding the knife he'd been given on the beach.

Rick turned around quickly and looked back up the wall. There was a hole where the boulder had once been. Maybe it was a way out? He turned back to Lash.

"I was waiting for you, Lash. I found the way out," he said.

The water raced towards them. It was now only a couple of feet behind Lash.

"De men took Megan," Lash repeated.

"Never mind Megan, she'll be okay and she'll find Rats and Mo. Megan's a good girl, you know that, Lash. Remember how she fixed my eye? She'll be alrigh' Lash. She's a good girl."

Rick pointed the torch to the top of the wall and the new hole. He had to get back up there and fast. The water ran over Lash's runners.

"Help me to get up there Lash and then you can follow me up. I need to get the backpack in first. Quick now, so it don't get wet."

"What about the Banshee, Rick?" said Lash stepping forward and out of the water. Rick had never seen Lash look so terrified.

"Quickly then. Help me up and then you come after. First the bag, then me, then you, okay? You're the best climber, aren't you?"

Rick removed the haversack and held it above his head. He stepped up on the boulder.

"Quickly. Lift me up," he said raising one knee and offering Lash his foot.

"Like a stirrup Lash, com' on, will you! You know how te do it."

Lash moved up to the wall and cupped his hands. Rick stepped forward and let Lash hoist him up.

The dislodged boulder had left a deep crevice, but nothing more than that. Rick worked out that it was just large enough for him and the haversack, but there would be no room for Lash.

Rick shoved the haversack deep into the opening and was surprised that it travelled in so far. Then it fell out of sight.

"Shit. Push me up Lash, so I can get the bag," he said.

Lash did so, but with little enthusiasm.

"Rick?" he said, "there's something in the water. Something touched my shoe."

Rick climbed into the crevice but found that the gap that the haversack had fallen through was not large enough for him. He turned the torch down into Lash's eyes.

"Stand on the boulder and your feet won't get wet. I'll try to make room."

Rick knew if Lash stood on the fallen rock he'd be out of touching distance.

Lash looked up at him with obvious distrust.

"You're a fuckin' liar, Rick," he said suddenly. His voice had changed. He no longer sounded like a simpleton. He sounded normal. He sounded angry and scared. He reached behind his back and pulled out the knife from under his belt. He pointed it at Rick.

What happened next, happened so quickly that Rick had to shake himself to be sure he had not been hallucinating.

Lash raised the knife above his head and got getting ready to pounce. There was a mad determination on his angry face. Rick could only cower and wait for the strike. When the black water rushed over Lash's shoes and socks he hesitated for a moment and looked down. Rick looked down too. Both saw the black shape in the water. Lash opened his mouth to scream but the sound had no time to escape. In an instant, and with a tremendous splashing, that continued down the tunnel and into the darkness, Lash was gone.

It happened in the blink of an eye.

"Oh fuck, fuck, fuck," screamed Rick, but there was no one now to hear him.

The water kept rising.

He tried to push himself further into the hole but it was no use. His hands were shaking and the torch light quivered and then went out.

"H...hey."

As the darkness crowded around, Rick tried to hold his breath. He began to cry. Something touched the front of his jacket and he heard a ripping sound.

"Is that you Meg? Please Meg...I'm sorry...don't...please..."

Rick Kavanagh screamed just before the claw took him by the face, snatched him out of his hidey-hole and dragged him down the tunnel after Lash.

Chapter 50.

Paul Creagan had been grilled for more than two hours by Chief Superintendent Sutton and then spent another half an hour in the presence of an American Special Agent named Theodore Brooks.

Superintendent Sutton spent the interview shouting at Paul, exposing, what he called, Paul's shortcomings as a police officer. Paul bore the assault and insults without argument. Sutton called him unprofessional and incompetent. At one point, he even accused Paul of treachery.

"Garda resources not good enough for a poncy Dublin whizz-kid like you Creagan? Think you're better than the rest of us, is that it, boyo? Well you're not as smart as that expensive suit of yours, that's for sure. And you can forget about fancy suits from now on. I'll be recommending a change of clothes and scenery for you. I have in mind a nice blue uniform with a matching peaked cap. Very fashionable on the streets of inner city Dublin. Garda Paul Creagan, queen of the traffic corp. I swear Creagan, before I'm finished with you and your Brit boyfriend, you'll both wish you were never born. And where did you say the cocky Cockney is? Potholing, is he? I understand they call him Horse. Horse? I don't think that's right, Creagan? No! Rat or mole would seem more appropriate. Yeh, that's it. A mole. What do you think, Creagan? The mole! Oh, ha ha ha."

Superintendent Sutton's laughter ended abruptly when a tall well-dressed black man opened the door and walked into the interview room without a word.

"Who, de fuck, are you? Can't you read? It says private on the door, doesn't it? That means, *private!*" snapped the Chief Superintendent.

"I am Special Agent Theodore Brooks of US Homeland Security. Surely you were told I was coming, Superintendent Sutton?" he said. He didn't offer Sutton his hand. The Superintendent stood up. The American was well over six-foot-three and, with his shiny bald head and handsome face, he reminded Paul of a basketball player whose name escaped him. Brooks walked right up to Sutton, so that they were no more than a foot apart, and for a moment Paul thought there might be a fight. The black man leaned forward and whispered something into Sutton's ear. Sutton stepped back. Brooks turned and faced Paul.

"So, you are Detective Paul Creagan, the one who brought us the letter? I've been looking forward to meeting you," he said. He offered his hand. Paul stood and shook it.

"Please, sit back down Detective. I would like to ask you a few questions, if you don't mind," he said.

Brooks turned back and looked at the Sutton.

"Thank you, Chief Superintendent. If you are finished, you may go. I need to speak with Detective Creagan in private, you understand?"

"I have been instructed to stay with Garda Creagan, while you interview him," said Sutton.

"I think you'll find your orders have changed, Superintendent. If you'd like to verify that with your Commissioner, please go ahead, but I am in a hurry and I need to speak with Paul urgently, and alone. So, if you wouldn't mind," he pointed to the door, "thank you, Chief Superintendent Sutton."

Sutton hesitated. The American lowered his head and stared at the Superintendent over a pair of imaginary spectacles. Sutton mumbled something, then gathered together his papers and headed for the door. In his haste, he slammed his leg into the corner of the table.

"Fuck," he said and groaned with pain. He gave Paul an evil look. "I'm not finished with you, Creagan," he said. He did not look at Brooks again and almost took the door off its hinges, when he slammed it behind him.

"I don't think you've made yourself a friend there," said Paul.

If he was expecting a smile from the American, he didn't get one.

"I don't need friends, Paul," said Special Agent Brooks.

Whilst they were talking Paul's mobile rang. When he saw the caller ID, he smiled.

"Oh, thank God. It's Inspector Hopkins. He's back from his adventures in the caves," he said.

"I see. Good. Where is he?" said Brooks.

"I'm not sure. He says he needs me to go get him, though."

"Good. Well, you do that, and then, bring him straight back here. Do you understand, Paul? Oh, and you will need to think about what to tell him."

"Yes. Of course," said Paul.

"Good. Well, go on then. Go get the Horse," said Theodore Brooks, smiling for the first time since entering the room.

*

Horse, Marie, Paddy and Megan climbed the fissure as quickly as they could, all the time keeping just ahead of the pursuing water. They shared the last of the oxygen as they went. The climb up proved much easier than the climb down. "Nothing like fear to motivate a person," thought Horse as he brought up the rear. Kevin was waiting at the top. Hughie was sitting beside him on the floor, with his back to the tunnel wall. He looked forlorn, but alive. His leg was badly swollen, but colour had returned to his cheeks. Horse thought he looked embarrassed. Hughie didn't seem to want to speak about what had happened to Denis. When pressed by Marie, he told her that he couldn't remember anything of the chamber or the ocean or of how he got his injury.

"Can you walk on that?" said Horse, pointing at his wounded leg.

"Yes. It looks worse than it feels. I think it's numb, but I can walk on it," said Hughie in a weak voice.

"Good. Where's the rest of the group? We need to get going. It's a long trek back," said Horse.

The three rescued students, Eric, Axel and Gitte, were not with Kevin and Hughie. Kevin told Horse that they had gone to investigate the rock slide because Gitte was convinced that some of their stuff may have been buried there. Professor Kearns had set up a supply camp in the general area, just before he and his party headed down to the beach. If Gitte was right, there may be useful supplies buried under the rocks. In the event, the three returned with nothing but a haversack that Axel had found at the top of the rubble wall. Paddy immediately identified it as being his bag. Stuffed inside, they found water, a canister of oxygen and a large quantity of, what Horse said was high grade cocaine.

At first Megan denied any knowledge of the drugs. Since leaving the beach she'd stuck close to Marie and avoided making eye contact with any of the others. After some gentle coaxing from Marie, she finally confided in Horse that the drugs belonged to her boyfriend, Rick Kavanagh, and that Rick had stolen them from Mr. G and some dangerous foreigner she referred to as the Creep. She told Horse about the secret cove and their escape through the caves, and how Rick had promised to take her away to a new life. She became vague when she spoke about what had happened in the hidden chamber, claiming that she had no idea what happened to Rick or the other two men who had escaped with them, called Lash and Mo. Horse didn't think Megan was telling the whole truth. She became extremely agitated when Horse threw the drug-laden haversack over his shoulder.

"Put dem back! That's Rick's stuff. He'll kill us fir takin' them," she yelled.

"Calm down. Nobody's going to kill anybody," said Horse.

Marie took Megan's arm and steered her away from the English detective, then they all headed back up the tunnel in single file, Horse at the front, Marie and Megan bringing up the rear. Horse's mind was racing. He was angry but knew he couldn't waste time pondering *what ifs*? His focus had to be on getting them back to the surface, as quickly as possible. He recognised Megan from the ferry. He wondered if she recognised him or if she remembered the man who had thrown-up on her shoes. Did she know it was the same man who had gone back for her on the poisoned beach, or that he had given his life to save hers?

Not long after leaving the entrance to the fissure there was another mini earthquake and the passage behind them collapsed in a hail of rocks, rubble and dust. There had been no warning. The walls and floor trembled and the aftershock moved the air so much that the force of it almost knocked them off their feet. Marie ventured back to investigate and found that the route to the fissure and hidden chamber was gone, sealed by a mountain of solid limestone. They had been extremely lucky. Had they stayed any longer at the entrance to the fissure they would have been buried alive or worse, trapped in the darkness until starvation or the poisonous air killed them.

"Get moving. Quick as you can. We need to get out of here, before the whole lot comes down on top of us," she said when she got back.

Horse didn't need to be told twice. They only stopped running when they reached the knotted end of the Professor's guide rope.

The earthquake had not only caused the roof collapse behind them, but it also tore open a massive hole in the side wall of the tunnel up ahead, in the widened section of the tunnel where, earlier in the day, Denis and Hughie had stormed off on their own. The hole was large enough to squeeze through and led into another network of tunnels. Whilst the others rested, Paddy and Kevin investigated and returned with good news. The new tunnels led to a chamber Paddy recognized, which was part of the cave system already mapped and explored, and which led directly to caves that were open to the public. The new tunnel would be a quicker route back to the surface, and much safer than trying to get back out through the Devils Throat.

Within an hour they were in a large chamber complete with hand rails, wall lights and a metal grid walkway.

The group of eight finally emerged, into a warm drizzly Skellig Éin afternoon, through a padlocked door which was an entrance into the cave system used by professional cavers, pot-holers and research students from the university. Horse and Paddy had had to kick the door off its hinges. Outside was a forest clearing at the bottom of one the tallest mountains on the island, and more than a mile and a half south of the Devil's Throat. A short path through thick trees led to the main road, which in turn led back to the town.

Horse watched on as, one by one, the rescued and the rescuers dropped onto the wet mossy ground. Bags and other gear were cast aside and jackets thrown off. They sat, slumped or lay flat on their backs, exhausted but relieved. Only Megan looked anxious. She clung to Marie's sleeve like a frightened child. No one spoke for a very long time. A warm rain fell on them and the air smelt sweet, of wood sap and new leaves. Horse turned his face to the sky and let the rain wash tears from eyes. He checked his mobile. He had two bars. He called Paul Creagan. Within twenty minutes there were vehicles stopping on the road beyond the trees. Not until the first of the emergency crew reached the clearing did any of the party make an effort to stand up.

*

Horse sat with his back to a set of French doors that opened out onto the back garden of the Tara Cove Hotel. The small conference room he had to himself was silent. Anyone watching him might have thought he was asleep. He held his hands on the table, palms down and sat as still as a statue, staring into the middle distance. He hardly blinked. He wondered if he *was* being watched, but there were no cameras he could see and no mirrored wall. He resisted a strong urge to drum his fingers.

He felt numb.

His partially completed report had been pushed to one side and his fountain pen had rolled away. It lay just out of reach, dangerously close to the front edge of the table. A mug of black coffee sat in front of him, going cold. He moved his eyes from the pen to the coffee. Something was causing the surface of the black liquid to quiver. The sight of it brought his mind back to the hidden beach, the inexorably rising tide and the memory of watching his friend drown.

Writing the official report of what had happened in the caves had been much more difficult than he had expected. He had written hundreds of such reports in his career as a detective and had always managed to remain precise, clear and coolly objective. But this time was different. His emotions had taken over and the effort required to keep himself focussed was exhausting. His account of what had happened, up to the point of reaching the hidden chamber, had been straightforward enough, but the rest had been clouded by the image of the rope snapping and of Michael sinking under the water. He stopped writing when he reached the moment of truth. He knew what he was going to write, but needed time to compose himself. He wondered if he stared at the mug of black coffee for long enough would dissolve into the air, along with the room, the report and the table, and that he'd wake up from the nightmare and there would be no collapsing caves, no monstrous unrelenting ocean, and no lost friend.

He sighed and squeezed his eye. "Snap out of it," he said to the empty room, "there were things to be done."

Finishing the report was just one of them. Once that was done, he would have to speak to Michael's brother, the Prior. Then there was Megan and the matter of the drugs investigation. From what Paul had managed to tell him in the car back to town, the investigation had taken a decisive turn and the authorities were now ready to pounce on a major international gang with connections to Central America, Eastern Europe and the Middle East. Megan was the key. She was willing to talk, but had insisted that she would only talk to Horse. Megan wanted to be put into what she called "one of those witness protection programs I seen on de TV, wi' a new name, a new face and a big house o' me own, somewhere in California, or somewhere like dat." Megan didn't have a criminal record and, because the American's seemed to have taken charge of the investigation, Horse thought that some kind of arrangement for her was likely.

Horse looked at the pen. He had resolved to lie for Michael, to protect those Michael loved. What Horse had witnessed in the flooded chamber he would take to his grave. No one needed to know what really happened. Horse was sure that Marie had not seen the knife. If she had, he was sure she would have said something to him. Only he knew that Michael had purposely cut the rope and, because he knew Michael, he knew why he'd done it. Had Michael not cut the link between them, both he and Marie would have died down there too. The water was rising incredibly quickly. Had Michael not cut the rope Marie, Paddy, Megan and Horse would never have made it out in time. Michael had sacrificed himself, knowing that by doing so they would have some chance of escape.

Horse reached for the pen and finished the report. Then he downed the cold coffee in one large mouthful and reread what he'd written.

The rope snapped and Michael Eustace was gone. The rope must have become frayed. The undercurrent was incredibly strong. The roped snapped and Michael was dragged under and then he was gone. Myself and Marie Joyce watched him go under. He never resurfaced. There was nothing either of us could do. Michael Eustace drowned in the caves and his body was not recovered.

When Horse was satisfied he signed and dated the report, then stood up. He walked over to the French doors and stared out into the garden as dusk began its slow approach. It looked like it was going to be a quiet evening on Skellig Éin.

Chapter 51.

Horse returned to the desk, reread the report one last time, then pushed the pages to one side and carefully screwed the top back onto his gold fountain pen. It was a very expensive pen and had been a present from his father for his eighteenth birthday. It was a family heirloom, one of the many family heirlooms Horse had received over the years, but the only one that he'd kept. He looked at it before slipping it into the inside pocket of his jacket. It felt comforting pressed against his heart. The fountain pen reminded him of the first time he'd met Michael. Michael had admired it and had recognised its value immediately.

Horse thought of Marie. He wondered if he'd see her again or if he should ask her out on a date. He could hear voices in the corridor outside and wondered if one of them was hers. There was a rap on the door. Before he had time to say anything or look up, it opened. He hoped it was Marie, changed into a blouse and skirt and looking more beautiful than ever. It wasn't her.

It was the tall black American who had interviewed him as soon as he'd got back to the hotel, who had introduced himself as Theodore Brooks and said he worked for the government of the United States of America. He hadn't stayed long and seemed satisfied with Horse's account. He'd ended the short interview with a small smile and a curt nod of his bald head. Horse suspected that Brooks had only been interested in the letter, and as soon as Horse made clear that he knew nothing about it, the interview was over, almost before it had begun.

Now Theodore Brooks was back, and he looked angry. He heeled the door shut behind him, walked over to the table and sat down. He put down a thick Manila folder which he turned to face the chair opposite.

"Sit down Inspector Hopkins. It seems we are not finished yet," he said.

"Oh?" said Horse.

Horse stayed standing.

"It seems that you have been holding back on me, Detective Inspector Hopkins."

"I beg your pardon?"

"You need to tell me about your friend Michael Eustace, and how he may be implicated in all this?"

Brooks fingered the cover of the file in front of him.

Horse walked over and sat down opposite him.

"Michael? Implicated? What are you talking about? Michael's not implicated in any of this. What in God's name are you talking about? If it wasn't for Michael I wouldn't be here talking to you. Implicated? What are you talking about?" said Horse.

"I'm talking about the fact that Michael Eustace has a criminal record and has a past so shady that even I have restricted access to parts of it. I thought I made myself quite clear, when we spoke earlier. The individual we are seeking, the owner of the fingerprint on that letter, is at the very top of the "Most Wanted" list of international criminals and when I said *tell me everything*, regardless of how seemingly insignificant, I meant *everything*. I assumed Inspector Hopkins that you, of all people, were smart enough to know that that included the fact that one of your caving party, someone you have confided in and whom you regarded as a close friend, had such a colourful background."

"I don't know what you're talking about?"

Horse looked down at the folder on the table. It was about two inches thick.

"Are you telling me you didn't know any of this? Michael was your friend and yet you want me to believe that he never mentioned any of this, or that you didn't do some background checking of your own? You knew nothing about his time in the army, or his time in Africa? He never discussed his wild teenager years or the fact that he almost battered another teenager to death in the school yard when he was fifteen? And then there are the questions of the relationship with his father, who, by the way, was a decorated policeman like yourself. Rumour has it that Michael Eustace brought on the heart attack that led to his father's untimely death. And that, Inspector Hopkins, is only the tip of the iceberg."

Theodore Brooks slid the folder closer to Horse.

"Maybe I should let you get reacquainted with your friend. I'll be back in fifteen minutes and we'll talk some more once your memory has cleared. I'd cancel any plans you have for this evening. I have a feeling you'll be here for a while."

"I need to talk to Michael's brother," said Horse.

"Don't worry about that. Your colleague Paul Creagan has contacted the Prior. He's on the way over. Fifteen minutes Inspector Hopkins. Then I'll be back. Then we will talk."

*

The first part of the report was a collection papers, stapled together and headed: North Western Africa, 1998. Clipped to the front was a photograph of a small group of soldiers standing together in a jungle clearing. On the reverse of the photograph there was one word, *nGangoot*. Six men dressed in light camouflage khaki with soft matching caps. None of them wore army insignia of any kind. They reminded Horse of a group of Airsoft enthusiasts, office workers who spend their weekends playing war games with fake guns and fake bullets. But Horse knew, by the way the men were standing and the look on their faces, that these were real soldiers with real guns and real bullets. They leered at the camera. The eyes that Horse could see, those not shaded by the peak of their caps or black face paint, were hollow and cold. The soldiers held their guns like trophies. Behind them a dense jungle loomed. Horse could almost hear the noisy chatter of wildlife in the trees beyond.

Horse recognised one of the soldiers. It was a young Michael Eustace. He stood apart from the other men and closer to the camera. His elbow rested on the lower branch of an old tree. At some point in the past the top surface of the thick branch had been worn flat and polished to form a shelf. It was an altar and on it had been placed a collection of two-inch high grotesque figurines, made of twisted wire, vines and coloured beads. The wire-dolls had big heads and skinny bodies. Their green eyes seemed to be staring up at Michael.

Horse began to read.

The first section was a potted history of a remote region of north-western Africa and ended with a page and a half on what was referred to as the Massacre at nGangoot. The report concluded that the massacre was a pivotal moment in the struggle for control of the region and ultimately led to the anti-government faction gaining the upper hand. When the isolated jungle village of nGangoot was razed to the ground and its, nearly two hundred, inhabitants slaughtered, (men, women and children) the rebels claimed that the massacre had been the work of a group of foreign mercenaries on the orders of corrupt local officials, facilitated by the USA and the United Kingdom.

The regional government also blamed the massacre on foreign insurgents, but denied any involvement in the killings, portraying it as a cynical ploy by the anti-government side to besmirch the good name of the army. As a sign of its bona fides the government offered a substantial financial reward for any information leading to the capture of the mercenary group, promising that they would pay for the heinous crimes perpetrated against the whole of the African continent. UN observers were unable to verify any of the facts but pointed out that the destruction of the village conveniently removed a major obstacle threatening the proposed route of a multi-million-dollar natural gas pipeline part-funded by a Russian oligarch and an American business consortium. The ancient village of nGangoot sat at a pinch-point along the proposed route of the pipeline. With the entire population of the village wiped out, the bull-dozers were free to continue as planned.

The massacre garnered international condemnation but was soon forgotten, as the international news cycle moved on to other matters closer to home.

At the top of the last page was a second photograph. Horse studied it. This one was in black and white and showed, in the foreground, three piles of what could have been the charred remains of human bodies, although they could have been three piles of burnt rubbish. It was impossible to say. In the background was the remains of the village, and behind that, the jungle. At the edge of the frame was the alter tree from the earlier photograph, the one that Michael had been leaning against, but the votive figures were no longer there. Horse studied the ground beneath the flat branch but could not tell if there were any figurines lying there. He flicked back to the first photograph. There was no doubt that the location was same in both photographs. Michael and his cohort of soldiers had been photographed standing at the outskirts of nGangoot, and at some time before the massacre occurred.

Horse began to look through the other sections of the file on Michael Eustace. He was no more than a page in, which dealt with Michael's time in the British Royal Marines, when the door opened and Theodore Brooks re-entered. This time he left the door wide open and Brian could see two people standing in the hallway outside. Father Francis was talking to Marie and she was smiling up at him. Horse noticed that she had changed into a blouse and skirt, as he'd imagined she would, and it pleased him greatly to see her. The knee-high cowboy boots were a surprise.

Brooks walked over, closed the file in front of Horse and lifted it off the table.

"It seems, Inspector Hopkins, you can go. There's been some sort of mix up. Thank you for your co-operation. You may go now."

"What?" said Horse. He stood up and stared at Brooks.

"I trust you understand that whatever you read in this is classified information," said Brooks.

"What? What do you mean mix up? What sort of mix up?"

"It appears that your friend is...as you suggested, not involved. I'm sorry for your loss."

It was cold and calculated and made Horse angry.

"What, the fuck?" said Horse.

Brooks turned and went to leave. At the door, he stopped and looked back.

"Whatever you read is classified. You are not to divulge what you read or saw to anyone. Do I make myself clear Inspector Hopkins?"

"I don't remember signing the US Official Secrets Act," said Horse.

Brooks stopped and closed the door. Horse faced down the American. When Brooks spoke again his tone was conciliatory.

"From one law enforcement officer to another, I am asking you Detective Inspector Hopkins, to keep whatever you saw in that file to yourself. It is a matter of the utmost importance that it remains confidential. We have all been compromised. I admit I made a mistake showing it to you. I apologise for being curt. We are on the same side, Detective Inspector Hopkins."

"Are we? I might have to think about that Agent Brooks."

"And the file?"

"I didn't get a chance to read any of it. And if I had I don't suppose there was anyone in it that I recognised. No one that I know."

"Thank you. I am truly sorry for the loss of your friend," said Brooks. He left, taking the folder with him.

Horse tried to compose himself. The door opened again. This time it was Father Francis. Marie was with him. The Prior looked crestfallen.

"Father Francis. I was hoping to speak with you before...about Michael but... I got stuck here with all this paperwork...I am so sorry."

"Marie told me everything Brian. It is sad sad news. For all of us. Are *you* alright, Brian?"

"Me?"

"Michael was your friend. I know that. He valued your friendship more than he'd ever have told you, and I know you valued his."

"I'm fine Father. We hadn't seen each other for a few years. If I'm honest, Father, I'm not sure I knew the real Michael," he said.

The Prior's face became stern.

"I can assure you, Brian, all your instincts about my brother were correct, no matter what anyone else says. You knew the real Michael, Brian. In fact, other than myself, I'd say you knew Michael better than anybody."

Chapter 52.

In a nightmare Michael saw the moment of his own death.

He lay, like a corpse, on a door-sized wooden raft floating in the middle of a vast, empty and turbulent ocean. He couldn't move or scream, but could feel the roll of the sea under him and hear the surf breaking all around. Icy water raced across the boards and wet his legs and bottom, and the back of his head.

His eyes were open and he stared up at a dark silvery starless sky. There were long flashes of lightening, but no rain.

The air was surprisingly dry.

When the lightening flashed, the sky became a mirror and Michael could see himself on the raft, a tiny lonely thing in the vastness of the dark angry ocean.

He could see other things too.

There were shapes in the water around the raft. Hundreds of enormous black creatures moving just beneath the surface, monstrous eels, coiling and uncoiling, slippery and excited. They began to circle the raft, forming a ring of oily blackness in the flashing sky above. A hollow formed in the centre and Michael felt himself sinking. Deeper and deeper he dropped into the swirling well as the shadows of the beasts rose around him. Finally, the wall of water collapsed in a thunderous roar and the raft, with Michael still clinging to it, sank under the maelstrom of writhing black bodies and was gone.

It was only a nightmare. Soon he would wake up.

*

Michael didn't open his eyes, so much as focus them. His mind went from unconscious to conscious in the blink of an eye, except that, he was sure he hadn't blinked. A camera-flash of yellow light had suddenly illuminated something that had been in complete darkness and what was revealed was so frightening that his first instinct was to close his eyes and pretend it wasn't there, but no matter how hard he tried, Michael couldn't make his eyelids do what he wanted. He couldn't will himself to close his eyes, nor could he work the muscles of his face to make it happen. All he could do was watch, with unblinking eyes.

It must be another nightmare. It had to be, and the silence was proof of it. There was absolute silence therefore, Michael contended, it must be a nightmare. Nightmares and dreams exist in silent places, sound only added afterwards, in recollection or retelling.

It must be another nightmare and yet, it seemed so real.

He was aware of something indistinct but familiar in the foreground, a blurred unmoving outline, no more than a foot from his face. Despite his best efforts he couldn't turn his eyes toward it, nor could he make sense of what it was. It was as if his head was held in a tight vice and his eyes had been super-glued into their sockets. All he could do was look straight ahead, at what was happening in the yellowy orange atmosphere twenty feet in front of him.

A man lay on his side on the ground. He was almost naked, his bare back turned toward Michael. Although Michael couldn't see the man's face he knew that it was Denis, the leader of the rescue party and Denis was being eaten by a giant black monster that towered over him. It brought to Michael's mind the vision of an eagle tearing apart the body of a tiny mouse.

What was left of Denis's clothes were shredded and blood stained and the flesh of his back was ripped and punctured. Part of his spinal column was visible and there was a hole in the back of his head the size of a fist, exposing a portion of his brain.

One of the Denis's arms was in the air, stretched out as if he was trying to grab at something, or waving at someone in the distance. The arm, like the rest of him, seemed frozen solid. He looked like he was made of plastic or wood, a life-like life-sized, deformed statue of himself, that had toppled over onto its side. Bits of Denis were missing. The lower half of his left leg was gone, as was his right buttock and two of the fingers from his out-stretched hand. Strings of bloody gristle and strips of skin trailed along the ground, where his flesh had been torn off.

Despite the terrible injuries, in Michael's new nightmare Denis was still alive. Blood still pumped through his heart and his tattered skin still pulsed with the living colours that only Michael could see. And the colours never lied. They were proof of identity and proof of life. Michael was reminded of the body in the woods.

The nightmare continued. The monster ignored Michael and continued to feed. There was very little blood. Michael considered how it was possible and conceded that either coagulation had happened at an incredible rate or the wounds had been cauterized in some way, soon after being inflicted.

The creature held Denis's supine body with the tip of a bony four fingered claw, which extended from the end of one of its massive black wings, and it picked at his innards with a white globular worm-like tongue. The tongue darted in and out of the creature's pointed beak which was packed, top and bottom, with rows of sharp serrated teeth.

As Michael watched, four more monsters arrived to join in the feast, their wings flapping silently as they landed unsteadily on strange bird-like legs. All of them were the same size as the one attacking Denis and were bigger than any animal or mammal Michael had ever seen. They looked like some sort of dinosaur, in some ways not unlike a pterodactyl, in others not at all. Besides having black wings and a pointy beak there were too many differences to suggest that the monsters in front of him were even long distant cousins of that prehistoric dinosaur. These creatures were not giant birds. They were part-fish, part-winged serpent and were the strangest, most terrifying thing Michael had ever set eyes on.

Except for their milky white eyes, the creatures were completely black. The eyes were triangular, and protruded from either side of a bulbous puffer-fish-like head. They had no discernible pupils and Michael wondered if the creatures were blind, which could explain why none of them seemed to be paying him any attention. They had scaly skin, which was shiny bluebottle-black, and their gigantic wings were see-through and looked like soot covered cobwebs. The tip of the wings ended in a four-fingered claw, each finger made up of a series of ever diminishing hooks, like rows of polished black rose thorns.

One of the monsters landed on the ground in front of Michael and yawned. From out of its gaping gullet emerged a long translucent milk-coloured tongue. To Michael it looked like a transparent caterpillar and it seemed to have a mind of its own. Its hollow tip seemed to sniff the air and then turn in Michaels direction, swaying in front of him for a little while before retracting back down the monster's throat. The monster lowered its head and huffed through two funnel-shaped nostrils like an angry horse.

One of the four newcomers lay down on the ground and fully retracted its massive wings to the side of its body. In a moment they were gone. Then the creature tucked its legs in under itself and they too vanished into the feathery folds of its undercarriage Suddenly the creature was transformed into an enormous snake. It was only when this happened that Michael first focussed on the creatures tail. In both forms, bird and snake, the creature held its tail in the air. When standing upright, the tail hovered just behind and above the beast's head, like the stinger of a scorpion. When in the form of a snake, the tail was held up like a rattle. It had a clubbed end, like a black medicine ball, which was covered in sharp barbs, exactly like the ebony coloured thorns that made up the creature's fingers. Michael noticed that one of these barbs was sticking out of Denis's neck. The monster feeding on Denis waved its tail erratically as a warning to the other four to stay back.

The snake monster between Michael and Denis opened its jaw impossibly wide and bellowed silently at the feeding beast, before turning around and slithering slowly in Michael direction. Michael tried to will himself to wake up, but couldn't. The snake monster kept coming. Michael tried not to look at it but it was impossible to look away, so he tried to think of what he'd been doing before the visions had started as a way of understanding what was going on.He remembered being in the cave with Marie and of a terrible pounding in his head. He remembered taking tablets. He couldn't remember how many, but was sure he'd taken more than he should. In the past his yellow pain relievers had caused him mild hallucinations, but never anything like this. He remembered that the pounding in his head had been unbearable.

Had he collapsed? he wondered. Had he fallen into a coma? Could that be it, he wondered? Was he in a coma? Is this what's it was like to be trapped in your own body, paralysed and hallucinating? It made perfect sense.

Maybe he was in hospital or still in the caves, lying on the floor with Marie fretting over him. He tried to focus on her beautiful face. He tried to hear her voice.

The image in front of him didn't change. The deadly silence continued. More monsters arrived. The snake-like creature came close to him but turned away at the very last moment.

Another memory came to him. He remembered thinking he was drowning, being pulled under water, not being able to breath, not being able to move, feeling his life slipping away. He remembered falling into darkness. Falling... falling and then...this.

In front of him the monster continued to feed on Denis and the air darkened as more of the horrible beasts arrived from the sky.

Three things happened suddenly and almost simultaneously to prove that what Michael was experiencing was no nightmare, no hallucination.

Firstly, feeling returned to his body.

It started with pins and needles in his legs, but the sensation quickly spread and intensified. Michael thought he had been electrocuted. Piercing cramps punched every muscle in his body. The spasms of pain caused him to twitch violently and then his legs gave out beneath him.

That was the second thing. Suddenly, he could move. He went from rigid to flexible in less time than it would take to swallow.

As soon as feeling and movement returned, he crumpled forward onto the ground. His right leg felt as if it was on fire. The unknown object that had evaded identification earlier, when his eyes were locked on the middle distance, turned out to be his own raised arm and outstretched hand. Once movement returned the arm flicked backwards and he slapped himself hard in the face.

Michael heard himself yelp, but only barely.

That was the third thing that indicated that this was not a dream or an hallucination.

Sound had returned and it was deafening.

into the folds of its scaly undercarriage All of the monsters were screeching.

The noise was so loud Michael thought his ear drums might burst. He wanted to curl up and cover his eyes and ears but the marshy ground was brittle and sticky and it stank of vomit and fish. The stench of rot was so bad that it made Michael cough and gag. As soon as he did so, the creatures nearest him stopped screaming.

Michael raised his head.

The monster feeding on Denis had stopped what it was doing and had turned its head in his general direction. The other monsters were looking straight at him.

Michael tried to hold his breath and hold back the urge to gag..

The snake-creature that, moments earlier, had turned away turned around and began to slither back toward him. Michael thought of getting to his feet and running for it, but he knew that it was no good. The monsters were too close, too big and there were too many of them. He wouldn't stand a chance.

The snake beast stopped four foot in front of him and raised its trumpet-like snout. It sniffed the air, then slowly opened its long beak, revealing a waiting, hungry tongue. At the same time its barbed tail began to rise and roll forward toward Michael.

Tongue and tail moved lazily, as if both had been woken from the same deep sleep. White sticky ooze leaked from an opening at the tip of the tongue, as it moved out beyond the beast's snout, thinning, stretching and dribbling as it approached Michaels prostrate form.

Michael tried to stand, but a piercing pain in his right ankle caused him to topple back to the ground. The pain was so bad that putting the slightest pressure on his right foot caused him agony. Somehow he resisted the urge to scream, knowing that to do so would attract the attention of other monsters and quickly seal his fate.

In a final desperate effort to get away, Michael shuffled on his backside, using his arms to drag himself backwards, to put as much distance between himself and the creatures, as quickly as he could. He hadn't gone ten feet when he backed into something solid. When he found the courage to turn around, he found that he was stopped against base of a cliff wall that rose upwards and in both directions, left and right, as far as he could see.

He was trapped, with no hope of escape.

He tried to close his eyes, but he couldn't, and this time it had nothing to do with his eyelids or the muscles of his face. He was transfixed by the horrors in front of him.

More and more of the giant black creature arrived from out of the mist and the ground shook as each one landed. The snake-like monster moved closer, its barbed tail hovering above its head, its tongue fully extended and searching.

Tail and tongue, poised to strike.

Terror or curiosity prevented Michael from screaming.

He knew this was the end of the nightmare and that he would either wake up or die.

Chapter 53.

When Hanna stepped between Michael and the monster she looked like an angel from a Renaissance painting. She shone. Her entire body was luminous. Michael tried to speak but he couldn't. All he could do was gape at her. The snake-creature drew back its head. Its barbed tail quivered but didn't strike. The white tongue retracted a little. The other creatures nearby hesitated too. Hanna raised her right arm. In her hand she held a compact camera. She pointed it at the nearest monster and calmly said, "Say cheese!" She pressed down on the shutter button and there was a flash of intense white light.

The reaction was immediate, the result staggering. The space exploded in terrible screaming as the monsters reacted to the light. The nearest creature almost fell backwards when the flash went off. It was as if it had been struck by a giant wrecking ball. The other monsters toppled back too. Those in flight dropped to the ground and cowered behind raised wings or the bodies of other beasts. Those in snake-like form did a one hundred and eighty-degree U-turn and headed back the way they'd come. Hanna waited a moment and then pressed the shutter again. The resulting noise was deafening. The second flash caused those that had not already done so to turn and flee. By the time Michael's eyes had readjusted from the glare of the flash, all the monsters were gone. Denis was gone too. It was as if the monsters had been vaporised into the yellow mist.

An eerie silence returned.

Michael could hear his own heartbeat. It pounded in his ears and made his wounded leg throb.

"What's happening?" he said, as much to himself as to Hanna. Hanna turned and looked at him.

"Can you hear me?" she said. Her voice was hollow and distant.

"Just about," he said.

His own voice sounded like it was coming out of an old radio.

"Can you move? We have to get off the ledge. They'll be back. If not them, then others. We need to move."

"What's happening?" said Michael.

"We need to move. Can you stand?"

"My leg, it's...I don't know...I think it's broken."

Hanna knelt in front of him. Every now and then she looked over her shoulder. He noticed she was in her underwear. Every bit of her was covered in an oily green luminous substance. It dripped from her shoulder length hair and from the tips of her long eyelashes. Only her eyeballs had been spared.

In the subdued yellowy light Hanna looked like a flame from a candle.

"Can you stand?" she said.

"I think so."

"Come on. You can lean on me. We have to get out of here, before they come back."

Michael used the cliff wall as support and raised himself up, putting all his weight onto his good leg, then leaned forward and fell into Hanna's outstretched arms. She was much shorter than him, so he had to crouch. She tucked herself under his left arm and pulled him away from the wall. The green substance from her body stained his jacket and when she held his hand the slippery slime got between his fingers. It was icy cold and it made his skin tingle.

She dragged him out into the mist. It was slow going. Hanna tugged and heaved, Michael hopped and winced. She was surprisingly strong. The marshy floor was soft but solid. At one point Hanna stopped, leaned forward and picked something up off the ground. Michael recognised it and another memory came back to him. It was a knife, the one he'd taken from the young woman on the beach, the same one he had used to cut the rope that had been his life-line to Horse and Marie.

"Am I...are we...dead?" he said.

Hanna looked up at him.

"We're not dead. Do you feel dead?" she said.

The pain in his leg answered for him.

He winched.

"No."

Hanna slipped the knife into one of his pockets and then continued on. She still held the camera, its strap secured around her slender wrist, her finger poised above the shutter button.

"It's not far. We're nearly there," she said.

After moving out for fifty yards, Hanna stopped. They had reached a cliff edge, beyond which was a dark abys. Michael shivered. He had no desire to go any closer or to look over the edge. Hanna steered him to the left and they continued along the cliff top until they came to the exposed roots of a large felled tree. The roots rose four feet from the soft ground in a tangle of dead wood. From a distance, it looked like a thick twisted bramble bush. When they got close to it, Michael saw that the felled tree and it's torn-out roots concealed a small hole in the ground, just large enough, he thought, for a person to climb into.

"We need to get in there. There's a bit of a drop. No more than four feet down. I'll go first and then you follow me. Don't dilly dally. Okay? I will help you once you are in. We'll be safe in there. Don't hesitate. Okay?" she said.

With a nod and a smile, Hanna let go of him, then dropped down onto all fours. Michael suddenly felt exposed, so he flopped down beside her.

"Feet first. Once you are over the hole, just push yourself in. Feet first, be quick okay? I'll be waiting."

With another nod, she shuffled backwards and was gone.

From somewhere beyond the cliff edge, a monster screamed.

They were coming back, Michael thought.

He turned onto his belly and scuttled backwards, ignoring the pain of his damaged leg, and followed Hanna down the hole.

He landed on his good leg and Hanna caught him before he put weight on the other.

"Good. Now we need to crawl. Follow behind me," she said.

He smiled and said "Thank you Hanna."

"Do you have a torch in any of those pockets," she said.

"Actually, I probably have a few."

"Good. Mine is nearly dead. Come on then. We need to get away from here. If they come back and hear us they might try to get in, or dig us out. We can crawl," she said.

Michael passed her a torch. She turned it on and pointed it at him.

"Do I know you? You look familiar," she said.

"I don't think we've ever met," he said throwing his arms up to shield his eyes from the light. His leg still hurt like hell and the pain was distracting. He lowered his head.

"You called me Hanna. How did you know who I am?"

"Oh that? Your mother asked me to find you. Your mother and I are old friends. I came here to find you, Hanna," he said.

"You've come to rescue me?" she said.

Michael noted the sarcasm in her voice. He ignored it.

"I usually do the finding, others do the rescuing."

"Well you've found me. When does the rescue party arrive, or was that it out there, been eating by one of the monsters?"

Hanna lowered the torch.

"Who did you say you were?" she said.

"Michael Eustace," he said.

"You definitely look familiar. Are you sure we haven't met?"

"I get mistaken for my brother all the time...and he for me. We're identical twins."

"How would I know *him*?"

"He's the parish priest on the island, the Prior of the monastery?"

Hanna thought for a minute.

"Yes. That must be it. Mum's gone all *Holy Mary* lately. I must have seen her talking to him after Mass once."

Michael was impressed by the Hanna's tough talking, but was sure he could sense fear behind the bravado.

"We need to get going, come on," she said. "Follow me. It's not far. Watch the floor. The rocks are sharp."

"Where are we going," he said.

"Somewhere away from them. Somewhere safer than here," she said.

Chapter 54.

Hanna and Michael crawled down a meandering rock burrow for about five minutes. The tunnel ended at the floor level of a small cavern where they could finally stand up. Hanna helped Michael to his feet. The floor of the chamber was level and dusty and the jagged ceiling, high above them, was covered in stubby ancient stalactites. The space was the size of a squash court and, in the torchlight, Michael could see two other exits from it, both on the opposite wall. One was tall and narrow, the same height as the chamber, the second looked like a low arched doorway. Whilst the room was bone dry, Michael could hear the sound of dripping water.

In the centre of the room there were the remains of a camp fire. Beside this was a makeshift bed, consisting of a single blanket and a haversack turned on its side for a pillow. Against one of the side walls was a pile of small fish laid out on a flat stone. The fish were the same luminous green colour as the paint that covered Hanna's body. Otherwise the chamber was empty.

"Well, Michael Eustace, welcome to my home, which will be your home for the duration of your stay in Monster World," said Hanna with a forced smile. Michael removed his haversack and dropped it to the floor with a sigh.

"You'd better take off your wet clothes. I'll light the fire. It will give us some heat and save on torch battery. Wait here. I'll be back in a couple of minutes," she said.

"I'm not going anywhere. Where would I go?" he said.

"Right," she said.

Hanna headed for the arched doorway. She brought the torch and its light with her and was soon out of sight. Michael stood looking after her. She couldn't have gone far as the light was still visible and sufficient for him to see what he was doing. He found the jacket impossible to remove. Not only did the pain in his leg force him to sit down, but the rope that Horse had tied around his chest was so tightly knotted that the only way to get free would be to cut it off. Hanna had put the knife in one of his pockets but he couldn't be bothered to look for it. He was exhausted. He decided to remove his boots instead. They were soaking wet and twice as heavy as they should be. This turned out to be a bad idea. He couldn't bend forward enough to get his hands to the laces without the pain in his right leg causing his whole body to spasm in agony.

He gave up.

Hanna returned, cleaned of all the luminous paint, wearing jeans and a tee-shirt. Her fiery red hair stood out against her pale skin. She was carrying a pile of dried tree root. She dropped it onto the blackened circle on the floor and knelt down. In among the twisted stalks she shoved a ball of cloth that was heavily stained with the luminous green paint. Michael assumed she had used the cloth to clean herself. When she lit the fire the cloth burned quickly but the stalks took their time to get going. When they did, they crackled and spat and gave off a great deal of light and heat, but very little smoke. The sound of the fire was comforting.

Hanna hunkered down in front of Michael.

"You okay?" she said.

"Tired, cold and possibly in an ante room of Hell, and I think my ankle is broken, but other than that, just great, thanks for asking. How are you?" he said sarcastically.

She smiled.

"We don't want to lose you, before the rescue party gets here," she said.

"I'm tired and all tied up. Can you cut this rope? It's killing me. I can't even get my bloody boots off."

"Okay. Relax. I'll help you. Then you can sleep. I've got a good fire going. The water won't be back down for many hours. I'll take a look at your ankle. I have a first-aid kit in my bag."

"I have some pain killers in my pocket. I'll take one," said Michael.

"Have you any food?" said Hanna.

"I've pockets full of boiled sweets," he said.

"Expecting to crash a children's birthday party, were you?" she said.

"Ha," he said and smiled at her for the first time. In her faded tee shirt and jeans, Hanna reminded Michael of a young Primrose. He couldn't help staring at her.

"What?" she said.

"Nothing...it's just...you look so much like your mother, now that you're not green anymore...and have clothes on."

They laughed.

The release of tension was good.

Hanna cut the rope around his chest and helped him out of his wet clothes, then she wrapped him in her bed blanket until he stopped shivering. Removing his trousers had been the worst part. She wanted to cut the material but he wouldn't let her. They were the only pair he had with him. Together they assessed the damage to his right leg. The wound above the ankle looked very bad. There was a black puncture hole with a white centre of boiling puss. Around this, the skin was grey and dry. It looked like charred timber. It reminded Michael of the wound he'd seen on the back of Denis's neck.

"You are very lucky. The dart must have fallen out or not broken off the creature's tail," she said.

"I don't feel lucky. You can't imagine the pain. I've never felt anything like it. It's almost beyond pain and it's not just in my leg either. It's in my blood, like acid pumping around my body, and my skin feels like it's on fire."

Michael rummaged in the pocket of his discarded jacket for his pills. How long had it been since he'd taken one, he wondered? He couldn't remember. He knew it was dangerous to take too many, but didn't care. He needed relief, something, *anything*, to take away the pain.

"Wait," said Hanna, "I have a better way."

She rose and went over to the flat rock containing the pile of luminous fish. She returned with one of them.

"Dinner can wait," she said.

"What are you going to do?" Michael asked.

"This stuff seems to have magical properties, when it comes to the demon venom. I'll show you," said Hanna.

Making sure both of her palms were fully coated with the luminous slime from the fish's body Hanna began to caress Michael's wound. He flinched at first, but then welcomed the icy touch. The tingling sensation he'd felt earlier, when his fingers were stained by the luminous paint, was now much more intense. It seemed to be competing with the pain for his attention. Michael couldn't concentrate on both sensations at the same time, so he focussed on the cold. Was he imagining it, he wondered, or was the pain receding? He relaxed and lay back against Hanna's haversack. Not long afterwards he fell into a long, deep and dreamless sleep.

*

Michael woke needing to pee. The fire was down to collapsing embers and the chamber was cold and full of dark spaces. It took a moment for him to remember where he was. Hanna lay beside him, sleeping. Her face was close to his and her breathing was steady and quiet. Her breath was warm and smelt of aniseed and lemon. Her right arm was draped across his chest. He didn't want to move or wake her, but his bladder insisted that he get up.

Carefully he lifted her arm and rolled his body away from her. She grumbled, but didn't wake up. Michael covered her with the blanket and then looked around. Everything was in shadow. He noticed a strange A-frame structure on the other side of the fire. It looked like a small tent but was in fact a make-shift clothes horse. It was constructed from the stripped branches of a gnarled unrecognisable tree. Michael's clothes hung from it. He stood up as quietly as he could. He had taken several steps toward the clothes horse before he noticed that the pain in his ankle was completely gone. When he moved about he noticed that he had no pain anywhere in his body and, in fact, felt better than he had done in years.

For the first time since his late teens, Michael felt healthy.

His clothes were dry, which made him wonder how long he had been sleeping. He dressed in silence. Even his boots, which had been tilted upright against two small stones close to the edge of the fire, were surprisingly dry. They had been stuffed with old bits of cloth which had soaked up all the wetness inside. The laces had been removed. He found them hanging next to his hi-viz jacket on the a-frame. He took his time tying up his boots and then, in the small beam of light from a pencil torch he found in one of the pockets, he moved quietly toward the doorway and the sound of the dripping water. He kept the light to the floor and avoided pointing it in Hanna's direction.

Once through the doorway he raised the torch.

He was in a square room, half the size of the main chamber, but with a much lower ceiling. There was no other entrance or exit, apart from a three-inch gap running along the length of the rear wall at floor level, just big enough for a crouching mouse to fit under. In one corner of the room there was a bath-sized pool of crystal clear water recessed into the floor. It looked quite deep. Water dripped from the ceiling into the pool and any overflow disappeared through the gap at the bottom of the wall. In the opposite corner was a small hollow that Hanna used as a toilet. It too was fed from above and drained under the wall. To one side of the entrance Michael saw a large pile of the dry seaweed and a small pile of torn clothes.

When he returned to the chamber Hanna was awake.

"I see you found the bathroom," she said.

"I see you found the boiled sweets," he said.

He added some seaweed to the dying embers of the fire.

"I didn't take many," she said.

"They were for you. A house-warming present," he said.

"Thanks. They were wonderful. They taste of home. If we ever make it out of here, I'll always keep a bag with me."

"*When* we make it out of here. Despite your wonderful home and hospitality, I have no intention of staying here any longer than I have to, and I'm taking you with me, Hanna Brennan."

"That may be easier said than done, Michael Eustace. After breakfast I'll show you where we are. Then you may not be so sure of yourself," she retorted.

"Well, I got this far didn't I, and I suddenly feel like I could do anything? I have no idea what you did, but my ankle is one hundred per cent better. No, make that one hundred and fifty per cent. I feel great."

"Magic hands or magic fish," she said, "which reminds me, it's time for breakfast. Hope you like fillet of luminous fish."

"Do I have a choice?" he said.

"Eh...no!"

Chapter 55.

Paul met Horse in the hotel lobby and, with a gentle hand on his back, directed the English detective towards the quiet sitting room they had used before. Once again the room was empty, so they settled into the same two armchairs at the window. Paul watched Horse for a while before saying anything.

"What a bloody awful mess," he finally said.

"That's for sure," said Horse.

He didn't look at Paul. Instead he looked out the window. The evening had turned to night. Pools of yellow light illuminated the front of the hotel and portions of the lawn. A taxi pulled up outside the window.

Everything seemed to move in slow motion.

"I shouldn't have brought that damned letter to the Americans. It was stupid of me. I don't know what I was thinking," said Paul, almost absent-mindedly.

Horse said nothing. He was still smarting from a conversation he'd just had with Chief Superintendent Sutton. They were off the case. Superintendent Sutton was now in charge and had made it quite clear that Hopkins and Creagan were no longer part of the team. Suttons words still rang in his ears.

"This has gone far enough and the Garda Commissioner agrees with me. We're taking down Mr G and he's going tell me where we can find that other cunt the Americans want so bad, if I have to beat it out of the little fucker myself. You and your boyfriend are off the case and when the dust settles I'd say Creagan will be looking for another career. As for you, New Scotland Yard is expecting you back tomorrow. You'll be leaving us in the morning Detective Inspector Hopkins."

Horse had tried to argue with Sutton that it might be wiser to *hold fire* for a little, to see where the dust settled. Mr G wasn't a fool and if the man the Americans were after, heard about a raid on Mr G's place, he'd most likely go underground and never be found.

"Showing our hand early is a mistake," Horse had said to Sutton

"You're not listening to me, are you Mr Scotland Yard? I am not interested in your fuckin' opinion. You can fuck off back to wherever it is you came from and leave this to people who know what they're doing? I'm in charge now, do you understand? I don't want to see you or hear from either of you. Do I make myself clear, Inspector Hopkins?"

The taxi outside the window pulled away. Horse turned and smiled weakly at Paul. He thought about what Paul had just said. He wasn't in any position to be judgemental. After all, he'd gone off with the rescue party when he should have remained focussed on the investigation.

"I would probably have done the same thing," he lied.

Before Paul said anything, Horse said,

"None of this makes any sense, Paul. A sleazy conniving accountant, a small-time Dublin criminal and the CIA's most-wanted? I don't see the connection, do you? As for the drugs we found in the caves, a big haul for the News at Six, but hardly enough to merit all this top-brass attention, is it? No, there's something else going on here - something we're missing. After all, it was the American's who gave you the information about Gregory Kelleher, then Kelleher gives you this letter which connects Mr G to some international terrorist. All rather convenient, isn't it? And what about the body in the woods? How does that fit in to all this?"

Paul said nothing.

"What did the letter say anyway?" said Horse.

"To be honest, I only read it once. I remember thinking it was the work of a sycophant. The tone all sickly sweet and fawning."

"The work of a sycophant? Did you swallow a dictionary while I was away? You'll have me thinking you're the intellectual half of this partnership, Creagan."

Paul frowned and shook his head.

"You English. You still think you're smarter than us, don't you?"

"It was a joke, Paul," said Horse defensively. "I only do it to wind you up. It's not my fault you're so easily offended."

"Well, it wasn't funny."

"Sorry."

Paul now stared out the window. Horse did too. Another taxi arrived.

Horse's thoughts returned to the cave. The rescue effort had been both a success and a disaster. They had saved the lives of four people who would certainly have died, but four others were still missing, presumed dead, two of whom were rescuers. Four for four. Not much of a success, he concluded.

Horse shook his head dramatically.

"I'll be fucked, Paul, if I'm goin' leave this island without knowin' what, the fuck, is goin' on. Try to remember anything you can about the letter. It might give us a clue as to who this guy is, or where he is."

"I think it was definitely a man writing to a woman although the handwriting was feminine. My dearest Jay and all that. Spelt J...A...Y, by the way. Another thing was the letter was visually beautiful. I mean straight lines and precise equal margins on both sides. If it had been typed it would have been edge-justified, you know?"

"You what?"

"You know. Both the left-hand and the right-hand edges are dead straight," said Paul.

"I know what you mean. Sounds like someone with OCD."

"And good quality paper too. Not lined. Thick and woven. I remember thinking that a great deal of effort had gone into the way the letter looked. There was a slight smudge in the bottom right hand corner and the paper had been scrunched up then flattened out again before being put in the plastic sleeve. The handwriting was flowery. Like I said, it looked feminine, but the content suggested a man writing to a woman."

Paul paused for a moment.

"I suppose it could have been written by a woman. That was the very first thing that crossed my mind, when Kelleher handed it to me, that the letter was in a woman's hand."

"That's very interesting. First impressions are very important...unless that's what you were meant to think," said Horse.

"Are you riling me again?"

"No, not at all. It is very interesting. It could be significant"

"I could be wrong. Men can have flowery writing too."

"Yes they can. Did you mention this to anyone else? The American agent Brooks or Superintendent Sutton?"

"No."

"Good."

Horse considered the idea. It might be nothing, but then again, it was certainly curious. His mind wandered. He started to think about Marie.

Paul coughed and Horse looked over at him.

"Sorry. I was miles away," he said, "Anything else? You said sycophantic. In what way?"

Paul closed his eyes.

"It was being sent to Ashford in Surrey. The whole thing seemed badly written, grammatically incorrect, which was very much at odds with the way it looked. One or two of the lines were twisted so they sounded like they were written by Yoda from Star Wars. You know what I mean? Sentences starting with a verb?"

"Speaking you are, Master Paul, in this fashion?" said Horse doing his best Yoda impression. It wasn't very good.

"Exactly."

"I could never understand how the *supposedly* most intelligent creature in the universe couldn't speak English properly. Even you Irish can speak English quite well, Creagan."

"Anyway," continued Paul, "the way it was written, I wondered if it was some kind of code."

"I'm sure you know Paul, that the structure of the sentence in the Irish language is such that the sentence begins with the verb. Just like Yoda, actually. Do you think the letter was a Google Translate from one originally written in Irish Gaelic?"

Paul narrowed his eyes.

"Where did *that* come from? You don't speak Irish, do you, Horse?"

"I saw a programme on the TV about how the Irish language is unlike any other European language. Gaelic is the only language in Western Europe to start its sentences with a verb."

"You're definitely smarter than you look, Horse."

"So, what do you think? Could it have been a bad translation?" said Horse.

"I suppose it could've been, but I don't think so," said Paul.

Horse gave him a questioning look.

"I remember one reference that I found particularly odd. He, or she, referred to the Monster House, or something like that. Written with capital letters, you know. Maybe it's a nightclub or something."

"Huh. It could mean anything," said Horse.

"The Monster *Mansion*. That was it. Something happened to someone called P in the Monster Mansion," said Paul.

"The Monster Mansion? Are you sure it was the Monster Mansion, Paul?"

"Yes I'm positive. What does it mean?"

"And you said the letter was addressed to Ashford in England?"

"Ashford. Yeah."

"The Monster Mansion is the nickname for HM Wakefield, a high security prison in Yorkshire. It is the home of some of the most dangerous criminals in the UK. There's an entire wing for high-risk sex offenders. Monsters, all of them."

"Fuck," said Paul.

"I've sent a few to that particular establishment myself," said Horse.

The door behind them opened and a little blond girl popped her head in, just below the handle. After a quick look around the room she smiled the two policemen then looked straight at Horse. Before he had time to say "hello", she stuck out her tongue and made a loud raspberry noise, then she withdrew her head and slammed the door as loudly as she could. They could hear her running across the lobby screaming with glee.

"All Irish women are as mad as 'atters. It starts in the womb, Creagan" said Horse.

They both started to laugh. The door opened again. Horse turned and stuck out his tongue in anticipation of the little girls' return.

It was Marie.

"That's nice," she said.

Paul looked at her.

"Oh fuck," he said Paul and stood up. He rummaged in his pocket, retrieved his mobile and said, "bollocks."

"That's *very* nice," said Marie looking from Horse to Paul and back again.

"I was expecting...I thought you were someone else," stammered Horse. He stood up to greet her. They both looked down at Paul who was still cursing at his phone.

Paul raised his head.

"Sorry. It's Henry. He's still out there, and my phone battery is dead. Sorry Miss Joyce, I didn't mean to curse."

"Who's Henry?" said Horse.

"Henry? He's...eh...one of the students. He's waiting for me, at the Devil's Throat. I forgot about him. Shit. I better head out there and get him."

"Well I suppose you'd better," said Horse.

Horse looked at Marie. She was smiling. Horse had noticed she'd been smiling at him a lot since they'd returned from the caves. He liked it. He smiled back.

"Sorry. We're slightly out of sorts at the moment Miss Joy...I mean, Marie. I thought you were someone else," he said again. She looked beautiful. She had changed again. She now wore a pale green taffeta dress.

"Do you normally stick your tongue out at people? Is it an English thing?" she said.

His smile broadened.

"Only at people I like," he said.

He thought she reddened slightly, but it might have been his imagination.

"I came in to ask if you two wanted to get something to eat, but if you've got other plans it doesn't matter," she said.

"No. I'd love to...I mean we...we're very hungry aren't we Paul?" said Horse.

Marie looked at Paul wide-eyed.

"Paul seems to have his own plans," she said with a mischievous grin. Paul said nothing.

"I know," Marie said, "Why don't I come with you, to the Devil's Throat? I'm sure Henry probably needs feeding too. We'll all go get him, clear the place up and then we can come back here. A foursome, as it were. What do you think Detective Creagan? The Dancing Lotus is surprisingly good."

Horse noticed a strange look pass between Paul and Marie.

"Why not," said Paul hesitantly.

A *foursome*, thought Horse, what's she on about?

"So, or you up for it, Englishman?" said Marie.

"Sounds perfect," he said.

"Well, come on then. It's getting late. It'll be dark soon. If we're going, we should go now," said Marie.

Paul was already at the door.

"Am I missing something?" said Horse to her, as they made their way across the hotel lobby to the front door.

"You're the bloody detective. You work it out," she said.

"Bags the front," said Marie, before climbing into the front passenger seat of Paul's car. When Horse squeezed into the back behind Paul Marie turned around in her seat and gave him a cheeky grin. She reminded him of the little girl from the hotel lobby, so much so, that he half expected her to stick out her tongue and blow him a raspberry.

"I suppose I don't really have a choice, do I?" he said sullenly.

"No. Not really," she said.

He mumbled something under his breath.

"What was that?" said Paul Creagan from the driver's seat.

"Nothing Paul. Just the ramblings of an idiot. Nothing that you're not used to by now, eh?" said Brian.

"Can't argue with you there, Englishman," said Paul, with a wink to Marie.

Chapter 56.

Father Francis had one more call to make before going back to the monastery for evening prayers. He had been to see Primrose and had stayed with her for as long as he could. Once she started fussing about in the kitchen, he thought he would have to stay with her for the night. Primrose was distraught and he could see that she needed something to take her mind of the reality of what he had come to tell her. He wasn't sure if she was cooking or just moving pots about.

It pained him to see her like that. She had been the one to come out the worst in all of this, and in the cruellest way. Not only had she lost her daughter but, in her eyes, she had sent an old friend to his death. In addition, she would not have her daughter's body to bury or a place to leave flowers. Hundreds of tonnes of solid rock and an ocean of icy water had made sure of that. Hanna was more lost now than she had been before.

"I will always be here for you Primrose, you know that, don't you?" he'd said.

"Will you? How can you be so sure, Father Francis?"

"I just am," he said.

"Oh yes, of course. You are a man of *faith*. That's it, isn't it? You have your faith. Well, where is your God now, Father Francis? Where was *He*, when the caves took my child and your brother?"

She was angry and afraid. She clenched and unclenched her fists, twisting and turning the tea-towel in her hand.

"I believe they are together and that they are with Him. I believe Michael found Hanna. I know it in my heart. I pray for them every day and will do so until we meet again, all of us, in the presence of Jesus."

"I don't want your prayers. I don't want your Jesus. I want Hanna. He said he'd find her. I believed him. She was so young, so alive."

Father Francis held her gaze. He reached out for her hand but she pulled away from him.

"I'm sorry. I'm so sorry, Primrose. You know he did everything he could. You know that, and that Hanna is with him. They are together, watching over each other...watching over us."

When the doorbell rang neither Father Francis nor Primrose reacted. It rang a second time.

"I'll get it," said the Prior.

It was a woman Father Francis didn't recognise. She seemed taken aback when he answered, but quickly regained her composure. She introduced herself as Eileen Fancy, the district nurse working with Dr Susan McCarthy. She carried a tray of food under clean tea towel.

"Eileen. Yes, of course. Dr McCarthy has spoken of you. It is kind of you to come over so quickly."

"Oh, as soon as I heard the terrible news I thought I should come over. Are they sure he is...I mean...they are really gone?" she said. Her voice was deep and hoarse and conveyed little emotion.

"I'm afraid so. Come in, please. Primrose is in the kitchen."

"Both of them?" said Eileen. She sounded annoyed.

"Yes," snapped the Prior, before apologising for being rude.

"I understand. It must be awful for you. I feel awful for your loss, Father Francis."

"Yes. Well, thank you, Eileen. Will you stay awhile with Primrose?"

"Of course I will. I'll stay, as long as necessary. That's why I came."

"God bless you, Eileen," he said with a forced smile, "Please, come in."

Eileen Fancy walked beside him down the hall. The Prnoticed that the odd-looking woman walked awkwardly and yet the tray of food remained perfectly still.

"Will you stay for a bite, Father? There's more than enough for two."

"No. I must get going. But thank you Eileen. Thank you."

Father Francis left soon after, promising Primrose that he would return later.

"I'm sure we'll meet again Eileen," he said before he left.

"I'm sure of it too," she said with a smile that did nothing to improve her appearance.

As the Prior made his way to his little car he wondered why he didn't feel like Primrose, why he wasn't suffering her grief. Was his faith *that* strong, or was he in denial?

Shouldn't I be feeling something? he wondered.

His brother was dead. Brian and Marie both said they'd seen Michael drown. The rescued students stated that Hanna and Professor Kearns had been swept away by the same rising waters and that they too were dead. So why did he not feel a terrible loss? Michael was his twin. They were more than just brothers – they had a special connection. Should he not feel broken? Should he not feel something…anything…guilt?

His car was cold and stayed that way for the entire journey between Primrose's house and Dr Susan McCarthy's surgery, despite the heater banging away at full blast all the way along. Father Francis didn't mind. The noisy racket of the heater was distracting. The little car gave off an air of loneliness. He wished that Brother Benjamin had been well enough to bring him around on his motor bike. Benji was good company and was happy to be the Prior's chauffeur. Although the home-made side-car terrified Father Francis, now he would have welcomed the sting of cold air on his face and the adrenalin rush of high speed.

The lights were still on in the surgery when he arrived. The carpark was empty, save for one car that he recognised as Susan's rental. He parked next to it and got out. He stood for a moment and looked out at the ocean. The night had not fully descended and if he squinted he could see the horizon as a thin line of fading lavender. Wispy clouds ran away to the west. They looked like lilac smoke. He thought of Michael and forced a smile.

"Sometimes the Man upstairs lets me see colours too, Bro," he whispered.

"What was that, Father Prior?" said Susan.

"Oh!" he said and turned around.

The surgery behind was now in darkness. Dr Susan McCarthy stood in front of him with her car keys in her hand.

"Sorry, I didn't mean to startle you Father. I was just locking up for the day. My receptionist had to leave unexpectedly, so I'm here later than usual. Is there something wrong? Do you need a consultation?"

"No. No. I'm fine. Actually, I came to see you. I met your receptionist, Mrs. Fancy, at Primrose's house."

"Oh? That's Hanna's mother, isn't it? The girl Michael has gone to find. Why did Eileen go there?"

"You haven't heard, Susan?"

"Haven't heard what?"

He hesitated before speaking again. He noticed he'd addressed her by her Christian name, which wasn't like him. She noticed it too.

Before he had a chance to find the right way of saying what he had to say, Susan spoke.

"Oh God, no!"

"I'm...sorry Susan. They rescued some of the students but not all them. Two of the rescuers were lost down there."

"M...Michael?" she stammered.

"Yes. I'm afraid so. My brother and another man, a much more experienced caver, drowned saving the others. Their bodies were not recovered."

"And...Hanna? Did he find Hanna?" she said.

"I'm afraid Hanna drowned too."

"Oh God."

Susan rocked a little on her feet and Father Francis feared that she might collapse. He stepped toward her. She looked up at him, raised her arms and backed away.

"I'm fine," she said. "I'm fine."

He knew she was lying. His lips were dry.

"I'm sorry," he said. "I came to tell you, so that you wouldn't hear it from someone else."

Susan moved away from him and toward the door of her car.

"If you don't mind Father, I have somewhere to be."

"Of course," he said. He turned to get back into his car."

"Wait. Father Francis."

"Yes."

"I'm so sorry. I'm so sorry for your loss. I'm sorry," she said. Her voice quivered.

"I know," he said. "Thank you Susan. Michael meant a great deal to both of us."

*

When Father Francis drove away Susan got into her car and slammed the door. She didn't turn on the engine or the lights. She sat and stared at a smudge on the windscreen. Her hands were shaking and she could hear herself breathing. She began to cry. She was confused, frightened and alone. For the first time, in as long as she could remember, she wished she was with her mother, in the house where she grew up. She needed to go home, back to the secrets and comfort of her old bedroom, back to the happy wasted hours on the garden swing, back to the smell of the turf fire and the noise the old cat made on the arm of the couch, before it found a warm seat on her lap. She needed to go home. She'd spend most of her adult life trying to escape from her past and the controlling grip of her mother and now, when she felt most alone, it was her mother and that familiar place that she needed.

It was Michael's fault. She'd let herself fall in love with him. He had disarmed her and she had fallen for him, hook, line and sinker. And now he was gone. To make things worse, when she looked at Father Francis she saw Michael. She knew that the Prior had only wanted to comfort her in the car park but she couldn't let him touch her. She couldn't let him hold her. Not now. Not ever. He was too like his brother. She had to get away. Canada wouldn't be far enough. She wiped her eyes on her sleeve, composed herself and then rummaged through her bag and found her mobile phone. She tapped the number of her mother's house.

"Mum. It's Susan," she said.

"Who?"

Susan waited.

"My daughter, the doctor? Who never phones, from one end of the week to the next? *That* Susan?"

"I need…you…mum," Susan stammered.

There was moment of silence.

"What is it, dear? Has something happened? Are you all right, Susan?" The sarcasm was gone from her mother's voice, replaced by genuine concern.

"I'm fine. I just need you. Can you come to the island?"

Susan began to cry again. She couldn't stop herself.

"I'll come now, dear. Immediately."

"The earliest flight is in the morning. I'll pick you up at the airport. The flight is from Galway at five to eleven."

"Right. Five to eleven. I'll be there."

"And mum?"

"Yes dear?"

"I want to come home."

Susan put the phone down and got out of the car. The black night and the icy air was welcome. She wiped her eyes on the sleeve of her jacket for the second time and then leaned against the car until she got her breath back. A lone seagull came in from the ocean, circled the car and squawked at her. She ignored it and after a while, it headed back out to sea.

Chapter 57.

Over breakfast Hanna and Michael talked. They told each other how they had ended up on the ledge and they tried to make sense out of how they had managed to survive when the others, like Denis and Professor Kearns, hadn't.

Hanna's went first.

She told Michael that she and Professor Kearns had separated from the others once they reached the beach. The Professor was excited and wanted to explore. Axel, Eric and Gitte stayed close to the entrance. Their job was to set up camp, erect the lights and prepare the scientific equipment. Hanna and the Professor went to take water samples from the ocean. There were four steps of bony sand leading down to the edge of the still water. The lowest step was saturated and Professor Kearns said that he feared quick sand and insisted that he and Hanna remain roped together. Being tied to him made climbing down from tier to tier awkward and exhausting. Hanna said she had difficulty breathing and had had to take oxygen from a canister strapped to her belt.

When they reached the water's edge Professor Kearns lobbed a gauge weight attached to one-hundred-foot of rope-line into the ocean. The weight sank quickly and took all of the rope with it.

The Professor was flabbergasted.

"Amazing," he said, "This place is amazing Hanna...beyond amazing!"

Hanna told Michael she remembers Kearns becoming quiet, which was not like him. She guessed he was short of breath too. He shared her oxygen. She could taste him on the mouthpiece.

When he did speak, it was to himself.

"It's an enormous scientific discovery. I will be famous, famous," he kept saying.

Hanna remembered being frightened. The place frightened her and so did Professor Kearns. He was becoming manic. When he suggested they go back and get the scuba gear, she'd told him she didn't want to go into the water. His response was almost violent. She thought he was going to strike her. Instead, he sneered at her. "You disappoint me Hanna," he'd said. "We've just made one of the most astounding scientific discoveries of our time and you are acting like a frightened child. You are such a disappointment to me."

The words were meant to sting her, and they did. Just before they turned to go back for the diving equipment Eric got the generator going and the beach was flooded with light. Professor Kearns stopped and pointed at something floating on the surface of the ocean. "Good Lord, look at that! There's life down here. Can you believe it?" he declared. He was pointing at something that looked like three fist-sized black carnations bobbing gently in the sea, above the spot where the gauge weight had been dropped in. At the time Hanna thought that the weight might have dislodged the strange flowers from the sea bed, and had sent them floating up to the surface. At the centre of each flower a single willowy stamen quivered and flickered in the air. Hanna said she remembered thinking at the time that the stamen looked worms burrowing into rancid flesh. One of the flowers floated in toward them and before she could stop him, Professor Kearns stepped forward, hunkered down and stretched out a hand to grab it.

Hanna remembered pleading with the Professor not to touch it, but he ignored her. As soon as the tip of his outstretched finger touched the waving stamen the black flower rose up and grabbed his hand and yanked him viciously into the water. In the seconds before she lost consciousness Hanna remembered seeing the Professor disappearing, at lightning speed, under the surface and then feeling the powerful tug on her waist as she was dragged in after him. When she returned to consciousness she was sitting on the same ledge where she'd found Michael, and was still tied to the Professor. He sat, rigid and upright, three feet in front of her and they were both soaking wet. Water dripped from her hair onto her face, pooled under her eyes and wet her lips. It tasted of iron. The air was dank and, at first, thick and clawing, but it had a sweet edge and soon her breathing slowed to a natural rhythm. It took her eyes a little longer to focus. When she looked upwards she thought she could see a reflection of an ocean in the sky above – dark, foreboding and impossibly large. Beneath the surface of the ocean she could see large shapes racing around. When she realised it wasn't a reflection but the impossible belly of a real ocean above her head she wanted to scream. The world had somehow turned itself upside-down. She looked at the Professor. He sat on the solid ground in front of her. It didn't make sense. How could they be sitting on the ground if an ocean was above their heads? Where was up? Where was gravity?

One of the Professor's arms was raised, as if poised to strike her. The outstretched hand was blackened and burnt, although she noticed that his wrist and the sleeve of his jacket were unmarked. He didn't move. She was sure he must be dead.

Although his body was facing away from her, his head was twisted so far around, that he was almost staring straight into her eyes. The skin on his neck was wrung so tight, it looked as if it was on the point of tearing apart. Although she was sure he couldn't be alive, she thought she saw tears in his eyes. She remembered thinking that he looked sad and frightened, and that she pitied him.

She reached out to him but as soon as she touched his sleeve he pulled away from her, and kept going until the rope between them became taut. Before she knew what was happening she too shunted forward. They slid along the sticky ground like a couple on an invisible snow sled, the Professor in front and Hanna behind, the strong rope keeping them linked together. Something powerful was dragging them forward. She tilted her body sideways to see what it was and came face to face with one of the giant black beasts. When she tried to scream only air came out.

Hanna told Michael that she remembered that she couldn't stop crying.

"We were being dragged toward the edge of a pit. I thought I was hallucinating. I tried to convince myself that it couldn't be true. But my tears were real. I knew it wasn't a dream, because my tears were real."

In the end, Hanna's instinct for survival kicked in and she knew what she must do. Her fingers found the crampon just as the monster toppled clumsily over the edge, dragging the

Professor's still rigid body after it. In the final seconds Hanna managed to undo the clasp and free herself from the rope, but the forward momentum dragged her on. She stopped inches from the precipice. A cacophony of noise rose from the pit beyond. She crawled to edge and looked over and what she saw made her scream. This time the sound did come out, loud and clear. It attracted the attention of other monsters. She pulled away from the edge and scuttled blindly on all fours back the way she'd come. In her scramble to escape she stumbled on the entrance to the burrow and without a second thought she clambered inside.

Hanna couldn't tell Michael how long she'd stayed curled up in a ball in the burrow or how long it had been before she first plucked up the courage to look back outside. She was sure she'd fallen asleep many times and each time terrible noises woke her. When she turned on her torch she found that she was dry but the floor of the burrow was wet. Around her were the bodies of a few of the luminous fish. The face of her wrist watch had been smashed in and water had destroyed the works. She had no idea what time it was or for how long she'd been in the burrow.

She very quickly realised that the burrow entrance, which was partly covered by a strange tree root, was hidden from the monster's view. Because of the tree roots she could raise her head, look about and still not be seen. Even when the monsters were on the ground in their snake-like form they were too large to notice the small opening.

She found watching the creatures strangely fascinating and she returned to the entrance often. She was convinced that understanding the creatures and their behaviour would be crucial, if she was to find a way of escaping from the place. So, she came and watched. What she noticed was that the world above the burrow changed at regular intervals. The upside down ocean rose and fell and it's movements seemed predictable. When the ocean rose up, the black monsters took to the air and entered the water, becoming snake-like in form, like giant sea serpents. Later, when the ocean began to come back down the beasts returned to ledge with their bounty and then to the pit to sleep. The full cycled took about four or five hours. Shoals of luminous fish were the only other creatures Hanna saw in the upturned ocean and these the serpents avoided. The monsters didn't like the small shiny fish. They didn't attack or eat them and they skirted around them if any of the fish landed on the ground. Even when the fish were dead, the monsters kept their distance. The luminous fish swam in the ocean unmolested.

Hanna used this knowledge to her advantage. Covering herself in the luminous oil that coated the little fish's bodies allowed her to explore the ledge unhindered. By placing piles of dead fish around the entrance to the burrow she ensured that none of the giant snakes ventured too close. The luminous pile also acted as a marker to help her find her way back to the safety of the burrow should she move too far away. Although never venturing very far from the mouth of the burrow, it soon became clear that there was no way out of the place and she resigned herself to the fact that she was trapped and could only hope that a rescue party would be sent to save her. So, she set up home in the cave beneath the burrow, and spent her waking hours watching the monsters on the ledge and waiting for the rescue party to arrive.

Sometimes when the monsters returned to the ledge from the ocean above, they carried people.

Hanna told Michael she saw three other people being brought down, one before he and Denis arrived and two more, not long after. The first man was brought down close to the entrance to the burrow and before he was dragged over the edge Hanna got to see his face. Like the Professor he looked paralysed and he too had a raised burnt hand, which she remembered was covered in rings. Hanna didn't recognise him. He wasn't dressed like a caver and certainly didn't seem like part of any rescue party. He had cropped white hair which looked dyed, and he was heavily tattooed, with piercings all over his face and neck. The other two were also men. They came down after Michael. They landed on the ledge on the other side of the burrow entrance. They didn't look like cavers either. Hanna was about to go over to them when she heard Michael cry out.

"Are you sure they were men?" said Michael, thinking of Horse and Marie. "Were they dressed like cavers?"

"No. They were wearing jeans and tee shirts. No they were not cavers."

Michael relaxed.

"By the time I got you to the burrow they were gone. Whoever they were, they are now gone. Like the Professor and your friend Denis, those other three guys are dead."

"You said the ocean moves up and down. What do you mean, Hanna?" Michael asked.

He picked a fish bone from between his teeth.

"I have a theory. I've been trying to make sense of all of this, of what's happening here."

She told Michael that she thought that they were in an oxygen filled space that existed underneath the ocean they'd discovered in the hidden chamber. A world under the water. An air pocket of unimaginable proportions. If the vast hidden chamber, with its tiered beach, existed above the ocean, then the ledge and the monster's world existed somewhere beneath it. The two places were separated from each other by billions of tons of water, and the ocean was constantly rising and falling like a giant mechanical lung. In the chamber with the tiered beach, the rising and falling appeared like an incoming and receding tide, whilst in the monster's world, it was the rising and falling of a liquid sky. In the underworld, when the water had dropped down to its lowest level, the ledge was fully submerged and the tide was fully out on the tiered beach above. When the belly of the ocean rose off the ledge, up as high as it could go, the tiered beach was fully submerged, and Professor Kearns' hidden chamber completely flooded. She admitted her theory was far-fetched, but it worked with the evidence before their eyes. The ocean rose and fell at regular and predictable intervals.

"But how could that be? If we are in an air pocket underneath a vast ocean, surely we could never survive the pressure. We'd be crushed to nothing," said Michael.

"Actually, if humans didn't have pockets of air inside us, in our lungs and other organs, we wouldn't be crushed at all. That's why fish can swim to great depths without being crushed, but I know, you're right, it doesn't make sense. I don't know what's going on. It doesn't make any sense. None of it does. The creatures, the ocean in the caves, the birds, the frozen people, none of it! It's like a scene from a Bruegel painting. It's like we're in Hell," Hanna said with a sigh.

Michael thought of Brother Benjamin's stories of St Áedán and Purgatory. He winced.

"So what's your story Michael Eustace? How did you end up in this fine mess and, more importantly, how did you survive when your friend didn't?"

Michael told Hanna everything, including the fact that he cut the rope.

"Why did you cut the rope, Michael?"

"If I hadn't they would have drowned too. I had no choice, Hanna. Something strong was pulling me under. It would have pulled Brian and Marie with me."

"Just like me and the Professor, you mean?" said Hanna.

"Yes, I suppose so," he said.

"So, your friends think you're dead. And my friends think I'm dead too. Kevin thinks I'm dead and no one will be coming back for us? Is that what you are telling me, Michael? There will be no more rescue attempts, will there?" she said.

"No, I don't think so," he admitted reluctantly. "I was the only one that was sure that you were still alive, Hanna," he said.

"You? How did you know I was still alive? How could you?" she said.

"I have a particular gift which makes me good at finding missing people, so long as they are alive. You were missing, but I knew you were alive, and I knew where to look!"

"What are you talking about?"

Michael told her what he'd told Kevin earlier. He told her how he could see the living colours of all the people around him and how these colours were individual to every single person.

"That's weird," she said.

"Yes, I know. I also think that the colours have meaning. They tell me what sort of person I was dealing with, like a window to the person's soul."

Hanna raised her eyebrows.

"At least that's how my brother sees it. He says that it's a gift from God. I'm not so sure. I'm not even sure I believe in a God or souls, or Hell for that matter. Although, following recent events I think I might have to revise my opinion on that score. I've told very few people about my gift. A few years back, I stupidly thought I could make money out of it, by becoming a TV psychic. I needed the money. It was a big mistake and ended badly."

"I still don't get it? How does being able to see fuzzy colours around people, help you find them if they are missing?" Hanna said.

"Sometimes people shed their colours, when they touch things. They leave their coloured mark on things, walls, a door handle, a piece of clothing, furniture, whatever. Not always and not everywhere or on everything. It's rather arbitrary, actually. There doesn't seem to be rhyme nor reason to it. Anyway, I see these marks and I can follow them. They slowly fade but never fully go away, not until the person dies. It seems at the moment of death all of the person's colour marks vanish. I've seen it happen. It's hard to watch. I also believe that marks can tell me if the person is close to death. I watched your colours weaken and then strengthen again. At one point I thought you were dying."

"Wow."

"Your mother knows about my gift, of course. We were best friends in college. That's why she asked me to find you. She knew if you were still alive I could find you and I did, didn't I?" said Michael.

Hanna widened her eyes.

"This gets weirder and weirder," she said eventually.

"Tell me more of your theory about this place, Hanna. There must be some way of getting out of here," he said.

"Well, as I said the ocean is constantly rising and falling, like a giant mechanical lung, and at regular intervals, every few hours. Its movement is fairly predictable and I think the up and down motion effects the air. It cleans it, oxygenates it. When the ocean is fully up, the beasts leave the pit and go searching for food. They are usually gone for a good while. They come back down when the tide turns. When the ocean is fully down, they sleep. Other things happen too but it's best you see for yourself. I will show you later. You'll see," she said.

"It seems impossible," he said.

"So," she continued, "the up and down motion draws in new oxygen and expels the poisonous gases, possibly into the space above the ocean. I think the air down here is oxygen rich. That would explain the size of the creatures and maybe also why we heal so quickly."

"I don't understand," said Michael.

"During the time of the dinosaurs the earth's atmosphere had far higher levels of oxygen than it has now, which is the reason everything was so big back then."

Michael stood up.

"I didn't know that. It makes sense. Do you think, Hanna, it could be possible that one of those creatures could have got out? Up to the surface, I mean?" he said.

"God no! I think someone would have noticed, don't you?"

"Hmm? I suppose," he said.

Chapter 58.

Paul, Horse and Marie arrived at the parking area near the Devil's Throat just as it was getting dark. Henry was sitting alone on the bonnet of Denis's locked car. In one hand, he held a pen torch, in the other a small book. He was reading. Around his feet was a neat pile of packed-up camping gear. When he saw the car approach he got down off the bonnet and carefully book-marked the page he was on.

"I thought you had forgotten me," he said, as soon as Paul got out of the car.

"No, I…sorry," said Paul.

"Are you here on your own?" said Horse when he and Mari got out.

"Yes. I've heard the news though. I'm sorry about your friends and …" he touched the side of the car he'd been sitting on. "Denis, was it?" he said, "He owns…I mean…owned this? It's locked. He didn't leave a key with any of you, did he?"

"Maybe his friend Hughie has a spare. If not, we'll get someone to come and tow it back into town in the morning," said Horse.

"How did you hear the news, Henry?" asked Marie.

"Carol Lenehan and a couple of the other students turned up. Apparently, it's all over the island: the rescue, the deaths and something about drugs. They helped me clear up all the stuff and left about half an hour ago."

"Why didn't they take you with them?" asked Paul, sounding slightly angry.

"Carol tried her best to persuade me to go with them, but they came in a very small car and we'd have to leave all this stuff behind. Anyway, I told her that you were coming back for me Paul."

"Sorry," Paul said again, in a small voice.

"You're grand. You came, didn't you," said Henry. He smiled at Paul and Paul smiled back.

The tops of the trees around the secluded car park swayed and creaked. Horse shivered.

"Right," he said, "let's pack up and get out of this Godforsaken place. How long have you been waiting Henry?"

"Not long. I haven't been bored," he said. "It's been all go around here, over the past half hour."

"Oh?" said Horse.

"What with ambulances and Garda cars zooming by, this way and that, and then, just when I thought it was all over, another car came flying over the hill going at a hundred miles an hour. It gave me such a fright, I can tell you. I was sure it wouldn't make the bend. Bloody idiot. I expected a squad car to come after it, you know, giving chase, but no one else came by. He was in a dreadful hurry, wherever he was going. Must have been trying to catch the last ferry or something."

"When was this?" asked Paul as he packed the camping gear into the back of the car.

"Not ten minutes ago," said Henry.

"Going that way? We should have passed it, shouldn't we?" said Horse.

"We didn't pass any other cars on the way here, Henry," said Marie.

"No we didn't," agreed Paul.

"Curious," said Horse. "Maybe they had to rush home to catch something on the television, ha ha."

"I don't think that can be right. There are no houses along that road. None for miles," said Marie.

"There is one around here," said Paul.

The other three looked at him.

"Remember Horse, your friend Michael stopped at a set of gates. The house was set-in, almost hidden from the road."

"You're right. The one with the security gates." Horse said.

Marie thought for a moment. She looked confused.

"It's a two storey house in a mock-Tudor style. Part brick, part painted plaster, with timber gables," said Horse

410

"Gerry Gallagher's farm? That's not on this road. It's on the old road from the University. Gerry is in his eighties. He has a very old Hyundai, four by four. Even if he'd wanted to drive fast he couldn't. His is the only house around here with security gates. His late wife Agnes had him build them, along with the English style house. She was from Surrey. Security cameras too. Gerry's been living on his own since she died. No children. Four or five years. He keeps to himself."

"Could the boy racer have been heading that way?" asked Horse.

"Suppose so. It's the only house out here. He could have been taking the back road to the University but that doesn't make sense. He'd have got there quicker if he continued on this road."

"Why *did* your friend stop at the gates that day, Horse?" said Paul.

"Dunno, but when I suggested I ring the buzzer, Michael got edgy. I remember thinking at the time that he looked frightened."

He smiled at the others.

"Watcha' say we take a detour over to Gerry Gallagher's farm? See if everything is okay?" he said.

"An adventure? Why not?" said Marie.

*

Paul had just turned the last corner when a dark saloon car, with a single occupant, pulled out from the recess in front of the gates to Gerry Gallagher's farm and headed off at high speed in the opposite direction.

"I think that's the car I saw earlier," said Henry from the back seat.

"That was not Gerry's car," said Marie.

"Should we follow him, Horse?" said Paul.

"No. Drive in, before the gates close. Quickly now, Paul."

Paul accelerated, then braked hard. The car skidded on the gravel in front of the gates. Henry toppled sideways onto Marie who sat beside him in the back. Marie had let Horse take the front passenger seat once they'd packed the boot with the last of Henry's camping gear.

Paul nudged the car forward until the front bumper crossed the invisible beam between the two stone pillars. The gates stopped closing and, after what seemed like an age, began to

411

slowly open. When there was just enough clearance between the gates Paul drove through and headed down the long sealed-gravel drive. The impressive two storey house was in total darkness.

"No one's home," said Henry.

"Doesn't seem so, no," said Horse.

Paul stopped the car outside the front door. For a moment, no one moved. The car went quiet.

Horse felt uneasy. He considered telling Henry and Marie to stay in the car. None of them seemed to be in a great hurry to get out. Marie's sudden lack of enthusiasm surprised him and he wondered if she felt the same way he did. The thought made him happy.

"Well, what are we waiting for? Let's go see if Gerry is in. Maybe you should ring the bell Marie. He knows you, doesn't he? I'll be beside you," said Horse.

"Okay," he said.

All four climbed out of the car. Paul and Henry stood back whilst Horse and Marie went to the door. Horse noticed that all the curtains were drawn. Through a slit in the curtains of the bay window to their right, they could see the weak flicker of orange light. In contrast, the outside of the house was so dark that they couldn't see their own feet.

There was an icy wind. Marie shivered. Horse wanted to put his arm around her. Instead, he pressed the bell. It sounded like a distant drill.

There was no sound from inside.

"Call through the door Marie. Identify yourself. Gerry might be frightened by strangers, at this time of night," Paul said.

"Hello! Gerry? It's Marie Joyce. It's Marie Joyce. Hello?"

Horse rang the bell again. He held his finger on the button for a good ten seconds. He guessed that inside the bell was loud enough to wake the dead.

A donkey brayed in a field down the valley and a large bird rose noisily from a nearby hedge, the flap of its wings sounded like someone moving heavy furniture across a timber floor.

Wooaw. Wooaw. Wooaw.

"Like Henry said, no one's home," said Paul.

Henry cupped his hands around his face and pressed them against the glass of the bay window so he could see into the room with the flickering light.

"What, the hell, is that?" he said.

The others gathered around the window and took turns to look through the narrow gap in the curtains.

"Oh fuck," said Horse.

The stuttering orange light was coming from a Bunsen burner that sat at the centre of a big writing desk at back of the room. A large can of lighter fuel had been positioned on a metal A-frame above the burner. The solid flame hammered at the base of the can which had turned black. Piles of loose paper had been stacked around the assembly, far enough away as not to be set alight by the flame, but close enough to ignite once the lighter fluid exploded.

Paul put his shoulder to the front door and heaved. When Horse added his weight the door gave way and swung inwards with a crunching sound. The two detectives toppled forward, Horse fell onto the hall floor, but managed to throw his arms out in time to land on the palms of his hands. He looked like he was about to begin a round of press-ups. The carpet was wet and smelt of petrol.

"Stay back, you two," he said, Horse when he got back to his feet. He wiped his wet hands on the front of his jacket, then opened the door of the room to his right and raced to the desk. Using a handkerchief, he snatched the burner from under the can of lighter fluid and flicked the valve key to cut off the supply of gas. The flame splutter away and the room fell into darkness. Even through the handkerchief the metal of the burner was red hot. Horse dropped the burner on the floor and yelled out in pain.

"Ouch. Fuck. Fuckin' ouch."

Paul went to the car and returned with two torches.

"Are you okay?" asked Marie.

"I'll live. Please stay back Marie. It's not safe in here."

As if to prove his point the can of lighter fuel cracked loudly. Everyone took a breath, the only sound being the volatile liquid bubbling away inside.

"Another few seconds and that would have gone up. It still might. Better not touch it," said Horse.

He backed away from the table. Paul handed him a torch but kept his own trained on the can.

"And don't touch the light switches or anything electrical. Let's see if we can find Gerry. We need to be as quick as we can but I think we should stick together. Paul, you check upstairs. Go with him, Marie. Henry, you're with me. We'll check down here. No light switches, remember."

"There's a basement too. There is a door off the kitchen," said Marie.

"Okay, we'll check the basement too. Be careful, you two, okay? Said Horse."

"Sure," said Paul.

"Will do, boss," said Marie with a smile.

Chapter 59.

After breakfast Hanna led Michael to a place she called the viewing gallery. They left the chamber through the second, taller exit. Despite their predicament Michael was excited and, now that he felt better, he was more than a little curious about the adventure ahead. Since he'd woken he'd become increasingly aware of how well he felt. Fit and fantastic, that's how. Not only had his leg fully healed but it was now almost impossible to see where he'd been injured. There was no mark and no latent pain. Added to that, his throat wasn't dry or sore, as it always was first thing in the morning, and there was none of the usual lethargy that enveloped him for at least a half an hour after he woke up. His muscles seemed energised. He had to fight the urge to run about. He wanted to climb things. He'd even thought about dropping to the floor and seeing how many press-ups he could do. Even his big luminous jacket and heavy climbing boots seemed surprisingly light. Once upright, Michael couldn't keep still. He bobbed up and down on his toes as if he was getting ready for a race. And he couldn't stop smiling.

"You okay?" asked Hanna. She looked at him with concern.

"Never better," he said, "never better!"

The most obvious change was in his head. The constant pulsing pain, that had driven him almost to distraction for so long, was suddenly and completely gone. After years of constant headaches, the absence of pain in his head was shocking and a little frightening. Where once there had been nothing but noise, now there was absolute silence. He couldn't decide whether the sudden absence of a headache was a good thing or bad thing. He settled on a *good thing* and so, followed Hanna into the tunnels with unusual gusto.

They moved freely at first, walking side by side, but soon the tunnel narrowed so much that Michael had to travel behind Hanna. At one point the walls were so close together that Michael didn't think he'd be able to fit through.

"I don't think I'll get in there," he said.

"Take off your coat."

"It's not that. I have a big head."

"Hadn't noticed, but I don't know you that well," Hanna said. She tossed her flaming head back and laughed out loud.

"Ha ha. Seriously though, Hanna, I really don't think I can fit through."

"Turn your head sideways and crouch down. The gap down there is a little wider. Once you get through, the tunnel widens again. This is the worst bit, I promise."

"You're much smaller than me. If I bend down that far my knees will stick out. I don't think I can fit. Honestly, I'd need to be a bloody contortionist," he said.

"Come on, you can do it, big head. Don't you want to see what I have to show you?"

It was a terrible struggle but, after several attempts, Michael eventually managed to squeeze through. He scraped both sides of his face on the rough rock wall in the process. It should have stung him, but it didn't.

"I wouldn't like to have to do that in a hurry," he said, once back on his feet.

"Hopefully you won't have to," she said, "You've cut your cheek. Here let me."

Hanna spat on a handkerchief and gently wiped the side of his face.

"Thanks," he said, adding, "You know you remind me so much of your mother, when she was your age, Hanna."

"The way I look?" she said.

"And act," he said

"How?" she asked.

"Oh, you know? So shy and unassuming."

Hanna raised an eyebrow.

"Really? Was mum shy and unassuming?"

"No. Not at all. I was joking. Your mother is a force of nature."

"Was she? Were you in love with her?" said Hanna.

"Of course. I still am."

He winked at her.

"Ha. You're pulling my leg. Come on, we better get going or we'll miss the main event," she said.

"Can't wait," he said.

They continued, always descending. The tunnel was always wide enough for Michael to easily squeeze through. He imagined that they were in an amusement park on the way to some underground attraction. Memories of his childhood came to him with surprising clarity. He thought about his brother. He tried to focus on him but his reminiscing was suddenly interrupted by a terrible racket coming from somewhere up ahead. It sounded like hundreds of angry seagulls squawking at each other.

"What the hell is making that racket?"

"You'll see," said Hanna, "come on."

They turned a corner and Hanna stopped. She turned off her torch.

"We won't be needing these from now on," she said.

Michael switched off his torch and, once his eyes had adjusted, the darkness was replaced by a soft orange yellowy glow.

"Follow my lead. Do what I say and prepare to astounded," she said.

"Are we back at the place where you found me?" Michael said.

"Kind of. Back then you were on the ledge. This is what you would have seen if you'd looked over the edge."

Up ahead was a large triangular opening in the side wall of the tunnel. It looked like a badly formed Gothic window. It's sill was three feet above the cave floor. Bright yellow light streamed in from outside and strange shadows danced on the wall of the tunnel opposite.

Hanna moved forward slowly and Michael followed her lead. When he was close enough, he could see shadows passing by the window, large enough to momentarily block out the yellow light. The sound of shrieking was almost deafening. Hanna ducked down below the sill and scurried on all fours to the other side. Once there she stood up and pressed her back against the wall.

"I call this window my viewing gallery. Don't let them see you," she shouted before taking a quick look out and then quickly withdrawing her head. Michael copied her. What he saw made his jaw drop. When he drew his head back in, he gasped. He looked over at Hanna.

"Oh my God. They can't get in here, can they?" he shouted across the opening.

"I think they're too big, but I can't be sure. In their snake-like form they might be able to. Just don't let them see you."

He nodded then stole another look. The scale of what he saw was astonishing.

The window looked down from a great height into a vast open plain. Michael estimated that it must be over a hundred feet from the viewing window to the ground. Everything beyond the window existed in an orange haze and, everywhere he looked, there were winged monsters, just like the ones on the ledge. They crowded the space between the ground and the low black liquid sky, hundreds of feet above the window. It was the first time that Michael had really looked at the sky and it was exactly as Hanna had described it. It was an upturned ocean. He thought it looked ready to burst.

Almost all of the monsters were in flight. They swooped, dived and wheeled left and right on their enormous wings. They weaved in and out, twisting and turning with amazing dexterity and skill. Michael could see hundreds and hundreds of them, each one following its own seemingly haphazard flight path, zipping past the others with only inches to spare. In parts of the sky the number of beasts was so great, and were moving so fast, that the mass of them blocked out the light. Michael thought of a covered stadium filled with enormous bats. He withdrew his head and tried to slow his breathing. The world outside the window stank of fish and offal. It made his eyes water.

Hanna shouted something he couldn't hear. She shouted louder.

"They have a routine. The ocean is almost all the way down. If we'd come earlier most of them would have been on the ground. Now they are all in the air. Soon the action will begin. You'll see. We're here at a good time." Michael stole another look outside. It seemed like the number of creatures had doubled since the last time he looked out.

He retreated again. After thinking for a moment he removed his luminous jacket and dropped it on the floor, then crossed to the other side of the tunnel and pressed his back against the wall, from where he had a ringside view of the goings-on outside.

Hanna stayed with her back against the wall beside the window. She looked terrified.

"Don't let them see you," she shouted.

"I won't," he said.

As he stared out into the orange abyss something happened that set off a terrifying and brutal chain reaction, and it happened so fast, that Michael almost missed the catalyst for the mayhem that followed.

One of the giant beasts, swooping at an almost leisurely pace, turned suddenly and acrobatically in mid-air. Without warning and with lightning speed it bent one of its enormous wings and plunged a sharp claw into the back of a beast flying by beneath it, catching its victim just below the neck. The barb dug deep into the scaly flesh and caused the surprised creature to jerk backwards like a darting fish caught on a hook, howling in shock and terror.

"Reeeeeeee..." it bellowed.

It was the call to war. From that first assault the world outside the window exploded into a frenzy of activity. More monsters joined the initial attack and within a matter of seconds the wounded beast had been torn to pieces. Swinging claws, snapping beaks and flying tails ripped and slashed. Globules of flesh and gristle were thrown up and out, only to be snatched from the air by passing beaks. White oily puss squirted and sprayed in all directions. The air around the fight became thick with blood and gristle, that fell like heavy rain toward the ground below. Very little of it reached the valley floor. Monsters flying closer to the ground raced each other for the last lumps of meat that had somehow managed to evade the jaw of those higher up.

Then there was another attack. And another. And another.

"Reeeeeeee..."

"Reeeeeeee..."

Everywhere Michael looked it was a case of kill, or be killed. It was mind blowing. Michael stood transfixed. Hanna shouted at him but he couldn't hear what she was saying.

Just when he thought that the fight would go on until all the monsters were dead, the battle ended. It was as if someone had blown a silent whistle that only the creatures could hear. It was over almost as quickly as it had begun. As the noise level abated and the sky cleared, a degree of calm returned. Soon Michael could hear nothing but the sound of his own heartbeat and the swishing of the giant wings of the victorious survivors, as they flew past the window. Now the vast space beyond Hanna's viewing gallery seemed almost empty, and the air thinner too. Michael stepped forward, leaned out the window and looked down into the valley below.

Hanna screamed.

"Get in, Michael. Don't let them see you."

When Michael didn't respond Hanna lunged at him. Her movement caused a monster flying close to the opening to turn its head in their direction. It bellowed and wheeled around to face them.

Hanna stood in front of Michael with her back to the approaching beast.

She shook him violently.

"Michael," she shouted.

The creature over her shoulder hovered close to the opening. Michael watched it as it slowly approached. It could see them. The creature lowered its head, opened its serrated beak and drew its wings forward. Michael knew that it was only a matter of seconds before it would strike.

"Please Michael, please," pleaded Hanna.

Other creatures approached, curious to see what was happening. Michael grabbed Hanna and shoved her behind him and against the back wall of the cave, his body shielding her completely from the beast outside the window.

"Stay behind me and don't move," he whispered as loudly as he could. She fell to the floor of the tunnel and he buried her under himself, then turned to face the creature, and braced himself in the event of a strike.

The monster stopped.

Michael stared into its triangular eyes. The creature looked confused. It flapped its massive wings and, rather than strike, moved back and away from the window. Other, smaller, monsters gathered around but none of them came close or tried to enter. One by one they flew away. The first beast was the last to leave. It followed all the others upwards toward the upturned ocean.

Hanna struggled from beneath Michael's body and got to her feet. Her eyes were red and she looked both angry and terrified. She stumbled away from him and away from the window. Michael grabbed his jacket and followed her. Once he was close enough she turned and slapped him hard across the face. The force of it almost knocked him over.

"What is wrong with you?" she screamed. "Are you on some sort of martyrdom trip, is that it? You want to die? Is that it?"

Tear welled up behind her eyelids, but she didn't look away. She looked like she might hit him again.

"No I...I..," he stuttered.

He looked back to the window, as if an explanation could be found there.

All the monsters were gone.

"They're gone to the ocean to lick their wounds and look for prey. They will be gone for hours. We can go down now and get some supplies before they come back," said Hanna.

Her voice was cold.

"I'm sorry Hanna," he said.

"Don't try and save me Michael by getting yourself killed. I promise you, if you leave me here on my own, I will kill myself. Do you understand? I will not stay here on my own. You will be responsible for my death. Do you understand?"

"I'm sorry Hanna," he said in a small voice, "I needed..."

"Don't be sorry! Don't be a fucking asshole!"

She turned away from him and switched back on her torch. It was the first time he'd heard Hanna curse. Primrose never cursed. In fact, Primrose detested bad language. He could tell Hanna didn't curse either and he was sorry that it was he who had caused her to do so now.

"I'm sorry," he said again, so quietly that only he could hear it.

The tunnel ahead was wide and tall and the floor stepped down in a series of long sloping platforms and continued like that for the forty minutes it took them to reach the valley floor.

Chapter 60.

Gerry Gallagher's farmhouse was eerily silent. The stink of petrol made it hard to breathe. Horse and Henry searched the ground floor as quickly as they could. All the rooms were empty and all had been doused with petrol. The front room, to the left of the front door, looked like a store for old furniture. Horse guessed that the upturned couch, the two arm chairs and the other odds and ends had originally been in the bay windowed room opposite, which now looked like a very untidy study. They found the door to the basement just where Marie had said it would be. The kitchen table, which was also piled with paper, had been pushed against it.

"Help me Henry. We'll have to lift it. We can move it over there. Don't drag the feet, they might be metal tipped. We don't want to cause a spark."

"Right."

"On the count of three. Ready?"

"Yep."

"One, two, three."

They carried the table away from in front of the door and placed it in the centre of the room. Horse opened the door to the basement. It was surprisingly heavy. A single flight of steep concrete steps led down into darkness. Horse went first. There was no handrail. He ignored the light switch inside the door. Henry stuck close behind him. The air at the bottom of the steps was clean, dry and chilly. There was no smell of petrol and, compared to the rest of the house, the air was almost fresh. Horse shone the torch about. The basement was a large room with a high bare concrete ceiling and smooth concrete block walls. Both the ceiling and walls had recently been painted white. The floor was covered in a grey vinyl sheet that also looked, and smelt, brand new. It had a clinical feel. There was another light switch on the wall at the bottom of the stairs.

A bank of nine computer monitors sat on a counter running along the back wall, all tilted to face a single keyboard and mouse in the middle. There was the only one chair in the room, with black leather, armrests and a high back. The only other thing in the room was a tall glass cabinet that stood on its own against the side wall opposite the stairs. Heavy red and black cables trailed along the floor between the monitors and the cabinet which was empty, save for a small black router the size of a cigar box that sat in the middle of the centre shelf. The front of the router had a row of tiny green LED lights which blinked on and off in a seemingly random and inexplicable sequence. Horse went over for a closer look. He noticed that the plastic router box showed signs of scorching along one side as if, at some time in the past, it had been placed too close to a fire.

"It's a computer room," said Henry, "or a security room, maybe."

"I think it would be okay to switch on the lights, Henry. There's no petrol down here."

After a moment of hesitation, Henry hit the switch. A series of spot lights came on over the counter. The rest of the room remained in subdued light. Horse walked over and touched one of the keys on the keyboard. One by one the monitors came to life. A green snowy image of the bay-windowed room upstairs filled the nearest screen. The view was of the desk and the cooling can of lighter fuel.

"A night-vision camera," said Henry confidently.

"If it is a security camera, surely it should be focussed on the window or door, shouldn't it? Why is it pointed at the desk?" said Horse.

When the next screen came to life two shadowy figures moved in the green snow. It was Paul and Marie on the stair landing.

"These images are live," said Horse.

On the next screen, there was a view of a bedroom. As they watched, the door opened and Paul entered with his torch. Horse and Henry saw the two mutilated bodies leaning against the back wall, before Paul did. The camera was pointing straight at them. Henry gasped.

424

Then the fourth screen came to life. This one was in full colour. The screen was split into four, each section showing a view of a different room. Three of the rooms Horse recognised. All of them were in the Tara Cove Hotel. One was the main conference hall. It was empty but all the lights were on. The image was so clear Horse could read the names of the delegates on the cards placed on the top table. Another image was of the hotel reception area. Horse could see the concierge talking to the night porter. The third was the interview room that he and Paul had been in for the last few hours, the room in which he'd written his report and where he'd been shown the disturbing file on Michael.

"Holy shit," said Horse, and shook his head in disbelief.

"What is it?" said Henry.

"It's the hotel. The Tara Cove."

"There must be sound with these," said Henry.

He leaned forward and pressed a key on the keyboard. The screen showing Paul and Marie in the bedroom upstairs buzzed and then they could hear Marie's voice.

"...but why would someone cut off their hands and their faces? Is that guy wearing a woman's corset, Paul?"

Horse noticed that Marie sounded only slightly spooked and not frightened at all.

"I need to take some photos. This is a crime scene Marie. Please don't touch anything. As for the mutilations, it is something the Russian mob is famous for. And...yes, it does appear that he is wearing a corset. God almighty, what's going on?" Horse heard Paul say, before Henry toggled between the *Ctrl* and *Tab* keys on the keyboard and Paul's voice was replaced by the hotel porter discussing a football match that was going to penalties, "...'sfuckin stupid overpaid prima donnas couldn't score in a brothel, overpaid and..." Henry toggled to the empty interview room. The fourth image was of a corridor. The five remaining screens remained dark.

"How do we turn these on Henry?"

Henry thought for a moment and then smiled.

"Maybe the monitors are just turned off?"

"It's possible," said Horse.

He located the button under the first screen and pressed it on. A tiny green light appeared and the screen came to life. He followed suit with the others.

Three of the screens were split into eight images, each one showing the interior of a bedroom, the camera focussed on the bed. Some of the bedrooms were occupied, some not. Horse scanned the thirty-two small screens and finally found his own empty room.

"Holy fuckin' shit," he said.

The fourth screen was split into four. Horse doubted it was the Tara Cove. One of the images was of a grimy bar and dance floor; the second the interior of a tattoo parlour; the third a large empty store room with bare brick walls and bunch of chairs arranged in a large circle around what appeared to be a stainless-steel trolley, containing tools of some sort, and the last showed a small neat office where a man sat behind a mahogany desk. The man was Mr. G.

"What is going on?" said Horse to himself.

"Huh?" said Henry.

When Horse didn't reply, Henry said,

"This is a very sophisticated surveillance system."

"That's an understatement, Henry."

"Where's that?" said Henry. They both watched as the last screen came into focus. This too was divided into four equal squares. One image was the interior of a church; the second a small room with cupboards and shelves and in which they could see, hanging on the back of a door, a priest's vestments.

The other two images Horse recognised. The first was the entrance hall of the priory and the other, Father Francis's oak-panelled study.

*

Horse turned his attention to the screen showing Mr G. The Dublin gangster looked anxious. Horse felt odd watching him. Without warning Mr G looked up at him. It was so blatant and direct that Horse wondered if Mr G could see him. Was it possible? Horse didn't think so. As if to prove him right Mr G casually looked away and mouthed something to someone out of view.

"Can you turn the sound up on that, Henry?"

"The guy in the office? Sure. I can do better than that."

Henry pressed a few keys and the four-image screen dissolved into one. Mr G's face grew in size. Another figure entered the frame just as the sound arrived.

"Whatcha want me to do about Kavanagh and dee others boss?"

"There's nothing to do, Stefan. With luck those three were buried alive. Is there nothing to be salvaged of the stash, Stefan?"

"No boss. What the beetch took, is now in the hands of Chief Superintendent Sutton."

Mr G put his face in his hands.

"Okay. Never mind. We will open tonight as usual Stefan. Now go away I need to think."

"Oh crap," said Henry.

"What?" said Horse, his attention still on Mr G.

"Look. The room upstairs is on fire."

Somehow the papers around the Bunsen burner had caught fire and a small fire was beginning to take hold. Horse knew it would very quickly become a very big blaze.

"We need to get out of here, right now Henry" said Horse.

There was a loud bang as the can of lighter fuel exploded. There was a slight delay between the actual sound of the explosion and the image reaching the screen. The blaze instantly consumed the room and obscured the view.

Horse moved to the glass cabinet.

"Do you think that's a recorder in there, Henry?" Horse pointed at the black box with the blinking green LED lights.

"Possibly?" said Henry.

"Right, well we'll take it with us then. How do you open this thing?"

"It's a fire cabinet. It looks very secure. There must be a key somewhere."

There was another bang from upstairs.

"Never mind," said Horse.

Horse picked up the chair, which was awkward and heavy, and flung it at the glass cabinet. It bounced off and crashed onto the floor. One of its casters flew off and ended up on the other side of the room.

"Fuck," said Horse.

"You'll need to use the point of something sharp. It's heat-toughened glass," said Henry.

Horse picked up the chair again, pointed the wheel-less leg toward the centre of the glass and then ran at the cabinet. The glass shattered with surprising ease. Small lumps of crystal cascaded through the open metal shelves of the cabinet. Without being asked Henry grabbed the router box and yanked it free of the cables, then followed Horse up the stairs.

The kitchen was clear but the hall was full of smoke. The front door was wide open. Paul and Marie were standing outside looking like they were about to come back in. When Marie saw Horse and Henry she shouted at them.

"Come on, come on."

As they ran out the door to the study cracked loudly and buckled. A torrent of thick hot smoke billowed into the hall. There was a dreadful whooshing sound as Henry and Horse crossed the threshold. The air outside was refreshing cold.

They piled into the car.

"Get us out here, Paul," shouted Horse.

There was another large explosion and the gravel driveway outside the front door turned bright red. The fire had reached the upper floor. Then a top window blew out and glass rained down on the bonnet of the car.

Paul accelerated quickly, jerked the steering wheel to the left and pulled up the hand brake. With a screech of rubber and a crunch of gravel the car turned one hundred and eighty degrees. As soon as it was pointing in the right direction, Paul released the handbrake and slammed the accelerator pedal to the floor. The car shot forward, almost got away from him, straighten up and, spitting gravel high into the air sped down the drive toward the gates.

The gates were closed so Paul had no option but to stop. He pulled the car onto the grass and parked it under the dense canopy of an ancient tree. Without being told, they all clambered out and crouched down behind the car, from where they watched the farmhouse burn. For a while Horse thought that the structure of the house might survive the blaze but then three enormous explosions, one after the other, took away one of the side gables and its chimney. Not long after that, the roof collapsed with a thunderous roar, followed quickly by the other side wall and its chimney. Within a half an hour it was over and Gerry Gallagher's English style farmhouse was gone, reduced to a smouldering heap of steaming sizzling rubble.

Five minutes after the last bit of the wall had fallen to the ground, the islands only fire truck arrived, with blaring sirens and flashing lights. Seeing the glow in the distance the engine driver proceeded to smash through the ornate iron gates, ripping one entirely from its gate post and sending it careering across the lawn. It was the final act in the destruction of Gerry Gallagher's English country farmhouse.

Chapter 61.

From the time they left the viewing gallery not much was said as they journeyed down the tunnel. Michael walked three or four paces behind Hanna. Every so often she would turn her head to check on him. When Michael caught sight of her pretty face in his torchlight he dropped his eyes to the floor. He wanted to say sorry again, or tell her what he was thinking, but instead he made much of watching where he put his feet. He felt shitty. Hanna was right. What had he been thinking, facing up to the monster like that, and all to test out one of his stupid theories? What if he'd been wrong? Like she'd said, he could have been killed. They both could have died, or something worse. What had he been thinking, risking their lives on a hunch? But he had to know and now that he did, the implications were intriguing, and might even prove to be their ticket out of this place. He would have to share his thoughts with her at some point but knew that right now was not the time.

Ever since he'd woken up, Michael had been thinking about why the monsters on the ledge hadn't attacked him. After all, just like Denis, he had been paralysed and unable to escape, yet the creatures on the ledge ignored him completely. It was not until Michael screamed out in agony that any of them reacted. Was it possible that the monsters couldn't see him? The more he thought about it, the more he came to believe that this was the only logical conclusion and, in his exaggerated good mood, Michael couldn't wait to test out his theory. The viewing gallery provided him with an opportunity to do just that.

Michael's first thought had been that the giant winged creatures were blind, and that the triangular eyes were not eyes at all. Maybe, like bats, the monsters didn't need to be able to see

431

to move about. Their breath-taking display of inch-perfect flying Michael of a large colony of bats leaving their cave at dusk. No two bats ever collided nor did any of them crash into tree branches or the walls of the cave. Michael knew that bats used a form of sophisticated sonar to steer clear of each other, and wondered if it was possible that the monsters used something similar.

But the idea that the monsters were blind didn't fit with what Michael had seen and heard. Firstly, he was convinced that the creature attacking Denis was looking at Denis as it did so, like a fat man slobbering over his dinner. The monster chose carefully where to put its trumpet-shaped snout and it moved its giant claws with the delicacy of a jeweller fixing a diamond into a ring setting. Then there was the fact that Hanna had had to cover herself in luminous fish-paint to deter the creatures. They turned their eyes away from her, just as they fled from the light of her camera flash. That meant that the monsters could see, they just couldn't see him. And Michael was sure he knew why!

The idea came from something Primrose had once said, many years before, when she and Michael were at university together. Her words had stayed with him and the memory remained vivid. They had just got back from a late-night study session in the library and were sitting on the floor of her sitting room, drinking cheap wine and discussing the state of the world. When they began to argue about politics Primrose changed the subject.

"I've been thinking about your gift. You know when you said the only human colours you can't see are your own? I think you might have it all wrong!" she'd said.

"What do you mean?" he'd said.

"I've been thinking about it. Maybe it's because you don't have any colours to see."

"But, everyone has colours, Primrose. Everyone!" he'd argued.

"How do you know? Or maybe your colours can't be seen. Invisible colours," she'd said with glee.

"Like the sounds only dogs can hear," he said.

"Maybe you're invisible" said Primrose, "the invisible man!"

"But that's no good, Primrose. Unless there is someone else who can see the colours like me, I'm only invisible to myself."

At the time, it had seemed like a joke, the ramblings of a drunken tongue. Now the notion of invisibility took on a different meaning altogether. Maybe the creatures could see him because they saw the world the same way he did. Maybe here, in this world beneath the upturned ocean, Michael *was* invisible. The monster hovering outside the viewing gallery was not there because it saw Michael, it was there because it heard Hanna when she shouted out and it was not until she stepped out in front of him that the creature moved toward them. It saw Hanna, but it didn't see him. When he stepped in front of her, she was hidden from the creature by his invisibility.

If he was right he knew it was something he could use to their advantage, something that could help them escape.

*

The floor levelled off and thirty yards further along the tunnel came to an end. They walked out into total darkness..

"Where are we?" Michael said.

"A forest," said Hanna. She turned on her torch.

All around them were the gnarled trunks of enormous trees that rose fifty feet into the air and supported a dense opaque canopy, as solid as rock. When Michael looked up tiny spots of yellow light winked at him from some the sky above.

"Come this way. We need to stay close to the cliff wall, if we are to be safe and find our way back later," said Hanna. "Take my hand and don't let go."

Michael did so without question. Her small hand was dry and warm.

"Where are we going?" asked Michael, using his free hand to direct the torch in every direction.

"To collect food and fire-wood, and so you can see exactly where we are," she said.

*

After walking for a little while they emerged from the shadow of the trees and moved into the familiar bright yellow world. Hanna turned off her torch but kept hold of Michael's hand. When they were a good distance from the forest, Michael turned and looked back.

"Oh my God, they're mushrooms. I thought they were trees," he said.

433

"This place is full of surprises. Those mushrooms produce the light down here. See the dust rising above them? It's luminous," she said.

A forest of impossibly large orange capped mushrooms hugged the cliff wall, and ran away into the interior of the world beneath the ocean. The space directly above their shiny convex lids pulsed in a bright ocre haze. It looked like the forest of mushrooms was on fire.

"Amazing," he said.

"Come on. I don't know how long we've got. Sometimes they stay up in the water for a long time, sometimes not. We should have the place to ourselves for at least a couple of hours. After the battle, they all go into the ocean," she said.

She tugged his hand. He followed her, step for step.

She led him out onto an open plain, moving further and further from the cliff wall and the relative safety of the mushroom forest. Although nothing moved and the place appeared empty, Michael felt anxious and exposed.

"Where are we going?"

"You'll see," she said, "come on, we should hurry."

He heard his heart beat beneath his hi-viz jacket. He tried to stay calm.

Despite the pungent odour, the air in the open plain was surprisingly easy to breath. Michael noticed a rumbling noise and, the further they went along, the louder the noise became. The ground was hard, dry and dusty and although relatively flat, every so often they had to skirt around deep hollows or leap across wide shallow trenches. The sides of the trenches were stained with a black oily substance and the bottom strewn with large clumps of what looked like gigantic animal droppings.

"Is this where the flying monsters land before changing into their snake-like form?" asked Michael.

"Yes," said Hanna, "but they nest in caves in the cliff wall. I will show you, some other time. We are not dressed for such an adventure today."

The ground rose in front of them.

"We need to creep now," she whispered, letting go of Michael's hand.

"There may be monsters in the water," she said. "and, if there are, we can't let them see us."

They dropped onto their hands and knees and crept up the rise. Michael cautiously looked over the edge and saw a wide fast flowing river was the source of the rumbling noise. The surface of the iron-coloured water lapped and bubbled as it raced by and the air above it stank of decay. The smell was cloying and poisonous. The river meandered across the open plain, disappearing around a sharp bend two hundred yards to their right. In the other direction it skirted the mushroom forest, halting its advance into the open plain.

Hanna stood at the top of the bank and looked in both directions. After a moment she pointed to a horseshoe shaped indent in the bank fifty yards away. Michael could see that she was pointing to a large pool of still water that had become isolated from the main flow.

"There," she said, "We can fish in there. We'll catch as many as we can. Stay close to me and don't go near the river's edge."

The circular pool had a gravelly bank all round and the water in it was much lower than the river running by. They carefully made their way down to the water's edge with line of scree chasing after them. The sound it made momentarily drowning out by the roar of the river. Michael wondered how easy it would be to scramble back up the bank if they had to get out in a hurry. He resolved that it was probably best not to think about it and so he concentrated on watching how Hanna went, and copying her movements.

The pool was about twenty feet in diameter and almost perfectly circular. It was separated from the raging river by a narrow gravel wall no more than three feet wide.

"Could there be creatures in the pool?" Michael asked.

"It's not big enough. But there should be fish," she said.

Hanna removed a net from her pocket. Michael recognised it as an insert from one of the haversacks. A wire had been stitched around the edge, which in turn was attached at four points to a length of thin rope. Hanna formed the wire into a neat ring and tested the rope.

"I need something heavy to weigh it down. Find me a smooth rock or a few stones, Michael. Not too heavy," she said.

Michael found some rounded stones among the scree and handed three of them to Hanna.

"That should do," she said.

She placed the stones at the bottom of the net and then tossed it into the pool. After a few moments she wrenched it out. When the net broke the surface, it trembled violently with frightened luminous fish. Against the muddy background, their luminosity was exaggerated and they sparkled like magic.

Hanna emptied the fish into a satchel she had with her.

"Can I have a go?" said Michael.

"Okay. You need to be quick and firm when you're hauling it in or they'll escape," she said.

Michael took hold of the weighted net. He thought he might cast it further out than Hanna had. He was sure he could make the centre of the pool, if he gave it a good swing. He was aware that she was watching him and that she could tell what he had in mind.

"Go for it," she said with a smile.

Michael spun the weighted net like a cowboy with a lasso and let go. The net rose in a slow elegant arc toward the centre of the pool. Just as it touched the surface of the water there was a deafening whoosh followed by a tremendous splash which caused almost the entire pool and its contents to be thrown into the air. The violent force of the wave of water drenched Michael and Hanna and threw them backwards onto the gravel bank which quickly became saturated and began to roll down toward the much-depleted pool, carrying Michael and Hanna with it. Another whoosh and splash tore down the wall of gravel that separated the river from the pool and in an instant the pool was gone, replaced by an eddy of swirling water.

Hanna somehow managed to scramble to her feet. The wet scree was like quicksand and she almost tumbled backwards, before steadying herself. She reached down and grabbed Michael's hand and with a great effort heaved him up. They scrambled together up the bank.

"What the hell?" he said.

"We need to run," Hanna shouted above the sound of the roaring river that now licked at their ankles. The ground trembled as more giant water bombs crashed to earth all across the open plains.

"What's happening?" he screamed.

They clambered over the top of the bank and stood up. Hanna stared up at the sky. Michael followed her gaze.

"Oh God," he said.

The sky was black with flying monsters returning from the ocean. As the creatures broke through the surface of the upturned sea they threw down gigantic globules of the black oily water which crashed to the ground, like enormous raindrops. Anything unlucky enough to be caught under one of them would be flattened by the weight of water.

"Run Michael," screamed Hanna, "we need to get to the cliff and then back to the forest."

Chapter 62.

Father Francis sat on his brother's bed and stared at his own reflection in the long mirror fixed to the front of their late mother's wardrobe. He felt odd. Since hearing the news of Michael's death, his mind had been unsettled. It didn't feel like grief. It didn't feel like anything. It was not a hollowness in his stomach nor a debilitating pain in his chest. It was neither sadness nor sorrow. The truth was that the Prior felt nothing, one way or another, and he knew feeling *nothing* wasn't right.

He'd wondered if it was could be a strange expression of grief. Since becoming a priest he'd witnessed grief on an almost daily basis and he understood that grief came in many different forms and was experienced differently by different people. He himself had experienced a terrible soul-searching grief after the death of their mother. As a child he'd suffered in very different ways following the death of his little sister and then his father. As a priest and confessor he'd witnessed people suffer in stoic silence or others, so physically wounded by the loss of a loved-one, that they could no longer function properly. He'd known people to grieve for years.

But this wasn't grief. He was sure of it.

He felt nothing and feeling nothing disturbed him. He wanted to feel something. He wanted to grieve, but the more he tried to focus on the idea that his brother was dead, the less real it seemed. It was only when he sat down on the edge of Michael's bed and looked at his own reflection in the mirror opposite that he began to understand why. Father Francis didn't believe that his brother was dead. Despite the evidence to the contrary, he was sure that Michael was still alive. If he was that meant he was trapped somewhere deep in the caves under Skellig Éin. Whilst the English detective had been adamant that Michael had drowned, and Marie Joyce was certain that there was no way he could have survived in the icy black waters of the cave, Father Francis wasn't convinced. After all, Michael was his twin brother. They'd shared a womb. He and his brother were connected in ways that others could not understand. He'd know if his brother was dead. He'd feel it. He'd be able to grieve.

But the living link between the brothers was not broken. Michael was still alive and the revelation was startling. In an instant, it explained so much.

From the start, doubts had whispered in the Prior's ear, but he'd chosen to ignore it. Even when he'd broken the news to Primrose, and then to Susan, he'd felt unusually uneasy, but couldn't think why. Now he knew. The uneasy feeling he'd had was a feeling of dishonesty. His words to Primrose and Susan had felt like lies.

Father Francis sat on his brother's bed and stared at the mirror image opposite.

"I'd know if you were dead," he whispered. "I'd know."

He snorted loudly like an angry bull. He stood up. The man in the mirror looked different. The look of uncertainty and emptiness had been replaced by one of determination. He would have to speak with the English detective as soon as possible. They would have to go back into the caves. He'd go himself if necessary, even if it meant going through the Devil's Throat. The detective would understand. Michael had told him that his friend Horse knew the importance of trusting an impulse, of acting on a hunch.

Father Francis didn't hear the gentle tap on the door.

"I'm sorry to disturb you Father Prior," said Brother Benjamin, "Father Bernard asked me to find you. He said he needs to speak to you urgently, about the rats in the cheese store."

The Prior looked up.

The young priest stood just beyond the threshold of the door. His eyes were red, his cheeks puffy. He'd been crying.

"Rats...? What? Oh, yes, of course. Father Bernard mentioned something about them at dinner. We'll need to get someone to come in, find the holes and seal them up. I'm sure they must be coming down through gaps around the boiler pipes," said the Prior distractedly.

"Em... it's not the boiler pipes, Father, em... it's the lower basement, the cheese store, em...but they can't, it's too far down, there are no pipes down there, Father, em...the lower basement, no pipes down there, em...no holes, no way into the lower basement Father Prior."

Brother Benjamin stuttered when he was upset.

Father Francis smiled at him.

"Of course, you are right Brother Benjamin. What was I thinking? The walls down there are solid rock and there are no pipes. You are right. How curious. They must be getting into the upper basement and finding some way down."

"Em...but Father Bernard said there's no way unless they opened the door. I...em... he said you'll need to come down and see. He told me to come and get you."

Father Francis tried not to look annoyed. Benji looked like he might start crying again. Benji looked around Michael's room, then at the Prior.

"Poor Michael," he said.

"It's fine Benji. It will all work out, I promise you. You'll see. Now listen, we have very important work to do, you and I. I will go down to see Father Bernard immediately, and help him sort out this rat problem. We can't have rats get in with our famous cheese, now can we? In the meantime, I have a very urgent errant for you to run for me. How are your feet? Are they better? Can you ride your motor bike, Benji? "

"Oh yes, Father Prior, much better now."

He dried his eyes on his sleeve.

"Really, Benji?" said Father Francis raising an eyebrow.

Brother Benjamin smiled.

"I'm fine Father Prior. I can easily ride the bike. It's easier than walking. Standing about is the worst thing. I'm fine Father Francis. You won't need to ask anyone else."

"Right then. Good."

Before Father Francis moved toward the door a small book on the bedside table caught his eye. It was The Life of St. Áedán. Michael must have been reading it before heading off to the caves. There was a thin leather bookmark three quarters way through.

"This is yours, Brother Benjamin, isn't it?" said the Prior, lifting it up and showing it to the young priest.

"Yes. I lent it to Michael. I won't take it back yet, he might not be finished it yet," he said quickly.

"Yes. Right. I'll leave it here then. You'll know where it is if you want it."

"He isn't finished it yet," repeated Brother Benjamin.

"No. Indeed. We better leave it then," said the Prior.

Father Francis wondered if maybe Benji felt the same way he did, believing that Michael was still alive, or was the young priest so grief stricken that he couldn't think straight. Before the Prior put the book back down, he flicked through it. The book was familiar to him and of little interest. It claimed to be a short history of St. Áedán and the island of Skellig Éin, but was nothing more than a cheap glossy memento, a book for pilgrims and the tourist market. It made much of the saint's reported miracles, his exceptionally long life and his monthly visits to Purgatory. It included lurid images, presented in full colour and in a hyper-realistic, painterly style. Father Francis opened the book at Michael's book-mark. There was a double page spread showing the saint rescuing sinners from the gates of Hell. In the picture the saint, depicted as a frail elderly man, knelt with his arms raised to heaven. His eyes were closed but his face was animated. He was enclosed in a large sphere of white light which seemed to emanate from his head and his hands. The kneeling saint was surrounded by naked tortured men and women. They crawled toward him out from the shadows beyond his bubble of light, pleading faces, imploring Saint Áedán to free them from the torments of Purgatory. Behind them, cowering in the darkness, was a wall of white triangular eyes. The demons looked frightened and angry. The image made Father Francis shudder. He thought of Michael, still alive and lost in the darkness. He closed the book and returned it to the bedside table.

"You must ride to the Tara Cove Hotel, Brother Benjamin, and find Detective Inspector Brian Hopkins. He's an English policeman. He's staying at the hotel. Ask Kathleen at reception. When you find him, tell him I need to speak with him urgently. Bring him here, if you have to. Do you understand Benji? As quickly as you can, now. Tell him it concerns Michael. Tell Detective Hopkins that I believe Michael is still alive and we must go back into the caves for him. Will you do that for me, Benji? As fast as you can?" said the Prior.

"Michael is alive?"

"I believe so, yes. Will you go now, Benji?"

"Yes of course Father Prior. Detective Inspector Brian Hopkins, at the Tara Cove. Michael is alive."

"Good man, and while you are away, I will go see about Father Bernard and his rats.

Chapter 63.

With one eye on the ground and the other watching the sky above they ran, hand in hand, towards the safety of the cliff. They stayed on the high ground, skirting the hollows and jumping the trenches. Hanna was panting and the further they went the slower her pace became. In stark contrast, Michael felt animated again. His muscles pulsated with energy and his senses were alive. His mind raced ahead of him. Suddenly he stopped dead, turned and grabbed Hanna as if he were about to assault her. He wrapped his arms around her and covered her with his body. Seconds later a water bomb crashed to the ground in the space they would have occupied, had they kept on going. The back of his heavy luminous jacket took most of the force of the splash. Hanna felt nothing more than a light thump as Michael was pushed into her. She looked up at him. There was terror in her eyes.

"Come on. Let's go," he said.

He looked over his shoulder and then up above them. The sky was packed with returning monsters. Some of them had already landed. Eventually, all would find a place on the ground.

"It's too late," said Hanna and she started to cry.

Michael looked in all directions. Hanna was right. It seemed hopeless. They were surrounded.

Michael took Hanna's wet face in his hands and looked into her eyes. She seemed smaller than before.

"Do you trust me, Hanna?" Before she answered, he removed his luminous jacket and put it around her shoulders.

"Do you trust me?" he said again. This time he had to shout. She looked at him as if he was mad.

"Put it on and pull up the hood. Make yourself as small as you can."

She began to shiver. Another water bomb crashed to the ground behind them. Michael pulled the coat around her.

"Come on, Hanna. Trust me. I will get us out of here. I promise. But you must trust me. Put the coat on. Okay?"

"How? What are you going to do? Don't leave me, Michael," she said in a small terrified voice.

"I won't leave you Hanna. I promise. Never!"

She put on his coat. Her fingers barely reached the cuffs.

"Good. Now tie up the hood and crouch down behind me. Hold onto my belt and don't let go and don't look up. Keep your head down. Do you hear me? We're going to walk to the cliff and with any luck none of the bastards will land on us. Okay?" he said. "It'll be okay, I promise."

"How?" she shouted at him. "How, Michael?"

"The creatures can't see me Hanna. They couldn't see me on the ledge and they couldn't see me at your viewing gallery. And they can't see me now! Don't ask me how, but they can't. With luck, they will think you are a shoal of luminous fish in that jacket and will keep their distance. If any of them get too close, I'll use the camera flash. They can't see me. Hold onto the back of my belt with both hands, keep your head down and I will lead us to the cliff."

Hanna said nothing. She just stared wide-eyed at him.

Michael smiled. He could see that she wanted to believe him.

"They can't see me. I promise. We will work together. I will be your eyes and you, in my Luminous Lenny suit, will keep them from landing on us. I'm your rescue party, remember? So, now I rescue you."

Hanna wiped her eyes.

"Trust me, Hanna," he shouted into her ear.

She nodded.

"Okay," she said.

"Good." He touched her cheek. "Then let's get going then," he said.

Michael turned, waited until he could feel her fingers grip the back of his trousers and then headed off toward the cliff.

*

Moving like a naked pantomime horse, Michael the head and front legs and Hanna, bent double and holding onto the back of his trousers, the hind quarters, they soon found a rhythm and stuck to it. As Michael suspected, the creatures ignored him and the large luminous jacket ensured they kept their distance. Once or twice Hanna stumbled, but she never let go of his belt. Once, when she stumbled and dropped to her knees, Michael stopped, crouched down and gently squeezed her hand in his. He found she was trembling and panting. After that Michael stopped regularly to allow Hanna to get her breath back.

"I'm okay. Keep going," she kept insisting.

In his effort to stay a far as possible from any of the landing creatures Michael was forced to steer them away from the mushroom forest, rather than closer. He had no choice. Getting them to the base of the cliff wall was his priority. Once under the cliff they could make their way to the forest without the fear of being crushed by the monsters. So long as they were in the open plain, Michael and Hanna were vulnerable.

During one of their short stops to allow Hanna catch her breath, Michael hunkered down and looked around.

"Are we there?" Hanna whispered from under the coat.

"No. Not yet. I need to rest and catch my breath," he lied.

Hanna let go of his belt, shuffled forward and wrapped her arms tightly around him.

"Don't leave me, Michael," she said.

"I won't," he said.

The bottom of the cliff was no more than one hundred and fifty yards away, but between them and the wall was a field of monsters. It reminded Michael of one of those wildlife programs on the TV, showing a beach jam-packed with reclining walruses, except that these walruses were the size of fully grown blue whales.

Once on the ground, the monsters lay down on their bellies and went to sleep, the only movement being the rise and fall of their enormous chests and the slow lazy swish of their vicious barbed tails. In places they were packed so close together that they were touching the monsters next to them and as more and more landed the possible routes to the wall diminished. Suddenly it looked desperate and the task impossible. Michael looked in all directions and finally spotted what seemed like the only route left to the cliff. It would not be easy and would mean making their way between two beasts that lay, side by side, head to toe, no more than four foot apart. Both looked to be asleep and both had their tails in the air. It was going to be extremely dangerous but if they could get through the gap, they would then have a relatively clear march to the wall.

Michael told Hanna it was time to go. Walking with her back bent had exhausted her but he knew that once they got going again they would have to keep on going and could not stop until they reached the base of the cliff. As he waited for her to assume her crouched position, he scanned the cliff wall. Half way up, between the ground and the bottom of the upturned ocean he could see the ledge. It ran to his left as far as he could see but, to his surprise, when he looked to his right he found that the ledge was not continuous, but stopped into the side of the cliff which, from then on, continued upwards, unabated into the upturned ocean.

Curious, thought Michael.

His eyes ran up the cliff and quickly found the triangular opening of Hanna's viewing gallery. It was below the level of the ledge but in the portion of wall that continued up through the ocean. It was also below the lowest water line, where the rock face was smooth, dry and barren. Above this line the face of the cliff was black, wet and pot-marked, with clumps of strange sea-moss sprouting out from various cracks and crevices. The cliff face was peppered with openings, some in the dry zone, such as the viewing gallery window, and many more in the wet zone above. Any cave in the wet zone would be flooded when the ocean dropped down and reached them. The opening into one of the caves in the wet zone caught his eye. It was no more than twenty feet above the top of the viewing gallery's triangular window. What attracted his attention were splashes of colour on the rock face all around its entrance. They sparkled on the wet walls and stood out in the yellow atmosphere.

Michael gasped.

The colours that covered the edges of the cave entrance were the marks left by living human beings. People had been through the entrance, people who were still alive! Michael wondered if the opening could be the entrance to a tunnel system that led back up to the hidden tiered beach or even, all the way to the surface? It was not beyond the bounds of possibility that the wall of rock kept on going, rising inexorably through the ocean and out the other side, rising and rising, until it became the rock ceiling of the enormous hidden chamber where they had found Hughie and the others. If that was the case, then the cave in the wet cliff wall could be their route out of this hell.

The colours winked at him and he began to formulate a new plan. He told Hanna they had to move quickly. She didn't object.

"Good," he said.

Michael felt exhilarated and confident and he ignored the niggling voice that whispered in his ear, warning him to be careful, and he pushed to the back of his mind the idea that the colours he could see, even from this distance, were colours he thought he recognised.

Chapter 64.

There were two reasons that the Prior rarely visited the cellars.

Firstly, the climb down was both unpleasant and, for those not used to it, dangerous, particularly for a tall man wearing a full-length cassock. Taking the first few steps was always difficult for the Prior. There were fifty-four of them in two straight flights separated from each other by a short landing half way down. The steps were steep and uneven. A curved stone ceiling followed the fall of the stairs, but in certain locations it bulged downward, reducing the head height by almost a foot, so that Father Francis had to duck down, to avoid hitting his head. Yellowing wall lights, linked together by a loose looping cable, provided weak pools of light between large areas of shadow. Some of the steps could only be located by feeling your way forward. The stair never widened enough to allow two people to pass, so traffic flow was always one-way. If two people met on the stairs one of them would have to politely turn around and go back the way they'd come. A thin wrought-iron handrail, fixed to one wall, provided the only support. Reaching the bottom always came as a great relief to the Prior and once there he tried not to think too much about the climb back up.

The second reason for not visiting the cellars was the cold reception the Prior received from Father Bernard whenever he was there. This was the Purser's domain and Father Bernard made it quite clear that he didn't like intruders of any sort. The Prior guessed that, as far as Father Bernard was concerned, he and the rats fell under the same definition of intruder.

"But today I'm here by invitation, am I not?" said the Prior to himself.

At the back of his mind he wondered if it was not more accurate to say he'd been summoned by the Purser, but as soon as this thought crossed his mind he felt guilty for thinking it.

Not very Christian of you Francis, a God-like imaginary voice whispered in his ear.

"Forgive me, Lord," he said, clasping the handrail a little tighter as he continued down.

By the time he reached the bottom he'd resolved to make a special effort with Father Bernard, although he knew it would not be easy. He could forgive Father Bernard for jealously guarding his territory, but not for his pompous intellectual snobbery. This was most pronounced in the way Father Bernard constantly belittled Brother Benjamin. Benji was young and lacked confidence, but he was not stupid, despite what the Purser liked to suggest. Intellectual snobbery was something the Prior despised. He'd always considered it a form of bullying. Recognising it in Father Bernard coloured his feelings for the man. The Prior could not tolerate bullies of any kind. But today he would make a special effort and maybe, God willing, the Purser would respond in kind.

At the bottom of the stairs there was a dim corridor which led to large ancient oak door. Over the years the door and the surrounding stone walls had faded and gathered a dusty coat, so much so, that now the two were almost the same colour. If the lights got any dimmer, thought the Prior, it would be hard to distinguish one from the other.

The door stood slightly ajar. From the brightly lit room beyond came a faint smell of garlic. The Prior could hear Father Bernard's voice. He was mumbling to himself. Father Francis rapped on the door. There was no response. He called out.

"Hello."

The mumbling stopped abruptly.

"Who's that?" snapped Father Bernard.

"Only me Father," said the Prior.

He pushed open the door and stepped onto the raised platform six feet above the cellar floor. A ship's galley ladder, to the right of the gantry, led down to the cellar. The Prior leaned on the railing and looked down.

Father Bernard stood in the centre of the room with a broom in his hand and looked up at the Father Francis, aghast.

"May I come down, Father Bernard?" said the Prior with a gentle smile.

"Father Prior?" said Father Bernard, "Of course. You are welcome. What brings you to the lowly basements of the Purser?"

Father Francis turned his back and climbed down the galley ladder. Once his feet touched the stone floor he turned around and dusted himself down with gusto, but when he looked up and saw the expression on Father Bernard's face he immediately regretted doing so. He gave the Purser a sheepish smile.

"Brother Benjamin said you needed to speak to me urgently, about an infestation of rats?"

"What? Oh really! That young man - he doesn't have the brains he was born with. I may have mentioned that I would have to discuss the vermin infestation with you, but there was no reason for you come all the way down. I must apologise Father Prior. Where is that silly young man, anyway?" Father Bernard raised his voice and turned his head from side to side, as if Brother Benjamin might magically appear from behind one of the many neatly stacked shelves. The Prior raised his eyebrows but held his tongue.

"I am so sorry to have put you to so much trouble, Father Prior, what with all that you have to deal with right now," said Father Bernard.

"Please, call me Francis," said the Prior and held his smile. "As for Brother Benjamin, I believe he is much smarter than most of us think. I believe Benji could see that I needed a distraction and proposed I immerse myself in the mundane matter of rat-catching, as a way of taking my mind of the other things. I find he has a very good heart, don't you Bernard? As for where he is, I've sent him on a most important errant to the village. With luck, he should be back within the hour, if not sooner. I know how you depend on him Father Bernard. He won't be too long, please God."

"Yes, well, of course. Maybe I can be, at times, too hard on him, but he must learn, Father Pri...Francis. He needs strict guidance. He is young and his head is in the clouds."

"Indeed. But we were all young once, were we not?" said the Prior. "Now, what about these rats, Bernard? Benji tells me they are in the lower basement. Is that possible?"

"They are, Father Francis. It is most unusual. Something has changed down there. The air is different. If you have the time, now that you are here, I can show you?" said Bernard.

"Please do. As I said, I would welcome the distraction."

Father Francis followed the Purser to the back of the cellar. As he went along the Prior noticed that the cellar was immaculately neat and uncluttered. It was a large oblong room with a barrel- vaulted stone ceiling which, at its highest point, was fifteen feet above the floor. The air was cool and a little stuffy because of a strong smell of crushed garlic. There was a constant hum emanating from a large red boiler in the far corner and the Prior found the sound strangely comforting.

The room was filled with rows of tall wooden double sided shelving units, running side by side from front to back. Every shelf was full and all were neatly stacked. Everything was ordered and clearly labelled. Food stuffs, such as shop-bought non-perishables sat next to jars of jam and marmalade made in the monastery kitchen, from fruit from the monastery garden and orchards. Boxes containing cereal, flour, sugar and salt occupied the higher shelves; cans of cooking oil and sauces on the shelves along the bottom. Nothing sat directly onto the stone floor. One entire row of shelves was given over to hundreds of jars of the famous monastery honey. The aisles between the shelves were empty and the floor was clear of everything except for the dust that Father Francis had carelessly brought with him.

The centre aisle was wider than the others and ran from the foot of the galley ladder to a low door in the middle of the end wall that, viewed from the ladder, appeared to be no more than three foot tall. This was a trick of the eye because the door sat in a four-foot recess in the floor. Seven crooked stone steps led down to a small space, wide enough for two people to stand side by side, in front of the door.

"Down, down, down," said the Prior, as they approached the hole.

"What was that, Father?" said Bernard.

"Nothing, Bernard. Nothing at all. I was just mumbling to myself."

To the right of the recess was the boiler, to the left a large and ancient dumb waiter that linked the cellar to the monastery kitchens at ground floor above.

"You've not been down to the cheese store before, have you?" said Father Bernard.

"On my first week here I stuck my head in, but I didn't climb down. I must say the cellar is a credit to you, Bernard. I envy your organisational skills. I don't know what our little community would do without you."

"Thank you Father Francis," said the Purser with pride.

Father Bernard skipped down the steps with confidence and unlocked the door with a big key, which he then dropped into his pocket. He pulled the door toward him. It moved silently on well-greased hinges. The Purser then leaned into the darkness and flicked on a light switch. The lower cellar exploded into bright white light as a series of fluorescent tubes snapped loudly into life. The Prior joined Father Bernard in the recess.

"Another climb down, Bernard," he said.

"Yes. I have been thinking about replacing the old ladder with steps, but they would take up too much space. Be careful going down, Father Prior."

The floor of the lower cellar was another five feet below the door threshold, the lower cellar roof no more than a foot above the head of the door.

"And I been thinking about getting the light switch moved to this side of the door, but I keep putting it off. Jimmy Potts is not very reliable and I don't like strangers down here," said Father Bernard.

The Prior leaned forward, as he had on his first visit to the cellars. It was like putting his face close to the open door of a freezer. The difference in temperature between the two rooms was startling.

"Will you be alright, Father Prior? The ladder is very sturdy and it's not difficult to climb onto. Just follow my lead and use the rubber grips. The metal is very cold," said Father Bernard.

"Oh I'll be fine. Lead the way, Bernard. I'll be fine."

Father Francis followed the Purser down the iron ladder fixed to the wall to the right of the door. The sides of the ladder had been wrapped with rubber pipe insulation. Where exposed, the bare iron bars felt like tubes of ice.

The lower cellar was half the size of the upper cellar in both width and length. Its sole purpose was as a storeroom for the monasteries famous garlic cheese. Row upon row of the wax covered wheels matured in the chilly air. If the cheese itself gave off any smell it could not be detected above the pong of garlic.

The Prior shivered.

Father Bernard checked a wall mounted thermometer.

"See? It's over seventeen degrees. It should be much colder. Closer to twelve, or no more than thirteen. Seventeen is much too high. And the humidity levels are fluctuating widely. It's very concerning, Father Prior."

"It seems mightily cold down here to me, but you know your business," said the Prior. He looked about. Other than the shelves containing the cheese, the room was empty. Unlike the floor in the upper room however the stone floor of the cheese store was dirty. There were small piles of what looked like animal droppings in various places.

Father Bernard followed the Prior's gaze and frowned.

"I really don't understand," he protested.

Father Francis looked around. He thought he saw something move under a tall timber shelving unit that ran the length of the back wall. He walked toward it, dropped onto his hands and knees and tried to see under. He immediately felt a draught of air kiss his face.

"What's behind these shelves, Bernard?"

"Nothing. Solid rock?"

"Well I'm sure I can feel a draught," said the Prior.

He shuffled closer, until his face almost touched the bottom shelf.

"Yes. I'm certain of it. I can feel a strong breeze at floor level. Come, tell me if I'm right."

The Purser joined Father Francis on the floor.

"Goodness me, you are right, Father Prior."

They stood up together and looked at the shelf unit.

"Can we move it, I wonder? I think we could, if we emptied the shelves," said Father Francis.

Father Bernard looked shocked by the suggestion.

"I'm not sure. We'd have to empty the shelves. Where will we put all the cheese? It all might get mixed up. Those cheeses are nearly ready. They all might get mixed up," said Bernard. Father Francis gently touched his arm.

"We'll be careful, Bernard. We'll stack them over there in, exactly, the same way they are stacked here on the shelves.

Exactly! Then, when we're finished, we'll put them back, just as they were. Okay?"

The purser nodded meekly.

"Okay," he said with a look of desperate resignation.

It took them some time to clear the shelves. Stacking the wheels of cheese, one on top of the other, didn't work very well and the neat piles soon toppled over, sending cheese rolling away in every direction.

"Oh never mind. I'll deal with them later," said Father Bernard tetchily. The Prior guessed that Bernard had concluded that dealing with the rats was more important than anything else and that sorting the cheeses could wait.

Once the shelves were empty, the Prior stood back.

"Right then, let see what's going on, shall we, Bernard? The unit looks to be in two halves. We'll pull one side and then the other, okay?" he said.

It was easier said than done. The tall shelves were heavy and had been bolted together in several places. Father Bernard went back to the upper basement and returned with a heavy wrench and then undid all the nuts, each of which he safely dropped into his pocket, beside the door key. It took all their strength to prise the two halves of the unit apart. They only stopped when there was a gap between the units wide enough to squeeze through.

"That was heavy work. Are you okay, Bernard?"

The Purser said nothing.

"Father Bernard? Are you okay?" repeated the Prior.

"They were never meant to be moved. Look at the mess we've made," he said nervously.

"Do you have a torch, Bernard?" said the Prior.

"Yes. Yes. I have two. I'll go get them."

Father Bernard went away and returned five minutes later with a big box torch and the heavy floor brush he'd been using earlier. The torch had a large diameter lens that was bigger than the rest of it. Father Bernard passed it to the Prior.

"I have a smaller one in my pocket. You take this, Father Prior. It's new. It's very bright."

The Prior switched it on. Even under the fluorescent lights of the lower cellar the glare from the torch was blinding.

"Indeed. Very powerful. Just the thing. Well then, let's take a look, shall we Bernard?"

He shone the torch between the two halves of the tall shelving unit and revealed an enormous hole in the stone wall behind, large enough for a man to pass through.

"Oh my God," said Father Bernard.

"It must have happened during the earthquake. The shelves prevented you from noticing it, Bernard. The wall's been ripped open and I think there's a cave back there."

Holding the torch in front of him Father Francis squeezed between the two shelves and then through the hole. A chilly breeze brushed his face. It was dry and fresh.

"Goodness me," he said.

He had entered a large, surprisingly cylindrical tunnel that ran to his left and right. His first thought was that it was an ancient sewer, but quickly decided it couldn't be a man-made. It was just too big. The ceiling was fifteen feet above the floor.

To his right the floor rose, whilst to his left it fell away. Tiny motes of stone dust danced and sparkled in the strong beam of white light. They could hear the rats scuttling in the shadows.

"Come see this, Bernard. I've found your vermin."

The Purser hesitated before entering the tunnel.

"Where are we?" he asked.

"I don't know," said the Prior. He shone the torch down the tunnel to his left.

"Can you hear that, Bernard?"

"What?"

"Listen," the Prior whispered.

They both stood very still.

"What is it?" said Bernard.

"I think I can hear moaning," said the Prior.

Chapter 65.

Horse and Paul spent two and a half hours in the make-shift interview room being interviewed by Brooks and a sour-faced Chief Superintendent Sutton. Garda Commissioner Whelan had joined them, via a video link, from his office in Dublin. The Garda Commissioner was particularly peeved and continually reminded everyone that he was supposed to be preparing his key-note speech for the closing session of the International Conference of Cross Border Co-Operation, "and not dealing with the fall-out from this almighty fuck up."

Nobody was pleased with how things had played out and everyone wanted someone to blame. Most of the spotlight seemed to be directed at Paul Creagan and his English colleague.

Mr G had been brought in for questioning. Although Sutton was claiming credit for capturing him, the truth was Mr G had given himself up. He'd marched into the Tara Cove Hotel with a short sweaty solicitor in toe, looking for "*the big black American guy who'd trespassed on my premises without a warrant*". Brooks questioned Mr G about the drugs and his relationship with the man at Gallagher's farm. Horse and Paul could only watch the proceeding from an adjoining room. They were not invited to participate in the questioning of the Dublin gangster.

Horse suspected that Mr G was enjoying himself. He was in a surprisingly good mood and seemed particularly pleased with the attention of the black agent.

Despite talking almost continuously for the entire thirty-minute interview, Mr G. said very little and nothing of any consequence, beyond what they already knew. As expected he admitted nothing.

"I am a businessman with legitimate business interests here on Skellig Éin. My relationship with the man at the farm was just that. Business. Legitimate business," he'd said.

"Oh? And what sort of business would that be?" snarled Sutton.

"Laundry business. I do...I mean I *did* Mr Parker's laundry. As I said, I'm shocked and saddened to hear of his early demise. He can't have been more than fifty. A heart attack, was it? Mind you, he was a prime candidate. Always looked pale, jah' know wha' I mean? Never saw 'im stand up. Always in that sitting room, always sittin' down, jah' know wha' I mean? I found him interesting. He was strange, for sure, but interesting too. Like you, Special Agent Brooks, he was *exotic*, jah' know wha' I mean? I took im' for a foreign gentleman."

Brooks raised a quizzical eye.

"Are you trying to be funny, Mr Gimple?" he said.

"Not at all, Special Agent Brooks. Just givin' you my opinion, jah' know wha' I mean?"

"You're honestly asking us to believe that your visits to this Parker creep, which by the way we have on tape, was to deliver his fucking laundry?" snarled Sutton.

"That's right, Sergeant Sutton," said Mr G with a toothy grin.

"It's *Chief Superintendent* Sutton, you lying little prick," spat Sutton.

"Now, now, that's not very nice, is it?" said Mr G.

Sutton rose from his seat and looked like he might launch himself across the table at Mr G.

Mr G. didn't flinch. He glanced at his lawyer, who immediately began to object, using phrases like harassment of my client; human rights violations; and police brutality.

"Brooks raised his hand and Sutton sat back down.

"You have him well trained," said Mr G.

Sutton's nostrils flared and his face turned puce.

"I told you what I know. You know where you find me. I'm not going anywhere," said Mr G.

When he stood up to leave, Brooks didn't move.

"We'll be watching you Mr Gimple," he said quietly.

"It seems these days, everybody's watching everybody, isn't that the case, Special Agent Brooks? Jah' know wha' I mean?"

Mr G looked up at the camera hanging from the ceiling. He smiled and winked.

Looking at the monitor in the adjacent room, Horse smiled back.

"Cheeky bugger," he said.

"Jah' know wha' I mean?" mimicked Paul Creagan.

They both laughed.

Horse had never actually met Mr G but he knew his type. He knew that Mr G was a smart and vicious crook, no more than one or two steps up from a thieving street thug who probably wouldn't think twice about murdering someone. He was definitely dangerous, the recordings retrieved from the computer hard drive included a beating Mr G had personally meted out on one of his underlings. The quality of the recording wasn't very good but sufficient to show that Mr G was a controlled and controlling psychopath. Horse also knew Mr G couldn't be trusted. He was certainly lying about his relationship with Sylvester Parker. But did that make him his killer? Of course, he could have given the order to have Parker killed, but for some reason Horse didn't think so. It just didn't feel right. Anyway, Mr G. had seemed genuinely surprised when Brooks told him that Sylvester Parker was dead. Surprised, pleased and relieved, thought Horse.

Just before he left the room Mr G turned back and said,

"By the way, the next time you two wise guys want to come into my nightclub, I'll be expecting you to pay the €10 cover charge. The good news is we do a two for one special for couples like you and Sergeant, sorry...Superintendent Sutton, jah' know wha' I mean?"

Horse could hear Mr G's loud guffaws all the way down the hall.

*

Marie and Henry were questioned together, as soon as Mr G had left. Once again Horse and Paul could only watch from the adjoining room. Henry had been coy and nervous. Marie was sarcastic and rude, aiming most of her vitriol at Sutton. When it was over she'd stormed out cursing under her breath. Horse stepped out into the hallway to intercept her, but she raced past without looking at him. It hurt him more than if she'd slapped him across the face. Before Henry left the interview room,

Brooks thanked him for saving the computer hard-drive from the basement of Gallagher's farmhouse.

"It has given us very valuable evidence for our investigations. Had you not got it out, as you did, it would have gone up in flames with the rest of that house."

"Actually Agent Brooks, I don't think it would have," said Henry.

"What do you mean, Henry?" asked Brooks.

"The cupboard it was in was a heavy-duty fire cabinet, specially designed to withstand a fire. The glass was nearly an inch thick. All the cables were protected too. It was the best I've ever seen. Better than the ones we have at the university. I bet if you went back there now, that cabinet is still standing amongst the charred rubble of the farm house." he said with a shrug of his shoulders.

"Is that so? Well maybe we'll check that out, but, nonetheless, thank you."

"Sure. No problem," said Henry with a sigh.

When Horse and Paul returned to the interview room they both baulked. It smelt like a rugby club locker room after a particularly sweaty match. The air was thick with fug and testosterone. Horse felt a headache coming on as soon as he sat down. Theodore Brooks seemed to have aged ten years since the last time they spoke. His skin no longer looked like ebony and the collar of his white shirt was no longer crisp. The knot of his tie had been fiddled with too many times and now looked like it had been tied in a hurry and without the use of a mirror. Most of all, Brooks looked exhausted.

On the other hand, Superintendent Sutton hadn't changed much since the last time Horse had met him. He still looked like a sunburnt walrus; all sweaty, angry and dangerous.

Brooks thanked them for their patience and said he was sure that the information on the hard-drive, which consisted of three and a half weeks of silent surveillance footage from the various CCTV cameras hidden around the island, would prove to be a treasure trove of information for his investigation. Brooks was satisfied that the unknown figure, whom Mr G identified as Sylvester Parker was the man he had been pursuing for the better part of a decade.

"I know we should be happy, but it all seems such a mess. I won't deny I wanted to catch the bastard alive, but at least we know he's gone," said Brooks.

"So you'll be returning to the States then?" said Paul.

"Yes. Back to Dublin this evening, then fly out tomorrow afternoon," said Brooks.

Horse thought Brooks looked relieved and found Paul's overly familiar approach rather peculiar. He had the odd impression that, just like Mr G before him, Paul was fawning in front of the American.

"I wish the recordings had sound. I'd like to have heard his voice. Mr G was no help. We enlisted the help of a lip reader from Deaf Studies at the university, to see if we could tell us what Parker was saying when he met Mr G. but Parker had an annoying habit of bringing his hands up to his mouth whenever he spoke, so only the odd word or short snippets of sentences could be discerned."

Brooks told Horse that the recordings had indicated that Sylvester Parker spent most of the three and a half weeks in the front room of Gallagher's farm, leaving only to use the bathroom or when he went to bed. He seemed to have a routine. He went to bed at the same time every night. He returned to his desk each morning at the same time too. For most of the day Parker just sat there looking at the computer monitor in front of him. Once in a while, he paced the room. Parker ate meals brought to him by an unseen accomplice (someone who managed to avoid being caught on any of the cameras in the farmhouse or anywhere else), and wrote letters, most of which he never finished. Almost all of them were scrunched up into angry balls and lobbed in the direction of the empty fireplace.

Horse and Paul had been let see small segments of the recordings from the farmhouse. Horse's first impressions was that Sylvester Parker appeared either anxious or bored, and whilst he certainly looked and acted the part of evil criminal mastermind, something didn't feel right. Parker's violent death and dismemberment suggested that whoever had him killed was anxious to ensure his identity remained a mystery. Burning the farm down was just finishing the job. Brooks stated that the faceless body in the bedroom was definitely Sylvester Parker. Sophisticated computer bone structure analysis of the footage of the man writing the letters, matched the man on the bedroom floor. The second man was clearly Parker's man servant, O'Hara, although nothing was known of him beyond what he looked like and how he dressed.

Horse could not help feeling they were missing something obvious.

"Well, you got what you came for. Your visit to Ireland has been a success," Paul said.

Brooks narrowed his eyes.

"Do you think so, Detective Creagan? What about you, Inspector Hopkins? Do you think we got what we came for?"

"Well, as I see it, there's still a lot of unanswered questions," said Horse.

"Such as," said Brooks.

"Well, for starters, who killed Parker and why? And why cut off his face and hands? And the other guy, O'Hara, the guy who likes wearing corsets, do we know anything about him or does he matter? And where's Gerry Gallagher? And who was the guy in the car, the one who started the fire, the one who presumably killed Parker and O'Hara? And then there's all that surveillance. What was all that for?"

"Seems fuckin' clear to me," snapped Sutton, "Mr G. or one of his henchmen killed Parker and Parker's pansy boyfriend too, and probably the farmer. You two jerk-offs probably watched the killer drive away from the crime scene."

Theodore Brooks said nothing. He kept his eyes focussed on Horse. Horse didn't blink.

Horse's unanswered questions were not the focus of the Garda Commissioner's mind when he joined them again via a Skype link from his office in Dublin.

The Commissioner didn't waste time with niceties either.

"How the fuck did these fuckers manage to bug our operations and God help us, even the closed-door discussions of the international conference? Holy Sweet Jesus, we'll be the laughing stock of Europe. How the fuck did this happen? That's what I'd like to know. And by the way, Mr Brooks, your superiors back home in Washington are asking the same questions. One of them called it a security breach to end all security breaches. It's fucking staggering, wouldn't you say Mr Brooks?"

Brooks didn't answer.

"As for you Garda Creagan, where exactly have you been all day? Whilst you were gallivanting about on a sight-seeing tour of the island, the man you were supposed to be watching was wandering around murdering and dismembering people like there's no tomorrow."

The Commissioner paused before he went on.

"And as for you, Detective Inspector Hopkins, what has Scotland Yard's contribution been to this fiasco? Sweet fuck all, if you ask me. If this thing goes public, Scotland Yard's involvement will not be brushed under the carpet, I can assure you of that. None of this will be forgotten. For now we need to contain this. We will focus on the successful drug seizure and highlight the fact that it was because of cross-border co-operation, between three police forces, that a major crime syndicated was broken up and a major crime thwarted. Do you understand? Superintendent Sutton..."

"Ye...s Commissioner?"

"I want a full report on my desk by eight tomorrow morning. Where are we in relation to charges being brought against Gimple? I want him charged. The girl from the cave, I want her charged too, with possession and involvement. I trust, Mr Brooks, that your people will assist Chief Superintendent Sutton?"

"Of course Garda Commissioner," said Brooks.

"And what about these fucking cameras?"

"The hotel has been thoroughly swept, all the devices have been located, neutralised and removed. Everywhere is clean," said Brooks.

"A bit late, aren't you? If you think I'm angry, Agent Brooks, wait until you get back home. It wouldn't surprise me if you get sent back to CIA school or wherever you guys come from," said the Commissioner. "And as for you Garda Creagan, your holiday is over. Give everything you have to the Chief Superintendent, and then head back to Dublin. I will decide what to do with you later."

With that the video link to Dublin was terminated.

Chapter 66.

Horse thought Brooks was surprisingly open with himself and Paul once the Garda Commissioner had logged off and Chief Superintendent Sutton had left the room. Horse wondered if this new, friendly approach, was a matter of professional courtesy or because the American felt guilty about how Paul was being made the scapegoat for everything that happened. After some reflection he concluded that neither was the case and, for the second time that day, felt that there was something he was missing. Horse knew that Theodore Brooks was a calculated man and that everything he did and said, he did and said for a reason. Horse suspected that Brooks was only being civil to them to be sure that they weren't holding anything back of their own. Horse didn't trust Brook and clearly, Brooks didn't trust him.

Brooks told them that a full analysis of the surveillance tapes would take months. The criminals had been much smarter than the Irish, British or Americans could have imagined. Having eyes *and ears* (all the bugs found were fitted with high-range microphones) in the interview room, the conference hall and the reception area of the Tara Cove Hotel, the bad guys were always at least two steps ahead of the authorities. From behind his ornate desk, Parker could watch and listen to the conference, to Mr G's day to day goings on and even listen into what the American's task force was up to. The level of infiltration was staggering. Brooks showed them various edited segments of the recordings found on the hard-drive.

"This is your international criminal mastermind?" asked Horse when he was shown footage of the curious dark eyed man sitting behind the desk in the front room of Gerry Gallagher's farm. Horse sounded sceptical. The man reminded Horse of a Hollywood version of a latter-day Devil. Parker was certainly strange looking and appeared to have multiple personalities. Whenever he met with Mr G he sat upright and looked manic and dangerous. When he was on his own he slumped in the big chair like a bored child. Whenever the man-servant was in the room Parker seemed obsequious.

"It would appear so," said Brooks with a sigh.

"And you think Mr G. had him killed?" said Paul Creagan.

"Superintendent Sutton believes so," said Brooks.

"It doesn't feel right," said Horse. "From what we know of Mr G, it's not his style. Carving off their faces and chopping off his hands, that's Russian Mafia behaviour, not the modus operandi of a Dublin pimp."

"Maybe Mr G has moved up a level, or maybe the drugs belonged to the Russians and they wanted to send a message," said Brooks.

"Mr G didn't seem worried. He looked surprised that Parker was dead. In fact, he looked relieved," said Horse.

Brooks tried to stare Horse down. In the end, he gave up.

"What about this other guy, the servant? Anybody know anything about him?" said Horse

"We haven't identified him yet, but we will. Mr G said he was known only as O'Hara. No first name. It's probably an alias. Does the name mean anything to either of you?"

"Not me," said Hopkins.

"And you, Paul?" said Brooks

"No," said Paul adding, "Mr G's description of him suggests he's the kind of fellow who'd stand out in a crowd. The corset, the white gloves, the unusual dress sense. A bit of a dandy, by all accounts. He must have stuck out like a sore thumb in Skellig Éin. Someone must have seen him. He must be picked up on CCTV somewhere around the island."

"We'll find out who he was," said Brooks, "but the important thing is that we've finally got Parker."

The American stared at Horse

"What are you thinking Superintendent Hopkins?" asked Brooks.

"It doesn't feel right. None of it. That's what I'm thinking Agent Brooks."

468

Horse thought about the man hanging in the woods, flayed and dismembered. Could the two mutilated bodies be connected, he wondered? He thought about Parker's reaction when the man-servant was in the room with him. What was the word for it?

"Supplicant," he suddenly said out loud.

"What?" said Brooks.

Paul looked at Horse.

"Sorry. Nothing. Just thinking of a word. It just came to me there."

"Has it anything to do with all this, Superintendent Hopkins?" asked Brooks.

"No. Just a word I've been thinking about. Supplicant. You know, it means submissive. Last word to complete a crossword puzzle," said Horse with a curious smile.

"What? You're thinking about crossword puzzles? For God sakes, Hopkins," said Brooks tetchily.

By the time they left the interview room it was after 10.30pm. Paul asked Horse if he'd like to get a drink at the bar, but Horse declined the offer.

"I'll give it a miss Paul. I need to shower. I'll probably clean out the mini bar in my room before I sleep. We'll meet at breakfast and arrange our return to Dublin then. Good night Paul," he said.

As he made his way to his room Horse thought about Megan and the group of young men who'd been with her on the ferry. He thought about Sylvester Parker and he thought about Michael. Most of all he thought about Marie.

*

Horse had just stepped out of the shower and was brushing his teeth at a steamed-up mirror, when there was a firm tap on the door.

"What now?" he sighed.

"Hold on a sec, I'm g'umfming" he shouted as he spat a mouthful of minty tooth paste into the bowl.

Could this day get any worse, he wondered?

The person rapped on his door again, even louder the second time.

"I'm coming. Hold on."

Horse found a complimentary hotel dressing gown hanging in the wardrobe and put it on, then opened the door.

Marie Joyce stood in the hallway looking up at him. She smiled.

"Are you alone?" she said.

"Marie? Yes. Absolutely."

"Well?"

"Em...?"

"Well are you going to invite me in or do you intend the whole hotel to see me like this?"

Marie began to open the top buttons of her blue taffeta dress.

"No. Come in, come in."

"I thought you were never going to ask?" she whispered.

They stood face to face behind the closed door. Horse looked into Marie's soft eyes. Without a word he leaned down and kissed her. Her lips came to meet his.

He wanted to say so much. He wanted to tell her how beautiful she was, how much he'd yearned for her from the moment he'd seen her on the ferry, how visions of her filled his head and constantly invaded his thoughts. He wanted to tell her how much he wanted her, wanted to be in her, to be one with her, naked in body and soul. He wanted to tell her all this and more, but he didn't speak.

He just kissed her.

He kissed her eyes and the tip of her nose and the rose of her cheeks. He kissed her head, her hair and the lobes of her ears. He kissed her neck and her shoulders. When he'd removed her dress he kissed her breastbone and the gauzy material of her white brassiere. When he undid the clasp at the back and the delicate bra fell to the floor he kissed her breasts and her erect nipples. She held his head between her hands and gently pushed him to his knees. He ran his tongue around the prickly warm skin of her stomach and poked it into the hollow of her small belly button. From there he traced a trail of saliva down to the front of her silk panties. He pushed his tongue into the puffed-out material and felt her pelvis respond. She gripped his hair and lifted his head.

"Make love to me, Englishman," she whispered.

He stood up and removed his dressing gown, then lifted her off the floor and carried her to the bed.

They made love slowly.

Horse had never felt anything like it. He had to work very hard to stop himself from ending it all, before it got started. He tried to think of something distracting, to take his mind off what his body was screaming to do, but it was no good. Marie smelt and tasted wonderful. She responded in a way he'd never experienced and when he entered her the feeling was so intense that he wanted to cry out. She dug her fingers into his back and she bit his bottom lip. She wrapped her legs around his and pulled him into to her. His hands explored her breasts and the tips of their tongues fumbled with each other like frantic dance partners. They came together and when they did, the bed moved with a thump against the wall. Marie jerked and jerked. She gripped him so tightly and shuddered so much that he felt that they had become conjoined; melded together into a single trembling whole.

Horse wrapped himself around her and closed his eyes.

"Never set me free," he whispered. She smiled and kissed him. "Can I ask you something, Marie?"

"Go ahead, but I'm not going to promise to answer you."

"Why me? I knew from the first day on the ferry that you liked me, but I can't think why. Why did you choose me, Marie?"

"Ha. Men! You are all the same. Always in competition with other men. If you must know, when I saw you on the ferry you reminded me of a boy I once knew. I thought I'd seen a ghost."

"I reminded you of an old boyfriend?"

"He's gone. He is from the past. Another time. Another world. Anyway, that was then. As I got to know you, you grew on me."

"Did I? Good. What was his name, this boyfriend?"

"Owen."

"Did you love him?"

"We were only children, so yes, as a child, I did."

"Will you love me?"

"I think so," she said.

"Good, because I've decided to love you too."

They lay together in the warmth of their combined body heat and would have slept like that all night, had the phone beside the bed not suddenly burred into life.

"Ignore it," she whispered.

"Sure," he said.

It burred again.

"It might be Paul. Something might have happened," he said.

"Answer it then," she said.

"I don't want to."

It burred again.

"Answer it," she said.

"Okay."

Horse prised himself free, sat up and answered the phone.

It wasn't Paul.

"Reception? Do you know what time it is? I was in bed," he said, trying to sound annoyed. The woman on the other end of the line said something.

"Who?" said Brian.

The woman repeated what she'd just said.

"Brother Benjamin? Here? Now? But it's after eleven O clock," said Horse.

After a long pause Horse spoke again.

"Hello Brother Benjamin. Yes, this is Inspector Hopkins. What's this all about?"

After another pause, he said,

"But that can't be right. What? Okay. Give me ten minutes. I'll be down to you in ten minutes. I need to get dressed. I'm in bed. Ten minutes. See you then, Brother Benjamin."

He carefully returned the phone to its cradle.

Marie gathered the bed sheet about her and sat up. She looked at him.

"A Brother Benjamin is waiting for me in reception. He is here to bring me to see Father Francis, Michael's brother. Apparently, it's most urgent. Father Francis seems to believe that Michael is still alive."

Marie didn't say anything. Horse furrowed his brow. The thought of Michael had destroyed his good mood.

"I think I should go. Will you wait for me, Marie?" he said.

"No," she said.

"What?"

She smiled.

"I'll come with you."

Chapter 67.

Making it to the base of the cliff wall was easier than Michael had anticipated. The beasts on the ground were all asleep. He even touched one as he passed by.

Since waking that morning Michael felt fearless and full of energy. In stark contrast, Hanna was exhausted and terrified. She became hysterical when Michael stretched out his arm and ran his hand across the oily hide of one of the monsters.

"They're asleep," he said in defence.

She tugged at his belt angrily until he withdrew his hand.

"Sorry," he said.

He waited until they got to the cliff before he told Hanna of his plan.

"Listen to me Hanna. We're not going to make it back to the forest."

"Why not?" she gasped.

"It's too far. There are too many of them. But I have an idea."

Hanna looked around and when she saw that the route to the forest was completely blocked she started to cry.

Michael thought she looked small and pathetic in his big luminous jacket. He felt awful.

"Listen to me, Hanna; I won't let anything happen to you. I promise you." He took her into his arms and hugged her tightly. She squeezed him.

"We can do this. We've come this far. You survived here on your own. Together we can do this," he said.

"Do what?" she whispered.

"Climb," he said, "up there."

He pointed to the cave in the cliff face twenty feet above the triangular viewing gallery window.

"Up there," he said again.

She followed the line of his finger and found the entrance he was pointing at.

"Why. What's up there?" she said.

"I think it's a way back to the hidden beach. If we can get back to the beach, then maybe we can find the trail of lights and make our way back home."

*

From where they were, the climb looked reasonably straightforward. The rock wall was covered in horizontal ledges that jutted out three or four feet from the cliff face. The ledges were stacked one on top of the other and were never more than five feet apart. From below, the wall looked like a giant's bookcase. Michael was sure that if he and Hanna could get onto the lowest ledge, they could quickly and easily climb the rest of the way up to the cave stained with the human colours. The only problem was getting onto the lowest ledge.

It was at least twelve feet above their heads and the cliff face up to it was flat and smooth, with no obvious grips or toe-holds. To make matters worse, the wall sloped outwards as it rose. Even with ropes and proper climbing gear, scaling it would be difficult; without them, it was virtually impossible. Michael looked around for another way up. He'd almost given up hope when he spotted something and an idea popped into his head. One of the larger creatures lay against the cliff wall, wedged between it and a outcrop of medium-sized boulders, and the top of the monster's scaly back was almost level with the lowest ledge. The beast was asleep. Its barded tail lay motionless just above the ground, and it's head was tucked under one wing.

"We need to get up to that ledge Hanna and then it will be an easy climb to the cave," Michael whispered.

Hanna had been watching him and she could tell what he was thinking. She shook her head dramatically.

"We can't," she said.

"We have to, but I'm sure it'll be all right. When I touched the creature, out on the field, it didn't feel me. Their hides are thick. Once on its back we can step onto the ledge and climb up to the cave. Honestly Hanna, the beast won't feel us. We'll be like flies on the back of an old dog."

She clung to his arm with both hands.

"We can't. It's madness," she said.

"Once we get onto the ledge we can get to the cave quite quickly. If it turns out to be a dead end, we can always make our way to the triangular window and back to your cave. We need to hurry Hanna. Even if we wanted to get back to the forest we'd never make it, you know that's true, Hanna. We have no choice."

She looked terrified.

"Come on Hanna, we can do this," he whispered.

He had to drag her forward. They made their way toward the sleeping monster, always careful not to get too close to any of the other beasts or their barbed tails. When they reached the boulders Michael led her up to the top of the tallest one, which put them level with the top of the beast's rump.

"I can't do this, Michael. Really, I can't. I'll fall," Hanna said.

"Yes you can. I'll go first and then you. I won't let you fall, I promise. Once on the tail we can climb up its back. Like ticks on the tail of a dog. I promise"

Hanna's grip on Michael's hand tightened.

"I can't," she sobbed.

"Yes you can. I won't let you fall."

Reluctantly, she loosened her grip.

"It will be fine," he said.

She let go of his hand. He touched her face, smiled at her and then winked.

"Good girl."

Michael turned and looked at the monster. Before he stepped out he looked over his shoulder at the field behind. He could see that some of the creatures had begun to stir. Time was running out. They'd have to go now. Michael took one large exaggerated step. The gap between the rock edge and the spine of the wide tail was no more than five feet. He landed solidly and then dropped onto all fours before straddling the tail. It felt like he had mounted an elephant. The beast didn't move. Its hide was rough and the black fish scales were course and rigid. They provided excellent hand-holds. Michael slipped his left hand under one and gripped on tight. He steadied himself before turning back to Hanna. She looked at him with wide-eyed terror and before he had a chance to say anything, or get himself ready to catch her, she jumped out with her arms and legs flailing widely.

Michael was caught totally off guard and braced himself for the inevitable collision.

It never happened.

Hanna didn't reach him. Her legs hit the up-slope of the curve of the tail and rather than crashing into him she toppled awkwardly backwards and slid down the side of the tail. She ended up on her back, wedged between the tail and the side of the rock she'd been standing on.

She began to scream.

Michael panicked.

"Stop screaming," he whispered.

The beast moved. The tail moved. Hanna slipped further down.

Gripping clumps of the beast's hide Michael scrambled down after her.

"Give me your hand," he yelled.

The tail moved again, threatening to crush Hanna between it and the rock. If the beast woke or moved again, she'd be killed.

She looked desperate. She tried to grab at the scales but, where she was, closer to the underside of the tail, they were shorter and more like thorny spikes. Along with that, they were wet and slippery.

Michael slid further down.

The beast rolled a little and the tail began to rise. With one last heave Michael grabbed for Hanna and by pure chance caught her by the wrist. The tail rose quickly and Michael and Hanna rose with it. Holding on to the tail with all his strength Michael dragged Hanna up to him. Somehow they managed to clamber onto the ridge of the rising tail just as the monster came to life.

Out on the plains Michael could see some of the beasts were rising and taking to the air.

The barbed end of the tail they were on, rose above them. Michael knew that if they let go it would mean certain death. They were now fifteen feet above the ground. Hanging on was getting harder and harder. Their only hope was to get onto the ledge.

Michael turned and looked toward the cliff. The ledge was close. The tail kept rising. The beast twisted and began to flex the tips of its unfolding wings. Michael knew that at any moment the beast would try to stand. To do that it would move away from the cliff wall and the opportunity to get onto the ledge would be gone. If they were going to jump it would have to be now.

"We've got to stand and jump," he screamed. "Stand up Hanna, we need to jump. We'll go together. Okay? Get ready. On the count of three."

They stood and wobbled but somehow remained upright. Michael put an arm around Hanna's waist and roughly turned her body so that she faced the cliff wall. With his other hand he gripped a twisted clump of thick feathers. They began to slide sideways as the tail began to curl in over the body of the beast.

The barbs at the tip hung menacingly over Michael and Hanna. The ledge came into view. It was wider than expected.

"One..."

The tail kept rising. The beast's body trembled violently as it shook off the short sleep.

"Two...."

The tail began to move away from the wall. Michael steadied himself for the jump. He felt Hanna tense.

"Three."

They jumped together just as the tail flicked and the beast stumbled upright. They were catapulted through the air. Michael hit the cliff wall with a tremendous crash and fell like a sack of potatoes onto the ledge. Hanna landed heavily on top of him.

The beast bellowed, dislodged itself from the wall, stretched out its enormous wings and rose awkwardly into the air.

Hanna scrambled to her feet as if woken from a trance.

"Get up Michael. We have to move."

Blood ran from the top of Michael's skull and trickled down cheek. For a moment he was disorientated and wobbled dangerously close to the edge. Hanna put her shoulder under his arm and dragged him back in.

"Come on Michael. We need to move."

His mind cleared slowly. As it did the pain on the crown of his head intensified.

"Ah!" he wailed.

"Come on. We'll see to that later. We need to move."

Blood trickled into his mouth.

He stumbled forward like he was drunk but Hanna kept him upright and somehow took his weight.

They climbed quickly. Just as Michael had hoped, the climb proved relatively easy. Soon they reached the mouth of the cave, by which time Michael had regained his senses and the pain in his head was completely gone.

"I'll go first," he insisted, adding a "just in case."

"Just in case of what?" said Hanna.

"Just...in case. They can't see me, remember? If there are any creatures in there they won't see me, but I can see them. They might see you though. So, I'll go first, just in case."

Hanna didn't argue. The sky behind them began to fill with waking monsters.

"Okay but hurry it up," she said.

"Right. Stay under the jacket Hanna."

"Don't worry about me. Just hurry up. I'll be right behind you."

Chapter 68.

Before entering the cave, Michael noticed it had started to rain. Large droplets of icy water spat at him from above.

When he looked up he saw that the gravity-defying ocean had begun to descend again. It looked bloated and seemed to strain with the effort of holding its enormous load in place. He started to wonder if climbing up to a cave that would very soon be under water, had been such a good idea.

He stepped over the threshold.

The entrance was stained with human colours - the roof, the side walls and the floor – and the living colours pulsed with a soft glow. A trail of colours led into the darkness.

The amount of colour visible to Michael bothered him. It was more than he'd expected. He hesitated.

"Well? What are you waiting for? This was your idea," said Hanna over his shoulder.

"Right. Yes. Okay," he whispered.

Michael stepped forward into the pitch-black cave and onto a steep ramp. He stumbled forward and only just managed to remain on his feet. As soon as he stopped moving, he held his breath. Nothing moved in the darkness and there was no sound, but he could see people in front of him. They were huddled together in small groups, ten or twelve in all.

"Hello," he said.

No one replied. He reached for his torch, but before he turned it on Hanna slid down the ramp and crashed into him. They fell over and Michael dropped the torch.

"Ouch," he cried.

"Sorry, but you could have told me that the floor wasn't level. I can't see a thing," she whispered.

"I dropped the torch," he said, "help me find it, Hanna."

They crawled about, on all fours.

Michael found the torch and switched it on.

Hanna had moved away from him and was holding onto someone else's arm. The man was on his knees and one side of his face was missing. When Hanna saw what she was doing, she jumped backwards and screamed. The man toppled forward and landed face down with his legs in the air.

"I thought it was you," she said shuffling up to him and grabbing his arm.

Michael shone the torch about. They were in a small chamber with no other entrance or exit. At the back of the space was a small group of people. Some were sitting, some lying and some in strange contorted poses. One or two could even have been described as standing. Several of them leaned on each other. They all looked frozen solid. Those that were turned toward Michael and Hanna stared past them with dead eyes. It was as if Michael and Hanna were witnessing at the final act of a hideous contemporary dance move.

They were all disfigured horribly. Most of their injuries looked serious, if not fatal. Some of them had been partially disembowelled, some had limbs missing and all of them had been flayed to some degree. They looked like deformed life-sized manikins moulded in the workshop of a madman. They reminded him of Denis and the man hanging from the tree.

His heart sank.

When Michael had first spotted the cave high on the cliff wall, and saw the colours of living human beings, he believed that it was proof that other people had found the world of monsters and had lived to tell the tale. At the time, he'd wondered if the cave was *their* viewing gallery, and if so then maybe part of a tunnel system that ran between the underworld of monsters and the hidden beach above the ocean. It had seemed like a reasonable proposition at the time and certainly worth exploring.

Now Michael knew the truth.

He had led Hanna into the monster's pantry. This was where the creature's stored and, most disturbingly, *preserved* their food. His hand shook and in the half-light the shadows of the torn and twisted men danced across the floor and up walls.

"Oh God," he whispered.

Hanna grabbed his arm.

"Are…are they all dead?" she gasped.

"I…I don't know," he lied in a hollow voice.

"They couldn't be, could they?" she said.

"No. Of course not."

Hanna looked away in disgust then tugged at his sleeve.

"Look at the roof Michael," she said.

Michael shone the torch upwards.

The roof of the cave was peppered with thick funnel-shaped formations that protruded two or three feet into the room, like upside down stone beehives. Michael and Hanna stepped under one and looked up. It was hollow. Inside was a vertical tubular shaft about four feet in diameter.

"They're like upside-down chimney pots," she said. "I wonder where they go."

"Up, I suppose" said Michael.

They moved to the next funnel making sure to watch where they put their feet. It was the same as the first.

"If they go up, I wonder how far?" he said.

One of the funnels caught his eye. It was larger than the others and different in other ways too. It's rim and shaft were stained with human colours. He moved toward it but before he got there something at the back of the chamber made a noise. Michael redirected the torchlight.

Hanna gasps.

"Oh God, what's that?".

From a roof funnel at the back of the cave something white had begun to emerge. It was large, bloated and wormlike. It whined as it squeezed its plump sticky body out of the vertical shaft.

"Reeeeeeee," it screeched, as it twisted free.

It had a trumpet-like snout and the same triangular eyes of the monsters outside. A gauzy outer layer of skin covered its bulbous head. When it opened its beak, it revealed two rows of small pointed teeth.

"It's a baby monster," gasped Hanna.

"This place is a nest," said Michael.

With one last push the white worm plopped noisily onto the floor then raised its head and waved its snout in their direction.

Michael and Hanna backed away.

"We need to get out of here Michael. Coming here was a mistake," shouted Hanna.

"I'm sorry, Hanna. You're right, I shouldn't have brought you here."

"Never mind that. We'll go back to the viewing gallery. We'll be safe in my tunnel," she said.

"Okay, let's go."

They turned toward the doorway but immediately stopped.

"Oh God, no," said Hanna.

Outside the cave a black winged monster hovered menacingly. It looked straight at them and screamed.

"Reeeeeeee."

"Fuck," said Michael.

He pulled Hannah to one side, away from the doorway, the worm on the floor and the funnels in the ceiling. When they reach the far corner they hunkered down.

The monster outside the entrance was too big to get in, so Michael kept the torchlight trained on the white worm on the floor. The baby monster was six feet long, from top of snout to tip of its small partly-formed barbed tail, and it was as thick as a fully-grown walrus. It moved like a slug towards the entrance.

"Reeeeeeee," it screamed.

"Reeeeeeee," bellowed the monster outside the cave.

More worms emerged from other funnels in the rock ceiling. Soon there were seven of them on the floor, all screaming like the first. The noise was deafening. It reverberated around the cave. Hanna tightened the hood of the luminous jacket around her ears and buried her head in Michael's side. Michael noticed that no worm emerged from the largest funnel. He wondered why. Suddenly, the winged monster outside the entrance threw itself at the cliff wall. The floor of the cave shook with the impact. Hanna buried her head further into Michael's side. Michael watched in horror as the monster, clinging to the cliff face, twisted its bulbous head and pushed its long beak into the chamber.

The baby monsters crawled toward the adult's snout.

"Reeeeeeee."

The mother beast sniffed the air and then moved her snout in Michael and Hanna's direction but moved her snout about only stopping when it reached the body of a man that Hanna had knocked over. The creature nudged the man with the tip of it's beak, almost gently. When nothing happened it nudged him again, this time with just enough force to roll the man onto his side, exposing a terribly mutilated torso. Michael watched in horror as the monster turned its head and opened its beak as wide as it could in the confined space, and a thin snake-like tongue emerged. As Michael watched the tip of the tongue buried itself into the petrified man's gut and began sucking on the his innards. He wanted to look away but he couldn't.

The tongue thickened.

The seven white worms stopped screaming and gathered in a semi-circle around the beak. After awhile the adult beast withdrew its tongue and raised the tip high into the air above the baby monsters who had gathered underneath. They raised their heads and opened their mouths, like hungry chicks in a crowded nest. With a pulsing motion the tongue discharged its load, showering the worms in a steaming milky spray. They snapped and swallowed and jostled each other for the best position under the tongue.

Michael thought he might throw up. He could hardly hold the torch steady. He thought about turning it off but the prospect of being left in total darkness frightened him even more than the horror that curiosity forced him to watch. He was glad Hanna wasn't interested in seeing what was happening. He pulled her tighter to him.

He was angry and frightened. He had surely led them to their death or possibly something far worse. He felt stupid and ashamed. They were doomed. It was only a matter of time before the seven baby monsters or the mother monster discovered them.

He shone the torch around the cave in a vain attempt to find a hidden crack in the back wall or an opening they may have missed at floor level. There were none. The torchlight rested on the large funnel. He stared at the colours.

None of the other funnels were stained in the same way.

As he pondered why this should be, there was a terrible crash and, with frightening force, the black monster yanked its beak out of the cave. The suddenness and force of it, dragged two of the feeding worms after it. Michael leaned forward to see what had happened. Through the entrance he saw that the battle above the plains had begun again and that the suckling mother had been one of the first monsters to be attacked. She had been ripped from the cliff wall by a much larger creature and then torn to pieces by an excited mob. The two worms that followed her out of the cave fell helplessly down the cliff wall, but neither made it to the ground. The remaining worms began to make their way up the ramp toward the entrance in search of their mother. One by one the plump babies were snatched up in the jaws of passing monsters, until all of them were gone.

Michael and Hanna remained huddled together until the focus of the battle moved away from their cave. Just as before, the battle ended as abruptly as it had begun. In the silence that followed, Michael tried to calm his pounding heart. He stood up, lifting Hanna to her feet. She kept her face buried in his side and her arms wrapped around him, no longer interested in seeing or knowing what was happening. Michael shuffled them toward the cave entrance. He knew if they were to survive they would have to climb down to the viewing gallery as quickly as possible, but when he looked out his heart sank.

Escape to Hanna's viewing gallery was no longer an option. Although the battle was over, the lowering ocean was almost completely down, its bulging black belly almost at the head of the cave entrance. Sheets of water ran down the cliff face and the ledge outside the entrance was now a river. If they stepped out onto it, they would be swept over the edge. But staying where they were, wasn't an option either. At any moment, the ocean would rush into the chamber. They had to do something.

Michael turned around and trained the torch at the base of the large funnel.

"Hanna. We need to move."

He prised her from his side and faced her.

"We need to go up," he said, pointing at the funnel.

"Up? Up where?" she said.

"Up one of the chutes," he said.

"Are you mad, Michael?"

"We have no choice. All the worm-monsters are gone. We need to go up one of the chutes and I think I know which one. Come on, I've no time to explain. If we don't go now, we'll drown."

As if to reinforce his point the ocean entered the chamber and thundered across the rock ceiling. It didn't take long for it to reach the bottom of the smaller funnels. The cave was filling up from the top down and at a frightening rate. Michael dragged Hanna under the largest funnel. Its mouth was lower and wider than the others and if they climbed up, there was enough room for both of them to fit inside. The rock edge around the mouth of the funnel was damaged and broken but there was no evidence of any worms. The walls of the tubular shaft, which rose vertically beyond the reach of Michael's torchlight, were smooth and shiny.

"Quickly now. I'll climb up and then pull you after me. Okay? Don't mess about. There are none of those worms up there. I'm sure of it," he said.

The look on Hanna's face surprised him.

"Don't worry about me," she said. Before Michael could say another word, she had scampered up the funnel.

Now he was alone. He turned the torch toward the people on the floor. They looked like broken discarded mannequins. One of them was staring at him, accusingly. The man's colours looked familiar. They were the same ones he'd noticed on the entrance to the cave on the upper ledge, when he and Marie first entered the tiered beach. He shone the torch directly at the man and noticed that one of his eyes was a different colour to the other. Although he recognised the man's colours, he couldn't remember where he'd seen them. Just before he clambered up the chute he thought he saw the man blink, but decided it was only a trick of the light.

Pressing against the smooth walls of the funnel with her hands and feet Hanna climbed as high as she could and then stopped and wedged herself there. When Michael reached her, he manoeuvred himself so that they were face to face. He shone the torch up the shaft. It seemed to go on forever.

"We'll never climb that," said Hanna.

"No," said Michael, "but we won't have to. Get ready to grab hold of me Hanna. We'll go up together."

The roar from the ocean below was suddenly replaced by a loud continuous moan as the water entered from below and forced the air upwards. In a matter of seconds the ocean was in the shaft and rushing upwards toward them. The head of the icy water caught Hanna and Michael at a tremendous rate, forced them together and then shot them up the chute, like peas up a wind pipe.

Up they went, into the darkness and into the unknown.

Part Five

"Aiséirí."
"Resurrection."

Chapter 69.

Mr G headed for the bar of the Tara Cove.

It had been an impulse decision. As he was leaving the hotel, after his fun with Agent Brooks and Superintendent Sutton, he saw someone in the lobby he recognised, so he turned around and went back in. The woman had smiled at him and the smile had been inviting. Seeing her again had seemed like a stroke of great fortune or maybe, he thought, a matter of fate. Whichever, luck or destiny, it gave Mr G the opportunity to satisfy a desire he'd had for some time. So instead of going back to his lonely office he turned around and followed her into the bar.

As he did so he thought of the first time he'd seen the strange woman and the strong, unusual feelings he'd had ever since.

He'd been on one of his long lunchtime walks through the lakeside park when the mysterious woman, literally, fell into his arms. They'd met on a narrowed stretch of footpath that ran between a dense copse of trees and the edge of the black lake. A low concrete wall had recently been built on the lake side to stop the footpath from flooding when the lake rose after heavy rain. The addition of the low wall reduced the width of the footpath and, for anyone not concentrating, the low wall presented a trip hazard.

Mr G had watched the woman approach. She was walking towards him and heading straight for the start of the low wall. She had her head held high above the raised collar of her heavy coat and strode with a confident air, lost in a private world, oblivious to the rest of the world and, more particularly, any trip hazard at footpath level.

Mr G called out to her and waved his arms in a frantic attempt to attract her attention. She ignored him and kept on toward the wall. Only at the very last moment did she register Mr G and only then did she see the low wall. She yelped and swerved sideways, but her momentum carried her forward. Her foot caught the edge of the wall, she stumbled and fell headlong into Mr G's waiting arms. He braced himself and somehow managed to stop her from falling to her knees.

She was heavier than he expected and felt unusually strong in his arms. He could feel her fingers pressing into his shoulders and experienced the heat of her perfumed skin on his face. A charge of electricity ran through his body. He was sure she must have felt it too because she responded by prising herself free and pushing him away from her. He remembered feeling inexplicably ashamed.

"I...I'm sorry, I was only...I didn't mean anything..." he'd pleaded.

The woman composed herself, patted down the front of her coat and then smiled. It was a coy, girlish smile.

"No, no. It was me. I am so sorry. I wasn't looking where I was going. How dreadful. I'm the one who should apologise. Please forgive me...," she said.

Her voice was husky, and she spoke just above a whisper.

Mr G remembered being lost for words.

She broadened her smile and, in doing so, revealed sharp, high cheekbones, then took one step forward and raised her eyebrows. Mr G stepped sideways to let her pass, backing himself into a thorny hedge.

"Please," he said, raising an open palm.

"Thank you. You have been a gentleman and I have been horrid. I'm so sorry. You have been a kind gentleman. Thank you," she said.

She lowered her head but continued to smile at him for a long time, before walking away.

Mr G felt weak at the knees. Her smile and strong sweet musty perfume lingered long after she was gone. She was fifty paces away before pulled himself free from the hedge. He considered following her, catching up and starting a conversation. He didn't. Instinctively he knew she would not appreciate such an approach. He decided it would be best to bide his time. He could only hope she wasn't a day-tripper or a weekend pilgrim. She certainly didn't dress like either. She looked poor, but proud. She reminded him of a younger version of his late mother. He fantasised about who she was and convinced himself that the curious woman had come to Skellig Éin to escape from something, or *someone*, and what she needed was a champion, a powerful man to look after her.

Since the incident by the lake the mysterious shy woman was never very far from Mr G's thoughts. He'd seen her again a week later, sitting on a park bench in the town square reading a small hard-backed book, which she held high in the air above her raised chin, like a model in a magazine holding a compact mirror. She wore large sun glasses that hid her eyes and a good deal of her face, but he knew it was her. She wore the same coat, the same black leather gloves and possibly all the same clothes she'd been wearing when they'd bumped into each other in the park. Mr G had wanted to go over and say hello but once again found he couldn't bring himself to do so. Instead, he slinked down a side street and watched her from the shadows. She returned the next day and the day after that, and Mr G returned too, watching and waiting for the right moment to make his move.

So, when he saw her entering the bar at the Tara Cove Hotel he decided that the time for action had arrived. He felt good after his little run-in with Sutton and the black American agent and he felt like fate was smiling on him.

The woman was seated at the bar with her back to the door, staring vacantly into the smoky mirror behind the counter. If she'd wanted to, she could watch Mr G approach. She toyed absent-mindedly with a half-finished green coloured cocktail. She still wore her soft gloves, one more thing he found unusual but endearing. No one sat near her. It was early evening and the lounge was not busy. The barman wasn't busy either, but he made no effort to converse with the woman. Mr G approached slowly. He looked at her reflection in the mirror. She could have been anywhere between her mid-thirties and early fifties. He was sure she dressed at least ten years older than her actual age and did so by choice. He liked the way she dressed. It was old-fashioned. Her woollen coat was good quality, as was the silk Paisley scarf knotted loosely to one side of her long neck. The scarf and coat reminded Mr G of how women dressed in the Seventies, when he was a boy. He liked her face too, although he was quite sure most men would find her features ugly. Her eyes were a dark brown and her nose unusually long. Her high cheekbones, which came alive when she smiled, were slightly masculine. She wore eye liner and rouge on her cheeks and a dark lipstick that widened her small mouth. Her front teeth were slightly prominent which puckered out her upper lip. He found the effect disarming. Up close she smelt of sweet talc and old perfume. She certainly wasn't beautiful, but there was something about her that appealed to him, as no woman had ever done before.

The attraction Mr G felt for the mysterious woman surprised and confused him. It was certainly physical, which didn't seem to make any sense because Mr G had never been physically interested in women. He would certainly never admit, even to himself, that he was sexually attracted to men. The idea that he might be homosexual made him angry and ashamed. Mr G was an avowed celibate and a virgin. But this woman had got to him. She had made him *feel* something. She had made him wonder.

He approached quietly and stood next to her.

"Is this seat taken?" he said.

The woman swivelled her stool and her long legs, which were crossed under the front of her closed coat, lightly touched off the side of his pants. A tingle of electricity ran up his leg.

"Oh, hello! It's you. The kind gentleman from the park. No, not at all. There will always be a seat beside me, for a gentleman," she said in her husky whisper. She forced a coy giggle. It sounded strange.

"It's very quiet in here tonight," said Mr G, and he climbed onto the stool next to her. He ignored the odd looks from the barman.

"Is it? I wouldn't know. I don't visit bars that often," she said.

"Actually, neither do I," he said with a chuckle. "May I get you another of those? What is that anyway? It looks interesting."

"Oh, thank you. How very kind. It's a Grasshopper. These days they serve it with vodka instead of cream. But I'm very old fashioned and insist. Well, Ireland does have the nicest cream in the whole wide world, don't you think? It would be a sin not to have it with cream, here of all places," she said.

"Two Grasshoppers please, with cream," said Mr G with a curt wave of his hand to the bored-looking barman. The barman turned, without a word, and reached for the recently opened bottle of Crème de menthe.

The woman leaned close to Mr G.

"He's not very polite, but I can forgive him because he makes an excellent Grasshopper," she whispered.

Mr G smiled.

"I'm Maurice Gimple," he said.

"Hello Maurice Gimple. I'm Eileen Fancy," she said offering him a gloved hand.

"Eileen Fancy? I knew a Fancy once. Monica was her name. A neighbour, when I was growing up. She was a good friend of my late mother. Are you from Dublin, Eileen?"

"No. I grew up in England and India," she said, "but, you'd never know, we may be related, your Monica and me. You should ask your mother if her friend had relations in Kent."

"My mother died earlier this year," he said. It was the first time he'd said the words out loud. He held her gaze. Her top front teeth bit into her bottom lip.

The barman returned with the two Grasshoppers, complete with a large mint leaf expertly balanced on the rim of each glass.

"Thank you," said Mr G. "Shall we drink these at a table Ms Fancy? There's one free near the window."

"Please call me Eileen."

"Eileen," he said.

"Thank you Maurice, I think sitting at the window would be just perfect."

After three more Grasshoppers Mr G felt a little tipsy and asked to be excused to use the men's room. When he returned, there were two more cocktails on the table.

"One for the road. I couldn't have you leave without buying you one. You have been too generous," said Eileen with a smile.

"I believe a lady shouldn't be expected to pay for her drinks," said Mr G.

"You are an exceptional gentleman. One in a million, I'd say. No, one in *ten* million. It's so nice to meet a real gentleman. You are a dying breed Maurice Gimple. Your mother would be so proud of you," she said.

Mr G beamed.

"To you, Ms Eileen Fancy. A true and beautiful lady," he said raising his glass.

Mr G downed the new Grasshopper in one mouthful. The effect was almost immediate. He widened his eyes and stared at Eileen Fancy, as if trying to focus on something on her forehead, and then collapsed forward. He would have cracked his face on the table had Eileen not casually leaned across, stretched out a strong hand to stop his forward momentum and then shoved him back into his seat, where he slouched like a sack of wet potatoes.

Chapter 70.

When Horse drove through the gates of the monastery, the front of the main building was alive with activity. All the outside lights were on and the large front doors leading into the main hall was wide open. Yellow light leaked out and washed over a group of monks standing on the doorstep. They looked like ghosts. Brother Benjamin stood at the front, slightly apart from the rest. He had removed his helmet and looked anxiously toward the approaching car.

Most of the men behind Benji were very old. Some were in their dressing gowns. In their company Brother Benjamin looked particularly young. He was at least two decades younger than the next youngest, and four decades younger than most.

The future of the Order, thought Horse.

"Quite a reception party, Brian," said Marie, "I hope we didn't miss the main event."

"And what would that be?" said Horse.

"Oh, I don't know, Detective Hopkins, maybe the second-coming of Michael Eustace?"

"Huh," scoffed Horse.

He had been wondering about the possibility of Michael being alive since Brother Benjamin had put the notion into his head, but no matter how much he wanted it to be true, he knew in his heart it wasn't remotely possible. Marie was right to be cynical. They'd both watched Michael drown. No matter what Brother Benjamin said or how Father Francis felt, the truth was undeniable. Michael was dead. Whatever was going on here was ludicrous fantasy.

Marie put her hand on his and squeezed it gently.

"I'm sorry. He was your friend and I liked him. Really, I did. Michael was nice. And he was the only person who ever got my paintings," she said.

Horse cut the engine. The priests on the doorstep stopped talking.

"Well, we're here now. I suppose we should go and see what this is all about." He said

Marie removed her hand from his.

"I'm glad you came with me, Marie. I'm glad you are here," he said.

"C'mon. We better get out. The natives are looking restless," she said with a smile.

"Hi there," she said Marie, as soon as she was out of the car. The group of priests said nothing. The atmosphere became awkward and uncomfortable. Only one of them looked at her. He seemed to be the oldest, a gaunt man with pale blue eyes that sparkled, the last remaining remnant of the younger man he'd once been. They made him look kindly.

"You are most welcome, my dear," he said giving her a generous smile.

Horse got out and joined Marie at the front of the car. He had to resist a sudden urge to put an arm around her shoulder. He felt compelled to explain her presence.

"Marie Joyce was with me when Michael, the Prior's brother...well...when he was lost in the caves. Marie led the expedition. She is a very experienced caver. None of us would have got out without her. Marie saved us all."

The gathered priests began to mumble and nod to each other. The oldest priest looked most impressed. She repaid him by returning his smile. Horse felt an irrational pang of jealousy. Brother Benjamin grabbed his arm.

"We need to go. Father Prior has found something and he's sure Michael is alive and he told me to get the English policeman, and I did. But we need to hurry. We need to go."

"Go where?" said Marie.

"Into the cellars and into the caves. We think the Prior has found St. Áedán's Bed."

*

496

"Come on Bernard, this way, we are nearly there," said Father Francis,

"Nearly where, Father Prior?" protested the Purser, who maintained a good ten paces behind.

They were still in the same tubular tunnel following the sound of moaning. Their progress was slow as the floor sloped downwards and was covered in a fine dusting of gravel. It was like walking on tiny marbles.

When they entered the tunnel the sound had been a low moan. The further down the tunnel they went, the louder it got and now sounded like a howl.

"Ahooohhh. Ahoooohhh. Ahooooohhh."

"Look Bernard, we've reached the end of the tunnel."

The floor levelled off quite suddenly and the change in gradient caught Father Francis by surprise. He stumbled and almost fell over.

"Blast," he said.

When he straightened up and raised the torch he saw that he was standing on a ledge, looking down into a very large chamber. The floor of the chamber was two storeys below him and the curved rock ceiling at least three-times that above his head. His first impression was that he'd entered the hollowed-out carcass of a giant rock monster, an illusion accentuated by rows of equally spaced pilasters that continued across the arched roof like ribs.

The howling noise, which seemed to be coming from somewhere at the far end of the space was amplified by the shape of the chamber. It echoed and reverberated like a winter gale through a derelict warehouse. But there was no wind. The air in the chamber was still, and bitterly cold.

"It's St Áedán's Bed," gasped Father Bernard when he reached the ledge, "the hidden cathedral he wrote about in his diaries."

The Prior knew what Father Bernard meant and immediately his imagined monster-carcass vanished and was replaced by the vision of the interior of an ancient church. The illusion was astonishing. The ribbed roof looked Gothic; the floor, which was smooth and wet, looked like polished marble with a mosaic pattern; and the two lines of long rectangular boulders, separated by a wide central aisle leading to a single slab of polished black stone, were unmistakably the church pews and altar. Adding to this was a row of tall fluted columns and arches along the back wall that suggested a dark and shadowy cloister. It was uncanny.

"Goodness! You might be right, Bernard. Come on, let's get down and take a look, find out what's making that noise."

"It's his cathedral. It is! It must be, Father Prior," exclaimed Bernard again.

If they had stumbled upon St. Áedán's Bed of legend, then the Prior knew that the find was of great significance, but for now his focus was on the source of the sound. It was calling to him and, although he could not explain why, he was sure it would lead him to his brother. It was telling him he had to hurry, that something was about to happen and time was running out.

"Come on, quickly Bernard, we must hurry," he said.

Climbing down was relatively easy and they reached the bottom in less than five minutes. The noise level continued to rise. The howling was coming from somewhere beyond the cloister.

"Come on Bernard, we need to get going."

Before heading down the central aisle Father Francis turned and shone his torch back up the ramped ledge. They had emerged from a wall of rock peppered with similar sized circular holes.

"Will you look at that, Bernard? How strange. There are so many. What could have made them, I wonder?"

"Water," said Father Bernard confidently. "Water and time moulds everything down here."

"I suppose you are right. But they seem so regular. Like enormous worm holes," said Father Francis.

"Rock-eating worms, Father Prior?" said Father Bernard scornfully.

"Well no! Obviously, I was letting my imagination get the better of me. We'd better mark which tunnel is ours. We could easily get lost. If we choose the wrong one, we might never find our way back to the cellar. Even now it's difficult to say which one we came from!"

"Is it wise for us to explore on our own, Father Prior? Maybe we should go back and get help, and get more torches," said Bernard. He had to raise his voice to be heard above distant but ever growing din.

The Prior considered the question. Father Bernard was probably right. It was foolhardy to explore on their own, dressed as they were, *inexperienced* as they were, but instinct had brought him this far and it was urging him on. He couldn't explain why he must keep going, neither to himself nor the Purser, but he knew Michael would understand and, if Michael was here, he would tell his brother to trust his instincts. A voice was whispering to him and it was loud enough to be heard above the terrible din. It had begun in Michael's bedroom and the further into the cave he'd come, the louder the voice had become.

"Save us, brother," the voice was saying, "Trust your instincts."

"You go back, Bernard. I need to see what's up ahead. I won't go far. I promise. You go back and get help."

"Please come with me, Father Prior. It is dangerous down here on your own."

"I'll be fine Bernard. I won't go far. I promise. Anyway, you will easily see me with my big torch. I won't go far."

"I really think we should both go back Father Prior," shouted Father Bernard. The Prior ignored him.

"Be back as quick as you can. Leave something to mark the cave entrance, just in case!" said the Prior.

Father Bernard frowned. Father Francis became impatient and his annoyance must have been clear on his face.

Father Bernard backed down.

"Go on now, Bernard. Tell the others what we've found and get them to tell Brother Benjamin where we are, then you come back down. God willing, Benji will have help with him. Be as quick as you can, Bernard. I'll be fine. Be as quick as you can."

With a look of resignation, Father Bernard left the Prior and climbed back up the wall to the tunnel entrance. When he reached it, he removed the white cord from around his waist and hung it over a rock nearby, so that it was clearly visible from below. When he turned back and looked down into the chamber Father Francis was gone.

Chapter 71.

When Mr G woke up, Eileen Fancy was gone.

He was dazed and his vision blurred. It took him a few moments to realize where he was. It didn't make sense. What was he doing in the big room next to the basement bar of his nightclub and why was there a strong white light shining in his face? It was hot and it burned the back of his corneas. He tried to close his eyes or just blink, but he couldn't manage either.

There was music playing.

At first it was muffled. Slowly the volume rose and the louder it became the clearer it became. It was an old Irish rebel song, sung with screaming venom, with a lot of roaring electric guitars and thumping drums. Soon the level of noise became unbearable. Mr G wanted to cover his ears but he couldn't feel where his hands were.

Someone moved in the shadows behind the source of light.

Mr G tried to focus on who it was. He wanted to call out but he couldn't make his mouth move or make any sound at all. The person moved in front of the lamp and knelt down in front of him. For a moment, he thought it was Eileen Fancy.

"Hello Maurice."

Mr G saw the mouth move, understood what was said but couldn't hear the voice, because the music was too loud. Slowly the rest of the face came into focus. O'Hara, Sylvester Parker's manservant smiled. He spoke again.

"Nice to have you join us, at last. We really did think that you were out for the night. But here we all are now."

O'Hara slowly tilted his head from one side to the other, smiling inanely.

"Don't you just love a good old rebel song? Fires up the anger? Makes you want to hurt someone, know what I mean?" he shouted, over the noise.

The music suddenly stopped and O'Hara head stopped rocking from side to side. He smiled sideways at Mr G. Mr G wanted to scream. He didn't. He couldn't.

"How are you feeling? Anything yet? Anything at all? No? Never mind. Soon enough you'll feel everything." O'Hara drew out the "everything" like he was savouring a particularly juicy morsel of food. Mr G tried to turn or even look away but he couldn't move. O'Hara straightened up, shuffled backwards and then stood upright. He seemed taller than Mr G remembered, and he no longer looked thin. He was dressed, top to toe, in white plastic overalls which were splashed red with, what looked like, blood. He looked like a worker in an abattoir. In one hand O'Hara held a scalpel, in the other a small electric disc saw. He continued to smile at Mr G.

"It's okay. I sowed dem up good Maurice, I swears I did. I stopped all dat bleedin' bleedin, g'ha know what I mean? I done a great job. Did I ever tell ye, me mammy was a seamstress, just like your mammy? Me mammy taught me all I knows about sowing. G'ha know what I mean? She'd be fuckin' proud me. Don't worry, I'll show yous later. Don't worry, Maurice. You'll see I done a great job with de stitchins."

O'Hara's inner-city Dublin accent was perfect. He tilted his head again and spoke with a low husky familiar voice.

"Has the kind gentleman got nothing to say to me? Has the pussy cat got his tongue? No! No! That can't be. That's not right. The pussy cat hasn't got the kind gentleman's tongue. I have it!"

It was Eileen Fancy's voice coming from O'Hara's mouth.

Mr G wanted to cry.

"Now where did I put the kind gentleman's tongue?"

O'Hara bent down and rummaged on the floor under Mr G's chair. He picked up a clump of bloody flesh and held it in front of the unblinking eyes of the Dublin gangster. It was too big to be a tongue. O'Hara rotated it so Mr G could see the toes at the end of the severed foot.

"No. Theeze iz not it."

The voice had changed again. Now it was the South American who had turned up at the nightclub two days earlier with instructions from the Cartel. Mr G had taken an instant dislike to the man and had dispatched him to the caves with Pete Mercer. O'Hara bent down again and returned with a severed hand with a large ring on the longest finger that looked familiar.

"No. Theeze iz not it, either. Maybe I don't have it, after all!"

O'Hara tossed the hand back onto the floor, gave Mr G a vacant look and then touched his lips with his index finger.

"Ju,no! I teeink we forgot to take out dee his tongue. We are soooo forgetful."

He cocked an ear dramatically. Mr G was sure there was no one else in the cellar.

"What's that? Why not take It now, before he starts screaming? Yes. Yes. That eeze a good idea. Take the tongue now, before the anaesthetic wears off!" he said with glee.

O'Hara was changing voices at will. First it was Eileen Fancy speaking, then the Latin American, then a voice that could have been any of his associates from Dublin.

He moved closer, with the scalpel poised, but stopped inches from Mr G's face. He cocked his ear again.

"Wha' was dat? Use de saw? I suppose we could...bu'...I don't know? There would be soooo much blood." The inner-city Dublin accent morphed into Eileen's husky whisper. O'Hara stared into Mr G's eyes. When he spoke again it was his own his voice. It sounded English with the hint of an Irish lilt.

"I think I've cut off enough, for now," he said.

He backed away and stepped behind the light. When he returned, he was man-handling one of the nightclubs round tables which he plonked noisily onto the floor beside the light. Then he set up three laptops on the table and turned them so they all faced Mr G. One by one they flickered into life.

"I guess you have a lot of questions, Mr G? I will try to answer them all, before the show begins. I must admit, though, I have a few questions of my own. For one thing, I'm curious to know what it was that attracted you to that rather plain Ms Eileen Fancy? What could it have been? Was it her curious manner? The way she dressed? It can't have been her stunning good looks? She was hardly what you'd call a conventional beauty, was she? If anything, I'd say she was a bit manly. And let me tell you Mr G, I should know if Eileen Fancy was manly or not, Gha know wha' I mean?"

He grabbed his crotch, grimaced and then gave Mr G a theatrical wink.

"Or maybe it was that rather awkward vulnerability that Eileen possessed? Was that it? Or maybe she reminded you of someone dear – someone close to your cold heart? The way she dressed? The way she held herself? The way she smelt? Did she smell like someone familiar Maurice? Maybe your dear old mammy? But I don't know! I think it was because Ms Eileen Fancy was more than a woman to you. Yes, I guess that's it. Because we all know that Maurice Gimple is a little queer, don't we? Yer daddy would be so proud."

O'Hara went away and when he returned he was wearing a wig and Paisley scarf. He spoke in Eileen Fancy's voice again.

"Oh how I fooled the nice gentleman. But you did make it so easy Maurice, didn't you? Of course, my Eileen had to be more than just manly, to turn your head. Eileen had to be more than just a man in a dress. She had to have that extra little "je ne se que" that would only appeal to Maurice Gimple. The photograph of your mammy, the one that you keep in the bottom drawer of your desk, was particularly useful. It was much harder than you might think to match your mother's coat and her favourite Paisley scarf. They just don't make 'em like that anymore. And the voice, well..." O'Hara cleared his throat, "I found *that* in a television interview from the RTE archives, from the Seventies. It was just the thing, don't you think? It's kind of working-class Dublin trying hard to be posh, but not quite pulling it off. I do think I nailed it, don't you? And the scarf served a double purpose, of course. Not only did it remind you of your dearly departed mother, but it also hid my Adam's apple."

Mr G wanted to cry. The revelation that O'Hara had been Eileen Fancy was like he'd soiled himself in public. He felt angry, guilty and ashamed. O'Hara stared at him.

"We're not losing you, are we? We couldn't allow that."

He flicked his finger under Mr G's right eye. Mr G didn't feel anything, nor did he blink.

"Still no feelings? That is odd. Never mind. While we're waiting, and we still have your full and undivided attention, I might as well explain what all this has been about. I see you are confused and our guests have not arrived yet. I can't say knowing any of this will give you much comfort, but at least it will pass the time, until the show begins."

O'Hara walked into the shadows and returned moments later with a chair which he placed in front of Mr G. He sat down and faced the Dublin pimp. Now he wore a white plastic cap to match his coat and Mr G noticed a face mask tucked under his chin. He reminded Mr G of a dentist about to start his examination.

O'Hara spoke in a lowered voice.

"You see, Maurice, I am evil incarnate. I am the great orchestrator of havoc. I am night and death and it has been my destiny to bring terror and destruction to the world. I am my father's son and I do his bidding. I am the Antichrist. I am the omega man. My mission has begun, starting here on the holy island of Skellig Éin. I will bring death and destruction, and my wrath will spread out across the world. I am the Lord of Death. I am Legion, the son of Satan, and I am here to do my father's bidding."

O'Hara paused. His face changed.

"Oh, you should just see your face. I'm joking. I'm not the son of Satan. I'm in it for the money! Oh, and revenge, of course. Maurice, Maurice, Maurice! You should see your face…or at least, what's left of your face! Ha ha. Son of Satan! Ha ha."

As if by magic the music started up again. It was not as loud as before but it was more disturbing. The rebel song was replaced by many people chanting. They sang in a strange language. The singers roared and bellowed like wild beasts. They keened and howled and behind the noise Mr G thought he could hear whispers and giggles, moaning and wailing.

"It's African music. The Handa are a tribe of cannibals from the remote jungles of the Cameroon. The women and children of the tribe sing this, while their men torture people unlucky enough to enter their territory. Frankly I think the singing is the worst part of the torture. Pretty awful, isn't it? But then again, who am I to tell people what they should like. My customers, sorry, I mean my guests, seem to like it. Sound track of their lives!"

A sharp pain ran up Mr G's right arm and his cheeks tingled.

O'Hara noticed the movement and leaned forward.

"I do believe you twitched, Mr G. Good. Can you speak?"

Mr G swallowed. His throat felt raw.

"If you don't, I *will* cut out your tongue."

Mr G said something.

"What was that?"

"Fuck you, O'Hara, you fucking little creep."

Anger coursed across O'Hara's face. It only lasted a moment.

"Bravo! At last, Mr G. gets to curse. Exhilarating, isn't it? Fuck. Fuck. Fuck. Fuck. Fuck. Fuck you, Mr G."

"What do you want, O'Hara?" whispered Mr G.

"Haven't you worked it out yet, Maurice. There is no O'Hara. I am Sylvester Parker. I am the man who contacted you. I am the man you did your deal with and I am the man you betrayed."

"What do you want?" said Mr G.

"I want to hurt you. I need to hurt you. And anyway, my customers are here now, and I've promised them a show."

Sylvester Parker pulled the face mask up over his nose and lowered the cap, so that only his eyes were visible. The he turned around and switched on the monitors, one after the other.

On the first screen, there was a heavy set man in a suit and tie sitting in an armchair. He smiled on the screen.

"Welcome John the twenty third," said Parker. The man in the suit just nodded. On the middle screen Mr G saw a group of people, men and women. They were all dressed in S&M gear. Most of them wore masks. They sat in couples on recliners and couches. They were drinking from wine glasses and they cheered when they saw Parker. He raised one hand and showed them a serrated hunting knife. They cheered again. On the last screen was an Arab. He was sprawled on a bed of satin sheets with his hands over his crotch. He looked bored.

"Welcome", said Parker. The Arab nodded curtly.

Parker stepped back and revealed Mr G. The group of masochists cheered again.

"Welcome to one and all, and thank you for your continued support. Tonight's show will begin in a moment and should last...," Parker looked at Mr G, "oh, I'd say, at least an hour."

Suddenly, feeling returned to the rest of Mr G's body, which quickly turned from tingling sensations to growing pain. His heart began to pound and his eyes watered. When his bowls loosened, he began to cry. In the distance, Mr G could hear a buzzing sound.

At first he didn't know what it was.

When Parker stepped closer and the buzzing got louder Mr G remembered the electric saw.

That was when he started to scream.

Chapter 72.

They made their way down the steep narrow stairs in single file. There was no room for two abreast. Brother Benjamin led the way, followed some way back, by Horse and then Marie. Behind Marie some of the elderly priests had ventured to the top of the stairs but none seemed inclined to follow her. Horse spent most of the journey with his chin on his chest and his shoulders bent back to avoid banging his forehead on the low sections of the curved stone ceiling. At the half-landing he stopped to catch his breath. He turned and asked Marie if she was okay.

"Oh, I'm fine, big man. I'm the caver here, remember?" she said with a chuckle.

"Ha. What's this about St. Áedán's Bed? Did the saint sleep in the cellars of the monastery?"

"Not likely," said Marie. "This monastery has only been here since the fifteenth century. St. Áedán was around in the fifth, sixth and possibly seventh century, if you believe that he lived to be one hundred and forty. Didn't you read up about St. Áedán before you visited the island? The full story is in the official guide, The History & Mysteries of Skellig Éin. There should be a copy in your hotel bedside locker, next to the Gideon Bible. Both are popular reading material with anyone having trouble sleeping."

"I didn't come here for a holiday or on pilgrimage, Marie. I have been working. I haven't had time to read the headline of a newspaper, never mind a history of St Áedán."

Horse began down the second flight of steps. There was no sign of Brother Benjamin ahead. Marie continued talking as they went. Horse didn't ask her to stop. He liked the sound of her voice.

"St. Áedán wrote a lot," she said, "and described finding a cathedral in the caves at the edge of a black lake. St. Áedán said that the lake was a mirror of the one on the island. He called it Thurloch Beag, which means "small lake". St. Áedán wrote about sleeping in a cave at the bottom of the lake. The cathedral and lake have never been found."

Horse stopped again. He was panting.

"What's this about...about Purgatory?" he managed to ask.

"I thought you policemen were supposed to be super-fit?"

"Ha. Actually luv, I've had a very strenuous evening," he said.

Marie thumped him gently on his shoulder.

"Shush, or you'll have me excommunicated," she whispered.

"You were telling me about Purgatory," he said.

"Oh yeh! Well St. Áedán claimed that he found Purgatory. He went there every full moon, or something like that, to do battle with the Devil and free the souls trapped there. He said that at the bottom of the black lake there was a gate that led from this world to the next. He said God built him a cathedral in the caves, a sanctuary, or *base camp* as I always imagined it, where the holy man planned his nightly expeditions, checked his Scuba gear and sub-marine and such like, before he set out on his soul-saving missions."

"What?" said Brian.

Marie giggled.

"Well I don't know, do I? It's been years," she said, adding, "We learnt about it in school. I played an angel in the school play, when I was eight or nine. There were angels with him when he went down to Purgatory, and the light of the Holy Spirit."

"You did school plays about Purgatory?" said Horse.

"Sure. You are in the West of Ireland now, Mr Englishman. Our nativity plays include flesh eating monsters, gratuitous torture and general mayhem. You should visit us at Halloween."

"I think I'll give that a miss, thanks," he said.

"Chicken," she said.

When they reached the bottom step Horse was out of breath but smiling. Brother Benjamin was waiting. He looked worried.

"Please, we must hurry," he said.

"Of course, I'm not as fit as I used to be," said Horse with a sigh.

Brother Benjamin led them down a corridor and into the first of the cellar rooms. Horse found the room hot and he could smell garlic and diesel, neither of which he particularly liked. He covered his mouth and nose with his hankerchief. Marie seemed unaffected by the smell or the heat.

They reached the next cellar through a door in the middle of the end wall, at the bottom of a rectangular pit in the floor.

The lower cellar was a mess. Wax covered wheels of cheese were strewn about the room, and Horse could see small piles of animal droppings in various places. It was also much colder than the upper room, but the air was fresh and there was no smell of garlic.

Benji and Horse climbed down the ladder fixed to the wall inside the door. Marie, in her taffeta dress, waited until both men had moved away from the ladder before climbing down.

"Father Bernard," Benjamin called out. No one responded.

"Father Prior," he shouted, louder this time. "I've brought the English detective and...," he glanced back at Marie, "...and my...torch."

Still no one responded.

Horse noticed that the two tall shelf units against the back wall had been pulled apart. As he drew near he could feel a breeze and could see air movement. When he reached the shelves he saw a gaping hole in the rear wall. The door to the upper cellar opened and the elderly priest popped his head into the room.

"You'll need these if you are going to follow them," he shouted down in a croaky voice. Horse turned to see the elderly priest looking down at them from the door to the upper basement. In his hand he held two torches. Marie went back to the foot of the ladder and the old priest stretched out a scrawny arm and passed her down a large box torch and then a smaller flashlight. It was the same priest who had spoken to Marie on the doorstep. Horse thought he must be close to ninety years old. He looked like a ghost in his white habit.

"Thank you, Father," said Marie.

"Father Raymond! You shouldn't be down here, you'll get your death," said Brother Benjamin reproachfully.

The old priest waved his arm in a dismissive gesture. He didn't take his eyes off Marie.

"It's this young lady who'll get her death, Brother Benjamin," he said. As if to prove his point, Marie shivered.

"Are you alright, my dear? I'm sorry if I frightened you just then. You are one of the Joyce girls, aren't you?" said Father Raymond.

"Yes. I am Marie Joyce. My sister is Martha," she said.

"I remember the two of you, when you were little girls. I knew your mother well, God rest her soul. Little rascals, the pair of you, if I remember. Wait there for a moment, my dear," he said. He vanished behind the door, returning moments later with a heavy sheepskin coat in one hand and a picnic rug in the other. He passed the items down one by one, all the time watching Marie with his pale blue eyes.

"This room has always been cold, my dear. Of course, that is why it's such a good place to store our famous cheese. But now it appears that we have unwanted visitors and a new door," he said.

Horse wondered how the old man had managed to carry the two torches, the coat and the rug all the way down the stairs, but then remembered seeing a small lift in the corner opposite the boiler, a dumb waiter, like the ones they have in hotel kitchens. Horse watched as Marie slipped on the coat. It was large, wool-lined and, he imagined, very warm. It was much too big for her, extending well below her knees, and her arms were lost up the sleeves.

"Under the circumstances, a very good fit I'd say, my dear," said Father Raymond.

"Thank you, Father. You are very kind," said Marie.

"Pah! It's not every day an old man like me gets the chance to impress a beautiful young lady."

Horse felt another pang of jealousy and batted it away with a shake of his head and a broad smile.

"Thank you, Father Raymond, it was very thoughtful of you," he said.

"Please, Father Raymond, do go back up to the warmth of the monastery. I'm sure we won't be long," said Brother Benjamin.

"Oh, don't you worry about me, Benji. I will sit on Father Bernard's chair beside the boiler and wait until you get back. Anyway, some fool left the front doors wide open and the whole place is like an icebox up there. No, I'll stay here next to the boiler. Besides, you may need my assistance when you get back from your adventures."

With a wink to Marie, Father Raymond backed away and let the door close with a loud clunk.

"Come on," said Horse, "we best go and see what this is all about."

All three squeezed between the shelving units and entered a large tubular tunnel. They could hear heavy breathing. After a moment, a figure in white appeared and hurried up the tunnel. It was the Purser. He looked distraught and slightly puzzled when he saw Marie. When he saw Horse he relaxed a little.

"Oh, thank God you've come," he said, "Father Prior has lost his senses. He's gone wandering about down there, all on his own. I've been back and forth. I don't know where he's gone now. We must go back for him. The Prior has lost his senses."

Chapter 73.

The Prior moved as quickly as he could.

The floor of the cavern was dry and level. Any dust he kicked up as he ran along soon settled back onto the floor behind him. The light from his torch cast shadows on the ceiling and floor and invaded ancient cracks and crevices that had never seen such light before. Now that he was alone, Father Francis felt small and vulnerable. In his mind, he imagined that the howling ahead of him was the gathering of demons, waiting in the darkness to devour him. Despite this, he kept going. He stopped only once, to consider the strange altar. It looked as if it had been hewn from a large chunk of onyx. It was jet-black and as smooth as a pool ball. It seemed to him to be very much out of place among all the limestone greys, but he didn't spend long thinking about it. How it had got there was a question that could wait for another time.

Behind the altar, a row of Gaudíesque arches added to the illusion of being inside an ancient church. He knew that the cloister had formed over millennia by the slow deposit of calcites from water dripping at curiously regular intervals along a seam in the rock ceiling. What began as separate bulbous stalagmites and pointed dripping stalactites, eventually became hour-glass in shape, and as time went by, the centre filled out to form the columns. They looked almost man-made. Behind the colonnade was a smooth flat wall, in the centre of which there was an eight-foot-wide opening that looked like a doorway. The deafening noise was coming from somewhere beyond.

The opening led into a second chamber, twice the size and height of the first, but the Prior didn't go in, because the room was totally flooded. Where there should have been a floor there was water and the water was as black and shiny as the altar. In the torchlight, it looked like a lake of treacle. The air in the second chamber stank of rotten eggs. Covering his nose he surveyed the new space with his torch. It was empty, save for a small island right in the middle, which looked like a miniature volcano, being almost perfectly conical, with steep sloping sides and a flat top. The howling sound, which was now ear-splitting, was coming from inside the volcano.

As the Prior considered what to do, the howling suddenly stopped. The silence that followed was disconcerting and eerie. Father Francis held his breath and stared at the island, more than a hundred yards away. His mouth felt dry and the torch, suddenly heavy. Time seemed to slow down. From across the water the Prior thought he could hear whispering which then became a constant hiss. The hissing grew louder and louder. Suddenly there was a tremendous whoosh sound as a column of water rushed upwards from the top of the volcano and cascaded out in every direction, sending gallons of water crashing into the lake. Ripples turned into small waves which raced outwards, crashing into the side walls of the chamber and across the threshold of the doorway. Icy water washed over the Prior's shoes and soaked his socks. Clouds of chilly spray filled the air and a freezing mist wet his cheeks and eyes.

The constant torrent from the enormous fountain continued to pound the surface of the lake. It sounded like the thunderous applause given at the end of a great performance, and in the middle of it all the Prior heard something heavy splash into the water, halfway between him and the island. Whatever it was flickered and flashed in his torchlight, before disappearing beneath surface. Father Francis shone the beam of light at the spot where the large object had entered the water but he could see nothing because of the hazy mist that was everywhere. He was sure it had been something luminous. Then he heard a second splash, somewhere on the blind side of the island.

The column of rising water continued unabated for another two, or three minutes. Then, and as quickly as it had started, it stopped.

When the water in the lake settled, Father Francis looked again at the spot where the first splash had occurred, and saw what appeared to be a large body in the water, inside a luminous high visibility jacket just like the one the rescuers had told him Michael had been wearing when he drowned.

Could it possibly be Michael, he wondered?

The jacket was drifting just beneath the surface.

Father Francis set the torch on the floor, directing its blinding white beam toward the body in the lake. Quickly he removed his habit and his wet shoes and socks, and then waded into the water. It was freezing and quickly deepened. As soon as he could, he began to swim. He was a strong swimmer and cut through the icy water with little effort, swimming down the lane of torchlight. When he reached the coat, he grabbed the collar and jerked the body upwards, turning it over as he did so. It was much heavier than he expected and he soon realised why. There were two people in the jacket, not just one, and it was Michael and Hanna.

"Oh God, please let them be alive," he cried.

They were clinging to each other, Hanna wearing the large coat with Michael wrapped in her arms. Somehow she's managed to fastened a few of the buttons behind Michael's back. Even if Michael had wanted to free himself from Hanna's embrace, he couldn't. It was like he was in a straight-jacket of Hanna's making. They were both blue and they looked dead.

"Please God, don't let me be too late."

The Prior pulled their faces close to his. Neither appeared to be breathing and both were as cold as ice. He knew if there was to be any hope, he would have to get them back to the shore. He lay on his back and, threading water, pulled them above him, then, kicking out as hard as he could, he dragged them back along the wide beam of light. It was difficult going, but he was strong. He noticed that the torchlight had weakened since he'd entered the water and he tried not to think of what would happen if it went out. Something moved in the water to his right which caused him to turn his head. He stopped swimming. There was something else in the lake with them. He remembered hearing the second splash and wondered what had come out of the volcano after Michael and Hanna.

"Hello," he shouted as loud as he could. No one replied. His head went under and he swallowed a mouthful of water. It tasted of iron. When he resurfaced, he noticed that the light was weaker than before. Michael and Hanna began to sink. The Prior kicked his legs and pounded with his free arm, then continued toward the shore now less than forty yards behind him.

Not long, he thought.

There was another splash, this time to his left. It sounded like a very large fish had risen in the shadows to catch an unseen fly. The Prior ignored the sound and kept on moving. The torchlight turned from pale white to soft cream. Something touched his right calf and clung momentarily to his trouser leg. He kicked out and it let go.

Thirty yards to the shore.

The light was turning pale yellow, its' reach shortening as it dimmed. There was another loud splash, this time from over his shoulder, in the space between him and torch. Father Francis slowed and turned his neck to see behind him and came face to face with someone looking back at him. Although he could only see the top of his bald head and the shadow of his different colour eyes, he was convinced that the thing in the water with him wasn't human. He thrashed out in shock and sank below the water. When he resurfaced, the creature was gone.

He coughed and gagged. Michael and Hanna sank and threatened to pull him under again. He knew he had to keep moving. There was now less than twenty yards to go.

He pushed on.

Fifteen yards.

Ten.

Suddenly Michael and Hanna got much heavier. At first Father Francis put it down to tiredness on his part so, to compensate, he put an extra burst of power into his legs. It made no difference. They were sinking and bringing him down with them. It didn't take him long to realise what was happening. The creature had got hold of Michael and Hanna and was trying to drag them back out. Without letting go of them, the Prior rolled sideways, pushed himself under and kicked out with all his might. His bare foot connected with something soft and fleshy. The creature released its hold on Michael and Hanna.

Father Francis resurfaced again and immediately pushed on with all the power as he could muster. No sooner had he regained his momentum when the thing in the water attacked again, this time with such ferocity that all three were dragged under. Father Francis kicked out blindly. A snort of bubbles escaped from his nose, releasing pressure from his burning lungs. He let go of his brother and swam up to the surface, desperate for air. As soon as he had regained his composure, he swam back down.

Everything under the surface was pitch black. He groped about and by sheer chance, clapped his hands onto his adversary's head. Before the creature had time to react Father Francis pushed his fingers into its eyes, causing it to twist and squirm in a spray of panicked bubbles. The Prior clung on, for as long as he could. When he finally let go, the creature darted away allowing the Prior to return to the surface for air. For a moment, he couldn't see Michael and Hanna. When he finally spotted them in the fading torchlight, they were fifteen yards back out toward the island.

He felt exhausted and sleepy. The rank smell of rotten eggs didn't help. He swam out slowly and somehow found the energy to turn Michael and Hanna over so that their heads were again above water, but the effort was exhausting. He had no energy left. They were twenty-five yards from the shore but it might as well have been two hundred and five. He knew that if the thing in the water was to attack them again there would be nothing he could do. The torchlight dropped to a mere flicker. Hope disserted him and he felt sadness and shame. He had failed.

So close and yet so far, he thought.

When the torch went out the darkness that replaced it was suffocating. Father Francis continued to thread water and continued to hold onto Michael and Hanna, but he could see nothing and had no idea if their faces were still above the water.

The darkness and the smell threatened to smothered him.

Michael and Hanna began to sink. Father Francis couldn't see them anymore and it took all his strength just to keep a hold of the collar of the luminous jacket. For the first time since childhood, the man who had become Father Francis and the Prior of the monastery of Skellig Éin, began to cry. He was frightened and wanted Hanna and Michael to make room for him in the coat, to hug him as they hugged each other.

The weight of them pulled him down. He had to tilt his head backwards to keep his nose and mouth out of the water. The sinking threatened to rip his arm from its socket and yet, despite the pain and knowing that they would ultimately drag him to his death, Father Francis refused to let go. In his last moment of consciousness, Father Francis began to pray.

"Bless your brothers and sister with thy grace Lord Jesus Christ, and the grace of God the Father and the Holy Spirit. Free us from our sins and raise us up to be by your side. Forgive me Lord for I am..."

His words were lost in the darkness as he sank beneath the water, still clinging to Michael and Hanna. Just before he blacked out he thought he heard a woman's voice. It sounded like it was their mother calling. Then, through the darkness, he saw a tunnel of light, much brighter than he could ever have imagined.

Chapter 74.

Marie was the first to start running. She ran past the altar and through the colonnade just in time to see the Prior go under for the last time.

"Over here. Hurry up. Come on Brian. Over here," she screamed.

"Look. There," she said, pointing to a circle of receding bubbles in the middle of the lake.

"Oh shit," said Horse. He dropped his torch and the blanket that Father Raymond had given him, removed his shoes, into which he placed his watch, his wallet and his mobile phone and, without a word, dived into the lake. When he resurfaced moments later he yelled out.

"Oooh shiiiit! It's...fuckin'...free...zing."

"Never mind that. Swim out before he drowns," yelled Marie

Marie held Horse in her powerful torchlight as he swam toward the receding bubbles. Behind her, Brother Benjamin quickly removed his habit and sandals.

"Excuse me please," he whispered apologetically. When she stepped aside, he dived into the water and followed the wake left by Horse. Brother Benjamin was a much better swimmer and soon caught up with English detective. Marie kept the torch focussed on the spot where she'd seen the Prior go under.

The bubbles had vanished.

"Hurry. There. Yes, just there," she shouted.

Father Bernard joined Marie and he trained his own torch on the two swimmers. The combined light was blinding. Bernard began to grumble again. Marie ignored him.

Like a pair of synchronised swimmers at the start of their routine Benji and Horse rose out of the water together before diving under. Marie and Father Bernard watched and waited in silence. Horse resurfaced moments later, took a gulp of the air and then went back down. The surface of the lake quickly returned to a sheet of mirrored glass. In the bright torchlight, it sparkled like black ice. Marie bit her lip. Nothing happened for an age and then, all of a sudden, the top of Father Francis's head broke the surface quite a distance from where he'd gone down, followed closely after, by Brother Benjamin.

"There," shouted Marie. Bernard turned his eyes and torch toward the Prior. With a practiced ease Benji manoeuvred himself behind and under the Prior, gently cupped one hand under his chin, tilted his head back with the other and with strong even strokes dragged Father Francis back to shore. Father Bernard followed the progress with his torch. Marie kept her torch focussed on the spot where she'd last seen Horse go down.

"Where's Brian?" she said.

This time Father Bernard ignored her. He was muttering something about telling the Prior not to go on alone.

"Where's Brian?" she shouted. There was desperation in her voice.

Marie knew how dangerous cave pools could be. They were unpredictable, with treacherous undercurrents lurking beneath a deceptively calm surface. Often they were cluttered with a forest of sharp rising rock columns that could snag a diver and trap them or damage their scuba equipment. No experienced caver would dare dive head first into an uncharted rock pool, as Horse and Benji had, and none would have gone exploring without lights, oxygen and ropes.

"Where's Brian?" she screamed again.

Just as she was about to jump in, Horse resurfaced. When she saw him she gasped.

"What...?"

Father Bernard looked up.

"Good God almighty. What...who...is that?" said Bernard.

Horse was clinging to something large and luminous.

"That's...impossible!" said Marie, "That's Michael."

Once the Prior was out of the water, Benji turned around and swam back out to help the Horse. Father Bernard attended to the Prior. Marie kept her torch on the men in the water. When they drew near she saw that there were two people wrapped in Michael's coat.

"I don't believe this!"

Marie helped the others carry Michael and Hanna out of the water. She stared Horse in disbelief.

"He found her. Michael found Hanna...but, it's impossible, Brian. I don't understand," she whispered, "We saw him drown."

"They need medical help and quickly," said Horse.

Horse and Benji carried Michael and Hanna into the cathedral chamber and laid them on the floor beside the black altar. Father Bernard had begun performing CPR on the Prior, but wasn't having much luck reviving him.

"I'll take over there, Father. We need a doctor, Marie," said Horse.

"I'll go," she said. "Daibhí lives nearby. I'll ring him from upstairs. He'll know what to do."

*

When Marie got back to the cathedral chamber with Daibhí French, Father Francis was kneeling next to the bodies of Michael and Hanna, who were still wrapped together in the large luminous coat. He was praying. Brother Bernard and Brother Benjamin stood behind him with their heads bowed. Horse sat on the floor a little way off, shivering violently. He watched Marie approached and saw a wave of emotion cross her beautiful face. She began to cry. Horse wanted to go to her, but couldn't find the energy to stand. He hoped she'd come to him.

The old doctor went over to Michael and Hanna and knelt in front of them. He didn't say anything. From his medical bag he removed a stethoscope and popped the ear plugs into his ears, then leaned forward and undid the top buttons of Hanna's blouse. He placed the cold disc over Hanna's heart and after listening for a little while, remove the disc and smiled.

"She's still alive. Can you open your brother's shirt, please Father."

"But..."

"Please Father," he said he said again.

Horse sat up straight. He could hardly believe what he was hearing. He scrutinised Daithí French. Had the old doctor lost his mind? Daithí went through the same routine with Michael.

"Him too. They are both alive. We need to warm them up, slowly."

"But how can that be?" said Marie.

"It's a miracle," said Brother Benjamin.

"It's a miracle," agreed the Prior.

"Actually, I've seen this phenomenon before, many years ago in Norway. We were on a training expedition in the northern forests. One of the young soldiers went missing. He fell down a ravine and was knocked unconscious. We didn't find him for more than two weeks. He was buried under four foot of snow. When I checked his vital signs, I found, just as I have now with these two, a faint heartbeat. The soldier had gone into a sort of mild coma and the packed snow around his mouth provided the water and minerals his body needed to survive. It seems that under the right conditions the human body can go into a kind of hibernation. There have been other cases too. We revived the young soldier and he made a full recovery. Last time I heard about him he was attending his daughter's graduation. He's a Lieutenant Colonel now I believe."

No one said anything.

"We need to warm them up. Can you carry them up to the boiler room?"

Horse stood up.

"Sure, anything to get away from that ruddy smell," he said.

"Smell?" said Daibhí.

"The rotten eggs? From the lake water. Back there where we found them," said Horse. He pointed toward the cloister.

Dr French stood up with surprising ease. He walked behind the altar and under the cloister. Marie followed him.

Horse noticed how tall the old man was and how upright his stance when he walked. Forever the army officer, he thought. The way the doctor carried himself reminded the detective of someone else, but he couldn't think who.

"Hmm," said Daibhí when he returned. "Interesting. And you found them in there?"

"Yes," said the Prior, "they were thrown out the top of that volcano."

Everyone looked at him.

"In a fountain of gushing water. It just started, spat them out and then soon after, stopped. A volcano of water," said Father Francis.

"Well the smell is hydrogen sulphide. It is also known as sleeping gas," said the doctor.

"Are you saying that they are asleep?" said Father Francis.

"We'll see. We need to get them warmed up and then get them proper medical attention."

"The air ambulance is on its way. I called the hospital in Galway too," said Marie.

"The helicopter can land in the courtyard," said Brother Benjamin excitedly.

Daibhí French turned to Horse.

"And you, sir, need to get out of those wet clothes before I have three patients to deal with."

Marie smiled at Horse, then she winked at the old doctor.

"Yes Sir!" said Horse, giving Daibhí a theatrical salute.

Always the army officer, thought Horse.

Chapter 75.

Daibhí led the group back up to the cellars. In one hand, he held a torch and in the other his medical bag. The three priests and the English policeman carried Michael and Hanna just as they were found, entwined in the luminous coat.

"Once we get to the boiler room we can separate them and get them dry and warm," Daithí had said. "It's best to keep them together for now."

Horse noticed that several times during the journey back the Prior looked over his shoulder, staring in the direction of the cloister.

"Are you okay, Father? Did you forget something?" Horse asked.

"No. I...," said Father Francis absent-mindedly, "No. It's nothing, Inspector Hopkins."

Carrying Michael and Hanna up the wall proved difficult. Getting from the lower cellar to the boiler room would have been almost impossible had Michael and Hanna not been frozen rigid. Horse held their weight whilst the others pulled them through the narrow door. Horse couldn't stop shaking.

Father Raymond, the elderly priest who'd given Marie the sheepskin coat, was waiting for them in the upper cellar. Whilst they were away he had somehow managed to bring down a large flask of steaming soup and a tray full of mugs. As soon as Horse climbed up Father Raymond took his arm and led him over to a chair beside the boiler.

"Come and sit down and have some chicken soup. Your young lady wouldn't be pleased if I let anything happen to you, now would she?"

Horse smiled and plonked down on the chair. Marie came over and touched his hand.

"You are a wonder, Father Raymond," said Father Francis taking one of the steaming mugs of soup.

"I'm very glad to see you back with us, Father Prior. You had us all very worried, I can tell you. Now drink up everyone, there is more coming down."

Father Raymond looked at Michael and Hanna.

"And you found your brother! It's a miracle. Our prayers have been answered."

The Prior smiled at the old man.

"It's a miracle, Raymond. A miracle," he repeated.

When Marie was sure that Horse was okay, she went back up to the hall. She returned ten minutes later to say the helicopter would be with them in twenty minutes.

"Right. We need to warm them up and get oxygen into them. But first we need to get them out of their wet clothes. Will you help me Marie? The rest of you get warm and dry," said Daibhí.

The prior remained beside Michael. Although still soaking wet he gave no indication that he was cold.

"You too, Father Prior, please. Myself and Marie can do this." "It's okay," said Marie to Father Francis. He relented and stepped back out of their way.

A low whining noise made everyone look up. It was coming from the lift in the corner.

"Ah good. Warm clothes and more soup," declared Father Raymond.

He walked over to the large dumb waiter, pulled open the timber shutters, ducked his head and stepped inside. Horse had never seen a dumb waiter so large. It was the same floor area of a small passenger lift but the lift car – a box of plain and polished packing timber - was only four foot high.

Father Raymond returned carrying a pile of priest's habits.

"Not the height of fashion but they are surprisingly warm," he said as he handed one to Horse.

"Cheers, Father," said Horse with a smile.

He avoided looking at Marie. He was sure if he did, she'd make a face and make him laugh.

Marie erected a privacy screen from a blanket and two chairs then helped Dr French to gently prise Michael and Hanna. Then

Marie removed Hanna's wet clothes, dried her, wrapped her in warm towels and dressed her in one the habits. Daibhí did the same with Michael

"How are we going to get them up those bloody stairs?" said Horse, once the work was complete.

"I'm sure you'll think of something Brother Brian," said Marie, stifling a giggle. Horse made a hang-dog face and then guffawed as loud as he could. Everyone, even Father Bernard, joined in.

"That's the spirit," said Father Raymond.

"We could send them up in the lift," said Brother Benjamin.

Father Bernard tutted noisily. "Oh don't be silly, Brother Benjamin, the dumb-waiter could never take the weight of a man."

The Prior looked at Horse and then spoke quickly before Brother Benjamin had time to say something he might later regret.

"Oh, I think Brother Benjamin might have something there Bernard. I'd say that old thing could easily take them up, one at a time, of course. It's worth a try. If it doesn't work, we will just have to carry them. There's a first time for everything, Bernard," said the Prior.

"Well, if you are sure, Father Prior," said Bernard, hesitantly.

"Yes. I think we should give it a go, don't you? If of course that's okay with the doctor?" said Horse.

"Yes. It's probably a good idea. Those stairs are treacherous."

"Good. That's settled then. Excellent idea, Brother Benjamin," said Father Francis with a smile.

Father Francis knew very well that the dumb-waiter could take the weight of a man and that, on occasions when Father Bernard was away and Benji was alone in the cellar, he regularly travelled in the dumb up to the kitchen. Father Francis had seen it with his own eyes, a few days after arriving at the monastery. The Purser was in Galway at the time and the new Prior had gone to the kitchen to speak to the cook about refreshments for an upcoming school governors meeting. The kitchen was empty but, just as he was about to leave, he heard the dumb-waiter approach. In the cellar the dumb-waiter stopped at floor level, in the kitchen it opened onto a wide stainless steel counter beside a bank of sinks. The Prior waited and watched, imagining that the cook must have called the lift and had then stepped out for a moment. When the dumb-waiter came to a stop and the doors opened on their own, the Prior was taken aback. As he watched, two large rolls of cheese emerged, pushed from behind by an unseen hand. These were followed by one of Brother Benjamin's gangly legs, and then the other. Rather than confront or embarrass Benji, the Prior quietly left the kitchen before the young priest had fully extricated himself from the wooden box.

The dumb-waiter carried Michael and Hanna up to the ground floor. By the time the air ambulance arrived they were in the entrance hall facing each other on separate leather couches at either side of the front doors. Neither of them had revived but a little colour was showing on both faces and, for the first time since being found, they looked alive. Curled up in their monk's habits they looked like oversized new-born babies in swaddling-clothes. Only their faces and feet were uncovered.

The paramedics took Hanna first to the helicopter and then returned for Michael. Dr French insisted that he and his assistant, Marie, travel with their patients. After a bit of arguing, the air ambulance crew reluctantly agreed and within ten minutes of landing, the helicopter was ready to leave.

Horse watched them go. Marie waved to him from the window.

He waved back.

Soon the whirr of the rotor blades faded into the distance and the helicopter became just another white speck in the star-filled sky. With the evenings excitement over the elderly priests headed for their beds. Father Bernard insisted on returning to his cellars to tidy up, despite being told by the Prior to "leave it till the morning".

"I need to do it now Father Prior. I will not sleep thinking about it."

"I will help you Father, and we will have it spick and span in a jiffy," said Brother Benjamin with a hearty smile.

"Thank you, Brother Benjamin, that is very kind of you" said Father Bernard giving the young monk a rare smile.

Chapter 76.

Having found proper clothes for Horse from his own wardrobe, Father Francis invited the English detective to warm himself by the fire in his study, before returning to his hotel.

"Will you take a glass of whiskey, detective Hopkins? Michael brought me a bottle of *Redbreast* when he arrived. It's the only indulgence I allow myself. Twelve year old. A single pot-still Irish whiskey. Something to be shared and we should celebrate should we not? This is a great occasion."

"Thank you, Father. Maybe a small one. It does seem like a miracle that you found them."

"Yes. A miracle indeed. How do you like your whiskey?"

"Neat or with a little water. No ice."

"This is best served neat. Ice in whiskey is a travesty, don't you think, or am I being a snob?" said the Prior.

"No, I totally agree. It was the Americans who started the fad of drinking whiskey on the rocks or possibly some shrewd Scottish salesman. Whiskey was a drink invented for cold climates."

As if to reinforce the point, Horse shivered.

The Prior carried two crystal tumblers of the pale golden liquid over to the detective who had taken one of the armchairs beside the fire, and handed Horse one of them.

"Cheers," said the Prior.

"Sláinte," said Brian in his strong English accent.

The Prior smiled a sat down in the other chair. He stared into the fire.

"Galway Crystal," he said before taking a sip, "they belonged to our mother. Michael didn't take much of anything after she died and I was the only other family member. The monastery has most of her stuff now."

Horse took a sip and then a bit more. Whether it was the quality of the whiskey or the fact that he was still feeling the effects of his swim in the icy cave pool, he thought it was the nicest thing he'd ever tasted. He swallowed it slowly and almost "umm'ed" like a child drinking sweet warmed milk before bed.

"This is exceptionally good, Father."

"Isn't it? Even my Scottish friends have had to admit as much, however reluctantly!"

"I thought you had a sister?" Horse said absent-mindedly, responding to the Prior's comment about his mother's furniture.

"Our sister died when she was eight," said the Prior.

Horse sat upright and stared at the priest.

"Oh God, I'm sorry. Michael told me and I'd forgotten. I'm sorry, Father Francis; I'm such a bloody clot."

"You have nothing to be sorry about. You saved my life and Michael's, not to mention Hanna's. You have nothing to be sorry about, Brian. Nothing."

For a while neither men spoke, both lost in their own thoughts.

Finally, Father Francis broke the silence.

"May I ask why they call you Horse?"

"Michael never told you? He is among a very small group who know the truth," said Horse with a smile. Father Francis raised an eyebrow.

"Oh it's not rude, Father, if that's what you are thinking, although most of my colleagues think it has something to do with the size of a certain bodily appendage. It hasn't, but, to be honest with you, I've never said anything to dissuade them from that view."

The Prior waited.

"Despite my accent, I come from a very, well..." he hesitated "...wealthy family."

"I see," said Father Francis.

"In fact," continued the Englishman, "and I trust you know I'm telling you this in the strictest confidence, I have a minor title. I am the 26th Earl of Thristlington, twice or three times removed."

The Prior's face showed a mixture awe and confusion.

"I never understood that twice removed thing," he said.

"It means that I'd have to kill off a load of uncles, all their male heirs and all of their sons, along with my own brother to ever become the Earl, and even then, I'm not even sure it's a legitimate title anymore. We are a catholic family and we lost most of our land and influence under Henry VIII in the sixteenth century."

"So are you very wealthy?"

The detective looked surprised at the question.

"My family still hold a good-sized estate in Norfolk."

"Oh? What size is good-sized?"

"I don't know. A couple o' hundred thousand acres," said Horse almost sheepishly.

"Not very large then?"

"Ha ha. I suppose it is a lot, isn't it?"

"Oh I don't know. Your family estate in Norfolk can't be much more than the size of county Galway."

They both laughed.

"I suppose when you put it that way...ha ha. Anyway, we had stables and horses when I was growing up. Race horses I mean - thoroughbreds."

"Of course," said the Prior.

They were both becoming skittish.

"Anyway, when I was a kid I was given the name Horse, because of my background. In the local comprehensive school my older brother was known as Posh-boy, something I still call him, by the way, and I got the nickname Horse. My nick-name somehow stuck with me."

"And the accent? Is it fake?" asked the Prior.

"No. Not anymore. I was the black sheep of the family, Father. When I was growing up I hung around with the local kids and started to talk the way they did. At first I was copying them, to make me fit in. It annoyed my parents too, which was a bonus. I laid it on thick at home just to get up their noses. Now I've spent so many years with people who speak like this, it's become part of me. I don't suppose I could speak posh now, even if I wanted too."

"I see. And joining the police force was part of the youthful rebellion too?"

"I suppose it was. It sounds stupid, doesn't it?"

"Michael told me you were an exceptional policeman."

Horse took another sip of his whiskey. It sent a warm tingle down his throat. Every inch of his skin was sore but the whiskey was taking effect, warming and numbing in equal measure.

"I hope he's okay. Michael never ceases to amaze me, Father. I know he'll pull through."

"God watches over him, even if he doesn't always believe it." The Prior emptied his glass.

"Do you think, Inspector Hopkins, that we might risk another small one?" he said, holding up his empty tumbler.

"No, I'd better not. I'd like to but I'd have to sleep here on the floor. It's late and I have to drive back to the hotel. Another time perhaps, Father Francis, all three of us? That was without doubt the finest whiskey I've ever tasted. To have a second might ruin the magic of the first."

He emptied his own glass and then rose from his chair slowly, with a show of discomfort. Something clicked behind his shoulder blades. He was stiff but the whiskey and the warm fire had revived him a little. He felt sleepy but much better.

"Right," said the Prior, rising with ease. "There is one matter I'd like to clear up before you go Brian."

"Oh?" said Horse with little enthusiasm.

"Earlier today you were told certain things about my brother."

Horse had to gather his thoughts before he recalled the interview and the Manila file with the photographs of the soldiers in the jungle. So much had happened since. It all seems so long ago.

"Oh that?" he said.

"I want you to know," continued the Prior, "that whatever was said about my brother is not true. You have my word. If you were told anything that may have changed your opinion of him, well I want you to know that whatever was said, whatever accusation were made against him, I want you to know that they were lies. Michael is as he seems, Brian. He is as you know him, as you have always known him. There is not, nor has there ever been anything dishonest or dishonourable about him."

Horse looked at the Prior wide eyed. It was not what he'd expected and Father Francis looked angry.

"You don't have to worry on that score Father. I wouldn't believe a single word that American agent said. He is not police.

He's a politician. That's what he is. And I know Michael and I am well able to tell the good guys from the bad guys."

"Of course you are."

The Prior's face softened again.

"You're sure I can't tempt you with another small glass, Inspector Hopkins?"

"No thank you Father, I'd best be off now. Please take my card. My number's is on the back. I'd appreciate it if you'd keep me informed of any developments."

"Of course."

Horse moved toward the door.

"Brian?"

Horse turned.

"I...I..," the Prior hesitated, "...as soon as I hear any news I will let you know. I will take the first ferry in the morning and be at the hospital before eight," he said.

"Are you alright, Father Francis?"

"Yes, of course. I am just exhausted from all the excitement. Let me show you out."

They walked to the front door in silence. Horse looked at his watch. It was after two thirty in the morning and had begun to rain. They could hear the loud pitter-patter on the glass of the skylight high above the stairs.

"I'll never get used to the sudden change of weather on this island. One minute it's sunny, with clear blue skies, and the next it's like hurricane season," said Horse.

"And now we have earthquakes too", said the Prior.

"Skellig Éin is a very strange place, Father. Here, it seems, anything is possible."

"Even miracles, Inspector Hopkins?"

"Even miracles, Father Prior."

"Good night Brian and thank you again, for everything."

"Good night, Father Francis."

No sooner was Horse through the gates of the monastery and his hire car rumbling down the dark wet road, when his mobile beeped and burred in his pocket. When he looked at the screen he saw that he had seven missed calls, all of them from Paul Creagan.

*

533

Father Bernard and Brother Benjamin worked in virtual silence, the only sound being the constant hum from the boiler in the upper room. Bernard "tutted" a lot, but that was the extent of it. Benji welcomed the silence and as usual he worked quickly and diligently. Together they tried to push the large shelf units back in place but could only get them part of the way. Father Bernard told Benji that any decision on what should be done about the hole in the back wall would be taken later by the Prior, but, for now, putting some semblance of order back was a priority.

They dusted the shelves and then re-stacked them with the wheels of cheese. Then they brushed the floor, pushing all the dust and droppings into a corner before bagging it all for the bin. It took them less than half an hour. Just as they finished and were about to leave, they heard a loud noise coming from the upper cellar.

"Now who can that be?" said Bernard angrily.

Brother Benjamin thought it might be Father Raymond or even the Prior, but he didn't offer an opinion. Instead he just shrugged his shoulders.

"Hello. Who's there?" shouted Bernard angrily.

When no one answered, the Purser marched to the ladder and began to climb.

Benji watched him go but stayed where he was, leaning on the brush. He secretly pitied whoever it was in the upper cellar. Father Bernard was back to his old self and was in a bad mood. Someone was about to get an earful, thought Benji.

The low door at the top of the metal ladder had been left slightly ajar and white light leaked out from the upper room.

"Hello," Bernard said again when he reached the top of the ladder.

Still no one answered.

With both his hands the Purser grabbed the vertical bar that had been fixed to the wall to help people on and off the ladder, and he swung around in a well-practised manoeuvre that would propel him into the upper room.

He didn't make it.

Just as he had reached the point of no return someone slammed the door in his face and knocked him off the ladder. He fell to the floor with a resounding thud, landing on his backside.

534

He yelped in agony. Brother Benjamin ran over and knelt down beside him.

"Are you all right, Father?"

"I'm...fine. I'm fine, Benji. Pl..lease don't fuss," he snapped.

He pushed Benji aside and got to his feet. He rubbed his bottom and winched in pain.

"I'm fine," he said again.

Father Bernard looked up at the door and frowned. Benji followed his eyes. From the upper cellar they could hear the sound of someone opening and closing the doors of the dumb-waiter.

"Someone is using the lift, Father Purser," whispered Benji.

"What is going on? I can't have this," cried Bernard almost in despair.

"I'll go see Father," said Benji.

Brother Benjamin went to the ladder and began to climb, all the time watching the door above.

"Be careful," said Father Bernard, almost under his breath.

Benji found the door unlocked. He pushed it open and let it swing in. The lights were off in the upper cellar. Benji hesitated. He thought of the monster in the toilet, and the whisperers in the corridor outside his bedroom, but then he thought of Michael and what he'd said him about monsters not being real. Brother Benjamin climbed up, swung sideways and stepped into the darkness. Although he couldn't see a thing he knew the room was empty. He heard the dumb waiter shuddered to a stop and the doors open in the kitchen above. Whoever had been in the cellar had taken the goods lift to get away.

Chapter 77.

Father Francis sat at Michael's bedside and watched his brother sleeping. It was early morning. The sun was above the eastern hills that skirted the city and the waters of Galway bay shimmered and steamed in its pale light. The choir of city birds were through their morning recital and had gone quiet. Seagulls wheeled and cawed above the recently returned trawlers. The city was awake, but most of its inhabitants had not yet reached their work desks.

The small hospital room was warm and comfortable. This part of the hospital was particularly quiet. Visitors wouldn't return for another two hours or so. Night duty staff had gone home and the day shift had begun its morning routine. Hanna was asleep in the next room. Primrose was with her, as she had been since the night of the rescue, also asleep, curled up in tight ball beneath a heavy blanket in an armchair next to her daughter's bed. There was a door between the two rooms, a throw-back from when this, the oldest part of the hospital, had been a Georgian house overlooking the bay.

The connecting door was closed.

Sleep threatened Father Francis. He'd been up all night and for much of the previous four days. He thought about standing up, stretching, or going down the hall to get himself another coffee, but he didn't move. Michael would wake soon and Father Francis needed to be there when he did. The coffee and sleep could wait. He yawned without covering his mouth. He apologised to the room and thought of his mother scolding him for it, just as she so often had when he was a little boy. "You'll catch flies," she'd say to him. The memory of their mother brought a sad smile to his tired face. He lowered his head and

537

shuffled through the pages of the small book he held in his lap. Brother Benjamin had dropped it in an hour earlier, on his way to morning mass in Galway cathedral. The little book was the key to freeing his brother from the madness. He was sure of it.

"It's time for you to come back to us," the Prior whispered, "time to come home, brother."

*

It had been four days since they'd found Michael and Hanna and both were on their way to a full physical recovery. The doctors said that the mental trauma of their ordeal could live with them for a long time. Hanna was to be discharged later that day. Michael was being kept in for a few more days, for a few more tests.

Hanna came back to life in the helicopter, slowly and without fuss. She just opened her eyes. By the time the helicopter touched down on the roof of the hospital, she was asking for water and her mother.

It took Michael much longer to come around. For a while it looked like he might not come back at all. Father Francis kept a constant bedside vigil, praying, and whispering to his sleeping brother. In the late afternoon of the second day Michael woke up suddenly, as if from a terrible nightmare. Blinking wildly, he sat bolt upright and started screaming. Father Francis, Horse and Marie were in the room at the time and Michael's sudden outburst made them all jump. He became so agitated that he had to be restrained and then sedated. He woke again later that evening, once the effects of the sedative had worn off. A young male nurse was present at the time, checking his blood pressure. Father Francis was at the window, having moved from his bedside chair to allow the nurse to do his job.

"Where's Hanna?" Michael said groggily.

"You're back with us then?" said the Prior with a smile.

Michael looked afraid.

The male nurse shone a pen torch into Michael's half opened eyes.

"How are you feeling Michael?" said the nurse.

"Thirsty," said Michael.

"Any pain?" asked the nurse.

"No, just tired and thirsty," he said.

The nurse brought the straw of a juice container to Michael's lips.

"Diluted orange juice," he said.

Michael sucked on the straw with his eyes closed. He drank too quickly and gagged. Orange juice dribbled down his chin. The nurse wiped it with a tissue and then returned the straw to Michael's mouth.

"Slowly," he said.

"Where's Hanna?" Michael asked after taking some more juice.

His voice was weak. Father Francis came over to him.

"Hanna is fine," he said. "You found her. I knew you would."

"Hanna..." said Michael.

"She's fine. You found her. You brought her back. She's fine."

Father Francis smiled at the male nurse.

After drinking half of the orange juice Michael turned his face away and fell back into a deep sleep.

Michael followed this pattern throughout the following day. He'd wake for a short period before dropping off again. Sometimes, when he stayed awake a bit longer, he started talking about monsters and would become distressed and would have to be sedated. Father Francis stayed with him always. He prayed while Michael was asleep and he spoke to him when he was awake. Michael seemed trapped, somewhere between sleeping and waking, between nightmares and reality.

*

Michael and Hanna's return from the dead had become a media sensation and everyone wanted to interview them. Reporter from local, national, and international news agencies camped out in the car park of the hospital and one or two even tried to gain access, pretending to be relatives.

Father Francis and Primrose went into protection mode. Primrose allowed only two police officers, Horse and Paul, to interview Hanna and only on the proviso that she could stay in the room during the interview and call a halt to it, should Hanna become distressed. Hanna repeated the story she'd told Primrose and Father Francis the previous day. Professor Kearns was dead.

She'd been with him when he slipped into the water and was dragged under by a powerful current. He drowned. There was nothing she could do for him. Denis was dead too. She'd seen his body. He must have drowned too or was poisoned by the toxic air. Hanna insisted that there was no way that she and Michael could have brought their bodies back out. She told them that she'd found Michael on the stepped beach, after the rising waters had subsided. He was unconscious, but alive. Like the other students, she had survived by climbing into an air pocket in one of the surrounding caves. She revived Michael and after searching the cliff wall, discovered a tunnel that led them out of the caves. She said that, at one point, the cave they were in became flooded and they were swept along, in a torrent of freezing water. All she could remember was the cold, the darkness and clinging to Michael. She thought that they would die down there. That was all that she could remember. She told them she must have blacked out and the next thing she remembered was waking up in the helicopter. When asked about how they had survived without food, Hanna said that they had water and they shared a bag of boiled sweets that Michael had brought with him.

Father Francis refused to let anyone interview Michael. Most of the time Michael was delirious. He insisted that there were monsters living in the caves, in a hidden world beneath an upturned ocean and claimed that Professor Kearns and Denis were still alive. He said that the monstrous creatures had trapped the two men, and that Denis, Kearns and other people were being kept alive as food for the monster's young.

When it became clear to him that no one, including his brother believed him and he got agitated and angry.

*

Michael woke just after midnight on the third day. The small recessed fluorescent tube behind his head, the only light in the room, gave everything a yellowish hue. Michael sat up wide-eyed and started screaming. The noise woke Father Francis who, despite his best efforts, had succumbed to exhaustion and had nodded off in the chair. The screaming also attracted the attention of a night orderly who had been patrolling the corridors. A young female registrar on night duty was paged and she came quickly. She sat on the bed and gathered Michael flailing arms. Although quite small she was strong. She forced him to look at her, before she spoke.

"It was just a nightmare, Michael" she said. Her voice was firm but kind, like a mother consoling her little boy. "It's not real. Do you understand? You're safe here. You are in hospital. Your brother is here. You are safe, Michael. It was only a nightmare."

She cupped his hands in hers and held his gaze.

"It was a nightmare. That's all. Do you understand Michael?"

He nodded and turned away.

"Good. It was a nightmare. That's all."

When the registrar left, Michael whispered something.

"What was that?" said the Prior.

"It was real. They're real and they're on the island."

"They? Who are Michael?" said Father Francis.

"The monsters. They are real and they are on the island. We have to warn people."

The Prior sighed.

"Ask Hanna. There are monsters in the caves and an upside-down world under an ocean. That's where I found Hanna. That's where she was. Denis too. The monsters have him. Giant winged scorpion-like monsters. They feed on humans. They poison them. Keep them alive. Keep them fresh. They mutilate them, but won't let them die. Half alive, half dead. Where's Hanna? She'll tell you. And they can change into snakes...giant snakes. They swim in the ocean. It's where they catch their prey. It's like Purgatory. There is air that we could breathe, and a forest of mushrooms, and vast open plains with rivers and valleys. A world under an ocean. There was a terrible battle, but they couldn't see me. I am invisible..."

"You are not making sense, Michael. You are safe. There are no monsters. They are all in your head," said Father Francis.

He went to stand up but Michael grabbed his arm.

"No. You don't understand. They got out. They've come to the surface. Brother Benjamin was attacked by one in the bathroom. And the body in the forest. That man was still alive. He shouldn't have been. Half his head was gone, but he was still alive. They got out. Don't you understand? We need to warn people. Ask Hanna, if you don't believe me. It's true."

"Michael. Hanna said she found you on a beach and that you got out through a cave. She never said anything about monsters or snakes or upturned oceans. Hanna said that Professor Kearns and Denis are dead. There are no monsters. They are in your head Michael. The monsters are all in your head."

|*

On the morning of fourth day Marie came to the hospital without Horse and was there when Michael woke up. She sat on the edge of the bed and spoke to him quietly. Father Francis watched her from the window. Sometimes Marie spoke so quietly he had to strain to hear her. Michael said nothing. He just stared at her and listened.

Father Francis was amazed at how gentle she was. He had heard stories about Marie from different people, none of them very complimentary. It seemed to be common knowledge that Marie Joyce was difficult and odd. One woman had referred to her as cold and dangerous. Another claimed Marie was a witch.

"Have you seen her art, Father? Nothing but blacks and greys. They say she's never been right in the head, since her parents died."

Father Francis felt guilty. Since getting to know Marie, he had been struck by her honesty, and he saw in her a restless energy that he recognised. Like most men, Father Francis was taken by her disarming beauty, but it was her spirit which he found most attractive. Watching her with Michael gave him hope.

Marie took Michael's hand.

"When I was fourteen, Michael, I got lost in the caves for nearly six hours. Myself and my boyfriend, Owen. He was very handsome. His eyes were soft, just like the Englishman's eyes."

"You told me this story. When we were in the caves," said Michael.

"You remember? When we had to stop because you had a terrible headache. You took some pills. I saw you. Lots of them. More than you should have, I think? Do you remember *that*, Michael?"

He lowered his eyes.

"Yes," he said, nodding.

"Good, well it seems you may have missed the point of my story, so if you don't mind, I tell it again."

Michael looked at her with frightened eyes. She went on.

"At first, I was only pretending to be lost, just to scare Owen. He was sweet and gullible. He had never been in the caves and I knew the caves well, and was confident I knew the way back out. I wanted to scare him. I never meant to..."

She stopped for a moment, before continuing. Michael squeezed her hand.

"We had only one torch between us and it was old. The batteries were old too. I turned it off, to scare Owen, but then I couldn't get it to turn back on. God, it was so dark, Michael. I swear, I couldn't see a thing, not even my hands in front of my face. You know what it's like, Michael. Owen panicked and he ran from me. I tried to stop him, but I couldn't see where he'd gone. I couldn't see anything. I was blind. I could hear him, but it took me ages to find him. When I finally did, I had no idea where we were. We were totally lost. All we could do was huddle together and hope someone would come for us. We were lost for six hours, Michael. It was a lifetime. If my sister Martha hadn't come to find us, I know we would have died down there."

Marie stopped again, but never took her eyes off Michael.

"In the darkness, we heard noises. Things touched us. Owen convinced me that he could hear a woman giggling. At first, I couldn't hear her, but he kept telling me to listen, listen, listen, and then I heard her too, and the more I concentrated, the louder her giggling became. She was as real to me as you are, Michael, and when Owen said he could see her, I saw her too. It was impossible. He described her long black hair, her cold hungry eyes and her cruel smile. He told me she had sharp teeth and that her fingers had claws. He said that she had seen us and that she was going to eat us. I tried not to look, I tried to cover my eyes because I knew if I looked, if I really looked, I'd see the Banshee looking back at me, see her racing toward us, down the pitch-black tunnel, coming to eat us."

Marie turned and looked at Father Francis. There was a shadow over her eyes. She turned back to Michael.

"Owen tried to pull away from me. He said that I was the witch. I had to cling on to him or he would have run away again. I was terrified. He hit me and kicked me and scratched me. And he screamed and screamed. Martha heard him and she found us. Just before Martha reached us, from the corner of my eye, I spotted a shape in the shadows. It was a crouching woman with long black hair and cold white eyes. She was scuttling away from

Martha's torchlight, like an enormous black spider. When Martha came with the others I told her about the Banshee. Martha said I was hallucinating. I showed her the marks on my arms and face, where the witch had scratched me."

Marie stopped again. Michael looked up.

"For almost a year I was convinced that everyone else was wrong and that there was a Banshee in the caves. I wouldn't listen to anybody, even Martha. I became distant and afraid. Owen was the same. We stopped seeing each other. We stopped seeing everybody. Owen and I became strangers and it broke my heart, Michael. About a year after we were rescued, Owen tried to take his own life and his parents had him committed to a psychiatric hospital in Dublin. He was only fifteen years old. I went to visit him once, but he didn't recognise me. I didn't recognise him either. Only the eyes were his, but the Owen I knew was gone. The caves and the darkness and the madness took him. Seeing Owen like that, saved me. When I left the hospital, I knew I had to choose between what was real and what was a figment of my imagination. The Banshee was in my head and if I didn't let her go, I knew I would end up just like Owen."

Marie wiped her eyes with the back of her hand. When she spoke again her voice quivered slightly.

"She seemed so real, Michael, the witch in the cave, the Banshee. But she wasn't real. She belongs in fairy tales and nightmares. If she had been real, do you really think that I would have gone back down there?"

Michael opened his mouth to speak but didn't. He just squeezed her hand again and looked away.

"Come back to us Michael," she said. "There is nothing in the caves except cold empty darkness and the madness of nightmares."

When Marie left, Michael fell asleep. After listening to Marie's story an idea came to the Prior. It was still early, just after two in the afternoon. The sky was clear. Father Francis ran down the corridor to the visitor's waiting room and rang the monastery. He asked for Brother Benjamin.

"Father Prior," said Benji, catching his breath.

"Have you been running Benji? You know you shouldn't, until your feet are better."

"I'm fine, Father Prior."

"Good. Well if you are up to it, I need you to bring something to the hospital for me. It's very important and I think it will help with Michael's recovery. I suppose it's too late for you to catch the evening ferry, so the morning ferry will have to do."

"I'll go out at dawn, with Padge Clancy. He will bring me across in his boat. He goes over every morning at five thirty," said Brother Benjamin.

"Well, if you are sure, Benji," said Father Francis.

"Oh yes, Father. If it's for Michael, I'll swim over, if I have to."

"Thank you, Benji. Thank you. Here's what I need you to get for me."

*

Michael woke and looked at his brother who was sitting on the side of his bed.

"You still here?" he said groggily.

Father Francis passed him the orange juice. Michael's strength was coming back. He sat up.

"I brought you something," said the Prior. "A book. You didn't get a chance to finish it, before you went on your grand adventure in the caves. I even found the page you were on."

Father Francis opened The Life of St. Áedán on the double page spread showing the kneeling saint in a ball of blinding light, surrounded by black demons hiding in the shadows.

"Do you recognise this, Michael?" he said.

Michael took the book and studied the image for a long time. Then he flicked through the other images in the book. After a while he started to cry.

"It seemed so real," he said.

Father Francis said nothing.

Michael shook his head.

"They seemed so real," he said, this time to himself.

"They were nightmares, that's all. Like all nightmares, they are anchored in a jumbled reality. Unconnected memories become connected, dissonant images are welded together and our brains try to make sense of it all. Our imagination builds a story. You always had a wild imagination, brother. Maybe you could write that horror novel you were always talking about, when you were in college. The Vampire Fish of Skellig Éin?" said the Prior with a broad smile.

Michael touched his brothers hand.

"I'm sorry. It seemed so real," he whispered.

The adjoining door opened and Primrose popped her head into the room. She looked exhausted, but happy.

"Hey there," said the Prior.

"I thought I heard voices. Is everything okay?" she said.

She looked at Michael.

"Yes, I think so," said the Prior with a smile, "everything seems to be back the way it should be. Michael has come back to us, Primrose, out of the darkness."

Chapter 78.

"Ah, there you are," said the doctor when he entered the room.

"Were you expecting me to be somewhere else?" said Michael dryly.

Michael was sitting up in the bed with his eyes closed. He had been thinking of Susan. He blinked and tried to focus on the man standing over him. He looked like a doctor, but Michael didn't recognise him. Father Francis was not in his usual chair by the window and Michael guessed his brother must have stepped out for a moment.

"I recognise you, don't I? Have we met before?" said the doctor.

"I don't know. Who are you?" said Michael groggily.

"I'm your doctor. Dr Aidan Kelleher, from the island."

"What? What about Susan...I mean, Dr McCarthy. She's my doctor on the island."

"Ah, I'm afraid Dr McCarthy is no longer with us, so you'll just have to put up with me, until a permanent replacement can be found."

"What do you mean, no longer with us?"

"On her way to Canada. Bigger and better things, for our Susan."

"She's already gone?" said Michael, now fully awake.

"Next Tuesday morning. Are you a friend?

"Yes, I am. What day is it?

"It's Friday of course. All day, ha ha," said Kelleher with a chuckle."

"So, she's still on the island now?"

"Well, I'm not sure. She said she'd be back this weekend for her things. She left in an awful hurry, and dropped me in it, if you must know. I only agreed to take her place for a couple of days, and now I'm stuck there, until a replacement can be found. At least that awful district nurse is leaving too. Bloody awful woman," said Dr Kelleher.

He tutted and then returned his attention to Michael.

"Are you sure we've never met? You look awfully familiar," he said again.

"I don't think so," said Michael.

"Well, I am your doctor now, and I'd like you to have some more tests, before we let you go."

"I don't want any more tests, or scans or psychological assessments. I'm fine. In fact, I'm ready to leave. Where is my brother?"

Before Dr Kelleher could respond, Father Francis came into the room.

"Well good morning doctor, and how's the patient today?"

Dr Kelleher wheeled around, looked at Father Francis and then did a double take.

"Aha!" he said, "twins. That explains it. I don't know you Michael, but I've met your brother before. Father..?"

"Francis," said the Prior.

"Yes indeed. I've seen you around town. The likeness is uncanny."

"Twins," said Michael and the Prior simultaneously.

"Ha. Very good. But really, you are the spitting image of each other. Usually by your age any differences are pronounced, identical twins are no longer identical. But with you two, well, quite uncanny," said the Dr, looking from one brother to the other, and back again.

Michael swung his legs out from under the covers and began to get out of bed. He looked at the Prior.

"I'm fine. I'm leaving. That's all right, isn't it Dr Kelleher?" he said.

"Well, I would like you to have a few more tests, just to make sure."

"Michael. You should listen to the doctor," said Father Francis.

"I'm fine," said Michael. He stood up and stretched. "See. I'm fine."

"Well if you want to leave, I can't stop you. In fact, I should be kicking you out, and not trying to keep you here. But I would ask you to call in and see me on Monday. You are returning to Skellig Éin?"

"Yes. Immediately," said Michael.

"Well, I have a free slot just after lunch on Monday. Two fifteen. You will come to the surgery?" said Dr Kelleher,

Michael frowned.

"He'll be there, doctor, if I have to drag him to you myself."

Michael found his clothes and started to dress, then stopped.

"I should shower and shave and then we'll go. Thank you, doctor. I'll see you on Monday," he said, before disappearing into the bathroom.

When he re-emerged, fifteen minutes later, Dr Kelleher was gone and his brother was back in his usual chair.

"What's your hurry, Michael?"

"If I'm lucky I can catch her, before she leaves."

"Susan?"

"Yes. Dr What's-his-face said she was leaving. I need to see her before she goes."

"Oh. Right. Well, we should be in time to catch the evening ferry, if we hurry," said the Prior.

"Ferry? You must be joking. I'm not going on any ferry. When is the next flight?"

"I believe there's one at four thirty," said the Prior.

"Good. We'll be on that one then."

Chapter 79.

Horse left behind the noise of Dublin's afternoon traffic, when he entered the quiet lobby of 64B Henrietta Street.

After identifying himself to the attractive dark haired receptionist he was directed to room 1131 on the second floor. He wandered up and down a plush empty corridor for several minutes before he finally found the room. The room numbering seemed to defy logic. He knocked firmly on the door and it opened almost immediately. Paul Creagan stood in front of him and gave him a weak smile.

"We thought you'd got lost."

Horse entered the large meeting room and balked. Sitting around the conference table were the last three people he expected to see. From the far side of the table Harry Buckingham raised a hand and gave him a toothy smile.

"Hey Horse," he said.

Buick's partner, Gerry Redinski, who was sitting opposite Harry with his back to Horse, turned and gave him a curt disinterested nod. Special Agent Theodore Brooks sat at the top of the table. He stood up when Horse entered and extended his hand.

"Welcome Detective Inspector Hopkins, it's good that you could join us."

"And where's Mr. Getys?" asked Horse.

Horse had received a call requesting him to attend a meeting with Paul and Donal Getys at the offices of Getys Mather & Moore Solicitors on Henrietta Street, before heading to the airport to catch his flight back to London. He assumed the meeting had something to do with signing confidentiality papers.

Seeing the three Americans didn't make sense.

"Mr Getys will not be joining us, but he has kindly given us permission to use his office," said Brook.

Paul closed the door and indicated that Horse should take the seat next to Red. Paul sat down on the chair opposite. Horse sat down.

"Could someone please tell me what, the fuck, is going on?" he said.

"That is why you are here. We owe you that. The evidence you managed to retrieve from Gerry Gallagher's farm, the footage from the hard-drive, has proved invaluable. Sylvester Parker is dead and, because Parker is dead, our work here in Ireland is complete and I am free to be open with you Detective Inspector Hopkins" said Brooks, sitting back down and smiling at him, like a cat that had just swallowed a canary.

*

Horse didn't settle. He sat forward in his chair and kept his hands together on the table. While Brooks spoke, Horse watched Paul. Paul held his gaze.

"Three years ago, Garda Paul Creagan was asked to assist an American led task-force, set up to capture an international terrorist named Sylvester Parker. Parker has been at the top of our Most Wanted list for nearly a decade. The task force was initiated by an Executive Order from the President himself."

Brooks looked at his American colleagues before continuing.

"Paul's involvement was, and had to be, top secret. Only one other person in the Garda Síochána knew of his involvement with us, the late Garda Commissioner, Patrick Howley. Paul's task was to watch Mr G. and to report everything, no matter how trivial, to Harry here."

"So, Harry was your mysterious American contact?" said Horse.

Paul nodded.

Horse looked at the big black Texan. The Buick shrugged and smiled at him.

Theodore Brooks continued.

"You need to understand who Sylvester Parker was and why we needed to be very, very careful. Why we are *still* being careful. Parker had friends everywhere. Maybe *friends* is the wrong word? People he controlled. Powerful and influential people. People who helped him to stay one step ahead of us. People who helped him to travel the world with impunity and to scupper any attempts to apprehend him. We think that some of these people even killed for him."

Brooks paused and took a mouthful of water before going on.

"Blackmail and coercion seemed to be his stock and trade. That's not to say he didn't attract disciples. He did, and many of them are still at large. That is why we had to use subterfuge to get you to come here. Getys Mather & Moore Solicitors are not involved and, obviously know nothing of this matter. Mr Getys is a friend of my family. He let me use the room for our meeting and this building is secure. By the time I'm finished, you will understand why we still need to be vigilant."

Horse said nothing. He'd spent his career going to police briefings and knew to hold his tongue until the main speaker was finished.

"You see, Horse, for Sylvester Parker, knowledge was power and he had highly sophisticated methods for obtaining it. Everyone has a dirty little secret, Inspector Hopkins, and Parker was particularly good at uncovering them. We believe that the recordings you found in Gerry Gallaher's farm is only a very small part of a much greater haul yet to be discovered. Only the tip of the iceberg, but now that he's dead we're sure that what we have uncovered will lead us to his lair and the rest of his organisation."

Brooks topped up his glass from a pitcher on the table and took another mouthful before he continued.

"Sylvester Parker was the worst kind of psychopath, Detective Inspector. He was vicious, clever, and cruel. A dangerous and deranged madman, who derived pleasure from the pain he inflicted on others. He liked to torture people, both physically and psychologically and he recorded everything he did, making sick videos which he sold to like-minded whack-jobs on the Dark Web. Snuff videos and torture porn are big business."

Horse broke his silence.

"He sounds just like every other psychopath I've ever encountered," said Horse dismissively. "It's only in Hollywood, or on U.S. television, that psychopaths are presented as dark anti-heroes or misunderstood souls. I've never met one who didn't get pleasure in the pain and horror he inflicted on his victims. In my experience psychopaths do what they do for self-gratification; to satisfy their twisted lust; and to prove that they are smarter than the rest of humanity. This Parker characters may have been sophisticated and techno-savvy, but he sounds just the same as all the rest. A sad twisted little fuck."

"I am aware of your experience in such matters, Inspector Hopkins, but I must disagree with you. Parker was not like anyone who have ever encountered."

Brook stretched out an elegant finger and touched the key pad of a laptop in front of him. An image of Sylvester Parker, sitting at the desk in the front room of the farmhouse on Skellig Éin, appeared on the white wall behind him. Horse recognized it as a still-shot from one of the recordings found in Gerry Gallagher's basement.

"Our guy was special; a unique and particularly twisted little fuck. Sylvester Parker, we assume it was not his real name, first came to our attention in 2003 in Houston Texas. What, at first, appeared to be the murder and brutal torture of a local pimp, soon took on a different colour when four more bodies turned up in four different cities along the east coast, all with the same, or strikingly similar, modus operandi. Once the local cops saw that they had a serial killer on their hands, who was plying his trade in several different States, the FBI were brought in."

"How close together were the murders?" asked Horse.

"No more than two weeks apart. Close enough to get noticed," said Brooks.

"So, Sylvester Parker, or whatever his name is, was announcing himself to the world?" said Horse.

"Yes, certainly it would seem that way. As I said the MO's were very similar. All the victims had been stripped naked, mutilated and left in a very public place, ensuring they'd be found quickly. And all the victims were...posed," said Brooks.

"Posed?" said Horse.

"Yes, posed and photographed by Parker, before he left the scene. Polaroids were found on or around the victims. The photographs were his calling cards. It was grotesque."

Brooks touched a key on the keyboard and the image on the wall behind him changed. A man sat on a park bench with his head in his lap, staring wide-eyed up at the place where his head used to be. His eyelids had been removed. He looked shocked. The image behind Brooks changed again. This one showed a man lying on his belly near a children's playground with his arms stretched out in front of him and what was left of his legs bent upwards behind him. A large triangle of skin from his back had been sown onto the stumps where his feet had once been. His nose was missing and half-moon slashes had been carved into his neck. The Polaroids left by Parker made him look like a humanfish.

"For obvious reasons, the details of the crimes were kept from the Press. At first, we thought there was nothing to link the victims, other than the M.O. Some of his victims were from the criminal fraternity, like the pimp in Houston, but others appeared to be ordinary citizens. The fish-guy was an accountant who had no criminal record. He'd been walking home from a movie when he was abducted. His mutilated body was found in a park in Boston two days later. Another, was the owner of a hardware shop. She was murdered in her own home, her face carved up to look like a demented clown. When the cops turned up, following an anonymous call to 911, they found bits of her cooking in the oven on a tray surrounded by neatly prepared vegetables. There was a note on the kitchen table for the cops. It read Dinner's in the Oven Boys."

"And you were never able to find a link between the victims?" said Horse.

"Not at first. But one of the pathologists noted something odd. She pointed out that two of the victims had a small piece of skin missing from the same place just above their right wrists and in her report, she suggested that the killer may have been removing a tattoo. We went back and checked all of the victims and found that the skin above the right wrist was missing on all of them."

Horse closed his eyes as if fighting a headache. He brought his hands up to his face, then dropped them back onto the table.

"So, you think the killer was removing evidence that could lead you to him?" he said.

"Exactly," said Harry.

"Like a gang tattoo?" said Horse.

"Obviously not. But they all had a mark which identified them as members of the same club," said Brooks.

"The Sylvester Parker appreciation society?" said Horse.

"Something like that," said Brooks.

"The mark of the Devil," said Red, without raising his head.

"Thanks to you and Paul, we now know what it was."

"You do?" said Horse.

"It was the tattoo of a snake. This is one of the images from the bedroom of Gerry Gallagher's farm."

A new image filled the screen. It was a close-up of an arm. The hand was missing. Just above the stump was a blurry tattoo of a snake."

"Were all of Parker's victim's part of his snake club then?" said Horse

"No. But all of the people murdered in the 2003 investigation probably were," said Brooks.

He looked over at Harry before continuing.

"The FBI investigation into those five murders in 2003 was led from the Houston office. The agent running the investigation was a top man and we were all confident that he'd catch the serial killer. Everyone thought that way. The killer appeared to have been an amateur. Along with the Polaroid photographs, he'd left forensic evidence at almost all the crime scenes. This led the investigating team to a seemingly legitimate Baltimore businessman named Sylvester Parker. Parker had an import/export business and he owned several warehouses in the docklands. He was registered as living there too, in one of the warehouse buildings."

Brooks paused and played with his water but didn't drink any. Horse noticed that Brooks looked at Harry Buckingham again. Buick looked grey. Horse had a strange feeling that Brooks was seeking the other agent's permission to continue. If he was, Buick made no gestures to suggest he had an opinion, one way or the other.

When Brooks began again, his voice was quieter.

"It turned out that the FBI's confidence was misplaced and that Parker had been playing them for fools. We now know that the evidence found at the crime scenes had been left there on purpose. Parker was leading them into a trap. At 5am on a Saturday morning the FBI and three units from the Baltimore SWAT surrounded the properties and moved systematically through the warehouses. All of them were empty. If Parker had an import/export business, it wasn't being run from Baltimore. In the last warehouse, they found a small electrical generator hooked up to a television and DVD player which was sitting on a table in the middle of the empty space. Beside the TV was an envelope addressed to the FBI agent leading the investigation. Inside the envelope was a card which read: Press PLAY for your viewing pleasure. It was signed SP."

Brooks stopped again.

"The agent shouldn't have pressed the button. God only knows what he was thinking. It could have been a bomb or anything. It was worse than a bomb. It was a recording made the previous evening, a video of the agent's wife and his two young children, gagged and naked, strapped to chairs in their own kitchen in Houston. A man wearing a face mask, rubber gloves and dressed in a white plastic abattoir coat moved between them. He had a hunting knife in one hand and a portable bone saw in the other. He whispered to his captors and he talked to the camera, to the agents watching in the warehouse in Baltimore. What he did to that family is beyond belief, beyond madness. It was evil incarnate."

Brooks stared at Horse.

"I too have met my fair share of psychopaths, Detective Inspector Hopkins, but I've never witnessed anything so cold, so fucking evil. I've seen the beheading of captured American soldiers in Afghanistan, I've seen footage of a CIA agent being burned to death with a blow torch in Columbia and a man crucified in the Congo with his balls in his mouth, but I swear to God, I've never seen anything like that. It was Sylvester Parker behind the mask, he was the man in the white coat and he was the one who murdered the agent's family. It took him over an hour. The little girl was five years old. Her brother was nine. The bastard arranged their chairs in a semi-circle so that they were facing each other and the camera. He left the mother 'til last. When he spoke to the camera he spoke directly to the agent and to the other agents investigating the murders. He named them all. Then he listed off their wives' names, the names, and ages of all their children, and where they lived and where the children went to school. He boasted about what he was going to do them. It was evil, Detective Inspector Hopkins, pure fucking evil."

Chapter 80.

For a long time, no one spoke. Horse found the silence uncomfortable. Brooks brought his hand to the side of his face but stopped short of touching it. He made a tight fist, then returned his hand to the table. He sighed.

"After Baltimore, the investigation stalled. The agents working the case, along with their families, were given around-the-clock protection. Those who wanted it, which amounted to virtually all of them, were fast-tracked into the witness protection programme, given new names, new homes and new lives."

"Good God Almighty," said Horse.

"After that, the search for Parker became political. Our current President is related to the wife of Houston agent, the woman who had to watch as her children were dismembered before her eyes. Back then our current President was a Texas Senator, but when he came into office he made the hunt for Parker a top priority. *Unfinished business* was how he saw it. A special task-force would be set up, small and tightknit. A three-man team. Very few, outside of the President himself, knew the names of those on the team. The President's instructions were clear. Find Parker and stop him, by whatever means necessary. It would be financed from the Homeland Security budget, but Homeland Security was not involved. The resources of every US law enforcement and intelligence agencies would be made available and the task force would be afforded full co-operation and untrammelled access to intelligence data. It was unprecedented, but an Executive Order is not to be ignored. Added to that, the three agents travelled the world on diplomatic passports and given consulate protection. No stone was to be left unturned, no obstacle to be put in the way of finding Sylvester Parker."

Brooks looked again at his two colleagues.

"We are that task force, Detective Inspector Hopkins."

"But you still didn't catch him?" said Horse. There was no sarcasm in his voice. It was just a statement of fact.

"No," said Buick, "he proved to be quite a slippery fucker. But we were getting closer and closer. It was only a matter of time."

"Four months ago, we got lucky," said Brooks. "We intercepted an international telephone call between Mr G. and some unknown person. There were things about the conversation that piqued our interest. Words were used that suggested that the unknown caller could be our target."

"How did you know it was Parker?" said Horse.

"We didn't, at first. It was only a suspicion, based on some key words used in their conversation. The nature of the call was unusual too. The unknown caller was making Mr G a curious offer. Part of the payment to Mr G for services rendered, was a piece of real estate on the island of Skellig Éin. Mr G's mother was from the island. Did you know that? That's why they went there every summer. She loved the place. She was very religious too. We don't think she ever knew what her only son did for a living. Anyway, along with a large quantity of cash Mr G was being offered the mothers old homestead. This was quite a prize. For years Mr G had tried, unsuccessfully, to acquire the six-acre site, but Galway University continually refused to sell. It seems someone had finally persuaded the University to change its mind."

"What did Mr G have to do for this?" said Horse.

"That was the curious thing. The mysterious caller's instructions were simple. Mr G was to take up residency on the island for the summer months, run his nightclub and other businesses and wait for further instructions. Nothing more."

"Why were you tapping Mr G's phone calls in the first place?" said Horse.

"We weren't," piped up Red. It was the first time he'd spoken since Horse had entered the room. He raised his head from the folder he'd been reading and gave Brooks a quizzical look. Brooks nodded at him. Red turned in his chair and looked directly at Horse.

"We monitor everything," he said, "All o' the time. All communications. Everything. We scan the internet, the Dark Net, social media and conventional airwaves, all across the planet, twenty-four hours a day, seven days a week, three hundred and sixty-five days a year. In the case of audio files, we look for certain words in certain combinations, sentence structure, known peculiarities, voice recognition, accents, and even tone inflections. Then we compare these with the things we know about the target - how Parker talked on the tape from Houston, for example. Even when a person tries to disguise their voice, they can't avoid usin' tell-tale words and phrases. If the analysing programme is sophisticated enough, it can spot these tell-tale signs. So, when the programme hits on something promising, it gives the sample a score, a number between one an' a hundred. If the numbers are high, over sixty-five say, then these samples are extracted for more detailed analysis. The system was designed to identify national and international security threats, such as ISIS, Al-Qaeda, an' here in Ireland, the Continuity IRA and the like. The system can be used to find anyone."

"Is that legal?" said Horse.

"When it's a matter of national or global security, it is. When it is on the direct orders of the President of the United States of America different rules apply. Like I said, whatever we had to do was sanctioned." interrupted Brooks.

"What did he want here in Ireland? Why was he on the island of Skellig Éin?" said Horse.

"I'll get to that. The point was, if Red was right, and it *was* Sylvester Parker talking to Mr G then, for the first time ever, the task-force had the upper hand. And we couldn't have asked for a better lead in Mr G."

"Oh? How's that?" said Horse.

"Mr G is a Luddite when it comes to computers and new technology. He doesn't do e-mails. We don't think he even has a cell phone. He writes letters and uses a pay phone in his brothel in Capel Street, probably the last pubic pay phone in Ireland. Parker had no choice but to contact him by letter or phone and he had no idea we were on to him," Brooks hesitated, "well, at least, not at first. Of course, now we know differently, but back then, we were excited. We knew we'd have to move carefully, but it was all systems go. The late Garda Commissioner Howley was very accommodating. He gave us permission to tap the pay phone in Capel Street. We didn't technically need it, but obviously, it was better for us to have an officially sanctioned wiretap. That way, whatever we got on Parker would be admissible in a court of law, if ever it got to that. Commissioner Howley believed that the Irish police force was assisting American law enforcement in an undercover operation to bust an international drugs ring. If the truth ever got out, we could claim that we were protecting him and his family from a deranged psychopath, which was partly true."

"So, you tapped the pay phone," said Horse impatiently.

"Yes. There were two further calls. Parker must have been writing to Mr G too, because they spoke of previous correspondence, which we knew nothing about. Anyway, during the first call Mr G got angry and referred to the man on the line as Mr Parker, at which point the caller hung up."

Brooks took another mouthful and swallowed slowly before going on.

"Our suspicions had proved correct, but now Parker was spooked. We were very concerned that it was over before it had begun and that Parker would fade back into the shadows and that would be the end of it. Our only hope was that, whatever Parker was planning was too big or too far along for him to pull out now. Our only option was to watch Mr G and to do that we needed a man on the ground, someone we could trust. That's where Paul came in. Paul was perfect, but the problem was he would have to work alone. Like I said, we needed to be very careful and smart. We knew that a detective working alone could look suspicious, if Parker had someone inside Garda HQ. We had to work on the assumption that every organisation was compromised. As you know from what you found in Gallagher's farm, Parker was meticulous in his information gathering. Finding someone we could trust to tag along with Paul and not ask too many questions, or become suspicious of Paul's extra-curriculum activities, seemed like an intractable problem until you came along, Detective Inspector Hopkins. When it was suggested that, as part of the cross-border co-operation initiative, a senior police officer from Scotland Yard would be seconded to Dublin's Serious Crime Unit, it seemed like a stroke of good fortune. You could investigate Mr G whilst not knowing the extra dimension to the investigation."

"I see. And of course, I was easy to keep in line, wasn't I?" scowled Horse.

"It was never about that, but we had to keep you in the dark. Paul needed a partner and you were exactly the sort of high profile cop we needed. The spotlight was on you, because you were the British cop in the Irish police force. Paul could hide in the shadow of your notoriety and if Parker had you investigated, he would see that you were clean."

"And that was the reason I was chosen?"

"It also helped that, like Paul, you were single. Keeping you in the dark was also a way of protecting you," said Brooks.

"Fuck you, Brooks. Fuck all of you," shouted Horse.

He pushed back his chair and went to stand up.

"Hold on, Brian. Hear them out, please," said Paul.

"You asked why Ireland, Inspector Hopkins. Well now we think we know," said Brooks, as if nothing had happened. Horse reluctantly sat back down, but remained on the edge of his seat.

"The footage from the hard disc you saved from the explosion at the farm confirmed it. A couple of weeks before the first call we intercepted between Parker to Mr G, the parliament of the European Union produced its calendar for the next three years. The calendar included which country would hold the presidency of the Union for the coming three years. Ireland would hold the presidency from March to August this year. A fortnight later the Irish government produced its programme of events for the six months of its presidency. One of the highlights would be the International Conference on Cross Border Co-operation, which would be held on the island of Skellig Éin. Justice Ministers and their high-ranking coterie, from across the world, would be in attendance. One week later Mr G got the phone call from Sylvester Parker with the offer of his mother's homestead, if he agreed to spend the summer on Skellig Éin."

Brooks gritted his teeth.

"We believe it was the conference that brought Sylvester Parker to the island, because it presented him with a most unique information-gathering opportunity and, as we now know, Parker managed to gain unrestricted access to the conference and everywhere else too."

"It was some set-up," said Red, without raising his head.

"Yes, it was. Fly-on-the-wall surveillance, eyes and ears everywhere, and all of it recorded. I don't need to tell you

Detective Inspector Hopkins, that matters discussed in the corridors and private meeting rooms of the Tara Cove Hotel would be priceless for a man like Sylvester Parker, as would the bedroom secrets of the high-profile delegates." said Brooks.

"You sound like you admire him," said Horse.

Brooks exploded with rage. He got to his feet and stabbed an accusatory finger at Horse.

"Watch your mouth, Hopkins. I despised Sylvester Parker. I hated everything about him. I only wish I could have been there to watch the sick bastard die. I hope they took off his face and hands before they killed him. I hope he died slowly and screaming."

Horse snorted. He turned to Red.

"How did he manage to get the bugs into the hotel? I couldn't move in there without being searched or scanned every five minutes," he said.

"The equipment Parker used was highly sophisticated," said Red, "All o' it plastic. A type of carbon fibre. The lenses, the cables, the microphones, everything, an' all of it shielded too. The security sweeps missed it all. We believe he got it in when the hotel was being up-graded, in preparation for the conference. Mr G may have provided the men or a' least the access to the building works."

"And you think that's how Mr G fit into all this?" said Horse.

"We think so," interrupted Brooks, who had sat back down. "Mr G was Parker's man on the ground. We think the drugs thing was a red herring or at least of secondary importance, to both men. Maybe the drugs were part of Mr G's payment. It's highly unlikely that Parker would have come all the way to Ireland for a shipment of drugs, no matter how large. We have little evidence that drug-dealing was part of what he did. That's not to say he didn't deal in drugs, it just wasn't his main source of income. Information was what he bought and sold. Parker was here on Skellig Éin for the conference, we are sure of that. Mr G was being played for a mug. Our guess is that Mr G found out that he was being duped and, with his Russian bodyguard, paid Parker and O'Hara an unscheduled visit, that night you turned up."

"Remember, Parker was spying on Mr G too," said Red.

"And we're sure Mr G knew he was being watched," added Brooks. "Mr G is our prime suspect in Parkers murder. Neither he nor his Russian bodyguard can be located."

Horse thought back to his time in Gerry Gallagher's basement, watching Mr G watching him. The memory sharpened, but rather than support the American's argument, it contradicted it. Mr G was in his office in Ballyhoary and therefore couldn't have been the one who left the farmhouse at high speed, the one who left the Bunsen burner under the can of lighter fuel. And if Mr G knew Parker was dead why would he still be looking at the concealed camera in his office? Why hadn't he ripped it down, along with all the others? It didn't make sense. Horse considered it for a while but decided to keep his thoughts to himself. Brooks was still talking.

"Mr G is a vicious thug and would not have taken kindly to an outsider muscling in on his territory. He had both motive and opportunity. We're convinced he's our man," said Brooks. He closed his laptop and smiled at Horse, "but Mr G and the Russian are someone else's problem. As far as I'm concerned, whoever killed Parker deserves a medal."

Brooks stood up again. He closed his laptop.

"We are finished here," he said, "We got what we came for. We fly back to Washington tonight."

"And that's it?" said Horse indignantly.

"That's it, Detective Inspector Hopkins. It wasn't my decision to extend you this courtesy. I'm only telling you all this because Paul asked me to, and because you too are returning home."

It was clear to Horse that Brooks was still smarting from his earlier comment.

"Thanks for extending me the courtesy. I feel privileged," said Horse sarcastically. He also stood up.

"In my opinion, Detective Inspector Hopkins," retorted Brooks, "you jeopardised our investigation and still have questions to answer of your own. But, as I said, we are finished here and none of that matters now, and I'm not interested in staying in this Godforsaken country a moment longer than I have to."

"What questions?" said Horse.

Brooks shrugged his shoulders.

"Well, for example, how was it that you and Paul just happened to end up at Gerry Gallagher's farm that night?"

"Fuck you, Brooks," said Horse. "You got what you came for and fuck the rest of us, is that it? Well before you climb onto your Presidential jet and head off across the Atlantic, ponder this, Agent Brooks. Sylvester Parker played you like a fucking violin from the start, played you like an Irish fiddle, and you, and your boys here, have danced to his merry tune. So, tell me something, Brooks. How are you so sure the music has stopped? What make you so sure that you're not still dancing to Parker's tunes now?"

With that, Horse walked out and slammed the door behind him.

Part Six

"Chughat an búidí mean!"
"The boogey-man is coming!"

Chapter 81.

Horse left 64B Henrietta Street and headed towards Dublin city centre at a determined pace. Paul chased after him.

"Wait up. Please," called Paul from over his shoulder. Horse stopped and turned around.

"Look Brian, calm down, will you? Brooks is an asshole. I only met him, for the first time, last week. All my dealings were with Harry. I couldn't tell you what was going on, what I was doing, you know that! I wanted to, but all this happened before you came over to Ireland, before I started working for you."

"Let's go get a pint, Paul. I need a pint and maybe a glass of fine Irish whiskey. What do you say?" said Horse, giving Paul a toothy grin.

They found a small pub at the bottom of a lane off George's Street. Outside the door, a skinny man was on one knee, fiddling with the handle of a trap door inset into the pavement. Horse reckoned it was the entrance into the keg store under the pub. They had to step over the man's legs to get to the door. He didn't look at them as they passed by.

The pub suited Horse perfectly. It was clean but tatty. Its interior was all fake leather and 1970's chrome furniture. Horse thought it was probably the career low of a less than capable interior designer, a place that would never become fashionable unless it was gutted and totally remodelled and painted a trendy grey. But Horse wanted privacy and for that the bar was perfect. He was quite certain Brooks or the other two Americans would never dream of darkening its door.

He led the way to a table away from the window.

"What'll you have, Horse?"

"Thank you, Paul, that's kind of you. I'll have a pint of Guinness and a Redbreast neat, if they serve it. Make sure it's the twelve-year-old."

"Redbreast? Right! I didn't know you liked Irish whiskey, Horse."

"I have been living in the darkness my son, but I have seen the light," he said in a mock-Texan drawl.

Horse watched Paul make his way to the bar. A big bruiser of a man stood behind counter playing with a pile of bear mats. His flat face and narrow eyes suggested a history of boxing or street fighting. He greeted Paul with a mixture of suspicion and contempt. After what seemed like an eternity, Paul returned with two beers and two whiskeys.

"He said they only serve Powers."

"Never mind. Nothing wrong with Powers. Sláinte," said Horse.

"Cheers," said Paul with a cautious smile.

After taking a large swig of his Guinness Horse licked his lips. After a couple more, he lowered the half empty pint and lifted the whiskey and took a sip.

"This is all bullshit, Paul. You know that, don't you?" he said

"I couldn't tell you, Brian. You know that?"

"Not that. I'm talking about all this Sylvester Parker crap. I don't believe it. Do you?"

"Sorry. I'm not with you, Horse?"

"Think about it. This supposedly brilliant criminal mastermind comes to Ireland to spy on a conference? Yeh? If 'e's that fackin' brilliant, why couldn't 'e have spied on the conference from wherever 'e lives? Why did 'e take the risk of comin' 'ere? So 'e could spend his days in front of a TV screen, in a shitty farmhouse in the middle of nowhere? I don't believe that for a minute. Do you?"

Horse emptied the whiskey glass.

"And another thing, Paul. Where's Gerry Gallaher?" he said.

"Probably dead and buried on the farm somewhere," said Paul, playing with his pint. He finally put it to his lips, opened wide and swallowed half the glass in one swallow.

Horse drank a large mouthful of his pint and then sucked air noisily between his teeth.

"Yeh, you're probably right. Okay, so they kill the farmer and take over 'is 'ouse. Parker and 'is manservant...eh..."

"O'Hara," said Paul.

"Yeh, O'Hara, and then Parker sits there all day starin' at a TV screen, scribblin' cryptic love letters to someone in prison in the UK. He sits there, looking all evil, being waited upon by his man servant O'Hara, a ponce in a corset? Does that sound like the actions of a master criminal to you? The only time he does anything interesting is when Mr G comes to visit. Then Sylvester Parker gets all angry an' animated, makin' real scary faces, like he's puttin' it on, just for Mr G."

Horse emptied his pint glass.

"And 'e never leaves that front room. He 'as his meals brought to 'im. Probably 'ad a piss-pot under that desk. It was like 'e was a fackin' prisoner, Paul. Super intelligent evil mastermind? I don't fackin' think so. This whole thing smells like shit."

"Where are you going with this, Horse?"

"What exactly did we see on that hard-drive we pulled from the basement, Paul? Maybe we saw what we were meant to see? Don't you think it's odd that all the monitors were in the basement, yet Parker had just one to look at? Who was doing the monitoring? I tell you who; O'Hara the manservant, or someone else. Maybe there is a third party? Maybe someone who likes setting fires, someone who likes drivin' his car at high speed around the island at night?"

Horse paused and held up his empty pint glass. His mind was racing. A third man! He caught the barman's eye, wiggled the empty glass at him and nodded.

"Same again mate," he shouted at him.

The big barman scowled at him.

"So, what are you saying, Horse?"

"I'm sayin' Brooks is full of shit. He's been so obsessed with catchin' this fucker 'e can't see the wood for the trees. I think that hard-drive we found, I think we were supposed to find it. Your friend Henry said that, even if we hadn't rescued it, it would have survived the fire. It was in a fire proof cabinet, remember? The fact the hard-drive was fire damaged, before the fire even started, has been bugging me from the beginning. It all seems very convenient. Don't you think it all seems staged, Paul?"

Paul Creagan furrowed his brow.

"I guess so. But what does it mean, Horse?"

"It means we're still dancing to someone else's tune. Someone would have found that hard-drive, eventually. An explosion of that size, so close to the international conference, that would have attracted the attention of more than just the local police force. Eventually, the stuff on the hard-drive would get back to Brooks, one way or another. And tell me Paul, what exactly did we find on the hard-drive? Just enough footage of the conference to set alarm bells going off. Then they'd find bits of interviews starring agent Theodore Brooks and the shit would really hit the fan. But that wasn't the end of it. There were scenes of angry meetings between Sylvester Parker and Mr G. No sound, but you wouldn't have to be Einstein to see the two men despised each other. And for the finale, the corpses in the bedroom. Parker and O'Hara. Someone got to them and gave them a bit of their own medicine. Maybe it was Mr G who killed them, or some Russian mob guys? Who cares? Sylvester Parker is dead. We can all go 'ome. It's a shame about all the loose ends and all the other evidence that is now a pile of soot but, so what? Case closed. Parker is dead. Everyone can go home."

"Good God," said Paul.

"Indeed. But, if I am right, where does it leave us? Nowhere, that's where. Who's the third person? Hell, we don't even know what O'Hara looked like, before 'e 'ad his face cut off."

The barman plonked the two new pints on the bar causing the creaming heads to spill down the side of the glasses, making it quite clear that he had no intention of bringing them to the table. Horse got up and went over.

"And the two whiskeys?" he enquired.

Before the barman could react, a door opened in the wall behind him and the skinny man from outside the front door joined him behind the counter. He had a kind face and he smiled at Horse."

"That's grand Eric, thanks. You can go back now and finish tidying the cellar."

The skinny man walked over to Horse and broadened his smile. His eyes sparkled.

"Now, can I get you anything else Sir?"

The boxer-faced barman left without a word.

"I was lookin' for a couple of whiskeys," said Horse

"What would you like, Sir?"

"You don't 'ave Redbreast, do you?"

"I do indeed. I'll have to warn you though; it's an expensive glass. I've only the twelve-year-old. No point in stocking any of the older ones in here. As I said, an expensive glass of whiskey, Sir."

"But worth it," said Horse.

"Every penny."

"May I ask you something? Are you the owner of this establishment?"

"I am indeed, as my father was before me, and his father before him."

"Ha, and I thought..." Horse stopped, "never mind. It's a grand place. I'll have two glasses of twelve-year-old Redbreast please, make them doubles and please have one for yourself."

"Thank you, that's very kind. I'll bring them down to your table."

"Cheers, and you'll have to take for the two pints of Guinness as well" said Horse, putting a fifty euro note on the bar.

"Will that cover it?" he asked

"I'm sure it will, Sir," said the owner of bar.

Horse returned to the table. He was smiling.

"You took your own photos at the farmhouse that night, didn't you Paul?"

"Only a few of the bedroom. I didn't have time for anywhere else"

"Do you still have them?"

"Yes. They're here on my phone."

"The wonders of modern technology eh? Can I see?" said Horse.

Paul fiddled with his smart phone, then handed it to Horse. Horse flicked through the photographs and stopped at one in particular.

"Did you show these to Brooks?"

"Eh, actually no, I didn't. There was so much footage on the hard-drive, I didn't think they were needed, and then it just slipped my mind."

"Tut, tut. Never mind, eh?" said Horse with a cheeky grin.

"Why?" said Paul.

The bar owner came to the table carrying a small tray on which sat two large whiskeys and a small jug of water.

"I took the liberty of putting them into our Waterford Crystal and I didn't bring ice. You don't want ice, do you?"

Horse looked at the Redbreasts and licked his lips.

"Ice? God no," said Horse with an air of indignation.

"Good man you are," said the bar owner.

The barman left a crisp ten euro note on the table. Horse hadn't expected any change.

"Cheers, Paul," said Horse.

"Cheers, Horse. You seem in a particularly good mood, all of a sudden, splashing out on expensive whiskey."

"Huh. Tomorrow we could all be dead," said Horse.

He went back to looking at the phone photos of the bodies in the bedroom.

"Well, well, well. Now that is very interesting."

"What is? What did I miss?" said Paul.

"Everything, it would seem, but it's not your fault, you've been spending far too much time with those Americans."

"Huh?"

Horse passed back the phone.

"What do you see, Paul?"

"Eh...O'Hara?"

"How do you know?"

"The flash three-piece suit? The unusually pointy shoes? The greasy hair? And then there's his exceptionally thin waist? Look, you can see he's wearing a corset."

"What about the ears?" said Horse.

Paul looked closely at the small screen.

"What about them? They're grey. He's definitely dead."

"Yes, he is Paul. By the colour of his ears, I'd guess he's been dead about two weeks, wouldn't you? Unless his ears were always grey, but then I imagine if they were, it's something Mr G would have mentioned when describing O'Hara."

"But the waist coat is covered in fresh blood? I saw it with my own eyes."

"Yes, it is. Now how can that be?"

Horse didn't wait for Paul to answer.

"My guess is, you are looking at the late Gerry Gallagher. The corset was put on after he was killed, along with the wig. I guess he was killed the day Parker took over his house. The blood on the waist coat belongs to the man lying beside him."

"Sylvester Parker?"

"No! Whoever that is, sitting beside Gerry Gallagher, I bet my left tit, it's not Sylvester Parker. Sylvester Parker set the fire, he left the evidence of his own death in the fire proof cabinet for the forensic boys to find, and then he drove like a bat out of hell from Gallagher's farm before it blew sky high."

"Fuck! You mean..."

"Yes. There is no third man. The man known to Mr G. as O'Hara, is the same Sylvester Parker that Brooks and the others have been trying to catch for more than a decade. Drink up, Paul. We need to get back to Skellig Éin immediately."

"Why?"

"Parker didn't go to the island to spy on the conference. Maybe he went to fake his own death or maybe to identify who was chasing after him. But I can't help thinking there is something else going on. We need to get back there and find out what it is."

"You think Parker is still there, on the island?"

"Yes I do Paul. And I also think that Father Francis and his brother, my curious friend Michael Eustace, may very well be able to cast some light on what exactly Sylvester Parker is up to."

Chapter 82.

The taxi pulled into the small car park just after six. There were still lights on in the surgery and two cars and a large white van parked in the car park. Michael recognised the larger of the two cars as Susan's hire car. He paid the fare and then hurried to the door. He felt invigorated and his mind was clear. In the madness of the caves and the terrors he'd experience when he woke from the coma, it had been thoughts of Susan that had sustained him. He'd focussed on her image, and the possibility of seeing her again was the motivation he'd needed to get better. When he heard that she planned to leave, he knew he had to act fast. He had never felt like this about any woman and he was determined to try to convince her not to go to Canada.

The door of the clinic was locked.

"Damn," he said.

He squinted through the mottled glass of the side screen. He could see the receptionist behind the desk. She was filling a box. All the cabinet drawers around her were open. She was clearing out. Michael rapped on the door with more vigour than he'd intended. The receptionist, a particularly ugly woman, looked up briefly.

"We're closed. Phone Dr Kelleher. His number is on the door," she shouted at him.

Michael knocked again, with less force this time.

"I need to speak with Dr McCarthy. It's a personal matter," he shouted through the glass.

The receptionist stopped what she was doing and rose reluctantly. Michael almost heard her "tut". She stomped over to the door and he braced himself for an earful of abuse, but as soon as the door opened her face lit up.

Michael thought it a strange reaction.

"I'm looking for Susan. Is she still here?" he said.

The receptionist put her hands behind her back, raised herself up onto the balls of her feed and gave him a large smile. The action didn't improve her appearance. Michael had to catch his breath. She reminded him of a pantomime witch. Her nose was particularly large and it looked as if it had been broken half way down its length at some point in the past. She was tall, for a woman, standing five ten or eleven, and her dark heavy clothes gave no hint of the shape of the body hidden beneath. She wore far too much make-up and Michael suspected that it had been applied in a hurry, or without the use of a mirror.

She let him stare at her, seemingly in no particular hurry to answer his question.

She wore a thick woollen knee-length skirt over matching tights and an even thicker woollen cardigan over a heavy cotton blouse. The blouse had a high floral collar which covered her neck completely. The collar made her head appear like a wigged and painted egg, perched on a floral coconut shy. She continued to smile at him. She made him uncomfortable. He dropped his eyes and noticed that she was wearing men's shoes, black brogues, polished to a mirror finish. The thought of being able to see up her skirt, in the reflection of the shoe leather, made him raise his head again. He felt inexplicably uneasy.

He tried to see the woman's colour aura but, with her hands behind her back and her face powdered and painted, there was very little exposed skin to see. What he could make out, around her eyes, was very dark.

"Come in, please," she said.

Michael hesitated. Something felt wrong. A noise from inside distracted him. Over the woman's shoulder a door with a name plate that read "Dr Susan McCarthy GP" opened and a tall muscular man with blond hair walked out. Michael thought he looked eastern European. The receptionist turned her head and gave the man a curious look, but said nothing. On seeing Michael, the big man took one step forward and, with a hand behind his back, quietly closed Susan's door.

"Do come in, please," said the woman again.

She stepped back. Despite his better judgement, Michael entered the surgery and the receptionist closed the door behind him. He thought he heard her twist the lock.

"We're officially closed, but I'm sure Dr McCarthy would be happy to see you, Michael," she said.

Michael turned and looked at the woman.

"Have we met before?" he said.

"No. I've never actually had the pleasure, but I've been waiting to meet you for ever so long," she said.

"Oh? Has Susan spoken to you about me?"

"Susan? No, she never did. Were you her secret date, Michael? How very interesting? It is such a pity I didn't know that. Oh well, never mind. Can't be expected to know everything, eh? Susan will just have to be for another day."

"What?"

"I'll explain later."

"Is Susan here?" asked Michael

"Alas no. It appears she left in a hurry, went back to the mainland with her mother."

Michael stared at the woman. She still had her hands behind her back, which caused her ample chest to rise when she spoke. He tried not to stare at it and instead concentrate on the faint colours around her eyes. There was something familiar about them. It only took him a moment to remember that they were the same ones he'd seen on the key pad on the farm gate post, on his way back from the university the previous week. They had caught his attention then, because they reminded him of something else that he still couldn't put his finger on, a distant, elusive memory.

"Are you sure we've never met?" said Michael.

"Absolutely sure," said the ugly woman.

"If Susan isn't here, then why did you say she was? Why did you invite me in?"

"Actually, I didn't say Susan was here, I just said she'd be happy to see you. But I'm playing with words. You're right, I lured you in, on false pretences. I know it was wrong but, well, I've waited so long to meet you, Michael. It's certainly not as I planned, but I pride myself on my ability to adapt. Maybe it was fate that brought you to me now."

"What are you talking about?" said Michael.

The blond man moved away from Susan's door and approached Michael.

"Quickly now Stefan, but be careful. Michael Eustace has a vicious streak."

"What..?" said Michael.

He was grabbed from behind and had his arms were pinned to his side, at the same moment the woman in front of him reached into her pocket and retrieved a small loaded syringe which she jabbed into his neck.

The poison took hold almost immediately.

The last thing Michael saw, before his legs went from under him, was the clear colour aura that pulsed around the ugly woman's manly hands. For an instant Michael was somewhere else, staring into the dark cold eyes of a beautiful woman. She was sitting opposite him, across a low coffee table, in a television studio in England. She was almost smiling.

Just before Michael passed out, a word popped into his head. The word was *obsidian*.

*

Father Francis got to the monastery just as Brother Benjamin was about to set off on his motor bike. The Prior called out to him so Benji cut the engine. It was past seven thirty and the evening sun was dropping behind the ancient roofs, casting a shadow across the courtyard. High above them, a gusty wind jostled large clumps of clouds, hastening the coming night, it's intermittent whistle, warning of imminent rain.

"Ah Benji, it's good that I caught you," said the Prior once he'd paid the taxi driver who had brought him in from town. Brother Benjamin looked surprised and bewildered.

"We weren't expecting you back this evening, Father Prior. We've all had dinner. Margaret and the rest of the kitchen staff have gone for the night."

"A change of plan, Benji. Michael was discharged and he was in a hurry to get back to the island."

Benji looked around. Knowing what Brother Benjamin was thinking the Prior said,

"Michael went to visit a friend. He may be back later tonight or tomorrow."

"Oh, right," said the young priest.

"Where are you off to Benji?"

"Into town for choir practice, in preparation for Sunday, but I'll stay, if you need me, Father Prior?"

"Not at all. Anyway, that's why I asked you to hang on. I'd like you to drop in to Mrs Primrose Brennan and tell her Michael is back. She's probably in her art studio. I've tried ringing the house but got no answer. The studio doesn't have a phone and her mobile is not responding either. She doesn't know he's been discharged and she may be planning to visit the hospital in the morning. I want to catch her before she does. You could call in and let her know, if you don't mind a slight detour."

"Oh right. Of course."

"Do you know where her studio is Benji?"

"Eh...yes. Yes, I do! I brought Michael there on his first day on the island. I'll go straight away. Don't worry, I'll find her and let her know that Michael is back home, eh, I mean, back on the island. But what about your dinner, Father Prior?"

"Oh, don't worry about that. I had a burger at the airport. Michael insisted on us having a burger. It was very nice," he lied.

He hadn't been able to eat more than a bite before returning it to the polystyrene carton. It was vile. It tasted like a slab of salted fat sandwiched between thin baps of stale bread. He had been looking forward to a proper meal. He thought about heading straight to the kitchen and the fridge. With luck, there'd be cold meats and some tomatoes.

Benji climbed onto the bike, but stopped before putting on his helmet.

"Oh gosh, I almost forgot. The builders came back, just an hour ago. They said they had to work in the basements overnight."

It was only then that the Prior noticed the white van backed up against the delivery doors to the kitchen.

"On a Friday night? That's odd," he said.

"Yes. One of them asked to speak with you and he was quite cross with us because you were not here to meet him. Then he told us that they had to spray the basement with something that was poisonous. It smells awful. He insisted that none of us go down there, for at least twenty-four hours. Father Bernard is in a foul mood. He is worried about his cheeses. The place is a mess and everywhere smells. We had dinner in the third-floor common room. We could still smell it up there, but it's not so bad. No one wants to come down. It smells unnatural."

"Okay, I'll see if I can find out what's going on. You go on now, Benji. I'll be fine."

"If you are sure Father Prior. I'm glad to be out in the air. How those two builders can stand it, I don't know. They don't even look like builders. The smaller man was cross when he couldn't speak to you. He must be the one in charge. He doesn't look like a builder."

"Well, I'll speak to him. Father Bernard and the others are upstairs, are they?"

"Yes. They don't want to come down."

"Okay. Ride carefully Benji."

"I will Father."

"God bless, Brother Benjamin."

"God bless, Father Prior."

Chapter 83.

Brother Benjamin had been right. Father Francis found the smell in the main hall obnoxious and unnatural. He covered his nose as he hurried down to the kitchen. As he went along he noticed that the door to the cellar stairs had been left open, so he reached out with his free hand and flicked it closed. The smell lessened slightly but still lingered in his nostrils and burnt the back of his throat. It reminded him of his school days and of the strange concoctions he and his classmates had made in the school science class when the teacher wasn't watching. The memory made him smile. The smell made him feel ill.

As soon as he reached the kitchen Father Francis went straight to the deliveries doors and opened them wide. He was met with a blast of fresh cold air and the back doors of the tall white van. After filling his lungs with the fresh night air, he stepped forward and squinted in the back window of the van. To his surprise inside was neat, tidy, and empty, save for a few lengths of rope and a carefully folded sheet of heavy tarpaulin. It didn't look much like a builder's van, he thought. His stomach rumbled reminding him he needed to eat. As he turned to go back inside, he caught a glimpse of movement behind him, reflected in the window of the van. He turned quickly and saw a muscular blond man moving silently across the kitchen toward him. The man hesitated and then stopped. He was very tall, the Prior guessed maybe six foot seven, and he looked Eastern European.

"Fadher Prior?" he said in broken English.

"Yes. I'm the Prior. Can I help you?"

"You must come. There haz been an accident. Your brudher."

"My brother? Oh, you mean one of the priests. What has happened?"

"In the cellar, Fadher. Your brudher. Bad accident. You need you to come now."

"In the cellar?"

"You come now. You'll see," said the blond.

"Okay. I will follow you."

The foreigner frowned.

"Well? Lead on," said the Prior. He walked back into the kitchen but left the doors to the yard open wide. The blond man hesitated but when he saw that the Prior was following him he left the kitchen and made his way to the door leading to the cellar stairs.

"You go down first Fadher. It's very dark and very narrow. You go first. I follow you Fadher."

"No. I will follow you. You lead the way. What is that smell?"

"Very bad poison, for killing the rats, Fadher."

"I see. Go on, now. I will be right behind you."

Once again, the big man hesitated. He clenched and unclenched his fists but finally relented and went through the door and down the first flight. The prior followed holding the handrail with one hand, his nose with the other.

On the half-landing the Prior noticed that the stone floor and the first few steps of the lower flight were shiny and wet. Before following the blond, he bent down, touched the liquid and then brought his finger up to his nose. He quickly drew back his head. The mysterious liquid was the cause of the obnoxious smell that permeated the ground floor of the monastery. The Prior wondered if the builders had carelessly spilt some of the rat poison on the way down. He felt like saying something, but the other man was already half way down the last flight and out of earshot. Father Francis wiped his fingers vigorously on the side of his habit and continued down. He noticed that the rest of the steps were dry. By the time he reached the corridor at the bottom, the rotten smell was all but a memory.

"What exactly is going on?" Father Francis called forward.

The man in front ignored him. Father Francis had to hurry to catch up. By the time he reached the gantry inside the door of the upper cellar, the blond was at the far end of the room, at the well leading down the lower cellar door.

"Big accident. Your brudher. You come see," he shouted back up at the Prior.

Father Francis climbed down the galley ladder and walked cautiously toward the foreigner.

"He's in dare, Fadher," said the man pointing down into the recessed well and the door that led to the lower basement. Father Francis stopped at the top of the short flight of steps. He looked up into the foreigner's eyes. The man stared back. The Prior smiled. The man dropped his eyes.

"What is your name?" said the Prior.

"St...tefan, Fadher."

"Are you a Christian, Stefan?"

"What? I...em, my modher was a Roman Catholic."

"Was?"

"She is...she died, many years ago."

"So, you are a Catholic too then, Stefan?"

The big man twitched uncomfortably.

"You know it's a sin to lie, and worse to lie to a Priest, don't you Stefan?"

"Big accident. Your brudher. You see. Big trouble," said Stefan.

Father Francis walked past Stefan and went down the steps. He hesitated before he opened the door. When he did, he found that the lower basement was in total darkness. He tried to remember what Father Bernard did to turn on the lights. He leaned forward.

Before he touched the switch, Stefan jumped into the well behind him and pushed him violently through the door. Father Francis fell forward into the darkness and down five feet onto the stone floor below. He landed with a loud thump and lay there until the lights came on.

With the lights came the sound of a generator and a man's unusual voice. The Prior exhaled quietly.

"I didn't mean for you to kill him Stefan, you fool. He'd better not be dead!"

In the moments before he closed his eyes, Father Francis took in as much as he could of the scene in front of him. What he saw frightened and disturbed him but instinct told him to do nothing and play at being unconscious, so he lay as still as he could and slowed his breathing. With his eyes closed he replayed and analysed what he'd seen in the room.

Four people sat at the back of the cellar in a semi-circle facing each other, like members of a support group or actor's preparing their lines for an up-coming play. In front of them stood a strange looking man holding a meat cleaver. He was wearing a long white oilskin apron over a bare chest, white plastic trousers and matching Wellington boots. His hands were covered in surgical gloves and he had a white face-mask pulled down under his chin. His other hand was on the on/off switch of the generator. He looked angry but excited. His eyes were dark and cold, the eyes of a killer. On a stainless steel two-tiered trolley beside him, there was a selection of knives, saws, and other implements.

The seated people were tied to their chairs. Although he could only see two of them clearly, because the other two were covered by white sheets, Father Francis was sure there was three men and one woman in the seated group. The woman had been stripped to her underwear. The person sitting between the two shrouded figures was fully clothed. It was his brother, Michael.

Father Francis recognised the woman as one of the women that Detective Inspector Brian Hopkins and Marie Joyce had rescued from the caves. He remembered that her name was Megan. He'd seen her briefly in the hotel, at the time of the interviews.

Michael and the woman had their mouths covered with wide black packing tape. Michael's face was covered in blood, which seemed to be trickling from his nose.

Next to Megan was an empty chair.

To one side of the group stood a sophisticated-looking video camera, perched on top of sturdy metal frame on rubber wheels. On the other side, on a long table next to the generator, was a bank of five computer monitors, which were switched off. An arc lamp on a tri-pod flooded the scene in blinding white light.

Father Francis focussed most of his attention on the man in white. By the way the man had spoken to the blond foreigner, the Prior was sure that he was the one calling the shots. The Prior didn't think there was anyone else. He remembered what Brother Benjamin had said about there being only two men.

Just before Father Francis closed his eyes he looked at Michael and Michael looked at him. It was a fleeting glance but enough to reassure each of them that the other was okay.

"Get down here, you big oaf, and get him up. Strip him and tie him to the chair so that I can get started. He needs to be fully conscious for this," snapped the man in white. He stepped away from the generator and moved the meat cleaver from hand to hand in an impatient manner. With the sound of the blond giant scampering down the steel ladder behind him, all the muscles in the Prior's body tensed, then relaxed and then tensed again.

Chapter 84.

ifteen minutes before the Prior made his dramatic entrance into the lower basement, Michael woke up with a fuzzy head and a jumble of disassociated images. He had been brought back to consciousness by another jab of a needle to his neck. The release from the induced sleep was brutal. The harsh light from the arc lamp hurt his eyes and the hum from the generator seemed much louder than it probably was. The sound of it made his body tremble. In the blur of half-opened eyes, he saw a strangely familiar man standing in front of him, dressed in white. Michael could just make out a syringe in the man's right hand and could see that the man was smiling.

Michael's first thought he was that he was back in the hospital. He blinked and shook his head. After a moment, the room came into sharp focus and Michael realised that the man in white was not a doctor, and he was not back in the hospital. When he tried to stand up, he found he couldn't move because he was tied, wrists and ankles, by means of stout leather straps, to the arms and front legs of his chair. The straps bit into his wrists and ankles.

He was in a cellar. There was a very faint smell of garlic. There were four other chairs arranged in a small semi-circle around him. Three of them were occupied. Two of the sitters were covered in white sheets. Michael was sure they were both men. The other person was a woman. Michael recognised her as the young woman from the ferry; the woman he'd gone back to save from the rising waters in the chamber with the tiered beach. She had been stripped to her underwear. She looked asleep. Her head was forward and her chin was resting on her chest bone.

Next to her was an empty chair and behind her stood the blond muscular man Michael had seen standing outside Dr Susan McCarthy's surgery door, the one who'd attacked him. The blond also held a syringe and, as Michael watched, he lifted the young woman's head and plunged the needle into her neck.

"Where am I? What's going on?" said Michael to the man in white.

"Shush. Relax. Don't trouble yourself Michael," said the man in a mock soothing voice. His smile broadened. He was nearly six-foot-tall and of slight build but his exposed arms looked muscular. He had a sharp handsome, rather boyish face framed in a thick crop of wavy black hair. He had an even tan on arms and face, suggesting a life lived in sunny climes. When he smiled crow's-feet gathered beneath his dark eyes, and Michael guessed the man was much older than he looked. Michael reckoned he was in his forties, maybe even closer to fifty. His hands would reveal the truth but they were hidden under white surgical gloves. He had slightly crooked teeth.

"Relax," the man in white said again.

Michael didn't relax.

"Who are you? What the hell is going on here?"

"Questions, questions, questions! Don't fret, Michael, all will be revealed, in due course. For now, don't go anywhere and make yourself comfortable."

He waved a theatrical hand in the air. He was wearing an almost full-length oiled butcher Mack and matching white Wellington boots. His hands were gloved but his arms were bare to the shoulder. Michael noticed a small snake tattoo on one wrist.

Behind the man in white there was a stainless-steel trolley with two shelves, containing a selection of knives, bone saws, meat cleavers and other items, Michael thought, likely to be found in an abattoir or a coroners operating theatre.

The man in white dropped the syringe he was holding onto the top shelf of the trolley and began fingering some of the other instruments. He took up a cleaver, held it to the light and inspected the blade.

Michael turned his attention to the blond man standing over the woman. As soon as he'd withdrawn the needle from her neck she woke up, just as dramatically as Michael had. When she saw where she was, she began to scream, which prompted the shrouded figure sitting on Michael right to groan. The person on his other side, who was also covered in a white sheet didn't move or make a sound. When Michael turned toward him he saw that he was dead.

"Scream all you like Megan. No one can hear you," shouted the man in the white coat.

"No one can 'ear you screeem," repeated the blond giant who then leaned forward and ran his tongue up the side of her face.

"Sheez not too bad looking," he said.

Megan tried to pull away but couldn't. She stared wide-eyed across the room at Michael. He wanted reassure her in some way, but couldn't think how.

Michael turned back to the man in white. He was sure they had met before, even though the man's face was not familiar, so he concentrated on what he could see of the man's colour aura. It was dark and was strongest about his hands.

The answer came to him slowly.

He'd seen the man's unusual colours on the keypad on a gatepost of a farmhouse on the road back from the university the week before, but that wasn't the first time he'd seen them, or something like them. He racked his brain. The answer danced annoyingly at the back of his sub-conscious, just beyond his reach. There was something frightening and dangerous about the man's colours. They were cold and cruel, like the darkness of the caves under Skellig Éin. A half memory whispered in his ear but made no sense.

"Gag the bitch, Stefan, she is annoying me. There will be plenty of time to scream later."

The blond man went to the trolley and took a roll of black packing tape from the bottom shelf. He tore off a long strip and went back to Megan. When he knelt in front of her she spat in his face and then shook her head from side to side to prevent him putting the tape over her mouth. He slapped her hard across the face, then viciously applied the tape. When she was gagged, he put one of his big hands between her legs and squeezed her crotch.

She winced wide-eyed in pain.

"I weel hurt you more later. Mr Parker said I can have you. I will enjoy cutting you up, you little beetch."

While this was going on, the man in white flicked a switch and one of the monitors sprang into life. He swivelled it around so that Michael could see the screen. The image was grainy and in black and white, but clear enough for Michael to see that it was live feed, showing a birds-eye view of the monastery entrance hall. The hall was empty.

"Our last guest will be here soon, and then we can begin. We can watch and wait together, Michael."

"What the hell is going on?"

"I'm sorry but I make it a rule never to kiss and tell."

"What are you talking about?"

The man in white smiled. There was no warmth in it. His eyes were like bubbles of dark brown mud. He didn't look human.

"Who, the fuck, are you?" said Michael.

"Tut tut tut, language, Michael. Your saintly brother would be shocked to hear you speak like that."

"Why won't you tell me?"

"Oh alright! I suppose I could, while the cameras are off and we're here on our own, just you and me. I suppose I have time to kill, before it's time to kill. Ha ha!"

The man in white looked again at the monitor showing the monastery entrance hall. The hallway was still empty.

"My name is Sylvester Parker, or at least that is what people call me. I have many names and many guises." He twisted his nose and raised his head.

"We're officially closed, but I'm sure Dr McCarthy would be happy to see you, Michael," he said in the voice of Susan's ugly receptionist.

"And I was such a comfort to your friend Primrose, when she thought that you were dead Michael." he said.

Michael baulked.

"Oh, don't worry. Primrose is fine, well for the moment, at least. I would have liked to have brought her, and her daughter too, to our little gathering tonight, but it was all so rushed. I had no time to extend the invitations. That's your fault, for turning up as you did, out of the blue. But I will have my moments with them soon enough. Another day, another Sylvester Parker production."

He turned again and looked down at the trolley.

"Now, where was I? Oh, yes. Who I am and why we are here? Well I've told you who I am or at least my name. But my name is not the question, is it? The question is what does Sylvester Parker want with Michael Eustace?" He paused for effect. "The answer is simple. Vengeance!"

Michael looked across at Megan.

"What have we ever done to you?" he said.

"We? Not *we*, Michael. You! Only you! This little tart Megan and, of course, our last guest, your saintly brother the Prior, they are your collateral damage. My vengeance is aimed solely at you, Michael Eustace. Their suffering will be part of that vengeance. As will be the torture of your friends, Horse and Primrose and Hanna and anyone else I can think of, who will suffer the same fate."

He pointed to the video camera.

"Oh, and I almost forgot. It will all be recorded, for posterity and the pleasure of my paying guests."

Sylvester Parker tapped the camera.

"I was thinking of calling tonight's show *Where is God when you need her?* What d'ya think, Michael? A good title? Maybe Father Prior could give me a couple of suggestions when he gets here?"

Michael tried to move his wrists but it was impossible. Parker continued to talk.

"Some people say vengeance is a weakness of character. I do not think that, Michael. I find vengeance liberating and my methods of meting it out, therapeutic. Simply put, and please excuse the vulgarity, torturing people gives me an almighty stiff one. It's a sexual experience, bordering on the spiritual. Another talking point for your brother, I think. Did you know, Michael, that in the Celtic pagan ritual of virgin sacrifice, practiced to ensure a good harvest and whatnot, the moment between life and death was considered magical, therefore the slower the death the happier were the Gods. Drawing out the moment of death for as long as possible would therefore render the sacrifice even more potent and ensure prosperity for the community. Did you know that Michael. It's nice to know that I am continuing in the footsteps of our Celtic forefather. Huh! The stuff you learn from the internet?"

"You're mad and you have the wrong man," said Michael.

"Really? I don't think so! Let me tell you something. When you entered my world, *Michael X*; when you disrupted my business affairs; when you tore my family apart; you set in train all of what will happen tonight. This is all your doing Michael."

"I don't know you. You have the wrong man."

"Have I, really? I don't think so. I know all about you and your English detective friend. I wish he was here too but, like Primrose and her lovely daughter Hanna, Detective Inspector Horse Hopkins will have his own night of pleasure, sometime in the not too-distant future. I have something very special planned for Lord Hopkins and his family, a real royal celebration, you might say."

"What in God's name are you talking about?" said Michael.

"God? God who? This is not about God. It's about you. You entered my world, you interfered with my business and you took something of mine, something most precious. And when you did that, you sealed your fate and the futures of all those you love."

Michael concentrated on the colour aura around Parker's hands. The half-memory teased him, flitting in and out of focus. Parker studied him and Michael held his stare.

"You don't know who I am, how could you? But I know everything about you," said Parker.

As Michael stared into Parker's eyes the answer came to him and he knew.

"You're Jane Wesley's father. Jane Wesley is your daughter, isn't she?" said Michael.

Sylvester Parker looked genuinely stunned. He almost toppled back on his heels and his jaw dropped.

"How the...how did you know that?" he stammered.

Michael didn't answer. It had been a leap of faith, an educated guess. Sylvester Parker became fidgety. Stefan looked confused.

"How did you know that? How could you know that?" snapped Parker. Michael thought he saw fear in the madman's face.

"Who else knows? You will tell me," he shouted. "You will tell me. You will talk, I promise you that. And, if you do not tell me what I want to know, where she is, it will be so much worse for the tart and your precious brother."

"Your daughter, Jane Wesley was making those CD's for you, wasn't she?" Michael said, ignoring Parker's threats. He had found leverage and had no intention of letting it go.

"It was a *family* business," said Parker.

"Well, if you want me to tell you where your daughter is, I am happy to do so. Jane Wesley is rotting in a maximum-security prison in the south of England, and as far as I know, she will be there for the rest of her life."

"My daughter! I know where my daughter is. Of course I do. Do I not write to her every week? I even send her presents. She'll receive a copy of this night's work. It's not my darling Jane I'm looking for."

"Who then?" said Michael, trying his best to remain calm.

"Allie, of course. That's what you will tell me, Michael Eustace, what you have done with my granddaughter. Where is my little sweetheart, Allison?"

"Your granddaughter? The little girl your psychopathic daughter and her psychotic husband tortured and abused for their own sexual pleasure, and probably the sexual pleasure of her equally psychopathic grandfather? Even if I did know, which I don't, I would never tell you."

Parkers face turned red with rage.

"How dare you. We would never hurt Allison. She was never harmed? What sort of people do you think we are? Allie is our own flesh and blood, our little star. Her mother pines for her every night and I know that, wherever Allison is, she pines for her mother and her grandfather too."

"You're fucking mad. Why would she look for you or her sick twisted mother?" said Michael.

"Why? Why?" Parker shouted at Michael, with wide-eyed delirium.

He reached for a saw from the trolley.

"You know nothing Michael Eustace. We are a family. Allie was a key part of our operation. How do you think we managed to abduct those little girls in broad daylight? Allie found the girls, groomed them and brought them to us. She is such a good little girl. She even stayed with them in the cage, pretended to be one of them, told them to co-operate. It was a game to her. She enjoyed it as much as we did. She stalked and studied like a good little huntress. Allison is her mother's daughter and the apple of her grandfather's eye."

Michael caught his breath. He knew he could not hide the shock on his face. What Parker had just revealed was worse than anything he could have imagined.

"Oh God," he whispered.

The words escaped before he could stop them.

Parker smiled again and returned the saw to the trolley.

"God? God who? There is no God."

Chapter 85.

Sylvester Parker kept looking at the monitor showing the empty hallway upstairs. Michael wondered what Parker would do if the Prior didn't return.

"I wonder," Parker said, still looking at the monitor, "will you plead for your life, Michael? I don't expect that you will. Will you plead for the life of Megan, the tart, or for the life of your brother? Will you beg me to kill them? I'm not sure that you will. You see, I know all about you, Michael Eustace. I have studied you. I know you and I know that you and I are not so unalike."

"I am nothing like you. You are a psychopath. You corrupted your daughter and your granddaughter. You are a monster," spat Michael.

"A monster? A curious word, coming from you. Isn't that what they called you and your band of merry men, when you were in Africa? The white monsters? Of course, that was before you became a soft-spoken caring television personality. Back then you were a vicious cold blooded murderer. People don't change. I've seen your military file. I've read about your escapades in the jungle. I know you, Michael Eustace, and I know that a murderer is *always* a murderer. It becomes part of the fabric of who you are."

"You don't know me at all," said Michael.

"Don't I? What about that classmate you beat unconscious when you were fourteen? Had that teacher not intervened you would have killed the boy, wouldn't you? That would have been your first kill. And then there is your army record. Hardly exemplary, is it? Constant reports of insubordination, disobedience and fighting your colleagues. One commanding officer described you as a *loose and dangerous cannon*. Mad Mick."

Parker widened his eyes.

"Tell me, Michael, was it a case of *like father like son*? I understand that your father liked on beating people too. Was he violent with you, Michael? Did he abuse you when you were a little boy? Did he beat your mother or that weakling brother of yours? Did he take out his anger on your little sister? Maybe he abused her in a different way? Is that it? I understand it was quite a common pastime in Ireland, years ago. A country of saints, scholars and paedophiles. I suspect, it still is today. Some of my most fervent clients are compatriots of yours. Was that why your father had to die? You were with him in the car when he had his accident, weren't you, Michael? Did you cause him to veer out in front of the other car, or did you make sure he was dead before the ambulance arrived? Maybe you covered his mouth and nose with your small hands, squeezed the life out of him. Was that how he died? There are things I will never know about you, Michael Eustace, but I can guess, because you and I are not so unalike. I know my kin and kind."

Parker gave Michael an ugly smile.

"Is that how you made the connection? Is that how you knew who I was? When you look at me, do you see a reflection of yourself?" he said.

"You don't know anything about me. You are a mad sick monster," said Michael.

"Am I really a monster, Michael? How can I be, if I have people I love, people who love me? My daughter Jane and my granddaughter Allison. I would kill for them. I *have* killed for them, and tonight I will *kill* for them again. And you? Tell me, Michael, would you kill for the people you love? I understand that you attacked the boy in school because he was bullying your brother. Would you have killed him, for your brother? If I unstrapped you now, would you kill me? Of course you would. And, if you are honest, it would give you pleasure. Admit it, Michael! You would like to take one of these knives and kill me, just as you killed all those people in Africa. You and I are so alike. The only difference is, I admit who I am. I embrace who I am. You? You hide who you are. You are a coward, Michael Eustace. A coward."

Parker moved over to Megan. He stared into her eyes until she looked away. He dropped his head onto one shoulder frowned dramatically before letting his mouth curl into a cruel crooked smile.

"What eeze dee matter. You no like me, Megan?"

Megan glared at him. The silly voice reminded Michael of a cartoon character but it caused Megan to shudder with fear and loathing. Parker smiled.

He turned back to Michael.

"This," he said with distain, "…I don't understand. You risked your life to save *this*? I must say, that is a surprise, Michael. I mean, look at the little slut," he turned up his nose dramatically; "was she, really, worth the trouble? Maybe your saintly brother has got to you? Is that it? I understand he was the one who rescued you from the savages in Africa. Did he change you? Did the good Father Francis make you see the error of your ways? Have you found God, Michael? Was saving this little drugged-up tramp, an act of contrition?"

Parker took hold of Megan's chin and roughly lifted her head so she had no option but to look at him. Along with fear, Michael saw defiance on Megan's face.

"I guess you are wondering why you are here, my dear," he said. His voice was soft but cruel. "Well, for two reasons. Firstly, as revenge for what your ignorant boyfriend, Rick Kavanagh did. Like Michael, Rick also took something that didn't belong to him, something that belonged to me. Alas, it appears Rick died in the caves. Had he not, he would have been here on this chair instead of you. You are his stand-in. You will take his punishment."

Parker released the grip on her chin and let his hand drop onto her left breast. He gently caressed the front of her bra.

"I will enjoy hurting you, once Stefan has had his fun. I have promised Stefan that he can do the skinning, but I will sprinkle the salt."

Megan started to cry.

Parker took his hand off her breast.

"But there is a second reason you are here, Megan. It's because of him," he said, pointing at Michael. "Your suffering will be part of my revenge. He saved you from the caves only to lead you here to me. Ironic really. Out of the frying pan, into the fire. I must say, I think it has a certain cruel beauty about the way it has panned out. He's to blame for all your pain."

Megan looked blankly at Parker through wet eyes.

"Leave her alone. I am the one you want. Let her go," said Michael.

"I don't think so. What I can do is let you see what I am going to do to Megan, and Father Francis and then you."

Parker walked over and lifted the white sheet covering the dead man, just high enough so that only Michael could see what was underneath. He was sorry he looked.

The person beneath the sheet had been flayed, just like the body hanging from the tree in the woods. Not only had large areas of skin been stripped away but chunks of the dead man's flesh were gone too. There were large gaping holes in his chest and under his arms, and his lower intestine had escaped from a deep gash across his belly and now sat, like a coiled white snake, in a pile on his lap. One of the man's hands had been chopped off and both of his feet were missing. The worst of it was the man's eyes. They were open wide, in a terrifying lifeless stare. The eyelids had been cut away.

Michael had to work hard not to throw up.

When Parker peeked under the sheet he cursed.

"That cheap Dublin bastard! He's dead! That cowardly little..."

Parker dropped the sheet and moved over to the other man and lifted the sheet before Michael had the chance to turn away.

"Never mind, Pete is still with us, aren't you Pete?"

Pete's head was turned toward Michael. With his free hand, Parker twisted Michael's head so he had to look at Pete.

"Look. Here eze one I prepared earlier. Theeze one iz steel warm, steel cooking away. You like how de gringo uses his knives, Michael? Pete didn't like, did you, Pete?"

Parker spoke in the same pigeon-Latino accent he'd used to taunt and terrify Megan. Michael had no idea who either of the men were, but the one called Pete, although as badly mutilated as the dead man, was still alive. Michael thought that Pete must be drugged because, although he looked to be in terrible pain and his face was wet with sweat and tears, he didn't move, nor did he make more than a weak gurgling noise. He looked pathetic. Bubbles of sticky saliva formed around the edge of his gaping toothy mouth that no longer had any lips. Pete gave Michael a pitiful pleading stare and Michael imagined that he was whispering and was sure that if he leaned over and put his ear close to Pete's mouth he could hear what he was trying to say.

Parker dropped the sheet back in place.

"Now you know what is in store for you and your brother and the slut," he said with venom in his voice.

Parker returned his attention to the black and white monitor.

"What is taking your brother so long? I need to be doing something, but I don't want to start until he gets here. What shall I do, Michael? What shall I do?"

Parker went back to the trolley and ran his hands over the implements again.

"I know. An aperitif. No one will object. A taster, to get thing going."

Stefan smiled.

Michael felt panic rise from his stomach.

"If I tell you where Allison is, will you let us go?" said Michael, trying to sound nonchalant.

Parker ignored him and continued to rummage through the implements on the trolley. When he turned around and faced Michael again he was holding a hammer.

"You broke my daughter's nose. She will want me to return the favour."

Without another word, Parker walked over and swung the hammer in a wide descending arc. The heavy head clipped the side of Michael's nose, which broke with a horrible crack, and the blow sent Michael reeling. Megan jolted backward in her seat and tried to cry out from behind the black packing tape.

Blood splattered onto the floor. Parker stepped back and swung again, this time using a backhand motion, like a tennis player returning a quick serve, hitting the nose from the other side and almost knocking Michael and his chair and into the dead man beside him. A large gash opened on Michael's right cheek and blood gushed from his nose. He moaned and gurgled. The pain was excruciating. Tears filled his eyes.

Parker wiped the head of the hammer on the sheet covering the dead man, before speaking to the dead man underneath.

"Maybe I should have borrowed your ring, Maurice? Taken his eye, while I was at it? You'd have approved of that Mr G, wouldn't you?"

Stefan spoke up.

"Look boss, de priest haz com back." He pointed at the grainy image on the black and white screen. Michael blinked. There was blood and tears in his eyes. The pain of his broken nose was blinding but he tried to ignore it and focus on the monitor in front of him.

"At last. Good. Can you see, Michael? Your brother has arrived. Soon we can begin."

Through a mist of tears and pain Michael watched as his brother made his way from the front door, down the hall and passed the door to the stairs leading down to the cellar. Michael watched as his brother paused, closed the door, and then headed toward the kitchen.

"Go get him, Stefan. Try to get him to come down on his own. Tell him there's been an accident. We'll wait for you in the dark. We'll all be very, very quiet. Won't we children?"

With a nod of his head Stefan climbed the short ladder and left the lower cellar to get Michael's brother.

As soon as he was out of sight Sylvester Parker wrapped a large strip of the packing tape over Michael's mouth. Michael winced when Parker's fingers touched the tip of his broken nose.

"Sorry about that Michael, but I can't have you screaming out and alerting your brother, now can I? Once the star guest is with us, I promise you I will remove everyone's gags, we'll wake up Pete and then we can all have a good long scream."

Chapter 86.

Father Francis lay, face down and as still as a stone in front of the man in the white apron. He felt angry and he the rage wash over him. He had no idea what was going on but knew that whatever it was, it would not be resolved by *talking it through.* As his mind raced, his senses heightened. He slowed his breathing until the beating of his heart was hardly perceptible. He re-ran in his mind what he'd seen, in the fleeting moments before closing his eyes, ordering and analysing the images. They crystallised before him.

The man in white was no more than eight feet away. He was medium height, five ten or eleven, and was of slim build. He had a hard, boyish face. In his left hand, he held a small butcher's meat cleaver. His other hand was empty. A few feet behind him was a stainless-steel trolley with two shelves, both loaded with other potential weapons. A table, containing several computer monitors, was positioned to one side and opposite it was a video camera on top of a heavy mobile tri-pod. Father Bernard's wheels of cheese had been dumped unceremoniously into a pile in one corner.

Given the way he'd spoken to the Eastern European, Father Francis was sure that the man in white was the one in charge, the one orchestrating whatever was going on.

Behind him, the Prior could hear Stefan's making his way down the ladder and he knew it wouldn't be long before the big man was standing over him. For the moment, he decided, Stefan was the greatest threat. Even though the man in white had a weapon, the Prior knew he would have to deal with Stefan first.

Stefan was muscular, looked very fit, and possibly trained in hand to hand combat. Back in the kitchen, the Prior had noticed something cold and distant in Stefan's eyes, and instantly knew what it meant. Stefan was a soldier and had the look of someone prepared to take a life. Like the man in white, the Prior was sure that Stefan was a killer. His size alone made him a formidable opponent. He was bigger than the Prior, both taller and heavier. He was mostly muscle and bone. It was likely he was a gym junkie and probably took steroids to add to his muscle mass. Father Francis doubted there was an ounce of fat on him.

Muscle and bone, and cold killer eyes.

Stefan would have to be taken out of the equation, quickly and comprehensively.

Before Stefan reached him, Father Francis turned his thoughts to the four people who sat in a semi-circle facing each other. The chairs were all carvers, taken from the dining room upstairs. The two people he recognised, were gagged, and tied to the arms and front legs of the chairs. The other two were covered in white sheets, like seated ghosts. Michael sat between them. A young woman sat across from him. There was a fifth, unoccupied chair next to her. Michael's face was covered in blood. For the briefest of moments, just before the Prior closed his eyes, he and Michael managed to look at each other. It was just a glance, but enough for the twins to communicate to each other. The look exchanged told Father Francis that Michael was okay, or, at least for the moment. The young woman, who was in her underwear seemed unhurt, but she was in a highly distressed state. The Prior knew her. Her name was Megan. She had been rescued from the caves by Detective Inspector Hopkins and Marie Joyce.

The two figures hidden under the sheets didn't move. The Prior considered the possibility that they were accomplices of the man in white, but thought this highly unlikely. He had a strong sense that one of them was dead. He resolved to accept that all four seated individuals were hostages and that the fifth, unoccupied chair, was reserved for him.

The room was brightly lit by a powerful arc lamp that sat on a frame to one side of the group, powered by a small mobile generator. Behind the seated figures was the camera on its tri-pod and the table containing the computer monitors.

The area of floor between the Prior and the man in white was clear. Room enough to fight, thought the Prior. He wouldn't need much room, but his movements would be hampered by his full-length habit. Getting out of that would take precious time, time for Stefan to defend himself and the man with the meat cleaver to attack. The Prior's only advantage would be the element of surprise. If he was lucky, that would be enough.

"He better not be dead, Stefan," said the man in white angrily.

"Heeze not. Problee unconscious, only, Mr Parker. I take off his gown."

"Habit."

"What?"

"It's called a habit, not a gown," said Parker.

Stefan came around and hunkered down in front of the Prior, blocking Parker's view. He nudged the Prior roughly on the shoulder. Father Francis didn't react. Stefan felt for a pulse in the priest's neck. It took him a moment or two but he finally declared,

"It'z okay, Mr Parker. He'z just unconscious. Must 'av banged 'eeze 'ead on de floor."

"Get him undressed and into the chair. Hurry now, Stefan!"

Stefan grabbed the Prior under the arms and turned his dead weight over into a sitting position, then tugged the habit lose and pulled it up over the Prior's head. Father Francis remained limp until his bare arms were released from the long woollen sleeves. Under his habit the Prior wore a white cotton vest and green chequered boxer shorts. The vest covered his back, shoulders, and chest, but not his upper arms. Because Stefan was crouched over him his large bulk blocked Parker's view of the priest and so Parker didn't see the tattoos that covered the Prior's now exposed skin. Had he seen the army insignia and the strange and disturbing African symbols that covered Father Francis's upper arms, Parker would have known that there was something wrong and, had he had the time to consider what the tattoos meant, he might have come to the conclusion that when Michael said "you have the wrong man," he had been telling the truth.

*

Once free of the habit, Father Francis moved with lightning speed. Before Stefan knew what was happening, the Prior was on his feet and had landed his first punch into Stefan's chest. Stefan toppled backwards and dropped the habit. The first punch surprised him, the second, to his lower abdomen, winded him and forced his upper body back toward the priest. The third punch, a right upper cut, was delivered with clinical precision and tremendous force. It smashed Stefan's lower jaw sending two of his bottom teeth through the hard pallet of his upper mouth. After a few more punches Stefan stopped trying to defend himself. The punches continued, hard and fast, a controlled but frenzied attack. Stefan finally lost consciousness and collapsed backwards, clattering into the nearest covered figure, the one sitting on Michael's right hand side, knocking the man and chair over. The sheet partially fell away. When Megan, who had somehow finally managed to work her mouth free of the gag, saw what was left of Pete Mercer, she began to scream hysterically.

Sylvester Parker scuttled backwards. His eyes flitted from side to side. In desperation, he flung the meat cleaver at Father Francis. It's sharp heavy blade struck the Prior's right shoulder, then clattered to the floor, taking a lump of the his flesh and a good splattering blood with it. The Prior winched and stumbled backwards. Parker saw his opportunity and grabbed a large knife from the trolley. He rushed forward, but the Prior caught himself before he fell over, quickly straightened up and then braced himself for Parker's assault. The psychopath hesitated and then stopped altogether. Father Francis clenched his fists and focussed on the man in front of him. His muscles tensed and the pain in his wounded shoulder melted away. Parker sensed the danger and instead of attacking the priest he turned sideways and grabbed Megan's hair.

"I'll cut her fuckin' head off, do you hear me? I'll cut her head off. I swear. If you take one step forward."

He pressed the knife to Megan's throat. Megan screamed and squirmed and the action caused the knife to break the skin.

"Stop moving, you stupid cunt," hissed Parker

He plunged the knife into her upper thigh until the tip hit bone, withdrew it quickly and returned it to her trembling throat.

"One more step and I swear I cut this fucking cunt's head off."

*

Michael heard the guttural sound before anyone else did. It was just audible above the hum of the generator and Megan's screams. It sounded like the growl of an angry tomcat or a

606

wounded fox. It echoed from somewhere to his left, from behind two tall shelving units standing at odd angles to each other against the back wall.

"Meaa."

Michael tried to block out Megan wailing and the generator hum and focus on new sound.

"Meeaa."

It was getting louder.

"Meeaa."

"Meeaa."

Megan suddenly stopped screaming and pricked up her ears. She turned her head slightly. Parker remained as he was, never taking his eyes off the Prior. Father Francis gave no indication that he'd heard anything, all of his focus was on Parker and the knife at Megan's throat.

"Meeaa. Meeaa. Meeaa. Meeaa."

Michael saw recognition on Megan's face. She whispered something. Parker heard what she said and looked shocked. He turned his head and looked over his shoulder. For a split second the point of the blade moved away from Megan's neck.

Father Francis pounced.

No sooner had the Prior crashed into Parker and sent him flying across the floor, when Michael saw the creature dart out from behind the shelves and slam down on the generator switch.

Darkness swallowed the room.

"Maaee," the creature bellowed in triumph.

Michael heard the two men hit the floor and the sound of Parker's knife clattering away. Following that there was sound of shuffling and a lot of heavy breathing. As his eyes adjusted in the pitch blackness Michael could see his brother's colour aura wrestling with Parkers. Parker was trying to pull away from the Prior. He kicked out and Michael saw his brother's colours fall backward and then, Parker scampering away on all fours, toward the back of the cellar.

The room fell silent. In the darkness even Megan seemed to be holding her breath.

"Kill him, Father. Kill the bastard," she whispered.

The Prior moved toward Michael and his hand touched his face. Gently he removed Michael's gag.

"Where is he, FX?" he whispered.

Michael turned his head.

Parker was standing with his back to the rear shelves. He had his arms out in front of him and was groping about in the dark.

"In front of you, six good paces. He's trying to locate the weapons on the trolley," said Michael, as quietly as he could.

Megan mumbled something.

"Trick?"

"There's someone else here," whispered Michael.

Parker turned his head at the sound of Michael's voice and his colour aura move forward, his outstretched arms still searching. Then there was a clatter of metal on metal. Parker had found the trolley and the weapons.

"Shit," said Michael.

Father Francis moved away and silently narrowed the gap between himself and Sylvester Parker.

"There," whispered Michael.

Parker heard Michael and began to swing his arms about in front of him.

"Be careful, he has weapons and he's swinging them ...." said Michael, but stopped mid-sentence.

"Meeaa."

The creature he'd seen run to the generator switch was standing right behind him. The point of something sharp was pressed into Michael's cheek and dragged down his face. He felt a warm trickle of blood on his chin and a feather-light breath kiss the back of his neck. It smelt rank and feral.

"Meeaa," the creature growled menacingly.

Cold clammy hands took hold of Michael's head and squeezed. Michael closed his eyes as the vice grip tightened.

"Is that you, Rick?" said Megan from across the room.

The pressure on Michael's head eased slightly.

"Rick?" she said again, louder this time, "Not him, Rick. The bastard in white."

Suddenly there was light.

It came from a mobile phone. The beam was powerful but very narrow. It could only illuminate a section of the room at any one time. The light surprised and frightened the creature and it let go of Michael's head. It backed away.

The phone-light belonged to Sylvester Parker.

He held it high in his left hand and he waved it about as he searched for Father Francis. In his right hand, he held a large chopping knife.

"Meeaa," screamed the creature and it ran behind a shelf unit, knocking over wheels of cheese as it darted for the shadows. Parker directed the phone light toward the sound.

When Michael saw his brother he diverted his eyes and looked at Megan."

"Look at me Megan," he shouted across the room, "Look at me. Father Francis has gotten away. He's gone for help. It will be over soon." Parker swung the light from Michael to Megan and then up to the door to the upper cellar, just as Michael had hoped. It gave his brother the opportunity he needed. Because Parker was pointing the phone upwards he didn't see that the Prior was hunkered down in the darkness behind him.

Michael held his breath.

It happened with lightning speed.

Father Francis sprang to his feet, grabbed Parker, turned him around and head-butted him hard between the eyes. Parker dropped to the floor like a sack of potatoes and, as he went down, the Prior delivered a powerful knee to his face and the phone and chopping knife went flying in different directions. The phone landed face down with the tiny torch pointing at the roof of the cellar.

Father Francis moved forward to finish Parker off, but was suddenly jostled sideways by Stefan, who had regained consciousness. They crashed into the camera, which toppled off its stand and clattered onto the floor. The Russian clambered on top of the Prior, wrapped his hands around his neck and begin to throttle him.

Megan screamed.

"Nooo. Someone stop him!" she shouted.

Meanwhile Parker stumbled to his feet. He looked groggy but managed to retrieve the phone and directed the light onto Stefan and Father Francis.

"Kill him Stefan and then ...we will ...kill the rest of them."

Parker coughed up blood.

Michael could only watch in horror as his brother tried in vain to push the blond giant off him.

After a while the Prior stopped pushing at Stefan's chest and his arms fell limply across the floor. Michael's heart sank. Megan screamed and screamed. Sylvester Parker began to laugh.

"Well done, well done, Stefan."

Stefan raised his head. He was panting and there was madness in his eyes.

"Dee priest, 'e caught me by surprise, Mr Parker, but I got 'im by surprise too."

Michael looked at his brother's limp body.

They were lost.

"I want his head, Stefan. You can practice your cutting skills on him. Cut off his head," said Parker.

Stefan, who was still straddling the Prior, smiled and turned to speak, but the words never left his mouth. With an almost detached nonchalance, Father Francis raised an outstretched hand, grabbed the heavy camera that had fallen to the floor and, in one powerful manoeuvre, drove it into the face of his attacker. Stefan had no time to react. Glass from the camera's shattered lens tore into his right eye, slicing his eyeball in two. More of the glass tore lumps of flesh from his jaw. The Russian howled in pain and confusion. When the camera crashed into his face for a second time, Stefan fell over. Megan cheered. Parker screamed, ran to the trolley, and grabbed another meat cleaver, then lunged at the Prior like a rabid dog. Father Francis tried to get up but couldn't because he was trapped under the unconscious body of the Russian. Before Parker could deliver, what would have been, a fatal blow, the creature raced forward, grabbed his arm, and yanked him backwards. Parker screamed and dropped the weapon, which clattered onto the floor, inches from Father Francis's face, but he held onto the phone.

Michael tried to reconcile what he was seeing.

It didn't make sense.

His first thought was that the intruder was not a man, but a very large monkey or a medium sized emaciated ape. He moved like a monkey, springing forward on a pair of crooked legs and he danced around Parker, like an enormous excited puppy, still clinging to his arm with his claw-like hands. Michael thought that, whatever it was, it was trying to avoid the light.

Parker began to hyperventilate.

"Maaee," his assailant screamed.

Parker raised the phone light and shone it into the creatures deformed face

"Eeeeee" bellowed the creature. It was a blood-curdling scream.

"What the fuck?" Parker stammered.

Parker stumbled backwards and dropped the phone. Once again, it landed with the torch pointing up and Michael got a fleeting glimpse of the deformed face that had frightened Parker.

It was a man, but not a man. It's head was hairless and milky white. One of his eyes was white too, like a stone. There was a chunk of his cheek missing as if he'd been bitten by a dog. He had no eyebrows or eyelashes. The skin that covered his face was lumpy and looked as if it had melted and cooled, melted and cooled, over and over again, so that the vertical ridges and troughs looked like lines of wax running down the side of a candle. His nose was thin and elongated and both his ears were gone. His lips were unnaturally thin and his teeth were black, some of which were pointed, as if they'd been sharpened on a flint stone.

"What...are...you?" stammered Parker.

"Maeee," screamed the man-creature and then leaned in and took a bite out of the side of Parker's face. Parker screamed in agony, tried to pull away but then just suddenly stopped.

The torchlight went out and darkness returned.

Michael refocused on Parker's colours. They moved toward the back of the cellar and then disappeared.

For a while no one spoke.

Michael looked at his brother, who was not moving, but was alive. Then Michael heard excited voices coming from the upper cellar. He heard Brian Horse Hopkins and then the voice of a woman. The door at the top of the ladder opened and a hand stretched in and flicked the light on.

Nothing happened.

"Have you a torch, Brother Benjamin?" Michael heard Horse say.

"We are saved," Michael said.

It was then that Megan started screaming again.

Chapter 87.

The torchlight brought shadows and hysterical voices. Once the generator switch was located the bright white light from the arc lamp brought clarity and shock. It took a little while before a degree calm descended on the lower cellar.

After climbing down and switching back on the arc light Horse took charge. Paul Creagan and Marie Joyce followed him down the ladder but Brother Benjamin stayed at the door.

Horse cuffed Stefan's hands behind his back, but left the Russian face down on the floor. The blond Russian was still out cold but was breathing. The damage to his face didn't look life-threatening. Then he told Paul to go back upstairs to call the emergency services and to get whatever Garda back-up he could muster. When Michael mentioned Sylvester Parker name, Horse told Paul that he should let the American's know too.

"And hurry back, will you Paul?" he said.

Once Paul was gone, Horse released Michael and then Megan. Whilst he was doing this Marie went to the upper basement and returned with some blankets. She went straight to Megan and covered her up. Megan started to cry. She looked pathetic and sad. Blood from the stab wound to her upper thigh ran down her leg and pooled around her bare feet. Luckily for Megan, Parker hadn't hit an artery but the wound was still deep and it would need stitches. Marie hugged Megan and stroked her hair.

"It's okay Megan, We're here now. You're safe," she said.

No one went near the two shrouded figures. Michael told Horse that both men were dead.

"Are you all right, Father?" said Horse to the Prior, who had said nothing since they'd come down to the cellar. Before the lights came back on Father Francis had managed to free himself from under the Stefan's dead weight, put his habit back on and plonk himself on the chair that Parker had set up for him.

"I'll be fine," said Father Francis, "I just needed to sit down." He was nursing his wounded shoulder. Horse could see blood seeping through his fingers.

"You're wounded, Father," he said.

"I'll be fine. It looks worse than it is," he said, giving Horse a weak smile.

"Where did Parker go Michael, did you see?" said Horse.

"There was someone else down here," said Michael.

"Who? One of Parker's accomplices?" he said.

"No. Whoever he was, he attacked Parker. They left together, but I think the other man took Parker against his will," said Michael.

Horse looked exasperated.

Michael sensed his frustration so he explained what he'd seen, gave a detailed account of what had taken place in the cellar, and then told him what Parker had said about this being revenge for Michael's involvement in the apprehension of Jane Wesley, and to force Michael to reveal where Allison Wesley had been taken. He also told Horse what Parker had said about his granddaughter's involvement in the child abductions.

"Fuck," said Horse.

He rubbed his face and then shook his head.

"Naw. I don't believe that."

"Maybe you don't *want* to believe, Brian. Parker seemed sincere," said Michael.

"Parker is a fucking madman, Michael. A manipulating madman."

"You're right," conceded Michael.

"What 'appened to this brute?" said Horse, prodding Stefan in the ribs with the toe of his boot.

"I caught him a lucky punch and then hit him with the camera," said the Prior without raising his head.

"Lucky punch? Right. Okay, but I still don't understand. Where did Parker and this other bloke go?" said Horse.

"They went behind those shelves," said Michael, pointing at the back wall.

"And you don't think he was an accomplice?" said Horse.

"No, I don't think so. Parker seemed genuinely surprised. He looked scared. What I do know is that if that man hadn't attacked Parker, we would all be dead," said Michael.

"So they've gone into the caves?" said Horse.

Michael's expression changed to one of puzzlement.

"What?"

Horse looked at him and smiled.

"There's an entrance to the caves behind those shelves. That's where your brother found you, Michael," he said.

Michael looked at the shelves.

"Whether 'e was an accomplice or not, I need to get after 'em," said Horse. He picked up the larger of the two torches and tested it. The light was blinding.

"When Paul gets back tell him where I've gone and tell him to follow me," he said to Michael.

"You are not going after them alone, are you?" said Marie.

"I don't have a choice. If I don't, they'll get away."

"I'll go with you. You'll need me," said Michael.

He picked up the other torch.

"No. You're hurt, mate. Have you seen your face?" said Horse quickly.

"I'm okay. It probably looks worse than it is," he said adding, "Anyway you'll need me. It's not save for you to go alone. There's two of them."

Horse hesitated.

"You really sure you want to go back in there?" he said.

"No, but you won't track them on your own. You know that. You'll probably get lost and then I'll have to go in anyway, just to find *you*," said Michael.

"Ha. Okay, but I promise you, Michael, the first mention of monsters, or any of that shit, and I'm sending you straight back, is that clear?"

"That's fair. There'll be no mention of monsters."

"Okay then. C'mon, we better get going."

Horse turned to Marie. She was still comforting Megan.

"Tell Paul to stay here. He's not to follow us, just in case this big lug wakes up and tries to cause more trouble."

Marie looked at the Prior.

"We'll be fine, won't we Father?" she said.

The Prior smiled weakly.

"Yes Marie, we'll be fine."

Marie looked at Horse.

"Be careful, Englishman," she said.

Horse nodded, then winked at her.

"Don't you worry. We'll be back before you know it," he said.

"Good," she said, "I'll be waiting."

Chapter 88.

The route taken by Parker and the other man was easy for Michael to follow. Parker left a trail of his dark colour marks mixed with splatters of blood on the dusty floor, like an oil leak from the sump of a car. There were fewer marks left by the other man, but what Michael could see looked familiar. It didn't bother him that he couldn't remember where he'd seen them before. He was sure it would come to him later.

They followed the tubular tunnel and arrived on a shelf that looked down into the church-like cavern.

Michael inhaled sharply. He remembered looking down onto the hidden tiered beach where they'd found Hughie and the others. Horse shone his torch at the arched ribbed ceiling and then down onto the floor. Michael followed the light like a compliant dog.

"Looks like a cathedral, doesn't it?" said Horse, "which way did they go, Michael?"

"Yes, yes it does look like church, doesn't it? They went down the centre, all the way to the end, past that slab of black stone."

"The altar, you mean? Looks like an altar, doesn't it? And those are the pews," said Horse with a wave of his hand. "Come on, let's go, before they get away."

They climbed down and hurried toward the altar.

"How did you know where we were, Brian? How did you know we were in trouble? Why did you come back? I thought you were heading back to London today?" said Michael.

"I came back on a hunch. Paul came along for the ride. We met Brother Benji in Ballyhoary. He'd gone to M & M's looking for your friend Primrose. When he told us about the builders and then described the big blond bloke, I suspected it must be Mr G and his henchman, so we rushed over. We came in Marie's car."

"On a hunch?" said Michael.

"Well, I've been thinking about the whole thing a lot lately. I was sure something was wrong and was convinced this Sylvester Parker fellow wasn't dead, as the American's thought. From the moment I got on the ferry, I had a feeling that things were not as they seemed. Even meeting you. It was strange. Then I kept thinking of you stopping at the gates of Gerry Gallagher's farm, that day on the way back from the university. It seemed significant. Why did you stop there, Michael?"

"Oh that? I stopped to look at the odd-looking house, I'd caught a glimpse of it on the way out, but then I saw a very unusual colour marks on the gate post, which I thought I recognised. I remember thinking I'd seen them before. Now I know it was the colour marks of Jane Wesley's father. It is very like her aura, but not exactly the same. That's why it took me so long to make the connection."

"It was his colour aura on the key pad? Sylvester Parker's finger prints?" said Horse.

"Yes. I know that now. Their colour auras share certain unique and unusual similarities. Both auras are mainly black, but it's not like black-black, its bright black, sorry blacks. Like overlapping blacks. Almost three dimensional."

"Sorry mate, you've lost me. Isn't black overlapping black just…well…black?"

"Not in my world," said Michael.

"I see. Well it's not surprising, is it? Black on black on black. The colour of evil," said Horse.

"I don't know, maybe," said Michael.

They reached the onyx altar. Horse stopped and raised his hand.

"Which way now?" he whispered.

"Back there, through the … cloister? You're right Brian, this place really looks like a church. It's weird, isn't it?"

"Yes, I know. Supposedly it's St. Áedán's bedroom or something. C'mon, I think I know where they're going."

"Oh?" said Michael.

"I've been here before and so have you, mate. Like I said, this is where we found you."

"Here?" said Michael.

618

"Well, no, actually, your brother found you and Hanna, floating face down in the black lake in the next chamber. This way, I'll show you," said Horse.

They entered the cloister.

When Horse reached the doorway leading into the next chamber, he stopped and gasped. Michael stopped beside him.

"Where' this lake you were telling me about Brian?"

"Bloody 'ell. This place was flooded the last time I was 'ere. I swear t' God," said Horse.

"Well, it's bone dry now," said Michael.

"I wonder where all the water went?" said Horse.

"Dunno, but look," said Michael, shining his torch into the distance, "there they are!"

He pointed the light toward the base of the mountainous structure at the centre of the massive cavern. Parker and the other man were already at least three hundred yards away.

"Is that a volcano?" said Michael.

"I 'ope not," said Horse.

"It looks like a volcano," said Michael running his torchlight up the steep sloping sides, all the way to its flat top. Horse focussed his torchlight on the two men ahead. They had begun to climb the mountain. It appeared that one of the men was carrying the other.

"They're moving fast, Michael. Come on we need to get going or they'll get away," said Horse.

Michael and Horse scrambled down a sloping bank of rocks to the floor of the chamber and then made their way to the base of the volcano as quickly as they could run. The flat dry plain was peppered with sink holes, which they skirted with care.

By the time they reached the base of the mountain, Parker and the other man had reached the top. When Horse directed his torchlight up at them, the ugly man hissed loudly at him, then turned and bellowed into Sylvester Parker face. It was a terrifying sound and it echoed around the massive chamber. Parker didn't react and, to Michael's surprise, didn't even move.

Horse took a hand gun from a holster concealed under his jacket.

"Stay where you are or I'll shoot," he shouted up at them.

Both men ignored him. As Michael and Horse watched the ugly man bent down and lifted Parker above his head as if he was as light as cardboard. Once again, Parker did nothing. Even from the bottom of the mountain Michael could see Sylvester Parker's face. He looked terrified yet made no attempt to struggle or get away. His body, which was in a strange lurching pose, looked as stiff as a plank of wood.

"Stay where you are or I'll shoot," yelled Horse again.

Once again, then men ignored him. With Parker's stiff form held above his head the ugly man jumped out of sight.

"Damn," said Horse. He re-holstered his pistol and clambered up the side of the mountain on all fours. Michael followed close on his heels.

They reached the top together, both panting noisily, and stood side by side in the spot where the other two men had just been. In front of them was a crater more than twenty feet in diameter, a black circular hole that fell into the hollowed-out mountain. The rim they were on was flat and wide enough to stand on, back from the edge of the precipice.

"Are you sure it's not a volcano, Brian? It sure looks like one," said Michael.

Horse said nothing. They both edged forward and looked down the dark shaft. It seemed to be perfectly cylindrical, much like the tunnel that had led them from the cellar to the cathedral chamber. It was like looking down into an enormous man-made well. Even with their powerful torches neither Michael nor Horse could see the bottom of it. Michael guessed that it must be what it felt like to look down one of those great Victorian brick chimneys that peppered the industrial countryside of northern England. Michael leaned further forward.

There was a faint smell of sulphur rising from the hole, with a hint of rotten eggs.

"Careful Michael. You don't want to fall in there," said Horse.

"Where did they go?" said Michael.

"You saw them. They jumped in there."

"But that would be suicide," said Michael.

Horse leaned out and scanned the sides of the shaft as far down as his torchlight could reach, but there were no ledges or openings in the shaft wall.

"How deep do you think it is?" said Horse.

"There's only one way to find out," said Michael.

He stepped closer to the edge, stretched out his arm as far as he could and let his torch drop into the well. They both watched it fall in silence, twisting and tumbling, getting smaller and smaller until it was nothing more than a pin-prick of blinking white in the blackness below. Then it was gone.

They waited for a splash or any noise, but none came.

"I owe Father Bernard a torch," said Michael.

"I'll tell him you dropped it by accident," said Horse.

"Thanks," said Michael.

A noise rose from the bottom of the shaft. It sounded like a moan.

"What the 'ell's that?" said Horse.

"I don't know Brian, but," said Michael and he backed away from the edge, "I think we need to go."

The noise rose quickly and dramatically.

"I think you might be right, mate," said Horse.

"I told you it was a volcano," shouted Michael as they scampered down the sloping sides of the mountain. By the time they reached the bottom, the moaning had got so loud it was almost deafening. As they started across the floor of the chamber they felt the ground shake.

"Not another fackin' earthquake?" shouted Horse.

"Run," said Michael.

When they were no more than thirty yards from the base of the mountain, water began to bubble out of the sink holes behind them. They picked up their pace, Horse lighting the way with the big torch. He moved faster than Michael and when he got too far ahead he stopped, turned and shone the torch back to light Michael's way. Over Michael's shoulder the water had become a torrent and was rushing after them.

"Fuck, shit, run, Michael, c'mon or we'll drown."

"Where's it coming from?" panted Michael as soon as he caught up?"

"Who, the fack, cares? Where's that fackin' doorway?"

"There," shouted Michael pointing ahead. It was twenty yards ahead but they would still have to climb up the sloping bank. Water smacked into them like an incoming tide and drenched their feet and ankles. It was icy cold. More visions from the hidden ocean invaded Michael's thoughts, but he dislodged them before they could take root. He tried not to think that there might be monsters in the water racing after them.

They reached the bottom of the slope together and kept running, using both hands and feet to climb up the bank. A six-foot wave followed them through the doorway and threw them forward in different directions. Horse ended up on his back against one of the cloister pillars, whilst Michael became fully submerged and only by grabbing hold of the edge of a boulder stopped himself being dragged back out into the second chamber, along with the receding tide. After a few smaller waves rushed in and out the water in the second chamber settled down, but the moaning continued, getting louder and louder.

Abruptly, the moaning stopped and the silence that followed, was both eerie and ominous.

Michael and Horse got to their feet and cautiously they made their way back to the doorway. As they watched, the top of the volcano exploded. A column of water, the diameter of the shaft, shot upwards with such a force that it slammed into the cavern roof thirty feet above. The whole chamber trembled with the force of it and as they watched, thousands of gallons of water cascaded down in every direction.

"Holy shit," said Horse, the torch trembling in his hand.

They looked at the roof of the chamber. Large cracks appeared across its surface, as the mighty head of water continued to pound away, the cracks growing longer and wider with every passing moment.

"Sweet God Almighty," said Horse.

The water level in the chamber bubbled and steamed and began to rise again at an alarming rate. Michael and Horse didn't move, both mesmerised by the spectacle in front of them. Eventually, the power of the water-shoot slowed and then petered out completely. Within minutes the water in the lake settling back down and silence returned. Michael could hear his heart pounding and thought that if he concentrated hard enough, he might even be able to hear Horse's heart too.

"Wow, that was something, wasn't it mate?" whispered Horse.

"Point the torch at the roof above the volcano, Brian," said Michael.

Horse did what he was told.

"Oh shit," he said.

There were cracks everywhere. The rock ceiling above the mountain was now divided into five or six large irregular segments, interspersed with smaller ones, like pieces of a giant inverted jig-saw puzzle. As they watched stone dust fell from the cracks between some of the segments and then, without warning, large lumps of the roof collapsed, first onto the mountain, and then, in a chain reaction and with thunderous reports, into newly formed the lake.

Michael and Horse turned and ran. Horse had the torch to guide them. Over their shoulders an explosion, followed by a powerful blast of air, knocked them off their feet. Rather than get back up, they crawled behind the nearest rock pew and kept their heads down.

"Sounds like the whole place in there is coming down," Horse shouted above the thunderous noise.

"Well I'm not going back to see," said Michael.

Horse trained the torch upwards. Without speaking he traced the length of the cathedral roof.

"It looks okay," said Horse.

"So did the one next door a couple of minutes ago," said Michael.

"True enough mate. Let's get the hell out of here."

They stood up. Before they moved off Horse turned the torch back toward the black altar. It was covered in a coating of fine dust. More dust billowed like smoke from the arches of the cloister.

"I don't suppose there is any point in looking for Parker now?" said Michael.

"No. I think it quite save to say Sylvester Parker is dead," said Horse.

"In that case, what are we waiting for? Let's get the hell out of here," shouted Michael.

Together they headed out of the cathedral chamber and didn't look back until they reached the safety of the cellar.

Part Seven

"Giorraíonn beart bother."
"A friend will shorten the road."

Chapter 89.

Michael sat in his brother's study and waited for the others to arrive. The room was warm and comforting, thanks to a quietly murmuring turf fire and the homely smell of floor polish. The sweet waxy aroma brought back memories of childhood and a simpler time, now gone forever.

It was now two weeks since that terrible night in the cellar, but the memory of it was still raw. In an unconscious gesture, Michael raised a finger and gently touched the bridge of his nose, which had been straightened and was healing at quite a remarkable rate. The bandages and nose splint had been removed after only five days. Susan had done the minor operation to straighten his nose. It had been her final act of doctoring, before leaving for her new job in Canada. He put his hand back on his lap and looked around, staring at nothing in particular.

Thinking of Susan helped to take his mind off Sylvester Parker, but thoughts of her always ended with the memory of them saying goodbye at Dublin Airport, which invariably made him sad. He didn't want her to go to Canada and was sure that if he'd asked her to stay, she would have. But he never asked, or even suggested it. Instead he told her that, for the moment, his place was on Skellig Éin with his brother who, he insisted, would need him more than ever now.

It was a lie.

Father Francis was fine. A wounded shoulder was not the worst thing his brother had endured in his life. The truth was Michael let Susan go because he was frightened for her safety. Being around him was dangerous. Sylvester Parker had targeted him and, more importantly, threatened the people closest to him, the people he loved. Until Michael was sure that Parker's reign of terror was over and that there were no accomplices, ready to fulfil the psychopath's wishes, Michael had resolved to keep a distance between himself and Susan. Canada was reassuringly far away.

Father Francis had called the meeting for eleven O' clock and had invited Michael, Horse Hopkins and Marie Joyce. He told them that he had something important to say and that it would be best to do it face to face and all together. Michael was both excited and anxious.

Three chairs had been arranged in front of the Prior's desk. Because he was early, Michael took the one furthest from the door, so that he could watch the others arrive. He heard them before he saw them.

Marie entered first, followed close behind by his brother and then Horse.

"Ah, so you got here before us, good, then we are all here," said the Prior when he saw Michael.

Michael stood and embraced Marie. Horse gave him a wide smile and shook his hand vigorously.

"Hey mate. How's the 'ooter?" said Horse.

"It's getting better, thanks for asking."

"So I see. That, my friend, is fanks to the lovely Dr Susan. Magic 'ands. Can't believe you let 'er get away, mate."

Marie reproached Horse with a scornful stare, then turned and smiled sadly at Michael. He thought she was going to hug him again. The idea aroused strange feelings in him so he lowered his eyes to the floor.

Marie had allowed her hair to grow since the last time Michael had seen her and she now wore it tied up into a small bun. She was wearing a silk blouse over a pleated skirt and, to Michael's great surprise, high-heel shoes. Her face seemed slightly fuller and her cheeks held a rosy hue that made her eyes sparkle. She looked older and yet younger, sexier, and more beautiful than he'd ever seen her. She also looked happy. For the briefest of moments Michael envied his English friend. The word around town was that Marie Joyce had found herself a boyfriend, and an Englishman to boot. Michael guessed that he was not the only man to look at Horse with a jealous heart.

"Who says I let her get away? Maybe she'd had enough of me. Anyway, Canada is not that far away. I was thinking I might take a holiday there, later in the year," he said.

"Good for you," said Marie. There was genuine warmth in her smile.

"You go get her mate, that's my advice," said Horse.

"Thanks, Aunty Brian," said Michael.

Marie chuckled.

There was a light tap on the door. Without been asked Brother Benjamin entered carrying a tray containing a large pot of tea and four cups along with a plate of fruit scones. He laid the tray on the Prior's desk.

"Thank you, Brother," said Father Francis.

Marie smiled at the young priest and he smiled back, and then at Michael before quietly leaving the room.

Father Francis sat down behind his desk.

He looked tired.

"Thank you both for coming," he said, "I know this is all very *cloak and dagger*, but once I've said what I have to say, I think you'll understand my reason for not explaining over the phone. I need to clear the air and you both deserve an explanation."

Horse and Marie looked at each other. Marie shrugged her shoulders.

"Maybe you could be mother Michael, and serve the tea?" said Father Francis, "I can recommend the scones. They are my favourite, pear and almond, home-made and from a wonderful café in Ballyhoary."

"I think I know the place. Run by a couple of crazy local women," said Horse.

Marie thumped him on the knee. They all laughed.

When everyone had their tea and had settled back in their chairs the Prior began.

"The last time we spoke in this room Brian, following your interview with the American FBI agent Theodore Brooks, I told you that the Michael you know, the man you see here beside Marie right now, was not the person in those files, was not the mercenary soldier photographed in Africa. What I didn't tell you then, what I should have told you was, that that soldier was me."

"What?" said Horse.

"You see Brian, I am Michael Eustace," said Father Francis.

"I'm sorry, Father, I don't understand. How can you be Michael?" said Horse. Michael said nothing. Marie turned her piercing gaze on him.

"Maybe this will help explain," said the Prior.

Father Francis placed the palm of his right hand flat on his desk and raised the sleeve of his woollen habit, all the way to the shoulder, exposing an upper arm covered in tattoos. Marie gasped. The lurid ink-work ran upwards from just below his elbow. The thick tail of a large rattle snake suggested the tattoos continued across the Prior's still covered chest and back. Mythical beasts and naked women vied for space with the snake's tail, each overlapping and entwining the others. Every square inch of skin was marked. High on the shoulder there was what looked like an army insignia inside an African tribal symbol.

"Most of my body is covered in tattoos. My brother says I'm more ink than skin."

He dropped his sleeve and then his eyes.

"I often dream of having them removed," he said, "but even if I could, I wouldn't. They are a permanent reminder of the life I left behind, when I became a priest."

The Prior seemed to ponder his last sentence then declared,

"There is one tattoo that I am proud of, one that I would never have removed."

He lifted the other sleeve, this time to a point below the elbow. He twisted his arm. Two inches above the wrist on the white skin of the back of his arm was a small tattoo showing the Sacred Heart, the symbol of Jesus Christ. It was beautiful and arresting. The crown of thorns that pierced the blue red heart was very realistic, as were the drops of blood that trickled from it. The heart tattoo seemed to pulsate. Beneath the it was a single word, in Gothic script: Francis.

"It represents my Lord and Saviour, Jesus Christ and my brother, Francis."

He looked at Michael.

Horse still looked puzzled.

"If you read that file Brian, the one the American showed you, you'd know that, from a young age, Michael Eustace was a trouble-maker and a fighter, with a violent and uncontrollable temper. He was expelled from two schools and was constantly in trouble. He brought shame on his family and heartache to his long-suffering mother," said Father Francis.

Michael shook his head and began to protest but the Prior raised his hand.

"Let me tell them," he said.

Michael acquiesced and Father Francis continued,

"Somewhere in that file it probably stated that the only thing Michael Eustace had in common with his identical twin brother Francis, was their physical appearance. Their personalities could not have been more different. Francis was a kind, sensitive and caring boy. Michael was none of those. He was selfish and full of himself, with an angry and violent temper."

He paused and when he continued, he did so in the first person.

"At the age of seventeen I, Michael Eustace, ran away from home, found my way to Dublin and got on a ferry to Liverpool. I lived rough and I mixed with unsavoury and dangerous characters. I had several run-ins with the police. I tried to get work but ended up stealing and begging just to survive. One morning I saw an army recruitment poster in the window of the local job-centre and, on the spur of the moment, I signed up. The military life suited me, and despite my natural dislike of authority and reluctance to be told what to do, I became the perfect soldier. I was a good fighter, a top marksman and fearless to the point of reckless. Looking back now, I think at the time I had a death wish.

"After serving for eight years in places like Iraq, Syria and Afghanistan, I was sent, as part of a six-man Special Forces team, to the jungles of Western Africa. Our mission was covert, with orders to infiltrate, disable and destroy any fledgling fundamentalist terror groups and their supporters. We set up a semi-permanent camp close to the border. We carried out lightening attacks, mostly at night, on unsuspecting villages and we left a trail of destruction behind us. We were feared and hated in equal measure. Mad mercenaries who brought death and terror wherever we went."

Father Francis composed himself before he continued.

"We became infamous and a bounty was offered for our capture, dead or alive. It was only a matter of time before we were betrayed and our hidden camp discovered. We were captured by a local warlord, a thug whose main business was human trafficking and drug smuggling. He knew us well and we knew him. We'd helped him earlier in the year in a dispute over territory with another drug smuggler. When the authorities refused to pay the reward, the warlord showed his anger in a terrible way. We were tortured and, one by one, killed. Ironically, for a man with a death wish, I was the only one to survive. He killed my compatriots slowly and desecrated their bodies. Severed heads were sent in parcels to the homes of the government officials who had reneged on the deal and dismembered torsos were stuffed with explosives and left on the road outside foreign embassies, known as infidel IED's.

"I don't know why the warlord kept me alive. He saw me as the leader, although I was not. Maybe it was because I had an Irish passport or maybe he kept me in the vain hope that the authorities would pay up. They didn't and there was no rescue party. I lived without hope of freedom and became a broken man."

The Prior stopped again. The room became unnaturally quiet. Michael watched Horse and Marie. Neither spoke.

"I think he would have killed me in the end, just like the others" said Father Francis at last, had my brother Francis Xavier not come to find me," said the Prior at last.

"Francis *Xavier*? Is that where Michael *X* came from? Isn't that what you were known as, when you were a television celebrity?" said Marie.

"Yes. It wasn't my idea, but the people at the BBC thought it was my name," said Michael.

"I see," said Horse, although not sounding convinced, "so Michael X, I mean Francis X came looking for you in the jungle?"

"Yes, he did, Brian, with the help of a Roman Catholic priest who ran a mission in the area, Brother Hugh O Mahoney, a native of County Kildare. My brother used his own unusual gift to find the warlord's hidden camp. With money from Ireland and more from the meagre coffers of Brother Hugh's mission, an inflated ransom was paid and I was released. Coming for me was an act of incredible bravery by both Francis and Brother Hugh. They risked their lives for me and they saved me. I was taken to a local hospital but when it became too dangerous to stay there, I was spirited away to the monastery. For nearly eight months Brother

Hugh and the other monks nursed me back to health. Francis stayed by my bedside all through my recovery."

Michael smiled at the Prior.

"Something happened during that eight months. You might say that I had a *Road to Damascus* moment. Whatever it was it changed me and the man who rose from the infirmary bed was not the same man who had been taken from the jungle. Like St Paul, my eyes had been opened. *Love* saved me. I renounced my past and sought forgiveness from Brother Hugh, from my brother Francis, and from all those that I'd hurt throughout my life. I made a promise to myself that, from then on, I would dedicate my life to Jesus Christ. It was not easy to convince the other monks of my conversion, but Brother Hugh believed in me. Hugh saw goodness in every man," the Prior paused, "even, I suppose, the men who dragged him out of his bed one night, not long after I left Africa, tied him to a tree outside the hospital and took his life."

"Good God," whispered Marie.

"It is because of Brother Hugh that I am a priest. I'm sorry Marie if I have been too graphic, but I want to be honest with you both. I have seen terrible things and I have done terrible things, but I have experienced incredible goodness and witnessed the power of total love. Brother Hugh was a great and modest man who lived the best life he could. He dedicated his life to others and I believe he is in heaven now. God willing, we will meet again in paradise, and he will be proud of me."

Michael looked at Marie and thought he saw a tear well up in her eye.

Seeing her discomfort, the Prior frowned.

"Finally, I get to the good bit," he said cheerfully.

Marie raised her eyes.

"Before my Rite of Ordination in Africa I was told that if I wished I could take a new name, the one by which I would be known as a priest. Many men keep the name they were christened with, but others choose to take a new name, like the name of a favourite saint or that of a pope. I had changed as a person and wanted so much to change my name. I considered choosing Hugh but on the night before my ordination my brother Francis came to me with an offer. He knew what I wanted to do so he offered to take my name, if I would take his. He said it was a two-way gift. He would become Michael and I Francis - Father Francis."

Horse looked at Michael.

"Why didn't you tell me?"

"I suppose I would have, at some point, but I guess I didn't think it was all that important. To you I am Michael and, well, I am Michael. My name does not define me. I'm sorry Brian; I guess I didn't think it was important."

"It seems it was very important to Sylvester Parker," said Marie.

"Indeed it was Marie," said Father Francis, "Because Sylvester Parker didn't know of our name-swap, very few people did, he assumed that Father Francis was of little threat to him or to his Russian muscle man. Parker thought he had Michael Eustace, the crazy ex-soldier, drugged and strapped to a chair. His mistake was our blessing and with God's help, I was able to deal with Stefan and hold Parker off until you arrived."

"A lucky punch?" said Marie with a cheeky grin.

The Prior blushed.

"But there was someone else in the cellar too, wasn't there? Who was that?" she asked Marie.

"I don't know," said Father Francis, "actually, I didn't see him. Michael was the only one who did. Maybe he was an enemy of Parker's. Whoever he was, he saved us. Had he not turned up God only knows what would have happened."

Michael didn't offer an opinion on who other man was. He had a feeling he knew, but didn't want to think about it or share his suspicions with them. It was taking all his energy not to think about Sylvester Parker.

"That's some story, Father," said Marie.

"Yes, I suppose it is. It's not something that we have told many people."

"Well, we won't tell anyone, will we Marie? Anyway, who'd believe us Father?" said Horse, "It's almost as unbelievable as Michael's cave monsters."

"Thanks, Horse," said Michael sardonically.

Michael made a face and they all laughed.

"It is a hellova story though, Father, that's for sure." said Horse.

Chapter 90.

May I ask you about Sylvester Parker and the investigation, Brian?" said Father Francis, "I can't deny, I'm more than a little intrigued."

They had moved over to the fire, the Prior insisting that Marie and Brian take the armchairs. He and Michael sat between them on two of the straight-backed carvers. The Prior had poured them each a generous glass of whiskey. Horse studied the golden liquid intensely before taking a small sip. He closed his eyes and sighed. A log in the fire crackled and hissed at him.

"Of course, Father. You deserve that, at least, for all you did. Paul Creagan has kept me updated, although I'm no longer involved in the case," said Horse mysteriously.

"Stefan, the Russian guy, sang like the proverbial canary, bu' only after he was given a written guarantee that 'e would not be extradited to the US or returned to Russia where, it seems, he's wanted for the murder of a security guard. He admitted that 'e' had been working for Parker, as a mole in Mr G's organisation."

Father Francis raised an inquisitive eyebrow.

"Mr who?"

"Mr G. Eh, Maurice Gimple. He is, I mean, he *was* a Dublin criminal with business interests on Skellig Éin. Myself and Paul were watching him. That's why we were here on the island. Mr G was the older of the two dead men in the cellar – the ones under the white sheets, Father. The other unfortunate bloke was one of his henchmen."

"Oh, I see. Please continue," said the Prior.

"Yes, well, Stefan told us that the man Mr G met at Gerry Gallagher's farm house was not Sylvester Parker at all, but, an unemployed actor from Dublin. The real Parker paid this actor to play the role of the Devil, in what the actor thought was a reality TV show. The real Sylvester Parker was in fact the manservant, O'Hara. I worked that one out for myself when I got back to Dublin. That's why I came back to the island. I knew whatever was going on wasn't finished, and I was sure it had something to do with Michael, although I didn't know what or why."

"So the manservant O'Hara was actually the real Sylvester Parker?" said Michael.

"Yes," said Horse, "and the man behind the desk was an out of work actor, a forty-five-year-old named Kieran Noonan, who really thought 'e was on TV, poor sod. The footage we saved from the fire at Gerry Gallagher's farm, the soundless images from the front room, was nothing more than an actor playing a part. Mr G was being duped."

"Wow," said Michael.

"Yeh. It was somethin' else, alright. Paul told me that Stefan found it all very funny. It seems Kieran Noonan was desperate for money. He'd not worked for over two years, was separated from his wife and was, by all accounts, very close to destitution. He was vulnerable and an easy target for Sylvester Parker to manipulate. We will never know why Noonan never tried to leave the farmhouse, but presumably Parker was paying him a lot of money for the gig, and of course, Noonan believed he was going to be on the television. He was quite a good actor, actually. Stefan said that he terrified Mr G. When confronted with the evidence that Kieran Noonan and Gerry Gallagher had been brutally murdered and mutilated, Stefan claimed he had no idea what Parker was really like, but when pushed, Stefan led the Gardaí to a modern penthouse apartment overlooking the main square in Ballyhoary. In a floor safe in the bedroom, they found lap-tops, CD's, photographs, videos and files, including details of over twenty different bank accounts and a collection of false passports used by Parker in his various guises, both male and female. Parker had masqueraded, at one time or another, as a district nurse, a man servant, a school teacher, a Latin American businessman, an Arab and even a priest. In fact, Sylvester Parker could have given Kieran Noonan a run for his money in the acting department. In the safe they also found several references to an innocuously sounding web site, *The Glitter Garden*. Parker ran the site. The techie boys at the Garda Computer Crime Investigation Unit managed to circumvent Parker's elaborate security protections and protocols. What they found was astounding. *The Glitter Garden* was only a doorway into a second, sister, site on the dark web. Like the Glitter Garden the sister-site was access-protected and members only. It took the GCCI a bit longer to crack its password protections but they are very good at what they do. The site was dedicated to every kind of twisted depravity, with an emphasis on child pornography and violent/murder erotica."

"Good God," said the Prior.

Horse continued.

"Entry to *The Glitter Garden* was by invitation only and only Parker sent out the invitations. The list of its members reads like an abridged version of Who's Who. They are the pillars of society; the rich, the powerful and the very influential. The roll call includes wealthy and prominent businessmen (and a few businesswomen too), politicians, members of the clergy and even members of law enforcement agencies. There is a famous Hollywood movie star, three Saudi oil sheiks and even a popular Christian evangelist in the US. Not only are these people very twisted but they are very gullible too. For Parker, the site controller and its convivial host, *The Glitter Garden* provided both business and pleasure. It was a place where he could share his own perversions with like-minded sickos, but it also offered him an opportunity to manipulate and control its members. Parker obtained a massive amount of wealth, information, and influence by blackmailing the members of *The Glitter Garden*. Whilst providing a *seemingly* safe and anonymous place for the perverts to meet, share their views and upload their obscene videos, the truth was that Parker knew who everyone was and he recorded everything they did and said on the site. Parker was the ring master of a circus of performing rats."

Horse stared into the fire before going on.

"Parker contributed to the website too, uploading snuff movies of his own making, most recently two separate recordings showing the gruesome torture of two Dublin gangsters, Mr G and his first lieutenant, a low-life named Pete Mercer. Mercer was the other man covered by the sheet in the cellar. It was stomach churning stuff. Unlike the other members of the club whenever Parker appeared on screen he wore a mask. And he got turned-on by what he did, if you know what I mean. Presumably, so did those watching it."

"It's awful," said the Prior.

"He was a very disturbed individual and he attracted very disturbed followers," Horse continued.

"So far the GCCIU has discovered over three hundred hours of recordings on that web site. It seems Parker insisted that each member of the Glitter Garden provide at least one home-made movie, as proof of their bona fides, and nothing but extreme hard-core violence was acceptable. These he used to blackmail the members. Once a member, always a member. Once in, there was no getting out. One in you belonged to Sylvester Parker. The members provided him with money, influence and information. He had eyes everywhere, even as you know Father Francis, in the monastery and the church sacristy."

"It's incredible and yet he still got it wrong, when it came to us," said Father Francis.

"No one is infallible. Psychopaths think they are, but they are not. Maybe he met his match when he crossed paths with the Eustace brothers?"

"And the man we found in the woods, was he one of Parker's victims too?" said Michael.

"Yes. It seems most likely. Megan told us that he was one of Mr G's men. Seánie Egan, better known as Rats. Apparently, he stole some of Parker's drug shipment. Bad idea. We think Rats was strung up as a brutal warning to anyone else who may be having similar ideas: cross Sylvester Parker and this is what will happen to you."

"What about Jane Wesley and all that stuff I told you Parker said about Allison? Is all that true?" said Michael.

"I was getting to that. In Parker's penthouse Paul found a box of unsent letters. All were written in different hands, and addressed to different inmates at Bronzefield Prison in Ashford in the Surrey. It's a woman's prison and it's home to some of the most violent and notorious women prisoners in the UK, including Jane Wesley. As I said, every letter was different: the colour of the pen, the type of pen used, the style of handwriting, the paper used and so on, but all had one thing in common, a small red squiggle that looked like an "S" somewhere on the envelope, and again on the letter. They all had it, a little squiggle. At first, it looked like the writers had been testing the pen, but Paul soon realised that it was some kind of secret signature, proof, as it were, that all the letters were coming from the same source. Once the prison authority was told of Paul's suspicions all the cells in Bronzefield were searched. They found a stack of similarly marked letters hidden in the metal legs of Jane Wesley's bed, all addressed to different inmates, but clearly all for Jane Wesley's attention. When the other inmates were interviewed they all told, more or less, the same story."

Horse stopped and took a sip of whiskey before continuing.

"Soon after Jane Wesley arrived at Bronzefield some of the other inmates received a visit from an unknown man or woman. Everyone described meeting a different person, but we think they were probably all Sylvester Parker, in one of his many disguises. The visitor told the inmates that if she did not do what she was told all of her loved-ones on the outside would be in mortal danger. To prove the point, the inmates were shown photographs – recent photographs – of husbands, children, parents, grandparents and friends, along with photographs of some of the victims from *The Glitter Garden.* They were told that this is what would happen if they did not co-operate. None of the prisoners doubted that the threat was genuine. The rules were simple. Every week one of the inmates would receive a hand written letter. Somewhere on the envelope there would be the squiggle mark. The letter was not to be removed or read, but immediately passed to Jane Wesley. Obviously, the letters were written in code so that neither the prison guards nor an inquisitive fellow inmate would know what was being said. Only Jane could decipher her father's messages."

Horse paused again. None of the others spoke, so he went on.

"Paul's people managed to crack the code. Most of the letters were about Parker's search for his granddaughter, but there was also stuff about his preparations to deal with Michael and the rest of us. In the most recent letter, a copy of which Paul received courtesy of the late Mr G, Parker was talking about the death of Jane's husband Peter, who had been knifed in the exercise yard of Strangeways Prison by a fellow prisoner, and, also, about mounting an appeal for her release. In a previous letter Parker told Jane that he'd elicited the help of one of the most prominent criminal lawyers in London who, as I'm sure you guessed, is an active member of *The Glitter Garden*. Paul assures me that Jane Wesley is not going anywhere soon. Since hearing of her fathers death she has been put in solitary confinement and on twenty-four-hour suicide-watch."

"And Allison, do we know what happened to her?" said Michael.

"Allison has a new name and a new family. She lives in Australia. Obviously, when you told us what Parker said, Scotland Yard had it checked it out. Allison was reassessed. Her psychologist says he is convinced that what Parker said was lies. Obviously, they will keep close tabs on her."

"What I don't understand," said Marie "was how he could get away with it all, and for so long, when everyone knew his name."

"There are two reasons for that, Marie," said Horse. "Firstly, Sylvester Parker was not his real name. The second reason was he was extremely wealthy. Extreme wealth can buy you anonymity, along with everything else. Once we knew he was related to Jane Wesley, finding out his real identity became a much easier task. Jane Wesley's maiden name is Jane Sylvester. After some digging we were able to locate the name of her father: Prenderville Kendrick Sylvester or PK to his friends. PK Sylvester grew up in Cornwall, the son of two doctors. He was an extremely clever young man and spent three years in Cambridge studying medicine. Unfortunately, it appears PK was a strange and volatile character, prone to angry violent outbursts. People remembered Prenderville, because they remembered not liking him. He didn't fit in and had few, if any, friends. He dropped out of medical school. One of his classmates said she thought he was suffering from depression and rumours at the time suggested PK was admitted to a mental institution for his own good. The next record of Prenderville was an accusation of the rape of a seventeen-year-old girl, the only daughter of a devout Catholic couple. When girl became pregnant the charges against PK were dropped. Because the family were devout Christians there was never a question of a termination. The young girl gave birth to a daughter. They called her Jane. Becoming a father seemed to change Prenderville and apparently he begged forgiveness from the girls parents. They were good Christian people and accepted Prenderville into their house and lives. He stayed with them for nearly two years, the doting father, the loving partner. A marriage was planned. Three days before the big day, Prenderville vanished, taking his baby daughter Jane with him. Despite having no obvious means of supporting the child, he managed to disappear completely and without trace. We now know he took baby Jane to Argentina."

"Argentina. How did he afford that?" said Marie.

"Well, this is the most bizarre fact about PK Sylvester. We think he won the National Lottery. Someone from that area won thirty-seven million pounds, five months before he and baby Jane disappeared. Getting out of the country with an eighteen-month old child, when every police force in the UK was looking for you, would have been near impossible, unless you had a lot of clout. Thirty-seven million pounds is a lot of clout. It's only a theory at this stage but it's looking promising. Scotland Yard are checking it out. The lottery board in the UK is not too keen on breaking any confidentiality clause they might have signed, even thirty-four years ago. A mysterious recluse named Senor Kendrick purchased a large remote cattle ranch in northern Argentina, close to the border with Paraguay. It was reckoned to have cost fourteen million US dollars thirty four years ago. At some point he returned to England with his daughter Jane and her husband Peter Wesley, the only child of a wealthy industrialist. Peter and Jane had only one child, Allison."

"So Parker was a psychopath with a lottery fortune, and his daughter married a wealthy like-minded freak?" said Michael.

"That's about the measure of it. Scary, isn't it?" said Horse.

He stared into the fire. This time it ignored him.

"How is Paul Creagan," asked Father Francis.

"He's very good. He got promoted. Since the arrest of Deputy Garda Commissioner Rowland and the very positive press coverage Paul has been receiving, not to mention the praise being heaped on him from the Americans for his outstanding contribution in ridding the world of one of their *most wanted*, it's hardly surprising."

"The Deputy Commissioner was arrested?" said Michael.

"Don't you read the newspapers, Michael?" said Horse.

"Not if I can avoid them."

"Rowland was in Parker's pocket too. He was a member of the Glitter Garden."

"You're joking," said Michael.

Horse didn't respond. He looked glum. Michael turned to Marie.

"Rowland was the one who arranged for Brian to be transferred from Scotland Yard to Dublin. He was Brian's confidante," she said.

641

"Oh," said Michael.

"I thought 'e was one of the good guys. Turns out he was a creep, just like Parker," said Horse.

"Is that why Garda Commissioner Whelan resigned?" asked Father Francis.

"Yes. His position, as they say, became untenable," said Horse with little enthusiasm.

"Shit," exclaimed Michael, "do you think Parker had a hand in you being transferred over here?"

"That's what the Americans think, and it does seem too much of a coincidence. All of it. You, me and the Americans, all turning up on the island, all at the same time. They think Parker orchestrated the lot," said Horse.

"It's quite unbelievable," said the Prior.

"Not really, when you have so much money and influence. The Americans told me they got lucky when they intercepted a phone call between Mr G and Parker. They had been trawling the air-waves for a sign of Parker for years. Suddenly Bingo. Mr G says his name. But I'm not sure they're right. I think that while the Americans were trawling for Parker, he was trawling for them. I think the phone call with Mr G was bait and the Americans took it, hook, line and sinker."

"Good God," said the Prior again.

"Yeh, well it gets better Father" said Horse, "It turns out that Deputy Commissioner Rowland was instrumental in bringing the International Conference in Cross Border Co-Operation to Skellig Éin too. I really misread that bastard, pardon the French, Father."

Horse blushed.

Marie smiled.

"It's perfectly understandable, Brian. Is there no end to this?" said the Prior.

"It would seem not. When they searched Mr G's nightclub they found a hidden door in the basement. It opened into another basement running under the three adjoining buildings linked by another door to the basement of a laundrette Mr G also owned. Mr G used it as a secret passage when he wanted to leave the nightclub unnoticed. The basements under the three middle building was basically one enormous space. Recently it had been used as a torture chamber by Sylvester Parker. It's where he recorded the mutilation of Mr G and Pete Mercer. It was also where he'd originally planned to wreck his vengeance on Michael and the rest of us. There were fourteen chairs arranged in a circle, with a bank of flat screen televisions on two walls and four studio cameras on mobile stands. I guess one of those chairs had my name on it. I shudder to think of what would have happened if it had all gone to Parker's plan. It seems likely that when Parker thought Michael had died in the caves he abandoned his grand scheme. He must have felt cheated, but thought the best option was to cut his losses, tie up all the loose ends and clear off back to Argentina, disguised as a nun or something. That meant killing Kieran Noonan and burning down Gerry Gallagher's farm, but leaving just enough evidence for the Americans to believe that Sylvester Parker and his manservant O'Hara had been murdered by Russian drug lords or by Mr G. Once that was taken care of, all that was left to do was deal with Mr G and Pete Mercer. When Michael resurfaced alive, Parker quickly arranged a new plan. It wouldn't be as dramatic as his original scheme, but it would do. As he told you Michael, he had plans to get to me and my family and loved-ones at a future date." Horse looked at Marie.

"Why did he come here to the monastery?" said Father Francis.

"Well for one thing he couldn't go back to the cellars under the night club. The Gardaí were all over Mr G's place. And he didn't have time to lure you anywhere else. The monastery basement was quiet and probably appealed to him because it was your home, Father. The Devil doing his evil work in the house of God. Parker was a showman and holding his theatre of horror in the monastery would have appealed to him on many levels. I'm happy he's dead and I hope he slowly rots in Hell."

"What did you mean Brian, when you said you were no longer involved in the investigation? Why is that?" said the Prior.

"I've resigned from the police force. Didn't Michael tell you?"

"No, he didn't," said Father Francis.

"I got the opportunity to take earlier retirement and, after all that had happened here, I decided the time was right. I'm moving over here. I've had enough of London."

"What will you do?"

"I've decided to go private," said Horse.

"You mean become a private investigator?" said the Prior.

"Yes Father. I'm looking at leasing of a small office in Galway. I just need to find the right partner, before I fully commit."

"I see," said Father Francis. He looked at Michael. Michael shrugged his shoulders.

"Horse wants me to join him in his business venture. Hopkins and Eustace PI."

"As I've told Michael many times before, Father Prior, his unusual gift is very useful in my line of business," said Horse.

"You are not looking for a partner, you're looking for a bloodhound. Is that what I'll be, Brian? The agency's bloodhound?" said Michael.

"No," pleaded Horse, "I'm looking for a partner, someone I can work with, someone I can trust. The fact that you have the ability to see through walls is a secondary consideration. Anyway, I think you're closer to a moth than a bloodhound, Michael."

"A moth?" said Michael indignantly. "A moth!"

"You may not know this, but many species of moth share your particular ability. For example, some moths can see ultra-violet light. Others can distinguish different colours, even in total darkness. So you see, you are much closer to a moth than you are to a bloodhound. The bloodhound uses his nose to find his prey. The moth uses its eyes. It sees colours that the rest of us can't see."

"That *is* very interesting, Brian," said Father Francis.

"So I'm to be a moth then, am I? And what if I fly too close to the flame? Isn't that how all moths end up? Burnt to a crisp?"

"Well that's what I'm here for, isn't it? To protect you, to reign in your impulses to go into places you shouldn't go. To stop you flying into the fire," said Horse with a smile.

"I, for one, think it's a great idea," said the Prior, "What do you think, Marie?".

"Giorraíonn beart bother," she said.

"Gur ram burt bow her? What does that mean?" said Horse.

"It means, two people shorten the road," she said, "or the journey is better when you have company."

Michael looked at her, then shrugged his shoulders.

"Well that seems settled then. When do we start?"

Chapter 91.

Michael sat on an old, but sturdy, wooden bench in the garden of the art gallery and waited for Hanna and Primrose to arrive. They had arranged to meet him at eleven thirty but he had got there forty-five minutes early. When he knocked on the back door and no one answered, rather than leave, he went and sat in the garden. He was happy and the sunny morning only added to his good mood. He'd borrowed Brother Benjamin's motor bike again and had taken it for a very long exhilarating spin around the island on the way to the gallery. He'd added at least ten unnecessary miles onto the journey but knew Brother Benjamin wouldn't mind. He would have done another circuit of the island had the petrol gauge not told him that the fuel tank was dangerously low. The contrast between the adrenalin rush of the bike ride and the stillness of the garden was startling.

Michael was excited, but anxious too. It would be the first time he and Hanna had met since they left the hospital. Primrose had only agreed to the meeting on the proviso that she accompany Hanna. Since Hanna had returned to her, Primrose had become particularly protective of her only child, and word about town was that, for the first time since her father died, Hanna seemed happy to accept her mother's wholehearted attention. They had been seen walking about the island arm in arm, like a couple of inseparable school girls.

This made Michael happy but, as far as he was concerned, there was still some unfinished business to attend to.

Michael needed to prove to them that he wasn't mad, nor a threat to either of them. He was here to declare that he accepted, wholeheartedly and without reservation, that the memories he had from their time in the caves were nothing more than distorted nightmares brought on by drugs, the darkness and an over-active imagination, primed by the lurid images from a gift-shop book. He was here to tell them that the monsters that he had been so convinced were real, were only elaborate hallucinations. Michael wanted Hanna and Primrose to know that he was free, that his headaches were gone and he'd been sleeping better than he'd ever slept in his life.

The sun warmed the side of Michael face. The sky above the garden was enormous, a wide expanse of hazy blue. There wasn't the hint of a cloud. Everything around him sparkled. He closed his eyes. He could hear seagulls squawking far out over the ocean and bees busy in the branches of the weeping willow behind him. The air smelt sweetly of new growth and drying seaweed. Brother Benjamin had told Michael that when the seagulls were far out to sea the good weather would last. Michael had spent enough time on Skellig Éin to know that the weather, on and around the island, paid little attention to the musings of the its inhabitants, and even less to the flying habits of the native seagulls. The only certainty about the weather on Skellig Éin was its unpredictability.

It had been nearly a month since he'd agreed to go into business with Horse and plans for their detective agency were slowly coming together. He had been tasked with coming up with a catchy name. The best he could come up with was H & E Investigators. Horse hated it and said it sounded like the title of a porn movie set in a fitness club. Michael had no idea what he meant. When Marie proposed Moth Investigations, calling to mind what Horse had said about Michael's abilities being closely related to certain varieties of moth, the Englishman was beside himself with enthusiasm.

"*Moth Investigations*. Bloody perfect," he'd declared.

Michael hadn't been sure if Marie was joking when she suggested it, but if she was, it didn't matter. Horse was hooked and Michael had to admit there was something mysterious about the name.

"Moth Investigations - from darkness into light," Horse had said, with rare poetic gusto.

Michael shuffled on the garden bench and smiled to himself. He tried to clear his mind but for the umpteenth time Susan invaded his thoughts. Now that things had settled down, he had made plans to visit her. He'd heard Montreal was particularly beautiful in Autumn.

Michael opened his eyes just as the gate latch rose and Primrose, followed closely by Hanna, entered the garden. At first, they didn't notice him, but when he stood up and the wooden bench creaked under his weight, Primrose turned around. When Hanna saw Michael she ran down the garden and, without a word, buried her head into his chest and hugged him with all her strength. He felt her body trembling and wondered if she was crying. He hugged her back, then gently prised her away, raised her chin with the tip of his finger and looked down at her.

"Let me look at you," he said.

Hanna stepped back, but took his hands in hers, as if to ensure he couldn't get away.

"You're beautiful," he said.

She was beautiful, he thought. Her hair, now long and curly, was flame red. It framed a slightly round but perfectly symmetrical face. Her freckled skin was ivory and her lips were the colour of a blood orange. She was smiling. She had her mother's eyes, the soft unusual brown that seemed to darken and lighten to the flicker of an unseen candle. She *had* been crying.

"Did you think I was ugly, Michael?" she said with false indignation.

"No. Not at all. It's just I don't remember you being so beautiful. It was dark down there," he said.

Hanna squeezed his hands.

"Mum told me you were easy to tease," she said, broadening her smile.

"And you still are, Michael," said Primrose.

"Ha! Well the last time I saw your lovely daughter she hadn't washed for at least a week," he said. He didn't add that he had a vague memory of seeing Hanna in her underwear.

"Ha ha! Very funny," said Hanna

They sat down on the bench together. It creaked again, but held their combined weight. Hanna kept a hold of one of Michael's hands. She kept smiling at him.

"How are you, Michael?" said Primrose.

"I'm great. My headaches have gone and I've got a new career. Did you hear, I'm going to become a private investigator?"

"Father Francis told me. So, you'll be staying around then?"

"Yes, for a while. It will take time to set up the business and we both need some time out, after all that has happened. Brian is looking after all the technicalities. I'm just hanging around," he said.

"We're going to Tuscany for the rest of the summer. Why don't you come with us, Michael? We have a beautiful villa in San Gimignano," said Hanna like an excited little girl.

"Tuscany," he said.

"You'd love it there. It is the most beautiful place in the world," she continued. "Please come, Michael."

"You are more than welcome," said Primrose.

"Well, I'll see. As I said, I've things to do regarding the business."

"That means you won't," scowled Hanna. She let go his hand.

"How long will you be in Tuscany?" said Michael.

"Until mid-September," said Primrose.

"Then I promise I will come, for a couple of weeks, in August. Okay?"

"You promise?" said Hanna.

"I promise," he said.

Hanna looked doubtful and turned to her mother.

Primrose smiled.

"You should know by now, Hanna, that when Michael makes you a promise, he always, *always*, keeps it."

After a little while ominous clouds gathered above the garden, quickly obliterating the sun and sky. The ocean gulls stopped their squawking and the bees in the willow tree headed away, probably back to the warmth and protection of the hive. When a chilly wind rose, Michael, Primrose and Hanna went inside. When the clouds opened and it began to rain Primrose and Hanna led Michael down the spiral staircase into the Rain Room, which was suddenly alive with sounds and movement and colour.

"Where there is rain, there is always an abundance of life!" Michael declared when his feet touched the floor. Primrose beamed at him.

"Do you like it, Michael?" she said.

"I love it. It's majestic. It's poetic. It's just so…you!" he said.

Primrose served tea and fruitcake, and they sank into the comfy armchairs and experienced the water-show for a long time without speaking. It was a spectacular success and Michael was moved by its beauty and stunned by Primroses' artistic ingenuity. Her Rain Room danced and sang and sparkled. Michael wondered if this was what it was like to be truly at peace. He felt warm and safe. The feeling was innocent and intense and it made him want to laugh out loud. He wished the show could go on forever.

As usual the weather over Skellig Éin did the unpredictable and, as if to answer the request of the strange Irish mystic, it rained steadily, nonstop, for the rest of the day.

The End

Epilogue.

Brother Benjamin swept the cellar floor slowly but with purpose. Father Bernard had gone to Ballyhoary on important business, and had left Benji with a list of things to do before he got back.

"Dust the shelves and all the surfaces and then thoroughly sweep the floor. And, *in that order*! Only sweep the floor once all the dusting is done. Do you understand, Brother Benjamin?" Father Bernard had said.

"Yes, of course, Father Bernard. Dust first and then sweep."

"And after that you can go upstairs and clean out the hearth in the Prior's study, and set a new fire for when he gets back this evening."

"Yes, Father Bernard."

Benji knew what Father Bernard meant by *thoroughly* when it came to sweeping the cellar floor. It meant sweeping not just the exposed parts but also the hidden parts, like under the shelves, the space behind the dumb waiter and under the boiler. Father Bernard didn't like dust.

Because it was awkward, Benji left the floor under the boiler to last.

The boiler sat on two steel runners, like railway tracks, that raised the machine four inches off the stone floor. Four inches was enough space for the head of the brush to run underneath if the brush was laid horizontal. It meant Benji had to drop to his knees and use the brush with a bent back. If someone came into the cellar and saw him, prostrate before the big red humming machine, they might have assumed he was praying.

With his sleeves rolled up to the elbows Benji pushed the brush all the way under the boiler then slowly dragged it back out, like a fisherman hauling in his net. Starting at one runner and moving along toward the second, one brush-head width at a time, Benji removed what little dust had found sanctuary in the cold dark space.

It was slow and tedious work, but he was so used to doing it he could almost do it with his eyes closed.

As he drew close to the second steel runner something snagged the head of the brush and, no matter how hard Benji tugged at it, he could not dislodge whatever it was. Finally, instead of pulling he came at the object from an angle, pushed it sideways and then hooked it with the brush head and dragged it out. It scraped along the floor as it came to him.

It was a small silver compact camera.

"Now how did you get under there?" he said to it.

He picked it up. It was cold and battered, and when he tried to switch it on he found that it was either broken or the battery was flat. He guessed the latter was the case. He turned the camera over in his hand. On the base someone had carefully scratched the initials *HB*.

"HB? Huh. HB?"

After considering it for a while, and deciding that he knew no one with those initials, he slipped the camera into the deep pocket of his habit and got back to finishing his work.

Before Brother Benjamin left the cellar he had made up his mind that he would not tell Father Bernard about his curious find but instead would bring the camera to the Prior, but only after he did some investigating of his own. Benji often fantasised about being a detective and now he had a real mystery to solve. He was sure he could do it; find out who owned the camera; find out who HB was. It should be quite easy. All he'd have to do was recharge the camera battery, and then look at some of the photos. If he was lucky there would be pictures of people he recognised.

Before turning off the lights and heading back up the stairs, Benji took one last look around the cellar. Instinctively he gently tapped the camera which nestled in the pocket of his habit.

He smiled to himself.

A little mystery, a small secret and maybe, just maybe, he thought, the start of a big adventure.

If you would like to contact the author or leave a review
please visit please visit
www.martingpjordan.com

Published in the Republic of Ireland by:

**DIGGY DUFFY
PUBLISHING**

Made in the USA
Columbia, SC
27 July 2017